Hippocrene Standard Dictionary

RUSSIAN-ENGLISH/ENGLISH-RUSSIAN

Hippocrene Standard Dictionary

RUSSIAN-ENGLISH
ENGLISH-RUSSIAN

Oleg and Ksana Beniukh

New, Revised Edition
with Business Terms

HIPPOCRENE BOOKS
New York

Other Dictionaries by Oleg and Ksana Beniukh

RUSSIAN-ENGLISH/ENGLISH RUSSIAN
CONCISE DICTIONARY
ISBN 0-7818-0132-X $11.95pb

RUSSIAN-ENGLISH/ENGLISH RUSSIAN
STANDARD DICTIONARY
ISBN 0-7818-0083-8 $16.95pb

ENGLISH-RUSSIAN STANDARD DICTIONARY
ISBN 0-87052-100-4 $11.95pb

ESTONIAN-ENGLISH/ENGLISH-ESTONIAN
CONCISE DICTIONARY
ISBN 0-87052-081-4 $11.95pb

UKRAINIAN-ENGLISH/ENGLISH UKRAINIAN
STANDARD DICTIONARY
ISBN 0-7818-0189-3 $16.95pb

UKRAINIAN PHRASEBOOK AND DICTIONARY
Available with cassettes
ISBN 0-7818-0188-5 $9.95pb
ISBN 0-7818-0191-5 $12.95 cassettes

For information, contact:
HIPPOCRENE BOOKS, INC.
171 Madison Avenue
New York, NY 10016

Printed in the United States of America.

Preface

This dictionary has been designed as a clear, convenient and concise reference book. It can be used both by those who speak fluent Russian and those who have just acquainted themselves with the Russian alphabet. It will be of interest and value to students of Russian, tourists, visitors to conferences, business men, and others, who may simply want to understand Russian menus, theatre programmes, street-signs, notices, etc. The dictionary contains over 12000 vocabulary entries, alphabetically arranged and supplied with the basic grammatical information. The verbs are given in the imperfective aspect, which is normally treated as the basic form of the simple verb.

This dictionary's innovative feature is the transliteration of every Russian word and expression, which the users will find most helpful. For this purpose the Editors have chosen the Library of Congress transliteration system, it being the least confusing while providing the necessary pronunciation guides.

CONTENTS

GEOGRAPHICAL NAMES

Абакан /abakán/ Abakan

Абу-Даби /abú-dabí/ Abu Dhabi

Абхазия /abkháziia/ Abkhazia

Аваруа /avarúa/ Avarua

Австралия /avstráliia/ Australia

Австрия /ávstriia/ Austria

Аганья /agán'ia/ Agana

Адамстаун /ádamstaun/ Adamstown

Аддис-Абеба /addís-abéba/ Addis Ababa

Аден /áden/ Aden

Аджария /adzháriia/ Adzharia

Адмиралтейства о-ва /ostrová admiraltéistva/ the Admiralty Islands

Адриатическое море /adriaticheskoe móre/ the Adriatic Sea

Адыгея /adygéia/ Adygei

Азербайджан /azerbaidzhán/ Azerbaijan

Азия /áziia/ Asia

Азовское море /azóvskoe móre/ the Sea of Azov

Азорские о-ва /azórskie ostrová/ the Azores

Аккра /ákkra/ Accra

Аландские о-ва /alándskie ostrová/ the Aland Islands

Албания /albániia/ Albania

Александрия /aleksandríia/ Alexandria

Алеппо /aléppo/ Aleppo

Алеутские о-ва /aleútskie ostrová/ the Aleutian Islands

Алжир /alzhír/ Algeria; Algiers

Аллеганские горы /allegánskie góry/ the Allegheny Mountains

Алма-Ата /almá-atá/ Alma-Ata

Алофи /alófi/ Alofi

Алтай /altái/ the Altai

Альпы /ál'py/ the Alps

Аляска /aliáska/ Alaska

Амазонка /amazónka/ the Amazon

Америка /amérika/ America

Амман /ammán/ Amman

Амстердам /amsterdám/ Amsterdam

Аму-Дарья /amú-dar'iá/ the Amu Darya

Амур /amúr/ the Amur

Ангара /angará/ the Angara

Англия /ángliia/ England

Ангола /angóla/ Angola

Андаманские о-ва /andamánskie ostrová/ the Andaman Islands

Андорра /andórra/ Andorra

Анды /ándy/ the Andes

Анкара /ankará/ Ankara

Антананариву /antananarívu/ Antananarivo

Антарктида /antarktída/ the Antarctic continent, Antarctica

Антарктика /antárktika/ the Antarctic

Антверпен /antvérpen/ Antwerp

Антигуа и Барбуда /antígua i barbúda/ Antigua and Barbuda

Антильские о-ва /antíl'skie ostrová/ the Antilles

Апеннинские горы, Апеннины /apennínskie góry, apenníny/ the Apennines

Апиа /ápia/ Apia

Аппалачские горы /appaláchskie góry/ the Appalachian Mountains

Аравийское море /aravíiskoe móre/ the Arabian Sea

Аравия /aráviia/ Arabia

Аральское море /arál'skoe móre/ the Aral Sea

Аргентина /argentína/ Argentina

Арденны /ardénny/ the Ardennes

Арктика /árktika/ the Arctic

Армения /arméniia/ Armenia

Аруба /arúba/ Aruba

Архангельск /arkhángel'sk/ Arkhangelsk

Астрахань /ástrakhan'/ Astrakhan

Асунсьон /asuns'ón/ Asuncion

Атлантический океан /atlanti̇́cheskii okeán/ the Atlantic (Ocean)
Атласские горы /atlásskie góry/ the Atlas Mountains
Афганистан /afganistán/ Afghanistan
Афины /afi̇́ny/ Athens
Африка /áfrika/ Africa
Ашхабад /ashkhabád/ Ashkhabad

Баб-эль-Мандебский пролив /bab-el'—mandébskii proli̇́v/ Bab el Mandeb
Бавария /baváriia/ Bavaria
Багамские Острова /bagámskie ostrová/ the Bahamas
Багдад /bagdád/ Bag(h)dad
Базель /bázel'/ Basel or Basle
Баирики /bairi̇́ki/ Bairiki
Байкал /baikál/ (Lake) Baikal
Баку /bakú/ Baku
Балеарские о-ва /baleárskie ostrová/ the Balearic Islands
Балканские горы /balkánskie góry/ the Balkan Mountains
Балканский п-ов /balkánskii polu+óstrov/ the Balkan Peninsula
Балканы /balkány/ the Balkan states, the Balkans
Балтийское море /balti̇́iskoe móre/ the Baltic Sea
Балтимор /baltimór/ Baltimore
Балхаш /balkhásh/ (Lake) Balkhash
Бамако /bamakó/ Bamako
Банги /bangi̇́/ Bangui
Бангкок /bangkók/ Bangkok
Бангладеш /bangladésh/ Bangladesh
Бандар-Сери-Бегаван /bándar-séri-begaván/ Bandar Seri Begawan
Бандунг /bandúng/ Bandung
Банжул /banzhúl/ Banjul
Барбадос /barbádos/ Barbados
Баренцево море /bárentsevo móre/ the Barents Sea
Барнаул /barnaúl/ Barnaul

Барселона /barselóna/ Barcelona
Бас-Тер /bas-ter/ Basse-Terre
Бастер /bastér/ Basseterre
Батуми /batúmi/ Batumi
Баффинов залив /baffi̇́nov zali̇́v/ Baffin Bay
Бахрейн /bakhréin/ Bahrain
Башкирия /bashki̇́riia/ Bashkiria
Бейрут /beirút/ Beirut or Beyrouth
Белград /belgrád/ Belgrade
Белое море /béloe móre/ the White Sea
Белоруссия /belorússiia/ Byelorussia
Белуджистан /beludzhistán/ Baluchistan
Бельгия /bél'giia/ Belgium
Бельмопан /bel'mopán/ Belmopan
Бенарес /benarés/ Benares
Бенгалия /bengáliia/ Bengal
Бенгальский залив /bengál'skii zali̇́v/ the Bay of Bengal
Бенин /beni̇́n/ Benin
Берингово море /béringovo móre/ the Bering Sea
Берингов пролив /béringov proli̇́v/ the Bering Strait
Берлин /berli̇́n/ Berlin
Бермудские о-ва /bermúdskie ostrová/ Bermuda
Берн /bern/ Berne
Бирма /bi̇́rma/ Burma
Бирмингем /birmingém/ Birmingham
Бисау /bisáu/ Bissau
Бискайский залив /biskáiskii zali̇́v/ the Bay of Biscay
Богота /bogotá/ Bogota
Болгария /bolgáriia/ Bulgaria
Боливия /boli̇́viia/ Bolivia
Бомбей /bombéi/ Bombay
Бонн /bonn/ Bonn
Борнео /bornéo/ Borneo; see Калимантан
Бородино /borodinó/ Borodino
Босния /bósniia/ Bosnia
Бостон /bóston/ Boston
Босфор /bosfór/ the Bosp(h)orus

Ботнический залив /botnícheskii zalív/ the Gulf of Bothnia
Ботсвана /botsvána/ Botswana
Браззавиль /brazzavíl'/ Brazzaville
Бразилиа /brazília/ Brasilia
Бразилия /brazíliia/ Brazil
Брайтон /bráiton/ Brighton
Братислава /bratisláva/ Bratislava
Братск /bratsk/ Bratsk
Бретань /bretán'/ Brittany
Бриджтаун /bridzhtáun/ Bridgetown
Бристоль /bristól'/ Bristol
Британские о-ва /británskie ostrová/ the British Isles
Брно /brno/ Brno
Бруней /brunéi/ Brunei
Брюгге /briúgge/ Bruges
Брюссель /briussél'/ Brussels
Брянск /briánsk/ Bryansk
Буг /bug/ the Bug
Будапешт /budapésht/ Budapest
Бужумбура /buzhumbúra/ Bujumbura
Булонь /bulón'/ Boulogne
Буркина-Фасо /burkína-fasó/ Burkina Faso
Бурунди /burúndi/ Burundi
Бурятия / Buriátiia/ Buryatia
Бутан /bután/ Bhutan
Бухарест /bukharést/ Bucharest
Буэнос-Айрес /buénos-áires/ Buenos Aires

Вадуц /váduts/ Vaduz
Валлетта /vallétta/ Valletta
Вальпараисо /val'paraíso/ Valparaiso
Ванкувер /vankúver/ Vancouver
Вануату /vanuátu/ Vanuatu
Варшава /varsháva/ Warsaw
Ватикан /vatikán/ Vatican City
Вашингтон /vashingtón/ Washington
Везувий /vezúvii/ Vesuvius
Великобритания /velikobritániia/ Great Britain
Веллингтон /véllington/ Wellington
Вена /véna/ Vienna

Венгрия /véngriia/ Hungary
Венесуэла /venesuéla/ Venezuela
Венеция /venétsiia/ Venice
Верден /verdén/ Verdun
Версаль /versál'/ Versailles
Верхнее озеро /vérkhnee ózero/ Lake Superior
Вест-Индия /vest-índiia/ the West Indies
Византия /vizantíia/ Byzantium
Виктория /viktóriia/ Victoria
Вила /víla/ Vila
Виллемстад /víllemstad/ Willemstad
Вильнюс /víl'nius/ Vilnius
Виндхук /víndhuk/ Windhoek
Виннипег /vínnipeg/ Winnipeg
Виргинские о-ва /virgínskie ostrová/ the Virgin Islands
Висла /vísla/ the Vistula
Виши /vishí/ Vichy
Владивосток /vladivostók/ Vladivostok
Вогезы /vogézy/ the Vosges
Волга /vólga/ the Volga
Волгоград /volgográd/ Volgograd
Вологда /vólogda/ Vologda
Волхов /vólkhov/ the Volkhov
Восточное Самоа /vostóchnoe samóa/ Eastern Samoa
Выборг /výborg/ Vyborg
Вьентьян /v'ent'ián/ Vientiane
Вьетнам /v'etnám/ Vietnam

Гаага /gaága/ The Hague
Габон /gabón/ Gabon
Габороне /gaboróne/ Gaborone
Гавайи /gaváii/ Hawaii
Гавайские о-ва /gaváiskie ostrová/ the Hawaiian Islands
Гавана /gavána/ Havana
Гавр /gavr/ Havre
Гаити /gaíti/ Haiti
Гайана /gaiiana/ Guyana
Галапагос /galapagós/ the Galapagos Islands

Гималаи /gimalái/ the Himalaya(s)
Гиндукуш /gindukúsh/ the Hindu Kush
Глазго /glázgo/ Glasgow
Гоа /góa/ Goa
Гоби /góbi/ the Gobi
Голландия /gollándiia/ Holland
Голубые горы /golubýe góry/ the Blue
 Mountains
Гольфстрим /gol'fstrím/ the Gulf Stream
Гондурас /gondurás/ Honduras
Гонконг /gonkóng/ Hong Kong
Гонолулу /gonolúlu/ Honolulu
Горн /Мыс/ /mys gorn/ Cape Horn
Гренада /grenáda/ Grenada
Гренландия /grenlándiia/ Greenland
Греция /grétsiia/ Greece
Гринвич /grínvich/ Greenwich
Грозный /gróznyi/ Grozny
Грузия /grúziia/ Georgia
Гуам /guám/ Guam
Гудзон /gudzón/ the Hudson
Галлиполи /gallípoli/ Gallipoli
Гамбия /gámbiia/ The Gambia
Гамбург /gámburg/ Hamburg
Гамильтон /gámil'ton/ Hamilton
Гана /gána/ Ghana
Ганг /gang/ the Ganges
Гваделупа /gvadelúpa/ Guadeloupe
Гватемала /gvatemála/ Guatemala
Гвиана /gviána/ Guiana
Гвинея-Бисау /gvinéia-bisáu/ Gui-
 nea-Bissau
Гданьск /gdan'sk/ Gdansk
Гебридские о-ва /gebrídskie ostrová/
 the Hebrides
Гент /gent/ Ghent
Генуя /génuia/ Genoa
Германия /germániia/ Germany
Герцеговина /gertsegovína/ Herzegovi-
na
Гибралтар /Gibraltár/ Gibraltar
Гибралтарский пролив /gibraltárskii
 prolív/ the Strait of Gibraltar

Гудзонов залив /gudzónov zalív/ Hud-
 son Bay
Гулль /gull'/ Hull
Гурон /gurón/ (Lake) Huron

Дагестан /dagestán/ Daghestan
Дакар /dakár/ Dakar
Дакка /dákka/ Dacca
Дамаск /damásk/ Damascus
Дания /dániia/ Denmark
Дарданеллы /dardanélly/ the Dardanel-
 les
Дар-эс-Салам /dar-es-salám/ Dar es
 Salaam
Даугава /daugáva/ the Daugava; see
 Западная Двина
Дели /déli/ Delhi
Детройт /detróit/ Detroit
Джакарта /dzhakárta/ Jakarta
Джеймстаун /dzheimstáun/ Jamestown
Джибути /dzhibúti/ Djibouti
Джомолунгма /dzhomolúngma/ Cho-
 molungma
Джорджтаун /dzhordzhtáun/ George-
 town
Днепр /dnepr/ the Dnieper
Днепропетровск /dnepropetróvsk/ Dne-
 propetrovsk
Днестр /dnestr/ the Dniester
Доминика /dominíka/ Dominica
Доминиканская Республика /domini-
 kánskaia respúblika/ the Dominican
 Republic
Дон /don/ the Don
Донбасс /donbáss/ the Donbas, the Do-
 nets Basin
Донец /donéts/ the Donets
Доха /dókha/ Doha
Дрезден /drézden/ Dresden
Дублин /dúblin/ Dublin
Дувр /duvr/ Dover
Дунай /dunái/ the Danube
Душанбе /dushanbé/ Dyushambe

Дьепп /d'epp/ Dieppe
Дюнкерк /diunkérk/ Dunkirk

Еврейская автономная область /evréiskaia avtonómnaia óblast'/ the Jewish Autonomous Region
Европа /evrópa/ Europe
Евфрат /evfrát/ the Euphrates
Египет /egípet/ Egypt
Елгава /élgava/ Jelgava
Енисей /eniséi/ the Yenisei
Ереван /ereván/ Yerevan

Желтое море /zhóltoe móre/ the Yellow Sea
Женева /zhenéva/ Geneva

Заир /zaír/ Zaire
Замбези /zambézi/ the Zambezi or Zambesi
Замбия /zámbiia/ Zambia
Западная Двина /západnaia dviná/ the Zapadnaya Dvina
Западное Самоа /západnoe samóa/ Western Samoa
Зеленоград /zelenográd/ Zelenograd
Земля Франца Иосифа /zemliá frántsa iósifa/ Franz Josef Land
Зимбабве /zimbábve/ Zimbabwe
Зунд /zund/ the Sound

Иерусалим /ierusalím/ Jerusalem
Ижевск /izhévsk/ Izhevsk
Измир /izmír/ Izmir
Израиль /izráil'/ Israel
Инд /ind/ the Indus
Индийский океан /indíiskii okeán/ the Indian Ocean
Индия /índiia/ India
Индокитай /indokitái/ Indochina
Индонезия /indonéziia/ Indonesia
Индостан /indostán/ Hindustan

Иоганнесбург /iogánnesburg/ Johannesburg
Ионическое море /ionícheskoe móre/ the Ionian Sea
Иордан /iordán/ the Jordan
Иордания /iordániia/ Jordan
Ипр /ipr/ Ypres
Ирак /irak/ Iraq
Иран /iran/ Iran
Ирландия /irlándiia/ Ireland
Иртыш /irtýsh/ the Irtysh
Исламабад /islamabád/ Islamabad
Исландия /islándiia/ Iceland
Испания /ispániia/ Spain
Иссык-Куль /issýk-kúl'/ Issyk Kul
Исфахан /isfakhán/ Isfahan
Италия /itáliia/ Italy

Йемен /iémen/ Yemen
Йокогама /iokogáma/ Yokohama
Йошкар-Ола /ioshkár-olá/ Yoshkar-Ola
Кабардино-Балкария /kabardíno-balkáriia/ Kabardino-Balkaria
Кабо-Верде /kábo-vérde/ Cape Verde
Кабул /kabúl/ Kabul
Кавказ /kavkáz/ the Caucasus
Кадис /kadís/ Cadiz
Казань /kazán'/ Kazan
Казахстан /kazakhstán/ Kazakhstan
Казбек /kazbék/ Kazbek
Каир /kaír/ Cairo
Кайенна /kaiénna/ Cayenne
Кале /kalé/ Calais
Калимантан /kalimantán/ Kalimantan
Калининград /kaliningrád/ Kaliningrad
Калмыкия /kalmýkiia/ Kalmykia
Калькутта /kal'kútta/ Calcutta
Кама /káma/ the Kama
Камбоджа /kambódzha/ Cambodia
Камерун /kamerún/ Cameroon
Кампала /kampála/ Kampala
Камчатка /kamchátka/ Kamchatka
Канада /kanáda/ Canada

Канарские о-ва /kanárskie ostrová/ the Canary Islands

Канберра /kanbérra/ Canberra

Каракалпакия /karakalpákiia/ Karakalpakia

Каракас /karakás/ Caracas

Каракумы /karakúmy/ the Kara Kum

Карачаево-Черкесская автономная область /karacháevo-cherkésskaia avtonómnaia óblast'/ the Karachai-Cherkess Autonomous Region

Карачи /karáchi/ Karachi

Кардифф /kardíff/ Cardiff

Карелия /karéliia/ Karelia

Карибское море /karíbskoe móre/ the Caribbean Sea

Каролинские о-ва /karolínskie ostrová/ the Caroline Islands

Карпаты /karpáty/ the Carpathians

Карское море /kárskoe móre/ the Kara Sea

Каспийское море /kaspíiskoe móre/ the Caspian Sea

Кастри /kástri/ Castries

Катар /kátar/ Qatar

Катманду /katmandú/ Kat(h)mandu

Каттегат /kattegát/ the Kattegat

Каунас /káunas/ Kaunas

Кашмир /kashmír/ Kashmir

Квебек /kvébek/ Quebec

Квинсленд /kvínslend/ Queensland

Кейптаун /keiptáun/ Cape Town or Capetown

Кельн /kiól'n/ Cologne

Кембридж /kémbridzh/ Cambridge

Кемерово /kémerovo/ Kemerovo

Кения /kéniia/ Kenya

Кигали /kigáli/ Kigali

Киев /kíev/ Kiev

Килиманджаро /kilimandzháro/ Kilimanjaro

Киль /kil'/ Kiel

Кингстаун /kingstáun/ Kingstown

Кингстон /kíngston/ Kingston

Киншаса /kinshása/ Kinshasa

Киото /kióto/ Kyoto or Kioto

Кипр /kipr/ Cyprus

Киргизия /kirgíziia/ Kirghizia

Кирибати /kiribáti/ Kiribati

Китай /kitái/ China

Кито /kíto/ Quito

Кишинев /kishinióv/ Kishinev

Клайпеда /kláipeda/ Klaipeda

Клондайк /klondáik/ the Klondike

Ковентри /kóventri/ Coventry

Коломбо /kolómbo/ Colombo

Колумбия /kolúmbiia/ Colombia

Кольский п-ов /kól'skii poluóstrov/ the Kola Peninsula

Коми /Республика/ /respúblika kómi/ the Komi Republic

Коморские Острова /komórskie ostrová/ the Comoro Islands

Комсомольск-на-Амуре /komsomól'sk-na-amúre/ Komsomolsk-on-the-Amur

Конакри /konákri/ Conakry

Конго /kóngo/ Congo; the Congo

Копенгаген /kopengágen/ Copenhagen

Кордильеры /kordil'éry/ the Cordilleras

Кордова /kórdova/ Cordoba

Корейская Народно-Демократическая Республика /koréiskaia naródno–demokratícheskaia respúblika/ the Democratic People's Republic of Korea

Корсика /kórsika/ Corsica

Корфу /kórfu/ Corfu

Коста-Рика /kósta-ríka/ Costa Rica

Кот-д'Ивуар /kot-d"ivuár/ Cote d'Ivoire

Краков /krákov/ Cracow

Краснодар /krasnodár/ Krasnodar

Красное море /krásnoe móre/ the Red Sea

Красноярск /krasnoiársk/ Krasnoyarsk
Крит /krit/ Crete
Кронштадт /kronshtádt/ Kronstadt
Крым /krym/ the Crimea
Куала-Лумпур /kuála-lúmpur/ Kuala Lumpur
Куба /kúba/ Cuba
Кубань /kubán'/ the Kuban
Кувейт /kuvéit/ Kuwait
Кузбасс /kuzbáss/ the Kuzbass, the Kuznetsk Basin
Куйбышев /kúibyshev/ Kuibyshev; see Samara
Кука о-ва /ostrová kúka/ Cook Islands
Курильские о-ва /kuríl'skie ostrová/ the Kuril(e) Islands
Кызылкум /kyzylkúm/ the Kizil Kum

Лабрадор /labradór/ Labrador
Лагос /lágos/ Lagos
Ладожское озеро /ládozhskoe ózero/ Lake Ladoga
Ла-Манш /la-mánsh/ the English Channel
Ланкашир /lankashír/ Lancashire
Лаос /laós/ Laos
Ла-Пас /la-pás/ La Paz
Ла-Плата /la-pláta/ La Plata
Лаптевых море /móre láptevykh/ the Laptev Sea
Латвия /látviia/ Latvia
Лахор /lakhór/ Lahore
Лейпциг /léiptsig/ Leipzig
Лена /léna/ the Lena
Ленинакан /leninakán/ Leninakan
Ленинград /leningrád/ Leningrad
Лесото /lesóto/ Lesotho
Либерия /libériia/ Liberia
Либревиль /librevíl'/ Libreville
Ливан /liván/ Lebanon
Ливерпуль /liverpúl'/ Liverpool
Ливия /líviia/ Libya
Ливорно /livórno/ Leghorn
Лилонгве /lilóngve/ Lilongwe

Лима /líma/ Lima
Лион /lión/ Lyons
Лиссабон /lissabón/ Lisbon
Литва /litvá/ Lithuania
Лихтенштейн /likhtenshtéin/ Liechtenstein
Ломе /lomé/ Lome
Лондон /lóndon/ London
Лос-Анжелес /los-ánzheles/ Los Angeles
Лотарингия /lotaríngiia/ Lorraine
Лофотенские о-ва /lofoténskie ostrová/ the Lofoten Islands
Луанда /luánda/ Luanda
Луара /luára/ the Loire
Лусака /lusáka/ Lusaka
Львов /l'vov/ Lvov
Льеж /l'ezh/ Liege
Люксембург /liuksembúrg/ Luxemb(o)urg

Магелланов пролив /magellánov prolív/ the Straits of Magellan
Магнитогорск /magnitogórsk/ Magnitogorsk
Мадагаскар /madagaskár/ Madagascar
Мадрас /madrás/ Madras
Мадрид /madríd/ Madrid
Македония /makedóniia/ Macedonia
Малави /malávi/ Malawi
Малайзия /maláiziia/ Malaysia
Малая Азия /málaia áziia/ Asia Minor
Мальта /mál'ta/ Malta
Манила /maníla/ Manila
Марийская АССР /maríiskaia á es es ér/ the Mari ASSR
Махачкала /makhachkalá/ Makhach-Kala
Мекка /mékka/ Mecca
Мексика /méksika/ Mexico
Мертвое море /miórtvoe móre/ the Dead Sea
Мехико /mékhiko/ Mexico City

Минск /minsk/ Minsk
Молдова /moldóva/ Moldova
Монголия /mongóliia/ Mongolia
Мордовия /mordóviia/ Mordovia
Москва /moskvá/ Moscow
Мурманск /múrmansk/ Murmansk
Мыс Доброй Надежды /mys dóbroi
  nadézhdy/ the Cape of Good Hope
Мюнхен /miúnkhen/ Munich

Нагорный Карабах /nagórnyi kara-
  bákh/ Nagorny Karabakh
Нальчик /nál'chik/ Nalchik
Нахичеванская АССР /nakhichleván-
  skaia á es es ér/ the Nakhichevan
  ASSR
Нахичевань /nakhicheván'/ Nakhiche-
  van
Нева /nevá/ the Neva
Неман /néman/ the Niemen
Нигер /níger/ Niger
Нигерия /nigériia/ Nigeria
Нидерланды /niderlándy/ the Nether-
  lands
Нижний Новгород /nízhnii nóvgorod/
  Nizhny Novgorod
Никарагуа /nikarágua/ Nicaragua
Никосия /nikosíia/ Nicosia
Новая Зеландия /nóvaia zelándiia/ New
  Zealand
Новая Земля /nóvaia zemliá/ Novaya
  Zemlya
Новороссийск /novorossíisk/ Novoros-
  siisk
Новосибирск /novosibírsk/ Novosibirsk
Норвегия /norvégiia/ Norway
Нюрнберг /niúrnberg/ Nuremberg

Объединенная Арабская Республика
  /ob"ediniónnaia arábskaia respúbli-
  ka/ the United Arab Republic
Объединенные Арабские Эмираты
  /ob"ediniónnye arábskie emiráty/
  United Arab Emirates

Обь /ob'/ the Ob
Огненная Земля /ógnennaia zemliá/
  Terra del Fuego
Одесса /odéssa/ Odessa
Ока /oká/ the Oka
Ольстер /ól'ster/ Ulster
Онежское озеро /onézhskoe ózero/
  Lake Onega
Осло /óslo/ Oslo
Охотское море /okhótskoe móre/ the
  Sea of Okhotsk

Пакистан /pakistán/ Pakistan
Палестина /palestína/ Palestine
Памир /pamír/ the Pamirs
Панама /panáma/ Panama
Парагвай /paragvái/ Paraguay
Париж /parízh/ Paris
Пекин /pekín/ Bejing
Пенджаб /pendzháb/ the Punjab
Пенза /pénza/ Penza
Персидский залив /persídskii zalív/ the
  Persian Gulf
Перу /perú/ Peru
Петрозаводск /petrozavódsk/ Petroza-
  vodsk
Печора /pechóra/ the Pechora
Польша /pól'sha/ Poland
Португалия /portugáliia/ Portugal
Прага /prága/ Prague
Приморский край /primórskii krái/
  Primorski Territory

Рейкьявик /reik'iávik/ Reykjavik
Рига /ríga/ Riga
Рижский залив /rízhskii zalív/ the Gulf
  of Riga
Рим /rim/ Rome
Российская Советская Федеративная
  Социалистическая   Республика
  /РСФСР/ /rossíiskaia sovétskaia fede-
  ratívnaia sotsialístícheskaia respúb-
  lika er es ef es er/ the Russian Soviet
  Federative Socialist Republic /RSFSR/

Россия /rossíia/ Russia
Румыния /rumýniia/ R(o)umania

Самара /samára/ Samara
Сан-Сальвадор /san-sal'vadór/ San
 Salvador
Саранск /saránsk/ Saransk
Саудовская Аравия /saúdovskaia árá-
 viia/ Saudi Arabia
Сахалин /sakhalín/ Sakhalin
Свердловск /sverdlóvsk/ Sverdlovsk
Севан /seván/ Sevang
Севастополь /sevastópol'/ Sebastopol
Северная Америка /sévernaia amérika/
 North America
Северная Двина /sévernaia dviná/ the
 Severnaya Dvina
Северная Земля /sévernaia zemliá/ Se-
 vernaya Zemlya
Северная Осетия /sévernaia osétiia/
 North Ossetia
Северное море /sévernoe móre/ the
 North Sea
Северный Ледовитый океан /sévernyi
 ledovítyi okeán/ the Arctic Ocean
Сеул /seúl/ Seoul
Сибирь /sibír'/ Siberia
Сирия /síriia/ Syria
Словакия /slovákiia/ Slovakia
Соединенное Королевство Велико-
 британии и Северной Ирландии
 /soediniónnoe korolévstvo veliko-
 británii i sévernoi irlándii/ United
 Kingdom of Great Britain and Nor-
 thern Ireland
Соединенные Штаты Америки /США/
 /soediniónnye shtáty amériki se she
 á/ the United States of America /USA/
Сомали /somalí/ Somali(a)
София /sofíia/ Sofia
Сочи /sóchi/ Sochi

Союз Советских Социалистических
 Республик /СССР/ /soíuz sovétskikh
 sotsialistícheskikh respúblik es eses
 er/ the Union of Soviet Socialist Re-
 publics /USSR/
Средиземное море /sredizémnoe móre/
 the Mediterranean (Sea)
Ставрополь /stávropol'/ Stavropol
Ставропольский край /stavrópol'skii
 krái/ Stavropol Territory
Стамбул /stambúl/ Istanbul
Стокгольм /stokgól'm/ Stockholm
Судан /sudán/ the Sudan
Сухуми /sukhúmi/ Sukhumi
Суэцкий канал /suétskii kanál/ the
 Suez Canal
Сыктывкар /syktyvkár/ Siktivkar
Сырдарья /syrdar'iá/ the Syr Daria

Таджикистан /tadzhikistán/ Tajikistan
Таймыр /taimýr/ Taimir
Таллинн /tállinn/ Tallinn
Танжер /tanzhér/ Tangier
Танзания /tanzániia/ Tanzania
Татарская АССР /tatárskaia á es es er/
 the Tatar ASSR
Ташкент /tashként/ Tashkent
Тбилиси /tbilísi/ Tbilisi
Тверь /tver'/ Tver
Тегеран /tegerán/ Teh(e)ran
Тель-Авив /tel'-avív/ Tel Aviv
Тибет /tibét/ Tibet, Thibet
Тихий океан /tíkhii okeán/ the Pacific
 (Ocean)
Токио /tókio/ Tokyo
Тувинская АССР /tuvínskaia á es es
 er/ the Tuva ASSR
Тунис /tunís/ Tunisia; Tunis
Туркмения /turkméniia/ Turkmenia
Турция /túrtsiia/ Turkey
Тянь-Шань /tian'-shán'/ Tien Shan

Уганда /ugánda/ Uganda
Удмуртия /udmúrtiia/ Udmurtiia

Узбекистан /uzbekistán/ Uzbekistan
Украина /ukraína/ the Ukraine
Улан-Батор /ulán-bátor/ Ulhan-Bator
Улан-Удэ /ulán-udé/ Ulhan-Ude
Ульяновск /ul'iánovsk/ Ulianovsk
Урал /urál/ the Urals
Уругвай /urugvái/ Uruguay
Уфа /ufá/ Ufa

Федеративная Республика Германии /ФРГ/ /federatívnaia respúblika germánii/ Federal Republic of Germany /FRG/
Филиппины /filippíny/ the Philippines
Финляндия /finliándiia/ Finland
Финский залив /fínskii zalív/ the Gulf of Finland
Фолклендские Острова /folkléndskie ostrová/ the Falkland Islands
Франция /frántsiia/ France
Фрунзе /frúnze/ Frunze

Хабаровск /khabárovsk/ Khabarovsk
Хабаровский край /khabárovskii krai/ Khabarovsk Territory
Ханой /khanói/ Hanoi
Харбин /kharbín/ Harbin
Харьков /khár'kov/ Kharkov
Хельсинки /khél'sinki/ Helsinki
Хибины /khibíny/ the Khibini Mountains
Хиросима /khirosíma/ Hiroshima

Чебоксары /cheboksáry/ Cheboksari
Челябинск /cheliábinsk/ Cheliabinsk
Черное море /chórnoe móre/ the Black Sea
Чехо-Словакия /chékho-slovákiia/ Czechoslovakia
Чечено-Ингушетия /chechéno-ingushétiia/ Checheno-Ingushetia
Чили /chíli/ Chile
Чувашия /chuváshiia/ Chuvashia
Чудское озеро /chudskóe ózero/ Lake Chudskoye

Чукотский полуостров /chukótskii poluóstrov/ Chukot(ski) Peninsula
Чукотское море /chukótskoe móre/ the Chuckchee Sea

Швейцария /shveitsáriia/ Switzerland
Швеция /shvétsiia/ Sweden
Шотландия /shotlándiia/ Scotland
Шпицберген /shpitsbérgen/ Spitsbergen
Шри-Ланка /shri-lanká/ Sri Lanka

Эверест /everést/ Everest
Эгейское море /egéiskoe móre/ the Aegean (Sea)
Эдинбург /edinbúrg/ Edinburgh
Эквадор /ekvadór/ Ecuador
Эстония /estóniia/ Estonia
Эфиопия /efiópia/ Ethiopia

Южная Осетия /iuzhnaia osétiia/ South Ossetia
Югославия /iugosláviia/ Yugoslavia
Южная Америка /iuzhnaia amérika/ South America
Южная Корея /iuzhnaia koréia/ South Korea
Южно—Африканская Республика /iuzhno-afrikánskaia respúblika/ Republic of South Africa
Ютландия /iutlándiia/ Jutland

Ява /iava/ Java
Якутск /iakútsk/ Yakutsk
Якутия /iakútiia/ Yakutia
Ялта /iálta/ Yalta
Ямайка /iamáika/ Jamaica
Япония /iapóniia/ Japan
Японское море /iapónskoe móre/ the Sea of Japan

List of Abbreviations

abbr.	abbreviation	mus.	musical
adj.	adjective	n.	neuter
adv.	adverb	num.	numeral
coll.	colloquial	obs.	obsolete
comp.	comparative	paren.	parenthesis
conj.	conjunction	part.	participle
electr.	electrical	phot.	photography
f.	feminine	pl.	plural
fig.	figurative	pred.	predicate
gram.	grammar	prep.	preposition
indecl.	indeclinable	pron.	pronoun
interj.	interjection	sl.	slang
m.	masculine	smb.	somebody
med.	medicine	smth.	something

Transliteration Guide

а - a	к - k	х - kh
б - b	л - l	ц - ts
в - v	м - m	ч - ch
г - g	н - n	ш - sh
д - d	о - o	щ - shch
е - e	п - p	ъ - "
ё - io	р - r	ы - y
ж - zh	с - s	ь - '
з - z	т - t	э - e
и - i	у - u	ю - iu
й - i	ф - f	я - ia

A

а /a/ conj. and, but; part. eh?

абажур /abazhúr/ m. lampshade

аббат /abbát/ m. abbot

абзац /abzáts/ m. paragraph

абонемент /abonemént/ m. subscription

абонент /abonént/ m. subscriber

аборт /abórt/ m. abortion; miscarriage

абрикос /abrikós/ m. apricot; apricot-tree

абстрактный /abstráktnyi/ adj. abstract

абсурд /absúrd/ m. nonsense, absurdity

авангард /avangárd/ m. vanguard

аванс /aváns/ m. advance payment

авантюра /avantíura/ f. adventure

авантюрист /avantiuríst/ m. adventurer

авантюрный /avantíurnyi/ adj. risky; shady

авария /aváriia/ f. crash, accident; breakdown

август /avgúst/ m. August

авиабаза /aviabáza/ f. air base

авиакомпания /aviakompániia/ f. airline

авианосец /avianósets/ m. aircraft carrier

авиасалон /aviasalón/ m. airshow

авиатрасса /aviatrássa/ f. air-route

авиационный /aviatsiónnyi/ adj. aviation

авиация /aviátsiia/ f. air force

авось /avós'/ adv. perhaps

аврал /avrál/ m. emergency work

австралиец /avstralíets/ m. Australian

австралийка /avstralíika/ f. Australian

австралийский /avstralíiskii/ adj. Australian

австриец /avstríets/ m. Austrian

австийка /avstríika/ f. Austrian

австрийский /avstríiskii/ adj. Austrian

автобаза /avtobáza/ f. motor depot.

автобиография /avtobiográfiia/ f. autobiography

автобус /avtóbus/ m. bus; coach

автогонки /avtogónki/ pl. motor race(s)

автозавод /avtozavód/ m. motor works, car factory

автомагистраль /avtomagistrál'/ f. motor-highway

автомат /avtomát/ m. automatic machine; slot machine; submachine gun

автоматизация /avtomatizátsiia/ f. automation

автомашина /avtomashína/ f. car, automobile

автономия /avtonómiia/ f. autonomy

автономный /avtonómnyi/ adj. autono mous

автопогрузчик /avtopogrúzchik/ m. fork-lift truck

автор /avtór/ m. author

автореферат /avtoreferát/ m. synopsis

авторитет /avtoritét/ m. authority

авторитетный /avtoritétnyi/ adj. authoritative

авторский /ávtorskii/ adj. author's; copyright

авторское (право) /ávtorskoie právo/ adj.+n.copyright

авторство /ávtorstvo/ n. authorship

авторучка /avtorúchka/ f. fountain pen

авуары /avuáry/ pl. assets; holdings

агат /agát/ m. agate

агент /agént/ m. agent

агентство /agéntstvo/ n. agency

агитатор /agitátor/ m. agitator

агитпункт /agitpúnkt/ m. campaign centre

агония /agóniia/ f. agony

аграрный /agrárnyi/ adj. agrarian

агрегат /agregát/ m. aggregate; unit

агрессивный /agressívnyi/ adj. aggressive

агрессия /agréssiia/ f. aggression

агрессор /agréssor/ m. aggressor

агрикультура /agrikul'túra/ f. agriculture

агроном /agronóm/ m. agronomist

агрономия /agronómiia/ f. agronomy

ад /ád/ m. hell
адаптация /adaptátsiia/ f. adaptation
адаптер /adápter/ m. adapter
адаптировать /adaptírovat'/ v. adapt
адвокат /advokát/ m. lawyer; barrister; advocate
адвокатура /advokatúra/ f. the Bar
административный /administratívnyi/ adj. administrative
администратор /administrátor/ m. administrator
администрация /administrátsiia/ f. administration
адмирал /admirál/ m. admiral
адмиралтейство /admiraltéistvo/ n. admiralty
адрес /ádres/ m. address
адресат /adresát/ m. addressee
адский /ádskii/ adj. infernal
адъютант /ad"iutánt/ m. aide
азарт /azárt/ m. excitement
азартный /azártnyi/ adj. reckless
азбука /ázbuka/ f. alphabet; the ABC
азербайджанец /azerbaidzhánets/ m. Azerbaijani(an)
азербайджанка /azerbaidzhánka/ f. Azerbaijani(an)
азербайджанский /azerbaidzhánskii/ adj. Azerbaijani(an)
азиат /aziát/ m. Asian
азиатский /aziátskii/ adj. Asian, Asiatic
азот /azót/ m. nitrogen
аист /aíst/ m. stork
айва /aivá/ f. quince; quince-tree
айсберг /áisberg/ m. iceberg
академик /akadémik/ m. academician
акация /akátsiia/ f. acacia
акваланг /akvaláng/ m. aqualung
акварель /akvarél'/ f. water-colour
аквариум /akvárium/ m. aquarium
акведук /akvedúk/ m. aqueduct
акклиматизировать /akklimatizírovat'/ v. acclimatize
аккредитив /akkreditív/ m. letter of credit

аккуратность /akkurátnost'/ f. neatness; punctuality; accuracy
аккуратный /akkurátnyi/ adj. tidy; punctual; exact
акр /ákr/ m. acre
акробат /akrobát/ m. acrobat
аксиома /aksióma/ f. axiom
акт /ákt/ m. act
актер /aktíor/ m. actor
актив /aktív/ m. assets; the activists
активизировать /aktivizírovat'/ v. intensify; activate
актуальный /aktuál'nyi/ adj. topical; urgent; pressing
акула /akúla/ f. shark
акустика /akústika/ f. acoustics
акушерка /akushérka/ f. midwife
акцент /aktsént/ m. accent
акционер /aktsionér/ m. shareholder
акционерный /aktsionérnyi/ adj. joint-stock
акция /áktsiia/ f. share; action
албанец /albánets/ m. Àlbanian
албанка /albánka/ f. Albanian
албанский /albánskii/ adj. Albanian
алгебра /álgebra/ f. algebra
алименты /aliménty/ pl. alimony
алкоголик /alkogólik/ m. alcoholic
аллея /alléia/ f. avenue
алмаз /almáz/ m. diamond
алтарь /altár'/ m. altar
алфавит /alfavít/ m. alphabet, the ABC
алчность /álchnost'/ f. greed
алый /ályi/ adj. scarlet
альбом /al'bóm/ m. album
альпинизм /al'pinízm/ m. mountaineering
альт /ál't/ m. viola; alto
алюминий /aliumínii/ m. aluminium
амбар /ambár/ m. barn
амбиция /ambítsiia/ f. arrogance
амбулатория /ambulatóriia/ f. dispensary, out-patient clinic
амвон /amvón/ m. pulpit
американец /amerikánets/ m. American

американка /amerikánka/ f. American
амнистировать /amnistírovat'/ v. amnesty
амортизатор /amortizátor/ m. shockabsorber
ампер /ampér/ m. ampere
ампутация /amputátsiia/ f. amputation
амфибия /amfíbiia/ f. amphibian
амфитеатр /amfiteátr/ m. amphitheatre; circle
анализ /análiz/ m. analysis
аналогичный /analogíchnyi/ adj. analogous
аналой /analói/ m. lectern
ананас /ananás/ m. pineapple
анархизм /anarkhízm/ m. anarchism
анатом /anátom/ m. anatomist
ангар /angár/ m. hangar
ангел /ángel/ m. angel
ангина /angína/ f. tonsillitis
английский /anglíiskii/ adj. English
англиканский /anglikánskii/ adj. Anglican
англичанин /anglichánin/ m. Englishman, Briton
англичанка /anglichánka/ f. Englishwoman
анекдот /anekdót/ m. anecdote
анемия /anemíia/ f. anaemia
анемон /anemón/ m. anemone
анестезия /anesteziia/ f. anesthesia
анисовый /anísovyi/ adj. anisic
анкета /ankéta/ f. questionnaire
аннексия /annéksiia/ f. annexation
аннулировать /annulírovat'/ v. cancel, annul
анод /anód/ m. anode
анонимный /anonímnyi/ adj. anonymous
ансамбль /ansámbl'/ m. ensemble
антарктический /antarktícheskii/ adj. antarctic
антенна /anténna/ f. aerial; antenna
антиквар /antikvár/ m. antiquarian
антилопа /antilópa/ f. antelope

антисемитизм /antisemitízm/ m. antiSemitism
антисептика /antiséptika/ f. antiseptics
антракт /antrákt/ m. interval
антрепренер /antrepreniór/ m. theatrical manager, impresario
антресоли /antresóli/ pl. mezzanine
анчоус /anchóus/ m. anchovy
аншлаг /anshlág/ m. full house;
спектакль идет с аншлагом /spektakl' idiot s anshlagom/ the show is sold out
апатия /apátiia/ apathy
апеллировать /apellírovat'/ v. appeal
апельсин /apel'sín/ m. orange
аплодировать /aplodírovat'/ v. applaud
апломб /apl'omb/ m. self-assurance
апогей /apogéi/ m. climax
апостол /apóstol/ m. apostle
аппарат /apparát/ m. apparatus; staff
аппетит /appetít/ m. appetite
аппликация /applikátsiia/ f. applique
апрель /aprél'/ m. April
аптека /aptéka/ f. drug store; chemist's
араб /aráb/ m. Arab
арабский /arábskii/ adj. Arabian, Arabic
аравийский /araviiskii/ adj. Arabian, Arabic
арбуз /arbúz/ m. water-melon
арбитр /arbítr/ m. arbiter; referee
аргумент /argumént/ m. argument
арена /aréna/ f. arena; scene
аренда /arénda/ f. lease
арендная (плата) /aréndnaia pláta/ adj.+f. rent
арендатор /arendátor/ m. leaseholder; tenant
арест /arést/ m. arrest
аристократ /aristokrát/ m. aristocrat
арифметика /arifmétika/ f. arithmetic
ария /áriia/ f. aria
арка /árka/ f. arch
аркан /arkán/ m. lasso
арктический /arktícheskii/ adj. arctic
армия /ármiia/ f. army
армянин /armianín/ m. Armenian
армянка /armiánka/ f. Armenian

армянский /armiánskii/ adj. Armenian
аромат /aromát/ m. aroma
арсенал /arsenál/ m. arsenal
артезианский (колодец) /arteziánskii kolódets/ adj.+m. artesian well
артель /artél'/ f. artel
артерия /artériia/ f. artery
артиллерия /artillériia/ f. artillery
артист /artíst/ m. actor
артрит /artrít/ m. arthritis
арфа /árfa/ f. harp
археолог /arkheólog/ m. archaeologist
археология /arkheólogiia/ f. archaeology
архив /arkhív/ m. archives
архиепископ /arkhiepískop/ m. archbishop
архипелаг /arkhipelág/ m. archipelago
архитектор /arkhitéktor/ m. architect
архитектура /arkhitektúra/ f. architecture
аспирант /aspiránt/ m. post-graduate student
ассамблея /assambléia/ f. assembly
ассигнация /assignátsiia/ f. currency bill, note
ассигнование /assignovánie/ n. allocation
ассистент /assistént/ m. assistant
ассортимент /assortimént/ m. assortment
ассоциация /assotsiátsiia/ f. association
астма /ástma/ f. asthma
астра /ástra/ f. aster
астролог /astrólog/ m. astrologer
астронавт /astronávt/ m. astronaut
астроном /astronóm/ m. astronomer
астрономия /astronómiia/ f. astronomy
асфальт /asfál't/ m. asphalt
атака /atáka/ f. attack
атаковать /atakovát'/ v. attack
атаман /atamán/ m. ataman, chieftain
атеизм /ateízm/ m. atheism
ателье /atel'é/ n. studio; fashion house
атлас /átlas/ m. atlas
атлас /atlás/ m. satin

атлет /atlét/ n. athlete
атмосфера /atmosféra/ f. atmosphere
атом /átom/m. atom
атомный /átomnyi/ adj. atomic
атомоход /atomokhód/ m. nuclear ship or ice-breaker
атрофия /atrofíia/ f. atrophy
атташе /attashé/ m. attache
аттестат /attestát/ m. certificate;
   а. зрелости /a. zrélosti/ school-leaving certificate
аттестовать /attestovát'/ v. give a reference; give a report
аттракцион /attraktsión/ m. side show
аудиенция /audiéntsiia/ f. audience
аудитория /auditóriia/ f. lecture room
аукцион /auktsión/ m. auction
афганец /afgánets/ m. Afghan
афганка /afgánka/ f. Afghan
афганский /afgánskii/ adj. Afghan
афера /afióra/ f. swindle, fraud
афинский /afínskii/ adj. Athenian
афиша /afísha/ f. bill, poster
афоризм /aforízm/ m. aphorism
африканец /afrikánets/ m. African
африканка /afrikánka/ mf. African
африканский /afrikánskii/ adj. African
аффект /affékt/ m. fit of passion
аффектация /affektatsiia/ f. affectation
ахать /ákhat'/ v. gasp; sigh
ацетилен /atsetilén/ m. acetylene
аэровокзал /aerovokzál/ m. air terminal
аэродром /aerodróm/ m. airfield, aerodrome
аэропорт /aeropórt/ m. airport
аэрозоль /aerozól'/ m. aerosol

Б

б-/b/-бы
баба /bába/ f. (old) woman; wife
бабочка /bábochka/ f. butterfly
бабье (лето) /báb'e léto/ adj.+n. Indian summer

бабушка /bábushka/ f. grandmother

багаж /bagázh/ m. baggage, luggage

багажная (квитанция) /bagázhnaia kvitántsiia/ adj.+f. luggage ticket

багажник /bagázhnik/ m. boot, luggage compartment

багажный (вагон) /bagázhnyi vagón/ m. luggage van

багровый /bagróvyi/ adj. crimson, purple

база /báza/ f. base, basis, foundation

базар /bazár/ m. market, bazaar

базарный /bazárnyi/ adj. market; vulgar

базировать /bazírovat'/ v. base

байдарка /baidárka/ f. canoe

байка / báika/ f. flannelette

бак /bák/ m. tank; seamen's mess

бакалавр /bakalávr/ m. bachelor

бакалейный /bakaléinyi/ adj. grocery

бакалейщик /bakaléishchik/ m. grocer

бакен /báken/ m. buoy

бакенбарды /bakenbárdy/ pl. side-whiskers

баклуши (бить б.) /bit' baklushi/ v. idle away, one's time

бактериология /bakteriológiia/ f. bacteriology

бактерия /baktériia/ f. bacterium

бал /bál/ m. ball

баланс /baláns/ m. balance

балбес /balbés/ m. dolt, simpleton

балдахин /baldakhín/ m. canopy

балет /balét/ m. ballet

балка /bálka/ f. beam; girder; gully

балканский /balkánskii/ adj. Balkan

балкон /balkón/ m. balcony

балл /báll/ m. mark, point

баллада /balláda/ f. ballad

балласт /ballást/ m. ballast

баллон /ballón/ m. cylinder

баллотироваться /ballotírovat'sia/v. be a candidate (for)

баловать /bálovat'/v. spoil; give a treat to

баловаться /bálovat'sia/ v. be naughty; indulge

баловень /báloven'/ m. pet, fabourite

балтийский /baltíiskii/ adj. Baltic

бамбук /bambúk/ m. bamboo

банан /banán/ m. banana

банда /bánda/ f. gang; band

бандаж /bandázh/ m. bandage, truss

бандероль /banderól'/ f. (postal) wrapper

бандит /bandít/ m. bandit

бандитизм /banditízm/ m. brigandage; gangsterism

банк /bánk/ m. bank

банка /bánka/ f. jar, can, tin

банкет /bankét/ m. banquet

банкир /bankír/ m. banker

банкнота /banknóta/ m. bank-note, bill

банкрот /bankrót/ m. bankrupt

бант /bánt/ m. bow

баня /bánia/ f. bath-house; public baths

бар /bár/ m.bar

барабан /barabán/ m. drum

барабанная (перепонка) /barabannaia pereponka/ adj.+f. ear-drum

барак /barák/ m. barrack, hut

баран /barán/ m. ram

бараний /baránii/ adj. sheep's; mutton

баранина /baránina/ f. mutton

баранка /baránka/ f. ring-shaped roll

барахло /barakhló/ n. junk

барашек /barashek/ m. lamb

баржа /bárzha/ f. barge

барометр /barómetr/ m. barometer

баррикада /barrikáda/ f. barricade

барс /bárs/ m. snow leopard

бархат /bárkhat/ m. velvet

барьер /bar'ér/ m. barrier

бас /bás/ m. bass

баскетбол /basketból/ m. basketball

баснословный /basnoslóvnyi/ adj. fabulous, incredible

басня /básnia/ f. fable

бассейн /basséin/ m. basin; pool

бастион /bastíon/ m. bastion, bulwark

бастовать /bastovát'/ v. strike

батальон /batal'ión/ m. battalion

батарейка /batařeika/ f. electric battery

батарея /bataréia/ f. battery; radiator

батист /batíst/ m. cambric
батон /batón/ m. long loaf
батрак /batrák/ m. farm hand
бахрома /bakhromá/ f. fringe
бацилла /batsílla/ f. bacillus
башенка /báshenka/ f. turret
башкир /bashkír/ m. Bashkir
башкирка /bashkírka/ f. Bashkir
башкирский /bashkírskii/adj. Bashkir
башня /báshnia/ f. tower
баюкать /baiúkat'/ v. lull
баян /baián/ m. accordion
бдительность /bdítel'nost'/ f. vigilance
бег /bég/ m. run, race
бегать /bégat'/ v. run
бегемот /begemót/ m. hippopotamus
беглец /begléts/ m. fugitive
беглость /béglost'/ f. fluency
беглый /béglyi/ adj. fluent, rapid; fugitive
беготня /begotniá/ f. running about
бегство /bégstvo/ n. flight, rout
бегун /begún/ m. runner
беда /béda/ f. misfortune
беднеть /bednét'/ v. become poor
бедность /bédnost'/ f. poverty
беднота /bednotá/ f. the poor
бедный /bédnyi/ adj. poor
бедняга /bedniága/ m. poor fellow
бедняк /bedniák/ m. poor man
бедро /bedró/ n. thigh, hip
бедственный /bédstvennyi/ adj. calamitous; disastrous
бедствие /bédstvie/ n. disaste
бежать /bezhát'/ v. run; escape, flee
бежевый /bézhevyi/ adj. beige
беженец /bézhenets/ m. refugee
без /bez/ prep. without
безаварийный /bezavaríinyi/ adj. accident-free
безалаберный /bezalábernyi/ adj. disorderly; slovenly
безалкогольный /bezalkogól'nyi/ adj. non-alcoholic
безатомный /bezátomnyi/ adj. atom-free

безбедный /bezbédnyi/adj. comfortable, well-to-do
безбилетный /bezbilétnyi/ adj. without a ticket
безбожие /bezbózhie/ n. atheism
безболезненный /bezboléznennyi/ adj. painless
безбоязненный /bezboiáznennyi/ adj. fearless
безветренный /bezvétrennyi/ adj. windless
безвкусица /bezvkúsitsa/ f. bad taste
безвкусный /bezvkúsnyi/adj. vulgar; insipid; tasteless
безвластие /bezvlástie/ n. anarchy
безвозмездный /bezvozmézdnyi/ adj. free, gratuitous
безволие /bezvólie/ n. lack of will
безвредный /bezvrédnyi/ adj. harmless
безвыездно /bezvýezdno/ adv. without going anywhere
безвыходный /bezvýkhodnyi/ adj. hopeless
безграмотный /bezgrámotnyi/ adj. illiterate; ignorant
безграничный /bezgraníchnyi/ adj. boundless
бездарный /bezdárnyi/ adj. ungifted
бездействие /bezdéistvie/ n. inactivity, inertia
безделушка /bezdelúshka/ f. trinket
безделье /bezdél'e/ n. idleness
бездельник /bezdél'nik/ m. idler
безденежный /bezdénezhnyi/ adj. penniless
бездетный /bezdétnyi/ adj. childless
бездеятельный /bezdéiatel'nyi/ adj. inactive
бездна /bézdna/ f. abyss
бездомный /bezdómnyi/ adj. homeless; stray
бездонный /bezdónnyi/ adj. bottomless
безжалостный /bezzhálostnyi/adj. merciless, ruthless
безжизненный /bezzhíznennyi/adj. feeble, lifeless

беззаботный /bezzabótnyi/ adj. carefree

беззаветный /bezzavétnyi/ adj. selfless

беззаконие /bezzakónie/ n. lawlessness

беззастенчивый /bezzasténchivyi/ adj. impudent, shameless

беззащитный /bezzashchítnyi/ adj. defenceless

беззвучный /bezzvúchnyi/ adj. soundless; silent

беззубый /bezzúbyi/ adj. toothless; impotent, harmless

безлюдный /bezliúdnyi/ adj. uninhabited

безмозглый /bezmózglyi/ adj. brainless

безмолвие /bezmólvie/ n. silence, stillness

безмятежный /bezmiatézhnyi/ adj. serene, tranquil

безнадежный /beznadiózhnyi/ adj. hopeless

безнадзорный /beznadzórnyi/ adj. uncared-for

безнаказанный /beznákazannyi/ adj. unpunished

безногий /beznógii/ adj. legless

безнравственный /beznrávstvennyi/ adj. immoral

безобидный /bezobídnyi/ adj. harmless

безоблачный /bezóblachnyi/ adj. cloudless

безобразие /bezobrázie/ n. outrage

безобразный /bezobráznyi/ adj. ugly

безоговорочный /bezogovórochnyi/ adj. unconditional, unqualified

безопасность /bezopásnost'/ f. security

безопасный /bezopásnyi/ adj. safe

безоружный /bezorúzhnyi/ adj. unarmed

безостановочный /bezostanóvochnyi/ adj. non-stop

безответственный /bezotvétstvennyi/ adj. irresponsible

безотказный /bezotkáznyi/ adj. unfailing, reliable

безотлагательный /bezotlagátel'nyi/ adj. pressing, urgent

безотчетный /bezotchótnyi/ adj. uncontrolled; unconscious

безошибочный /bezoshíbochnyi/ adj. unerring, correct

безработица /bezrabótitsa/ f. unemployment

безработный /bezrabotnyi/ m. unemployed

безразличие /bezrazlíchie/ n. indifference

безрассудный /bezrassúdnyi/ adj. reckless, rash

безудержный /bezúderzhnyi/ adj. unrestrained

безукоризненный /bezukoríznennyi/ adj. impeccable

безумец /bezúmets/ m. madman

безумие /bezúmie/ n. madness

безумный /bezúmnyi/ adj. mad

безупречный /bezupréchnyi/ adj. irreproachable, faultless

безусловный /bezuslóvnyi/ adj. absolute, indisputable, unconditional

безуспешный /bezúspeshnyi/ adj. unsuccessful

безустанный /bezustánnyi/ adj. tireless

безыдейный /bezydéinyi/ adj. lacking principles and ideals

безымянный /bezymiánnyi/ adj. nameless, anonymous; (б. палец) /b. pálets/ ring-finger

безысходный /bezyskhódnyi/ adj. hopeless, desperate

бекон /bekón/ m. bacon

белеть /belét'/ v. grow white

белизна /belizná/ f. whiteness

белила /belíla/ pl. ceruse

беличий /bélichii/ adj. squirrel

белка /bélka/ f. squirrel

беллетрист /belletríst/ m. fiction writer

беллетристика /belletrístika/ f. fiction, belles-lettres

белок /belók/ m. white (of eye, egg)

белокровие /belokróvie/ n. leukaemia

белокурый /belokúryi/ adj. fair-haired

белорус /belorús/ m. Byelorussian

белоруска /belorúska/ f. Byelorussian

белорусский /belorússkii/ adj. Byelorussian

белуга /belúga/ f. white sturgeon

белый /bélyi/ adj. white; б. медведь /b. medvéd'/. polar bear; б. свёт /b. svét/ the wide world; б. стихи /b. stikhí/ blank verse

бельгиец /bel'gíets/ m. Belgian

бельгийка /bel'gíika/ f. Belgian

бельгийский /belgíiskii/ adj. Belgian

белье /bel'ió/ n. linen; washing; нижнее б. /nízhnee b./ underwear

бельмо /bel'mó/ n. wall-eye

бельэтаж /bel'etázh/ m. dress circle

бензин /benzín/ m. petrol

бензобак /benzobák/ m. petrol tank

берег /béreg/ m. bank; shore; coast

береговой /beregovói/ adj. waterside, coastal, riverside

бережливый /berezhlívyi/ adj. thrifty

бережный /bérezhnyi/ adj. careful

береза /berióza/ f. berch

беременеть /berémenet'/ v. be(come) pregnant

беременная /berémennaia/ adj. pregnant

беречь /beréch'/ v. take care of, keep; spare

беречься /beréch'sia/ v. beware (of)

берлога /berlóga/ f. den, lair

берцовая (кость) /bertsóvaia kóst'/ adj.+f. shin-bone

бес /bés/ m. devil, demon

беседа /beséda/ f. conversation, talk

беседка /besédka/ f. summer-house

беседовать /besédovat'/ v. talk, chat

бесить /besít'/ v. enrage

беситься /besít'sia/ v. be(come) mad, furious

бесклассовый /besklássovyi/ adj. classless

бесконечность /beskonéchnost'/ f. infinity

бескорыстие /beskorýstie/ n. unselfishness

бескровный /beskróvnyi/ adj. bloodless, anaemic

беспамятный /bespámiatnyi/ adj. forgetful

беспамятство /bespámiatstvo/ n. unconsciousness

беспартийный /bespartíinyi/ adj. nonparty

бесперебойный /besperebóinyi/ adj. uninterrupted, constant

б咳пересадочный /besperesádochnyi/ adj. through, direct

бесперспективный /besperspektívnyi/ adj. without prospects; hopeless

беспечный /bespéchnyi/ adj. careless

бесплатный /besplátnyi/ adj. free

беспокоить /bespókoit'/ v. worry; trouble

бесполезный /bespoléznyi/ adj. useless

беспомощный /bespómoshchnyi/ adj. helpless

беспородный /besporódnyi/ adj. mongrel

беспорядок /besporiádok/ m. disorder

беспорядочный /besporiádochnyi/ adj. irregular; unsystematic

беспосадочный (перелет) /besposádochnyi pereliót/ adj.+m. non-stop flight

беспочвенный /bespóchvennyi/ adj. groundless

беспошлинный /bespóshlinnyi/ adj. duty-free

бесправие /besprávie/ n. lawlessness; lack of rights

бесправный /besprávnyi/ adj. without any rights

беспрекословный /besprekoslóvnyi/ adj. absolute, unquestioning

беспрерывный /besprerývnyi/ adj. continuous, ceaseless

беспрецедентный /bespretsedéntnyi/ adj. unprecedented

беспризорник /besprizórnik/ m. waif

беспризорный /besprizórnyi/ adj. homeless, neglected

беспримерный /besprimérnyi/ adj. unparalleled
беспринципный /besprintsípnyi/ adj.
unscrupulous
беспричинный /bespríchinnyi/ adj.
groundless, without motive
беспробудный (сон) /besprobúdnyi
són/ adj.+m. deep sleep
бессвязный /bessviáznyi/ adj. incoherent
бесследный /bessédnyi/ adj. without a
trace
бессменный /bessménnyi/ adj. permanent
бессмертие /bessmértie/ n. immortality
бессмысленный /bessmýslennyi/ adj.
senseless
бессмыслица /bessmýslitsa/ f. nonsense
бессовестный /bessóvestnyi/ adj. shameless; outrageous
бессодержательный /bessoderzhátel'-
nyi/ adj. empty; shallow
бессознательный /bessoznátel'nyi/ adj.
unconscious; instinctive
бессонница /bessónnitsa/ f. insomnia
бессонный /bessónnyi/ adj. sleepless
бессрочный /bessróchnyi/ adj. permanent; termless
бесстыдный /besstýdnyi/ adj. shameless
бессчетный /besschótnyi/ adj. innumerable, countless
бестактный /bestáktnyi/ adj. tactless
бестия /béstiia/ f. rogue
бестолковый /bestolkóvyi/ adj. muddle-
headed, stupid; incoherent
бесхарактерный /beskharákternyi/ adj.
weak-willed
бесхребетный /beskhrebétnyi/ adj. spineless
бесцветный /bestsvétnyi/ adj. colour-
less, insipid
бесцельный /bestsél'nyi/ adj. aimless,
pointless
бесценный /bestsénnyi/ adj. priceless

бесчеловечный /beschelovéchnyi/ adj.
inhuman
бесчестный /beschéstnyi/ adj. dishonourable
бесшабашный /besshabáshnyi/ adj. reckless
бесшумный /besshúmnyi/ adj. noiseless
бетон /betón/ m. concrete
бетономешалка /betonomeshálka/ f.
concrete-mixer
бешенство /béshenstvo/ n. rage: hydrophobia
бешеный /béshenyi/ adj. rabid, frantic;
terrific
библейский /bibléiskii/ adj. biblical
библиотека /bibliotéka/ f. library
бивень /bíven'/ m. tusk
бидон /bidón/ m. can; churn
билет /bilét/ m. ticket, pass, card;   б.
обратный /obrátnyi b./ return ticket
биллион /billión/ m. billion
бинокль /binókl'/ m. binoculars
бинт /bint/ m. bandage
биография /biográfiia/ f. biography
биржа /bírzha/ f. stock exchange
биржевой маклер /birzhevói mákler/
adj.+m. stockbroker
бирюза /biriuzá/ f.. turquoise
бис /bis/ int. encore!
бисер /bíser/ m. beads
бисквит /biskvít/ m. sponge-cake
бита /bíta/ f. bat
битва /bítva/ f. battle
битком (набитый) /bitkóm nabítyi/
adv. crammed full
биток /bitók/ m. meat ball
бить /bit'/ v. hit, beat; strike; smash
биться /bít'sia/ v. fight; beat; struggle
(with)
бифштекс /bifshtéks/ m. steak
бич /bich/ m. whip; scourge
благовещение /blagovéshchenie/ n. Annunciation
благовоние /blagovónie/ n. fragrance
благодарить /blagodarít'/ v. thank

благодаря /blagodariá/ conj. thanks to, owing to

благодушие /blagodúshie/ n. gentleness, good humour

благожелательный /blagozhelátel'nyi/ adj. well-disposed, favourable

благозвучный /blagozvúchnyi/ adj. harmonious

благонамеренный /blagonamérennyi/ adj. loyal

благополучие /blagopolúchie/ n. well-being, prosperity

благоприятный /blagopriiátnyi/ adj. favourable

благоразумие /blagorazúmie/ n. prudence, discretion

благородный /blagoródnyi/ adj. noble

благословение /blagoslovénie/ n. blessing

благословлять /blagoslovliát'/ v. bless

благотворительность /blagotvorítel'-nost'/ f. charity

благоустроенный /blagoustróennyi/ adj. comfortable

благоухание /blagoukhánie/ n. fragrance

бланк /blank/ m. form

блат /blat/ m. pull, protection

бледнеть /blednét'/ v. grow pale

блеск /blesk/ m. brilliance

блеф /blef/ m. bluff

ближайший /blizháishii/ adj. nearest, next

близко /blízko/ adv. near, close

близнец /bliznéts/ m. twin

близорукий /blizorúkii/ adj. short-sighted

близость /blízost'/ f. closeness

блин /blin/ m. pancake

блиндаж /blindázh/ m. dug-out, shelter

блок /blok/ m. bloc; pulley

блокада /blokáda/ f. blockade

блокнот /bloknót/ m. writing pad

блондин /blondín/ m. fair-haired person

блоха /blokhá/ f. flea

блуждать /bluzhdát'/ v. rove, wander

блузка /blúzka/ f. blouse

блюдечко /bliúdechko/ n. saucer

боб /bob/ m. bean

бобр /bobr/ m. beaver

бог /bog/ m. god; боже, боже мой! /bózhe moi/ int. my goodness!; ей богу! /ei bógu/ int. really and truly; сохрани бог /sokhraní bog/ God forbid!

богатеть /bogatét'/ v. grow rich

богатство /bogátstvo/ n. wealth

богатый /bogátyi/ adj. rich

богатырь /bogatýr'/ m. hero, strong man

богач /bogách/ m. rich person

богиня /bogínia/ f. goddess

богоматерь /bogomáter'/ f. Mother of God

богомолец /bogomólets/ m. pilgrim

богородица /bogoróditsa/ f. Our Lady

богослов /bogoslóv/ m. theologian

богослужение /bogosluzhénie/ n. divine service

бодать /bodát'/ v. butt

бодрствовать /bódrstvovat'/ v. keep awake

бодрый /bódryi/ adj. cheerful; active

боевик /boevík/ m. hit

боевой /boevói/ adj. battle; fighting

боеголовка /boegolóvka/ f. warhead

боеспособный /boesposóbnyi/ adj. efficient

боец /boéts/ m. figher, warrior

божественный /bozhéstvennyi/ adj. divine

божество /bozhestvó/ n. divinity

божий /bózhiy/ adj. God's; divine

бой /bói/ m. battle

бойкий /bóikii/ adj. shrewd, sharp; lively

бойкот /boikót/ m. boycott

бойня /bóinia/ f. slaughter-house; massacre

бок /bok/ m. side

бокал /bokál/ m. glass, goblet

боковой /bokovói/ adj. side; lateral

бокс /boks/ m. boxing

боксер /boksiór/ m. boxer

болван /bolván/ m. blochead, fool
болгарин /bolgárin/ m. Bulgarian
болгарка /bolgárka/ f. Bulgarian
болгарский /bolgárskii/ adj. Bulgarian
более /bólee/ adj., adv. more; более или
менее /bólee ili ménee/ more or less;
более того /bólee togó/ moreover
болезненный /boléznennyi/ adj. ailing,
unhealthy; painful
болезнь /bolézn'/ f. illness, disease
болельщик /bolél'shchik/ m. fan
болеть /bolét'/ v. be ill; ache, become
sore
болеутоляющий   /boleutoliáiushchii/
adj. sedative
болт /bolt/ m. bolt
болтать /boltát'/ v. chatter
болтун /boltún/ m. chatterrbox
боль /bol'/ f. pain
больница /bol'nitsa/ f. hospital
больше /ból'she/ adj. bigger; adv. more
большевизм /bol'shevízm/ m. Bolshevism
большинство /bol'shinstvó/ n. majority
большой /bol'shói/ adj. big, large
бомба /bómba/ f. bomb
бомбардировщик /bombardiróvshchik/
m. bomber
бомбить /bombit'/ v. bomb
бомбоубежище /bomboubézhishche/ n.
air-raid shelter
борец /boréts/ m. champion, fighter;
wrestler
боржом /borzhóm/ m. Borzhom mineral
water
борзой /borzói/ adj. borzoi; борзая
собака /borzáia sobáka/ Russian
wolfhound, greyhound
бормотать /bormotát'/ v. mumble, mutter
борода /borodá/ f. beard
бороться /borót'sia/ v. struggle, fight,
wrestle
борт /bort/ m. side (of ship); на борту /na
bortú/ on board; за бортом
/za bortóm/ overboard

бортпроводник /bortprovodnik/ m. airline steward
борщ /borshch/ m. borshch
борьба /bor'bá/ f. struggle, fight; wrestling
босиком /bosikóm/ adv. barefoot
босоножка /bosonózhka/ f. sandal
бот /bot/ m. boat
ботаник /botánik/ m. botanist
ботанический /botanícheskii/ adj. botanical
бочка /bóchka/ f. barrel
бочком /bochkóm/ adv. sideways
бочонок /bochónok/ m. cask, keg
боярышник /boiáryshnik/ m. hawthorn
бояться /boiát'sia/ v. fear, be afraid (of)
бравый /brávyi/ adj. gallant
бразилец /brazílets/ m. Brazilian
бразильский /brazíl'skii/ adj. Brazilian
бразильянка /brazil'iánka/ f. Brazilian
брак /brak/ m. marriage; spoilage, waste
браковать /brakovát'/ v. reject as defective
браконьер /brakon'er/ m. poacher
брандспойт /brandspóit/ m. fire pump;
nozzle
браслет /braslét/ m. bracelet
брасс /brass/ m. breast stroke
брат /brat/ m. brother
брать /brat'/ v. take
брачный /bráchnyi/ adj. marriage
бред /bred/ m. delirium
бредить /brédit'/ v. rave; be mad (on)
брезгать /brézgat'/ v. be squeamish (about)
брезгливый /brezglívyi/ adj. fastidious
брезент /brezént/ adj. tarpaulin
брезжить /brezzhít'/ v. glimmer
брелок /brelók/ m. pendant, charm
бретелька /bretél'ka/ f. shoulder-strap
бригада /brigáda/ f. brigade, team, crew
бригадир /brigadír/ m. brigadier, team-leader; foreman
бриллиант /brilliánt/ m. diamond
британец /británets/ m. Briton
британка /británka/ f. Briton

британский /británskii/ adj. British
бритва /brítva/ f. razor; blade
брить /brit'/ v. shave
бровь /brov'/ f. brow, eyebrow
брод /brod/ m. ford
бродить /brodít'/ v. roam, wander
бродяга /brodiága/ m. tramp
бронза /brónza/ f. bronze
бронзовый /brónzovyi/ adj. bronze
бронировать /bronírovat'/ v. reserve
    (seats)
бронировать /bronirovát'/ v. armour
броня /brónia/ f. reserved quota, reser-
    vation
броня /broniá/ f. armour
бросать /brosát'/ v. throw
броситься /brósit'sia/ v. rush, dash
брошка , брошь /bróshka, brósh/ f.
    brooch
брошюра /broshiúra/ f. booklet, pamph-
    let
брусника /brusníka/ f. cow-berry
брусок /brúsok/ m. bar
брутто /brútto/ adj., adv. gross (weight)
брызгать /brýzgat'/ v. splash, sprinkle
брыкать /brýkat'/ v. kick
брюзга /briúzga/ f. grumbler
брюква /briúkva/ f. swede
брюки /briúki/ pl. trousers
брюнет /briunét/ m. dark-haired man
брюссельская   (капуста) /briussél's-
    kaia kapústa/ adj.+f. Brussels sprouts
брюхо /briúkho/ n. belly
бряцать /briatsát'/ v. clank; jingle ; б.
    оружием /b. orúzhiem/ rattle the sabre
бубен /búben/ m. tambourine
бубенец /bubenéts/ m. bell
бугор /bugór/ m. hillock; за бугрóм /za
    bugróm/ sl. abroad
будильник /budíl'nik/ m. alarm clock
будить /budit'/ v. wake
будка /búdka/ f. booth
будто /búdto/ conj. as if, as though
будущее /búdushchee/ n. the future
будущий /búdushchii/ adj. future

буженина /buzhenína/ f. cold boiled
    pork
бузина /buziná/ f. elder (bush)
буй /búi/ m. buoy
буйвол /búivol/ m. buffalo
буйный /búinyi/ adj. wild, violent
бук /buk/ m. beech
буква /búkva/ f. letter
буквальный /bukvál'nyi/ adj. literal
букварь /bukvár'/ m. primer, ABC book
букет /bukét/ m. bouquet
букинист /bukiníst/ m. second-hand
    bookseller
буксир /buksir/ m. tugboat
булавка /bulávka/ f. pin; английская б.
    /anglíiskaia b./ safety pin
булка /búlka/ f. roll
булочка /búlochka/ f. bun
булочная /búlochnaia/ f. baker's
булыжник /bulýzhnik/ m. cobble-stone
бульвар /bul'vár/ m. avenue, boulevard
бульварная   пресса /bul'várnaia prés-
    sa/ adj.+f. gutter press
бульон /bul'ón/ m. broth, clear soup
бум /bum/ m. sensation; boom
бумага /bumága/ f. paper
бумажник /bumázhnik/ m. wallet
буран /burán/ m. snowstorm
буревестник /burevéstnik/ m. stormy
    petrel
буржуазия /burzhuazíia/ f. bourgeoisie
бурлак /burlák/ m. barge-hauler
бурный /búrnyi/ adj. stormy
бурый /búryi/ adj. greyish-brown
буря /búria/ f. storm, tempest
бутерброд /buterbród/ m. open sand-
    wich
бутон /butón/ m. bud
бутсы /bútsy/ pl. football boots
бутылка /butýlka/ f. bottle
буфер /búfer/ m. buffer, bumper
буфет /bufét/ m. sideboard; buffet, bar
буфетчик /bufétchik/ m. barman
буханка /bukhánka/ f. loaf
бухгалтер /bukhgálter/ m. accountant

бухгалтерия /bukhgaltériia/ f. book-keeping
бухта /búkhta/ f. bay
бушевать /bushevát'/ v. rage
бывалый /byvályi/ adj. experienced
бывать /byvát'/ v. be, happen; visit
бывший /bývshii/ adj. former, ex-
бык /byk/ m. bull, ox
быстрота /bystrotá/ f. speed
быстрый /býstryi/ adj. quick
быт /byt/ m. way of life
быть /byt'/ v. be
бюджет /biudzhét/ m. budget
бюллетень /biulletén'/ m. bulletin; избирательный б. /izbирátel'nyi b./ ballot-paper
бюро /biuró/ n. bureau; office
бюрократ /biurokrát/ m. bureaucrat
бюст /biust/ m. bust
бюстгальтер /biustgál'ter/ m. brassiere

В

в /v/ prep. into; within; on; at
вагон /vagón/ m. carriage, coach
вагон-ресторан /vagón-restorán/ m. restaurant-car
важничать /vázhnichat'/ v. put on airs
важность /vázhnost'/ f. importance
ваза /váza/ f. vase
вазелин /vazelín/ m. vaseline
вакансия /vakánsia/ f. vacancy
вакантный /vakántnyi/ adj. vacant
вакса /váksa/ f. (shoe) polish
вакуум /vákuum/ m. vacuum
вакцина /vaktsína/ f. vaccine
валенок /válenok/ m. felt boot
валерьянка /valer'iánka/ f. tincture of valerian
валет /valét/ m. knave, Jack
валик /válik/ m. roller
валить /valít'/ v. throw down; в. вину на другого /v. vinú na drugógo/ lump the blame on someone else

валовой /valovói/ adj. gross
валторна /valtórna/ f. French horn
валун /valún/ m. boulder
вальдшнеп /vál'dshnep/ m. woodcock
вальс /vál's/ m. waltz
вальсировать /val'sírovat'/ v. waltz
валюта /valiúta/ f. currency
валютный (курс) /valiútnyi kúrs/ adj.+m. rate of exchange
ваниль /vaníl'/ f. vanilla
ванна /vánna/ f. bath
ванная /vánnaia/ f. bathroom
варвар /várvar/ m. barbarian
варежка /várezhka/ f. mitten
варенки /variónki/ pl., sl. faded (stone-washed) jeans
вареный /variónyi/ adj. boiled
варенье /varén'e/ n. jam
вариант /variánt/ m. version
варить /varít'/ v. boil, cook
варьете /var'eté/ n. variety (show)
варьировать /var'írovat'/ v. vary
варяг /variág/ m. Varangian
василек /vasiliók/ m. cornflower
вассал /vassál/ m. vassal
вата /váta/ f. wadding; cotton wool
ватерлиния /vaterliniia/ f. water line
ватерпас /vaterpás/ m. water level
ватник /vátnik/ m. quilted jacket
ватный /vátnyi/ adj. wadded, quilted
ватрушка /vatrúshka/ f. curd tart; cheesecake
ватт /vátt/ m. watt
вафля /váflia/ f. waffle
вахта /vákhta/ f. watch
ваш /vash/ pron. your(s)
ваяние /vaiánie/ n. sculpture
вбивать /vbivát'/ v. drive or hammer in
вблизи /vblizí/ adv. closely
вброд (переходить в.) /perekhodít' vbrod/ v.+adv. ford
введение /vvedénie/ n. introduction
вверх /vverkh/ adv. up, upward(s); в. дном /v. dnom/ upside down
вверху /vverkhú/ adv. above, overhead

вверять /vveriát'/ v. entrust
ввиду /vvidú/ adv. in view (of)
вводить /vvodít'/ v. introduce; bring in
ввоз /vvoz/ m. import(s)
вволю /vvóliu/ adv. to one's heart's content
ввысь /vvys'/ adv. up, upward(s)
ввязываться /vviázyvat'sia/ v. get involved (in)
вглубь /vglub'/ adv. deep into
вдалеке /vdaleké/ adv. far off
вдаль /vdal'/ adv. into the distance
вдвое /vdvóe/ adv. double, twice; в. больше /v. ból'she/ twice as big/ as much; уменьшить в. /umén'shit' v./ halve
вдвоем /vdvóiom/ adv. the two together
вдвойне /vdvoiné/ adv. twice, double; платить в. /platit' v./ pay double
вдобавок /vdobávok/ adv. in addition (to)
вдова /vdova/ f. widow
вдовец /vdovéts/ m. widower
вдоволь /vdóvol'/ adv. in abundance, enough
вдогонку /vdogónku/ adv. in pursuit of; броситься в. /brósit'sia v./ rush after
вдоль /vdol'/ prep. along; в. и поперек /v. i poperiók/ far and wide
вдох /vdokh/ m. inhalation
вдохновение /vdokhnovénie/ n. inspiration
вдохновенный /vdokhnovénnyi/ adj. inspired
вдохновлять /vdokhnovliát'/ v. inspire
вдруг /vdrug/ adv. suddenly
вдувать /vduvát'/ v. blow into
вдумчивый /vdúmchivyi/ adj. thoughtful
вдыхать /vdykhát'/ v. breathe in
вегетарианец /vegetariánets/ m. vegetarian
ведать /védat'/ v. be in charge of; (obs.) know
ведение /védenie/ n. authority, competence

ведение /vedénie/n. conducting, running
ведомость /védomost'/ f. list, register; платежная в. /platiózhnaia v./ pay-roll
ведомственный /védomstvennyi/ adj. departmental
ведомство /védomstvo/ n. department
ведро /vedró/ n. bucket
ведущий /vedúshchii/ adj. leading, basic
ведь /ved'/ conj. you see, you know; why, well
ведьма /véd'ma/ f. witch
веер /véer/ m. fan
вежливый /vézhlivyi/ adj. polite
везде /vezdé/ adv. everywhere
везти /veztí/ v. carry, drive; have luck
век /vek/ m. age; century; lifetime; на моем веку /na moióm vekú/ in my lifetime
веко /véko/ m. eyelid
вековой /vekovói/ adj. age-old
вексель /véksel'/ m. bill of exchange
велеть /velét'/ v. order, command
великан /velikán/ m. giant
великий /velikii/ adj. great
великодержавный /velikoderzhávnyi/ adj. great-power
великодушный /velikodúshnyi/ adj. magnanimous
великолепный /velikolépnyi/ adj. magnificent
великоросс /velikoróss/ m. Great Russian
великорусский /velikorússkii/ adj. Great Russian
величавый /velichávyi/ adj. stately, majestic
величественный /velichestvennyi/ adj. majestic
величество /velíchestvo/ majesty; ваше в. /váshe v./ Your Majesty
величие /velíchie/ n. grandeur, greatness
величина /velichiná/ f. size
велогонка /velogónka/ f. cycle race
велосипед /velosipéd/ m. bicycle, cycle
велосипедист /velosipedíst/ m. cyclist

вельвет /vel'vét/ m. corduroy
вена /véna/ f. vein
венгерка /vengérka/ f. Hungarian
венгерский /vengérskii/ adj. Hungarian
венгр /vengr/ m. Hungarian
венерический /venerícheskii/ adj. venereal
веник /vénik/ m. broom
венок /venók/ m. wreath, garland
вентилятор /ventiliátor/ m. ventilator, fan
вентиляция /ventiliátsia/ f. ventilation
венчание /venchánie/ n. wedding ceremony
вепрь /vepr'/ m. wild boar
вера /verá/ f. faith, belief
веранда /veránda/ f. veranda
верба /vérba/ f. willow
верблюд /verbliúd/ m. camel
вербное воскресенье /vérbnoe voskresénie/ adj.+n. Palm Sunday
вербовать /verbovát'/ v. recruit
веревка /verióvka/ f. rope, string
вереница /verenítsa/ f. row, file
вереск /verésk/ m. heather
верить /verít'/ v. believe; я не верю своим ушам /iá ne vériu svoím ushám/ I can't believe my ears
вермишель /vermishél'/ f. vermicelli
верноподданный /vernopóddannyi/ m. loyal subject
верность /vérnost'/ f. faithfulness, loyality
вероисповедание /veroispovedánie/ n. religion; creed
вероломный /verolómnyi/ adj. perfidious, treacherous
веротерпимость / veroterpímost'/ f. tolerance
вероятно /veroiátno/ adv. probably
вероятность /veroiátnost'/ f. probability
вероятный /veroiátnyi/ adj. probable
версия /vérsiia/ f. version
вертеть /vertét'/ v. turn, twist

вертикальный /vertikál'nyi/ adj. vertical
вертолет /vertoliót/ m. helicopter
верующий /veruiúshchii/ m. believer
верфь /verf'/ f. shipyard
верх /verkh/ m. top; summit
верховая (езда) /verkhováia ezdá/ adj.+f.riding
верховный /verkhóvnyi/ adj. supreme
верховье /verkhóv'e/ n. upper reachers
верхом /verkhóm/ adv. on horseback
вершина /vershína/ f. summit, peak
вес /ves/ m. weight
веселить /veselít'/ v. cheer, gladden
веселиться /veselít'sia/ v. enjoy oneself, be merry
веселый /vesiólyi/ adj. gay, merry
весенний /vesénnii/ adj. spring
весить /vésit'/ v. weigh
веский /véskii/ adj. weighty
весло /véslo/ n. oar
весна /vesná/ f. spring
веснушки /vesnúshki/ pl. freckles
вести /vestí/ v. lead, guide; в. себя /v. sebia/ behave
вестибюль /vestibiúl'/ m. entrance hall
вестник /véstnik/ m. messenger; bulletin
весть /vést'/ f. news
весы /vesý/ pl. scales
весь /ves'/ pron. all, whole
весьма /ves'má/ adv. very, extremely
ветвистый /vetvístyi/ adj. branchy
ветер /véter/ m. wind
ветеринар /veterínar/ m. veterinary surgeon
ветерок /veterók/ m. breeze
ветка /vétka/ f. branch, twig
вето /véto/ n. veto
ветошь /vétosh/ f. rags
ветреный /vétrenyi/ adj. windy; flippant
ветхий /vétkhii/ adj. old, dilapidated
ветчина /vetchiná/ f. ham
веха /vékha/ f. landmark
вечер /vécher/ m. evening
вечеринка /vecherínka/ f. party
вечность /véchnost'/ f. eternity.

вечный /véchnyi/ adj. eternal; perpetual

вешалка /véshalka/ f. peg, rack

вещественный /veshchéstvennyi/ adj. material

вещество /veshchestvó/ n. substance

вещь /veshch/ f. thing

веялка /véialka/ f. winnowing machine

взад /vzad/ adv. back (wards); в. и вперед /v. i vperiód/ back and forth

взаимность /vzaímnost'/ f. reciprocity

взаимовыгодный /vzaimovýgodnyi/ adj. mutually advantageous

взаймы /vzaimý/ adv.: брать в. /brat' v./ borrow; давать в. /davát' v./ lend

взамен /vzamén/ adv. instead of

взбалмошный /vzbálmoshnyi/ adj. extravagant

взбалтывать /vzbáltyvat'/ v. shake up

взбегать /vzbegát'/ v. run up

взбивать /vzbivát'/ v. beat up; shake up

взбираться /vzbirát'sia/ v. climb up

взвешивать /vzvéshivat'/ v. weigh, weigh up

взвизгивать /vzvízgivat'/ v. scream, yelp

взвинчивать /vzvínchivat'/ v. excite; inflate (prices)

взвод /vzvod/ m. platoon

взволнованный /vzvolnóvannyi/ adj. excited

взгляд /vzgliad/ m. look, stare; на мой в. /na moi v./ in my opinion; на первый в. /na pérvyi v./ at first sight

взгромоздиться /vzgromozdít'sia/ v. clamber

вздор /vzdor/ m. nonsense

вздох /vzdokh/ m. sigh

вздрагивать /vzdrágivat'/ v. shudder

вздремнуть /vzdrémnut'/ v. nap

вздутие /vzdútie/ n. swelling

вздымать /vzdymát'/ v. raise

вздыхать /vzdykhát'/ v. sigh; pine (for)

взламывать /vzlámyvat'/ v. break open

взлет /vzliot/ m. flight, take-off

взлохмаченный /vzlokhmáchennyi/ adj. dishevelled

взмах /vzmakh/ m. flap, wave (of hand)

взмахивать /vzmákhivat'/ v. flap, wave

взморье /vzmór'e/ n. seaside

взнос /vznos/ m. payment, dues

взор /vzor/ m. look, gaze

взрослый /vzróslyi/ m. adult

взрыв /vzryv/ m. explosion; outburst

взрывать /vzryvát'/ v. blow up

взъерошенный /vz"eróshennyi/ adj. dishevelled

взывать /vzyvát'/ v. appeal (to)

взыскание /vzyskánie/ n. penalty

взять /vziat'/ v. take

взятка /vziátka/ f. bribe

вибрация /vibrátsiia/ f. vibration

вид /vid/ m. sight, view; appearance, look; kind, sort; иметь в виду /imet' v vid'u/ bear in mind; терять из виду /teriát' iz vídu/ lose sight of

видеокассета /videokasséta/ f. video cassette

видеомагнитофон /videomagnitofón/ m. video recorder

видеть /vídet'/ v. see

видимость /vídimost'/ f. visibility; outward appearance

виднеться /vidnét'sia/ v. be visible

видный /vídnyi/ adj. visible; eminent

видоизменение /vidoizменénie/ n. modification

виза /víza/ f. visa

византийский /vizantíiskii/ adj. Byzantine

визг /vizg/ m. scream

визит /vizít/ m. visit

визитная (карточка) /vizítnaia kártochka/ adj.+f. visiting card

викторина /viktorína/ f. quiz

вилка /vílka/ f. fork; electric plug

вилы /víly/ pl. pitchfork

вилять /viliát'/ v. wag; prevaricate

вина /viná/ f. fault, guilt

винегрет /vinegrét/ m. Russian salad

винительный (падеж) /vinítel'nyi pad+ézh/ adj.+m. accusative (case)

винить /vinít'/ v. blame (for)

винный /vínnyi/ adj. wine; в. камень /v. kámen'/ tartar; винная ягода /vinnaia iagoda/ dried figs

вино /vinó/ n. wine

виноватый /vinovátyi/ adj. guilty (of)

виновник /vinóvnik/ m. culprit

виноград /vinográd/ m. vine; grapes

виноградарство /vinográdarstvo/ n. winegrowing

виноградник /vinográdnik/ m. vineyard

виноделие /vinodélie/ n. winemaking

виноторговец /vinotorgóvets/ m. wine merchant

винт /vint/ m. screw

винтовка /vintóvka/ f. rifle

винтовой /vintovói/ adj. screw; spiral; винтовая лестница /vintováia léstnitsa/ spiral stairs

виолончель /violonchél'/ f. cello

виртуоз /virtuóz/ m. virtuoso

вирус /vírus/ m. virus

вирусный /vírusnyi/ adj. virus

виселица /víselitsa/ f. gallows

висеть /visét'/ v. hang

виски /víski/ n. whisky

вискоза /viskóza/ f. viscose

висмут /vísmut/ m. bismuth

виснуть /vísnut'/ v. hang

висок /visók/ m. temple

високосный /visokósnyi/ adj.: в. год /v. god/ leapyear

вист /vist/ m. whist

висячий /visiáchii/ adj. hanging; в. замок /v. zamók/ padlock; в. мост /v. most/ suspension bridge

витамин /vitamín/ m. vitamin

витрина /vitrína/ f. shopwindow

вить /vit'/ v. twist, weave

вихрь /vikhr'/ m. whirlwind

вице-адмирал /vítse-admirál/ m. vice-admiral

вице-президент /vítse-president/ m. vice-president

вишневый /vishnióvyi/ adj. cherry

вишня /vishniá/ f. cherry

вкалывать /vkályvat'/ v. stick in; work hard

вкатывать /vkátyvat'/ v. roll in

вклад /vklad/ m. contribution (to); deposit (in bank)

вкладчик /vkládchik/ m. depositor

вклеивать /vkléivat'/ v. glue in, stick in

вколачивать /vkoláchivat'/ v. drive or hammer in

вконец /vkonéts/ adv. completely

вкрадчивый /vkrádchivyi/ adj. ingratiating

вкратце /vkráttse/ adv. briefly

вкривь и вкось /vkriv' i vkos'/ adv. pellmell; amiss

вкрутую (яйцо в.) /iaitsó vkrutúiu/ n.+adv. hard-boiled egg

вкус /vkus/ m. taste

влага /vlága/ f. moisture

владелец /vladélets/ m. owner, proprietor

владение /vladénie/ n. ownership, possession; property

владеть /vladét'/ v. own, possess

владыка /vladýka/ m. lord, sovereign

владычество /vladýchestvo/ n. rule, sway

влажность /vlázhnost'/ f. humidity

влажный /vlázhnyi/ adj. humid, damp

вламываться /vlámyvat'sia/ v. break into

властвовать /vlástvovat'/ v. hold sway (over)

властелин /vlastelín/ m. ruler, master

властный /vlástnyi/ adj. imperious, commanding

власть /vlast'/ f. power, authority

влево /vlévo/ adv. to the left

влезать /vlezát'/ v. climb in, into, up

влечение /vlechénie/ n. inclination, attraction

вливать /vlivát'/ v. pour in

влияние /vliiánie/ n. influence

влиятельный /vliiátel'nyi/ adj. influential

влиять /vliiát'/ v. affect, have influence (on)

вложение /vlozhénie/ n. enclosure; investment

влюбленный /vliublió nnyi/ m. lover
влюбляться /vliubliát'sia/ v. fall in love (with)
вменяемый /vmeniáemyi/ adj. responsible, liable
вместе /vméste/ adv. together; в. с тем /v. s tem/ at the same time
вместимость /vmestímost'/ f. capacity
вместо /vmésto/ prep. instead of
вмешательство /vmeshátel'stvo/ n. interference, intervention
вмещать /vmeshchát'/ v. contain, accomodate
вмиг /vmig/ adv. in an instant
вмятина /vmiátina/ f. dent
внаем /vnaióm/ adv.; отдáть в. /otdát' v./ let, hire out; взять в. /vziat' v./ hire, rent
вначале /vnachále/ adv. at first
вне /vne/ prep. outside, out of
внебрачный /vnebráchnyi/ adj. extramarital; illegitimate
внедрение /vnedrénie/ n. introduction
внедрять /vnedriát'/ v. introduce; inculcate
внезапный /vnezapnyi/ adj. sudden
внеклассный /vneklássnyi/ adj. out of school; extra-curricular
внеочередной /vneocherednói/ adj. extraordinary
внешний /vnéshnii/ adj. outer, external; внешняя политика /vnéshniaia politika/ foreign policy
вниз /vniz/ adv. down (wards)
внизу /vnizú/ adv. below, at the bottom
вникать /vnikát'/ go carefully (into)
внимание /vnimánie/ n. attention
внимательный /vnimátel'nyi/ adj. attentive
вничью (сыграть в.) /sygrát' vnich'iú/ draw (a game)
вновь /vnov'/ adv. again; newly
вносить /vnosít'/ v. carry or bring in; contribute
внук /vnuk/ m. grandson

внутренний /vnútrennii/ adj. inner, internal
внутренности /vnútrennosti/ pl. internal organs
внутри /vnutrí/ adv. inside, within
внутрь /vnutr'/ adv. into
внучка /vnuchka/ f. granddaughter
внушать /vnushát'/ v. inspire; в. ему уважение /v. emú uvazhénie/ fill him with respect
внушительный /vnushítel'nyi/ adj. impressive
внятный /vniátnyi/ adj. distinct
вовлекать /vovlekát'/ v. involve
вовремя /vóvremia/ adv. in time
вовсе /vóvse/ adv. completely, quite; вовсе не/vóvse ne/ not at all
вовсю /vovsiú/ adv. with all one's might
во-вторых /vo-vtorýkh/ adv. second(ly)
вогнутый /vógnutyi/ adj. concave
вода /vodá/ f. water
водворять /vodvoriát'/ v. settle, install, establish
водевиль /vodevíl'/ m. musical comedy
водитель /voditel'/ m. driver
водить /vodít'/ v. lead, conduct; drive
водка /vódka/ f. vodka
водный /vódnyi/ adj. water
водобоязнь /vodoboiázn'/ f. hydrophobia
водоворот /vodovorót/ m. whirlpool
водоем /vodoióm/ m. water body
водоизмещение /vodoizmeshchénie/ n. displacement
водолаз /vodoláz/ m. diver; Newfoundland (dog)
водонепроницаемый /vodonepronitsáemyi/ adj. waterproof
водопад /vodopád/ m. waterfall
водопровод /vodoprovód/ m. water pipe
водопроводчик /vodoprovódchik/ m. plumber
водород /vodoród/ m. hydrogen
водоросль /vódorosl'/ f. seaweed
водосточная (труба) /vodostóchnaia trubá/ adj.+f. drainpipe

водохранилище /vodokhranílishche/ n. reservoir

водружать /vodruzhát'/ v. hoist, erect

воевать /voevát'/ v. wage war

военачальник /voenachál'nik/ m. military leader

военно-воздушный/voénno-vozdúshnyi/ adj. air-force

военно-морской /voénno-morskói/ adj. naval

военнопленный /voennoplénnyi/ m. prisoner-of-war

военно-полевой (суд) /voénno-polevói sud/ adj.+m.court-martial

военнослужащий /voennoslúzhashchii/ m. serviceman

военный /voénnyi/ adj. military, war

военное положение /voénnoe polozh+énie/ adj.+n.. martial law

вожак /vozhák/ m. leader

вожатый /vozhátyi/ m. Young Pioneer leader

вождь /vozhd'/ m. leader

воз /voz/ m. cartload

возбудимый /vozbudímyi/ adj. excitable

возбуждать /vozbuzhdát'/ v. excite, arouse

возведение /vozvédenie/ n. raising, erection

возвеличивать /vozvelíchivat'/ v. glorify, exalt

возвещать /vozveshchát'/ n. announce, proclaim

возврат /vozvrát/ m. return, repayment

возвышать /vozvyshát'/ v. raise, elevate

возглавлять /vozglavliát'/ v. head

возглас /vózglas/ m. exclamation

возгораемый /vozgoráemyi/ adj. inflammable

воздавать /vozdavát'/ v. reward

воздвигать /vozdvigát'/ v. erect

воздействие /vozdéistvie/ n. influence

воздействовать /vozdéistvovat'/ v. have influence (on)

возделывать /vozdélyvat'/ v. till, cultivate

воздержание /vozderzhánie/ n. abstention, temperance

воздерживаться /vozdérzhivat'sia/ v. abstain, refrain (from)

воздух /vózdukh/ m. air

воздушный /vozdúshnyi/ adj. air; в. шар /v. shar/ balloon

воззвание /vozzvánie/ n. apeal, manifesto

возить /vozít'/ v. carry, drive, transport

возлагать /vozlagát'/ v. lay, place; в. надежду на /v. nadézhdu na/ place hopes on

возле /vózle/ adv. near

возлюбленный /vozliúblennyi/ adj. beloved

возмездие /vozmézdie/ n. retribution

возмещать /vozmeshchát'/ v. compensate

возможно /vozmózhno/ adv. possibly

возможность /vozmózhnost'/ f. possibility

возмужалый /vozmuzhályi/ adj. mature

возмутительный /vozmútitel'nyi/ adj. disgraceful, scandalous

вознаграждать /voznagrazhdát'/ v. reward

вознесение /voznesénie/ n. Ascension (Day)

возникать /voznikát'/ v. arise, crop up

возня /vozniá/ f. fuss

возобновлять /vozobnovliát'/ v. renew, resume

возражать /vozrazhát'/ v. object (to)

возражение /vozrazhénie/ n. objection

возраст /vózrast/ age; в возрасте пяти лет /v vózraste piatí let/ at the age of 5

возрождать /vozrozhdát'/ v. revive

возрождение /vozrozhdénie/ n. Renaissance

воин /vóin/ m. soldier, warrior

воинский /vóinskii/ adj. military, martial; воинская повинность /voinskaia povinnost'/ conscription воинственный /voínstvennyi/ adj. martial, bellicose

вой /voi/ m. howl

войлок /vóilok/ m. thick felt

война /voiná/ f. war

войско /vóisko/ n. army, troops

вокальный /vokál'nyi/ adj. vocal

вокзал /vokzál/ m. railroad station

вокруг /vokrúg/ adv. (a)round

вол /vol/ m. ox

волан /volán/ m. flounce; shuttlecock

волдырь /voldýr'/ m. blister

волевой /volevói/ adj. strong-willed

волейбол /voleiból/ m. volleyball

волей-неволей /vólei-nevólei/ adv. willy-nilly

волжский /vólzhskii/ adj. (on the) Volga

волк /volk/ m. wolf

волкодав /volkodáv/ m. wolfhound

волна /volná/ f. wave

волнение /volnénie/ n. excitement

волноваться /volnovát'sia/ v. be excited

волокита /volokíta/ f. red tape

волокнистый /voloknístyi/ adj. fibrous

волокно /voloknó/ n. fibre

волос /vólos/ m. hair

волосатый /volosátyi/ adj. hairy

волхв /volkhv/ m. wizard, magician

волчий /vólchii/ adj. wolf, lupine

волчица /volchítsa/ f. she-wolf

волчок /volchók/ m. top (toy)

волчонок /volchónok/ m. wolf cub

волшебник /volshébnik/ m. magician; wizard

волшебный /volshébnyi/ adj. magic, fairy

волшебство /volshebstvó/ n. magic, enchantment

вольно! /vól'no/ adv. stand at ease

вольнодумец /vol'nodúmets/ m. freethinker

вольность /vól'nost'/ f. liberty, freedom

вольный /vól'nyi/ adj. free, unrestricted

вольт /vol't/ m. volt

воля /vólia/ f. will; freedom

вон /von/ adv. away; over there; пошел вон! /poshól von/ go away!

вонзать /vonzát'/ v. thrust, plunge

вонь /von'/ f. stink

вонючий /voniúchii/ adj. stinking

вонять /voniát'/ v. stink

воображать /voobrazhát'/ v. imagine

воображение /voobrazhénie/ n. imagination

вообразимый /voobrazímyi/ adj. imaginable

вообще /voobshché/ adv. in general

воодушевление /voodushevlénie/ n. enthusiasm

воодушевлять /voodushevliát'/ v. inspire

вооружать /vooruzhát'/ v. arm

вооружение /vooruzhénie/ n. armament; arms

воочию /voóchiiu/ adv. with one's own eyes

во-первых /vo-pérvykh/ adv. first(ly)

вопить /vopít'/ v. howl; yell

вопиющая несправедливость /vopii+úshchaya nespravedlívost'/ adj.+f. crying injustice

воплощать /voploshchát'/ v. embody

воплощение /voploshchénie/ n. incarnation

вопль /vopl'/ m. wail, cry

вопреки /vorpekí/ prep. in spite of

вопрос /voprós/ m. question

вопросительный /voprosítel'nyi/ adj. interrogative; в. знак /v. znak/ question mark

вор /vor/ m. thief

ворковать /vorkovát'/ v. coo

воробей /vorobéi/ m. sparrow

воровать /vorovát'/ v. steal

ворожить /vorozhít'/ v. tell fortunes

ворон /vóron/ m. raven

ворона /voróna/ f. crow

вороненый /voroniónyi/ adj. blued; вороненая сталь /voroniónaia stal'/ blue steel

воронка /vorónka/ f. funnel; crater

вороной /voronói/ adj. black

ворота /voróta/ pl. gate(s)

воротник /vorotník/ m. collar

ворох /vórokh/ m. pile, heap

ворочать /voróchat'/ v. move, turn

ворошить /voroshít'/ v. stir, turn

ворс /vors/ m. pile

ворчать /vorchát'/ v. grumble

восемнадцать /vosemnádtsat'/ num. eighteen

восемь /vósem'/ num. eight

восемьдесят /vósem'desiat/ num. eighty

восемьсот /vosem'sót/ num. eight hundred

воск /vosk/ m. wax

восклицание /vosklitsánie/ n. exclamation

восклицательный /vosklitsatel'nyi/ adj. exclamatory

восклицать /vosklitsát'/ v. exclaim

восковой /voskovói/ adj. wax(en)

воскресенье /voskresén'e/ n. Sunday

воскрешать /voskreshát'/ v. revive, resuscitate

воспаление /vospalénie/ n. inflammation; в. легких /v. liógkikh/ pneumonia

воспаленный /vospaliónnyi/ adj. inflamed

воспитание /vospitánie/ n. upbringing, education

воспоминание /vospominánie/ n. recollection

восприимчивый /vospriímchivyi/ adj. susceptible (to)

воспринимать /vosprinimát'/ v. take (up); conceive

воспроизведение /vosproizvedénie/ n. reproduction

воспроизводить /vosproizvodít'/ v. reproduce

воспрянуть /vosprίanut'/ v. cheer up

воссоединение /vossoedinénie/ n. reunification

воссоединять /vossoediniát'/ v. reunite

воссоздавать /vossozdavát'/ v. recreate

восстанавливать /vosstanávlivat'/ v. restore

восстание /vosstánie/ n. insurrection

восстановление /vosstanovlénie/ n. restoration, reconstruction

восток /vostók/ m. east, orient

востоковед /vostokovéd/ m. orientalist

восторг /vostórg/ m. delight, rapture

восточный /vostóchnyi/ adj. eastern, oriental

востребование (до востребования) /do vostrébovaniia/ poste restante

восхваление /voskhvalénie/ n. praising, eulogy

восхвалять /voskhvaliát'/ v. praise, extol

восхитительный /voskhitítel'nyi/ adj. delightful

восхищение /voskhishchénie/ n. delight

восход /voskhód/ m.sunrise

восшествие (на престол) vosshéstvie na prestól/ n.+prep.+m. accession to the throne

восьмигранник /vos'migránnik/ m. octahedron

вот /vot/ part. here (is)

вотум /vótum /m. vote; в. (не)доверия /v. (ne)dovériia/ vote of (no)confidence

вошь /vosh/ f. louse

воюющий /voiúiushchii/ adj. belligerent

впадать /vpadát'/ v. fall in(to)

впервые /vpervýe/ adv. for the first time

вперед /vperiód/ adv. forward, ahead; часы идут в. /chasý idút v./ the clock isfast; платить в. /platít' v./ pay in advance

впереди /vperedí/ adv. in front (of), before

вперемежку /vperemézhku/ adv. alternately

впечатление /vpechatlénie/n. impression

впечатлительный /vpechatlítel'nyi/ adj. sensitive

вписывать /vpísyvat'/ v. enter, insert

впитывать /vpítyvat'/ v. absorb

вплавь /vplav'/ adv. by swimming

вплетать /vpletát'/ v. plait (into)
вплотную /vplotnúiu/ adv. close by
вплоть до /vplot' do/ adv. (right) up to
вполголоса /vpolgólosa/ adv. in a low voice
вползать /vpolzat'/ v. creep or crawl in (to)
вполне /vpolné/ adv. quite, fully
впопыхах /vpopykhákh/ adv. in a hurry
впору /vpóru/ adv. just right
впоследствии /vposlédstvii/ adv. subsequently; afterwards
впотьмах /vpot'mákh/ adv. in the dark
вправе (быть в.) /byt' vpráve/ have the right
вправо /vprávo/ adv. to the right
впредь /vpred'/ adv. henceforth
вприпрыжку /vpriprýzhku/ adv. hopping, skipping
вприсядку (плясать в.) /pliasát' vprisi÷ádku/ v.+adv. dance squatting
впроголодь /vprógolod'/ adv. half-starving
впрок /vprok/ adv. in store
впросак (попасть в.) /popást' vprosák/ v.+adv. make a fool of oneself
впрочем /vpróchem/ conj. however
впрыгивать /vprýgivat'/ v. jump in (to)
впрыскивание /vprýskivanie/n. injection
впрягать /vpriagát'/ v. harness
впрямь /vpriam'/ adv. really
впускать /vpuskát'/ v. let in, admit
впустую /vpustúiu/ adv. to no purpose
впутывать /vpútyvat'/ v. entangle
враг /vrag/ m. enemy
вражда /vrazhdá/ f. enmity
враждебный /vrazhdébnyi/ adj. hostile
вразброд /vrazbród/ adv. separately, in disunity
вразвалку (ходить в.) /khodít' vrazválku/ v.+adv. waddle
вразрез /vrazréz/ adv.; идти в. /idti v./ be contrary (to)
вразумительный /vrazumítel'nyi/ adj. intelligible
вранье /vran'ió/ n. lies, nonsense
врасплох /vrasplókh/ adv. unawares

врассыпную /vrassypnúiu/ adv. in all directions
врастать /vrastát'/ v. grow in (to), take root in
вратарь /vratar'/ m. goalkeeper
врать /vrat'/ m. lie
врач /vrach/ m. doctor
врачебный /vrachébnyi/ adj. medical
вращать /vrashchát'/ v. turn, rotate; в. глазамиЁ /v. glazami/ roll one's eyes
вред /vred/ m. harm
вредитель /vredítel'/ m. pest; saboteur
вредить /vredít'/ v. harm, damage
вредный /vrédnyi/ adj. harmful
врезать /vrezát'/ v. cut in (to)
временной /vremennói/ adj. temporal
временный /vrémennyi/ adj. temporary
время /vrémia/ n. time; в то в. как /v to v. kak/ whilst; за последнее в. /za poslédnee v./ recently; временами /vremenámi/ (every) now and then; сколько времени? /skól'ko vremeni/ What's the time?
вроде /vróde/ adv. like; such as
врожденный /vrozhdiónnyi/ adj. innate
врозь /vroz'/ adv. separately, apart
врукопашную /vrukopáshnuiu/ adv. hand to hand
врун /vrun/ m. liar
вручать /vruchát'/ v. hand over, deliver
вручение /vruchénie/ n. presentation
вручную /vruchnuiu/ adv. by hand
врываться /vryvát'sia/ v. burst in (to)
вряд ли /vriád li/ adv. hardly
всадник /vsádnik/ m. rider
всаживать /vsázhivat'/ v. stick or thrust in
всасывать /vsásyvat'/ v. suck in
всевозможный /vsevozmózhnyi/ adj. of all kinds of
всевышний /vsevýshnii/ m. the Most High
всегда /vsegdá/ adv. always
всего /vsevó/ adv. in all
вселенная /vselénnaia/ f. universe
вселяться /vseliát'sia/ v. move in (to)
всемерный /vsemérnyi/ adj. utmost

всемирный /vsemírnyi/ adj. world, universal

всемогущество /vsemogúshchestvo/ n. omnipotence

всенародный /vsenaródnyi/ adj. national, nationwide

всенощная /vsénoshchnaia/ f. Vespers

всеобщий /vseóbshchii/ adj. general, universal

всеобъемлющий /vseob'émliushchii/ adj. all-emgracing

всероссийский /vserossíiskii/ adj. all-Russian

всерьез /vser'ióz/ adv. in earnest, seriously

всесоюзный /vsesoiúznyi/ adj. all-Union

всесторонний /vsestoronnii/ adj. all-round

все-таки /vsió-takí/ conj. and part. nevertheless

всеуслышание (во в.) /vo vseuslýshanie/ n. for all to hear; in public

всецело /vsetsélo/ adv. entirely, wholly

вскакивать /vskákivat'/ v. leap up (into, on to; from)

вскармливать /vskármlivat'/ v. rear, nurse

вскачь /vskach/ adv. at full gallop

вскидывать /vskídyvat'/ v. throw up

вскользь /vskol'z'/ adv. casually, in passing

вскоре /vskóre/ adv. soon, before long

вскружить (голову) /vskruzhít' gólovu/ v.+f. turn someone's head

вскрывать /vskrývat'/ v. open; reveal

всласть /vslast'/ adv. to one's heart's content

вслед /vsled/ adv. (right) after; following

вследствие /vslédstvie/ adv. in consequence of

вслепую /vslepúiu/ adv. blindly, at random

вслух /vslukh/ adv. aloud

всмятку (яйцо в.) /iaitsó vsmiátku/ n.+adv. soft-boiled egg

всплеск /vsplesk/ m. splash

всплывать /vsplývat'/ v. rise to the surface; emerge

вспоминать /vspominát'/ v. remember, recall

вспорхнуть /vsporkhnút'/ v. fly up

вспыхивать /vspýkhivat'/ v. flash; blush

вставать /vstavát'/ v. stand up; get up

вставной /vstavnói/ adj. double (windows); false (teeth)

встревоженный /vstrevózhennyi/ adj. alarmed

встрепенуться /vstrepenút'sia/ v. rouse oneself

встречаться /vstrechát'sia/ v. meet; occur, happen

встреча /vstrécha/ f. meeting

встряска /vstriáska/ f. shock

вступать /vstupát'/ v. enter; join

вступительный /vstupítel'nyi/ adj. entrance, introductory

всхлипывать /vskhlípyvat'/ v. sob

всходы /vskhódy/ pl. (corn) shoots

всюду /vsiúdu/ adv. everywhere

всякий /vsiákii/ adj. any

всяческий /vsiácheskii/ adj. all kinds of; sundry

втайне /vtáine/ adv. in secret

втирать /vtirát'/ v. rub in

втихомолку /vtikhomólku/ adv. on the quiet

вторгаться /vtorgát'sia/ v. invade, penetrate

вторник /vtórnik/ m. Tuesday

второпях /vtoropiákh/ adv. in a hurry

второстепенный /vtorostepénnyi/ adj. secondary

в-третьих /v-trét'ikh/ adv. third(ly)

втридорога /vtrídoroga/ adv. at an exorbitant price; втрое /vtróe/ adv. three times; втроем /vtroióm/ adv. three together; втройне /vtroiné/ adv. three times as much

втулка /vtúlka/ f. plug

втягивать /vtiágivat'/ v. draw in

вуаль /vuál'/ f. veil

вуз /vuz/ abbr. m. higher educational institution

вулкан /vulkán/ m. volcano

вульгарный /vul'gárnyi/ adj. vulgar

вход /vkhod/ m. entrance

входить /vkhodít'/ v. go in, enter

входной /vkhodnói/ adj. entrance, admission

вчера /vcherá/ adv. yesterday

вчетверо /vchétvero/ adv. four times (as...)

вчитываться /vchítyvat'sia/ v. read carefully

вшивать /vshivát'/ v. sew in (to)

вшивый /vshívyi/ adj. lousy

вширь /vshir'/ adv. in breadth

въезд /v"ezd/ m. entrance

въезжать /v"ezzhat'/ drive in

вы /vy/ pron. you

выбалтывать /vybáltyvat'/ v. blurt, let out

выбегать /vybegát'/ v. run out

выбивать /vybivát'/ v. knock out

выбирать /vybirát'/ v. choose; elect

выбор /výbor/ m. choice; selection; option; всеобщие выборы /vseóbshchie výbory/ general election

выбрасывать /vybrásyvat'/ v. throw out

выбывать /vybyvat'/ v. leave, quit

вываливать /vyválivat'/ v. throw out

выведывать /vyvédyvat'/ v. find out

вывертывать /vyviórtyvat'/ v. unscrew

вывеска /výveska/ f. sign (board)

вывешивать /vyvéshivat'/ v. hang out, put up

вывинчивать /vyvínchivat'/ v. unscrew

вывих /vývikh/ m. dislocation

вывихнуть /vývikhnut'/ v. sprain

вывод /vývod/ m. withdrawal; conclusion

выводить /vyvodít'/ v. take out; remove; hatch, grow; conclude, infer

вывоз /vývoz/ m. export(s)

выгадывать /vygádyvat'/ v. gain, save

выгиб /výgib/ m. arch, curve

выглядеть /výgliadet'/ v. look, appear

выглядывать /vygliádyvat'/ v. look out, peep out

выговаривать /vygovárivat'/ v. pronounce; rebuke

выгода /výgoda/ f. advantage; profit

выгон /výgon/ m. pasture

выгонять /vygoniát'/ v. drive out

выгружать /vygruzhát'/ v. unload

выдавать /vydavát'/ v. hand out, distribute; betray; extradite

выдавливать /vydávlivat'/ v. squeeze out

выдалбливать /vydálblivat'/ v. hol low out

выдача /výdacha/ f. delivery, distribution, payment; extradition

выдвигать /vydvigát'/ v. put forward, propose, promote

выдворять /vydvoriát'/ v. evict

выделка /výdelka/ f. manufacture; workmanship

выделять /vydeliát'/ v. pick out; detach; allot; emphasize; apportion; secrete

выдергивать /vydiórgivat'/ v. pull out

выдержанный /výderzhannyi/ adj. self-possessed; ripe, seasoned

выдерживать /vydérzhivat'/ v. sustain; pass (exams.)

выдержка /výderzhka/ f. self-control; exposure (phot.)

выдирать /vydirát'/ v. tear out

выдох /výdokh/ m. exhalation

выдра /výdra/ f. otter

выдувать /vyduvát'/ v. blow out

выдумка /výdumka/ f. invention

выдыхать /vydykhát'/ v. breathe out

выдыхаться /vydykhát'sia/ v. become stale; exhaust oneself

выезд /výezd/ m. departure; exit

выезжать /vyezzhát'/ v. leave, depart; drive or ride out

выживать /vyzhivát'/ v. survive

выжигать /vyzhigát'/ v. burn out

выжидать /vyzhidát'/ v. wait for or till

выжимать /vyzhimát'/ v. squeze out

выздоравливать /vyzdorávlivat'/ v. recover

вызов /výzov/ m. call; challenge

вызревать /vyzrevát'/ v. ripen

вызубривать /vyzúbrivat'/ v. learn by rote

вызывать /vyzyvát'/ v. call, summon; rouse; evoke

выигрывать /vyígryvat'/ v. win

выигрыш /výigrysh/ m. benefit, gain

выигрышный /vʌýigryshnyi/ adj. advantageous, profitable

выкапывать /vykápyvat'/ v. dig out

выкармливать /vykármlivat'/ v. bring up, rear

выкачивать /vykáchivat'/ v. pump out

выкидывать /vykídyvat'/ v. throw out; hoist (up); miscarry

выкидыш /výkidysh/ m. miscarriage, abortion

выключатель /vykliuchátel'/ m. switch

выключать /vykliuchát'/ v. switch off

выковывать /vykóvyvat'/ v. forge; mould

выколачивать /vykoláchivat'/ v. beat out; dust

выкорчевывать /vykorchóvyvat'/ v. root out

выкраивать /vykráivat'/ v. cut out

выкрик /výkrik/ m. yell

выкройка /výkroika/ f. pattern

выкуп /výkup/ m. ransom; redemption

выкуривать /vykúrivat'/ v. smoke out

вылезать /vylezát'/ v. climb out

вылет /výlet/ m. flight, take-off

вылетать /vyletát'/ v. fly out; take off

вылечивать /vyléchivat'/ v. cure, heal

выливать /vylivát'/ v. pour out, empty

вымачивать /vymáchivat'/ v. soak

выменивать /vyménivat'/ v. exchange

вымерший /výmershii/ adj. extinct

выметать /vymetát'/ v. sweep out

вымирать /vymirát'/ v. die out, become extinct

вымогательство /vymogátel'stvo/ n. extortion, blackmail

вымогать /vymogát'/ v. extort

вымокать /vymokát'/ v. wet through

вымолвить /vymolvit'/ v. say, utter

вымпел /výmpel/ m. pennant

вымывать /vymyvát'/ v. wash (out)

вымысел /výmysel/ m. invention; fabrication

вымя /výmia/ n. udder

вынашивать /vynáshivat'/ v. bear (a child)

вынимать /vynimát'/ v. take out, produce

выносить /vynosít'/ v. carry out; endure

вынуждать /vynuzhdát'/ v. force, compel

вынужденный /výnuzhdennyi/ adj. forced

вынырнуть /výnyrnut'/ v. come to surface; emerge

вынюхивать /vyniúkhivat'/ v. smell, sniff out

выпад /výpad/ m. lunge; thrust; attack

выпаливать /vypálivat'/ v. shoot; blurt out

выпалывать /vypályvat'/ v. weed (out)

выпаривать /vypárivat'/ v. evaporate

выпекать /vypekát'/ v. bake

выпивать /vypivát'/ v. drink (off)

выпивший /výpivshii/ adj. drunk

выпиливать /vypílivat'/ v. saw out

выписка /výpiska/ f. writing out; extract

выпихивать /vypíkhivat'/ v. push out

выплата /výplata/ f. payment

выплевывать /vyplióvyvat'/ v. spit out

выплескивать /vyplióskivat'/ v. splash out

выплывать /vyplyvát'/ v. swim out

выполнять /vypolniát'/ v. carry out, implement

выпрашивать /vypráshivat'/ v. elicit by begging

выпрыгивать /vyprýgivat'/ v. jump out

выпрямлять /vypriamliát'/ v. straighten, rectify

выпуклый /výpuklyi/ adj. protuberant; bulging

выпуск /výpusk/ m. issue; output; discharge

выпускной (экзамен) /vypusknói ekzámen/ adj.+m. final exams

вырабатывать /vyrabátyvat'/ v. make, produce; develop

выравнивать /vyrávnivat'/ v. make even, level

выражать /vyrazhát'/ v. express

выражение /vyrazhénie/ n. expression

выразительный /vyrazítel'nyi/ adj. expressive

вырастать /vyrastát'/ v. grow (up)

вырез /výrez/ m. cut

вырезать /vyrezát'/ v. cut out; carve

вырезка /výrezka/ f. cutting-out; tenderloin

выродок /výrodok/ m. degenerate

выронить /výronit'/ v. drop

вырубать /vyrubát'/ v. cut down, fell

выручать /vyruchát'/ v. rescue, help out; gain

вырывать /vyryvát'/ v. pull or tear out; extort

высадка /výsadka/ f. disembarkation, landing

высасывать /vysásyvat'/ v. suck out; в. из пальца /v. iz pál'tsa/ invent, fabricate

высверливать /vysvérlivat'/ v. drill, bore

высвобождать /vysvobozhdát'/ v. set free

высекать /vysekát'/ v. carve, cut

выселение /vyselénie/ n. eviction

выселять /vyseliát'/ v. evict, expel

высиживать /vysízhivat'/ v. hatch

выситься /výsit'sia/ v. rise, tower

выскабливать /vyskáblivat'/ v. scrub clean; erase

высказывать /vyskázyvat'/ v. state, say

высказываться /vyskázyvat'sia/ v. speak out

выскакивать /vyskákivat'/ v. jump out, leap out

выскальзывать /vyskál'zyvat'/ v. slip out

выскребать /vyskrebát'/ v. scratch out

выслеживать /vyslézhivat'/ v. track down, shadow

выслуга /výsluga/ f. period of service

выслушивать /vyslúshivat'/ v. listen, hear out; sound (med.)

высмеивать /vysméivat'/ v. ridicule

высморкаться /výsmorkat'sia/ v. blow one's nose

высовывать /vysóvyvat'/ v. put out, push out

высовываться /vysóvyvat'sia/ v. lean out

высокий /vysókii/ adj. high, tall; lofty

высоковольтный /vysokovól'tnyi/ adj. high-voltage

высококачественный /vysokokáchestvennyi/ adj. high-quality

высококвалифицированный /vysokokvalifitsírovannyi/ adj. highly, skilled

высота /vysotá/ f. height; altitude

высохший /výsokhshii/ adj. dried up; withered

высочайший /vysocháishii/ adj. highest; imperial

высочество /vysóchestvo/ n. Highness

выставка /výstavka/ f. exhibition

выстраивать /vystráivat'/ v. draw up, parade

выстрел /výstrel/ m. shot

выступ /výstup/ m. prominence; projection

высушивать /vysúshivat'/ v. dry (up)

высчитывать /vyschítyvat'/ v. calculate

высший /výsshii/ adj. superior; highest

высылать /vysylát'/ v. send out; banish

высыпать /vysypát'/ v. pour out

высыпаться /vysypát'sia/ v. have a good sleep

высыхать /vysykhát'/ v. dry up

вытаскивать /vytáskivat'/ v. take out, pull out

вытекать /vytekát'/ v. flow out; flow from; follow, result

вытеснять /vytesniát'/ v. force out; oust, expel

вытирать /vytirát'/ v. wipe, dry

вытряхивать /vytriákhivat'/ v. shake out

выть /vyt'/ v. howl

вытягивать /vytiágivat'/ v. draw out; stretch

выучивать /vyúchivat'/ v. learn; teach

выхаживать /vykházhivat'/ v. nurse; bring up

выхватывать /vykhvátyvat'/ v. snatch out

выхлоп /výkhlop/ m. exhaust

выход /výkhod/ m. going out; exit; yield; publication

выходить /vykhodít'/ v. go or come out; withdraw; be published

выхоленный /výkholennyi'/ adj. well-groomed

выцветать /vytsvetát'/ v. fade, wither

вычеркивать /vychórkivat'/ v. cross out

вычерчивать /vychérchivat'/ v. draw

вычисление /vychislénie/ n. calculation

вычитание /vychitánie/ n. subtraction

вычитать /výchitat'/ v. subtract

вычищать /vychishchát'/ v. clean (up, out)

вышвыривать /vyshvýrivat'/ v. fling out

выше /výshe/ adj. higher, beyond, above

вышивание /vyshivánie/ n. embroidery; needlework

вышина /vyshiná/ f. height

вышка /výshka/ f. tower; sl. death sentence

выявлять /vyiavliát'/ v. expose, reveal

вьетнамец /v'etnámets/ m. Vietnamese

вьетнамка /v'etnámka/ f. Vietnamese

вьетнамский /v'etnámskii/ adj. Vietnamese

вьюга /v'iúga/ f. snowstorm, blizzard

вьюк /v'iuk/ m. pack, load

вьюнок /v'iunók/ m. bindweed

вьючное животное /v'iúchnoe zhivótnoe/ adj.+n. beast of burden

вьющийся /v'iúshchiisia/ adj. curly (hair)

вяжущий /viázhushchii/ adj. astringent

вяз /viaz/ m. elm

вязание /viazánie/ n. knitting

вязанка /viazánka/ f. bundle

вязаный /viázanyi/ adj. knitted

вязать /viazát'/ v. bind; knit, crochet; be astringent

вязкий /viázkii/ adj. sticky; swampy

вяленый /viálenyi/ adj. dried

вялый /viályi/ adj. flabby, flaccid; sluggush, inert

вянуть /viánut'/ v. fade; droop

Г

г /g/ abbr., m. gram(me)

га /ga/ abbr., m. hectare

гавань /gávan'/ f. harbour

гагара /gagára/ f. loon, diver

гагачий (пух) /gagáchii pukh/ adj.+m. eiderdown

гад /gad/ m. reptile; vile creature

гадалка /gadálka/ f. fortune-teller

гадание /gadánie/ n. fortune-telling

гадать /gadát'/ v. tell fortunes; guess

гадить /gádit'/ v. foul, dirty; make mischief

гадкий /gádkii/ adj. foul, nasty; bad

гадюка /gadiúka/ f. viper

гаечный (ключ) /gáechnyi kliuch/ adj.+m. spanner

газ /gaz/ m. gas

газета /gazéta/ f. newspaper

газетный (киоск) /gazétnyi kiósk/ adj.+m. newsstand

газетчик /gazétchik/ m. newsman

газированная (вода) /gaziróvannaia vodá/ adj.+f. soda water

газон /gazón/ m. lawn

газопровод /gazoprovód/ m. gas pipe

ГАИ /gaí/ abbr., n. State Motor-vehicle Inspectorate

гайка /gáika/ f. nut, female screw

галактика /galáktika/ f. galaxy

галантерея /galanteréia/ f. notions store; haberdashery

галантный /galántnyi/ adj. gallant, courtly

галерея /galeréia/ f. gallery

галка /gálka/ f. jackdaw

галлюцинация /galliutsinátsiia/ f. hallucination

галоп /galóp/ m. gallop

галочка /gálochka/ f. tick, mark

галоши /galóshi/ pl. galoshes, rubbers

галстук /gálstuk/ m. (neck)tie

галушка /galúshka/ f. dumpling

галька /gál'ka/ f. pebble(s)

гам /gam/ m. din, row, rumpus

гамак /gamák/ m. hammock

гамма /gámma/ f. gamut; range

гангрена /gangréna/ f. gangrene

гантель /gantél'/ f. dumb-bell

гараж /garázh/ m. garage

гарантировать /garantírovat'/ v. guarantee

гарантия /garántiia/ f. guarantee

гардероб /garderób/ m. cloakroom; wardrobe; clothes

гардина /gardína/ f. curtain

гармонировать /garmonírovat'/ v. harmonize

гармоника /garmónika/ accordion; губная г. /gubnáia g./ mouth organ

гарнизон /garnizón/ m. garrison

гарнир /garnír/ m. garnish; vegetables

гарнитур /garnitúr/ m. set, suite; спальный г. /spál'nyi g./ bedroom suite

гарпун /garpún/ m. harpoon

гарь /gar'/ f. burning; cinders

гасить /gasít'/ v. extinguish

гаснуть /gásnut'/ v. go out, die away

гастролер /gastroliór/ m. guest actor or artist

гастролировать /gastrolírovat'/ v. tour, give performance(s) on a tour

гастроли /gastróli/ pl. starring (performance)

гастроном /gastronóm/ m. food store or shop

гашиш /gashísh/ m. hashish

гвардеец /gvardéets/ m. guardsman

гвардия /gvárdiia/ f. Guards

гвоздика /gvozdíka/ f. carnation

гвоздь /gvozd'/ m. náil

где /gde/ conj. where; где-либо, где-нибудь, где-то /gde-libo, gde-nibud', gde-to/ any-, somewhere

гегемония /gegemóniia/ f. hegemony

гейзер /géizer/ m. geyser

гектар /gektár/ m. hectare

гелий /gélii/ m. helium

гемоглобин /gemoglobín/ m. haemoglobin

ген /gen/ m. gene

генеалогия /genealógiia/ f. genealogy

генерал /generál/ m. general; г.-майор /g.-maiór/ major-general

генеральный /generál'nyi/ adj. general; генеральная репетиция /generál'naia repetitsiia/ dress rehearsal

генератор /generátor/ m. generator

генетика /genétika/ f. genetics

гениальный /geniál'nyi/ adj. of genius, brilliant

гений /geníi/ m. genius

географ /geógraf/ m. geographer

географический /geografícheskii/ adj. geographical

география /geográfiia/ f. geography

геолог /geolog/ m. geologist

геология /geológiia/ f. geology

геометрический /geometrícheskii/ adj. geometrical

геометрия /geométriia/ f. geometry

георгин /georgín/ m. dahlia

геофизика /geofízika/ f. geophysics

герань /gerán'/ f. geranium

герб /gerb/ m. coat of arms

германский /germánskii/ adj. German

герметический /germetícheskii/ adj. hermetic

героизм /geroízm/ m. heroism

героиня /geroínia/ f. heroine

героический /geroícheskii/ adj. heroic

герой /gerói/ m. hero

герцог /gértsog/ m. duke

герцогиня /gertsogínia/ f. duchess

гетры /gétry/ pl. gaiters

гиацинт /giatsint/ m. hyacinth

гибель /gibél'/ f. destruction

гибкий /gíbkii/ adj. flexible, supple

гиблый /gíblyi/ adj. wretched, ruinous

гибнуть /gíbnut'/ v. perish

гибрид /gibríd/ m. hybrid
гигант /gigánt/ m. giant
гигантский /gigántskii/ adj. gigantic
гигиена /gigiéna/ f. hygiene
гигиенический /gigienícheskii/ adj. hygienic, sanitary
гид /gid/ m. guide
гиена /giéna/ f. hyena
гильза /gíl'za/ f. (cartridge) case
гимн /gimn/ m. hymn; anthem; государственный г. /gosudárstvennyi g./ national anthem
гимнаст /gimnást/ m. gymnast
гимнастика /gimnástika/ f. gymnastics
гинеколог /ginekólog/ m. gynaecologist
гипербола /gipérbola/ f. hyperbole
гипноз /gipnóz/ m. hypnosis
гипотеза /gipóteza/ f. hypothesis
гипотенуза /gipotenúza/ f. hypotenuse
гиппопотам /gippopotám/ m. hippopotamus
гипс /gips/ m. gypsum; plaster
гирлянда /girliánda/ f. garland
гиря /giria/ f. weight
гитара /gitára/ f. guitar
глава /glavá/ f. head, chief; chapter
главнокомандующий /glavnokomanduiushchii/ m. commander-in-chief
главный /glavnyi/ adj. chief, main; главным образом /glávnym óbrazom/ mainly
глагол /glagól/ m. verb
гладить /gládit'/ v. iron
глаз /glaz/ m. eye; на глазок /na glazók/ approximately; смотреть во все глаза /smotrét' vo vse glazá/ be all eyes; за глаза /za glazá/ behind someone's back; с глазу на глаз /s glázu na glaz/ tete-a-tete
глазунья /glazún'ia/ f. fried eggs
глазурь /glazúr'/ f. syrup, icing; glaze
гланды /glándy/ pl. tonsils
гласность /glásnost'/ f. glasnost; openness
глетчер /glétcher/ m. glacier
глина /glína/ f. clay

глинозем /glinozióm/ m. alumina
глиняная (посуда) /glínianaia posúda/ adj.+f. earthenware
глиссер /glísser/ m. speed-boat
глисты /glistý/ pl. worms
глицерин /glitserín/ m. glycerine
глициния /glitsíniia/ f. wistaria
глобус /glóbus/ m. globe
глотать /glotát'/ v. swallow
глотка /glótka/ f. throat
глоток /glotók/ m. gulp
глохнуть /glókhnut'/ v. grow deaf
глубина /glubiná/ f. depth
глубокий /glubókii/ adj. deep, profound; глубокой осенью /glubókoi ósen'iu/ in the late autumn
глумиться /glumít'sia/ v. sneer, mock
глупеть /glupét'/ v. become stupid
глупец /glupéts/ m. fool, blockhead
глупость /glúpost'/ f. stupidity
глупый /glúpyi/ adj. stupid
глухарь /glukhár'/ m. wood grouse
глухой /glukhói/ adj. deaf
глухонемой /glukhonemói/ adj. deaf-mute
глухота /glukhotá/ f. deafness
глушитель /glushítel'/ m. muffler
глушить /glushít'/ v. muffle; jam; suppress
глушь /glush/ f. backwoods
глыба /glýba/ f. clod; block
глюкоза /gliukóza/ f. glucose
глядеть /gliadét'/ v. look, glance (at)
глянец /gliánets/ m. polish, gloss
гнать /gnat'/ v. drive; pusue, chase
гнев /gnev/ m. anger
гневный /gnévnyi/ adj. angry
гнедой /gnedói/ adj. chestnut (horse)
гнездиться /gnezdit'sia/ v. nest; nestle
гнездо /gnezdó/ n. nest
гнет /gniot/ m. oppression; press(ure)
гниение /gniénie/ n. rotting
гнилой /gnilói/ adj. rotten
гноиться /gnoit'sia/ v. fester, suppurate
гной /gnoi/ m. pus
гнойник /gnóinik/ m. abscess

гном /gnom/ m. gnome
гнусный /gnúsnyi/ adj. vile, base
гнуть /gnut'/ bend; bow
гобелен /gobelén/ m. tapestry
гобой /gobói/ m. oboe
говеть /govét'/ v. fast
говор /góvor/ m. dialect
говорить /govorít'/ v. speak or talk; говорят /govoriat/ they say; г. по-русски /g. po-rússki/ speak Russian; иначе говоря /ináche govoriá/ in other words
говядина /goviádina/ f. beef
гогот /gógot/ m. cackle
год /god/ m. year; в этом (прошлом) году /v étom (próshlom) godú/ this (last) year; круглый г. /krúglyi g./ all the year round; из года в год /iz góda v god/ year in year out
годиться /godít'sia/ v. be fit (for), be of use
годичный /godíchnyi/ adj. annual
годный /gódnyi/ adj. fit, suitable
годовалый /godovályi/ adj. one-year-old
годовой /godovói/ adj. annual
годовщина /godovshchína/ f. anniversary
гол /gol/ m. goal; забивать г. /zabivat' g./ score a goal
голенастый /golenástyi/ adj. long-legged
голландец /gollándets/ m. Dutchman
голландка /gollándka/ f. Dutchwoman
голландский /gollándskii/ adj. Dutch
голова /golová/ f. head; как снег на голову /kak sneg na gólovu/ all of a sudden; на свою голову /na svoiú gólovu/ to one's own harm
головастик /golovástik/ m. tadpole
головка /golóvka/ f. head (pin, nail, etc.)
головной /golovnói/ adj. head; головная боль Ё/golovnáia bol'/ headache
головокружение /golovokruzhénie/ n. giddiness, dizziness
головоломка /golovolómka/ f. puzzle
голод /gólod/ m. hunger; famine
голодать /golodát'/ v. starve
голодный /golodnýi/ adj. hungry
голодовка /golodóvka/ f. hunger-strike

гололедица /gololéditsa/ f. ice-covered ground
голос /gólos/ m. voice; vote; право голоса /právo gólosa/ suffrage; во весь голос /vo ves' gólos/ at the top of one's voice
голосовать /golosovát'/ v. vote
голубец /golubéts/ m. stuffed cabbage
голубой /golubói/ adj. (sky- blue)
голубь /gólub'/ m. pigeon, dove
голый /gólyi/ adj. naked; bare
гомеопатия /gomeipátiia/ f. homoeopaty
гонение /gonénie/ n. persecution
гонец /gonéts/ m. messenger
гонорар /gonorár/ m. fee
гонорея /gonoréia/ f. gonorrhoea
гончар /gonchár/ m. potter
гончая /gónchaia/ f. hound
гонять /goniát'/ f. drive, chase
гора /gorá/ f. mountain, hill; идти в/на гору /idtí v/na góru go uphill/; под гору /pod góru/ downhill; стоять горой за /stoiát' gorói za/ stand by, defend
гораздо /gorázdo/ adv. much, far
горб /gorb/ m. hump
горбатый /gorbátyi/ adj. humpbacked
горбушка /gorbúshka/ f. crust, heel of loaf
горделивый /gordelívyi/ adj. haughty
гордиться /gordít'sia/ v. be proud (of)
гордость /górdost'/ f. pride
гордый /górdyi/ adj. proud
горе /góre/ n. sorrow, grief
горевать /gorevát'/ v. grieve
горелый /gorélyi/ adj. burnt
горение /gorénie/ n. burning
гореть /gorét'/ v. burn; glow, gleam
горец /górets/ m. mountaineer
горечь /górech/ f. bitter taste; bitterness
горизонт /gorizónt/ m. horizon

горизонтальный /gorizontál'nyi/ adj. horizontal

горлица /górlitsa/ f. turtle-dove

горло /górlo/ n. throat

гормон /gormón/ m. hormone

горн /gorn/ m. bugle

горничная /górnichnaia/ f. housemaid

горностай /gornostái/ m. ermine

горный /górnyi/ adj. mountainous; mining

горняк /gorniák/ m. miner

город /górod/ m. town, city

горожанин /gorozhánin/ m. townsman; pl. townspeople

горох /gorókh/ pea(s)

горсовет /gorsovet/ m. city or town soviet (council)

горсть /gorst'/ f. handful

гортань /gortán'/ f. larynx

гортензия /gorténzia/ f. hydrangea

горчица /gorchítsa/ f. mustard

горшок /gorshók/ m. pot

горький /gór'kii/ adj. bitter

горючее /goriúchee/ n. fuel

горячий /goriáchii/ adj. hot; cordial, fervent

Госбанк /gosbánk/ m. State Bank

госпиталь /góspital'/ m. hospital

Госплан /gosplán/ m. State Planning Committee

господи /góspodi/ int. good heavens! good Lord!

господин /gospodín/ m. gentleman; Mr.

господство /gospódstvo/ n. supremacy; rule

господь /gospód'/ m. Lord, God

госпожа /gospozhá/ f. lady; Mrs.; Miss

гостеприимный /gostepriímnyi/adj. hospitable

гостеприимство /gostepriímstvo/ n. hospitality

гостиная /gostínaia/ f. drawing-room

гостиница /gostínitsa/ f. hotel

гостить /gostít'/ v. be on a visit, stay with

государственный /gosudárstvennyi/ adj. State

государство /gosudárstvo/ n. state

государь /gosudár'/ m. sovereign

гот /got/ m. Goth

готический /gotícheskii/ adj. Gothic

готовальня /gotovál'nia/ f. case of drawing instruments

готовить /gotóvit'/ v. prepare (for)

готовность /gotóvnost'/ f. readiness

готовый /gotóvyi/ ready

ГПУ /gepeú/ abbr., n. G.P.U. (State Political Administration)

грабеж /grabiózh/ m. robbery

грабитель /grabítel'/ m. robber

грабить /grábit'/ v. rob

грабли /grábli/ pl. rake

гравер /graviór/ m. engraver

гравий /grávii/ m. gravel

гравировать /gravirovát'/ v. engrave, etch

гравировка /graviróvka/ f. engraving

гравюра /graviúra/ f. print, etching

град /grad/ m. hail

градус /grádus/ m. degree

градусник /grádusnik/ m. thermometer

гражданин /grazhdanín/ m. citizen

гражданство /grazhdánstvo/ m. citizenship

грамзапись /gramzápis'/ f. recording

грамм /gramm/ m. gram(me)

грамматика /grammátika/ f. grammar

грамота /grámota/ f. reading and writing; official document

грамотность /grámotnost'/ f. literacy

грампластинка /gramplastínka/ f. record

гранат /granát/ m. pomegranate; garnet

граната /granáta/ f. grenade

грандиозный /grandióznyi/ adj. grandiose

граненый /graniónyi/ adj. cut, faceted

гранит /granít/ m. granite

граница /granítsa/ f. boundary, frontier; ехать за границу /ékhat' za granitsu/ go abroad

гранка /gránka/ f. galley(proof)

грань /gran'/ f. border, verge; brink; side, edge

граф /graf/ m. count
график /gráfik/ m. diagram
графин /grafín/ m. decanter
графиня /grafínia/ f. countess
графство /gráfstvo/ n. county
грациозный /gratsióznyi/ adj. graceful
грач /grach/ m. rook
гребенка /grebiónka/ f. comb
гребец /grebéts/ m. oarsman
греза /grióza/ f. (day)dream
грек /grek/ m. Greek
грелка /grélka/ f. hot-water bottle
греметь /gremét'/ v. thunder
гремучая (змея) /gremúchaia zmeiá/ adj.+f. rattlesnake
гренки /grénki/ pl. toast(s)
грести /grestí/ v. row; scull
греть /gret'/ warm, heat
грех /grekh/ m. sin
грецкий (орех) /grétskii orékh/ adj.+m. walnut
гречанка /grechánka/ f. Greek
греческий /grécheskii/ adj. Greek
гречиха /grechíkha/ f. buckwheat
гриб /grib/ m. mushroom
грибок /gribók/ m. fungus
грива /gríva/ f. mane
грим /grim/ m. make-up
гримаса /grimása/ f. grimace
грипп /gripp/ m. influenza
грифель /grífel'/ m. slate pencil
гроб /grob/ m. coffin
гробница /grobnítsa/ f. tomb
гроза /groza/ f. (thunder)storm
гроздь /grozd'/ f. bunch
грозить /grozít'/ v. threaten, menace
гром /grom/ m. thunder
громить /gromít'/ v. rout
громкий /grómkii/ adj. loud
громоздкий /gromózdkii/ adj. bulky
громоотвод /gromootvód/ m. lightning-conductor
громыхать /gromykhát'/ v. rattle
грот /grot/ m. grotto
гротескный /grotésknyi/ adj. grotesque
грохот /grókhot/ m. rumble

грош /grosh/ m. half-kopeck piece; farthing
грошовый /groshóvyi/ adj. dirt-cheap; trifling
грубить /grubít'/ v. be rude
грубый /grúbyi/ adj. coarse; rude
груда /grúda/ f. heap
грудинка /grudínka/ f. bacon
грудной /grudnói/ adj. breast
грудь /grud'/ f. breast
груз /gruz/ m. load, cargo
грузин /gruzín/ m. Georgian
грузинка /gruzínka/ f. Georgian
грузинский /gruzínskii/ adj. Georgian
грузить /gruzít'/ v. load
грузный /grúznyi/ adj. massive
грузовик /gruzovík/ m. truck
грузоподъемность /gruzopod"iómnost'/ f. carrying capacity
грузчик /grúzchik/ m. stevedore
грунт /grunt/ m. ground; soil
группа /grúppa/ f. group
грустить /grustít'/ v. be sad
грустный /grústnyi/ adj. sad
грусть /grust'/ f. sadness, melancholy
груша /grúsha/ f. pear
грыжа /grýzha/ f. hernia, rupture
грызня /gryzniá/ f. squabble
грызть /gryzt'/ v. gnaw; crack (nuts)
грызун /gryzún/ m. rodent
гряда /griadá/ f. ridge, range
грядка /griádka/ f. (flower-)bed
грядущий /griadúshchii/ adj. future, coming
грязелечебница /griazelechébnitsa/ f. mud baths
грязнить /griaznít'/ v. make dirty
грязный /griáznyi/ adj. dirty, sordid
грязь /griaz'/ f. dirt, mud
губа /gubá/ f. lip; bay
губернатор /gubernátor/ m. governor
губительный /gubítel'nyi/ adj. pernicious
губить /gubít'/ v. destroy, ruin
губка /gúbka/ f. sponge
гувернантка /guvernántka/ f. governess
гудеть /gudét'/ v. buzz

гудок /gudók/ m. hoot

гул /gul/ m. rumble; hum

гулянье /gulián'e/ n. walking

гулять /guliát'/ v. go for a walk, stroll

ГУМ /gum/ abbr., m. State department store

гуманизм /gumanízm/ m. humanism

гуманитарный /gumanitárnyi/ adj. of the humanities

гуманность /gumánnost'/ f. humaneness

гуманный /gumánnyi/ adj. humane

гумно /gumnó/ n. threshing-floor

гусеница /gúsenitsa/ f. caterpillar

гусенок /gusiónok/ m. gosling

гусиный /gusínyi/ adj. goose; гусиная кожа /gusínaia kózha/ goose-flesh

густеть /gustét'/ v. thicken

густой /gustói/ adj. thick, dense; deep, rich (colour, sound)

гусыня /gusýnia/ f. goose

гусь /gus'/ m. goose

гуськом /gus'kóm/ adv. in single file

гуталин /gutalín/ m. shoe polish

гуща /gúshcha/ f. thicket; centre, heart

гэльский /gél'skii/ adj. Gaelic

ГЭС /ges/ abbr., f. hydroelectric power station

Д

да /da/ part. yes; conj. and; but; да и /da i/ and besides

давать /davát'/ v. give; grant, let; давайте /daváite/ let us

давить /davít'/ v. press; crush, run over

давка /dávka/ f. throng, jam

давление /davlénie/ n. pressure

давний /davnii/ adj. old, ancient

давно /davnó/ adv. long ago

даже /dázhe/ adv. even

далее /dálee/ adv. further, later; и так д. /i tak d./ and so on

далекий /daliókii/ adj. distant

далеко /dalekó/ adv. far (off, away); д. за полночь /d. zá polnoch/ long after midnight; д. не /d. ne/ far from, by no means

даль /dal'/ f. distance

дальневосточный /dal'nevostóchnyi/ adj. Far Eastern

дальнейший /dal'néishii/ adj. further

дальний /dál'nii/ adj. distant, remote

дальнобойный /dal'nobóinyi/ adj. long-range

дальновидный /dal'novídnyi/ adj. far-sighted

дальнозоркий /dal'nozórkii/ adj. long-sighted

дальше /dál'she/ adv. further, farther

дама /dáma/ f. lady; queen (cards)

дамба /dámba/ f. dam, dike

дамский /dámskii/ adj. ladies'

данный /dánnyi/ adj. given

данные /dánnye/ pl. data, facts

дантист /dantíst/ m. dentist

дань /dan'/ f. tribute, contribution

дар /dar/ m. gift

дарить /darít'/ v. present

дарование /darovánie/ n. gift, talent

даровитый /darovítyi/ adj. gifted

даровой /darovói/ adj. gratis, free

даром /dárom/ adv. gratis, free

дата /dáta/ f. date

дательный /dátel'nyi/ adj. dative

датировать /datírovat'/ v. date

датский /dátskii/ adj. Danish

датчанин /datchánin/ m. Dane

датчанка /datchánka/ f. Danish woman

дача /dácha/ f. dacha, summer residence; на даче /na dache/ out of town, in the country

два /dva/ num. two

двадцатилетний /dvadtsatilétnii/ adj. twenty-year-old

двадцать /dvádtsat/ num. twenty

дважды /dvázhdy/ adv. twice

двенадцать /dvenádtsat'/ twelve

дверной /dvernói/ adj. door

дверь /dver'/ f. door

двести /dvésti/ num. two hundred
двигатель /dvígatel'/ m. motor, engine
двигать /dvígat'/ v. move, push, drive; further; motivate
движение /dvizhénie/ n. muvement; traffic
движимость /dvízhimost'/ f. movable property
двое /dvóe/ num. two
двоебрачие /dvoebráchie/ n. bigamy
двоеточие /dvoetóchie/ n. colon
двойка /dvóika/ f. two; pair
двойник /dvoiník/ m. double
двойной /dvoinói/ adj. double
двойня /dvóinia/ f. twins
двойственный /dvóistvennyi/ adj. dual; double-faced
двор /dvor/ m. court; yard; farm(stead)
дворец /dvoréts/ m. palace
дворник /dvórnik/ m. street cleaner; windshield (windscreen) wiper
дворняжка /dvorniázhka/ f. mongrel
дворянство /dvoriánstvo/ n. nobility
двоюродный (брат), двоюродная (сестра) /dvoiúrodnyi brat, dvoiúrodnaia sestrá/ adj.+m., f. cousin
двоякий /dvoiákii/ adj. double, of two kinds
двубортный /dvubórtnyi/ adj. double-breasted
двукратный /dvukrátnyi/ adj. double, done twice
двуличный /dvulíchnyi/ adj. two-faced, hypocritical
двусмысленный /dvusmýslennyi/ adj. ambiquous
двуспальная (кровать) /dvuspal'naia krovat'/ adj.+f. double bed
двустволка /dvustvólka/ f. double-barrelled gun
двусторонний /dvustorónnii/ adj. two-way; bilateral
двухгодовалый /dvukhgodovályi/ adj. two-year-old
двухдневный /dvukhdnévnyi/ adj. of two days

двухколейка /dvukhkoléika/ f. double-track railway
двухколесный /dvukhkoliósnyi/ adj. two-wheeled
двухлетний /dvukhlétnii/ adj. biennial; two-year-old
двухместный /dvukhméstnyi/ adj. two-seated
двухмесячный /dvukhmésiachnyi/ adj. two months', two-month-old
двухнедельный /dvukhnedél'nyi/ adj. two-week-old, fortnightly
двухэтажный /dvukhetázhnyi/ adj. two-storeyed
двуязычный /dvuiazýchnyi/ adj. bilingual
дебатировать /debatírovat'/ v. debate, discuss
дебаты /debáty/ pl. debate
дебет /débet/ m. debit
дебри /débri/ pl. dense forest; maze, labyrinth
дебют /debiút/ m. debut
дева (старая д.) /stáraia déva/ adj.+f. spinster
девальвация /deval'vátsia/ f. devaluation
девать /devát'/ v. put; place; mislay
деваться /devát'sia/ v. get to, disappear to
девиз /devíz/ m. motto
девица /devítsa/ f. girl, maid
девка /dévka/ f. wench; whore
девочка /dévochka/ f. (little) girl
девушка /dévushka/ f. girl; miss
девяносто /devianósto/ num. ninety
девятка /deviátka/ f. nine
девятнадцать /deviatnádtsat'/ num. nineteen
девять /déviat'/ num. nine
девятьсот /deviat'sót/ num. nine hundred
дегенерат /degenerát/ m. degenerate
деготь /diógot'/ m. tar
дегустация /degustátsiia/ f. tasting
дед, дедушка /ded, dédushka/ m. grandfather; old man
деепричастие /deeprichástie/ n. gerund, adverbial participle

дееспособный /deesposóbnyi/ adj. energetic, active; capable

дежурить /dezhúrit'/ v. be on duty

дежурство /dezhúrstvo/ n. duty

дезавуировать /dezavuírovat'/ v. disavow

дезертир /dezertír/ m. deserter

дезинфекция /dezinféktsiia/ f. disinfection

дезорганизщация /dezorganizátsiia/ f. disorganization

дезориентировать /dezorientírovat'/ v. confuse, mislead

действенный /déistvennyi/ adj. effective, active

действие /déistvie/ n. action; act; operation

действительный /deistvítel'nyi/ adj. actual, real; valid

действительность /deistvítel'nost'/ f. reality

действовать /déistvovat'/ v. act, operate, function; have effect (on)

действующий /déistvuiushchii/ adj. acting in force; действующее лицо /deistvuiúshchee litsó/ character; действующие лица /déistvuiushchie lítsa/ dramatis personae

декабрь /dekábr'/ m. December

декабрьский /dekábr'skii/ adj. December

декада /dekáda/ f. ten days; (ten-day) festival

декан /dekán/ m. dean

деквалификация /dekvalifikátsiia/ f. loss of professional skill

декламация /deklamátsiia/ f. recitation

декламировать /deklamírovat'/ v. recite

декларация /deklarátsiia/ f. declaration

декольтированный /dekol'tírovannyi/ adj. low-necked

декоративный /dekoratívnyi/ adj. decorative, ornamental

декоратор /dekorátor/ m. scene-painter

декорация /dekorátsiia/ f. scenery

декрет /dekrét/ m. decree

декретный (отпуск) /dekretnyi otpusk/ adj.+m. maternity leave

деланный /delannyi/ adj. affected, forced

делать /délat'/ v. make; нечего делать /néchevo délat'/ it can't be helped

делаться /délat'sia/ v. become, grow, turn; happen; что с ним сделалось? /chto s nim sdélalos'?/what has become of him?

делегат /delegát/ m. delegate

делегация /delegátsiia/ f. delegation

дележ /deliózh/ m. distribution, sharing

деление /delénie/ n. division; point (scale)

делец /deléts/ m. (sharp) businessman

деликатес /delikatés/ m. dainty

деликатный /delikátnyi/ adj. delicate, tactful

делитель /delítel'/ m. divisor

делить /delít'/ v. divide, share

делиться /delít'sia/ v. exchange; confide; be divisible

дело /delo/ n. matter, business, affair; deed; говорить д. /govorít/ d./ talk sense; на самом деле /na sámom déle/ in reality, in fact

деловитый /delovítyi/ adj. efficient, business-like

деловой /delovói/ adj. business-like

делопроизводитель /deloproizvodítel'/ m. secretary

дельный /dél'nyi/ adj. competent; sensible

дельта /dél'ta/ f. delta

дельфин /del'fín/ m. dolphin

демагог /demagóg/ m. demagogue

демагогия /demagógia/ f. demagogy

демаркационный /demarkatsiónnyi/ adj. demarcation

демилитаризация /demilitarizátsiia/ f. demilitarization

демобилизация /demobilizátsiia/ f. demobilization

демократ /demokrát/ m. democrat

демократический /demokratícheskii/ adj. democratic

демократия /demokrátiia/ f. democracy

демон /démon/ m. demon

демонстрант /demonstránt/ m. demonstrator

демонстрация /demonstrátsiia/ f. demonstration

демонтировать /demontírovat'/ v. dismantle

деморализация /demoralizátsiia/ f. demoralization

денатурат /denaturát/ m. methylated spirits

денежный /dénezhnyi/ adj. money, pecuniary

денонсировать /denonsírovat'/ v. denounce

день /den'/ m. day; на днях /na dniákh/ the other day; три часа дня /tri chasa dnia/ 3 p.m.

деньги /dén'gi/ pl. money

департамент /departáment/ m. department

депозит /depozít/ m. deposit

депрессия /depréssia/ f. depression

депутат /deputát/ m. deputy

депутация /deputátsiia/ f. deputation

дергать /diórgat'/ v. pull, tug

деревенский /derevénskii/ adj. rural

деревня /derévnia/ f. village; country(side)

дерево /dérevo/ n. wood; tree; красное д. /krásnoie d./ mahogany; черное д. /chórnoe d./ ebony

деревянный /dereviánnyi/ adj. wooden

держава /derzháva/ f. power, state

держать /derzhát'/ v. hold, keep; д. себя /d. sebiá/ behave

держаться /derzhát'sia/ v. hold (onto); holt out, stand; д. в стороне /d. v storoné/hold aloof

дерзать /derzát'/ v. dare, venture

дерзкий /dérzkii/ adj. impudent; bold, daring

дерзость /dérzost'/ f. impudence, cheek

дерн /diórn/ m. turf

десант /desánt/ m. landing

десерт /desért/ m. dessert

десна /desná/ f. gum

деспот /déspot/ m. despot

десятиборье /desiatibór'e/ n. decathlon

десятилетие /desiatilétie/ n. decade; tenth anniversary

десятилетка /desiatilétka/ f. ten-year secondary school

десятилетний /desiatilétnii/ adj. ten-year-old

десятина /desiatína/ f. tithe

десятичный /desiatíchnyi/ adj. decimal

десятка /desiátka/ f. ten; ten-rouble note

десять /désiat'/ num. ten

деталь /detál'/ f. detail; component

детальный /detál'nyi/ adj. detailed, minute

детвора /detvorá/ f. children, kids

детдом /detdóm/ m. (orphan) boarding school

детектив /detektív/ m. detective; detective story

детеныш /detiónysh/ m. young one, cub

дети /déti/ pl. children

детский (сад) /detskii sad/ adj.+m. kindergarten

детство /détstvo/ n. childhood

дефект /defékt/ m. defect

дефективный /defektívnyi/ adj. defective ; handicapped

дефектный /deféktnyi/ adj. faulty

дефицит /defitsít/ m. shortage

дефицитный /defitsítnyi/ in short supply, scarce

децентрализовать /detsentralizovát/ v. decentralize

дешеветь /deshevét'/ v. become cheap

дешевизна /deshevízna/ f. cheapness

дешевый /deshóvyi/ adj. cheap

дешифровать /deshifrovát'/ v. decipher

деятель (политический д.) /politícheskii déiatel'/ adj.+m. politician; государственный д. /gosudárstvennyi d./ statesman; общественный д. /obshchéstvennyi d./ public figure
деятельность /déiatel'nost'/ f. activity
деятельный /déiatel'nyi/ adj. active
джаз /dzhaz/ m. jazz
джем /dzhem/ m. jam
джемпер /dzhémper/ m. jumper, pullover
джунгли /dzhúngli/ pl. jungle
диабет /diabét/ m. diabetes
диагноз /diágnoz/ m. diagnosis
диагональ /diagonál'/ f. diagonal
диаграмма /diagrámma/ f. diagram
диадема /diadéma/ f. diadem
диалект /dialékt/ m. dialect
диалектика /dialéktika/ f. dialectic(s)
диалог /dialóg/ m. dialogue
диаметр /diámetr/ m. diameter
диапазон /diapazón/ m. range, compass
диапозитив /diapozítiv/ m. slide
диафрагма /diafrágma/ f. diaphragm
диван /diván/ m. settee; divan; sofa
диверсант /diversánt/ m. saboteur
диверсия /divérsiia/ f. diversion; sabotage
дивизия /divíziia/ f. division
дивный /dívnyi/ adj. wonderful
диво /dívo/ n. wonder, marvel
диета /diéta/ f. diet
дизель /dízel'/ m. diesel engine
дизентерия /dizenteríia/ f. dysentery
дикарь /dikár'/ m. savage
дикий /díkii/ adj. wild; shy
дикобраз /dikobráz/ m. porcupine
диковинка /dikóvinka/ f. wonder; something strange
диктант /diktánt/ m. dictation
диктатор /diktátor/ m. dictator
диктаторский /diktátorskii/ adj. dictatorial
диктатура /diktatúra/ f. dictatorship
диктовать /diktovát'/ v. dictate
диктор /díktor/ m. announcer
дилемма /dilémma/ f. dilemma

дилетант /diletánt/ m. amateur, dilettante
динамика /dinámika/ f. dynamics
динамит /dinamít/ m. dynamite
динамический /dinamícheskii/ adj. dynamic
династия /dinástiia/ f. dynasty
динозавр /dinozávr/ m. dinosaur
диплом /diplóm/ m. diploma
дипломат /diplomát/ m. diplomat; sl. attaché case
дипломная (работа) /diplómnaia rabóta/ adj+f. graduation/ degree thesis
директива /direktíva/ f. instruction, directive
директор /diréktor/ m. director, manager
дирекция /diréktsiia/ f. management; board of directors
дирижабль /dirizhábl'/ m. airship
дирижер /dirizhór/ m. conductor
диск /disk/ m. disc; discus
дискант /diskánt/ m. treble
дисквалифицировать /diskvalifitsírovat'/ v. disqualify
дискредитировать /diskreditírovat'/ v. discredit
дискриминация /diskriminátsiia/ f. discrimination
дискриминировать /diskriminírovat'/ v. discriminate against
дискуссия /diskússiia/ f. discussion, debate
дискутировать /diskutírovat'/ v. discuss, debate
диспансер /dispánser/ m. clinic, health centre
диспетчер /dispétcher/ m. controller
диспут /dísput/ m. public debate
диссертация /dissertátsiia/ f. thesis, dissertation
дистанция /distántsiia/ f. distance
дистиллировать /distillírovat'/ v. distil
дисциплина /distsiplína/ f. discipline
дитя /ditiá/ n. child
дифтерит /difterít/ m. diphtheria

дифференциальное (исчисление) /differentsiál'noe ischislénie/ adj.+n. differential calculus

дичать /dichát'/ v. grow wild

дичь /dich/ f. game, wild fowl; nonsense

длина /dliná/ f. length

длинный /dlínnyi/ adj. long

длительный /dlítel'nyi/ adj. prolonged

длиться /dlít'sia/ v. last

для /dlia/ prep. for; для того чтобы /dlia tovó chtóby/ in order to

дневник /dnevník/ m. diary

дневной /dnevnói/ adj. daily

дно /dno/ n. bottom; ground; пей до дна! /pei do dna/ bottoms up!

до /do/ prep. up to, until, before; мне не до /mne ne do/ don't feel like, I'm not in the mood for; мне не до шуток /mne ne do shútok/ I'm not in the mood for jokes

добавка /dobávka/ f. addition, supplement

добавлять /dobavliát'/ v. add

добивать /dobivát'/ v. finish off

добиваться /dobivát'sia/ v. achieve, obtain; д. своего /d. svoevó/ gain one's end добираться /dobirát'sia/ v. get to, reach; д. до сути дела /d. do súti déla/ get to the root of the matter

доблестный /dóblestnyi/ adj. valiant

доблесть /dóblest'/ f. valour

добрачный /dobráchnyi/ adj. pre-marital

добро /dobró/ n. good; д. пожаловать! /d. pozhálovat'!/ welcome (to)!

доброволец /dobrovólets/ m. volunteer

добровольный /dobrovól'nyi/ adj. voluntary

добродетель /dobrodétel'/ f. virtue

добродушие /dobrodúshie/ n. good-nature

доброжелательный /dobrozhelátel'nyi/ adj. benevolent

доброкачественный /dobrokachestvennyi/ adj. of high quality; benign

добросовестный /dobrosóvestnyi/ adj. conscientious

добрососедский /dobrososédskii/ adj. neighbourly, friendly

доброта /dobrotá/ f. goodness, kindness

добротный /dobrótnyi/ adj. of high quality

добрый /dóbryi/ adj. good, kind; в добрый час! /v dóbryi chas!/ good luck!; по доброй воле /po dóbroi vóle/ of one's own free will

добывать /dobyvát'/ v. get, obtain

добыча /dobýcha/ f. output; booty, loot; extraction, mining

доверенное (лицо) /dovérennoe litsó/ adj.+n. agent, proxy

доверенность /dovérennost'/ f. warrant, power of attorney

доверие /dovérie/ n. confidence, trust

доверить /dovérit'/ v. entrust (to)

доверху /dóverkhu/ adv. to the top

доверчивый /dovérchivyi/ adj. trusting, credulous

довершать /dovershát'/ v. complete

доверять /doveriát'/ v. trust, confide (in); д. ему тайну /d. emú táinu/ take him into one's confidence

довесок /dovésok/ m. makeweight

довод /dóvod/ m. reason, argument

доводить /dovodít'/ v. lead, bring (to)

довоенный /dovoénnyi/ adj. pre-war

довозить /dovozít'/ v. take (to, as far as)

довольно /dovól'no/ adv. enough; rather

довольный /dovól'nyi/ adj. pleased, content (with)

довыборы /dovýbory/ pl. by-election

дог /dog/ m. Great Dane

догадка /dogádka/ f. conjecture

догадливый /dogádlivyi/ adj. quick-witted

догадываться /dogádyvat'sia/ v. guess

догма /dógma/ f. dogma

догматический /dogmatícheskii/ adj. dogmatic

договаривать /dogovárivat'/ v. finish telling

договариваться /dogovárivat'sia/ v. come to an agreement; talk (to the point of)

договор /dogovór/ m. agreement, contract, treaty

договорный /dogovórnyi/ adj. contractual, agreed

догола /dogolá/ adv. stark naked

догонять /dogoniát'/ v. catch up

догорать /dogorát'/ v. burn down *or* out

доделывать /dodélyvat'/ v. finish

додумываться /dodúmyvat'sia/ v. hit (upon)

доедать /doedát'/ v. eat up

доезжать /doezzhát'/ v. reach, arrive (at)

дожаривать /dozhárivat'/ v. fry to a turn

дождевик /dozhdevík/ m. raincoat; puffball

дождливый /dozhdlívyi/ adj. rainy

дождь /dozhd'/ m. rain

доживать /dozhivát'/ v. live till; live out

дожидаться /dozhidát'sia/ v. wait for

доза /dóza/ f. dose

дозволять /dozvoliát'/ v. allow

дозвониться /dozvonit'sia/ v. ring till one gets an answer; ring through

дозировка /doziróvka/ f. dosage

дознание /doznánie/ n. inquiry; inquest

дозор /dozór/ m. patrol

дозревать /dozrevát'/ v. ripen

доигрывать /doígryvat'/ v. finish (playing)

доисторический /doistorícheskii/ adj. prehistoric

доить /doít'/ v. milk

док /dok/ m. dock

доказательный /dokazátel'nyi/ adj. conclusive

доказательство /dokazátel'stvo/ n. proof, evidence

доказывать /dokázyvat'/ v. prove

доканчивать /dokánchivat'/ v. finish

докапываться /dokápyvat'sia/ v. find out

докер /dóker/ m. docker

доклад /doklád/ m. report

докладчик /dokládchik/ m. speaker

докладывать /dokládyvat'/ v. make a report

докрасна /dokrasná/ adv. red-hot

доктор /dóktor/ m. doctor; physician

доктрина /doktrina/ f. doctrine

документ /dokumént/ m. document

документальный (фильм) /dokumentál'nyi film/ adj.+m. documentary film

долбить /dolbít'/ v. chisel; sl. repeat

долг /dolg/ debt; брать в д. /brat' v d./ borrow; давать в д. /dávat' v d./ lend

долгий /dólgii/ adj. long

долго /dólgo/ adv. for a long time

долговременный /dolgovrémennyi/ adj. lasting, permanent

долговязый /dolgoviázyi/ adj. lanky

долголетие /dolgolétie/ n. longevity

долгота /dolgotá/ f. length; longitude

долетать /doletát'/ v. fly (as far as), reach

должник /dolzhník/ m. debtor

должность /dólzhnost'/ f. post, position

доливать /dolivát'/ v. add, pour in addition

долина /dolina/ f. valley

доллар /dóllar/ m. dollar

долой /dolói/ adv. down with

дольше /dól'she/ adv. longer

доля /dólia/ f. portion, share; fate

дом /dom/ m. house; building

дома /dóma/ adv. at home

домашний /domáshnii/ adj. domestic

доминион /dominión/ m. dominion

домино /dominó/ n. dominoes

домкрат /domkrát/ m. jack

домна /dómna/ f. blast furnace

домовладелец /domovladélets/ m. house-owner; landlord

домовой /domovói/ m. house-spirit

домогательство /domogátel'stvo/ n. solicitation; importunity

домой /domói/ adv. home, homewards

доморощенный /domoróshchennyi/ home-bred; homespun

домработница /domrabótnitsa/ f. domestic servant

донага /donagá/ adv. stark naked

донесение /donesénie/ n. report, message
донизу /dónizu/ adv. to the bottom; сверху д. /svérkhu d./ from top to bottom
донимать /donimát/ v. harass, weary
донос /donós/ m. denunciation
доносить /donosít/ v. report, inform (against)
доносчик /donóschik/ m. informer
донской /donskói/ adj. (of the river) Don
допивать /dopivát/ v. drink up
дописывать /dopísyvat/ v. finnish writing
доплата /dopláta/ f. extra payment; excess fare
доплачивать /dopláchivat/ v. pay the remainder; pay in addition
дополнение /dopolnénie/ n. addition, supplement
дополнительный /dopolnítel'nyi/ adj. additional
дополнять /dopolniát/ v. supplement
допрашивать /dopráshivat/ v. question, interrogate
допрос /doprós/ m. interrogation
допуск /dópusk/ m. admittance
допускать /dopuskát/ v. admit
допустимый /dopustímyi/ adj. permissible, possible
дорабатывать /dorabátyvat/ v. elaborate, develop
дореволюционный /dorevoliutsiónnyi/ adj. pre-revolutionary
дорога /doróga/ f. road, way; железная д. /zheléznaia d./ railway, railroad; туда ему и д. /tudá emú i d./ it serves him right!
дороговизна /dorogovízna/ f. high prices
дорогой /dorogói/ adj. dear; expensive
дорожать /dorozhát/ v. rise in price
дорожить /dorozhít/ v. value
дорожка /dorózhka/ f. path; track; strip (of carpet)
досада /dosáda/ f. vexation, disappointment

доска /doská/ f. board; slab
доскональный /doskonál'nyi/ adj. thorough
дословный /doslóvnyi/ adj. word-forword, literal
досрочный /dosróchnyi/ adj. ahead of schedule
доставать /dostavát/ v. get, obtain; suffice; reach; touch
доставка /dostávka/ f. delivery
достаток /dostátok/ m. prosperity
достаточный /dostátochnyi/ adj. sufficient, enough
достигать /dostigát/ v. reach, achieve
достижение /dostizhénie/ n. achievement
достоверный /dostovérnyi/ adj. authentic
достоинство /dostóinstvo/ n. dignity; merit
достойный /dostóinyi/ adj. worthy (of)
достопримечательность /dostoprimechátel'nost'/ f. sight; осматривать (достопримечательности /osmátrivat' dostoprimechatel'nosti/ go sightseeing
достояние /dostoiánie/ n. property
достраивать /dostráivat/ v. finish building
доступ /dóstup/ m. access
доступный /dostúpnyi/ adj. accessible
досуг /dosúg/ m. leisure; на досуге /na dosúge/ in one's spare time
досуха /dósukha/ adv. dry
досыта (есть д.) /est' dósyta/ v.+adv. eat one's fill
досягаемый /dosiagáemyi/ adj. attainable
дотация /dotátsia/ f. State grant, subsidy
дотла /dotlá/ adv. completely; сгорать д. /sgorát' d./ burn to the ground
дотрагиваться /dotrágivat'sia/ v. touch
доход /dokhód/ m. income
доходный /dokhódnyi/ adj. profitable

доходчивый /dokhódchivyi/ adj. intelligible, easy to understand

доцент /dotsént/ m. associate professor; senior lecturer

дочерний /dochérnii/ adj. daughter's; branch

дочиста /dóchista/ adv. clean; completely

дочка, дочь /dóchka, doch/ f. daughter

дошкольник /doshkól'nik/ m. child under school age

дошкольный /doshkól'nyi/ adj. preschool

дощатый /doshchátyi/ adj. made of planks

дощечка /doshchéchka/ f. small plank; door-plate, name-plate

доярка /doiárka/ f. milkmaid

драгоценность /dragotsénnost'/ f. jewel

драгоценный /dragotsénnyi/ adj. precious

дразнить /draznít'/ v. tease

драка /dráka/ f. fight

дракон /drakón/ m. dragon

драма /dráma/ f. drama

драматический /dramatícheskii/ adj. dramatic

драматург /dramatúrg/ m. playwright

драп /drap/ m. thick, woollen cloth

драть /drat'/ v. tear; flog

драться /drát'sia/ v. fight

драчливый /drachlívyi/ adj. pugnacious

дребезжать /drebezzhát'/ v. jingle

древесина /drevesína/ f. wood; wood-pulp

древнерусский /drevnerússkii/ adj. Old Russian

древний /drévnii/ adj. ancient

дрезина /drezína/ f. trolley

дрейф /dreif/ m. drift

дремать /dremát'/ v. doze

дремота /dremóta/ f. drowsiness

дремучий /dremúchii/ adj. dense

дрессировать /dressirovát'/ v. train (animals)

дрессировщик /dressiróvshchik/ m. trainer

дробь /drob'/ f. fraction

дрова /drová/ pl. firewood

дрогнуть /drógnut'/ be chilled; waver, falter

дрожать /drozhát'/ v. shiver, tremble

дрожжи /drózhzhi/ pl. yeast, leaven

дрожь /drozh/ f. trembling

дрозд /drozd/ m. thrush

друг /drug/ m. friend; друг друга /drug drúga/ each other; друг с другом /drug s drúgom/ with each other

другой /drugói/ adj. other, different; и тот и д. /i tot i d./ both; ни тот ни д. /ni tot ni d./ neither

дружба /drúzhba/ f. friendship

дружелюбный /druzheliúbnyi/ adj. amicable

дружеский /drúzheskii/ adj. friendly

дружить /druzhít'/ v. be friends

дружный /drúzhnyi/ adj. harmonious; concerted

дряблый /driáblyi/ adj. flabby

дрязги /driázgi/ pl. squabbles

дрянной /driannói/ adj. worthless

дрянь /drian'/ f. rubbish

дряхлый /driákhlyi/ adj. decrepit

дуб /dub/ m. oak

дубина /dubína/ f. cudgel, club; blockhead

дубинка /dubínka/ f. truncheon, club

дубить /dubít'/ v. tan

дуга /dugá/ f. arc; shaft-bow

дудка /dúdka/ f. pipe; плясать под его д. /pliasát' pod evó d./ dance to his tune

дуло /dúlo/ n. muzzle

дупло /dupló/ n. hollow (tree); cavity (tooth)

дура /dúra/ f. fool

дурак /durák/ m. fool, ass

дурацкий /durátskii/ adj. foolish

дурачиться /duráchit'sia/ v. play the fool

дурь /dur'/ f. nonsense; foolishness

дутый /dútyi/ adj. hollow; exaggerated

дуть /dut'/ v. blow

дуться /dut'sia/ v. sulk, pout (at)

дух /dukh/ m. spirit; breath; mind; spectre, ghost; захватывает дух /zakhvátyvaet dukh/ it takes one's breath away; присутствие духа /prisútstvie dúkha/ presence of mind; о нем ни слуху ни духу /o niom ni slúkhu ni dukhú/ nothing has been heard of him

духи /dukhí/ pl. perfume

духовенство /dukhovénstvo/ n. clergy

духовка /dukhóvka/ f. oven

духовный /dukhóvnyi/ adj. spiritual; inner; ecclesiastical

духовой /dukhovói/ adv. wind; д. инструмент /d. instrumént/ wind instrument

душ /dush/ m. shower(-bath)

душа /dushá/ f. soul; у меня душа в пятки ушла /u meniá dushá v piátki ushlá/ I was terrified; она в нем души не чает /oná v niom dushí ne cháet/ she dotes on him

душевнобольной /dushevnobol'nói/ adj. insane

душевный /dushévnyi/ adj. mental, psychical; sincere

душистый /dushístyi/ adj. fragrant

душить /dushít'/ v. smother, stifle, strangle; scent, perfume

душный /dúshnyi/ adj. stuffy

дуэль /duél'/ f. duel

дуэт /duét/ m. duet

дыбом /dýbom/ adv. on end; волосы у него стали д. /vólosy u nevó stáli d./ his hair stood on end

дым /dym/ m. smoke

дымить /dymít'/ v. smoke

дымка /dýmka/ f. haze

дымоход /dymokhód/ m. flue

дымчатый /dýmchatyi/ adj. smoke-coloured

дыня /dýnia/ f. melon

дыра /dyrá/ f. hole

дырокол /dyrokól/ m. hole-puncher

дырявый /dyriávyi/ adj. full of holes

дыхание /dykhánie/ n. breathing; breath

дыхательный /dykhátel'nyi/ adj. respiratory; дыхательное горло /dykhátel'noe górlo/ windpipe

дышать /dyshát'/ v. breathe

дьявол /d'iávol/ m. devil

дьявольский /d'iávol'skii/ adj. devilish

дьякон /d'iákon/ m. deacon

дюжина /diúzhina/ f. dozen

дюйм /diúim/ m. inch

дюна /diúna/ f. dune

дядя /diádia/ m. uncle

дятел /diátel/ m. woodpecker

Е

Евангелие /evángelie/ n. the Gospels

евнух /évnukh/ m. eunuch

евразийский /evraziískii/ adj. Eurasian

еврей /evréi/ m. Jew; Hebrew

еврейка /evréika/ f. Jewess

еврейский /evréiskii/ adj. Jewish

европеец /evropéets/ m. European

европейский /evropéiskii/ adj. European

египетский /egípetskii/ adj. Egyptian

египтянин /egiptiánin/ m. Egyptian

египтянка /egiptiánka/ f. Egyptian

еда /edá/ f. food, meal

едва /edvá/ adv. hardly, just, scarcely; е. не /e. ne/ nearly, all but

единица /edinítsa/ f. one; unit; individual

единичный /ediníchnyi/ adj. single, isolated

единогласие /edinoglásie/ n. unanimity

единодушие /edinodúshie/ n. unanimity

единомыслие /edinomýslie/ n. agreement of opinion

единообразие /edinoobrázie/ n. uniformity

единственный /edínstvennyi/ adj. only, sole

единство /edínstvo/ n. unity

единый /edínyi/ adj. united, common;
single
едкий /édkii/ adj. caustic, pungent
еж /iozh/ m. hedgehog; морской еж
/morskói iózh/ sea urchin
ежевика /ezhevíka/ f. blackberries
ежегодник /ezhegódnik/ m. year-book
ежегодный /ezhegódnyi/ adj. annual
ежедневный /ezhednévnyi/ adj. daily
ежемесячник /ezhemésiachnik/ m.
monthly (magazine)
еженедельник /ezhenedél'nik/ m. weekly (newspaper, magazine)
ежечасный /ezhechásnyi/ adj. hourly
ежиться /iózhit'sia/ v. huddle oneself up
езда /ezdá/ f. ride
ездить /ézdit'/ v. ride, drive, go
ей-богу /ei-bógu/ int. really and truly
елка /iólka/ f. fir(-tree); рождественская
е. /rozhdéstvenskaia io./ Christmas-
tree
ель /el'/ f. fir-tree
енот /enót/ m. raccoon
епархия /epárkhia/ f. diocese
епископ /epískop/ m. bishop
ересь /éres'/ f. heresy
еретик /eretík/ m. heretic
ерунда /erundá/ f. nonsense
ерш /iorsh/ m. ruf (fish); sl. mixture of beer
and vodka
если /ésli/ conj. if; е. не /e. ne/ unless
естественный /estéstvennyi/ adj. natural
естествознание /estestvoznánie/ n. natural science
есть /est'/ v. eat; there is, there are ; у меня
е. /u meniá e./ I have
есть! /est'!/ int. yes, sir; aye-aye
ефрейтор /efréitor/ m. lance-corporal;
private first class
ехать /ékhat'/ v. go, drive, ride
ехидный /ekhídnyi/ adj. malicious; venomous
еще /eshchió/ adv. still, yet; е. раз /e. raz/
once more, again

Ж

ж /zh/ - же
жаба /zhába/ f. toad; грудная ж. /grud-
náia zh./ angina pectoris
жабры /zhábry/ pl. gills
жаворонок /zhávoronok/ m. lark
жадность /zhádnost'/ f. greed
жадный /zhádnyi/ adj. greedy (for)
жажда /zházhda/ f. thirst
жакет /zhakét/ m. (ladies') jacket
жалеть /zhalét'/ v. feel sorry (for); regret
жалить /zhálit'/ v. sting
жалкий /zhálkii/ adj. pitiful, pathetic,
wretched
жало /zhálo/ n. sting
жалоба /zháloba/ f. complaint
жалобный /zhálobnyi/ adj. plaintive;
жалобная книга /zhálobnaia kniga/
complaints book
жалованье /zhálovan'e/ n. salary
жаловаться /zhálovat'sia/ v. complain
(of, about)
жалость /zhálost'/ f. pity
жаль /zhal'/ as pred. (it is a) pity; ему жаль
сестру /emu zhal' sestrú/ he is sorry for
his sister
жанр /zhanr/ m. genre
жар /zhar/ m. heat, fever
жара /zhará/ f. heat
жаргон /zhargón/ m. slang
жареный /zhárenyi/ adj. fried, grilled,
roasted
жарить /zhárit'/ v. fry, grill
жаркий /zhárkii/ adj. hot
жаркое /zharkóe/ n. roast (meat)
жатва /zhátva/ f. harvest; reaping
жать /zhat'/ v. press, squeeze; be too tight;
reap
жвачка /zhváchka/ f. chewing-gum
жвачное (животное) /zhváchnoe zhi-
vótnoe adj.+n. ruminant
жгут /zhgut/ m. plait

жгучий /zhgúchii/ adj. burning
ждать /zhdat'/ v. wait (for)
же /zhe/ conj. as for, but; after all
же /zhe/ emphatic particle: когда же они
приедут? /kogdá zhe oni priédut?/
whenever will they come?
же /zhe/ particle expressing identity: тот
же /tot zhe/ the same; там же /tam zhe/
in the same place
жевать /zhevát'/ v. chew
жезл /zhezl/ m. rod; crozier
желание /zhelánie/ n. wish, desire
желанный (гость) /zhelánnyi gost'/
adj.+m. welcome visitor
желательный /zhelátel'nyi/ adj. desirable
желать /zhelát'/ v. wish
желвак /zhelvák/ m. tumour
желе /zhelé/ n. jelly
железа /zhelezá/ f. gland
железнодорожник /zheleznodórozhnik/
m. railwayman
железный /zheléznyi/ adj. iron; железная дорога /zheléznaia doróga/ railway
железо /zhelézo/ n. iron
железобетон /zhelezobetón/ m. reinfor-
ced concrete
желоб /zhólob/ m. gutter
желтеть /zheltét'/ v. turn yellow, show up
yellow
желток /zheltók/ m. yolk
желтуха /zheltúkha/ f. jaundice
желтый /zhóltyi/ adj. yellow
желудок /zhelúdok/ m. stomach
желудочный /zhelúdochnyi/ adj. stomach, gastric
желудь /zhólud'/ m. acorn
желчный /zhólchnyi/ adj. bilious; bitter;
ж. пузырь /zh. puzýr'/ gall-bladder
желчь /zhelch/ f. bile, gall
жемчуг /zhémchug/ m. pearl(s)
жемчужный /zhemchúzhnyi/ adj. pearl
жена /zhená/ f. wife

женатый /zhenátyi/ adj. married
женитьба /zhenit'ba/ f. marriage
жениться /zhenit'sia/ v. marry, get married
жених /zhenikh/ m. fiancé
женский /zhénskii/ adj. female, feminine
женственный /zhénstvennyi/ adj. womanly
женщина /zhénshchina/ f. woman
жердь /zherd'/ f. pole
жеребенок /zherebiónok/ m. foal
жеребец /zherebéts/ m. stallion
жерло /zherló/ n. muzzle; crater
жернов /zhórnov/ m. millstone
жертва /zhértva/ f. victim
жертвовать /zhértvovat'/ v. sacrifice
жертвоприношение /zhertvoprinoshé-
nie/ n. sacrifice
жест /zhest/ m. gesture
жесткий /zhóstkii/ adj. hard, rigid
жестокий /zhestókii/ adj. cruel
жестокость /zhestókost'/ f. cruelty
жесть /zhest'/ f. tin(-plate)
жетон /zhetón/ m. counter
жечь /zhech/ v. burn
живой /zhivói/ adj. living, alive
живописец /zhivopísets/ m. painter
живописный /zhivopísnyi/ adj. picturesque
живость /zhívost/ f. liveliness
живот /zhivót/ m. abdomen, belly
животноводство /zhivotnovódstvo/ n.
cattle-breeding
животное /zhivótnoe/ n. animal
живучий /zhivúchii/ adj. hardy, tough;
enduring
живьем /zhiv'ióm/ adv. alive
жидкий /zhídkii/ adj. liquid; thin
жидкость /zhídkost'/ f. liquid; fluid
жизненный /zhíznennyi/ adj. vital, living; ж. уровень /zh. uroven'/ standard
of living
жизнеспособный /zhiznesposóbnyi/ adj.
viable

жизнь /zhizn'/ f. life
жила /zhíla/ f. vein
жилет /zhilét/ m. waistcoat
жилец /zhiléts/ m. tenant, lodger
жилище /zhilíshche/ n. dwelling
жилищные (условия) /zhilíshchnye uslóviia/ adj.+pl. housing conditions
жилой /zhilói/ adj. dwelling; ж. дом /zh. dom/ dwelling house
жилплощадь /zhilplóshchad'/ f. housing, accomodation
жилье /zhil'ió/ n. dwelling
жимолость /zhímolost'/ f. honeysuckle
жир /zhir/ m. fat, grease
жираф /zhiráf/ m. giraffe
жиреть /zhirét'/ v. grow fat
жирный /zhírnyi/ adj. fat; rich; greasy
житейский /zhitéiskii/ adj. everyday; worldly
житель /zhítel'/ m. inhabitant, resident
жительство /zhítel'stvo/ n. residence
житие /zhitié/ n. life (of a saint)
житница /zhítnitsa/ f. granary
жить /zhit'/ v. live
житье /zhit'ió/ n. life, existence
жмуриться /zhmúrit'sia/ v. screw up one's eyes
жнец /zhnets/ m. reaper
жребий /zhrébii/ m. lot; ж. брошен /zh. bróshen/ the die is cast
жрец /zhrets/ m. priest
жужжание /zhuzhzhánie/ n. buzz
жук /zhuk/ m. beetle
жулик /zhúlik/ m. swindler
жульничать /zhúl'nichat'/ v. cheat
журавль /zhurávl'/ m. crane
журнал /zhurnál/ m. periodical, magazine, journal
журналист /zhurnalíst/ m. journalist
журчание /zhurchánie/ n. murmur
журчать /zhurchát'/ v. babble
жуткий /zhútkii/ adj. terrible; мне жутко /mne zhútko/ I am terrified

жюри /zhurí/ n. jury

З

за /za/ prep. behind, beyond; at; for; after; because of; за городом /za górodom/ aut of town; за столом /za stolom/ at the table; за работой /za rabótoi/ at work; ехать за город /ekhat' za górod/ go out of town; ему за 50 лет /emu za 50 let/ he is over 50; далеко за полночь /daleko zá polnoch/ long after midnight; за 100 км от /za 100 km ot/ 100 km from...; за последние пять лет /za poslédnie piat' let/ for the past five years; за два дня до этого /za dva dniá doétovo/ two days before that; покупать за 10 руб. /pokupat' za 10 rublei/ buy for 10 roubles; я расписался за него /ia raspisálsia za nevó/ I have signed for him; за и против /za i protiv/ pros and cons; взять за руку /vziat' zá ruku/ take by the hand
забава /zabáva/ f. amusement
забавлять /zabavliát'/ v. amuse, entertain
забастовка /zabastóvka/ f. strike
забег /zabég/ m. heat, race
забегать /zabegát'/ v. drop in (to see); з. вперед /z. vperiód/ run ahead; anticipate
забеременеть /zaberémenet'/ v. become pregnant
забивать /zabivát'/ v. drive in; score (a goal)
забинтовывать /zabintóvyvat'/ v. bandage
забирать /zabirát'/ v. take away
забираться /zabirát'sia/ v. climb up, get (into)
заблаговременный /zablagovrémennyi/ adj. timely

заблудиться /zabludít'sia/ v. get lost
заблуждаться /zabluzhdát'sia/ v. be mistaken
заблуждение /zabluzhdénie/ n. error; ввести в з. mislead
забой /zabói/ m. (pit-)face
заболевать /zabolévat'/ v. begin to ache; fall ill
забор /zabór/ m. fence
забота /zabóta/ f. care
заботиться /zabótit'sia/ v. take care of
заботливый /zabótlivyi/ adj. considerate, solicitous
забрасывать /zabrásyvat'/ v. shower (with); throw; abandon
заброшенный /zabróshennyi/ adj. neglected
забывать /zabyvát'/ v. forget
забывчивый /zabývchivyi/ adj. forgetful
заваливать /zaválivat'/ v. heap up, block up; overload
заваривать (чай) /zavárivat' chai/ v.+m. brew tea
заведение /zavedénie/ n. establishment
заведовать /zavédovat'/ v. manage
заведомо/zavédomo/ adv. deliberately; admittedly
заведомый /zavédomyi/ adj. notorious
заведующий /zavéduyushchii/ m. manager, head
завертеть /zavertét'/ v. begin to twirl
завертывать /zaviórtyvat'/ v. wrap in; turn off
завершать /zavershát'/ v. complete, conclude
заверять /zaveriát'/ v. assure; certify; з. кого-либо в своей дружбе /z. kovólibo v svoéi drúzhbe/ assure someone of one's friendship
завеса /zavésa/ f. curtain
завет /zavét/ m. behest; Ветхий, Новый з. /vétkhii, nóvyi z./ the Old, the New Testament

заветный /zavétnyi/ adj. cherished; secret
завешивать /zavéshivat'/ v. curtain, cover
завещание /zaveshchánie/ n. testament, will
завещать /zaveshchát'/ v. bequeath
завивать /zavivát'/ v. wave; curl
завивка /zavívka/ f. waving; (hair-)wave
завидный /zavídnyi/ adj. enviable; ему завидно /emu závidno/ he is envious
завидовать /zavídovat'/ v. envy
завинчивать /zavínchivat'/ v. screw up
зависеть /zavíset'/ v. depend (on)
зависимость /zavísimost'/ f. dependence
зависимый /zavísimyi/ adj. dependent
завистливый /zavístlivyi/ adj. envious
зависть /závist'/ f. envy
завитой /zavitói/ adj. curled; waved
завком /zavkóm/ m. factory committee
завладеть /zavladét'/ v. take possession of; seize
завлекать /zavlekát'/ v. entice, lure
завод /zavód/ m. factory, works; stud (-farm); winding up
заводить /zavodít'/ v. bring, lead; acquire; establish; wind up
заводной /zavodnói/ adj. clockwork
завоевание /zavoevánie/ n. conquest; achievement
завоеватель /zavoevátel'/ m. conqueror
завоевывать /zavoióvyvat'/ v. conquer, win
завозить /zavozít'/ v. convey, deliver
заволакивать /zavolákivat'/ v. cloud, obscure
завораживать /zavorázhivat'/ v. bewitch
заворачивать /zavoráchivat'/ v. wrap up; turn; drop in
завтра /závtra/ adv. tomorrow
завтрак /závtrak/ m. breakfast
завтрашний /závtrashnii/ adj. tomorrow's
завуч /závuch/m. and f. director of studies
завхоз /zavkhóz/ m. bursar, steward
завывать /zavyvát'/ v. howl

завязнуть /zaviáznut'/ v. stick, get stuck
завязывать /zaviázyvat'/ v. tie up; start
завязь /záviaz'/ f. ovary
загадка /zagádka/ f. enigma, riddle
загадочный /zagádochnyi/ adj. mysterious
загадывать /zagádyvat'/ v. make, plans, look ahead; з. загадки /z. zagádki/ ask riddles
загаживать /zagázhivat'/ v. soil, dirty
загар /zagár/ m. (sun-)tan
загвоздка /zagvozdka/ f. snag, obstacle
загибать /zagibát'/ v. bend; sl. exaggerate
заглавие /zaglávie/ n. title, heading
заглавный (лист) /zaglávnyi list/ adj.+m. title page; заглавная буква /zaglávnaia búkva/ capital letter; заглавная роль /zaglávnaia rol'/ title role
заглаживать /zaglázhivat'/ v. press; make up (for)
заглушать /zaglushát'/ v. muffle, jam (broadcast); soothe (pain)
заглядывать /zagliádyvat'/ v. peep in; call on
загнивание /zagnivánie/ n. decay
загнивать /zagnivát'/ v. rot
заговаривать /zagovárivat'/ v. begin to speak; cast a spell over
заговариваться /zagovárivat'sia/ v. ramble
заговор /zágovor/ m. plot; exorcism
заговорщик /zagovórshchik/ m. conspirator
заголовок /zagolóvok/ m. heading, title; headline
загон /zagón/ m. pen
загонять /zagoniát'/ v. drive in
загораживать /zagorázhivat'/ v. enclose; obstruct
загорать /zagorát'/ v. become sunburnt
загораться /zagorát'sia/ v. catch fire; have a buning desire
загорелый /zagorélyi/ adj. sunburnt
загородный /zágorodnyi/ adj. country, out-of-town

загон /zagón/ m. pen
загонять /zagoniát'/ v. drive in
загораживать /zagorázhivat'/ v. enclose; obstruct
загорать /zagorát'/ v. become sunburnt
загораться /zagorát'sia/ v. catch fire; have a buning desire
загорелый /zagorélyi/ adj. sunburnt
загородка /zagoródka/ f. fence, enclosure
загородный /zágorodnyi/ adj. country, out-of-town
заготавливать /zagotávlivat'/ v. lay in, store
заграждать /zagrazhdát'/ v. obstruct
заграждение /zagrazhdénie/ n. blocking; obstacle
заграница /zagranítsa/ f. foreign countries; поехать за границу /poékhat' za granítsu/ go abroad
заграничный /zagraníchnyi/ adj. foreign
загребать /zagrebát'/ v. rake up; з. деньги /z. dén'gi/ rake in the shekels
загривок /zagrívok/ m. withers; nape (of the sneck)
загробный /zagróbnyi/ adj. beyond the grave
загромождать /zagromozhdát'/ v. block up
загружать /zagruzhát'/ v. load; feed (machine); keep fully occupied
загрызать /zagryzát'/ v. bite, worry to death
загрязнять /zagriazniát'/ v. pollute
загс /zags/ abbr., m. registry office
зад /zad/ m. back; buttocks; задом /zádom/ with one's back (to); з. наперед /z. naperiód/ back to front
задавать /zadavát'/ v. give, set
задаваться (целью) /zadavát'sia tsél'iu/ v.+f. set oneself (to)
задание /zadánie/ n. task

задаток /zadátok/ m. advance, deposit; природные задатки /priródnye zadátki/ instincts, inclinations

задача /zadácha/ f. problem, task

задвигать /zadvigát'/ v. push, bolt, bar

задвижка /zadvízhka/ f. bolt

задевать /zadevát'/ v. touch; offend, wound

заделывать /zadélyvat'/ v. do up, close up

задергивать /zadiórgivat'/ v. pull, shut

задеревенелый /zaderevenélyi/ adj. numbed

задержание /zaderzhánie/ n. detention

задерживать /zadérzhivat'/ v. hold back; arrest

задерживаться /zaderzhivat'sia/ v. stay too long

задержка /zadérzhka/ f. delay

задира /zadíra/ m. and f. trouble-maker

задирать /zadirát'/ v. lift up; з. нос /z. nos/ cock one's nose

задний /zádnii/ adj. back, rear; з. план /z. plan/ background

задолго /zadólgo/ adv. long before

задолженность /zadólzhennost'/ f. debts

задор /zadór/ m. fervour

задорный /zadórnyi/ adj. provoking, teasing

задувать /zaduvát'/ v. blow (out); extinguish

задумчивый /zadúmchivyi/ adj. thoughtful

задумывать /zadúmyvat'/ v. plan, intend

задумываться /zadúmyvat'sia/ v. become lost in thought

задушевный /zadushévnyi/ adj. sincere; intimate

задыхаться /zadykhát'sia/ v. choke, suffocate

заедать /zaedát'/ v. bite to death; torment; jam; take (with); он заел пилюлю сахаром /on zaél piliúliu sákharom/ he took the pill with sugar

заездить /zaézdit'/ v. wear out; override (a horse)

заезжать /zaezzhát'/ v. call (at)

заезженный /zaézzhennyi/ adj. worn out; hackneyed

заем /zaióm/ m. loan

заживать /zazhivát'/ v. heal; begin to live

заживо /zázhivo/ adv. alive

зажигалка /zazhigálka/ f. lighter

зажигательный /zazhigátel'nyi/ adj. inflammatory, incendiary

зажигать /zazhigát'/ v. set fire to;light

зажигаться /zazhigát'sia/ catch fire; inflame

зажим /zazhím/ m. clamp

зажимать /zazhimát'/ v. suppress; clutch

зажиточный /zazhítochnyi/ adj. prosperous

заздравный /zazdrávnyi/ adj. to the health (of); они выпили з. тост за посла /oni výpili z. tost za poslá/ they drank the ambassador's health

зазеваться /zazevát'sia/ v. gape (at)

заземление /zazemlénie/ n. earthing (electr.)

заземлять /zazemliát'/ v. earth

зазнаваться /zaznavát'sia/ v. give oneself airs

зазубривать /zazúbrivat'/ v. learn by rote

зазубрина /zazúbrina/ f. notch

заигрывать /zaígryvat'/ v. wear out (cards, etc.); flirt (with)

заика /zaíka/ m. and f. stammerer

заикаться /zaikát'sia/ v. stammer, slutter

заимствовать /zaímstvovat'/ v. borrow

заинтересовывать /zainteresóvyvat'/ v. interest

заискивать /zaískivat'/ v. ingratiate oneself (with)

зайчик /záichik/ m. little hare; reflection of a sunray

зайчиха /zaichíkha/ f. doe-hare

закабалять /zakabaliát'/ v. enslave

закавказский /zakavkázskii/ adj. Transcaucasian

закадычный (друг) /zakadýchnyi drug/ adj.+m. bosom friend

заказ /zakáz/ m. order

заказной /zakaznói/ made to order; заказное письмо /zakaznóe pis'mó/ registered letter

заказчик /zakázchik/ m. client, customer

заказывать /zakázyvat'/ v. order

закалывать /zakályvat'/ v. stab; pin (up)

закалять /zakaliát'/ v. temper

заканчивать /zakánchivat'/ v. finish

закапывать /zakápyvat'/ v. bury; fill up

закармливать /zakármvlivat'/ v. overfeed

закаспийский /zakaspiiskii/ adj. Transcaspian

закат /zakát/ m. sunset

закатывать /zakátyvat'/ v. roll up, wrap in

закатываться /zakátyvat'sia/ v. roll; set (of heavenly bodies)

закваска /zakváska/ f. ferment

закидывать /zakídyvat'/ v. shower (with); throw (out, away)

закипать /zakipát'/ v. begin to boil

закисать /zakisát'/ v. turn sour; become apathetic

заклад /zaklád/ m. pawning; биться об з. /bít'sia ob z./ bet

закладка /zakládka/ f. bookmark

закладная /zakladnáia/ f. mortgage

закладывать /zakládyvat'/ v. put (behind); block up; lay (the foundation of); pawn

заклеивать /zakléivat'/ v. glue up

заклепка /zakliópka/ f. rivet

заклинание /zaklinánie/ n. incantation; exorcism

заклинатель (змей) /zaklinátel' zméi/ m.+pl. snake-charmer

заключать /zakliuchát'/ v. conclude; infer; close, finish; contract; contain; imprison

заключаться /zakliuchát'sia/ v. consist (in)

заключение /zakliuchénie/ n. conclusion; imprisonment

заключенный /zakliuchónnyi/ m. prisoner

заключительный /zakliuchítel'nyi/ adj. final

заклятие /zakliátie/ n. pledge

заклятый (враг) /zakliátyi vrag/ adj.+m. sworn enemy

заковывать /zakóvyvat'/ v. chain

заколачивать /zakoláchivat'/ v. drive in; nail up

заколка /zakólka/ f. hairpin

закон /zakón/ m. law

законность /zakónnost'/ f. legality

законный /zakónnyi/ adj. legal, legitimate

законодательный /zakonodátel'nyi/ adj. legislative

законодательство /zakonodátel'stvo/ n. legislation

закономерность /zakonomérnost'/ f. regularity, conformity with a law

закономерный /zakonomérnyi/ adj. regular, natural

законопроект /zakonoproékt/ m. bill

закоренелый /zakorenélyi/ adj. inveterate

закостенелый /zakostenélyi/ adj. inveterate

закоулок /zakouílok/ m. back street

закоченелый /zakochenélyi/ adj. numb with cold

закрадываться /zakrádyvat'sia/ v. steal in, creep in

закрепление /zakreplénie/ n. fastening, fixing; consolidation закреплять /zakrepliát'/ v. fasten, fix; consolidate; allot

закрепощать /zakreposhchát'/ v. enslave

закройщик /zakróishchik/ m. cutter (of clothes)

закруглять /zakrugliát'/ v. make round; з. фразу /z. frázu/ round off a sentence

закручивать /zakrúchivat'/ v. twist; turn tight

закрывать(ся) /zakryvát'(sia)/ v. close, shut

закрытие /zakrýtie/ n. closing

закрытый /zakrýtyi/ adj. shut, closed; private

закулисный /zakulísnyi/ adj. secret; underhand

закупать /zakupát'/ v. buy up (wholesale)

закупка /zakúpka/ f. purchase

закупоривать /zakupórivat'/ v. cork

закупорка /zakúporka/ f. corking; thrombosis

закуривать /zakúrivat'/ v. light up (cigarette, etc.)

закуска /zakúska/ f. hors-d'oeuvre; snack

закусочная /zakúsochnaia/ f. snack bar

закусывать /zakúsyvat'/ v. have a snack

закутывать /zakútyvat'/ v. wrap up, muffle

зал /zal/ m. hall; (reception) room

заламывать (цену) /zalámyvat' tsenu/ v.+f. ask an exorbitant price

заледенелый /zaledenélyi/ adj. covered with ice

залеживаться /zaliózhivat'sia/ v. lie too long; find no market; become stale

залежь /zálezh/ f. deposit, bed

залезать /zalezát'/ v. climb (up, onto), creep (into)

залетать /zaletát'/ v. fly (into)

залетная (птица) /zaliótnaia ptítsa/ adj.+f. bird of passage

залечивать /zaléchivat'/ v. cure, heal

залив /zalív/ m. bay, gulf

заливать /zalivát'/ v. flood; quench; extinguish

заливной /zalivnói/ adj. jellied; з. луг /z. lug/ water-meadow

зализывать /zalízyvat'/ v. lick clean

залог /zalóg/ m. deposit; security; voice (gram.)

заложник /zalózhnik/ m. hostage

залп /zalp/ m. volley, salvo; выпить залпом /výpit' zálpom/ drink at one draught

замазка /zamázka/ f. putty

замазывать /zamázyvat'/ v. paint over; putty; soil

замалчивать /zamálchivat'/ v. hush up

заманивать /zamánivat'/ v. entice

заманчивый /zamánchivyi/ adj. tempting

заматывать /zamátyvat'/ v. roll up

замахиваться /zamákhivat'sia/ v. lift one's arm threateningly

замачивать /zamáchivat'/ v. wet

замашка /zamáshka/ f. manner, way

замедление /zamedlénie/ n. slowing down

замедлять /zamedliát'/ v. slow down

замена /zaména/ f. substitution

заменять /zameniát'/ v. substitute, replace

замерзание /zamerzánie/ n. freezing; точка замерзания /tóchka zamerzániia/ freezing point

замертво /zámertvo/ adv. as good as dead

заместитель /zamestítel'/ m. deputy, assistant, vice-...

заметать /zametát'/ v. sweep up; cover (up)

заметка /zamétka/ f. note, notice

заметный /zamétnyi/ adj. appreciable; noticeable; visible

замечание /zamechánie/ n. remark

замечательный /zamechátel'nyi/ adj. remarkable

замечать /zamechát'/ v. notice, observe, remark

замешательство /zameshátel'stvo/ n. embarrassment

замешивать /zaméshivat'/ v. involve; implicate; mix; з. тесто /z. tésto/ knead dough

замещать /zameshchát'/ v. replace

замещение /zameshchénie/ n. substitution

заминка /zamínka/ f. hitch; hesistation (in speech)

замирание /zamiránie/ n. dying out or down; с замиранием сердца /s zamirániem sérdtsa/ with a sinking heart

замирать /zamirát'/ v. die away

замкнутость /zámknutost'/ f. reserve

замкнутый /zámknutyi/ adj. exclusive; reserved

замок /zámok/ m. castle

замок /zamók/ m. lock

замолвить (словечко за) /zamólvit' slovéchko za/ put in a word (for)

замолкать /zamolkát'/ v. fall silent

замораживать /zamorázhivat'/ v. freeze

заморозки /zámorozki/ pl. (light) frosts

заморский /zamórskii/ adj. foreign, overseas

замочная (скважина) /zamóchnaia skvázhina/ adj.+f. keyhole

замуж (выдавать з.) /vydavát' zámuzh/ v.+adv. give in marriage (to); выходить з. /vykhodít' z./ get married (to)

замужем /zámuzhem/ adv. married (to)

замужняя /zamúzhniaia/ adj. married

замша /zámsha/ f. suede

замывать /zamyvát'/ v. wash off

замыкание (короткое з.) /korótkoe zamykánie/ adj.+n. short circuit

замыкать /zamykát'/ v. lock, close

замысел /zámysel/ m. project, plan

замышлять /zamyshliát'/ v. plan; contemplate

замять (разговор) /zamiat' razgovor/ v.+m. change the subject

занавес /zánaves/ m. curtain

занавеска /zanavéska/ f. curtain

занимательный /zanimátel'nyi/ adj. entertaining

занимать /zanimát'/ v. occupy; engage; interest

заниматься /zanimát'sia/ v. be occupied (with); be engaged (in); study

заново /zánovo/ adv. anew

заноза /zanóza/ f. splinter

занос /zános/ m. snow-drift

заносчивый /zanóschivyi/ adj. arrogant

занятие /zaniátie/ n. occupation

занятный /zaniátnyi/ adj. entertaining, amusing

занятой /zaniatói/ adj. occupied, busy

заоблачный /zaóblachnyi/ adj. beyond the clouds

заострять /zaostriát'/ v. sharpen; emphasize

заочник /zaóchnik/ m. external student

заочный (курс) /zaóchnyi kurs/ adj.+m. correspondence course

запад /západ/ m. west

западный /západnyi/ adj. western

западня /zapadniá/ f. trap

запаздывать /zapázdyvat'/ v. be late

запаковывать /zapakóvyvat'/ v. pack, wrap up

запал /zapál/ m. fuse

запальчивый /zapál'chivyi/ adj. quick-tempered

запанибрата (быть з. с кем-либо) /byt' zapanibráta s kem-líbo/ be hailfellow-well-met with someone

запас /zapás/ m. stock, supply

запасать /zapasát'/ v. store

запасаться /zapasát'sia/ v. provide one self (with)

запасливый /zapáslivyi/ adj. thrifty

запасной /zapasnói/ adj. spare, reserve

запах /zápakh/ m. smell

запев /zapév/ m. introduction (to song)

запевала /zapevála/ m. and f. leader (of choir)

запевать /zapevát'/ v. set the tune

запеканка /zapekánka/ f. baked pudding

запекать /zapekát'/ v. bake

запечатлевать /zapechatlevát'/ v. impress, imprint

запечатывать /zapechátyvat'/ v. seal up

запивать /zapivát'/ v. wash down

запить /zapít'/ v. take to drinking

запинаться /zapinát'sia/ v. stammer, falter

запирать /zapirát'/ v. lock

запираться /zapirát'sia/ v. be locked; lock oneself up

записка /zapíska/ f. note

записывать /zapísyvat'/ v. note; enter; record

записываться /zapísyvat'sia/ v. register, enroll

запись /zapis'/ f. writing down; entry; record, recording

запихивать /zapíkhivat'/ v.cram into

заплаканный /zaplákannyi/ adj. tear-stained

заплакать /zaplákat'/ v. start crying

заплата /zapláta/ f. patch

заплеванный /zaplióvannyi/ adj. bespattered (with spittle); dirty

заплесневелый /zaplesnevélyi/ adj. mouldy

заплетать /zapletát'/ v. braid, plait

заплывать /zaplyvát'/ v. swim far out; sailaway; be bloated

заповедник /zapovédnik/ m. preserve; reserve

заповедь /zápoved'/ f. commandment

заподозрить /zapodózrit'/ v. suspect (of)

запоздалый /zapozdályi/ adj. belated

заползать /zapolzát'/ v. crawl, creep (in)

заполнять /zapolniát'/ v. fill in, fill up

запоминать /zapominát'/ v. memorize

запонка /záponka/ f. cuff-link

запор /zapór/ m. lock, bolt; constipation

запорожец /zaporózhets/ m. Dnieper Cossack

запотевший /zapotévshii/ adj. misted, dim

заправка /zaprávka/ f. seasoning; refuelling

заправлять /zapravliát'/ v. season; trim; refuel

заправочная (станция) /zaprávochnaia stántsiia/ adj.+f. filling (gas) station

заправский /zaprávskii/ adj. real, true

запрашивать /zapráshivat'/ v. inquire

запрет /zaprét/ m. interdiction

запретный /zaprétnyi/ adj. forbidden

запрещать /zapreshchát'/ v. forbid

запрещение /zapreshchénie/ n. prohibition

запрокидывать /zaprokídyvat'/ v. throw back

запрос /zaprós/ m. inquiry; pl. spiritual needs

запруда /zaprúda/ f. dam

запруживать /zaprúzhivat'/ v. dam

запрягать /zapriagát'/ v. harness

запрятывать /zapriátyvat'/ v. hide

запугивать /zapúgivat'/ v. intimidate

запуск /zápusk/ m. launching

запускать /zapuskát'/ v. start, launch; neglect

запутывать /zapútyvat'/ v. tangle, confuse

запутываться /zapútyvat'sia/ v. become entangled

запутанный /zapútannyi/ adj. intricate

запущенный /zaplushchennyi/ adj. neglected

запыленный /zapyliónnyi/ adj. covered in dust

запыхаться /zapykhát'sia/ v. be out of breath

запястье /zapiást'e/ n. wrist

запятая /zapiatáia/ f. comma

зарабатывать /zarabátyvat'/ v. earn

заработная (плата) /zárabotnaia pláta/ adj.+f. wage, pay

заработок /zárabotok/ m. earnings

заравнивать /zarávnivat'/ v. level, even up

заражать /zarazhát'/ v. infect, contaminate

заражаться /zarazhát'sia/ v. be infected; catch

заражение /zarazhénie/ n. infection

зараза /zaráza/ f. infection, contagion

заразительный /zarazítel'nyi/ adj. infectious

заразный /zaráznyi/ adj. infectious, contagious

заранее /zaránee/ adv. beforehand

зарево /zárevo/ n. glow

зарез (до зарезу) /do zarézu/ prep.+m. desperately

зарезывать /zarézyvat'/ v. kill, slaughter

зарекаться /zarekát'sia/ v. promise to give up

зарекомендовать (себя) /zarekomendovát' sebiá/ v.+pron. show oneself (to be)

заржавленный /zarzhávlennyi/ adj. rusty

зарисовка /zarisóvka) f. sketch

зарница /zarnítsa/ f. summer lightning

зародыш /zaródysh/ m. embryo

зарождать /zarozhdát'/ v. engender

зарождение /zarozhdenie/ n. conception; origin

зарок /zarók/ m. pledge, vow

заронить /zaronít'/ v. drop; arouse (doubts)

заросль /zárosl'/ f. thicket

зарплата /zarpláta/ f. pay, wages

зарубать /zarubát'/ v. notch; kill; заруби себе это на носу/лбу! /zarubí sebé eto na nosu/lbu!/ put that in your pipe and smoke it!

зарубежный /zarubézhnyi/ adj. foreign

зарубцеваться /zarubtsevát'sia/ v. cicatrize

заручаться /zaruchát'sia/ v. secure; з. поддержкой /z. poddérzhkoi/ enlist support зарывать /zaryvát'/ v. bury

заря /zariá/ f. dawn, daybreak; sunset

заряд /zariád/ m. charge

зарядка /zariádka/ f. loading; physical exercises

заряжать /zariazhát'/ v. load; charge

засада /zaslada/ f. ambush

засаливать /zasálivat'/ v. salt, pickl;: make greasy

засасывать /zasásyvat'/ v. suck in

засахариваться /zasákharivat'sia/ v. candy

заседание /zasedánie/ n. session

заселять /zaseliát'/ v. populate; settle

засилье /zasíl'e/ n. domination, sway

заскакивать /zaskákivat'/ v. jump; drop in

заслонка /zaslónka/ f. oven-door

заслонять /zasloniát'/ v. shield

заслуга /zaslúga/ f. merit

заслуженный /zaslúzhennyi/ adj. honoured

заслуживать /zaslúzhivat'/ v. deserve

заслушивать /zaslúshivat'/ v. listen to

засов /zasóv/ m. bolt

засорять /zasoriát'/ v. litter

засохший /zasókhshii/ adj. withered

заспанный /zaspánnyi/ adj. sleepy

заспиртовывать /zaspirtóvyvat'/ v. preserve in alcohol

застава /zastáva/ f. frontier post

заставлять /zastavliát'/ v. make, compel; block up

застегиваться /zastiógivat'sia/ v. button oneself up

застежка /zastiózhka/ f. clasp; з.-молния /z.-mólniia/ zip fastener

застеклять /zastekliát'/ v. glaze

застенчивый /zasténchivyi/ adj. shy

застигать /zastigát'/ v. catch, take unawares

застилать /zastilát'/ v. cover (with)

застой /zastói/ m. stagnation

застраивать /zastráivat'/ v. build (over, on, up)

застраховывать /zastrakhóvyvat'/ v. insure

застревать /zastrevát'/ v. get stuck

застрелить /zastrelít'/ v. shoot (dead)

застрелиться /zastrelít'sia/ v. shoot oneself

застужать /zastúzhat'/ v. aggravate by exposure, to cold

заступ /zástup/ m. spade

заступаться /zastupát'sia/ v. intercede (for); stand up for

заступник /zastúpnik/ m. defender, patron

застывать /zastyvát'/ v. harden; be stiff with cold

засуха /zásukha/ f. drought

засушивать /zasúshivat'/ v. dry up

засчитывать /zaschítyvat'/ v. take into account

засыпать /zasýpat'/ v. fill up

засыпать /zasypát'/ v. fall asleep

засыхать /zasykhát'/ v. dry up

затапливать /zat1aplivat'/v. light (a stove)

затаптывать /zatáptyvat'/ v. trample down

затаскивать /zatáskivat'/v. wear out; pull (in)

затасканный /zatáskannyi/ adj. threadbare

затачивать /zatáchivat'/ v. sharpen

затвор /zatvór/ m. bolt, bar

затворять /zavtoriát'/ v. shut

затевать /zatevát'/ v. venture

затекать /zatekát'/v. flow (into, behind); become numb

затем /zatém/ adv. then

затемнение /zatemnénie/ n. black-out

затенять /zateniát'/ v. shade

затея /zatéia/ f. venture

затискиватьЁ/zatískivat'/ v. squeeze

затихать /zatikhát'/ v. calm down

затишье /zatísh'e/ n. lull

затмение /zatménie/ n. eclipse

зато /zató/ conj. but on the other hand

затоваривание /zatovárivanie/ n. glut (of goods)

затон /zatón/ m. backwater

затопление /zatóplenie/ n. flooding

затор /zatór/ m. (traffic) jam

затрагивать /zatrágivat'/ v. affect

затрата /zatráta/ f. expenditure

затрачивать /zatráchivat'/ v. spend

затребовать /zatrébovat'/ v. require; ask for

затруднение /zatrúdnenie/ n. difficulty

затруднять /zatrudniát'/ v. hamper

затуманивать /zatumánivat'/ v. dim; obscure

затуплять /zatupliát'/ v. blunt

затухать /zatukhát'/ v. be extinguished

затушевывать /zatushóvyvat'/ v. shade

затхлый /zátkhlyi/ adj. stuffy

затыкать /zatykát'/ v. stop up; plug

затылок /zatýlok/ m. back of the head

затычка /zatýchka/ f. plug

затягивать /zatiágivat'/ v. tighten; drag down

затяжка /zatiázhka/ f. delay; inhaling (in smoking)

затяжной /zatiazhnói/ adj. protracted

заурядный /zauriádnyi/ adj. ordinary, mediocre

заусеница /zausénitsa/ f. agnail

заутреня /zaútrenia/ f. matins

заучивать /zaúchivat'/ v. learn by heart

зафрахтовывать /zafrakhtóvyvat'/ v. charter

захват /zakhvát/ m. capture

захватить /zakhvatít'/ v. seize, capture

захватчик /zakhvátchik/ m. aggressor

захлебываться /zakhlíobyvat'sia/ v. choke

защита /zashchíta/ f. defence

защитник /zashchítnik/ m. defender

защитный /zashchítnyi/ adj. protective

защищать /zashchishchát'/ v. protect

заявка /zaiávka/ f. claim

заявление /zaiavlénie/ n. application

заявлять /zaiavliát'/ v. declare

заядлый /zaiádlyi/ adj. inveterate

заяц /zaiáts/ m. hare

звание /zvánie/ n. rank

званый обед /zványi obed/ adj.+m. dinner party

звать /zvat'/ v. call; name; как вас зовут? /kak vas zovút?/ what is your name)

звезда /zvezdá/ f. star

звездный /zviózdnyi/ adj. starry, stellar

звенеть /zvenét'/ v. ring; jingle

звено /zvenó/ n. link; team

зверинец /zverínets/ m. menagerie

звероводство /zverovódstvo/ n. furfarming

зверский /zvérskii/ adj. brutal

зверствовать /zvérstvovat'/ v. commit atrocities

зверь /zver'/ m. wild beast

звон /zvon/ m. peal

звонить /zvonít'/ v. ring; з. в колокол /z. v kólokol/ toll a bell; з. по телефону /z. po telefónu/ give (smb.) a ring

звонок /zvonók/ m. bell

звук /zvuk/ m. sound

звукозапись /zvukozápis'/ f. recording

звуконепроницаемый /zvukopronitsáemyi/ adj. sound-proof

звучать /zvuchát'/ v. sound

звучный /zvúchnyi/ adj. sonorous

звякать /zviákat'/ v. tinkle

зга (ни зги не видно) /ni zgi ne vídno/ it is pitch dark

здание /zdánie/ n. building

здесь /zdes'/ adv. here

здешний /zdéshnii/ adj. local

здороваться /zdoróvat'sia/ v. greet

здоровенный /zdorovénnyi/ adj. strong; big

здорово! /zdórovo!/ int. well done!; adv. splendidly

здоровый /zdoróvyi/ adj. healthy

здоровье /zdoróv'e/ n. health

здравомыслие /zdravomýslie/ n. common sense

здравомыслящий /zdravomýsliashchii/ adj. sensible, judicious

здравоохранение /zdravookhranénie/ n. public health

здравствовать /zdrávstvovat'/ v. be well; да здравствует! /da zdrávstvuet/ long live!

здравствуйте /zdrávstvuite/ how do you do

здравый /zdrávyi/ adj. sensible; з. смысл /z. smysl/ common sense/

зевака /zeváka/ m. and f. idler

зевать /zevát'/ v. yawn

зеленеть /zelenét'/ v. become green

зеленщик /zelénshchik/ m. greengrocer

зеленый /zeliónyi/ adj. green

зелень /zélen'/ f. greenery

зелье /zél'e/ n. poison
земельный /zemél'nyi/ adj. land
землевладелец /zemlevladélets/ m. landowner
земледелец /zemledélets/ m. farmer
земледелие /zemledélie/ n. agriculture
землетрясение /zemletriasénie/ n. earthquake
землистый /zemlístyi/ adj. earthy
земля /zemliá/ f. earth; land
земляк /zemliák/ m. fellow-countryman
земляника /zemlianíka/ f. strawberry
земляной /zemlianói/ adj. earthen
земной /zemnói/ adj. earthly; з. шар /z. shar/ globe
зенит /zenít/ m. zenith
зенитный /zenítnyi/ adj. anti-air-craft
зеркало /zérkalo/ n. mirror
зернистый /zernístyi/ adj. grainy; unpressed (caviar)
зерно /zernó/ n. grain
зефир /zefír/ m. zephyr; marshmallow
зигзаг /zigzág/ m. zigzag
зиждиться (на) /zizhdit'sia (na)/ v. be based on
зима /zimá/ f. winter
злак /zlak/ m. cereal
злить /zlit'/ v. irritate
злиться /zlít'sia/ v. be angry, annoyed
зло /zlo/ n. evil
злоба /zlóba/ f. anger; malice
злобный /zlóbnyi/ adj. malicious
злободневный /zlobodnévnyi/ adj. topical
зловещий /zlovéshchii/ adj. ominous
зловонный /zlovónnyi/ adj. stinking
зловредный /zlovrédnyi/ adj. harmful
злодей /zlódei/ m. villain
злодейство /zlodéistvo/ n. evil deed
злодеяние /zlodeiánie/ n. crime
злой /zloi/ adj. vicious; cruel; malicious

злокачественный /zlokáchestvennyi/ adj. malignant
злоключение /zlokliuchénie/ n. misadventure
злонамеренный /zlonamerénnyi/ adj. ill-intentioned
злопамятный /zlopámiatnyi/ adj. unforgiving
злополучный /zlopolúchnyi/ adj. ill-fated
злорадный /zlorádnyi/ adj. gloating
злорадство /zlorladstvo/ n. malicious, joy
злословие /zloslóvie/ n. scandal
злостный /zlóstnyi/ adj. malicious
злость /zlost'/ f. malice
злоумышленник /zloumýshlennik/ m. malefactor
злоупотребление /zloupotreblénie/ n. abuse
злоупотреблять /zloupotrebliát'/ v. abuse
злюка /zliúka/ m., f. malicious person
змеевидный /zmeevídnyi/ asj. serpentine
змей /zmei/ m. serpent; kite
змея /zmeiá/ f. snake
знак /znak/ m. sign, symbol, mark
знакомить /znakómit'/ v. introduce; acquaint
знакомиться /znakómit'sia/ v. make acquaintance (of)
знакомство /znakómstvo/ n. acquaintance
знакомый /znakómyi/ adj. familiar; m. acquaintance
знаменатель /znamenátel'/ m. denominator
знаменательный /znamenátel'nyi/ adj. significant
знаменитость /znamenítost'/ f. celebrity
знаменитый /znamenítyi/ adj. famous
знаменовать /znamenovát'/ v. signify
знаменосец /znamenósets/ m. standard-bearer

знамя /známia/ n. banner, flag

знание /znánie/ m. knowledge

знатный /znátnyi/ adj. notable; noble

знаток /znatók/ m. expert, connoisseur

знать /znat'/ v. know

знахарка /znakhárka/ f. sorceress

знахарь /znákhar'/ m. quack

значение /znachénie/ n. significance; meaning

значительный /znachítel'nyi/ adj. important

значить /znáchit'/ v. mean

значок /znachók/ m. badge

знобить /znobít'/ v. меня знобит /meniá znobít/ I fell feverish

зной /znoi/ m. intense heat

знойный /znóinyi/ adj. sultry

зоб /zob/ m. crop; goitre

зов /zov/ m. call

зодчество /zódchestvo/ n. architecture

зодчий /zódchii/ m. architect

зола /zolá/ f. ashes

золовка /zolóvka/ f. sister-in-law (husband's sister)

золотистый /zolotístyi/ adj. golden

золото /zóloto/ n. gold

золотуха /zolotúkha/ f. scrofula

золоченый /zolochónyi/ adj. gilt

Золушка /zólushka/ f. Cinderella

зона /zóna/ f. zone

зонд /zond/ m. probe

зонт /zont/ m. umbrella

зоолог /zoólog/ m. zoologist

зоологический /zoologícheskii/ adj. zoological

зоопарк /zoopárk/ m. zoo

зоркий /zórkii/ adj. keen-sighted

зорька /zór'ka/ f. dawn

зрачок /zrachók/ m. pupil (of the eye)

зрелище /zrélishche/ n. spectacle; sight

зрелость /zrélost'/ f. maturity

зрелый /zrélyi/ adj. ripe

зрение /zrénie/ n. sight; с точки зрения /s tóchki zréniia/ from the point of view

зреть /zret'/ v. ripen; mature

зритель /zrítel'/ m. spectator

зрительный /zrítel'nyi/ adj. visual; з. зал /z. zal/ auditorium

зря /zria/ adv. to no purpose, in vain

зрячий /zriáchii/ adj. able to see

зуб /zub/ m. tooth

зубастый /zubástyi/ adj. sharp-tonged

зубной /zúbnoi/ adj. dental

зубоврачебный /zubovrachébnyi/ adj. dental; dentist's

зубочистка /zubochístka/ f. toothpick

зубр /zubr/ m. aurochs

зубрежка /zubriózhka/ f. swotting

зубрила /zubríla/ m. and f. crammer

зубрить /zubrit'/ v. cram

зуд /zud/ m. itch

зыбкий /zýbkii/ adj. unstable

зыбучий /zybúchii/ adj. quick (sand)

зычный /zýchnyi/ adj. stentorian

зюйд /ziuid/ m. south; southerly wind

зябкий /ziábkii/ adj. chilly

зяблик /ziáblik/ m. finch

зябнуть /ziábnut'/ v. be chilled

зябь /ziab'/ f. autumn ploughing

зять /ziat'/ m. son-in-law (daughter's husband); brother-in-law (sister's husband)

И

и /i/ conj. and

иберийский /iberíiskii/ adj. Iberian

ибо /íbo/ conj. for

ива /íva/ f. willow

иван-да-марья /iván-da-már'ia/ f.
cow-wheat
иван-чай /iván-chai/ m. rose-bay,
willow-herb
иволга /ívolga/ f. oriole
игла /iglá/ f. needle
игнорировать /ignorírovat'/ v. ignore
иго /igo/ n. yoke
иголка /igólka/ f. needle
игольное (ушко) /igól'noe úshko/
adj.+n. eye of a needle
игорный /igórnyi/ adj. gambling
игра /igrá/ f. game; play; performance
играть /igrát'/ v. play; act
игривый /igrívyi/ adj. playful
игристый /igrístyi/ adj. sparkling
игрок /igrók/ m. player, gambler
игрушечный /igrúshechnyi/ adj. toy
игрушка /igrúshka/ f. toy
игумен /igúmen/ m. Father Superior (of a
monastery)
игуменья /igúmen'ia/ f. Mother Superior
(of a convent)
идеал /ideál/ m. ideal
идейный /idéinyi/ adj. ideological
идентичный /identíchnyi/ adj.
identical
идеолог /ideólog/ m. ideologist
идеологический /ideologícheskii/ adj.
ideological
идея /idéia/ f. idea; concept
идиллический /idillícheskii/ adj.
idyllic
идиома /idióma/ f. idiom
идиот /idiót/ m. idiot
идиотский /idiótskii/ adj. idiotic
идол /idól/ m. idol
идолопоклонник /idolopoklónnik/ m.
idolater
идти /idtí/ v. go, be going
иезуит /iezuít/ m. Jesuit
иерархия /ierárkhiia/ f. hierarchy

иероглиф /ieróglif/ m. hieroglyph
иждивенец /izhdivénets/ m. dependant
из /iz/ prep. out of, from
изба /izbá/ f. hut, peasant house
избавлять /izbavliát'/ v. save
избаловать /izbálovat'/ v. spoil (children)
избегать /izbegát'/ v. avoid, evade
избиратель /izbirátel'/ m. elector,
voter
избирательный /izbirátel'nyi/ adj.
electoral; и. округ /i. ókrug/, и.
участок /i. uchástok/ electoral district,
constituency
избирать /izbirát'/ v. choose, elect
избитый /izbítyi/ adj. well-worn; beaten
избрание /izbránie/ n. election
избранник /izbránnik/ m. the chosen one
избыток /izbýtok/ m. surplus; abundance
изверг /izvérg/ m. monster
извержение /izvérzhenie/ n. eruption
известие /izvéstie/ n. news
известность /izvéstnost'/ f. fame
известный /izvéstnyi/ adj. known; popular
известняк /izvestniák/ m. limestone
известь /ízvest'/ f. lime
извещать /izveshchát'/ v. inform
извещение /izveshchénie/ n. notification
извивать /izvivát'/ v. twist
извилина /izvílina/ f. bend
извинение /izvinénie/ n. apology
извинять /izviniát'/ v. excuse;
извините! /izviníte!/ excuse me!
I'm sorry
извиняться /izviniát'sia/ v. apologize
извлекать /izvlekát'/ v. extract
извне /izvné/ adv. from without
изворотливый /izvorótlivyi/ adj. resourceful
извращать /izvrashchát'/ v. distort
изгиб /izgíb/ m. bend, curve
изгнание /izgnánie/ n. exile

изголовье /izgolóv'e/ n. head of the bed

изголодаться /izgolodát'sia/ v. be starving

изгонять /izgoniát'/ v. banish

изгородь /ízgorod'/ f. fence; живая и. /zhivaia i./ hedge

изготавливать /izgotávlivat'/ v. manufacture

издавать /izdavát'/ v. publish

издавна /ízdavna/ adv. since long ago

издалека /izdaléka/ adv. from afar

издание /izdánie/ n. edition

издатель /izdátel'/ m. publisher

издательство /izdátel'stvo/ n. publishing house

издевательство /izdevátel'stvo/ n. mockery

издеваться /izdevát'sia/ v. scoff (at), mock

изделие /izdélie/ n. make; article

издержки /izdérzhki/ pl. outlay

издревле /izdrevle/ adv. from time immemorial

издыхать /izdykhát'/ v. die (of animals)

изживать /izzhívat'/ v. get rid of

изжога /izzhóga/ f. heartburn

из-за /iz-za/ prep. from behind; because of

излагать /izlagát'/ v. set forth; state

излечение /izlechénie/ n. recovery

излечивать /izléchivat'/ v. cure

излечимый /izlechímyi/ adj. curable

изливать /izlivát'/ v. pour out

излишек /izlíshek/ m. surplus

излишество /izlíshestvo/ n. excess

изложение /izlózhenie/ n. exposition; rendering

излом /izlom /m. break

изломать /izlomát'/ v. break to pieces

излучать /izluchát'/ v. radiate

излучина /izlúchina/ f. bend

излюбленный /izlíublennyi/ adj. pet, favourite

измазывать /izmázyvat'/ v. smear

изматывать /izmátyvat'/ v. exhaust

измена /izména/ f. treason

изменение /izmenénie/ n. change

изменник /izménnik/ m. traitor

изменять /izmeniát'/ v. change, alter; be unfaithful to, betray

измерение /izmerénie/ n. measuring

измерять /izmeriát'/ v. measure

изморозь /ízmoroz'/ f. hoar-frost

изморось /ízmoros'/ f. drizzle

измученный /izmúchennyi/ adj. exhausted

измышление /izmyshlénie/ n. fabrication

изнасилование /iznasílovanie/ n. rape

изнашивание /iznáshivanie/ n. wear and tear

изнемогать /iznemogát'/ v. be(come) exhausted

изнеможение /iznemozhénie/ n. exhaustion

изнервничаться /iznérvnichat'sia/ v. become a nervous wreck

изнурение /iznurénie/ n. exhaustion

изнурительный /iznurítel'nyi/ adj. exhausting

изнурять /iznuriát'/ v. wear out; overwork

изнутри /iznutrí/ adv. from within

изнывать /iznyvát'/ v. languish; pine away

изобилие /izobílie/ n. abundance

изобличать /izoblichát'/ v. expose

изобличение /izoblichénie/ n. exposure

изображать /izobrazhát'/ v. depict, portray

изобретатель /izobretátel'/ m. inventor

изобретать /izobretát'/ v. invent

изобретение /izobreténie/ n. invention

изолировать /izolírovat'/ v. isolate; insulate

изолятор /izoliátor/ m. insulator
изорванный /izórvannyi/ adj. ragged
изотерма /izotérma/ f. isotherm
изотоп /izotóp/ m. isotope
из-под /iz-pod/ prep. from under
изразцовый /izraztsóvyi/ adj. tiled
израильский /izráil'skii/ adj. Israeli
изредка /ízredka/ adv. now and then
изрытый /izrýtyi/ adj. pitted
изрядный /izriádnyi/ adj. fairly good
изувечивать /izuvéchivat'/ v. maim, mutilate
изумительный /izumítel'nyi/ adj. amazing
изумление /izumlénie/ n. astonishment
изумлять /izumliát'/ v. amaze
изумруд /izumrúd/ m. emerald
изучать /izuchát'/ v. study
изучение /izúchenie/ n. study
изъявительный /iz"iavítel'nyi/ adj. indicative
изъявлять /iz"iavliát'/ v. express
изъян /iz"ián/ m. defect
изымать /izymát'/ v. withdraw
изюм /iziúm/ m. raisins
изящество /iziáshchestvo/ n. grace; elegance
икать /ikát'/ v. hiccup
икона /ikóna/ f. icon
иконописец /ikonopísets/ m. icon-painter
икра /ikrá/ f. caviar
икс-лучи /iks-luchi/ pl. X-rays
ил /il/ m. silt
или /íli/ conj. or
иллюзия /illiúziia/ f. illusion
иллюминатор /illiuminátor/ m. porthole
иллюминация /illiuminátsiia/ f. illumination
иллюстратор /illiustrátor/ m. illustrator
иллюстрация /illiustrátsiia/ f. illustration

имбирь /imbír'/ m. ginger
имение /iménie/ n. estate
именины /imeníny/ pl. name-day
именительный /imenítel'nyi/ adj. nominative
именно /ímenno/ adv. namely; precisely
именной /imennói/ adj. inscribed
именовать /imenovát'/ v. name
иметь /imet'/ v. have; и. дело /i. délo/ have dealings (with); и. место /i. mésto/ take place
имитация /imitátsiia/ f. imitation
иммигрант /immigránt/ m. immigrant
иммунизировать /immunizírovat'/ v. immunize
иммунитет /immunitét/ m. immunity
император /imperátor/ m. emperor
императрица /imperatrítsa/ f. empress
империализм /imperializm/ m. imperialism
империя /impériia/ f. empire
импозантный /impozántnyi/ adj. imposing
импонировать /imponírovat'/ v. impress
импорт /ímport/ m. import
импровизация /improvizátsiia/ f. improvisation
импульс /ímpul's/ m. impulse
имущество /imúshchestvo/ n. property
имя /imiá/ n. name
иначе /ináche/ adv. differently, otherwise; так или и. /tak ili i./ in any case
инвалид /invalíd/ m. invalid
инвалидность /invalídnost'/ f. disablement
инвалютный /invaliútnyi/ adj. foreign currency
инвентарь /inventár'/ m. inventory; stock
ингалятор /ingaliátor/ m. inhaler
индеец /indéets/ m. American Indian
индейка /indéika/ f. turkey

индекс /índeks/ m. index
индианка /indiánka/ f. Indian ; American Indian
индивидуальный /individuálnyi/ adj. individual
индиец /indíets/ m. Indian
индийский /indíiskii/ adj. Indian
индоевропейский /indoevropéiskii/ adj. Indo-European
индонезиец /indonezíets/ m. Indonesian
индонезийка /indonezíika/ f. Indonesian
индонезийский /indoneziískii/ adj. Indonesian
индус /indús/ m. Hindu
индуска /indúska/ f. Hindu
индусский /indússkii/ adj. Hindu
индустриализация /industrializátsiia/ f. industrialization
индустрия /industríia/ f. industry
индюк /indiúk/ m. turkey (-cock)
индюшка /indiúshka/ f. turkey (-hen)
иней /ínei/ m. hoar-frost
инерция /inértsiia/ f. inertia
инженер /inzhenér/ m. engineer
инжир /ínzhir/ m. fig
инициал /initsiál/ m. initial
инициатива /initsiatíva/ f. initiative
инквизитор /inkvizítor/ m. inquisitor
инкубатор /inkubátor/ m. incubator
иноверец /inovérets/ m. adherent of different faith
иногда /inogdá/ adv. sometimes
иной /inói/ adj. different, other
иносказательный /inoskazátel'nyi/ adj. allegorical
иностранец /inostránets/ m. foreigner
иностранный /inostránnyi/ adj. foreign
инспектировать /inspektírovat'/ v. inspect
инстанция /instántsiia/ f. instance
инстинкт /instínkt/ m. instinct
институт /institút/ m. institute

инструктировать /instruktírovat'/ v. instruct
инсулин /insulín/ m. insulin
инсценировать /instsenírovat'/ v. dramatize, stage
интеллектуальный /intellektuál'nyi/ adj. intellectual
интеллигент /intelligént/ m. intellectual
интендант /intendánt/ m. quartermaster
интенсивный /intensívnyi/ adj. intensive
интервал /intervál/ m. interval
интервенция /intervéntsiia/ f. intervention
интервью /intervi'iú/ n. interview
интерес /interés/ m. interest
интересный /interésnyi/ adj. interesting
интересовать /interesovát'/ v. interest
интернат /internát/ m. boarding school
интернациональный /internatsionál'nyi/ adj. international
интерьер /inter'ér/ m. interior
интимный /intímnyi/ adj. intimate
интрига /intríga/ f. intrigue
интуиция /intuítsiia/ f. intuition
инфекционный /infektsiónnyi/ adj. infectious
инфекция /inféktsiia/ f. infection
инфляция /infliátsiia/ f. inflation
информатор /informátor/ m. informer
инфракрасный /infrakrásnyi/ adj. infra-red
инцидент /intsidént/ m. incident
инъекция /in"éktsiia/ f. injection
ион /ión/ m. ion
ирландец /irlándets/ m. Irishman
ирландка /irlándka/ f. Irishwoman
ирландский /irlándskii/ adj. Irish
иронический /iroshícheskii/ adj. ironic
ирония /iróniia/ f. irony
иррациональный /irratsionál'nyi/ adj. irrational
ирригация /irrigátsiia/ f. irrigation

иск /isk/ m. suit
искажать /iskazhát'/ v. distort
искать /iskát'/ v. seek, look for
исключать /iskliuchát'/ v. exlude;
   expel
исключение /iskliuchénie/ n.
   exception; elimination
исключительный /iskliuchítel'nyi/
   adj. exclusive
ископаемое /iskopáemoe/ n. fossil; mineral
искоренение /iskorenénie/ n.
   eradication
искоса /ískosa/ adv. sideways
искра /ískra/ f. spark
искренний /ískrennii/ adj. sincere
искристый /iskrístyi/ adj. sparkling
искриться /iskrít'sia/ v. sparkle
искусный /iskúsnyi/ adj. skilled
искусственный /iskússtvennyi/ adj.
   artificial
искусство /iskússtvo/ n. art
искушать /iskushát'/ v. tempt,
   seduce
ислам /islám/ m. Islam
исландец /islándets/ m. Iselander
исландка /islándka/ f. Icelander
исландский /islándskii/ adj. Icelandic
испанец /ispánets/ m. Spaniard
испанка /ispánka/ f. Spansh woman
испанский /ispánskii/ adj. Spanish
испарение /isparénie/ n. evaporation
испарина /ispárina/ f. perspiration
испачкать /ispáchkat'/ v. dirty
исповедовать /ispovédovat'/ v. profess
   (a faith); confess
исповедь /íspoved'/ f. confession
испокон веков /ispokón vekóv/ from
   time immemorial
исполин /ispolín/ m. giant
исполком /ispolkóm/ m. executive
   committee

исполнение /ispolnénie/ n. fulfilment
исполнительный /ispolnítel'nyi/ adj.
   executive; efficient
исполнять /ispolniát'/ v. fulfil
использование /ispól'zovanie/ n. use
испорченный /ispórchennyi/ adj.
   rotten
исправительный /ispravítel'nyi/
   adj. reformatory
исправление /ispravlénie/ n. correction
исправлять /ispravliát'/ v. correct
исправный /isprávnyi/ adj. in good
   repairs; zealous
испуг /ispúg/ m. fright
испытание /ispytánie/ n. trial
испытанный /ispýtannyi/ adj. proved
испытатель /ispytátel'/ m. tester
испытывать /ispýtyvat'/ v. try, test;
   feel, experience
исследование /isslédovanie/ n.
   research
исследователь /isslédovatel'/
   m. investigator
исследовать /isslédovat'/ v. explore
исступление /isstúplenie/ n. frenzy
иссушать /issushát'/ v. dry up
истекать /istekát'/ v. elapse; и. кровью
   /i. króv'iu/ bleed profusely
истекший /istékshii/ adj. past
истерика /istérika/ f. hysterics
истец /istéts/ m. plaintiff
истина /ístina/ f. truth
истинный /ístinnyi/ adj. true
истлевать /istlevát'/ v. rot
истовый /ístovyi/ adj. fervent
исток /istók/ m. source
истолкование /istolkovánie/ n.
   interpretation
историк /istórik/ m. historian
исторический /istorícheskii/ adj.
   historical
история /istóriia/ f. history

источать /istochát'/ v. exhale, emit
источник /istóchnik/ m. source;
  spring
истошный /istóshnyi/ adj. heart-
  rending
истощать /istoshchát'/ v. exhaust,
  wear out
истребитель /istrebítel'/ m. destroyer;
  fighter (aircraft)
истреблять /istrebliát'/ v. destroy;
  exterminate
истязание /istiazánie/ n. torture
исход /iskhód/ m. outcome
исходить /iskhodít'/ v. proceed;
  walk all over
исходный /iskhódnyi/ adj. initial
исхудалый /iskhudályi/ adj. emaciated
исцарапывать /istsarápyvat'/ v.
  scratch all over
исцеление /istselénie/ n. healing
исцелять /istseliát'/ v. cure
исцеляться /istseliát'sia/ v. recover
исчезать /ischezát'/ v. disappear
исчерпывать /ischérpyvat'/ v. exhaust;
  complete
исчисление /ischislénie/ n.
  calculation
исчислять /ischisliát'/ v. estimate
итак /iták/ conj. and so
итальянец /ital'iánets/ m. Italian
итальянка /ital'iánka/ f. Italian
итальянский /ital'iánskii/ adj.
  Italian
итог /itóg/ m. total; result
иудейство /iudéistvo/ n. Judaism
ишак /ishák/ m. donkey
ищейка /ishchéika/ f. bloodhound
июль /iiúl'/ m. July
июнь /iiún'/ m. June

Й

йод /iod/ m. iodine
йог /iog/ m. yogi
йодистый (калий) /iódistyi kálii/
  adj.+m. potassium iodide
йота /ióta/ f. iota; ни на йоту /ni na
  iótu/ not a whit

К

к /k/ prep. to, for; by
кабан /kabán/ m. boar
кабачок /kabachók/ m. vegetable mar-
  row
кабель /kábel'/ m. cable
кабина /kabína/ f. booth,
  cabin
кабинет /kabinét/ m. study;
  cabinet (of ministers)
каблук /kablúk/ m. heel
кавалерия /kavalériia/ f. cavalry
кавказец /kavkázets/ m. Caucasian
кавказский /kavkázskii/ adj. Caucasian
кавычки /kavýchki/ pl. quotation
  marks
кадет /kadét/ m. Cadet (Constitutional
  Democrat)
кадило /kadílo/ n. censer
кадка /kádka/ f. tub
кадр /kadr/ m. still; personnel
кадык /kadýk/ m. Adam's apple
каемка /kaiómka/ f. edging
каждый /kázhdyi/ adj. every,
  each
кажущийся /kázhushchiisia/ adj.
  apparent
казак /kazák/ m. Cossack
казарма /kazárma/ f. barracks

казаться /kazát'sia/ v. seem

казах /kazákh/ m. Kazakh

казашка /kazáshka/ f. Kazakh

казахский /kazákhskii/ adj. Kazakh

казино /kazinó/ n. casino

казна /kazná/ f. treasury

казнить /kaznít'/ v. execute

казнь /kazn'/ f. execution

кайма /kaimá/ f. edging

как /kak/ adv. how; conj. as

какао /kakáo/ n. cocoa, cacao

как-либо /kák-libo/ adv. anyhow

как-нибудь /kák-nibud'/ adv. anyhow, somehow

как-никак /kak-nikák/ adv. after all

какой /kakói/ pron. what

как-то /kák-to/ adv. somehow; one day

кактус /káktus/ m. cactus

каланча /kalanchá/ f. watch-tower

калека /kaléka/ m.and f. cripple

календарь /kalendár'/ m. calendar

калибр /kalíbr/ m. calibre

калий /kálii/ m. potassium

калина /kalína/ f. snow ball-tree

калитка /kalítka/ f. wicket-gate

калория /kalóriia/ f. calory

калоша /kalósha/ f. galosh

калька /kál'ka/ f. tracing-paper

калькулировать /kal'kulírovat'/ v. calculate

калькуляция /kal'kuliátsiia/ f. calculation

кальсоны /kal'sóny/ pl. drawers

кальций /kál'tsii/ m. calcium

камбала /kámbala/ f. flounder

камвольный /kamvól'nyi/ adj. worsted

каменистый /kamenístyi/ adj. stony

каменноугольный /kamennoúgol'nyi/ adj. coal

каменный /kámennyi/ adj. stone

каменоломня /kamenolómnia/ f. quarry

каменщик /kámenshchik/ m. stone-mason

камень /kámen'/ m. stone

камера /kámera/ f. cell; camera; к. хранения /k. khranéniia/ cloak-room

камерный /kámernyi/ adj. chamber

камертон /kamertón/ m. tuning-fork

камешек /kámeshek/ m. peb

камин /kamín/ m. fire-place

кампания /kampániia/ f. campaign

камфора /kámfora/ f. camphor

камыш /kamýsh/ m. reed

камышовый /kamyshóvyi/ adj. cane

канава /kanáva/ f. ditch

канадец /kanádets/ m. Canadian

канадка /kanádka/ f. Canadian

канадский /kanádskii/ adj. Canadian

канал /kanál/ m. canal; channel

канализация /kanalizátsiia/ f. sewerage

канарейка /kanaréika/ f. canary

канат /kanát/ m. rope

канатоходец /kanatokhódets/ m. rope-walker

канва /kanvá/ f. canvas

кандалы /kandalý/ pl. shackles

кандидат /kandidát/ m. candidate

каникулы /kaníkuly/ pl. vacation, holidays

канителиться /kanitélit'sia/ v. dawdle

канитель /kanitél'/ f. gold thread, silver thread; long-drawn-out procee-dings

канифоль /kanifól'/ f. rosin

канонада /kanonáda/ f. cannonade

канонерка /kanonérka/ gunboat

канонизировать /kanonizírovat'/ v. canonize

канун /kanún/ m. eve

канцелярия /kantseliáriia/ f. office

канцелярщина /kantseliárshchina/
f. red tape
капать /kápat'/ v. drip
капелла /kapélla/ f. choir
капеллан /kapellán/ m. chaplain
капельмейстер /kapel'méister/ m.
conductor
капельница /kápel'nitsa/ f. dropper
(med.)
капилляр /kapilliár/ m. capillary
капитал /kapitál/ m. capital
капитализм /kapitalízm/ m. capitalism
капиталовложение /kapitalovlozhénie/
n. investment
капитан /kapitán/ m. captain
капитулировать /kapitulírovat'/ v.
capitulate
капкан /kapkán/ m. trap
капля /kapliá/ f. drop, drip
капот /kapót/ m. bonnet, hood
каприз /kapríz/ m. whim
капризничать /kapríznichat'/ v.
be capricious
капсула /kápsula/ f. capsule
капуста /kapústa/ f. cabbage;
брюссельская к. /brussél'skaia k./
Brussels sprouts; кислая к. /kíslaia
k./ sauerkraut
капюшон /kapiushoń/ m. hood
карабкаться /karábkat'sia/ v.
clamber
каравай /karavái/ m. round loaf
караван /karaván/ m. caravan;
convoy (ships)
каракатица /karakátitsa/ f.
cuttle-fish
каракулевый /karákulevyi/ adj.
astrakhan
карамель /karamél'/ f. caramel
карандаш /karandásh/ m. pencil
карантин /karantín/ m. quarantine
карась /karás'/ m. crucian carp

карательный /karátel'nyi/ adj. punitive
караул /karaúl/ m. watch; почетный к.
/pochótnyi k./ guard of honour
карачки /karáchki/ in: на карачках
/na karáchkakh/ on all fours
карболовый /karbólovyi/ adj. carbolic
карбункул /karbúnkul/ m. carbuncle
карбюратор /karbiurátor/ m. carburettor
кардиограф /kardiógraf/ m.
cardiograph
карельский /karél'skii/ adj. Karelian
карета /karéta/ f. coach
карий /kárii/ adj. hazel
карикатура /karikatúra/ f.
caricature
каркать /kárkat'/ v. croak
карлик /kárlik/ m. dwarf
карман /karmán/ m. pocket
карнавал karnavál/ m. carnival
карниз /karníz/ m. cornice
карп /karp/ m. carp
карта /kárta/ m. map; card
картавить /kartávit'/ v. burr
картежник /kartiózhnik/ m. gambler
картель /kartél'/ f. cartel
картина /kartína/ f. picture;
scene
картинный /kartínnyi/ adj.
picturesque
картография /kartográfiia/ f.
cartography
картон /kartón/ m. cardboard
картотека /kartotéka/ f. card
index
картофелина /kartófelina/ f.
potato
картофель /kartófel'/ m. potatoes
карточка /kártochka/ f. card,
photograph
карточная система /kártochnaia
sistéma/ adj.+f. rationing system
картошка /kartóshka/ f. potato

карусель /karusél'/ f. merry-go-
round
карцер /kártser/ m. punishment cell
карьера /kar'éra/ f. career
карьерист /kar'erist/ m. careerist
касание /kasánie/ n. contact
касаться /kasát'sia/ v. touch;
concern
каска /káska/ f. helmet
каспийский /kaspiiski/ adj.
Caspian
касса /kássa/ f. box-office
кассета /kasséta/ f. cassette
кассир /kassir/ m. cashier
кассировать /kassirovat'/ v.
annul; reverse (legal)
каста /kásta/ f. caste
кастет /kastét/ m. knuckle-duster
касторка /kastórka/ f., касторовое
масло /kastórovoe máslo/ n.
castor oil
кастрюля /kastriúlia/ f. saucepan
каталог /katalóg/ m. catalogue
катание /katánie/ n. ride; к. на
коньках /k. na kon'kákh/ skating
катар /katár/ m. catarrh
катаракта /katarákta/ f. cataract
катастрофа /katastrófa/ f.
catastrophe
катать /katát'/ v. drive; roll
кататься /katát'sia/ v. go for
a ride
катафалк /katafálk/ m. catafalque
категорический /kategorícheskii/
adj. categorical
категория /kategória/ f. category
катер /káter/ m. patrol boat
катить /katit'/ v. roll
катод /katód/ m. cathode
каток /katók/ m. skating-rink
католик /katólik/ m. Roman Catholic
каторга /kátorga/ f. hard labour

каторжник /kátorzhnik/ m. convict
катушка /katúshka/ f. bobbin,
reel
каурый /kaúryi/ adj. light
chestnut
каучук /kauchúk/ m. rubber
кафе /kafé/ n. cafe
кафедра /káfedra/ f. chair;
rostrum; department
кафель /káfel'/ m. glazed tile
кафетерий /kafetérii/ m. cafeteria
качалка /kachálka/ f. rocking-chair
качать /kachát'/ v. swing
качели /kachéli/ pl. swing
качество /káchestvo/ n. quality
качка /káchka/ f. tossing (at sea)
каша /kásha/ f. porridge
кашлять /káshliat'/ v. cough
каштан /kashtán/ m. chestnut
каюта /kaiúta/ f. cabin
кают-компания /kaiút-kompánia/ f.
wardroom; saloon
каяться /káiat'sia/ v. repent; confess
квадрат /kvadrát/ m. square
квакать /kvákat'/ v. croak
квалификация /kvalifikátsiia/ f.
qualification
квантовый /kvántovyi/ adj.
quantum
квартал /kvartál/ m. block; district
квартет /kvartét/ m. quartet
квартира /kvartira/ f. flat,
apartment
квартирант /kvartiránt/ m. tenant
квартирная плата /kvartirnaia pláta/
adj.+f. rent
кварц /kvarts/ m. quartz
квас /kvas/ m. kvass
квасцы /kvastsý/ pl. alum
кверху /kvérkhu/ adv. up(wards)

квитанция /kvitántsiia/ f. receipt
ticket
кворум /kvórum/ m. quorum
кегельбан /kegel'bán/ m. bowling-
alley
кедр /kedr/ m. cedar
кеды /kédy/ pl. light sports boots
кекс /keks/ m. cake
кельт /kel't/ m. Celt
кельтский /kél'tskii/ adj. Celtic
келья /kél'ia/ f. cell
кенгуру /kengurú/ m. kangaroo
кепка /képka/ f. cap
керамика /kerámika/ f. ceramics
кесарево сечение /késarevo sechénie/
adj.+n. Caesarean operation
кета /ketá/ f. Siberian salmon
кетовая икра /ketóvaia ikrá/ f.
red caviar
кефир /kefír/ m. yoghurt
кибернетика /kibernétika/ f.
cybernetics
кивать /kivát'/ v. nod
кидать /kidát'/ v. throw
кий /kii/ m. cue
кикимора /kikímora/ f. goblin; fright
кило /kiló/ n. kilogram
киловатт /kilovátt/ m. kilovatt
киль /kil'/ m. keel
кильватер /kil'váter/ m. wake
килька /kil'ka/ f. sprat
кинематография /kinematográfiia/ f.
cinematography
кинжал /kinzhál/ m. dagger
кино /kinó/ n. cinema
киножурнал /kinozhurnál/ m.
newsreel
кинозвезда /kinozvezdá/ f. film
star
киносъемка /kinos'iómka/ f. filming
киоск /kiósk/ m. stall

кипа /kípa/ f. pile
кипарис /kiparís/ m. cypress
кипение /kipénie/ n. boiling
кипеть /kipét'/ v. boil
кипучий /kipúchii/ adj. seething
кипятильник /ripatíl'nik/ m. boiler
кипяток /kipiatók/ m. boiling
water
кипяченый /kipiachiónyi/ adj.
boiled
киргиз /kirgíz/ m. Kirghiz
киргизка /kirgízka/ f. Kirghiz
киргизский /kirgízskii/ adj.
Kirghiz
кириллица /kiríllitsa/ f. Cyrillic
alphabet
кирка /kirká/ f. pick-axe
кирпич /kirpích/ m. brick
кисель /kisél'/ m. jelly
кисет /kisét/ m. tobacco-pouch
кисея /kiseiá/ f. muslin
кислород /kisloród/ m. oxygen
кислота /kislotá/ f. acid
кислый /kíslyi/ adj. sour
киста /kistá/ f. cyst
кисть /kist'/ f. brush; cluster;
hand
кит /kit/ m. whale
китаец /kitáets/ m. Chinese
китайский /kitáiskii/ adj.
Chinese
китаянка /kitaiánka/ f.
Chinese
китель /kítel'/ m. tunic
китобой /kitobói/ m. whaler
китовый /kitóvyi/ adj. whale
кишечник /kishéchnik/ m. bowels
кишечный /kishéchnyi/ adj.
testinal
кишка /kishká/ f. gut
клавиатура /klaviatúra/ f.
keyboard

клавиш /klávish/ m. key
клад /klad/ m. treasure
кладбище /kládbishche/ n. cemetery
кладовая /kladováia/ f. store-
room
кланяться /klániat'sia/ v. bow
клапан /klápan/ m. valve
кларнет /klárnet/ m. clarinet
класс /klass/ m. class
классик /klássik/ m. classic
классифицировать /klassifitsírovat'/
v. classify
класть /klast'/ v. put; lay
клев /klióv/ v. biting
клевать /klevát'/ v. peck, bite
клевер /kléver/ m. clover
клевета /klevetá/ f. slander
клеенка /kleiónka/ f. oilcloth
клеить /kléit'/ v. glue, gum,
paste
клейкий /kléikii/ adj. sticky
клеймить /kleimít'/ v. brand
клеймо /kleimó/ n. mark; stamp
клейстер /kléister/ m. paste
клен /klión/ m. maple
клепать /klepát'/ v. rivet
клетка /klétka/ f. cage; check
(on fabric)
клешня /kleshniá/ f. claw
клещ /kleshch/ m. tick
клещи /kléshchi/ pl. tongs;
pincers
клиент /kliént/ m. client
клиентура /klientúra/ f. clientele
клизма /klízma/ f. enema
клика /klíka/ f. clique
климат /klímat/ m. climate
клин /klin/ m. wedge
клиника /klínika/ f. clinic
клинок /klinók/ m. blade
клирос /klíros/ m. choir (part of
church)

клич /klich/ m. call
кличка /klíchka/ f. nickname
клок /klok/ m. shred
клокотать /klokotát'/ v. gurgle
клонить /klonít'/ v. bend; tend
(towards)
клоп /klop/ m. bug
клоун /klóun/ m. clown
клочок /klochók/ m. shred
клуб /klub/ m. club (house)
клубень /klúben'/ m. tuber
клубиться /klubít'sia/ v. curl
клубника /klubníka/ f. strawberries
клубничное варенье /klubníchnoe
varén'e/ adj.+n. strawberry jam
клубок /klubók/ m. ball
клумба /klúmba/ f. flower-bed
клык /klyk/ m. fang
клюв /kliúv/ m. beak
клюква /kliúkva/ f. cranberries
ключ /kliúch/ m. key; spring
ключица /kliuchítsa/ f. collar-bone
клюшка /kliúshka/ f. club
клякса /kliáksa/ f. blot
кляп /kliáp/ m. gag
клясться /kliást'sia/ v. swear,
vow
клятва /kliátva/ f. oath
клятвопреступление /kliatvoprestuplé-
nie/ n. perjury
кляуза /kliáuza/ f. cavil
книга /kníga/ f. book
книгопродавец /knigoprodavéts/ m.
bookseller
книзу /knízu/ adv. downwards
кнопка /knópka/ f. press-button
кнопочное управление /knopóchnoe
upravlénie/ adj.+n. pushbutton
control
кнут /knut/ m. whip
княгиня /kniagínia/ f. princess
князь /kniáz'/ m. prince

коалиция /koalítsiia/ f. coalition
кобальт /kóbal't/ m. cobalt
кобель /kobél'/ m. (male) dog
кобура /koburá/ f. holster
кобыла /kobýla/ f. mare
коварство /kovárstvo/ n. deceit;
    treachery
ковать /kovát'/ v. forge; shoe
ковбойка /kovbóika/ f. checked shirt
ковер /koviór/ m. carpet
коверкать /kovérkat'/ v. mangle,
    distort
ковчег /kovchég/ m. ark
ковш /kovsh/ m. scoop
ковыль /kovýl'/ m. feather-grass
ковылять /kovyliát'/ v. hobble;
    toddle
ковырять /kovyriát'/ v. pick
когда /kogdá/ pron. when
коготь /kógot'/ m. claw
код /kod/ m. code
кодеин /kodeín/ m. codeine
кодекс /kódeks/ m. code (law)
коечный больной /kóechnyi bol'nói/
    adj.+m. in-patient
кожа /kózha/ f. skin
кожаный /kózhanyi/ adj. leather
кожевенный /kozhévennyi/ adj.
    tanning
кожура /kozhurá/ f. peel
коза /kozá/ f. she-goat
козел /koziól/ m. billy goat
козни /kózni/ pl. intrigues
козырек /kozyriók/ m. peak (of cap)
козырь /kózyr'/ m. trump (card)
койка /kóika/ f. berth; bed
кокетка /kokétka/ f. coquette
кокетничать /kokétnichat'/ v. flirt
коклюш /kokliúsh/ m. whooping cough
кокон /kókon/ m. cocoon
кокос /kokós/ m. coco; coconut
кокс /koks/ m. coke

коктейль /koktéil'/ m. cocktail
колба /kólba/ f. flask
колбаса /kolbása/ f. sausage
колготки /kolgótki/ pl. tights
колдовство /koldovstvó/ n. sorcery
колдун /koldún/ m. wizard
колдунья /koldún'ia/ f. sorceress
колебать /kolebát'/ v. shake
колебаться /kolebát'sia/ v. hesitate
коленкор /kolenkór/ m. calico
колено /koléno/ n. knee
коленчатый /kolénchatyi/ adj.
    cranked
колесить /kolesít'/ v. rove
колесница /kolesnítsa/ f. chariot
колесо /kolesó/ n. wheel
колея /koleiá/ f. track
колики /kóliki/ pl. colic
количество /kolíchestvo/ n. number,
    quantity
колкий /kólkii/ adj. prickly
коллега /kolléga/ m. colleague
коллегия /kollégiia/ f. board
колледж /kólledzh/ m. college
коллектив /kollektív/ m. collective
    (body)
колодец /kolódets/ m. well
колокол /kólokol/ m. bell
колокольня /kolokól'nia/ f.
    belfry
колокольчик /kolokól'chik/ m. bell;
    bluebell
колония /kolóniia/ f. colony
колонка /kolónka/ f. column;
    petrol pump
колонна /kolónna/ f. column
колос /kólos/ m. ear (corn)
колотить /kolotít'/ v. bang, beat
колотый сахар /kólotyi sákhar/
    adj.+m. lump sugar
колоть /kolót'/ v. prick
колпак /kolpák/ m. nightcap

колхоз /kolkhóz/ m. kolkhoz,
  collective farm
колыбель /kolybél'/ f. cradle
колыбельная песня /kolybél'naia
  pésnia/ adj.+f. lullaby
колье /kol'é/ n. necklace
кольцо /kol'tsó/ n. ring
колючка /koliúchka/ f. thorn
коляска /koliáska/ f. carriage
команда /kománda/ f. order; team
командир /komandír/ m. commander
командировать /komandirovát'/ v.
  send on
командировка /komandiŕovka/ f.
  business trip
командировочные /komandiŕóvochnye/
  pl. travelling expenses
комар /komár/ m. mosquito
комбайн /kombáin/ m. combine
комбинация /kombinátsiia/ f.
  combination; slip
комбинезон /kombinezón/ m.
  overalls
комбинировать /kombinírovat'/ v.
  combine
комедия /komédiia/ f. comedy
комендант /komendánt/ m. commandant
комета /kométa/ f. comet
комик /kómik/ m. comic (actor)
комиссар /komissár/ m. commissar
комиссионер /komissionér/ m. agent,
  broker
комиссионный /komissiónnyi/
  adj. commission; к. магазин /k.
  magazín/ second-hand shop
комиссия /komíssiia/ f. comission
комитет /komitét/ m. committee
комкать /kómkat'/ v. crumple
коммерсант /kommersánt/ m.
  businessman
коммерческий /kommércheskii/ adj.
  commercial

коммуна /kommúna/ f. commune
коммунизм /kommunízm/ m.
  communism
коммуникация /kommunikátsiia/ f.
  communication
коммунист /kommuníst/ m.
  communist
коммутатор /kommutátor/ m.
  switchboard
коммюнике /kommiuniké/ n.
  communique
комната /kómnata/ f. room
комод /komód/ m. chest of drawers,
  locker
комок /komók/ m. lump
компактный /kompáktnyi/ adj.
  compact
компания /kompániia/ f.
  company
компаньон /kompan'ón/ m. partner
компартия /kompártiia/ f.
  communist party
компас /kómpas/ m. compass
компенсация /kompensátsiia/ f.
  compensation
компенсировать /kompensírovat'/ v.
  compensate
компетентный /kompeténtnyi/ adj.
  competent; authorized
компетенция /kompeténtsiia/ f.
  competence, sphere
компилировать /kompilírovat'/ v.
  compile
комплекс /kómpleks/ m. complex
комплект /komplékt/ m. set
комплектовать /komplektovát'/ v.
  staff
комплекция /kompléktsiia/ f.
  build
комплимент /komplimént/ m.
  compliment

композитор /kompozítor/ m.
composer

компресс /kompréss/ m. compress

компрометировать /komprometírovat'/
v. compromise

компромисс /kompromíss/ m.
compromise

компьютер /komp'iúter/ m. computer

компьютеризация /komp'iuterizátsiia/
f. computerization

комсомол /komsomól/ m. Young
Communist League, Komsomol

комфорт /komfórt/ m. comfort

комфортабельный /komfortábel'nyi/
adj. comfortable

конвейер /konvéier/ m. production
line, belt

конвенция /konvéntsiia/ f. convention

конвергенция /konvergéntsiia/ f.
convergence

конверсия /konvérsiia/ f. conversion

конверт /konvért/ m. envelope

конвоировать /konvoírovat'/ v.
escort

конвой /konvói/ m. escort

конвульсия /konvúl'siia/ f.
convulsion

конгресс /kongréss/ m. congress

конденсатор /kondensátor/ m.
condenser

кондитерская /kondíterskaia/ f.
confectioner's shop

кондиционирование /konditsionírova-
nie/ n. conditioning; к. воздуха /k.
vózdukha/ air-conditioning

кондуктор /kondúktor/ m. conductor

коневодство /konevódstvo/ n. horse
breeding

конезавод /konezavód/ m. stud

конец /konéts/ m. end

конечно /konéchno/ part. of course;
sure

конечный /konéchnyi/ adj. final;
ultimate

конкретный /konkrétnyi/ adj.
specific, concrete

конкурент /konkurént/ m. competitor

конкуренция /konkuréntsiia/ f.
competition

конкурировать /konkurírovat'/ v.
compete

конкурс /kónkurs/ m. competition

конница /kónnitsa/ f. cavalry

конопля /konopliá/ f. hemp

коносамент /konosamént/ m. bill of
lading

консерватор /konservátor/ m.
conservative

консерватория /konservatóriia/
f. conservatoire

консервировать /konservírovat'/
v. can, bottle

консервный нож /konsérvnyi nozh/
adj.+m. tinopener

консервы /konsérvy/ pl. canned food

консилиум /konsílium/ m.
consultation

консорциум /konsórtsium/ m.
consortium

конспект /konspékt/ m. synopsis

конспиративный /konspiratívnyi/ adj.
secret

конспиратор /konspirátor/ m.
conspirator

констатировать /konstatírovat'/ v.
ascertain; note

конституционный /konstitutsiónnyi/
adj. constitutional

конституция /konstitútsiia/ f.
constitution

конструкция /konstrúktsiia/ f.
construction, design

консул /kónsul/ m. consul

консульский /kónsul'skii/ adj.
consular
консульство /kónsul'stvo/ n.
consulate
консультант /konsul'tánt/ m.
consultant
консультация /konsul'tátsiia/
f. consultation
консультировать /konsul'tírovat'/
v. advise; consult
контакт /kontákt/ m. contact
контейнер /kontéiner/ m. container
контекст /kontékst/ m. context
контингент /kontingént/ m.
contingent
континент /kontinént/ m. continent
контора /kontóra/ f. office
контрабанда /kontrabánda/ f.
contraband
контрабандист /kontrabandíst/
m. smuggler
контрабас /kontrabás/ m. double-
bass
контр-адмирал /kontr-admirál/ m.
rear admiral
контракт /kontrákt/ m. contract
контраст /kontrást/ m. contrast
контратака /kontratáka/ f. counter-
attack
контрибуция /kontribútsiia/ f.
contribution
контрнаступление /kontrnastuplénie/
n. counter-offensive
контролер /kontroliór/ m. inspector
контролировать /kontrolírovat'/ v.
check
контроль /kontról'/ m. control
контрпретензия /kontrpreténziia/ f.
counter-claim
контрразведка /kontrrazvédka/ f.
counter-expionage; security service

контрреволюция /kontrrevoliútsiia/
f. counter-revolution
контузить /kontúzit'/ v. shell-
shock
контур /kóntur/ m. outline
конус /kónus/ m. cone
конфедерация /konfederátsiia/ f.
confederation
конферансье /konferans'é/ m. master
of ceremonies
конференция /konferéntsiia/ f.
conference
конфета /konféta/ f. sweet,
candy
конфиденциальный /konfidentsiál'nyi/
adj. confidential
конфискация /konfiskátsiia/ f.
confiscation
конфликт /konflíkt/ m. conflict
конфорка /konfórka/ f. burner
(on cooker)
конформизм /konformízm/ m.
konformism
концентрация /kontsentrátsiia/
f. concentration
концепция /kontséptsiia/ f.
conception
концерн /kontsérn/ m. concern;
enterprise
концерт /kontsért/ m. concert
концертмейстер /kontsertméister/
m. leader of orchestra
концессия /kontséssiia/ f.
concession
концовка /kontsóvka/ f. tail-
piece; ending
кончать /konchát'/ v. finish
конь /kon'/ m. horse, steed
коньки /kon'kí/ pl. skates; роликовые
к. /rólikovye k./ roller-skates
коньяк /kon'iák/ m. cognac
конюх /kóniukh/ m. groom

конюшня /koniúshnia/ f. stable
копать /kopát'/ v. dig
копейка /kopéika/ f. kopeck
копи /kópi/ pl. mines
копилка /kopílka/ f. money-box
копирка /kopírka/ f. carbon-
paper
копировать /kopirovát'/ v. copy;
imitate
копить /kopít'/ v. accumulate
копия /kópiia/ f. copy
копна /kopná/ f. shock
копоть /kópot'/ f. soot
коптеть /koptét'/ v. smoke
копченый /kopchiónyi/ adj. smoked
копыто /kopýto/ n. hoof
копье /kop'ió/ n. spear, lance
кора /korá/ f. bark
кораблекрушение /korablekrúshenie/
n. shipwreck
кораблестроение /korablestroénie/
n. shipbuilding
корабль /korábl'/ m. ship
коралл /koráll/ m. coral
кореец /koréets/ m. Korean
корейка /koréika/ f. brisket
корейский /koréiskii/ adj. Korean
коренастый /korenástyi/ adj. thickset
коренной /korennói/ adj. radical
корень /kóren'/ m. root
коренья /korén'ia/ pl. culinary roots
кореянка /koreiánka/ f. Korean
woman
корзинка /korzínka/ f. basket
коридор /kirodór/ m. corridor
корица /korítsa/ f. cinnamon
коричневый /koríchnevyi/ adj.
brown
корка /kórka/ f. crust
корм /korm/ m. forage
корма /kormá/ f. stern

кормилец /kormílets/ m. bread-
winner
кормилица /kormílitsa/ f. wet-
nurse
кормить /kormít'/ v. feed
коробить /koróbit'/ v. warp
коробка /koróbka/ f. box
корова /koróva/ f. cow
коровка /koróvka/ f. little cow;
божья к. /bózh'ia k./ ladybird
королева /koroléva/ f. queen
королевский /korolévskii/ adj.
royal
королевство /korolévstvo/ n.
kingdom
король /koról'/ m. king
корона /koróna/ f. crown
коронка /korónka/ f. crown (on
tooth)
коростель /korostél'/ m. corncrake
короткий /korótkii/ adj. short
коротковолновый /korotkovolnóvyi/
adj. short-wave
корпорация /korporátsiia/ f.
corporation
корпус /kórpus/ m. building;
corps
корректировать /korrektírovat'/ v.
correct
корректор /korréktor/ m. proof-
reader
корректура /korrektúra/ f. proofs
корреспондент /korrespondént/ m.
correspondent
корреспонденция /korrespondéntsiia/
f. correspondence; report
коррозия /korróziia/ f. corrosion
коррупция /korrúptsiia/ f.
corruption
корсет /korsét/ m. corset
корт /kort/ m. (tennis) court
кортик /kórtik/ m. dirk

корточки /kórtochki/ pl. *in:* сидеть
  на корточках /sidét' na kórtochkakh/
  v. squat
коршун /kórshun/ m. kite
корыстолюбие /korystoliúbie/ n.
  mercenary spirit
корь /kor'/ f. measles
коса /kosá/ f. plait; scythe
косвенный /kósvennyi/ adj.
  indirect
косилка /kosilka/ f. mowing-machine
косинус /kósinus/ f. cosine
косить /kosit'/ v. twist;
  squint; mow
косичка /kosichka/ f. pigtail
косматый /kosmátyi/ adj. shaggy
косметика /kosmétika/ f.
  cosmetics
космический /kosmicheskii/ adj.
  space
космодром /kosmodróm/ m.
  spacedrom
космонавт /kosmonávt/ m.
  spaceman
космополит /kosmopolit/ m.
  cosmopolitan
космос /kósmos/ m. space
косный /kósnyi/ adj. stagnant,
  inert
косой /kosói/ adj. slanting
косолапый /kosolápyi/ adj.
  in-toed; clumsy
костер /kostiór/ m. bonfire
костистый /kostistyi/ adj. bony
костлявый /kostliávyi/ adj.
  bony
костный /kóstnyi/ adj. bone
костыль /kostýl'/ m. crutch
кость /kost'/ f. bone
костюм /kostiúm/ m. suit
косынка /kosýnka/ f. scarf
косяк /kosiák/ m. door-post;
  shoal

кот /kot/ m. tom-cat
котел /kotiól/ m. boiler
котелок /kotelók/ m. kettle;
  bowler (-hat)
котельная /kotél'naia/ f. boiler-
  room
котенок /kotiónok/ m. kitten
котик /kótik/ m. seal; sealskin
котиться /kotit'sia/ v. give
  birth to kittens
котлета /kotléta/ f. cutlet,
  chop
котлован /kotlován/ m. pit,
  excavation (for foundations)
котловина /kotlovina/ f.
  hollow
который /kotóryi/ pron. which,
  who
коттедж /kottédzh/ m. cottage
кофе /kófe/ m. coffee
кофеин /kofein/ m. caffeine
кофейник /koféinik/ m. coffee-
  pot
кофта /kófta/ f. cardigan
кофточка /kóftochka/ f. blouse
кочан /kochán/ m. head (e.g. of
  cabbage)
кочевник /kochévnik/ m. nomad
кочегар /kochegár/ m. fireman
коченеть /kochenét'/ v. become
  numb.
кочерга /kochergá/ f. poker
кочка /kóchka/ f. hillock
кошелек /kosheliók/ m. purse
кошка /kóshka/ f. cat
кошмар /koshmár/ m. nightmare
кощунство /koshchúnstvo/ n.
  blasphemy
коэффициент /koeffitsiént/ m.
  coefficient
краб /krab/ m. crab
крага /krága/ f. legging

краденый /krádenyi/ adj. stolen
кража /krázha/ f. theft; к. со взломом
/k. so vzlómom/ burglary
край /krai/ m. edge; brink; land;
territory
крайний /kráinii/ adj. extreme;
по крайней мере /po kráinei mere/
at least
кран /kran/ m. crane
крановщик /kranovshchík/ m.
crane-driver
крапива /krapíva/ f. nettle
крапинка /krápinka/ f. speck(le)
красавец /krasávets/ m. handsome man
красавица /krasávitsa/ f. beauty
красильня /krasíl'nia/ f. dyeworks
красить /krásit'/ v. paint, dye
краска /kráska/ f. colour,
paint, dye
краснеть /krasnét'/ v. go red
красноречие /krasnoréchie/ n.
eloquence
краснуха /krasnúkha/ f. German
measles
красный /krásnyi/ adj. red; красное
дерево /krásnoe dérevo/ mahogany
красота /krasotá/ f. beauty
красочный /krásochnyi/ adj.
colourful
красть /krast'/ v. steal
кратер /kráter/ m. crater
краткий /krátkii/ adj. brief
краткость /krátkost'/ f. brevity
кратковременный /kratkovrémennyi/
adj. short; short-lived
краткосрочный /kratkosróchnyi/
adj. short-term, short-dated
крах /krakh/ m. crash
крахмал /krakhmál/ m. starch
креветка /krevétka/ f. shrimp
кредит /kredít/ m. credit

крейсер /kréiser/ m. cruiser
крем /krem/ m. cream
крематорий /krematórii/ m.
crematorium
кремация /kremátsiia/ f.
cremation
кремень /kremén'/ m. flint
кремль /kreml'/ m. Kremlin
крен /kren/ m. list
креп /krep/ m. crepe
крепить /krepít'/ v. strenghthen
крепкий /krépkii/ adj. firm
кресло /kréslo/ n. armchair
крест /krest/ m. cross
крестить /krestít'/ v. christen
креститься /krestít'sia/ v. be
christend; cross oneself
крестьянин /krest'iánin/ m.
peasant
крестьянка /krest'iánka/ f.
peasant woman
кривляться /krivliát'sia/ v.
grimace
кривой /krivói/ adj. crooked
кризис /krízis/ m. crisis
крик /krik/ m. cry, shout
крикет /krikét/ m. cricket
криминальный /kriminál'nyi/ adj.
criminal
критерий /kritérii/ m. criterion
критик /krítik/ m. critic
кричать /krichát'/ v. shout
кров /krov/ m. shelter
кровавый /krovávyi/ adj.
bloody
кровать /krovát'/ f. bed
кровля /króvlia/ f. roof
кровный /króvnyi/ adj. blood
кровожадный /krovozhádnyi/ adj.
blood-thirsty
кровоизлияние /krovoizliiánie/
n. haemorrhage

кровообращение /krovoobrashchénie/ n. circulation

кровоостанавливающий /krovoostanáv-livaiushchii/ adj. styptic

кровопийца /krovopiitsa/ m. and f. bloodsucker

кровоподтек /krovopodtiók/ m. internal bruise

кровопролитие /krovoprolitie/ n. bloodshed

кровопускание /krovopuskánie/ n. blood-letting

кровотечение /krovotechénie/ n. blooding; haemorrhage

кровь /krov'/ f. blood

кроить /kroit'/ v. cut out (dress)

крокодил /krokodil/ m. crocodile

кролик /królik/ m. rabbit

кроме /króme/ prep. except; besides, apart from

кромка /krómka/ f. edge

кромсать /kromsát'/ v. shred

крона /króna/ f. top (of tree); crown (coin)

кросворд /krosvórd/ m. crossword

крот /krot/ m. mole

кроткий /krótkii/ adj. gentle

крошить /kroshit'/ v. crumble; chop; mince

крошка /króshka/ f. crumb

круг /krug/ m. circle

круглосуточный /kruglosútochnyi/ adj. round-the-clock

круглый /krúglyi/ adj. round

кругом /krugóm/ adv. round, about

кругообразный /krugoobráznyi/ adj. circular

кругосветный /krugosvétnyi/ adj. round-the-world

кружево /krúzhevo/ n. lace

кружить /kruzhit'/ v. spin, whirl

кружка /krúzhka/ f. mug

кружок /kruzhók/ m. small circle; group

крупа /krupá/ f. groats; cereals

крупинка /krupinka/ f. grain

крупица /krupitsa/ f. grain

крупный /krúpnyi/ adj. large

крутить /krutit'/ v. twist; twirl

крутой /krutói/ adj. steep

круча /krúcha/ f. steep slope

крушение /krushénie/ n. downfall

крушить /krushit'/ v. destroy

крыжовник /kryzhóvnik/ m. gooseberry

крыло /kryló/ n. wing

крыльцо /kryl'tsó/ n. porch

крымский /krýmskii/ adj. Crimean

крыса /krýsa/ f. rat

крысиный яд / krysinyi iad/ adj.+m. rat poison

крыть /kryt'/ v. cover; roof

крыша /krýsha/ f. roof

крышка /krýshka/ f. lid

крюк /kriúk/ m. hook

крючок /kriuchók/ m. hook; catch

крюшон /kriushón/ m. cold fruit-punch

крякать /kriákat'/ v. quack

кряква /kriákva/ f. wild duck

кстати /kstáti/ adv. by the way

кто /kto/ pron. who

куб /kub/ m. cube

кубизм /kubizm/ m. cubism

кубинец /kubinets/ m. Cuban

кубинка /kubinka/ f. Cuban woman

кубинский /kubinskii/ adj. Cuban

кубический /kubícheskii/ adj.
cubic
кубок /kúbok/ m. cup
кубометр /kubométr/ m. cubic metre
кувшин /kuvshín/ m. pitcher
кувыркаться /kuvyrkát'sia/ v.
turn somersaults
кувырком /kuvyrkóm/ adv. head-
over-heels
куда /kudá/ adv. where
кудахтать /kudákhtat'/ v. cackle
кудри /kúdri/ pl. curls
кузен /kuzén/ m. cousin
кузина /kuzína/ f. cousin
кузнец /kuznéts/ m. blacksmith
кузнечик /kuznéchik/ m. grasshopper
кузов /kúzov/ m. body (of car)
кукиш /kúkish/ m. fig (rude
sign)
кукла /kúkla/ f. doll
кукольный /kúkol'nyi/ adj. puppet
кукуруза /kukurúza/ f. corn
кукушка /kukúshka/ f. cuckoo
кулак /kulák/ m. fist
кулебяка /kulebiáka/ f. pie
кулек /kuliók/ m. bag
кулик /kulík/ m. snipe
кулинарный /kulinárnyi/ adj.
culinary
кулиса /kulísa/ f. wing; за кулисами
/za kulísami/ behind the scenes
кулуары /kuluáry/ pl. lobby
кульминация /kul'minátsiia/ f.
culmination
культ /kul't/ m. cult
культивировать /kul'tivírovat'/ v.
cultivate
культура /kul'túra/ f. culture
кумир /kumír/ m. idol
кумыс /kumýs/ m. koumiss
куница /kunítsa/ f. marten
купальный /kupál'nyi/ adj. bathing

купаться /kupát'sia/ v. bath(e)
купе /kupé/ n. compartment
купель /kupél'/ f. font
купец /kupéts/ m. merchant
куплет /kuplét/ m. couplet
купля /kúplia/ f. purchase
купол /kúpol/ m. dome
купорос /kuporós/ m. vitriol
купюра /kupiúra/ f. note
курить /kurít'/ v. smoke
курица /kúritsa/ f. hen, chicken
курносый /kurnósyi/ adj. snub-nosed
курок /kurók/ m. trigger
куропатка /kuropátka/ f. partridge
курорт /kurórt/ m. health resort
курс /kurs/ m. course; rate of
exchange
курсант /kursánt/ m. student
курсив /kursív/ m. italics
курсировать /kursírovat'/ v. ply
курсы /kúrsy/ pl. school; college
куртка /kúrtka/ f. jacket
курьер /kur'ér/ m. messenger
кусать /kusát'/ v. bite
кусачки /kusáchki/ pl. nippers
кусок /kusók/ m. piece; morsel
куст /kust/ m. bush
кустарь /kustár'/ m. artisan
кутать /kútat'/ v. wrap up
кухарка /kukhárka/ f. cook
кухня /kúkhnia/ f. kitchen
куча /kúcha/ f. heap
кушанье /kúshan'e/ n. dish
кушать /kúshat'/ v. eat
кушетка /kushétka/ f. couch
кювет /kiuvét/ m. ditch

Л

лабиринт /labirínt/ m. labyrinth

лаборатория /laboratóriia/ f.
laboratory

лава /láva/ f. lava

лаванда /lavánda/ f. lavender

лавина /lavína/ f. avalanche

лавка /lávka/ f. shop

лавочник /lávochnik/ m. shopkeeper

лавр /lavr/ m. laurel

лагерь /láger'/ m. camp

лад /lad/ m. harmony

ладан /ládan/ m. incense

ладно /ládno/ adv., part. all right, O.K.

ладонь /ladón'/ f. palm

лаз /laz/ m. manhole

лазарет /lazarét/ m. hospital

лазейка /lazéika/ f. loophole

лазить /lázit'/ v. climb

лазурный /lazúrnyi/ adj. azure

лазутчик /lazútchik/ m. spy

лай /lai/ m. barking

лайка /láika/ f. husky

лайнер /láiner/ m. liner

лак /lak/ m. lacquer

лакей /lakéi/ m. lackey

лаковый /lákovyi/ adj. varnished

лакомиться /lákomit'sia/ v.
treat oneself (to)

лаконичный /lakoníchnyi/ adj.
concise, laconic

лампа /lámpa/ f. lamp; valve

лампада /lampáda/ f. icon lamp

лангуста /langústa/ f. spiny lobster

ландшафт /landsháft/ m. scenery

ландыш /lándysh/ m. lily of the valley

ланцет /lantsét/ m. lancet

лань /lan'/ f. fallow-deer; doe

лапа /lápa/ f. paw

лапша /lapshá/ f. noodles

ларек /lariók/ m. stall

ласка /láska/ f. caress; weasel

ласкать /laskát'/ v. fondle

ласковый /láskovyi/ adj. affectionate;
tender; gentle

ласточка /lástochka/ f. swallow

латвийский /latvíiskii/ adj.
Latvian

латинский /latínskii/ adj. Latin

латунь /latún'/ f. brass

латынь /latýn'/ f. Latin

латыш /latýsh/ m. Latvian

латышка /latyshka/ f. Latvian

латышский /latýshskii/ adj.
Latvian

лауреат /laureát/ m. prizewinner

лацкан /látskan/ m. lapel

лаять /láiat'/ v. bark

лгать /lgat'/ v. tell lies

лебедка /lebiódka/ f. winch

лебедь /lébed'/ m. swan

лев /lev/ m. lion

левкой /levkói/ m. gillyflower

левша /levshá/ m. left-hander

левый /lévyi/ adj. left

легенда /legénda/ f. legend

легкий /liógkii/ adj. easy;
light

легкоатлет /legkoatlét/ m. athlete

легковой автомобиль /legkovói
avtomobíl'/ adj.+m. car

легкое /iiógkoe/ n. lung

легкомысленный /legkomýslennyi/ adj.
thoughtless; frivolous

лед /liód/ m. ice

леденеть /ledenét'/ v. freeze

леденец /ledenéts/ m. lollipop;
rock

лезвие /lézvie/ n. blade

лезть /lezt'/ v. climb; push
forward

лейка /léika/ f. watering-can

лейтенант /leitenánt/ m. lieutenant

лекарство /lekárstvo/ n. medicine

лен /lión/ m. flax
ленивый /lenívyi/ adj. lazy
лениться /lenít'sia/ v. be lazy
лента /lénta/ f. ribbon
лентяй /lentiái/ m. lazybones
лень /len'/ f. idleness
лепить /lepít'/ v. model
лес /les/ m. forest
леска /léska/ f. fishing-line
лесник /lesník/ m. forester
лестница /léstnitsa/ f. staircase;
ladder
лесть /lest'/ f. flattery
летать /letát'/ v. fly
лето /léto/ n. summer
летопись /létopis'/ f. chronicle
летчик /liótchik/ m. pilot
летчик-испытатель /liótchik-
ispytátel'/ m. test pilot
лечебница /lechébnitsa/ f.
hospital
лечебный /lechébnyi/ adj. medical
лечение /lechénie/ n. treatment
лечить /lechít'/ v. treat (for)
лещ /leshch/ m. bream
лжесвидетельство /lzhesvidetél'stvo/
n. false evidence
лжец /lzhets/ m. liar
лживый /lzhívyi/
adj. false; untruthful
ли /li/ part. whether
либерал /liberál/ m. liberal
либо /líbo/ part. or либо ... либо...
/líbo... líbo.../ conj. either... or...
ливень /líven'/ m. downpour
ливер /líver/ m. liver
лига /líga/ f. league
лидер /líder/ m. leader
лизать /lizát'/ v. lick
ликвидация /likvidátsiia/ f.
liquidation
ликер /likiór/ m. liqueur

ликовать /likovát'/ v. rejoice
лилия /líliia/ f. lily
лиловый /lilóvyi/ adj. lilac
лиман /limán/ m. estuary
лимит /limít/ m. limit
лимон /limón/ m. lemon
лимонад /limonád/ m. lemonade
лимфа /límfa/ f. lymph
лингвист /lingvíst/ m. linguist
линейка /linéika/ f. ruler
линза /línza/ f. lens
линия /líniia/ f. line
линкор /linkór/ m. battleship
линовать /linovát'/ v. line, rule
линолеум /linóleum/ m. linoleum
линчевать /linchevát'/ v. lynch
линь /lin'/ m. tench
линять /liniát'/ v. moult; fade
липа /lípa/ f. lime
липнуть /lípnut'/ v. stick
лирик /lírik/ m. lyric, poet
лиса /lisá/ f. fox
лисица /lisítsa/ f. fox
лист /list/ m. sheet; leaf
лиственница /lístvennitsa/ f. larch
листовка /listóvka/ f. leaflet
листопад /listopád/ m. fall
литейщик /litéishchik/ m. foundryman
литератор /literátor/ m. man of
letters
литература /literatúra/ f.
literature
литовец /litóvets/ m. Lithuanian
литовка /litóvka/ f. Lithuanian
литовский /litóvskii/ adj.
Lithuanian
литой /litói/ adj. cast
литр /litr/ m. litre
литургия /liturgíia/ f. liturgy
лить /lit'/ v. pour
лиф /lif/ m. bodice
лифт /lift/ m. elevator; lift

лифчик /lífchik/ m. brassiere
лихорадка /likhorádka/ f. fever
лицевой /litsevói/ adj. front;
л. счет /l. schiot/ personal account
лицей /litséi/ m. lyceum
лицемер /litsemér/ m. hypocrite
лицемерие /litsemérie/ n. hypocrisy
лицо /litsó/ n. face; person
личина /lichína/ f. mask
личинка /lichínka/ f. larva
лично /líchno/ adv. personally
личность /líchnost'/ f. personality
личный /líchnyi/ adj. private
лишай /lishái/ m. herpes
лишать /lishát'/ v. deprive of
лишний /líshnii/ adj. superfluous;
unnecessary
лишь /lish/ part. only; conj.
as soon as
лоб /lob/ m. forehead
ловить /lovít'/ v. catch
ловкий /lóvkii/ adj. adroit;
smart
ловля /lóvlia/ f. catching; рыбная л.
/rýbnaia l./ fishing
ловушка /lovúshka/ f. trap
логарифм /logarífm/ m. logarithm
логика /lógika/ f. logic
лодка /lódka/ f. boat
лодочник /lódochnik/ m. boatman
лодыжка /lodýzhka/ f. ankle
лодырничать /lódyrnichat'/ v. loaf
about
ложа /lózha/ f. box; masonic
lodge
ложбина /lózhbina/ f. hollow
ложиться /lozhít'sia/ v. lie down
ложка /lózhka/ f. spoon
ложный /lózhnyi/ adj. false
ложь /lozh/ f. lie
лоза /lozá/ f. vine; willow
лозунг /lózung/ m. slogan

локаут /lokáut/ m. lock-out
локомотив /lokomotív/ m.
locomotive
локон /lókon/ m. lock
локоть /lókot'/ m. elbow
лом /lom/ m. crowbar
ломаный /lómanyi/ adj. broken
ломать /lomát'/ v. break
ломбард /lombárd/ m. pawnshop
ломберный стол /lómbernyi stol/
adj.+m. card-table
ломкий /lómkii/ adj. fragile
ломота /lomóta/ f. rheumatic pain
ломоть /lomót'/ m. chunk
ломтик /lómtik/ m. slice
лопасть /lópast'/ f. blade
лопата /lopáta/ f. shovel; spade
лопатка /lopátka/ f. shoulderblade
лопаться /lópat'sia/ v. burst;
collapse
лопух /lopúkh/ m. burdock
лосина /losína/ f. elk meat;
chamois leather
лоскут /loskút/ m. shred
лосниться /losnít'sia/ v. glisten
лосось /losós'/ m. salmon
лось /los'/ m. elk
лотерея /loteréia/ f. lottery
лоток /lotók/ m. tray
лотос /lótos/ m. lotus
лоханка /lokhánka/ f. tub; почечная л.
/póchechnaia l./ renal pelvis
лохматый /lokhmátyi/ adj. shaggy
лохмотья /lokhmót'ia/ pl. rags
лоцман /lótsman/ m. pilot
лошадь /lóshad'/ f. horse
лощина /loshchína/ f. dell
лояльный /loiál'nyi/ adj. loyal
луг /lug/ m. meadow
лужа /lúzha/ f. puddle
лужайка /luzháika/ f. lawn
лук /luk/ m. onions; bow

лукавый /lukávyi/ adj. cunning;
roguish
луковица /lúkovitsa/ f. onion;
bulb
луна /luná/ f. moon
лунатик /lunátik/ m. sleepwalker
лунка /lúnka/ f. socket
лупа /lúpa/ f. magnifying glass
луч /luch/ m. ray
лучезарный /luchezárnyi/ adj.
radiant
лучше /lúchshe/ adj., adv. better
лучший /lúchshii/ adj. best
лыжи /lýzhi/ pl. ski
лысеть /lysét'/ v. go bald
львица /l'vítsa/ f. lioness
льгота /l'góta/ f. privilege
льдина /l'dína/ f. ice-floe
льнуть /l'nút'/ v. cling (to)
льняной /l'nianói/ adj. flax,
linen
льстить /l'stít'/ v. flatter
любезничать /liubéznichat'/ v. pay
complements
любезность /liubéznost'/ f. courtesy
любимец /liubímets/ m.
favourite
любительский /liubítel'skii/ adj.
amateur
любить /liubít'/ v. love; like
любоваться /liubovát'sia/ v.
admire
любовник /liubóvnik/ m. lover
любовница /liubóvnitsa/ f.
mistress
любовь /liubóv'/ f. love
любознательный /liuboznátel'nyi/ adj.
curious
любой /liubói/ adj. any
любопытный /liubopýtnyi/ adj. curious;
interesting

любопытство /liubopýtstvo/ n.
curiousity
люд /liud/ m. folk
люди /liúdi/ pl. people
людный /liúdnyi/ adj. crowded
люк /liuk/ m. hatchway; manhole
люкс /liúks/ m. de-luxe
люстра /liústra/ f. chandelier
лютеранин /liuteránin/ m. Lutheran
лютик /liútik/ m. buttercup
лютня /liútnia/ f. lute
лютый /liútyi/ adj. ferocious
лягать /liagát'/ v. kick
лягушка /liagúshka/ f. frog
ляжка /liázhka/ f. thigh
лязг /liázg/ m. clank
лямка /liámka/ f. strap

М

мавзолей /mavzoléi/ m. mausoleum
магазин /magazín/ m. shop
магистраль /magistrál'/ f. highway
магия /mágiia/ f. magic
магнат /magnát/ m. magnate
магний /mágnii/ m. magnesium
магнит /magnít/ m. magnet
магнитофон /magnitofón/ m. tape-
recorder
мадера /madéra/ f. Madeira wine
мадьяр /mad'iár/ m. Magyar
мадьярка /mad'iárka/ f. Magyar
мадьярский /mad'iárskii/ adj.
Magyar
мазать /mázat'/ v. paint; smear;
oil
мазут /mazút/ m. black oil
мазь /maz'/ f. ointment
май /mái/ m. May

майка /máika/ f. sports-shirt
майор /maiór/ m. major
майский /máiskii/ adj. May;
  м. жук /m. zhuk/ cock-chafer
мак /mak/ m. poppy
макароны /makaróny/ pl. macaroni
макать /makát'/ v. dip
макет /makét/ m. model, mock-up
маклер /mákler/ m. broker
макрель /makrél'/ f. mackerel
максимум /máksimum/ m. maximum
макулатура /makulatúra/ f. waste
  paper
макушка /makúshka/ f. top
малайский /maláiskii/ adj. Malayan
малейший /maléishii/ adj. smallest
маленький /málen'kii/ adj. little;
  small
малина /malína/ f. raspberry
мало /málo/ adv. little, few;
  not much; not many
маловажный /malovázhnyi/ adj. of little
  importance
маловероятный /maloveroiátnyi/ adj.
  improbable
малознакомый /maloznakómyi/ adj.
  unfamiliar
малоизвестный /maloizvéstnyi/ adj.
  little-known
малоимущий /maloimúshchii/ m.
  needy, poor
малокровие /malokróvie/ n. anaemia
малолетний /malolétnii/ adj.
  young; m. juvenile
малолюдный /maloliúdnyi/ adj.
  thinly pupulated
малонаселенный /malonaseliónnyi/
  adj. thinly populated
малоподвижный /malopodvízhnyi/
  adj. slow, inactive
малопродуктивный /maloproduktívnyi/
  adj. unproductive

малосемейный /maloseméinyi/ adj.
  with a small family
малоубедительный /maloubedítel'nyi/
  adj. not very convincing
малоурожайный /malourozháinyi/
  adj. low-yield
малыш /malýsh/ m. kiddy
мальчик /mál'chik/ m. boy
малютка /maliútka/ m., f. baby
маляр /maliár/ m. house-painter
малярия /maliaríia/ f. malaria
мама /máma/ f. mummy
мамонт /mamónt/ m. mammoth
мангуста /mangústa/ f. mongoose
мандарин /mandarín/ m. tangerine
мандат /mandát/ m. mandate
маневр /manióvr/ m. manoeuvre
манекен /manekén/ m. tailor's
  dummy
манекенщик /manekénshchik/
  m. model
манекенщица /manekénshchitsa/
  f. model
манера /manéra/ f. manner
манжета /manzhéta/ f. cuff
маникюр /manikiúr/ m. manicure
манипулировать /manipulírovat'/
  v. manipulate
манить /manít'/ v. attract;
  beckon; lure
манифест /manifést/ m. manifesto
манифестация /manifestátsiia/
  f. demonstration
манишка /maníshka/ f. shirt front
мания /mániia/ f. mania; м. величия
  /m. velíchiia/ megalomania
манная каша /mánnaia kásha/
  adj.+f. (boiled) semolina
манометр /manómetr/ m. pressure-
  gauge
маньяк /man'iák/ m. maniac
марать /marát'/ v. dirty

марганец /márganets/ m. manganese
маргарин /margarín/ m. margarine
маргаритка /margarítka/ f.
  daisy
мариновать /marinovát'/ v. pickle
марионетка /marionétka/ f.
  puppet
марка /márka/ f. stamp; mark;
  brand; make
маркий /márkii/ adj. easily
  soiled
марксизм /marksízm/ m. Marxism
марля /márlia/ f. gauze
мармелад /marmelád/ m. fruit
  sweets
март /mart/ m. March
марш /marsh/ m. march
маршрут /marshrút/ m. route
маска /máska/ f. mask
маскарад /maskarád/ m. fancy-
  dress ball
маскировать /maskirovát'/ v. mask;
  disguise; camouflage
масленица /máslenitsa/ f. Shrovetide
масленка /masliónka/ f. butter-
  dish
маслина /maslína/ f. olive
масло /máslo/ n. butter; oil
масон /máson/ m. freemason
масса /mássa/ f. mass
массаж /massázh/ m. massage
массив /massív/ m. massif
массировать /massírovat'/ v.
  massage
массовый /mássovyi/ adj. mass
мастер /máster/ m. master; expert
мастерить /masterít'/ v. make
мастерская /masterskáia/ f. workshop
мастерство /masterstvó/ n. skill
мастика /mastíka/ f. floor polish
маститый /mastítyi/ adj. venerable

масть /mast'/ f. colour, coat
  (animals); suit (cards)
масштаб /masshtáb/ m. scale
мат /mat/ m. checkmate; floor mat
математика /matemátika/ f. mathematics
материал /materiál/ m. material
материк /materík/ m. continent
материнство /materínstvo/ n.
  maternity
материя /matériia/ f. fabric
матрас /matrás/ m. mattress
матрешка /matrióshka/ f.
  matryoshka
матрос /matrós/ m. sailor;
  seaman
матч /match/ m. match
мать /mat'/ f. mother
махать /makhát'/ v. wave
махинация /makhinátsiia/ f.
  trick, machination
маховое колесо /makhovóe kolesó/
  adj.+n. fly-wheel
мачеха /máchekha/ f. step-mother
мачта /máchta/ f. mast
машина /mashína/ f. machine; car
машинист /mashiníst/ m. engine-
  driver
машинистка /mashinístka/ f.
  typist
машинка /mashínka/ f. typewriter
маяк /maiák/ m. lighthouse
маятник /máiatnik/ m. pendulum
мгновение /mgnovénie/ n. moment
мебель /mébel'/ f. furniture
мед /miód/ m. honey
медаль /medál'/ f. medal
медведица /medvéditsa/ f.
  she-bear; Большая М. /bol'sháia
  m./ the Great Bear; Малая М. /málaia
  m./ the Little Bear
медведь /medvéd'/ m. bear

медик /médik/ m. doctor
медикамент /medikamént/ m. medicine,
  drug
медицина /meditsína/ f. medicine
медленный /médlennyi/ adj. slow
медлить /médlit'/ v. linger;
  delay
медный /médnyi/ adj. brass
медосмотр /medosmótr/ m. medical
  examination
медпомощь /medpómoshch/ f. medical
  service
медпункт /medpúnkt/ m. surgery
медсестра /medsestrá/ f. nurse
медуза /medúza/ f. jellyfish
медь /med'/ f. copper
между /mézhdu/ prep. between,
  amongst
междугородный /mezhdugoródnyi/
  adj. inter-city
международный /mezhdunaródnyi/
  adj. international
межконтинентальный
  /mezhkontinentál'nyi/ adj.
  intercontinental
мезонин /mezonín/ m. mezzanine
мел /mel/ m. chalk
меланхолия /melankhóliia/ f.
  melancholy
мелеть /melét'/ v. become shallow
мелиорация /meliorátsiia/ f.
  land-reclamation
мелкий /mélkii/ adj. fine; small;
  petty; shallow
мелодия /melódiia/ f. melody, tune
мелочь /méloch/ f. trifle; small
  change (money)
мель /mel'/ f. sandbank
мелькать /mel'kát'/ v. flash
мельком /mél'kom/ adv. in passing
мельник /mél'nik/ m. miller

мельница /mél'nitsa/ f. mill
мельчайший /mel'cháishii/ adj.
  smallest
мелюзга /meliuzgá/ f. small fry
меморандум /memorándum/ m.
  memorandum
мемориальный /memoriál'nyi/
  adj. memorial
мемуары /memuáry/ pl. memoirs
менее /ménee/ adv. less
меньше /mén'she/ adv. smaller,
  less, fewer
меньшинство /men'shinstvó/ n.
  minority
меню /meniú/ n. menu
менять /meniát'/ v. change
мера /méra/ f. measure
мерещиться /meréshchit'sia/
  v. seem
мерзавец /merzávets/ m.
  scoundrel
мерзкий /mérzkii/ adj. vile
мерзнуть /miórznut'/ v. freeze
мерин /mérin/ m. gelding
мерить /mérit'/ v. measure; try on
мерка /mérka/ f. measure
мертвец /mertvéts/ m. dead man
мертворожденный /mertvorozhdiónnyi/
  adj. still-born
мертвый /miórtvyi/ adj. dead
мерцать /mertsát'/ v. glimmer,
  twinkle
месить /mesít'/ v. knead
мести /mestí/ v. sweep
местность /méstnost'/ f. locality
место /mésto/ m. place; site;
  seat
местожительство /mestozhítel'stvo/
  n. residence
местонахождение /mestonakhozhdénie/
  n. whereabouts

месторождение /mestorozhdénie/
n. deposit

месть /mest'/ f. revenge

месяц /mésiats/ m. month; moon

металл /metáll/ m. metal

металлист /metallíst/ m. metal-
worker

металлический /metallícheskii/
adj. metallic; metal

металлургия /metallurgíia/ f.
metallurgy

метан /metán/ m. methane

метафизика /metafízika/ f. metaphysics

метафора /metáfora/ f. metaphor

метель /metél'/ f. snowstorm

метеор /meteór/ m. meteor

метеоролог /meteorólog/ m.
meteorologist

метеорология /meteorológiia/ f.
meteorology

метис /metís/ m. mongrel

метить /métit'/ v. mark

метла /metlá/ f. broom

метод /métod/ m. method

метр /metr/ m. metre

метрика /métrika/ f. birth
certificate

метро /metró/ n. metro,
underground

мех /mekh/ m. fur

механизм /mekhanízm/ m.
mechanism

механик /mekhánik/ m. mechanical
engineer

меч /mech/ m. sword

мечеть /mechét'/ f. mosque

мечта /mechtá/ f. dream

мечтатель /mechtátel'/ m. dreamer

мечтать /mechtát'/ v. dream

мешалка /meshálka/ f. mixer

мешать /meshát'/ v. mix; hinder

мешаться /meshát'sia/ v. meddle
(in)

мешок /meshók/ m. sack

мещанин /meshchanín/ m.
Philistine

мещанский /meshchánskii/ adj.
vulgar

миг /mig/ m. moment

мигать /migát'/ v. blink, wink

миграция /migrátsiia/ f. migration

мигрень /migrén'/ f. migraine

мизинец /mizínets/ m. little
finger/toe

микроб /mikrób/ m. microbe

микрон /mikrón/ m. micron

микроскоп /mikroskóp/ m.
microscope

микрофон /mikrofón/ m. microphone

микстура /mikstúra/ f. mixture

милая /mílaia/ f. sweetheart

милитаризм /militarízm/ m.
militarism

миллиардер /milliardér/ m.
multi-millionaire

миллиметр /millimétr/ m.
millimetre

миллион /millión/ m. million

миллионер /millionér/ m.
millionaire

миловать /mílovat'/ v. pardon

миловидный /milovídnyi/ adj.
pretty

милосердие /milosérdie/ n.
charity

милостыня /mílostynia/ f.
alms

милость /mílost'/ f. favour

милый /mílyi/ adj. dear, sweet;
m. darling

миля /mília/ f. mile

мимика /mímika/ f. mime

мимо /mímo/ adv. past; by
мимолетный /mimoliótnyi/ adj.
  fleeting
мимоходом /mimokhódom/ adv.
  in passing
мина /mína/ f. mine
миндаль /mindál'/ m. almonds
минерал /minerál/ m. mineral
миниатюра /miniatiúra/ f.
  miniature
минимум /mínimum/ m. minimum
министерство /ministérstvo/ n.
  ministry
министр /minístr/ m. minister
минога /minóga/ f. lamprey
минувший /minúvshii/ adj.
  past
минус /mínus/ m. minus
минута /minúta/ f. minute
мир /mir/ m. world; peace
мираж /mirázh/ m. mirage
мирить /mirít'/ v. reconcile
мирный /mírnyi/ adj. peaceful
мировой /mirovói/ adj. world
мироздание /mirozdánie/ n. universe
миролюбивый /miroliubívyi/ adj.
  peace-loving
миска /míska/ f. basin
миссионер /missionér/ m.
  missionary
миссия /míssiia/ f. mission
мистика /místika/ f. mysticism
митинг /míting/ m. meeting
митрополит /mitropolít/ m.
  Metropolitan
миф /mif/ m. myth
мичман /míchman/ m. midshipman
мишень /mishén'/ f. target
младенец /mladénets/ m. infant
младший /mládshii/ adj. junior
млекопитающее /mlekopitáiushchee/
n. mammal

Млечный Путь /mléchnyi put'/
  adj.+m. Milky Way
мнение /mnénie/ n. opinion
мнимый /mnímyi/ adj. imaginary;
  illusory
мнительный /mnítel'nyi/ adj.
  health-conscious; suspicious
многие /mnógie/ adj. many
много /mnógo/ adv. much; many;
  a lot
многобрачие /mnogobráchie/ n.
  polygamy
многовековой /mnogovekovói/
  adj. ancient, centuries-old
многогранный /mnogogránnyi/ adj.
  many-sided
многодетная семья /mnogodétnaia
  sem'iá/ adj.+f. large family
многократный /mnogokrátnyi/ adj.
  repeated
многолетний /mnogolétnii/ adj.
  many years' standing
многолюдный /mnogoliúdnyi/ adj.
  crowded
многообразный /mnogoobráznyi/ adj.
  varied
многосторонний /mnogostorónnii/
  adj. ersatile; multilateral
многострадальный /mnogostradál'nyi/
  adj. long-suffering
многоточие /mnogotóchie/ n.
  (three) dots
многоуважаемый /mnogouvazháemyi/
  adj. respected; dear (in letter)
многоугольник /mnogougól'nik/
  m. polygon
многоцветный /mnogotsvétnyi/ adj.
  multicoloured
многочисленный /mnogochíslennyi/
  adj. numerous
многоэтажный /mnogoetázhnyi/ adj.
  many-storeyed

многоязычный /mnogoiazýchnyi/
adj. polyglot
множественный /mnózhestvennyi/
adj. plural
множество /mnózhestvo/ n. great
number
множить /mnózhit'/ v. multiply
мобилизовать /mobilizovát'/
v. mobilize
могила /mogíla/ f. grave
могучий /mogúchii/ adj. mighty
могущество /mogúshchestvo/
n. power
мода /móda/ f. fashion
модель /modél'/ f. pattern,
model
модернизировать /modernizírovat'/
v. modernize
модифицировать /modifitsírovat'/
v. modify
модный /módnyi/ adj. fashionable
может быть /mózhet byt'/ paren.
perhaps
можжевельник /mozhzhevél'nik/
m. juniper
можно /mózhno/ v. it is possible;
можно (мне)..? /mózhno mne/
may I..?
мозаика /mozáika/ f. mosaic
мозг /mozg/ m. brain
мозговой /mozgovói/ adj.
cerebral; brain
мозоль /mozól'/ f. corn
мой /mói/ pron. my
мойка /móika/ f. washing; sink
мокрица /mokrítsa/ f. wood-
louse
мокрота /mokróta/ f. phlegm
мокрота /mokrotá/ f. damp
мокрый /mókryi/ adj. moist,
wet

молва /molvá/ f. rumour;
дурная м. /durnáia m./ bad
reputation
молдаванин /moldavánin/ m.
Moldavian
молдаванка /moldávanka/ f.
Moldavian
молдавский /moldávskii/ adj.
Moldavian
молебен /molében/ m. church
service; thanksgiving
молекула /molékula/ f. molecule
молитва /molítva/ f. prayer
молитвенник /molítvennik/
m. prayerbook
молить /molít'/ v. pray
моллюск /molliúsk/ m. shellfish
молния /mólniia/ f. lightning
молодежь /molodiozh'/ f.
young people
молодеть /molodét'/ v. get
younger
молодец /molodéts/ m. fine,
fellow; молодец! paren. well
done!
молодить /molodít'/ v. make
(smb.) look younger
молодожены /molodozhióny/ pl.
newly-weds
молодой /molodói/ adj. young
молодость /mólodost'/ f.
youth
молоко /molokó/ n. milk
молокосос /molokosós/ m.
greenhorn
молот /mólot/ m. hammer
молотилка /molotílka/ f.
threshing machine
молотить /molotít'/ v. thresh
молоток /molotók/ m. hammer

молочная /molóchnaia/ f.
dairy
молочница /molóchnitsa/ f.
milkwoman
молчание /molchánie/ n.
silence
молчать /molchát'/ v. be silent
моль /mol'/ f. moth
мольберт /mol'bért/ m. easel
момент /momént/ m. moment
моментальный /momentál'nyi/
adj. instant
монарх /monárkh/ m. monarch
монархия /monárkhiia/ m.
monarchy
монастырь /monastýr'/ m.
monastery; convent
монах /monákh/ m. monk
монахиня /monákhinia/ f.   nun
монгол /mongól/ m. Mongol
монголка /mongólka/ f.
Mongol
монгольский /mongól'skii/
adj. Mongol
монета /monéta/ f. coin
монография /monográfiia/ f.
monograph
монолитный /monolítnyi/
adj. monolithic
монолог /monológ/ m.
monologue
монополизировать /monopolizí-
rovat'/ v. monopolize
монополия /monopóliia/ f.
monopoly
монотонный /monotónnyi/ adj.
monotonous
монтаж /montázh/ m. mounting
монтажная работа /montázhnaia
rabóta/ adj.+f. installation work

монтер /montiór/ m. fitter
монтировать /montírovat'/
v. assemble
мопс /mops/ m. pug dog
мораль /morál'/ f. moral
мораторий /moratórii/ m.
moratorium
морг /morg/ m. morgue
моргать /morgát'/ v. blink
море /móre/ n. sea
мореплавание /moreplávanie/
n. navigation
мореходный /morekhódnyi/
adj. nautical; seaworthy
морж /morzh/ m. walrus
морить /morít'/ v. exterminate
морковь /morkóv'/ f. carrots
мороженое /morózhenoe/ n.
ice-cream
мороз /moróz/ m. frost
морозоустойчивый /morozoustói-
chivyi/ adj. frost-resistant
моросить /morosít'/ v. drizzle
морошка /moróshka/ f.
cloudberry
морской /morskói/ adj. sea, maritime;
морская звезда /morskáia zvezdá/
starfish; м. болезнь /m. bolézn'/ sea-
sickness
морфий /mórfii/ m. morphine
морщина /morshchína/ f.
wrinkle
морщиться /mórshchit'sia/ v.
wrinkle
моряк /moriák/ m. sailor
москвич /moskvích/ m. Muscovite
москвичка /moskvíchka/ f.
Muscovite
москит /moskít/ m. mosquito
мост /most/ m. bridge

мостовая /mostováia/ f.
pavement; roadway
мотать /motát'/ v. reel
мотель /motél'/ m. motel
мотив /motív/ m. motive
мотивировать /motivírovat'/
v. motivate
мотогонки /motogónki/ pl.
motor-races
моток /motók/ m. ball
мотор /motór/ m. motor,
engine
мотоцикл /mototsíkl/ m. motor-
cycle
мотыга /motýga/ f. hoe
мотылек /motylіók/ m. moth;
butterfly
мох /mokh/ m. moss
мохнатый /mokhńatyi/ adj.
furry; bushy
моцион /motsión/ m. exercise
моча /mochá/ f. urine
мочалка /mochálka/ f. wisp; bast
мочевой пузырь /mochevói puzýr'/
adj.+m. bladder
мочить /mochít'/ v. soak, wet
мочиться /mochít'sia/ v. urinate
мочка /móchka/ f. lobe of ear
мочь /moch'/ v. be able
мошенник /moshénnik/ m. rogue,
swindle
мошенничать /moshénnichat'/ v.
cheat
мошка /móshka/ f. midge
мощеный /moshchiónyi/ adj.
paved
мощи /móshchi/ pl. relic (of
saint); живые м. /zhivýe m./
walking skeleton
мощность /móshchnost'/ f.
capacity
мощь /moshch/ f. power

мразь /mraz'/ f. filth
мрак /mrak/ m. gloom
мракобес /mrakobés/ m.
obscurantist
мрамор /mrámor/ m. marble
мрачный /mráchnyi/ adj.
gloomy
мститель /mstítel'/ m. avenger
мстить /mstit'/ v. avenge;
have revenge on
мудрец /mudréts/ m. sage
мудрость /múdrost'/ f. wisdom
мудрый /múdryi/ adj. wise
муж /muzh/ m. husband
мужество /múzhestvo/ n. courage
мужик /muzhík/ m. peasant;
man (coll.)
мужской /muzhskói/ adj.
masculine; male, men's
мужчина /muzhchína/ m. man
муза /múza/ f. muse
музей /muzéi/ m. museum
музыка /múzyka/ f. music
музыкант /muzykánt/ m.
musician
мука /múka/ f. torment
мука /muká/ f. flour
мул /mul/ m. mule
мультипликационный (фильм)
/mul'tiplikatsiónnyi fil'm/
adj.+m. cartoon film
мумия /múmiia/ f. mummy
мундир /mundír/ m. dress-coat;
tunic
муниципальный /munitsipál'nyi/
adj. municipal
муравей /muravéi/ m. ant
муравейник /muravéinik/
m. ant-hill
муравьед /murav'éd/ m. ant-
eater

муравьиная кислота /murav'ínaia kislotá/ adj.+f. formic acid
мурлыкать /murlýkat'/ v. purr
мускат /muskát/ m. muscatel
мускул /múskul/ m. muscle
мускус /múskus/ m. musk
муслин /muslín/ m. muslin
мусор /músor/ m. refuse
мусульманин /musul'mánin/ m. Moslem
мутить /mutít'/ v. stir up
мутный /mútnyi/ adj. muddy
муха /múkha/ f. fly
мучение /muchénie/ n. torment
мученик /múchenik/ m. martyr
мучитель /muchítel'/ m. tormentor
мучительный /muchítel'nyi/ adj. agonizing
мучить /múchit'/ v. torture
мчать /mchat'/ v. rush
мы /my/ pron. we
мылить /mýlit'/ v. soap
мыло /m'ylo/ n. soap
мыльница /mýl'nitsa/ f. soap-dish
мыльный /mýl'nyi/ adj. soap(y); мыльная пена /mýl'naia péna/ foam
мыс /mys/ m. cape
мысленный /mýslennyi/ adj. mental
мыслить /mýslit'/ v. think
мысль /mysl'/ f. idea; thought
мыть /myt'/ v. wash
мычать /mychát'/ v. moo; mumble
мышеловка /myshelóvka/ f. mousetrap
мышца /myshtsá/ f. muscle
мышь /mysh/ f. mouse
мышьяк /mysh'iák/ m. arsenic
мягкий /miágkii/ adj. soft; fresh, gentle; mild
мякина /miakína/ f. chaff

мясник /miasník/ m. butcher
мясо /miáso/ n. meat; flesh
мясорубка /miasorúbka/ f. mincing-machine
мята /miáta/ f. mint
мятеж /miatézh/ m. revolt
мятежник /miatézhnik/ m. mutineer
мятежный /miatézhnyi/ adj. rebellious
мять /miát'/ v. crush; crumple
мятый /miátyi/ adj. crumpled; rumpled
мяукать /miaúkat'/ v. mew
мяч /miách/ m. ball

Н

на /na/ prep. on; in; for (period of time); to; by; at; during
на /na/ part. here; на, возьми! /na voz'mí/ here, take this!
набег /nabég/ m. raid
набережная /náberezhnaia/ f. embankment
набивать /nabivát'/ v. stuff
набивной /nabivnói/ adj. printed
набирать /nabirát'/ v. gather; make up
наблюдатель /nabliudátel'/ m. observer
наблюдать /nabliudát'/ v. watch; observe; keep an eye on
набожный /nábozhnyi/ adj. pious
набок /nábok/ adv. awry
наболевший /nabolévshii/ adj. sore
набор /nabór/ m. recruitment; enrolment

наборщик /nabórshchik/ m.
type-setter
набрасывать /nabrásyvat'/ v.
sketch; heap up
набросок /nabrósok/ m. draft
набухать /nabukhát'/ v. swell
наваливать /naválivat'/
v. pile up
навек /navék/ adv. for ever
наверно(е) /navérno(e)/ adv.
probably
наверняка /naverɲiaká/ adv.
for certain
наверстывать /naviórstyvat'/
v. make up (for)
навертывать /naviórtyvat'/
v. screw on
наверх /náverkh/ adv. upstairs;
up
навешивать /navéshivat'/ v.
hang up
навещать /naveshchát'/ v. visit
навзничь /návznich/ adv.
backwards; on one's back
навигация /navigátsiia/ f.
navigation
нависать /navisát'/ v.
(over) hang
наводнение /navodnénie/ n.
flood
наводнять /navodniát/ v.
inundate
навоз /navóz/ m. manure
наволока /návoloka/ f.
pillowcase
навряд (ли) /navriád(li)/ adv.
hardly
навсегда /navsegdá/ adv.
for ever
навстречу /navstréchu/ adv.
in: идти н. /idtí n./ meet smb.
half-way

навыворот /navývorot/ adv.
inside out
навык /návyk/ m. habit
навытяжку /navýtiazhku/ adv.
at attention
навязчивый /naviázchivyi/
adj. obsessive; tiresme
навязывать /naviázyvat'/ v.
tie (on); impose; thrust (on)
нагайка /nagáika/ f. whip
нагибать /nagibát'/ v. bend
нагибаться /nagibát'sia/ v. stoop
наглухо /náglukho/ adv. tight(ly)
наглый /náglyi/ adj. impudent
наглядный /nagliádnyi/ adj.
graphic
нагнетать /nagnetát'/ v. force
нагноение /nagnoénie/ n.
suppuration
наговаривать /nagovárivat'/ v.
slander
нагой /nagói/ adj. naked
наголо /nagoló/ adv. bare
наготове /nagotóve/ adv. at the
ready
награда /nagráda/ f. reward;
decoration; prize
награждать /nagrazhdát'/ v.
award
нагревать /nagrevát'/ v. heat
нагрудник /nagrúdnik/ m. (child's) bib
нагружать /nagruzhát'/ v. load
над /nad/ prep. over, above
надавливать /nadávlivat'/ v.
press
надбавка /nadbávka/ f. increment
надвигать /nadvigát'/ v. push (on)
надвигаться /nadvigát'sia/ v.
approach; be imminent
надводный /nadvódnyi/ adj.
surface
надвое /nádvoe/ adv. in two

надгробный /nadgróbnyi/ adj.
tomb
надевать /nadevát'/ v. put on
надежда /nadézhda/ f. hope
надежный /nadiózhnyi/ adj.
reliable
надеяться /nadeiát'sia/ v. hope
надзиратель /nadzirátel'/ m.
supervisor
надзирать /nadzirát'/ v.
oversee
надменный /nadménnyi/ adj.
arrogant
надо /nádo/ v. it is necessary
надобность /nádobnost'/ f.
need, necessity
надоедать /nadoedát'/ v. pester;
bother
надоедливый /nadoédlivyi/
adj. tiresome
надой /nadói/ m. yield (of
milk)
надолго /nadólgo/ adv. for a long
time
надписывать /nadpísyvat'/ v.
inscribe
надпись /nádpis'/ f. inscription;
superscription
надрез /nadréz/ m. incision
надругаться /nadrugát'sia/
v. outrage
надстройка /nadstróika/ f.
superstructure
надтреснутый /nadtrésnutyi/
adj. cracked
надувать /naduvát'/ v. inflate;
swindle, cheat
надуманный /nadúmannyi/ adj.
far-fetched
надушенный /nadúshennyi/ adj.
scented

наедине /naediné/ adv. in private
наездник /naézdnik/ m. rider
наезжать /naezzhát'/ v. run
(into)
наем /naióm/ m. hiring; renting
наемник /naiómnik/ m. mercenary
наемный /naiómnyi/ adj. hired
наждак /nazhdák/ m. emery
нажива /nazhíva/ f. gain
наживать /nazhivát'/ v. acquire
наживаться /nazhivát'sia/ v. make
a fortune
наживка /nazhívka/ f. bait
нажим /nazhím/ m. pressure
нажимать /nazhimát'/ v. press
назад /nazád/ adv. backwards;
back
название /nazvánie/ n. name
наземный /nazémnyi/ adj. ground
назло /nazló/ adv. out of spite
назначать /naznachát'/ v. appoint
назначение /naznachénie/ n.
appointment
назревать /nazrevát'/ v. mature
называть /nazyvát'/ v. name
называться /nazyvát'sia/ v. be called
наиболее /naibólee/ adv. the most
наибольший /naiból'shii/ adj.
the greatest, the largest
наивный /naívnyi/ adj. naive
наивысший /naivýsshii/ adj.
the highest
наигранный /naígrannyi/ adj.
affected
наизнанку /naiznánku/ adv.
inside out
наизусть /naizúst'/ adv. by heart
наилучший /nailúchshii/ adj.
the best
наименее /naiménee/ adv.
the least

92

наименование /naimenovánie/
n. name
наименьший /naimén'shii/ adj.
the least
наимоднейший /naimodnéishii/
adj. trendy
наискось /náiskos'/ adv. obliquely
наихудший /naikhúdshii/ adj.
the worst
найденыш /naidiónysh/ m.
foundling
наказ /nakáz/ m. mandate
наказание /nakazánie/ n.
punishment
наказывать /nakázyvat'/ v.
punish
накаленный /nakaliónnyi/ adj.
overheated; tense
накалывать /nakályvat'/ v. pin
down
накануне /nakanúne/ adv. the day
before; prep. on the eve
накапливать /nakáplivat'/ v.
accumulate
накачивать /nakáchivat'/ v. pump
накидка /nakídka/ f. cushion-
cover; cape
накидывать /nakídyvat'/ v.
throw on
накипь /nákip'/ f. scum
накладная /nakladnáia/ f.
invoice
наклеивать /nakléivat'/ v.
stick on
наклейка /nakléika/ f. label
наклонный /naklónnyi/ adj.
sloping
наклонять /nakloniát'/ v. incline;
tilt
наклоняться /nakloniát'sia/
v. bend

наковальня /nakovál'nia/ f. anvil
наколенник /nakolénnik/ m. knee-
cap
наконец /nakonéts/ adv. at last;
finally
наконечник /nakonéchnik/ m. tip
накоплять /nakopliát'/ v. accumulate
накрапывать /nakrápyvat'/ v. drizzle
накрахмаленный /nakrakhmálennyi/
adj. starched
накрепко /nákrepko/ adv. fast
накрест /nákrest/ adv. crosswise
накрывать /nakryvát'/ v. cover;
н. на стол /n. na stol/ lay the table
накурить /nakurít'/ v. fill with
smoke
налаживать /nalázhivat'/ v.
adjust; organize
налево /nalévo/ adv. to the left
налегке /nalegké/ adv. light
налет /naliót/ m. raid; hold up
налетчик /naliótchik/ m. robber
наливать /nalivát'/ v. pour out;
fill
налим /nalím/ m. burbot
налицо /nalitsó/ adv. present;
availabe
наличие /nalíchie/ n. availability
наличность /nalíchnost'/ f. cash
налог /nalóg/ m. tax
налогоплательщик /nalogoplatél'-
shchik/ m. taxpayer
наложенным платежом /nalózhennym
platezhóm/ adj.+m. cash on delivery
намазывать /namázyvat'/ v. spread
наматывать /namátyvat'/ v. wind on
намачивать /namáchivat'/ v. wet
намек /namiók/ m. hint
намекать /namekát'/ v. hint (at)
намереваться /namerevát'sia/ v.
intend

93

намечать /namechát'/ v. plan;
outline
намного /namnógo/ adv. by far
намокать /namokát'/ v. get wet
намордник /namórdnik/ m.
muzzle
намыливать /namýlivat'/ v. soap
нанизывать /nanízyvat'/ v. string
нанимать /nanimát'/ v. hire; rent
наоборот /naoborót/ adv. the
other way round; paren. on the
contrary
наобум /naobúm/ adv. at random
наотмашь /naótmash'/ in: ударить н.
/udárit' n./ deal smb. a smashing
blow
наотрез /naotréz/ adv. point- blank
нападать /napadát'/ v. attack; assault
нападение /napadénie/ n. attack
нападки /napádki/ pl. attacks
напаивать /napáivat'/ v. make drunk
наперед /naperiód/ adv. in advance
наперекор /naperekor/ adv. counter
to
наперерез //napereréz/ adv. cutting
across
наперсток /napiórstok/ m. thimble
напиваться /napivát'sia/ v. get
drunk
напильник /napíl'nik/ m. file
напиток /napítok/ m. drink
напихивать /napíkhivat'/ v. stuff
наплевать /naplevát'/ v. spit;
мне н. /mne n./ coll
I couldn't care less
наподобие /napodóbie/ adv. like;
resembling
напоказ /napokáz/ adv. on show,
for show
наполнять /napolniát'/ v. fill

наполовину /napolovínu/ adv. half
напоминать /napominát'/ v. remind
напор /napór/ m. pressure
напоследок /naposlédok/ adv. by way
of farewell
направление /napravlénie/ n.
direction
направо /naprávo/ adv. to the right
напрасный /naprásnyi/ adj. vain
например /naprimér/ paren. for example
напрокат /naprokát/ adv. for hire
напролет /naproliót/ adv. right
through; весь день н. /ves' den' n./
all day long
напротив /naprótiv/ adv. on the
contrary; opposite
напрягать /napriagát'/ v. brace
напряженный /napriazhiónnyi/ adj.
tense; strained
напрямик /napriamík/ adv. straight
напуганный /napúgannyi/ adj. scared
напускной /napusknói/ adj. affected
напыщенный /napýshchennyi/ adj.
pompous
наравне /naravné/ adv. on equal
terms
нарастать /narastát'/ v. increase
нарасхват /naraskhvát/ adv. like
hot cakes
нарезать /narezát'/ v. cut
наречие /naréchie/ n. dialect;
adverb
нарицательный /naritsátel'nyi/
adj. nominal
наркоз /narkóz/ m. narcosis
наркоман /narkomán/ m. drug
addict
наркотик /narkótik/ m. dope
народ /naród/ m. people, nation
нарочитый /narochítyi/ adj.
deliberate

нарочно /naróchno/ adv. on
purpose
наружный /narúzhnyi/ adj.
external
наружу /narúzhu/ adv. outside
наручники /narúchniki/ pl. handcuffs
наручный /narúchnyi/ adj. wrist
нарушать /narushát'/ v. break,
infringe
нарушение /narushénie/ n.
infringement
нарушитель /narushítel'/ m. disturber;
trespasser
нарцисс /nartsíss/ m. daffodil
наряд /nariád/ m. dress
нарядный /nariádnyi/ adj. smart
наряду /nariadú/ adv. together
with; on a level with
наряжать /nariazhát'/ v. dress
up
насаждение /nasazhdénie/ n.
plantation
насвистывать /nasvístyvat'/ v. whistle
наседать /nasedát'/ v. press (on)
наседка /nasédka/ f. brood-hen
насекомое /nasekómoe/ n. insect
население /naselénie/ n. population
населять /naseliát'/ v. settle
насиживать /nasízhivat'/ v. hatch
насилие /nasílie/ n. violence
насиловать /nasílovat'/ v. rape
насилу /nasílu/ adv. with difficulty
насильственный /nasíl'stvennyi/
adj. forced; violent
насквозь /naskvóz'/ adv. through
наскоро /náskoro/ adv. hastily
наскучить /naskúchit'/ v. bore
наслаждаться /naslazhdát'sia/ v. delight
насладиться /nasladít'sia/ v. enjoy
наследие /naslédie/ n. legacy
наследник /naslédnik/ m. heir

наследный /naslédnyi/ adj. crown (prince)
наследовать /naslédovat'/ v. inherit
наследственность /naslédstvennost'/
f. heredity
наследственный /naslédstvennyi/ adj.
hereditary
наслушаться /naslúshat'sia/ v.
hear a lot of
насмерть /násmert'/ adv. to death
насмехаться /nasmekhát'sia/ v.
mock
насморк /násmork/ m. cold
насос /nasós/ m. pump
наспех /náspekh/ adv. in a hurry
настаивать /nastáivat'/ v. insist
(on)
настежь /nástezh'/ adv. wide open
настенный /nasténnyi/ adj. wall
настигать /nastigát'/ v. overtake
настойчивый /nastóichivyi/ adj.
persistent
настолько /nastól'ko/ adv. so much
настольный /nastól'nyi/ adj. table;
настольная книга /nastól'naia kníga/
adv. handbook
настороже /nastorozhé/ adv. on the
alert
настоятель /nastoiátel'/ m. abbot;
dean
настоящий /nastoiáshchii/ adj.
real, genuine
настраивать /nastráivat'/ v. tune; adjust
настроение /nastroénie/ n. mood
настройщик /nastróishchik/ m. tuner
наступательный /nastupátel'nyi/ adj.
offensive
наступать /nastupát'/ v. come
наступление /nastuplénie/ n. offensive
настурция /nastúrtsiia/ f. nasturtium
насухо /násukho/ adv. dry

насущный /nasúshchnyi/ adj. vital
насчет /naschiót/ prep. about
насчитывать /naschítyvat'/ v. count
наталкивать /natálkivat'/ v. incite;
н. на мысль /n. na mysl'/ suggest
the idea
натирать /natirát'/ v. rub
натиск /nátisk/ m. onslaught
натощак /natoshchák/ adv.
on an empty stomach
натравливать /natrávlivat'/
v. set smb. against
натрий /nátrii/ m. sodium
натрое /nátroe/ adv. in three
натура /natúra/ f. nature
натуральный /naturál'nyi/ adj.
natural
натурщик /natúrshchik/ m. model
натюрморт /natiurmórt/ m. still life
натягивать /natiágivat'/ v. stretch
натянутый /natiánutyi/ adj. tight
наугад /naugád/ adv. at random
наука /naúka/ f. science
наутро /naútro/ adv. on the
morrow
научный /naúchnyi/ adj.
scientific
наушник /naúshnik/ m. ear-phone
нахал /nakhál/ m. impudent person
нахлебник /nakhlébnik/ m. hanger-on
нахлынуть /nakhlýnut'/ v. rush
нахмуривать /nakhmúrivat'/ v. frown
находить /nakhodít'/ v. find
находиться /nakhodít'sia/ v. be situated
находка /nakhódka/ f. find
находчивый /nakhódchivyi/ adj.
quick; resourceful
нацеливать /natsélivat'/ v. aim
национализация /natsionalizátsiia/
f. nationalization

национализм /natsionalízm/ m.
nationalism
национальность /natsionál'nost'/
f. nationality
нация /nátsiia/ f. nation, people
начало /náchalo/ n. beginning
начальник /nachál'nik/ m. chief
начальный /nachál'nyi/ adj. elementary
начальство /nachál'stvo/ n. authorities
начерно /nácherno/ adv. rough(ly)
начинать /nachinát'/ v. begin
начинка /nachínka/ f. stuffing
начисто /náchisto/ adv. clean
начистоту /nachistotú/ adv. frankly
начитанный /nachítannyi/ adj. well-read
наш /nash/ pron. our
нашатырь /nashatýr'/ m. sal-
ammoniac
нашествие /nashéstvie/ n. invasion
нашивать /nashivát'/ v. sew on
нащупать /nashchúpat'/ v. grope
(for) and find; find
не /ne/ part. not
небезызвестно /nebezyzvéstno/
adv. it is no secret
небесный /nebésnyi/ adj. celestial; heavenly
небо / nébo/ n. sky; heaven
небо /nióbo/ n. palate
небольшой /nebol'shói/ adj. small, little
небосвод /nebosvód/ m. firmament;
небосклон /nebosklón/ m. horizon
небоскреб /neboskriób/ m. skycraper
небось /nebós'/ adv. it is most likely
небрежный /nebrézhnyi/ adj. careless
небывалый /nebyvályi/ adj. unprecedented
небылица /nebylítsa/ f. untruth; fantasy
небьющийся /neb'iúshchiisia/ adj. unbreakable
неважно /nevázhno/ adv. poorly

неважный /nevázhnyi/ adj. unimportant

невдалеке /nevdaleké/ adv. not far off

неведение /nevédenie/ n. ignorance

невежда /nevézhda/ m., f. ignoramus

невежливый /nevézhlivyi/ adj. rude, impolite

неверие /nevérie/ n. lack of faith

невероятный /neveroiátnyi/ adj. incredible

невеста /nevésta/ f. bride; fiancee

невестка /nevéstka/ f. daughter- in-law (son's wife), sister-in- law (brother's wife)

невзирая на /nevziráia na/ prep. regardless of

невзначай /nevznachái/ adv. by chance

невзрачный /nevzráchnyi/ adj.plain

невидимый /nevídimyi/ adj. invisible

невинность /nevínnost'/ f. innocence

невод /névod/ m. net

невозможный /nevozmózhnyi/ adj. impossible

неволить /nevólit'/ v. compel

невольник /nevól'nik/ m. slave

невольно /nevól'no/ adv. unintentionally; involantarily

невообразимый /nevoobrazímyi/ adj. inconceivable

невооруженный /nevooruzhiónnyi/ adj. unarmed; naked (eye)

невпопад /nevpopád/ adv. not to the point

невралгия /nevralgíia/ f. neuralgia

неврастеник /nevrasténik/ m. neurotic

невредимый /nevredímyi/ adj. unharmed; intact

невроз /nevróz/ m. neurosis

невыгодный /nevýgodnyi/ adj. unprofitable; unfavourable

невыносимый /nevynosímyi/ adj. unbearable

невыполнимый /nevypolnímyi/ adj. impracticable

негатив /negatív/ m. negative

негашеная известь /negashiónaia ízvest'/ adj.+f. quicklime

негде /négde/ adv. nowhere

негласный /neglásnyi/ adj. secret

негодный /negódnyi/ adj. worthless

негр /negr/ m. Black

неграмотный /negrámotnyi/ adj. illiterate

негритянка /negritiánka/ f .Black

недавний /nedávnii/ adj. recent

недавно /nedávno/ adv. lately

недаром /nedárom/ adv. not for nothing

недвижимость /nedvízhimost'/ f. real estate

неделимый /nedelímyi/ adj. indivisible

неделя /nedélia/ f. week

недоверие /nedovérie/ n. distrust

недовольство /nedovól'stvo/ n. displeasure

недоглядеть /nedogliadét'/ v. overlook

недоедание /nedoedánie/ n. malnutrition

недолгий /nedólgii/ adj. brief, short

недомогание /nedomogánie/ n. indisposition

недомогать /nedomogát'/ v. be unwell

недомолвка /nedomólvka/ f. reservation

недооценивать /nedootsénivat'/ v. underestimate

недопустимый /nedopustímyi/ adj. inadmissible

недоразвитый /nedorázvityi/ adj. underdeveloped

недоразумение /nedorazuménie/ n. misunderstanding

недорогой /nedorogói/ adj. inexpensive

недосмотр /nedosmótr/ m. oversight

недоставать /nedostavat'/ v. lack

недостаток /nedostátok/ m. lack; defect; fault

недостижимый /nedostizhímyi/ adj. inattainable

недостойный /nedostóinyi/ adj. unworthy

недоступный /nedostúpnyi/ adj. inaccessible; incomprehensible

недоумевать /nedoumevát'/ v. be perplexed

недра /nédra/ pl. bowels

недруг /nédrug/ m. enemy

недуг /nedúg/ m. illness

недурной /nedurnói/ adj. not bad; quite pretty

нежданный /nezhdánnyi/ adj. unexpected

нежность /nézhnost'/ f. tenderness

нежный /nézhnyi/ adj. gentle

незабудка /nezabúdka/ f. forget-me-not

незавидный /nezavídnyi/ adj. unenviable; mediocre

независимость /nezavísimost'/ f. independence

незадолго /nezadólgo/ adv. shortly (before)

незаконнорожденный /nezakonnoрózhdennyi/ adj. illegitimate

незаменимый /nezamenimýi/ adj. irreplaceable

незапамятный /nezapámiatnyi/ adj. immemorial

незваный /nezványi/ adj. uninvited

нездоровиться /nezdoróvit'sia/ v. мне нездоровится /mne nezdoróvitsia/ I don't fell well

незнакомец /neznakómets/ m. stranger

незнакомый /neznakómyi/ adj. unknown

незнание /neznánie/ n. ignorance

незрелый /nezrélyi/ adj. unripe; immature

незримый /nezrímyi/ adj. invisible

неизбежный /neizbézhnyi/ adj. inevitable

неизлечимый /neizlechímyi/ adj. oncurable

неизменный /neizménnyi/ adj. invariable; constant

неимоверный /neimovérnyi/ adj. increidible

неимущий /neimúshchii/ adj. indigent

неинтересный /neinterésnyi/ adj. uninteresting; dull

неискушенный /neiskushiónnyi/ adj. unsophisticated; inexperienced

неисполнимый /neispolnímyi/ adj. impracticable

неисправимый /neispravímyi/ adj. irreparable

неисправный /neisprávnyi/ adj. defective

неиссякаемый /neissiakáemyi/ adj. inexhaustible

неисчислимый /neischislímyi/ adj. innumerable

нейлон /neilón/ m. nylon

нейтралитет /neitralitét/ m. neutrality

нейтрон /neitrón/ m. neutron

некий /nékii/ pron. a certain

некогда /nékogda/ in: мне н. /mne n./ I have no time

некоторый /nékotoryi/ pron. a certain; some

некрасивый /nekrasívyi/ adj. ugly; unattractive; unseemly

некролог /nekrológ/ m. obituary

некуда /nékuda/ pron. nowhere

некурящий /nekuriáshchii/ adj. nonsmoker

нелегкий /neliógkii/ adj. difficult; not easy

нелепость /nelépost'/ f. absurdity

неловкий /nelóvkii/ adj. awkward
нельзя /nel'ziá/ adv. (it is) impossible
немало /nemálo/ adv. quite a lot of
немедленный /nemédlennyi/ adj. immediate
неметь /nemét'/ v. become dumb
немец /némets/ m. German
немецкий /némétskii/ adj. German
немилость /nemílost'/ f. disgrace
неминуемый /neminúemyi/ adj. inevitable
немка /némka/ f. German woman
немногие /nemnógie/ pl. few
немного /nemnógo/ adv. a little
немой /nemói/ adj. dumb
немыслимый /nemýslimyi/ adj. unthinkable; impossible
ненавидеть /nenavídet'/ v. hate
ненападение /nenapadénie/ n. nonaggression
ненастье /nenást'e/ m. wet or rainy weather
ненасытный /nenasýtnyi/ adj. insatiable
необдуманный /neobdúmannyi/ adj. rash
необитаемый /neobitáemyi/ adj. uninhabited
необоснованный /neobosnóvannyi/ adj. groundless
необратимый /neobratímyi/ adj. irreversible
необузданный /neobúzdannyi/ adj. unbridled
необходимость /neobkhodímost'/ f. necessity
необъективный /neob"ektívnyi/ adj. biased
необыкновенный /neobyknovénnyi/ adj. extraordinary; uncommon
неограниченный /neograníchennyi/ adj. unlimited

неоднократный /neodnokrátnyi/ adj. repeated
неожиданный /neozhídannyi/ adj. unexpected
неон /neón/ m. neon
неопределенный /neopredeliónnyi/ adj. indefinite; vague
неопровержимый /neoproverzhímyi/ adj. irrefutable
неосмотрительный /neosmotrítel'nyi/ adj. imprudent
неосуществимый /neosushchestvímyi/ adj. impracticable
неоспоримый /neosporímyi/ adj. irrefutable
неосторожный /neostorózh nyi/adj. careless
неотвратимый /neotvratímyi/ adj. inevitable
неотделимый /neotdelímyi/ adj. inseparable
неотесанный /neotiósannyi/ adj. rough; not polished
неоткуда /neótkuda/ adv. from nowhere
неотложный /neotlózhnyi/ adj. urgent
неотразимый /neotrazímyi/ adj. irresistible
неотъемлемый /neot"émlemyi/ adj. inalienable
неоценимый /neotsenímyi/ adj. invaluable
непереводимый /neperevodímyi/ adj. untranslatable
неплатежеспособный /neplatiozhesposóbnyi/ adj. insolvent
непобедимый /nepobedímyi/ adj. invincible
неповторимый /nepovtorímyi/ adj. inimitable
непогода /nepogóda/ f. bad weather
непогрешимый /nepogreshímyi/ adj. infallible

неподалеку /nepodalióku/ adv. not far (away *or* off)

неподвижный /nepodvízhnyi/ adj. motionless

неподкупный /nepodkúpnyi/ adj. incorruptible

неподходящий /nepodkhodiáshchii/ adj. unsirtable

неподчинение /nepodchinénie/ n. insubordination

непоколебимый /nepokolebímyi/ adj. steadfast

неполадка /nepoládka/ f. defect

непоправимый /nepopravímyi/ adj. irreparable

непорочный /neporóchnyi/ adj. immaculate

непорядочный /neporiádochnyi/ adj. dishonourable

непосвященный /neposviashchiónnyi/ adj. uninitiated

непослушание /neposlushánie/ n. disobedience

неправда /neprávda/ f. untruth

неправильный /neprávil'nyi/ adj. incorrect

непредвиденный /nepredvídennyi/ adj. unforeseen

непременно /nepreménno/ adv. certainly

непреодолимый /nepreodolímyi/ adj. insuperable; irresistible

непререкаемый /neprerekáemyi/ adj. indisputable

непрерывный /neprerývnyi/ adj. continuous

непривычный /neprivýchnyi/ adj. unusual

неприличный /neprilíchnyi/ adj. improper

непримиримый /neprimirímyi/ adj. irreconcilable

непринужденный /neprinuzhdiónnyi/ adj. relaxed, easy

неприступный /nepristúpnyi/ adj. inacessible

неприязненный /nepriiáznennyi/ adj. hostile

неприятель /nepriiátel'/ m. enemy

непроизводительный /neproizvodítel'- nyi/ adj. unproductive

непроизвольный /neproizvól'nyi/ adj. involuntary

непромокаемый /nepromokáemyi/ adj. waterproof

непроницаемый /nepronitsáemyi/ adj. impenetrable

непротивление /neprotivlénie/ n. nonresistance

непроходимый /neprokhodímyi/ adj. impassable

непрошеный /nepróshenyi/ adj. uninvited

неравенство /nerávenstvo/ n. inequality

неравный /nerávnyi/ adj. unequal

неразбериха /nerazberíkha/ f. mess

неразлучный /nerazlúchnyi/ adj. inseparable

неразрешимый /nerazreshímyi/ adj. insoluble

нерв /nerv/ m. nerve

нервничать /nérvnichat'/ v. be nervous

нерешительный /nereshítel'nyi/ adj. irresolute

нержавеющий /nerzhavéiushchii/ adj. stainless (steel)

нерушимый /nerushímyi/ adj.inviolable

неряха /neriákha/ m., f. sloven

неряшливый /neriáshlivyi/ adj. slovenly

несбыточный /nesbýtochnyi/ adj. unrealizable

несварение /nesvarénie/ n. indigestion

несгибаемый /nesgibáemyi/ adj. inflexible

несгораемый /nesgoráemyi/ adj. fireproof

несколько /néskol'ko/ pron. several, some

неслыханный /neslýkhannyi/ adj. unprecedented

несметный /nesmétnyi/ adj. innumerable

несмотря (на) /nesmotriá na/ adv.+prep. in spite of

несовершеннолетний /nesovershennolétnii/ adj. under age; m. minor

несовместимый /nesovmestímyi/ adj. incompatible

несогласие /nesoglásie/ n. disagreement

несокрушимый /nesokrushímyi/ adj. indestructible

несомненно /nesomnénno/ adv. undoubtedly

несоответствие /nesootvétstvie/ n. discrepancy

несправедливый /nespravedlívyi/ adj. unjust

нестерпимый /nesterpímyi/ adj. unbearable

нести /nestí/ v. carry; bear

несчастный /neschástnyi/ adj. unhappy; н. случай /n. slúchai/ accident

несчастье /neschast'e/ n. misfortune

нет /net/ part. no; not; nothing

нетерпение /neterpénie/ n. impatience

нетерпимый /neterpímyi/ adj. intolerant

нетрудоспособный /netrudosposóbnyi/ adj. disabled

нетто /nétto/ adj. net

неуверенный /neuvérennyi/ adj. uncertain

неудача /neudácha/ f. failure

неудачный /neudáchnyi/ adj. unsuccessful

неудобный /neudóbnyi/ adj. inconvenient

неужели /neuzhéli/ part. really?

неуклюжий /neukliúzhii/ adj. clumsy

неумение /neuménie/ n. inability

неустойка /neustóika/ f. forfeit

неустойчивый /neustóichivyi/ adj. unstable

неутолимый /neutolímyi/ adj. unquenchable

неутомимый /neutomímyi/ adj. indefatigable

неуч /néuch/ m. ignoramus

неуязвимый /neuiazvímyi/ adj. invulnerable

нефтедобыча /neftedobýcha/f. oil output

нефтеналивное (судно) /neftenalivnóe sudno/ adj.+n. oil tanker

нефтеперегонный (завод) /nefteperegónnyi zavod/ adj.+m. oil refinery

нефть /neft'/ f. oil, petroleum

нефтяная (скважина) /neftianáia skvázhina/ adj.+f. oil well

нехватка /nekhvátka/ f. shortage

неходовой /nekhodovói/ adj. unmarketable

нехотя /nékhotia/ adv. unwillingly

нецензурный /netsenzúrnyi/ adj. obscene (language)

нечаянный /necháiannyi/ adj. unexpected; accidental

нечестный /nechéstnyi/adj. dishonest

нечетный /nechótnyi/ adj. odd

нечто /néchto/ pron. something

неявка /neiávka/ f. failure to appear

ни /ni/ conj. not a; nor;

ни... ни... /ni... ni.../ neither... nor

нигде /nigdé/ adv. nowhere

нижний /nízhnyi/ adj. lower;

нижнее белье /nízhnee bel'ió/ underclothes, underwear

низ /niz/ m. bottom

низвергать /nizvergát'/ v. overthrow

низкий /nízkii/ adj. low, mean

никак /nikák/ adv. in no way
никакой /nikakói/ pron. no
никель /níkel'/ m. nickel
никогда /nikogdá/ adv. never
никотин /nikotín/ m. nicotine
никто /niktó/ pron. nobody, no one
никуда /nikudá/ adv. nowhere
никчемный /nikchiómnyi/ adj.
    good-for-nothing
нимало /nimálo/ adv. not in
    the least
ниоткуда /niotkúda/ adv. from
    nowhere
нитка /nítka/ f. thread
ничего /nichevó/ pron. nothing;
    adv. so-so; passably
ничей /nichéi/ pron. nobody's
ничто /nichtó/ pron. nothing
ничуть /nichút'/ adv. not a bit
ничья /nichiá/ f. draw, drawn game
ниша /nísha/ f. niche
нищета /nishchetá/ f. poverty
нищий /níshchii/ m. beggar
но /no/ conj. but, and
новелла /novélla/ f. short story
новинка /novínka/ f. novelty
новичок /novichók/ m. novice
новобранец /novobránets/ m. recruit
новорожденный /novorozhdiónnyi/
    adj. new-born
новоселье /novosél'ie/ n. house-
    warming
новозеландец /novozelándets/ m. New
    Zealander
новозеландка /novozelándka/ f. New
    Zealander
новозеландский /novozelándskii/ adj.
    New Zealand
новость /nóvost'/ f. news
новый /nóvyi/ adj. new
нога /nogá/ f. foot, leg
ноготь /nógot'/ m. nail

нож /nozh/ m. knife
ножницы /nózhnitsy/ pl. scissors
ноздря /nozdriá/ f. nostril
нокаутировать /nokautírovat'/ v. knock
    out (sport)
ноль /nol'/ m. nought; zero; nil
номенклатура /nomenklatúra/ f. no-
    menclature
номер /nómer/ m. number; size; (hotel)
    room
норвежец /norvézhets/ m. Norwegian
нора /norá/ f. burrow; hole
норвежка /norvézhka/ f. Norwegian
норвежский /norvézhskii/ adj.
    Norwegian
норд /nord/ m. north; north wind
норка /nórka/ f. mink
норма /nórma/ f. standard
нормальный /normál'nyi/ adj. normal
нормандец /normándets/ m. Norman
нормандка /normándka/ f. Norman
нож /nozh/ m. knife
ножницы /nózhnitsy/ pl. scissors
ноздря /nozdriá/ f. nostril
нокаутировать /nokautírovat'/ v. knock
    out (sport)
ноль /nol'/ m. nought; zero; nil
номенклатура /nomenklatúra/ f. no-
    menclature
номер /nómer/ m. number; size; (hotel)
    room
норвежец /norvézhets/ m. Norwegian
нора /norá/ f. burrow; hole
норвежка /norvézhka/ f. Norwegian
норвежский /norvézhskii/ adj.
    Norwegian
норд /nord/ m. north; north wind
норка /nórka/ f. mink
норма /nórma/ f. standard
нормальный /normál'nyi/ adj. normal
нормандец /normándets/ m. Norman
нормандка /normándka/ f. Norman

нос /nos/ m. nose

носилки /nosílki/ pl. stretcher

носильщик /nosíl'shchik/ m. porter

носитель /nosítel'/ m. bearer; repository

носить /nosít'/ v. carry; wear

носиться /nosít'sia/ v. rush

носовой /nosovói/ adj. nasal;
н. платок /n. platók/ handkerchief

носок /nosók/ m. toe (of boot or stocking); sock

носорог /nosoróg/ m. rhinoceros

нота /nota/ f. note

ночевать /nochevát'/ v. spend the night

ночлег /nochlég/ m. lodging for the night

ночник /nochník/ m. night-light

ночь /noch/ f. night

ноябрь /noiábr'/ m. November

нрав /nrav/ m. temper

нравиться /nrávit'sia/ v. please

ну /nu/ int. well now!

нужда /nuzhdá/ f. want, straits; need

нужный /núzhnyi/ adj. necessary

нутрия /nútriia/ f. nutria

нырять /nyriát'/ v. dive

ныть /nyt'/ acke; whine

нюанс /niuáns/ m. nuance

нюх /niúkh/ m. scent

нюхать /niúkhat'/v. sniff

нянчить /niánchit'/ v. nurse

нянчиться /niánchit'sia/ v. fuss (over)

O

о /o/ prep. about; with; on; against

оазис /oazis/ m. oasis

оба /óba/ num. m., n. both

обалдеть /obaldét'/ v. sl. be stunned

обаяние /obaiánie/ n. charm

обаятельный /obaiátel'nyi/ adj. fascinating

обвал /obvál/ m. landslide

обветренный /obvétrennyi/ adj. weather-beaten

обветшалый /obvetshályi/ adj. decrepit

обвешивать /obvéshivat'/ v. cheat (in weighing goods)

обвинение /obvinénie/ n. accusation

обвинитель /obvinítel'/ m. prosecutor

обвинительный (акт) /obvinítel'nyi akt/ adj.+m. indictment

обвинять /obviniát'/ v. accuse (of)

обводнять /obvodniát'/ v. irrigate

обвораживать /obvorázhivat'/v. bewitch

обворожительный /obvorozhítel'nyi/ adj. fascinating

обвязывать /obviázyvat'/ v. tie round

обгонять /obgoniát'/ v. outstrip

обгорать /obgorát'/ v. be scorched

обдумывать /obdúmyvat'/ v. consider

обе /óbe/ num. f. both

обед /obéd/ m. dinner

обедать /obédat'/ v. have dinner

обеднение /obednénie/ n. impoverishment

обедня /obédnia/ f. mass

обезболивать /obezbólivat'/ v. anaesthetize

обезвоживать /obezvózhivat'/ v. dehydrate

обезвреживать /obezvrézhivat'/ v. render harmless

обеззараживать /obezzarázhivat'/v. disinfect

обезопасить /obezopásit'/ v. secure (against)

обезоруживать /obezorúzhivat'/ v. disarm

обезуметь /obezúmet'/ v. go mad

обезьяна /obez'iána/ f. monkey

обезьянничать /obez'iánnichat'/ v. ape

обелять /obeliát'/ v. whitewash; vindicate

оберегать /oberegát'/ v. guard

обертка /obiórtka/ f. wrapper

обертывать /obiórtyvat'/ v. wrap up

обескураживать /obeskurázhivat'/ v. dishearten

обеспечение /obespechénie/ n. guaranteeing

обеспечивать /obespéchivat'/ v. provide for

обессилеть /obessílet/ v. lose strength

обессмертить /obessmértit'/ v. immortalize

обесценивать /obestsénivat'/ v. devalue

обет /obét/ m. vow

обетованный (земля обетованная) /zemliá obetovánnaia/ f.+adj. the Promised Land

обещание /obeshchánie/ n. promise

обещать /obeshchát'/ v. promise

обжалование /obzhálovanie/ n. appeal

обжаловать /obzhálovat'/ v. appeal against

обжигать /obzhigát'/ v. burn

обжигаться /obzhigát'sia/ v. burn oneself

обжора /obzhóra/ m., f. glutton

обзаводиться /obzavodit'sia/ v. provide oneself (with)

обзор /obzór/ m. review

обзывать /obzyvát'/ v. call someone names

обивать /obivát'/ v. upholster

обида /obída/ f. offence

обидный /obídnyi/ adj. offensive

обидчивый /obídchivyi/ adj. touchy

обижать /obizhát'/ v. offend

обилие /obílie/ n. abundance

обитаемый /obitáemyi/ adj. inhabited

обкрадывать /obkrádyvat'/ v. rob

облава /obláva/ f. raid

облагать (налогом) /oblagát' nalógom/ v.+m. tax

облагораживать /oblagorázhivat'/ v. ennoble

обладать /obladát'/ v. possess

облако /óblako/ n. cloud

областной /oblastnói/ adj. regional

область /óblast'/ f. region; province; sphere

облегчать /oblegchát'/ v. facilitate; ease

обледенелый /obledenélyi/ adj. ice-covered

облезлый /oblézlyi/ adj. mangy; shabby

облетать /obletát'/ v. fly (round)

обливать /oblivát'/ v. pour (over); spill (over)

облигация /obligátsiia/ f. bond

облизывать /oblízyvat'/ v. lick (all over)

облизываться /oblízyvat'sia/ v. smack one's lips

облик /óblik/ m. appearance

облицовка /oblitsóvka/ f. facing; lining

облицовывать /oblitsóvyvat'/ v. face (with)

обличать /oblichát'/ v. expose

обличение /oblichénie/ n. denunciation

обложка /oblózhka/ f. cover

облокачиваться /oblokáchivat'sia/ v. lean

обломок /oblómok/ m. fragment

облысеть /oblysét'/ v. grow bold

обмакивать /obmákivat'/ v. dip

обман /obmán/ m. deception

обманчивый /obmánchivyi/ adj. deceptive

обманщик /obmánshchik/ m. fraud

обманывать /obmányvat'/ v. deceive

обматывать /obmátyvat'/ v. wind

обмахивать /obmákhivat'/ v. fan

обмен /obmén/ m. exchange

обмениваться /obménivat'sia/ v. exchange; swop

обмолвиться /obmólvit'sia/ v. make a slip (in speaking)

обмолвка /obmólvka/ f. slip of the tongue

обмолот /obmolót/ m. threshing

обмороженный /obmorózhennyi/ adj. frost-bitten

обморок /óbmorok/ m. faint; swoon

обмотка /obmótka/ f. winding

обмундирование /obmundirovánie/ n. uniform, outfit

обмывать /obmyvát'/ v. bathe, wash

обнадеживать /obnadiózhivat'/ v. reassure

обнажать /obnazhát'/ v. bare; lay bare

обнародовать /obnaródovat'/ v. promulgate

обнаруживать /obnarúzhivat'/ v. reveal; display

обнаруживаться /obnarúzhivat'sia/ v. come to light

обнимать /obnimát'/ v. embrace

обнищалый /obnishchályi/ adj. impoverished

обнов(к)а /obnóv(k)a/ f. new acquisitiony, new dress

обновление /obnovlénie/ n. renewal, renovation

обносить /obnosít'/ v. enclose, serve round

обобщать /obobshchát'/ v. summarize

обобщение /obobshchénie/ n. generalization

обогащать /obogashchát'/ v. enrich

обоготворять /obogotvoriát'/ v. deify

обогреватель /obogrevátel'/ m. heater

обод /óbod/ m. rim

ободрять /obodriát'/ v. encourage

обожать /obozhát'/ v. adore

обожествлять /obozhestvliát'/ v. deify, worship

обоз /obóz/ m. string of carts; transport

обознаться /oboznát'sia/ v. take someone for someone else

обозначать /oboznachát'/ v. designate

обои /obói/ pl. wall-paper

обойма /obóima/ f. cartridge clip

обойщик /obóishchik/ m. upholsterer

оболочка /obolóchka/ f. cover; shell; радужная о. /ráduzhnaia o./ iris

обольстительный /obol'stítel'nyi/ adj. seductive

обольщать /obol'shchát'/ v. seduce

обонять /oboniát'/ v. smell

оборачиваться /oboráchivat'sia/ v. turn (round)

оборка /obórka/ f. flounce

оборона /oboróna/ f. defence

оборонительный /oboronítel'nyi/ adj. defensive

оборонять /oboroniát'/ v. defend, protect

оборот /oborót/ m. turn

оборотный /oborótnyi/ adj. reverse; working (capital)

оборудование /oborúdovanie/ n. equipment

оборудовать /oborúdovat'/ v. equip, fit out; arrange

обоснование /obosnovánie/ n. basis, ground

обосновывать /obosnóvyvat'/ v. substantiate

обострение /obostrénie/ n. aggravation

обострять /obostriát'/ v. sharpen; aggravate

обочина /obóchina/ f. edge; side

обоюдный /oboiúdnyi/ adj. mutual

обоюдоострый /oboiudoóstryi/ adj. double-edged

обрабатывать /obrabátyvat'/ v. process; till

образ /óbraz/ m. image; mode, manner; icon

образец /obrazéts/ m. model, pattern

образный /óbraznyi/ adj. figurative; graphic

образование /obrazovánie/ n. education

образовывать /obrazóvyvat'/ v. form

образцовый /obraztsóvyi/ adj. model; exemplary

обрамлять /obramliát'/ v. frame

обратимый /obratímyi/ adj. reversible

обратно /obrátno/ adv. back(wards)

обратный /obrátnyi/ adj. return; reverse

обращать /obrashchát'/ v. turn; pay (attention)

обращение /obrashchénie/ n. address; appeal; treatment

обрез /obréz/ m. edge; sawn-off gun

обрезать /obrezát'/ v. cut off; clip, trim

обрезки /obrézki/ pl. scraps

обременять /obremeniát'/ v. burden

обретать /obretát'/ v. find

обреченный /obrechiónnyi/ adj. doomed

обрисовывать /obrisóvyvat'/ v. outline

обронить /obronít'/ v. drop; let fall

обрубать /obrubát'/ v. chop off

обруч /óbruch/ m. hoop

обручальное (кольцо) /obruchál'noe kol'tsó/ adj.+n. engagement ring

обрушиваться /obrúshivat'sia/ v. collapse

обрыв /obrýv/ m. precipice

обрывать /obryvát'/ v. tear off; cut short

обрывистый /obrývistyi/ adj. steep; disconnected

обрызгивать /obrýzgivat'/ v. sprinkle

обрюзглый /obriúzglyi/ adj. flabby

обряд /obriád/ m. rite

обсерватория /observatóriia/ f. observatory

обследование /obslédovanie/ n. enquiry, inspection; investigation

обследовать /obslédovat'/ v. examine; investigate

обслуживание /obslúzhivanie/ n. service

обстановка /obstanóvka/ f. conditions, situation; furniture

обстоятельный /obstoiátel'nyi/ adj. thorough

обстоятельство /obstoiátel'stvo/ n. circumstance; adverbial modifier

обстрел /obstrél/ m. firing

обсчитывать /obschítyvat'/ v. cheat, overcharge

обтекаемый /obtekáemyi/ adj. streamlined

обтирать /obtirát'/ v. wipe dry

обтрепанный /obtriópannyi/ adj. shabby

обуваться /obuvát'sia/ v. put on one's shoes/boots

обувь /óbuv'/ f. footwear

обуза /obúza/ f. burden

обуздывать /obúzdyvat'/ v. bridle

обух /óbukh/ m. butt

обучать /obuchát'/ v. teach, train

обучаться /obuchát'sia/ v. learn

обучение /obuchénie/ n. instruction; teaching

обхватывать /obkhvátyvat'/ v. clasp

обход /obkhód/ m. roundabout way; evasion

обходительный /obkhodítel'nyi/ adj. pleasant

обчищать /obchishchát'/ v. clean, brush; sl. rob

обшаривать /obshárivat'/ v. ransack

обшивать /obshivát'/ v. edge; plant; make clothes for

обшивка /obshívka/ f. edging; panelling, boarding; plating

обширный /obshírnyi/ adj. vast

обшлаг /obshlág/ m. cuff

общаться /obshchát'sia/ v. associate (with)

общедоступный /obshchedostúpnyi/ adj. popular; of moderate price

общежитие /obshchezhitie/ n. hostel

общеизвестный /obshcheizvéstnyi/ adj. generally known

общенародный /obshchenaródnyi/ adj. public, national

общение /obshchénie/ n. intercourse; relations

общепринятый /obshchepríniatyi/ adj. generally accepted

общесоюзный /obshchesoiúznyi/ adj. all-Union

общественность /obshchéstvennost'/ f. the community, the public

общественный /obshchéstvennyi/ adj. public, social; общественное мнение /obshchéstvennoe mnénie/ public opinion

общество /óbshchestvo/ n. society; company

общеупотребительный /obshcheupotrebítel'nyi/ adj. in general use

общий /óbshchii/ adj. general, common; в общем /v óbshchem/ in general

община /obshchína/ f. commune

общительный /obshchítel'nyi/ adj. sociable

общность (интересов) /óbshchnost' interésov/ f.+pl. community of interests

объединение /ob"edinénie/ f. unification; union

объедки /ob"édki/ pl. leavings

объезд /ob"ézd/ m. detour

объект /ob"ékt/ m. object

объектив /ob"ektív/ m. lens

объем /ob"ióm/ m. volume

объявление /ob"iavlénie/ n. announcement; notice

объявлять /ob"iavliát'/ v. declare, announce

объяснение /ob"iasnénie/ n. explanation

объяснять /ob"iasniát'/ v. explain

объятие /ob"iátie/ n. embrace

обыватель /obyvátel'/ m. philistine

обыгрывать /obýgryvat'/ v. beat; win

обыденный /obýdennyi/ adj. ordinary, everyday

обыкновенный /obyknovénnyi/ adj. ordinary

обыск /óbysk/ m. search

обычай /obýchai/ m. custom

обычный /obýchnyi/ adj. usual

обязанность /obiázannost'/ f. duty, obligation

овальный /ovál'nyi/ adj. oval

овация /ovátsiia/ f. ovation

овдоветь /ovdovét'/ v. become a widow(er)

овес /oviós/ m. oats

овладевать /ovladevát'/ v. seize, take; master

овод /óvod/ m. gadfly

овощи /óvoshchi/ pl. vegetables

овраг /ovrág/ m. ravine

овсянка /ovsiánka/ f. oatmeal porridge

овца /ovtsá/ f. sheep

овцеводство /ovtsevódstvo/ m. sheepbreeding

овчарка /ovchárka/ f. Alsatian

овчина /ovchína/ f. sheepskin

огибать /ogibát'/ v. bend round; skirt

оглавление /oglavlénie/ n. contents

огласка /ogláska/ f. publicity

оглушать /oglushát'/ v. deafen; stun

оглушительный /oglushítel'nyi/ adj. deafening

оглядываться /ogliádyvat'sia/ v. glance back

огневой /ognevói/ adj. fire

огнемет /ognemiót/ m. flame-thrower

огненный /ógnennyi/ adj. fiery
огнеопасный /ogneopásnyi/ adj. inflammable
огнестрельное (оружие) /ognestrél'noe orúzhie/ adj.+n. firearm(s)
огнетушитель /ognetushítel'/ m. fire-extinguisher
огнеупорный /ogneupórnyi/ adj. fire-proof
оговорка /ogovórka/ f. reservation; slip of the tongue
оголтелый /ogoltélyi/ adj. unbridled; frenzied
оголять /ogoliát'/ v. strip
огонек /ogoniók/ m. small light
огонь /ogón'/ m. fire; light
огораживать /ogorázhivat'/ v. fence in, enclose
огород /ogoród/ m. kitchen-garden
огорчать /ogorchát'/ v. grieve, pain
огорчительный /ogorchítel'nyi/ adj. distressing
ограбление /ograblénie/ n. robbery
ограда /ográda/ f. fence
ограждать /ograzhdát'/ v. protect
ограничение /ogranichénie/ n. restriction
ограниченный /ograníchennyi/ adj. narrow-minded; limited
огромный /ogrómnyi/ adj. huge
огрызаться /ogryzát'sia/ v. snap at
огрызок /ogrýzok/ m. bit, end; stump
огульный /ogúl'nyi/ adj. indiscriminate
огурец /oguréts/ m. cucumber
ода /óda/ f. ode
одалживать /odálzhivat'/ v. lend; borrow (from)
одаренный /odariónnyi/ adj. gifted
одаривать /odárivat'/ v. give presents (to); endow (with)
одевать /odevát'/ v. dress
одеваться /odevát'sia/ v. dress (oneself)

одежда /odézhda/ f. clothes
одеколон /odekolón/ m. eau-de-Cologne
одергивать /odiórgivat'/ v. call to order, silence; pull down, straighten
одеревенелый /oderevenélyi/ adj. numb
одерживать (верх) /odérzhivat' verkh/ v.+m. gain the upper hand; о. победу /о pobédu/ gain a(the) victory
одержимый /oderzhímyi/ adj. possessed
одеяло /odeiálo/ n. blanket
один /odín/ num. and pron. one; only; certain; о. на о. /о. na o./ in private
одинаковый /odinákovyi/ adj. identical, the same
одиннадцать /odínnadtsat'/ num. eleven
одинокий /odinókii/ adj. lonely
одиночество /odinóchestvo/ n. loneliness
одиозный /odióznyi/ adj. odious
одичавший /odichávshii/ adj. wild
однажды /odnázhdy/ adv. once
однако /odnáko/ adv. however
однобокий /odnobókii/ adj. one-sided
однобортный /odnobórtnyi/ adj. single-breasted
одновременный /odnovreménnyi/ adj. simultaneous
одноглазый /odnoglázyi/ adj. one-eyed
однозвучный /odnozvúchnyi/ adj. monotonous
одноименный /odnoimiónnyi/ adj. of the same name
одноколейный /odnokoléinyi/ adj. single-track
однокурсник /odnokúrsnik/ m. fellow-member of course
однолетний /odnolétnii/ adj. annual
одноместный /odnoméstnyi/ adj. single-seater
одноногий /odnonógii/ adj. one-legged
однообразие /odnoobrázie/ n. uniformity
однообразный /odnoobráznyi/ adj. monotonous

однородный /odnoródnyi/ adj. homogeneous

однорукий /odnorúkii/ adj. one-armed

односпальная (кровать) /odnospál'naia krovát'/ adj.+f. single bed

односторонний /odnostorónnii/ adj. one-sided

однофамилец /odnofamílets/ m. namesake

одноэтажный /odnoetázhnyi/ adj. one-storeyed

одобрение /odobrénie/ n. approval

одолевать /odolevát'/ v. overcome

одомашнивать /odomáshnivat'/ v. domesticate

одуванчик /oduvánchik/ m. dandelion

одурачивать /oduráchivat'/ v. make a fool of

одурелый /odurélyi/ adj. dulled, besotted

одурманивать /odurmánivat'/ v. stupefy, drug

одурь /ódur'/ f. stupefaction

одутловатый /odutlovátyi/ adj. puffy

одухотворять /odukhotvoriát'/ v. inspire

одушевлять /odushevliát'/ v. animate

одышка /odýshka/ f. short breath

ожерелье /ozherél'ie/ n. necklace

ожесточенный /ozhestochiónnyi/ adj. embittered; violent

оживать /ozhivát'/ v. come to life, revive

ожидание /ozhidánie/ n. expectation; зал ожидания /zal ozhidánia/ waiting-room

ожидать /ozhidát'/ v. wait for, expect

ожирение /ozhirénie/ n. obesity

ожог /ozhóg/ m. burn

озаглавливать /ozaglávlivat'/ v. entitle

озадачивать /ozadáchivat'/ v. perplex, puzzle

озарять /ozariát'/ v. illumine, light up

озверелый /ozverélyi/ adj. brutal

озеленять /ozeleniát'/ v. plant with trees and gardens

озерный /oziórnyi/ adj. lake

озеро /ózero/ n. lake

озимый /ozímyi/ adj. winter (crops)

озлобление /ozloblenie/ n. animosity

ознакомлять /oznakomliát'/ v. acquaint (with)

означать /oznachát'/ v. mean

озноб /oznób/ m. shivering; chill

озон /ozón/ m. ozone

озорник /ozorník/ m. mischievous child

озорничать /ozornichát'/ v. be naughty

оказывать (помощь) /okázyvat' pómoshch/ v.+f. render assistance; о. влияние /o. vliianie/ exert influence (upon)

окаймлять /okaimliát'/ v. border

окантовка /okantóvka/ f. mount (for picture, etc.)

оканчивать /okánchivat'/ v. finish

окапывать /okápyvat'/ v. dig round

океан /okeán/ m. ocean

оккупант /okkupánt/ m. invader

оккупация /okkupátsiia/ f. occupation

оклад /oklád/ m. salary; framework (of icon)

оклеивать /okléivat'/ v. paste over

оклик /óklik/ m. call

окно /oknó/ n. window

оковы /okóvy/ pl. fetters

околдовывать /okoldóvyvat'/ v. bewitch

около /ókolo/ prep. around; by, near; about

окончание /okonchánie/ n. termination

окончательный /okonchátel'nyi/ adj. final

окоп /okóp/ m. trench

окорок /ókorok/ m. ham

окраина /okráina/ f. outskirts

окраска /okráska/ f. colouring

окрестность /okréstnost'/ f. environs

окроплять /okropliát'/ v. (be)sprinkle

окрошка /okróshka/ f. cold kvass soup

округ /ókrug/ m. district

округлять /okrugliát'/ v. round off

окружать /okruzhát'/ v. encircle, surround

окружение /okruzhénie/ n. encirclement; surrounding

окружной /okruzhnói/ adj. district

окружность /okrúzhnost'/ f. circumference

октава /oktáva/ f. octave

октябрь /oktiábr'/ m. October

октябрьский /oktiábr' skii/ adj. October

окулист /okulíst/ m. oculist

окунать /okunát'/ v. dip

окунь /ókun'/ m. perch (fish)

окупать /okupát'/ v. repay

окурок /okúrok/ m' cigarette end.

окутывать /okútyvat'/ v. wrap up.

окучивать /okúchivat'/ v. earth up.

оладья /olád'ia/ f. pancake

оледенелый /oledenélyi/ adj. frozen

оленеводство /olenevódstvo/ n. reindeer-breeding

оленина /olenína/ f. venison

олень /olen'/ m. deer

олива /olíva/ f. olive

олигархия /oligárkhiia/ f. oligarchy

олимпиада /olimpiáda/ f. Olympiad, Olympic Games

олицетворение /olitsetvorénie/ n. embodiment

олицетворять /olitsetvoriát'/ v. personify

олух /olukh/ m. blockhead

ольха /ol'khá/ f. alder (-tree)

ом /om/ m. ohm

омар /omár/ m. lobster

омерзительный /omerzítel'nyi/ adj. loathsome, sickening

омлет /omlét/ m. omelette

омолаживать /omolázhivat'/ v. rejuvenate

омрачать /omrachát'/ v. darken

омут /ómut/ m. whirlpool

омывать /omyvát'/ v. wash

он,Ёона, оно, они Ё/on, oná, onó, oní/ pron. he, she, it, they

ондатра /ondátra/ f. musquash

онкология /onkológiia'/ f. oncology

ООН /oon/ abbr. U.N.O.

опаздывать /opázdyvat'/ v. be late

опал /opál/ m. opal

опальный /opál'nyi/ adj. disgraced

опасаться /opasát'sia/ v. fear

опасность /opásnost'/ f. danger

опасный /opásnyi/ adj. dangerous

опека /opéka/ f. trusteeship

опекун /opekún/ m. guardian

опера /ópera/ f. opera

оперативный /operatívnyi/ adj. efficient; operative

оператор /operátor/ m. cameraman

операция /operátsiia/ f. operation

опережать /operezhát'/ v. outstrip; forestall

оперение /operénie/ n. plumage

оперировать /operírovat'/ v. operate (upon)

опечатка /opechátka/ f. misprint

опечатывать /opechátyvat'/ v. seal up

опираться /opirát'sia/ v. lean (on)

описание /opisánie/ n. description

описка /opíska/ f. slip of the pen

опись /ópis'/ f. inventory; list; о.имущества /o. imúshchestva/ distraint

оплакивать /oplákivat'/ v. mourn

оплата /opláta/ f. payment

оплачивать /opláchivat'/ v. pay

оплодотворять /oplodotvoriát'/ v. fertilize, impregnate

оплот /oplót/ m. stronghold

оповещать /opoveshchát'/ v. notify

опоздание /opozdánie/ n. delay

опознавательный (знак) /opoznavátel'-nyi znak/ adj. + m. landmark

ополаскивать /opoláskivat'/ v. rinse

оползень /ópolzen'/ m. landslide
ополчаться /opolchát'sia/ v. take up
arms; be up in arms
ополчение /opolchénie/ n. militia; home
guard
опомниться /opómnit'sia/ v. come to
one's senses
опора /opóra/ f. support
опорный /opórnyi/ adj. bearing; supporting
опорожнить /oporozhnít'/ v. empty
опошлять /oposhliát'/ vulgareze
оппозиционный /oppozitsiónnyi/ adj.
opposition (al)
оппозиция /oppozítsia/ f. opposition
оппортунизм /opportunízm/ m. opportunism
оправа /opráva/ f. setting; rim, frame
оправдание /opravdánie/n. justification;
acquittal; оправдательный (приговор)
/opravdátel'nyi prigovór/ adj. + m.
verdict of "not guilty"
оправдывать /oprávdyvat'/ v. justify; acquit
опрашивать /opráshivat'/ v. question
определение /opredelénie/ n. definition;
(gram.) attribute
определенный /opredeliónnyi/ adj. definite; fixed
определять /opredeliát'/ v. determine
опреснять /opresniát'/ v. distil; desalinate
опровергать /oprovergát'/ v. refute
опровержение /oproverzhénie/ n. denial
опрокидыватьЁ/oprokídyvat'/ v. overturn
опрометчивый /oprométchivyi/ adj. hasty, rash
опрометью /ópromet'iu/ adj. headlong
опротестовывать (вексель) /oprotestóvyvat' véksel'/ v.+m. protest a bill
опрыскивать /oprýskivat'/ v. spray, sprinkle
опрятный /opriátnyi/ adj. tidy

оптика /óptika/ f. optics
оптимизм /optimízm/ m. optimism
оптический /optícheskii/ adj. optical
оптовый /optóvyi/ adj.wholesale
оптом /óptom/ adv. wholesale
опубликование /opublikovánie/ n. publication
опускать /opuskát'/ v. lower; post (letter); omit; turn down (collar)
опускаться /opuskát'sia / v. sink; fall; у
него руки опустились /u nevó rúki
opustilis'/ he has lost heart
опустошать /opustoshát'/ v. devastate
опутывать /opútyvat'/ v. entangle
опухать /opukhát'/ v. swell
опухоль /ópukhol'/ f. swelling, tumour
опыление /opylénie/ f. pollination
опыт /ópyt/ m. experiment, test
опытный /ópytnyi/ adj. experienced; experimental
опьянение /op'ianénie/ n. intoxication
опять /opiát'/ adv. again
оранжевый /oránzhevyi/ adj. orange
оранжерея /oranzheréia/ f. hothouse, greenhouse
оратор /orátor/ m. orator
ораторияЁ/oratóriia/ f. oratorio
орать /orát'/ v. yell
орбита /orbíta/ f. orbit
орган /órgan/ m. organ; agency
орган /orgán/ m. (mus.)/ organ
организатор /organizátor/ m. organizer
организация /organizátsiia/ f. organization
организм /organízm/ m. organism
организовывать /organizóvyvat'/ v. organize
органический /organícheskii/ adj. organic
оргияЁ/órgiia/ f. orgy
орда /ordá/ f. horde
орден /órden/ m. order; decoration
ордер /órder/ m. order warrant
ординарец /ordinárets/ m. orderly

ординатор /ordinátor/ m. house-surgeon
орелЁ/oriól/ m. eagle; o. или решка /o. ili réshka/ heads or tails
ореол /oreól/ m. halo
орех /orékh/ m. nut
оригинал /originál/ m. original; eccentric person
ориентация /orientátsiia/ f. orientation
оркестр /orkéstr/ m. orchestra, band
оркестровать /orkestrovát'/ v. orchestrate
орнамент /ornáment/ m. ornament
оросительный /orosítel'nyi / adj. irrigation
орудие /orúdie/ n. instrument, tool; gun
орудовать /orúdovat'/ v. handle
оружие /orúzhie/ n. weapons, arm(s)
орфография /orfográfiia/ f. spelling
оса /osá/ f. wasp
осада /osáda/ f. siege
осадка /osádka/ f. settling (of soil building); draught (of ship)
осадок /osádok/ m. sediment; after-taste.; pl. precipitation
осанка /osánka/ f. bearing, carriage
осваиватьЁ/osváivat'/ v. master, assimilate
освоитьсяЁ/osvóit'sia/ v. feel at home
освежать /osvezhát'/ v. refresh
освещать /osveshchát'/ v. light up; elucidate
освидетельствоватьЁ/osvidétel'stvovat'/v. examine, inspect
освободитель /osvoboditel'/ m. liberator
освобождать / osvobozhdát'/ v. free, liberate
освящать Ё /osviashchát'/ consecrate
осел /osiól/ m. donkey; ass
оселок /oselók/ m. touchstone
осенний /osénnii/ adj. autumn (al)
осень /ósen'/ f. autumn
осетин /osetín/ m. Ossetian
осетинка /osetínka/ f. Ossetian
осетинский /osetínskii/ adj. Ossetian

осетр /osiótr/ m. sturgeon
осетрина /osetrína/ f. (flesh of) sturgeon
осечка /oséchka/ f. misfire
осина /osína/ f. asp(en)
осквернять /oskverniát'/ v. profane
осколок /oskólok/ m. splinter
оскорблениеЁ /oskorblénie/ n. insult
ослабевать /oslabevát'/ v. weaken
ослеплять /oslepliát'/ v. blind; dazzle
осложнение /oslozhnénie/ n. complication
осматривать /osmátrivat'/ v. examine
осмеивать /osméivat'/v. ridicule
осмеливаться /osmélivat'sia/ v. dare
осмотр /osmótr/ m. inspection
осмысленный /osmýslennyi/ adj. intelligent
основа /osnóva/ f. base
основатель /ocnovátel'/m. founder
основной /osnovnói/ adj. fundamental; principal
особа /osóba/ f. person
особенно /osóbenno/ adv. especially
особенность /osóbennost'/ f. peculiarity
особенныйЁ/osóbennyi/ adj.(e)special, particular
особо /osóbo/ adv. especially
осознавать /osoznavát'/ v. realize
осока /osóka/f. sedge
оспа /óspa/ f. smallpox; ветряная о. /vetrianáia o./ chicken-pox
оспаривать /ospárivat'/ v. dispute
оставаться /ostavát'sia/ v. remain, stay
оставлять /ostavliát'/ v. leave, abandon; о. за собой право /o. za sobói právo'/ reserve the right
останавливать /ostanávlivat'/ v. stop
останки /ostánki/pl. remains, relics
остановка /ostanóvka/ f. stop
остаток /ostátok/ m. remainder
остерегаться /osteregát'sia/ v. beware (of)
остов /óstov/ m. skeleton; frame

осторожность /ostorózhnost'/ f. care; caution

осторожный /ostorózhnyi/ adj. cautious

остригаться /ostrigát'sia/ v. have one's hair cut

острие /ostriió/ m. point; spike

острить /ostrít'/ v. crack jokes

остров /óstrov/ m. island

островитянин /ostrovitiánin/ m. islander

острога /ostróga/ f. harpoon

остроугольный / ostrougól'nyi/ adj. acute-angled

остроумие /ostroúmie/ n. wit

острый /óstryi/ adj. sharp

остывать /ostyvát'/ v. cool down

осуждать /osuzhdát'/ v. condemn

осуществлять /osushchestvĺiat'/ v. carry out

осуществляться /osushchestvliát'sia/ v. come true

осчастливливать /oschastlívlivat'/ v. make happy

ось /os'/ f. axis

осьминог /os'minóg/ m. octopus

осязаемый /osiazáemyi/ adj. tangible

осязание /osiazánie/ n. touch

от /ot/ prep. from

отара /otára/ f. flock (of sheep)

отбелить /otbelít'/ v. bleach

отбивать /otbivát'/ v. beat (off), repulse

отбивная (котлета) /otbivnáia kotléta/ adj. + f. chop

отбирать /otbirát'/ v. take away

отблеск /ótblesk/ m. reflection

отбор /otbór/ m. selection

отбрасывать /ootbrásyvat'/ v. throw off, cast away

отвага /otvága/ f. courage

отвар /otvár/ m. brew

отваривать /otvárivat'/ v. boil

отведывать /otvédyvat'/ v. taste

отвергать /otvergát'/ v. reject

отверженный /otvérzhennyi/ adj. outcast

отверстие /otvérstie/ n. opening

отвертка /otviórtka/ f. scredriver

отвесный /otvésnyi/ adj. perpendicular; steep

ответ /otvét/ m. answer

ответственность /otvétstvennost'/ f. responsibility

ответчик /otvétchik/ m. defendant

отвечать /otvechát'/ v. answer

отвешивать /otvéshivat'/ v. weigh out

отвиливать /otvilivát'/ v. dodge

отвинчивать /otvínchivat'/ v. unscrew

отвисать /otvisát'/ v. hang down; sag

отвислый /otvíslyi/ adj. sagging

отвлекать /otvlekát'/ v. distract

отвлеченный /otvlechiónnyi/ adj. abstract

отводный (канал) /otvodnói kanál/ adj. + m. drain

отвоевывать /otvoióvyvat'/ v. win back

отворачивать /otvoráchivat'/ v. turn on (tap); unscrew

отворачиваться /otvoráchivat'sia/ v. turn away

отворот /otvorót/ m. lapel, flap

отворять /otvoriát'/ v. open

отвратительный /otvratitel'nyi/ adj. disgusting

отвыкать /otvykát'/ v. get out of the habit of

отвязывать /otviázyvat'/ v. untie

отгадка /otgádka/ f. answer (to a riddle)

отгибать /otgibát'/ v. bend back

отглагольный /otglagól'nyi/ adj. verbal

отглаживать /otglázhivat'/ v. iron (out)

отговаривать /otgovárivat'/ v. dissuade

отгораживать /otgorázhivat'/ v. fence off

отгружать /otgruzhát'/ ship, dispatch

отдавать /otdavát'/ v. give back, return

отдаление /otdalénie/ n. distance

отдаленный /otdaliónnyi/ adj. remote

отдача /otdácha/ f. return; efficiency, performance

отдел /otdél/ m. department

отделывать /otdélyvat'/ v. finish, trim
отделываться /otdélyvat'sia/ v. get rid (of)
отдельный /otdél'nyi/ adj. separate
отделять /otdeliát/ v. separate
отдирать /otdirát'/v. rip off
отдуваться /otduvát'sia/ v. puff; take the rap (for)
отдушина /otdúshina/ f. air-hole
отдых /otdýkh/ m. rest; relaxation
отекать /otekát'/ v. swell
отель /otél'/ m. hotel
отец /otéts/ m. father
отеческий /otécheskii/ adj. paternal
отечественный /otéchestvennyi/ adj. native, home; patriotic (war)
отечество /otéchestvo/ n. fatherland
отзвук /ótzvuk/ m. echo
отзыв /ótzyv/ m. opinion
отзыв /otzýv/ m. recall
отзывчивый /otzývchivyi/ adj. responsive
отказ /otkáz/ m. refusal
откапывать /otkápyvat'/ v. dig up
откармливать /otkármlivat'/ v. fatten
откачивать /otkáchivat'/ v. pump out
откашливатьсяЁ /otkáshlivat'sia/ v. clear one's throat
откидной /otkidnói/ adj. folding
откладывать /otkládyvat'/ v. put aside
откланиваться /otklánivat'sia/ v. take one's leave
отклик /ótklik/ m. comment
откликаться /otklikát'sia/ v. respond (to)
отклонение /otklonénie/ n. deviation
откомандировывать /otkomandiróvyvat'/ v. send (on a mission)
откос /otkós/ m. slope
откровение /otkrovénie/ n. revelation
откровенный /otkrovénnyi/ adj. frank
открывать /otkryvát'/ v. open
открытие /otkrýtie/ n. discovery
открыткаЁ /otkrýtka/ f. postcard
открытый /otkrýtyi/ adj. open; frank

откуда /otkúda/ adv. where from whence
откупоривать /otkupórivat'/ v. uncork
откусывать /otkúsyvat'/ v. bite off
отламывать /otlámyvat'/ v. break off
отлет /otliót/ m. flying away; departure
отлив /otlív/ m. ebb. ebb-tide
отличать /otlichát'/ v. distinguish
отличаться /otlichát'sia/ v. differ
отличие /otlíchie/ n. difference; decoration
отличный /otlíchnyi/ adj. excellent; different (from)
отлучка /otlúchka/ f. absence
отлынивать /otlýnivat'/ v. shirk
отмель /ótmel'/ f. sandbank
отменять /otmeniát'/ v. abolish, annul
отмеривать /otmérivat'/ v. measure off
отметка /otmétka/ f. note; mark
отмечать /otmechát'/ v. mark
отмирать /otmirát'/ v. die out
отмыкать /otmykát'/ v. unlock
отмычкаЁ /otmýchka/ f. picklock
отнекиваться /otnékivat'sia/ v. deny, disavow
отнимать /otnimát'/ v. take away
относительно /otnosítel'no/ adv. relatively; prep. concerning
относительность /otnosítel'nost'/ f. relativity
относить /otnosít'/ v. take, carry away
относиться /otnosít'sia/ v. concern; treat
отношение /otnoshénie/ n. attitude
отображать /otobrazhát'/ v. reflect; represent
отовсюду /otovsiúdu/ adv. from every quarter
отогревать /otogrevát'/ v. warm
отодвигать /otodvigát'/ v. move aside
отождествлять /otozhdestvliát'/ v. identify
отопление /otoplénie/ n. heating
отпарывать /otpáryvat'/ v. rip off
отпевание /otpevánie/ f. burial service
отпетый /otpétyi/ adj. inveterate

отпечаток /otpechátok/ m. imprint
отпирать /otpirát'/ unlock
отпихивать /otpíkhivat'/ v. push off
отплачивать /otpláchivat'/ v. pay back
отплывать /otplyvát'/ v. sail
отповедь /ótpoved'/ f. reproof
отползать /otpolzát'/ v. crawl away
отпор /otpór/ m. rebuff
отправитель /otpravítel'/ m. sender
отправка /otprávka / f. dispatch
отправляться /otpravliát'sia/ v. set off
отпрашиваться /otpráshivat'sia/ v. ask (for) leave
отпрыск /ótprysk/ m. offspring
отпрянуть /otpriánut'/ v. recoil
отпугивать /otpúgivat'/ v. frighten away
отпуск /ótpusk/ m. leave; holiday
отпускать /otpuskát'/ v. let go
отпущение (грехов) /otpushchénie grekhóv / n. + pl. absolution; козел отпущения / koziól otpushchéniia/ scapegoat
отрабатывать /otrabátyvat'/ v. work off (a debt, etc.)
отрава /otráva/ f. poison
отрада /otráda/ f. joy
отражать /otrazhát'/ reflect; repulse
отрасль /ótrasl'/ f. branch, sphere
отрастать /otrastát'/ v. grow
отребье /otréb'e/ n. rabble
отрез /otréz/ m. cut; length (of material)
отрезать /otrezát'/ v. cut off
отрезвлять /otrezvliát'/ v. sober
отрезок /otrézok/ m. piece; section
отрекаться /otrekát'sia/ v. renonnce; о. от престола /o. ot prestóla/ abdicate
отречение /otrechénie/ n. renunciation
отрицание /otritsánie/ n. denial
отрицательный /otritsátel'nyi/ adj. negative
отрицать /otritsát'/ v. deny
отрог /otróg/ m. spur
отросток /otróstok/ m. shoot; appendix
отроческий /otrócheskii/ adj. adolescent

отрубать /otrubát' v. chop off;
отруби /ótrubi/ pl. bran
отрыв /otrýv/ m. breaking off; tearing off; isolation
отрывать /otryvát'/ v.tear off
отрываться /otryvát'sia/ v. come off; take off
отрывистый /otrývistye/ adj. abrupt
отрывной (календарь) /otryvnói kalendár'/ adj. + m. tear-off calendar
отрывок /otrývok/ m. excerpt
отрывочный /otrývochnyi/ adj. scrappy
отрыжка /otrýzhka/ f. belch
отряд /otriád/ m. detachment
отряхивать /otriákhivat'/ v. shake down
отсвет /ótsvet/ m. reflection
отсвечивать /otsvéchivat'/ v. shine
отсев /otssév/ m. sifting
отсекать /otsekát'/ v. cut off
отскабливать /otskáblivat'/ v. scrape off
отскакивать /otskákivat'/ v. jump aside
отсоветовать /otsovétovat'/ v. dissuade
отсрочивать /otsróchivat'/ v. postpone;
отсрочка /otsróchka/ f. delay
отставать /otstavát'/ v. lag behind, be slow (of a clock or watch)
отставка /otstávka/ f. resignation
отставной /otstavnói/ adj. retired
отстаивать /otstáivat' v. defend, stand up for
отсталость /otstálost'/ f. backwardness
отстегивать /otstiógivat'/ v. unbutton
отстирывать /otstíryvat'/ v. wash off
отстраивать /otstráivat'/ v. finish building
отстранение /otstranénie/ n. dismissal
отстранять /otstraniát'/ v. push aside
отстраняться /otstraniát'sia/ v. keep aloof (from)
отстреливаться /otstrélivat'sia/ v. return fire
отстригать /otstrigát'/ v. cut off
отступление /otstuplénie/ n. retreat
отсутствие /otsútstvie/ n. absence

отсутствовать /otsútstvovat'/ v. be absent

отсчитывать /otschítyvat'/ v. count off

отсылать /otsylát'/ v. send back; refer (to)

отсыпать /otsypát'/ v. pour off; measure off

отсырелый /otsyrélyi/ adj. damp

отсыхать /otsykhát'/ v. dry up; wither

отсюда /otsiúda/ adv. from here; hence

оттаивать /ottáivat'/ v. thaw out

отталкивать /ottálkivat'/ v. push away

отталкивающий /ottálkivaiushchii/ adj. repulsive

оттаскивать /ottáskivat'/ v. pull aside

оттачивать /ottáchivat'/ v. sharpen

оттенок /otténok/m. shade

оттепель /óttepel'/ f. thaw

оттеснять /ottesniát'/ v. push aside

оттирать /ottirát'/ v. rub off

оттого /ottovó/ adv. that is why

оттуда /ottúda/ adv. from there

отхлынуть /otkhlýnut'/ v. flood back

отход /otkhód/ m. withdrawal

отходить /otkhodít'/ v. move away (from)

отходы /otkhódy/ pl. waste

отцветать /ottsvetát'/ v. fade

отцовский /ottsóvskii/ adj. paternal

отцовство /ottsóvstvo/ n. paternity

отчаиваться /otcháivat'sia/ v. despare (of)

отчаливать /otchálivat'/ v. cast off; push off

отчасти /otchásti/ adv. partly

отчаяние /otcháianie/ n. despair

отчаянный /otcháiannyi/ adj. desperate

отчего /otchevó/ adv. why

отчеканивать /otchekánivat'/ v. coin; rap out (one's words)

отчеркивать /otchiórkivat'/ v. mark off

отчество /ótchestvo/ n. patronymic

отчет /otchiót/ m. account

отчетливый /otchiótlivyi/ adj. distinct

отчетность /otchiótnost'/ f. book-keeping

отчизна /otchízna/ f. native country

отчим /ótchim/ m. step-falher

отчислять /otchisliát'/ v. deduct

отчитывать /otchítyvat'/ v. rebuke

отчитываться /otchítyvat'sia/ v. give a report

отчищать /otchishchát'/ v. clean off

отшатываться /otshátyvat'sia/ v. start back

отшельник /otschél'nik/ m. hermit

отщепенец /otshchepénets/ m. renegade

отщеплять /otshchepliát'/ v. chip off

отщипывать /otshchípyvat'/ v. nip off

отъезд /ot"ézd/ m. departure

отъявленный /ot"iávlennyi/ adj. inveterate

отыгрывать /otýgryvat'/ v. win back

отыскивать /otýskivat'/ v. find

отягощать /otiagoshchát'/ v. burden

офицер /ofitsér/ m. officer

официальный /ofitsiál'nyi/ adj. official;

официант /ofitsiánt/ m. waiter

официантка /ofitsiántka/ f. waitress

оформление /oformlénie/ n. official registration

оформлять /oformliát'/ v. register officially; legalize

оформляться /oformliát'sia/ v. take shape; be registered; be taken on thestaff

охапка /okhápka/ f. armful

охать /ókhat'/ v. moan

охватывать /okhvátyvat'/ v. envelop; involve

охлаждать /okhlazhdát'/ v. cool

охлаждение /okhlazhdénie/ n. cooling

охота /okhóta/ f. hunt(ing)

охотник /okhótnik/ m. hunter

охотно /okhótno/ adv. willingly

охра /ókhra/ f. ochre

охрана /okhrána/ f. guard; protection

оценивать /otsénivat'/ v. evaluate

оценка /otsénka/ f. estimate

оценщик /otsénshchik/ m. valuer

оцеплять /otsepliát'/ v. surround; cordon off

очаг /ochág/ m. hearth

очарование /ocharovánie/ n. charm

очаровательный /ocharovátel'nyi/ adj. charming

очевидец /ochevídets/ m. eye - witness

очевидный /ochevídnyi/ adj. obvious

очень /óchen'/ adv. very; very much

очередной /ocherednói/ adj. next in turn; periodical; regular

очередь /óchered'/ f. turn; queue, line

очерк /ócherk/ m. essay

очертание /ochertánie/ n. outline

очерчивать /ochérchivat'/ v. outline

очистка /ochístka/ f. cleaning

очистки /ochístki/ pl. peelings

очищать /ochishchát'/ v. clean

очки /ochkí/ pl. spectacles

очко /ochkó/ n. pip; point

очковтирательство /ochkovtirátel'stvo/ n. eyewash

очковая (змея) /ochkóvaia zmeiá/ adj. + f. cobra

очнуться /ochnút'sia/ v. come to oneself, regain consciousness

очумелый /ochumélyi/ adj. mad, off one's head

очутиться /ochutít'sia/ v. find oneself

ошейник /oshéinik/ m. collar

ошибаться /oshibát'sia/ v. make a mistake

ошибка /oshíbka/ f. mistake, error

ошибочный /oshíbochnyi/ adj. erroneous

ошпаривать /oshpárivat'/ v. scald

ощетиниваться /oshchetínivat'sia/ v. bristle up

ощипывать / oshchípyvat'/ v. pluck

ощупывать /oshchúpyvat'/ v. feel

ощупь (идти на о.) /idtí na óshchup'/ v.+ adv. grope one's way

ощутимый /oshchutímyi/ adj. tangible

ощущать /oshchushchát'/ v. feel, sense

ощущение /oshchushchénie/ n. feeling

П

павильон /pavil'ón/ m. pavilion

павлин /pavlín/ m. peacock

паводок /pávodok/ m. flood

падаль /pádal'/ f. carrion

падать /pádat'/ v. fall

падеж /padézh/ m. (gram.) case

падучая /padúchaia/ f. epilepsy

падчерица /pádcheritsa/ f. step-daughter

паек /paiók/ m. ration

паж /pazh/ m. page

пазуха /pázukha/ f. bosom; за пазухой /za pázukhoi/ in one's bosom

пай /pái/ m. share

пайщик /páishchik/ m. shareholder

пакгауз /pakgáuz/ m. warehouse

пакет /pakét/ m. parcel, package

пакистанец /pakistánets/ f. Pakistani

пакистанка /pakistánka/ f. Pakistani

пакистанский /pakistánskii/ adj. Pakistani

паковать /pakovát'/ v. pack

пакт /pakt/ m. pact; п. о ненападении /p.o nenapadénii/ non-aggression pact

палата /paláta/ f. chamber, house

палатка /palátka/ f. tent

палехский /pálekhskii/ adj. (made in) Palekh

палец /pálets/ m. finger; toel

палисадник /palisádnik/ m. front garden

палитра /palítra/ f. palette

палка /pálka/ f. stick

паломник /palómnik/ m. pilgrim

палтус /páltus/ m. halibut

палуба /páluba/ f. deck

пальба /pal'bá/ f. firing

пальма /pál'ma/ f. palm (tree)

пальто /pal'tó/ n. (over)coat

памфлет /pamflét/ m. lampoon

памятка /pámiatka/ f. memorandum

памятник /pámiatnik/ m. monument

памятный /pámiatnyi/ adj. memorable
память /pamiát'/ f. memory
панацея /panatséia/ f. panacea
панегирик /panegírik/ m. panegyric
панель /panél'/ f. panel
паника /pánika/ f. panic
паникер /panikiór/ m. alarmist
панихида /panikhída/ f. office for the dead
панорама /panoráma/ f. panorama
пансион /pansión/ m. boarding-house
панталоны /pantalóny/ pl. drawers, knickers
пантера /pantéra/ f. panther
пантомима /pantomíma/ f. pantomime
панцирь /pántsir'/ m. armour
папа /pápa/ m. dad, daddy; pope
паперть /pápert'/ f. church-porch
папироса /papirósa/ f. cigarette
папка /pápka/ f. file; document case
папоротник /páporotnik/ m. fern
папский /pápskii/ adj. papal
пар /par/ m. steam
пара /pára/ f. pair
параграф /parágraf/ m. paragraph
парад /parád/ m. parade
парадный /parádnyi/ adj. full (dress)
парадное /parádnoe/ n. front door
паразит /parazít/ m. parasite
парализовать /paralizovát'/ v. paralyse
паралич /paralich/ m. paralysis
параллель /parallél'/ f. parallel
паранойя /paranóia/ f. paranoia
парашют /parashút/ m. parachute
парень /páren'/ m. guy; fellow
пари /parí/ n. bet
парижанин /parizhánin/ m. Parisian
парижанка /parizhánka/ f. Parisian
парижский /parízhskii/adj. Parisian
парик /parík/ m. wig
парикмахер /parikmákher/ m. hairdresser
парикмахерская /parikmákherskaia/ f. hairdresser's

паритет /paritét/ m. parity
парить /párit'/ v. steam out, sweat out
парить /parít'/ v. soar
парк /park/ m. park
паркет /parkét/ m. parquet
парламент /parláment/ m. parliament
парник /parník/ m. hotbed
парной /parnói/ adj. fresh
паровоз /parovóz/ m. locomotive
пародия /paródiia/ f. parody
пароль /paról'/ m. password
паром /paróm/ m. ferry
пароход /parokhód/ m. steamer
парта / párta/ f. (school) desk
партер /partér/ m. the stalls; pit
партизан / partizán/ m. partisan
партитура /partitúra/ f. score (mus.)
партия /pártiia/ f. party; game
партнер /partniór/ m. partner
парус /párus/ m. sail
парфюмерия /parfiumériia/ f. perfumery
парча /parchá/ f. brocade
пасечник /pásechnik/ m. beekeeper
пасквиль /páskvil'/ m. lampoon
пасмурный /pásmurnyi/ adj. gloomy
паспорт /pásport/ m. passport
пассажир /passazhír/ m. passenger
пассат /passát/ m. trade-wind
пассив /passív/ m. liabilities
пассивный /passívnyi/ adj. passive
паста /pásta/ f. paste
пастбище /pástbishche/ n. pasture
пастель /pastél'/ f. pastel
пасти /pastí/ v. graze
пастух /pastúkh/ m. shepherd
пастырь /pástyr'/ m. pastor
пасха /páskha/ f. Easter
пасынок /pásynok/ m. stepson
патент /patént/ m. patent
патока /pátoka/ f. syrup
патриарх /patriárkh/ m. patriarch
патриот /patriót/ m. patriot
патриотизм /patriotizm/ m. patriotism
патрон /patrón/ m. patron; cartridge

патруль /patrúl'/ m. patrol
пауза /páuza/ f. pause
паук /paúk/ m. spider
паутина /pautína/ f. spider's web.
пафос /páfos/ m. enthusiasm; говорить
с пафосом /govorít's páfosom/ speak
with inspiration
пах /pakh/ m. groin
пахарь /pákhar'/ m. ploughman
пахать /pakhát'/ v. plough
пахнуть /pákhnut'/ v. smell
пахотный /pákhotnyi/ adj. arable
пахучий /pakhúchii/ adj. fragrant
пациент /patsiént/ m. patient
пачка /páchka/ f. bundle
пачкать /páchkat'/ v. dirty
паштет /pashtét/ m. pate. paste
паюсная икра /páiusnaia ikrá/ adj.+f.
pressed caviare
паяльник /paiál'nik/ m. soldering-iron
паять /paiát'/ v. solder
паяц /paiáts/ m. buffoon
певец /pevéts/ m. singer
пегий /pégii/ adj. skewbald
педагог /pedagóg/ m. teacher
педаль /pedál'/ f. pedal
пейзаж /peizázh/ m. landscape
пекарня /pekárnia/ f. bakery
пекарь /pékar'/ m. baker
пеленать /pelenát'/ v. swaddle
пеленка /peliónka/ f. nappie
пеликан /pelikán/ m. pelican
пена /péna/ f. foam
пенал /penál/ m. pencil-case
пениться /pénit'sia/ v. foam
пенициллин /penitsillín/ m. penicillin
пенка /pénka/ f. skin (on milk)
пенсионер /pensionér/ m. pensioner
пенсия /pénsiia/ f. pension
пень /pen'/ m. stump
пеня /pénia/ f. fine
пепел /pépel/ m. ashes
первенец /pérvenets/ m. first-born
первичный /pervíchnyi/ adj. primary

первобытный /pervobýtnyi/ adj. primitive; prehistorie
первоначальный /pervonachál'nyi/ adj
original; initial
первосортный /pervosórtnyi/ adj. first
class
первостепенный /pervostepénnyi/ adj.
paramount
первый /pérvyi/ adj. first
переадресовывать /pereadresóvyvat'/ v.
readdress
перебегать /perebegát'/ v. desert; run
across
перебежчик /perebézhchik/ m. deserter
перебивать /perebivát'/ v. interrupt
перебирать /perebirát'/ v. sort out
перебой /perebói/ m. stoppage
перебороть /pereborót'/ v. overcome
перебранка /perebránka/ f. squabble
перевал /perevál/ m. crossing; (mountain) pass
перевертывать /pereviórtyvat'/ v. turn
over
перевод /perevód/ m. transfer; translation
переводной /perevodnói/ adj. translated;
переводная бумага /perevodnáia bu-
mága/ carbon paper; переводной
рубль /perevodnói rubl'/ transferable
rouble
переводчик /perevódchik/ m. translator,
interpreter
перевозить /perevozít'/ v. transport
перевооружать /perevooruzhát'/ v.
rearm
переворот /perevorót/ m. coup
перевоспитывать /perevospítyvat'/ v. re-
educate; reform
перевыполнять /perevypolniát'/ v. over-
fulfil
перевязка /pereviázka/ f. bandaging
перевязочный пункт /pereviázochnyi
punkt/ adj. + m. first-aid station

переглядываться /peregliádyvat'sia/ v. exchange glances

перегной /peregnói/ m. humus

переговорить /peregovorít'/ have a talk

переговоры /peregovóry/ pl. negotiations

перегородка /peregoródka/ f. partition

перегревать /peregrevát'/ v. overheat

перегружать /peregruzhát'/ v. overload

перед /péred/ conj. before; in front of

перед /periód/ m. front

передавать /peredavát'/ v. pass; transmit; convey; hand over

передатчик /peredátchik/ m. transmitter

передача /peredácha/ f. transfer; broadcast

передвигать /peredvigát'/ v. move

передвижение /peredvizhénie/ n. movement

передвижной /peredvizhnói/ adj. mobile

переделка /peredélka/ f. alteration

переделывать /peredélyvat'/ v. remake

передний /perédnii/ adj. front

передник /perédnik/ m. apron

передняя /perédniaia/ f. hall

передовица /peredovítsa/ f. editorial

передовой / peredovói/ adj. leading; advanced, progressive

передразнивать /peredráznivat'/ v. mimic; mock

передумывать /peredúmyvat'/ v. change ones mind

передышка /peredýshka/ f. respite

переезд /pereézd/ m. move; crossing

пережевывать /perezhióvyvat'/ v. chew

переживание /perezhivánie/ n. experience

переживать /perezhivát'/ v. endure

пережиток /perezhítok/ m. remnant

перезаключать /perezakliuchát'/ v. renew (e.g. contract)

перезрелый /perezrélyi/ adj. overripe

переигрывать /pereígryvat'/ v. play again; overdo

переизбирать /pereizbirát'/ v. re-elect

переиздавать /pereizdavát'/ v. reprint

переименовывать /pereimenóvyvat'/ v. rename

переиначивать /pereináchivat'/ v. alter

перекармливать /perekármlivat'/ v. overfeed

перекись /pérekis'/ f. peroxide

перекладина /perekládina/ f. crossbeam; horizontal bar (sport)

перекликаться /pereklikát'sia/ v. call to one an other

перекличка /pereklíchka/ f. roll-call

переключать /perekliuchát'/ v. switch (over)

перекрашивать /perekráshivat'/ v. repaint

перекрестный /perekrióstnyi/ adj. cross; п.допрос /p. doprós/ cross-examination

перекресток /perekrióstok/ m. crossroads

перекупщик /perekúpshchik/ m. second-hand dealer; middleman

переламывать /perelámyvat'/ v. break in two; conquer

перелезать /perelezát'/ v. climb over

перелесок /perelésok/ m. copse

перелет /pereliót/ m. flight; transmigration

перелетная птица /pereliótnaia ptítsa/ adj.+f. bird of passage

переливать /perelivát'/ v. pour, transfuse;

переливаться /perelivát'sia/ v. overflow

перелистывать /perelístyvat'/ v. look through

перелом /perelóm/ m. break; turning-point

переманивать /peremánivat'/ v. entice

перематывать /peremátyvat'/ v. (re)wind

перемежать(ся) /peremezhát'sia/ v. alternate

перемена /pereména/ f. interval; break; change

перемешивать /pereméshivat'/ v. mix; shuffle

перемещать /peremeshchát'/ v. transfer

перемещенные лица /peremeshchiónnye litsa/ adj.+pl. displaced persons

перемигаваться /peremigivat'sia/ v. wink

перемирие /peremirie/ n. truce

перемывать /peremyvát'/ v. wash

перенапрягать /perenapriagát'/ v. overstrain

перенаселенный /perenaseliónnyi/ adj. overpopulated

перенасыщенный /perenasýshchennyi/ adj. oversaturated

перенимать /perenimát'/ v. adopt; п. привычку /p. privýchku/ take (catch) the habit

перенос /perenós/ m. transfer

переносить /perenosit'/ v. carry across; put off; endure

переносица /perenósitsa/ f. bridge of nose

переносный /perenósnyi/ adj. portable; figurative

переносчик /perenóschik/ m. carrier

переоборудовать /pereoborúdovat'/ v. re-equip

переобуваться /pereobuvát'sia/ v. change ones footwear

переодевать /pereodevát'/ v. change (someone's clothes)

переодетый /pereodétyi/ adj. disguised

переоценивать /pereotsénivat'/v. overestimate

переоценка /pereotsénka/ f. revaluation

перепел /pérepel/ m. quail

перепечатывать /perepechátyvat'/ v. reprint; type

перепивать /perepivát'/ v. drink to excess

переписка /perepiska/ f. correspondence

переписывать /perepisyvat'/ v. copy

перепись /pérepis'/ f. census

переплачивать /perepláchivat'/ v. overpay

переплет /perepliót/ m. binding; cover

переплывать /pereplyvát'/ v. swim across

переподготовка /perepodgotóvka/ f. retraining

переползать /perepolzát'/ v. crawl

переполнять /perepolniát'/ v. fill (smth.) to overflowing; overwhelm; overcrow

переполох /perepolókh/ m. commotion, panic

перепонка /perepónka/ f. membrane

переправа /perepráva/ f. crossing

перепродавать /pereprodavát'/ v. resell

перепродажа /pereprodázha/ f. resale

перепроизводство /pereproizvódstvo/ n. overproduction

перепрыгивать /pereprýgivat'/ v. jump over

перепутывать /perepútyvat'/ v. confuse; process

перерастать /pererastát'/ v. outgrow

перерасход /pereraskhód/ m. overexpenditure

перерезывать /pererézyvat'/ v. cut

перерождаться /pererozhdát'sia/ v. degenerate

перерубать /pererubát'/ v. cut in two

перерыв /pererýv/ m. interval

пересадка /peresádka/ f. transplantation; change

пересаживать /peresázhivat'/ v. give another seat; move; transplant; repot, plant out

пересаживаться /peresázhivat'sia/ v. change (trains etc.)

пересдавать /peresdavát'/ v. resit (examination); sublet

пересекать /peresekát'/ v. cross

переселенец /pereselénets/ m. settler; immigrant

переселять /pereseliát/ v. move

пересечение /peresechénie/ n. intersection

пересиливать /peresílivat'/v. overpower

пересказывать /pereskázyvat'/ v. retell

пересматривать/ peresmátrivat'/ v. review

переспелый /perespélyi/ adj. overipe

переспорить /perespórit'/ v. beat (smb.) in argument

переспрашивать /perespráshivat'/ v. ask again

переставать /perestavát'/ v. stop

переставлять /perestavliát'/ v. rearrange

перестановка /perestanóvka/ f. rearrangement

перестраивать /perestráivat'/ v. rebuild

перестраиваться /perestráivat'sia/ v. reform

перестраховывать /perestrakhóvyvat'/ v. reinsure

перестреливать /perestrélivat'/ v. shoot

перестрелка /perestrélka/ f. exchange of fire

перестройка /perestróika/ f. perestroika; reorganization

переступать /perestupát'/ v. overstep

пересушивать /peresúshivat'/ v. overdry

пересчитывать /pereschítyvat'/ v. count again; recalculate

пересылать /peresylát'/ v. send

пересыхать /peresykhát'/ v. become (too) dry

перетаскивать /peretáskivat'/ v. carry over

перетасовка /peretasóvka/ f. reshuffle

перетирать /peretirát'/ v. rub

перетрясать /peretriasát'/ v. shake up

переубеждать /pereubezhdát'/ v. convince

переулок /pereúlok/ m. by-street; lane

переутомлять(ся) /pereutomliát'sia/ v. overstrain

переучет /pereuchiót/ m. inventory

переучивать /pereúchivat'/v. learn smth. over again

перефразировать /perefrazírovat'/ v. paraphrase

перехватывать /perekhvátyvat'/ v. intercept

перехитрить /perekhitrit'/ v. outwit; be too smart

переход /perekhód/ m. passage

переходить /perekhodít'/ v. cross

переходный /perekhódnyi/ adj. transition(al)

переходящий (кубок) /perekhodiáshchii kúbok/ adj. + m. challenge cup

перец /pérets/ m. pepper

перечень /pérechen'/ m. list

перечеркивать /perechiórkivat'/ v. cross out

перечислять /perechisliát'/ v. enumerate; transfer (fin.)

перечница /pérechnitsa/ f. pepper-pot

перешагивать /pereshágivat'/ v. step across

перешеек /pereshéek/ m. isthmus

перешивать /pereshivát'/ v. alter (clothes)

переэкзаменовка /pereekzamenóvka/ f. re-examination

перила /períla/ pl. (hand) rail

перина /perína/ f. feather-bed

период /períod/ m. period

периодика /periódika/ f. periodicals

перистые (облака) /péristye oblaká/ adj.+pl. cirrus

периферия /periferíia/ f. periphery

перламутр /perlamútr/ m. mother-of-pearl

перловая крупа /perlóvaia krupá/ adj. + f. pearl-barley

пернатый /pernátyi/ adj. feathered

перо /peró/ n. feather; pen

перочинный нож /perochínnyi nozh/ adj. + m. penknife

перпендикуляр /perpendikuliar/ m. perpendicular
перрон /perrón/ m. platform
перс /pers/ m. Persian
персидский /persidskii/ adj. Persian
персик /pérsik/ m. peach
персиянка /persiiánka/ f. Persian
персона /persóna/ f. person
персонаж /personázh/ m. character
персонал /personál/ m. staff
персональный /personál'nyi/ adj. personal
перспектива /perspektíva/ f. prospects
перстень /pérsten'/ m. ring
перуанец /peruánets/ m. Peruvian
перуанка /peruánka/ f. Peruvian
перуанский /peruánskii/ adj. Peruvian
перхоть /pérkhot'/ f. dandruff
перчатка /perchátka/ f. glove
песец /peséts/ m. polar fox
пескарь /peskár'/ m. gudgeon
песня /pésnia/ f. song
песок /pesók/ m. sand; сахарный п. /sákharnyi p./ granulated sugar
петиция /petítsiia/ f. petition
петлица /petlítsa/ f. buttonhole
петля /petliá/ f. loop
петрушка /petrúshka/ f. parsley
петух /petúkh/ m. cock, rooster
петь /pet'/ v. sing
пехота /pekhóta/ f. infantry
печалить /pechálit'/ v. sadden
печаль /pechál'/ f. sorrow; grief
печатать /pechátat'/ v. print; type
печататься /pechátat'sia/ v. be printed
печать /pechát'/ f. seal; the press
печенка /pechiónka/ f. liver
печеный /pechiónyi/ adj. baked
печень /péchen/ f. liver
печенье /pechén'e/ n. biscuit; cookies
печь /pech/ f. stove; v. bake
пешеход /peshekhód/ m. pedestrian
пешка /péshka/ f. pawn (chess)
пешком /peshkóm/ adv. on foot

пещера /peshchéra/ f. cave
пианино /pianíno/ n. piano
пианист /pianíst/ m. pianist
пивная /pivnáia/ f. pub; tavern
пиво /pívo/ n. beer
пивоваренный завод /pivovárennyi zavód/ adj. + m. brewery
пигмей /pigméi/ m. pigmy
пиджак /pidzhák/ m. jacket, coat
пижама /pizháma/ f. pyjamas
пик /pik/ m. peak; час п. /chas p./ rush hour
пикантный /pikántnyi/ adj. piquant
пикет /pikét/ m. picket
пики /píki/ pl. spades (cards)
пикник /pikník/ m. picnic
пикули /píkuli/ pl. pickles
пила /pilá/ f. saw
пиленый /piliónyi/ adj. sawn; п.сахар /p. sákhar/ lump sugar
пилить /pilít'/ v. saw
пилот /pilót/ m. pilot; высший пилотаж /výsshii pilotázh/ aerial acrobatics
пилюля /piliúlia/ f. pill
пион /pión/ m. peony
пионер /pionér/ m. pioneer
пипетка /pipétka/ f. dropper
пир /pir/ m. feast
пирамида /piramída/ f. pyramid
пират /pirát/ m. pirate
пирог /piróg/ m. pie
пирожное /pirózhnoe/ n. pastry
писатель /pisátel'/ m. writer, author
писать /pisát'/ v. write
писк /pisk/ m. squeck; peep
пистолет /pistolét/ m. pistol
писчая бумага /píschaia bumága/ adj. + f. writing paper
писчебумажный   магазин /pischebumázhnyi magazín/ adj. + m. stationer's shop
письмена /pis'mená/ pl. characters; letters
письменность /pis'mennost'/ f. writing; literature

письменный /pís'mennyi/ adj. written
письмо /pis'mó/ n. letter
питание /pitánie/ n. feeding
питательный /pitátel'nyi/ adj. nutritious
питать /pitát'/ v. nourish; feed
питомник /pitómnik/ m. nursery (for plants)
питон /pitón/ m. python
пить /pit'/ v. drink
питьевой /pit'evói/ adj. drinking, drinkable
пихать /pikhát'/ v. push, shove
пихта /pikhta/ f. fir
пишущий /píshushchii/ adj. writing;
пишущая машинка /píshushchaia mashinka/ typewriter
пища /píscha/ f. food
пищеварение /pishchevarénie/ n. digestion
пищевод /pishchevód/ m. gullet
пищевой /pishchevói/ adj. food
пиявка /piiávka/ f. leech
плавание /plávanie/ n. sailing; voyage; swimming
плавать /plávat'/ sail; swim
плавленый (сыр) /plávlenyi syr/ adj. + m. processed cheese
плавник /plavník/ m. fin
плавный /plávnyi/ adj. smooth
плагиат /plagiát/ m. plagiarism
плакат /plakát/ m. poster
плакать /plákat'/ v. weep, cry
плакса /pláksa/ f., m. cry-baby
плакучий /plakúchii/ adj. weeping (willow)
пламенный /plámennyi/ adj. fiery; ardent
пламя /plámia/ m. flame(s)
план /plan/ m. plan
планер /planiór/ m. glider
планета /planéta/ f. planet
планетарий /planetárii/ m. planetarium
планировать /planírovat'/ plan; glide
планировка /planiróvka/ f. planning; laying out

планка /plánka/ f. plank
пласт /plast/ m. layer
пластика /plástika/ f. plastic art; sense of rhythm
пластинка /plastínka/ f. plate; record; disc
пластический /plastícheskii/ adj. plastic
пластмасса /plastmáss/ f. plastic
пластырь /plástyr'/ m. plaster
плата /pláta/ f. pay
платан /platán/ m. platan
платеж /platiózh/ m. payment
платина /plátina/ f. platinum
платить /plat'it'/ v. pay
платный /plátnyi/ adj. paid
плато /pláto/ n. plateau
платок /platók/ m. kerchief
платформа /platfórma/ f. platform
платье /plát'e/ n. dress
плацдарм /platsdárm/ m. base
плацкарта /platskárta/ f. reserved-seat ticket
плашмя /plashmiá/ adv. flat
плащ /plashch/ m. raincoat
плебисцит /plebistsít/ m. plebiscite
плевать /plevát'/ v. spit
плеврит /plevrít/ m. pleurisy
плед /pled/ m. rug, plaid
племя /plémia/ n. tribe
племянник /plemiánnik/ m. nephew
племянница /plemiánnitsa/ f. niece
плен /plen/ m. captivity
пленительный /plenítel'nyi/ adj. fascinating
пленка /pliónka/ f. film; tape
пленник /plénnik/ m. prisoner
пленум /plénum/ m. plenary session
плесень /plésen'/ f. mould
плескать /pleskát'/ v. splash
плести /plestí/ v. weave
плетеный /pletiónyi/ adj. wicker
плеть /plet'/ f.lash
плечо /plechó/ n. shoulder
плешивый /pleshívyi/ adj. balding

плинтус /plíntus/ m. plinth
плита /plitá/ f. slab; stove
плитка /plítka/ f. tile
плов /plov/ m. pilau
пловец /plovéts/ m. swimmer
плод /plod/ m. fruit
плодить /plodít'/ v. breed; bring forth; multiply
плодородие /plodoródie/ n. fertility
пломба /plómba/ f. filling (in tooth); seal
пломбир /plombír/ m. ice-cream
пломбировать /plombírovat'/ v. fill (tooth); seal
плоский /plóskii/ adj. flat
плоскогорье /ploskogór'e/ n. plateau
плоскогубцы /ploskogúbtsy/ pl. pliers
плот /plot/ m. raft
плотва /plotvá/ f. roach
плотина /plotína/ f. dam
плотник /plótnik/ m. carpenter
плотный /plótnyi/ adj. tense, thick, tight; hearty (dinner)
плоть /plot'/ f. flesh
плохой /plokhói/ adj. bad
площадка /ploshchádka/ f. ground
площадь /plóshchad'/ f. square; area
плуг /plug/ m. plough
плыть /plyt'/ v. swim; sail
плюс /pliús/ m. plus
плюш /pliúsh/ m. plush
плющ /pliúshch/ m. ivy
пляж /pliázh/ m. beach
плясать /pliasát'/ v. dance
пневматический /pnevmatícheskii/ adj. pneumatic
по /po/ prep. along; through; by; on
побег /pobég/ m. flight; escape; shoot
победа /pobéda / f. victory
победитель /pobedítel'/ m. victor
побеждать /pobezhdát'/ v. conquer; defeat; win
побелка /pobélka/ f. whitewashing
побережье /poberézh'e/ n. coast
поблизости /poblízosti/ adv. closeby

побывать /pobývat'/ v. visit; be
побыть /pobýt'/ v. stay
повар /póvar/m. cook, chef
поведение /povedénie/ n. behaviour
повелевать /povelevát'/ v. rule
поверенный /povérennyi/ m. attorney; п. в делах /p. v. delákh/ charge d'affaires
повертывать /poviórtyvat'/ v. turn
поверх /povérkh/ adv. over
поверхностный /povérkhnostnyi/ adj. surface; superficial
поверхность /povérkhnost'/ f. surface
повесить /povésit'/ v. hang (up)
повествование /povestvovánie/ n. narrative
повестка /povéstka/ f. summons
повесть /póvest'/ f. story
по-видимому /po-vídimomu/ paren. apparently, evidently
повидло /povídlo/ n. jam
повинность /povínnost'/ f. duty; воинская п. /vóinskaia p./ military service
повиноваться /povinovát'sia/ v. obey
повисать /povisát'/v. hang; droop
повод /póvod/ m. bridle-rein; occasion; ground
повозка /povózka/ f. waggon, cart
поворачивать /povoráchivat'/ v. turn
поворотный /povorótnyi/ adj. turning; crucial
повреждать /povrezhdát'/ v. damage
повременить /povremenít'/ v. wait a while (with)
повседневный /povsednévnyi/ adj. everyday
повсеместный /povseméstnyi/ adj. general
повсюду /povsiúdu/ adv. everywhere
повторение /povtorénie/ n. repetition
повторять /povtoriát'/ v. repeat; revise
повышать /povyshát'/ v. raise

повышение /povyshénie/ n. rise; increase; promotion

повязка /poviázka/ f. bandage

поганка /pogánka/ f. toadstool

погибать /pogibát'/ v. perish

поглаживать /poglázhivat'/ v. stroke

поговорка /pogovórka/ f. saying

погода /pogóda/ f. weather

поголовный /pogolóvnyi/ adj. general; house-to-house

поголовье /pogolóv'e/ n. livestock

погоня /pogónia/ f. chase

погреб /pogréb/ m. cellar

погружать /pogruzhát'/ dip; plunge

погрузка /pogrúzka/ f. loading

под / pod/ prep. under

подавать /podavát'/ v. give; serve

подавлять /podavliát'/ v. suppress

подагра /podágra/ f. gout

подарок /podárok/ m. present, gift

подбегать /podbegát'/ v. run up (to)

подбирать /podbirát'/ v. pick up; choose

подбодрять /podbodriát'/ v. cheer up

подбор /podbór/ m. selection

подбородок /podboródok/ m. chin

подбрасывать /podbrásyvat'/ v. toss up

подвал /podvál/ m. basement; cellar

подвергать /podvergát'/ v. subject; expose

подвертывать /podviórtyvat'/ v. tighten; tuck up

подвешивать /podvéshivat'/ hung up

подвиг /pódvig/ m. exploit

подвигать /podvigát'/ v. move

подвинчивать /podvínchivat'/ tighten up; screw up

подводить /podvodít'/ v. lead; bring; let down

подводный /podvódnyi/ adj. underwater;

подводная лодка /podvódnaia lódka/ submarine

подвозить /podvozít'/ v. bring; give a lift to

подвязка /podviázka/ f. garter

подвязывать /podviázyvat'/ v. tie up

подгибать /podgibát'/ v. turn up

подглядывать /podgliádyvat'/ v. peep

подгорать /podgorát'/ v. get burnt

подготавливать /podgotávlivat'/ v. prepare (for)

поддакивать /poddákivat'/ v. agree

подданный /póddannyi/ adj. subject

подданство /póddanstvo/ n. citizenship

подделка /poddélka/ f. forgery; fake

подделывать /poddélyvat'/ v. forge; counterfeit

поддельный /poddél'nyi/ adj. false, fake; artificial

поддерживать /poddérzhivat'/ v. support

поддразнивать /poddráznivat'/ v. tease

подержанный /podérzhannyi/ adj. second hand

поджаривать /podzhárivat'/ v. fry; grill; roast; toast

поджигатель /podzhigátel'/ m. arsonist; instigator

поджигать /podzhigát'/ v. set on fire

поджидать /podzhidát'/ v. wait

поджимать /podzhimát'/ v. п. губы /p. gúby/ purse one's lips; п. ноги /p. nógi/ cross one's legs

поджог /podzhóg/ m. arson

подзаголовок /podzagolóvok/ m. subheading

подзадоривать /podzadórivat'/ v. encourage ; egg on

подзащитный /podzashchítnyi/ m. client (law)

подземелье /podzemél'e/ n. dungeon; vault

подзорная труба /podzórnaia trubá/ adj. + f. telescope

подзывать /podzyvát'/ v. call; beckon (to)

подкатывать /podkátyvat'/ v. drive up

подкидывать /podkídyvat'/ v. throw up

подкладка /podkládka/ f. lining

подключать /podkliuchát'/ v. put (smth.) in, connect up

подкова /podkóva/ f. horseshoe

подкожный /podkózhnyi/ adj. hypodermic

подкомитет /podkomitét/ m. subcommittee

подкрадываться /podkrádyvat'sia/ v. creep up (to)

подкрашивать /podkráshivat'/ v. touch up; colour

подкреплять /podkrepliát'/ v. support; reinforce

подкуп /pódkup/ m. bribery

подкупать /podkupát'/ v. bribe

подлезать /podlezát'/ v. crawl under

подлетать /podletát'/ v. fly up (to)

подлец /podléts/ m. scoundrel

подливать /podlivát'/ v. pour in

подливка /podlívka/ f. gravy

подлинник /pódlinnik/ m. original

подлог /podlóg/ m. forgery

подлокотник /podlokótnik/ m. elbowrest

подмазывать /podmázyvat'/ v. grease; oil

подмастерье /podmastér'e/ n. apprentice

подмена /podména/ f. substitution

подметка /podmiótka/ f. sole (of shoe)

подмечать /podmechát'/ v. notice

подмешивать /podméshivat'/ v. add; mix in

подмигивать /podmígivat'/ v. wink

подмога /podmóga/ f. help

подмывать /podmyvát'/ v. wash; undermine

подмышка /podmýshka/ f. armpit

подневольный /podnevól'nyi/ adj. dependent; forced

поднимать /podnimát'/ v. raise; lift

подновлять /podnovliát'/ v. renovate

подножие /podnózhie/ n. foot (of hill); pedestal

подножка /podnózhka/ f.footboard; back heel (sport)

подножный корм /podnózhnyi korm/ adj.+ m. pasture

поднос /podnós/ m. tray

подносить /podnosít'/ v. bring

подобать /podobát'/ v. become

подобающий /podobáiushchii/ adj. proper

подобный /podóbnyi/ adj. similar (to)

подогревать /podogrevát'/ v. warm up

пододвигать /pododvigát'/ v. move up (to)

пододеяльник /pododeiál'nik/ m. blanket cover

подозревать /podozrevát'/ v. suspect (of)

подозрение /podozrénie/ n. suspicion

подоконник /podokónnik/ m. windowsill

подол /podól/ m. hem

подолгу /podólgu/ adv. for a long time

подонки /podónki/ pl. riff-raff

подоплека /podoplíoka/ f. hidden motive

подопытный /podópytnyi/ adj. experiment al; п. кролик /p. królik/ (fig.) guinea-pig

подорожник /podorózhnik/ m. plantain

подоспеть /podospét'/ v. arrive in time

подотчетный /podotchiótnyi/ adj. accountable

подоходный (налог) /podokhódnyi nalóg/ adj. + m. income tax

подошва/podóshva/f. sole (of foot, shoe)

подпевала /podpevála/ m. f. yes-man

подпирать /podpirát'/ v. prop up

подписка /podpíska/ f. subscription

подписчик /podpíschik/ m. subscriber

подписывать /podpísyvat'/ v. sign

подпись /pódpis'/ f. signature

подплывать /podplyvát'/ v. swim up (to)

подползать /podpolzát'/ v. crawl up (to)

подполковник /podpolkóvnik/ m. lieutenant-colonel

подполье /podpól'e/ n. basement; underground

подпор(к)а /podpór(k)a/ f. support, prop

подпоясывать /podpoiásyvat'/ v. belt

подправлять /podpravliát'/ v. put (smth.) right, adjust

подпрыгивать /podprýgivat'/ v. jump up and down; bob

подрабатывать /podrabátyvat'/ v. work up; earn a little extra

подражать /podrazhát'/ v. imitate

подразделять /podrazdeliát'/ v. subdivide

подразумевать /podrazumevát'/ v. mean

подрастать /podrastát'/ v. grow up

подрастающее (поколение) /podrastáiushchee pokolénie/ adj.+n. the rising generation

подрезать /podrezát'/ v. cut, trim

подрисовывать /podrisóvyvat'/ v. touch up

подробность /podróbnost'/ f. detail

подросток /podróstok/ m. teenager

подруга /podrúga/ f. (girl-) friend; school-mate

по-дружески /po-drúzheski/ adv. friendly

подрыв /podrýv/ m. blasting; undermining

подрывать /podryvát'/ v. blow up

подрывной /podrývnoi/ adj. blasting; subversive

подряд /podriád/ m. contract; adv. in suc cession

подрядчик /podriádchik/ m. contractor

подсаживать /podsázhivat'/ give a hand up; v. help to a seat; give a lift

подсвечник /podsvéchnik/ m. candlestick

подсекция /podséktsiia/ f. sub-section

подсказывать /podskázyvat'/ v. prompt; suggest

подскакивать /podskákivat'/ v. run up (to); jump up and down

подслащивать /podsláshchivat'/ v. sweeten

подследственный /podslédstvennyi/ adj. under investigation

подслеповатый /podslepovátyi/ adj. weak-sighted

подслушивать /podslúshivat'/ v. eavesdrop; overhear

подсматривать /podsmátrivat'/ v. spy on; spot

подсмеиваться /podsméivat'sia/ v. make fun (of)

подснежник /podsnézhnik/ m. snowdrop

подсобный /podsóbnyi/ adj. auxiliary; subsidiary

подсовывать /podsóvyvat'/ v. put under; slip

подсознательный /podsoznátel'nyi/ adj. subconscious

подсолнечник /podsólnechnik/ m. sunflower

подспудный /podspúdnyi/ adj. hidden, latent

подставка /podstávka/ f. support; prop

подставлять /podstavliát'/ v. put under

подставной /podstavnói/ adj. false

подстаканник /podstakánnik/ m. glassholder

подстанция /podstántsiia/ f. sub-station; local telephone exchange

подстилать /podstilát'/ v. spread

подстрекатель /podstrekátel'/ m. instigator

подстрекать /podstrekát'/ v. incite (to); instigate

подстригать /podstrigát'/ v. trim

подстрочный перевод /podstróchnyi perevód/ adj.+m. word-for-word translation; подстрочное примечание /podstróchnoe primechánie/ footnote

подступать /podstupát'/ v. get near; approach

подсудимый /podsudímyi/ m. defendant

подсчет /podschót/ m. calculation; counting

подсчитывать /podschítyvat'/ v. count up

подсылать /podsylát'/ v. send for a (secret) purpose

подсыпать /podsypát'/ v. add, slip (smth.) in secretly

подсыхать /podsykhát'/ v. dry a little

подталкивать /podtálkivat'/ v. push; shove; prompt

подтаскивать /podtáskivat'/ v. drag up (to)

подтасовывать /podtasóvyvat'/ v. fiddle; garble

подтачивать /podtáchivat'/ v. sharpen; undermine

подтверждать /podtverzhdát'/ v. confirm

подтекст /podtékst/ m. implication

подтягивать /podtiágivat'/ v. tighten

подтяжки /podtiázhki/ pl. suspenders

подтянутый /podtiánutyi/ adj. smart; efficient

подушка /podúshka/ f. pillow

подхалим /podkhalím/ m. toady

подхватывать /podkhvátyvat'/ v. pick up; catch

подхлестывать /podkhlióstyvat'/ v. whip up

подходить /podkhodít'/ come up (to)

подходящий /podkhodiáshchii/ adj. suitable; proper

подчеркивать /podchórkivat'/ v. underline; emphasize

подчинять /podchiniát'/ v. subjugate; subordinate

подчищать /podchishchát'/ v. clean up; erase

подшипник /podshípnik/ m. bearing

подшучивать /podshúchivat'/ v. mock; make fun of

подъезд /pod"ézd/ m. entrance

подъем /podióm/ m. rise

подъемник /pod"iómnik/ m. elevator

подыскивать /podýskivat'/ v. seek out

подытоживать /podytózhivat'/ v. sum up

поединок /poedínok/ m. duel

поезд /póezd/ m. train

поездка /poézdka/ f. trip; journey

пожаловать /pozhálovat'/ v. come; добро п. /dobró p./ welcome

пожалуй /pozhálui/ adv. perhaps

пожалуйста /pozháluista/ part. please

пожар /pozhár/ m. fire

пожатие /pozhátie/ n. shake (of hand)

пожелание /pozhelánie/ n. wish

пожертвование /pozhértvovanie/ n. donation

пожизненный /pozhíznennyi/ adj. lifelong; life

пожилой /pozhilói/ adj. elderly

пожимать /pozhimát/press; п. плечами /p. plechámi/ shrug one's shoulders

пожинать /pozhinát'/ v. reap

пожирать /pozhirát'/ v. devour

поза /póza/ f. pose

позавчера /pozavcherá/ adv. the day before yesterday

позади /pozadí/ adv., prep. behind

позапрошлый /pozapróshlyi/ adj. before last

позволять /pozvoliát'/ v. allow

позвоночник /pozvonóchnik/ m. spine

поздний /pózdnii/ adj. late

поздравлять /pozdravliát'/ v. congratulate

поземельный (налог) /pozemél'nyi nalóg/ adj.+m. land tax

позже /pózzhe/ adv. later

позировать /pozírovat'/ v. pose

позитивный /pozitívnyi/ adj. positive

позиция /pozítsiia/ f. position

познавать /poznavát'/ v. cognize; get to know

позолота /pozolóta/ f. gilding

позор /pozór/ m. shame

позорить /pozorít'/ v. disgrace

позорный /pozórnyi/ adj. shameful; disgraceful

поименно /poimiónno/ adv. by name

поимка /poímka/ f. capture

поимущественный (налог) /poimúshchestvennyi nalóg/ adj.+m. property tax

по-иному /po-inómu/ adv. differently

поиск /póisk/ m. search

поистине /poístine/ adv. indeed

поить /poít'/ v. give a drink; п. чаем /p. cháem/ give smb. tea

поймать /poimát'/ v. catch

пока /poká/ adv. meanwhil for the time being; conj. while, till; coll bye-bye!; so long

показ /pokáz/ m. show

показание /pokazánie/ n. testimony; evidence

показатель /pokazátel'/ m. index

показывать /pokázyvat'/ v. show; demonstrate

покатость /pokátost'/ f. slope

покатый /pokátyi/ adj. slanting; sloping

покачивать /pokáchivat'/ v. rock; totter

покаяние /pokaiánie/ n. confession; repentance

поквитаться /pokvítat'sia/ v. get even

покидать /pokidát'/ v. desert; leave

поклон /poklón/ m. bow; regards

поклонение /poklonénie/ n. worship

поклонник /poklónnik/ m. admirer

покой /pokói/ m. quietness; peace

покойник /pokóinik/ m. the deceased

поколение /pokolénie/ n. generation

покончить /pokónchit'/ v. finish off; п. с собой /p. s sobói/ commit suicide

покорный /pokórnyi/ adj. obedient; humble

покорять /pokoriát'/ v. conquer; subjugate

покос /pokós/ m. haymaking

покров /pokróv/ m. cover

покровитель /pokrovítel'/ m. patron

покровительство /pokrovítel'stvo/ n. protection

покрой /pokrói/ m. cut (of clothes)

покрывало /pokryválo/ n. cloth; veil

покрывать /pokryvát'/ v. cover

покупатель /pokupátel'/ m. customer

покупать /pokupát'/ v. buy

покупка /pokúpka/ f. purchase

покушаться /pokushát'sia/ v. attempt

пол /pol/ m. floor; sex

пол- /pol-/ half

полагать /polagát'/ v. think; suppose

полагаться /polagát'sia/ v. rely; depend

полвека /polvéka/ m. half a century

полгода /polgóda/ m. half a year

полдень /pólden'/ m. midday

поле /póle/ n. field; ground; margin; brim (of hat)

полезный /poléznyi/ adj. useful

полемика /polémika/ f. polemics

полено /poléno/ n. log

полет /poliót/ m. flight

ползать /polzát'/ v. crawl

ползком /polzkóm/ adv. on all fours

поливать /polivát'/ v. water; pour

полигон /poligón/ m. proving ground; test range

полиграфия /poligráfiia/ f. printing industry

поликлиника /poliklínika/ f. polyclinic

полировать /polirovát'/ v. polish

полис /pólis/ m. policy (e.g. insurance)

политехникум /politékhnikum/ m. poly technic

политик /politik/ m. politician

политика /politika/ f. politics

политикан /politikán/ m. intriguer

полицейский /politséiskii/ adj. police; m. policeman

полиция /politsiia/ f. police

полк /polk/ m. regiment

полка /pólka/ f. shelf

полковник /polkóvnik/ m. colonel

полководец /polkovódets/ m. military leader

полнеть /polnét'/ v. put on weight

полновесный /polnovésnyi/ adj. full-weight; weighty

полновластный /polnovlástnyi/ adj. sovereign

полнокровный /polnokróvnyi/ adj. full-blooded

полнолуние /polnolúnie/ n. full moon

полномочие /polnomóchiie/n. authority; (full) power

полномочный /polnomóchnyi/ adj. pleni-potentiary

полноправный /polnoprávnyi/ adj. enjoying; full rights; equal

полностью /pólnost'iu/ adv. completely

полнота /polnotá/ f. corpulence; п. власти /p. vlásti/ fullness of power

полноценный /polnotsénnyi/ adj. valuable

полночь /polnóch/ f. midnight

полный /pólnyi/ adj. full, complete; stout, plump

половина /polovína/ f. half

половинчатый /polovínchatyi/ adj. ambivalent

половодье /polovód'e/ n. high water

половой /polovói/ adj. floor; sexual

положение /polozhénie/ n. situation

положенный /polózhennyi/ adj. given, appointed, fixed

положительный /polozhítel'nyi/ adj. positive; affirmativel

поломка /polómka/ f. breakage

поломойка /polomóika/ f. charwoman

полоса /polosá/ f. strip

полосатый /polosátyi/ adj. striped

полоскать /poloskát'/ v. rinse

полость /pólost'/ f. cavity

полотенце /poloténtse/ n. towel

полотер /polotiór/ m. floor-polisher

полотно /polotnó/ n. linen

полоть /polót'/ v. weed

полпути /polputí/ m. half-way

полтора /poltorá/ num. one and half

полу- /polu-/ semi-, half-

полугодие /polugódie/ n. half-year

полугодовалый /polugodovályi/ adj. six-month-old

полугодовой /polugodovói/ adj. half-yearly

полуграмотный /polugrámotnyi/ adj. semi-literate

полуденный /polúdennyi/ adj. midday

полузащитник /poluzashchítnik/ m. half-back (sport)

полукруг /polukrúg/ m. semicircle

полумесяц /polumésiats/ m. crescent

полумесячный /polumésiachnyi/ adj. fortnightly

полуостров /poluóstrov/ m. peninsula

полупроводник /poluprovodník/ m. semiconductor

полуфабрикат /polufabrikát/ m. half-finished product; convenience foods

полуфинальная (игра) /polufinál'naia igrá/ adj.+f. semi-final

получасовой /poluchasovói/ adj. half-hourly

получатель /poluchátel'/ m. recipient

получать /poluchát'/ v. receive; obtain

полушарие /polushárie/ n. hemisphere

полчаса /polchasá/ m. half an hour

полый /pólyi/ adj. hollow

полынь /polýn'/ f. wormwood

польза /pól'za/ f. use; profit

пользоваться /pól'zovat'sia/ v. make use (of)

полька /pól'ka/ f. Pole (woman); polka

польский /pól'skii/ adj. Polish

полюс /poliús/ m. pole

поляк /poliák/ m. Pole

поляна /poliána/ f. forest meadow

поляризация /poliarizátsiia/ f. polarization

полярник /poliárnik/ m. polar explorer

помада /pomáda/ f. lipstick

помазание /pomázanie/ n. anointing
помазанник /pomázannik/ m. anointed sovereign
помахивать /pomákhivat'/ v. wag
поместительный /pomestítel'nyi/ adj. spacious
поместье /pomést'e/ n. estate
помесь /pómes'/ f. cross-breed
помесячный /pomésiachnyi/ adj. monthly
пометка /pométka/ f. mark
помеха /pomékha/ f. obstacle
помечать /pomechát'/ v. mark
помешанный /poméshannyi/ adj. mad, crazy
помещать /pomeshchát'/ v. place, accommodate; п. капитал /p. kapitál/ invest
помещение /pomeshchénie/ n. premises
помещик /poméshchik/ m. landowner
помидор /pomidór/ m. tomato
помиловать /pomílovat'/ v. pardon
помимо /pomímo/ prep. besides
поминать /pominát'/ v. mention; pray for
поминки /pomínki/ pl. funeral repast
помирать /pomirát'/ v. coll. die
помнить /pómnit'/ v. remember; keep in mind
помножать /pomnozhát'/ v. multiply (by)
помогать /pomogát'/ v. assist; aid; help
по-моему /po-móemu/ adv. in my opinion
помолвить /pomolvít'/ v. engage
помост /pomóst/ m. platform
помочи /pómochi/ pl. braces
помощник /pomóshchnik/ m. assistant
помощь /pómoshch/ f. assistance; aid; help; первая п. /pérvaia p./ first aid
помпа /pómpa/ f. pump; pomp
помятый /pomiátyi/ adj. crumpled
понапрасну /ponaprásnu/ adv. coll. in vain

понаслышке /ponaslíshke/ adv. by hearsay
поневоле /ponevóle/ adv. willy-nilly
понедельник /ponedél'nik/ m. Monday
понижать /ponizhát'/ v. lower, reduce
поникать /ponikát'/ v. droop
понимать /ponimát'/ v. understand, comprehend
понос /ponós/ m. diarrhoea
поносить /ponosít'/ v. carry or wear for awhile; abuse, curse
понтон /pontón/ m. pontoon
понуждать /ponuzhdát'/ v. force; compel
понурый /ponúryi/ adj. downcast, depressed
пончик /pónchik/ m. doughnut
понятие /poniátie/ n. idea; concept; outlook
понятный /poniátnyi/ adj. clear; intelligible
поодиночке /poodinóchke/ adv. one at a time
поочередный /poocheriódnyi/ adj. taken in turn
поощрять /pooshchriát'/ v. encourage, stimulate
поп /pop/ m. priest
попадать /popadát'/ v. hit; get (into); reach
попадья /popad'iá/ f. priest's wife
попарно /popárno/ adv. in pairs
поперек /poperiók/ adv. across
попеременно /popereménno/ adv. alternately
поперечина /poperéchina/ f. cross-beam
поперечник /poperéchnik/ m. diameter
поперхнуться /poperkhnút'sia/ v. choke
попечение /popechénie/ n. care, charge
попирать /popirát'/ v. violate; trample
поплавок /poplavók/ m. float
поплин /poplín/ m. poplin
попойка /popóika/ f. drinking-bout; spree
пополам /popolám/ adv. in half

пополнение /popolnénie/ n. replenishment; reinforcement

пополнять /popolniát'/ v. replenish

попона /popóna/ f. horse-cloth

поправка /poprávka/ f. correction; amendment; recovery

поправлять /popravliát'/ v. correct; mend; adjust

поправляться /popravliát'sia/ v. improve; recover, get well; put on weight

по-прежнему /po-prézhnemu/ adv. as be fore

попрекать /poprekát'/ v. reproach

попросту /póprostu/ adv. simply

попрошайка /poprosháika/ f. and m. beggar

попугай /popugái/ m. parrot

популярный /populiárnyi/ adj. popular

попусту /pópustu/ adv. in vain

попутчик /popútchik/m. fellow-traveller

попытка /popýtka/ f. attempt

пора /porá/ f. pore

пора /porá/ f. time; as pred. it is time

порабощать /poraboshchát'/ v. enslave

поравняться /poravniát'sia/ v. come up (with)

поражать /porazhát'/ v. strike a blow; defeat; astonish

поражение /porazhénie/ n. defeat

поразительный /porazítel'nyi/ adj. striking, wonderful

пораньше /porán'she/ adv. a little sooner

порез /poréz/ m. cut

пористый /póristyi/ adj. porous

порицать /poritsát'/ v. blame

порка /pórka/ f. flogging

поровну /pórovnu/ adv. equally

порог /poróg/ m. threshold

порода /poróda/ f. breed

порождать /porozhdát'/ v. give birth (to)

порожний /porózhnii/ adj. empty

порознь /pórozn'/ adv. separately

порой /porói/ adv. at times

порок /porók/ m. vice

поросенок /porosiónok/ m. piglet

порох /pórokh/ m. (gun-) powder

порочить /poróchit'/ v. discredit

порочный /poróchnyi/ adj. vicious

порошок /poroshók/ m. powder

порт /port/ m. port

портативный /portatívnyi/ adj. portable

портвейн /portvéin/ m. port (wine)

портик /pórtik/ m. portico

портить /pórtit'/ v. spoil; ruin; corrupt (smb.)

портниха /portníkha/ f. dressmaker

портной /portnói/ m. tailor

портовик /portovík/ m. docker

портрет /portrét/ m. portrait

портсигар /portsigár/ m. cigarette-case, cigar-case

португалец /portugálets/ m. Portuguese

португалка /portugálka/ f. Portuguese

португальский /portugál'skii/ adj. Portuguese

портфель /portfél'/ m. brief-case; portfolio

портьера /port'éra/ f. door-curtain

порука /porúka/ f. guarantee; взять на поруки /vziat' na poruki/ bail (out)

по-русски /po-rússki/ adv. in Russian

поручать /poruchát'/ v. charge; entrust

поручение /poruchénie/ n. assignment; mission; errand

поручень /póruchen'/ (usually pl.) handrail

поручитель /poruchítel'/ m. guarantor; sponsor

поручительство /poruchítel'stvo/n. guarantee

порхать /porkhát'/ v. flutter

порция /pórtsiia/ f. portion, helping

поршень /pórshen'/ m. piston

порыв /porýv/ m. gust (of wind); fit (of passion)

порывать /poryvát'/ v. break off

порядковый /poriádkovyi/ adj. ordinal

порядок /poriádok/ m. order

порядочный /poriádochnyi/ adj. decent, honest; considerable

посадка /posádka/ f. planting; landing; boarding; posture

по-своему /po-svóemu/ adv. in one's own way

посвящать /posviáshchat'/ v. dedicate

посев /posév/ m. crop

посевной /posevnói/ adj. sowing

поселенец /poselénets/ m. settler

поселять /poseliát'/ v. settle

посередине /poseredíne/ adv. in the middle (of)

посетитель /posetítel'/ m. visitor

посещать /poseshchát'/ v. visit; call; attend

поскользнуться /poskol'znút'sia/ v. slip

поскольку /poskól'ku/ conj. since; inasmuch as

послабление /poslablénie/ n. indulgence

посланец /poslánets/ m. messenger

послание /poslánie/ n. message

посланник /poslánnik/ m. envoy

после /pósle/ adv. later; prep. after

последний /poslédnii/ adj. last; the latest

последователь /poslédovatel'/ m. follower

последствие /poslédstvie/ n. consequence

послезавтра /poslezávtra/ adv. the day after tomorrow

послесловие /posleslóvie/ n. epilogue

пословица /poslóvitsa/ f. proverb

послушный /poslúshnyi/ adj. obedient

посменный /posménnyi/ adj. by shifts

посмертный /posmértnyi/ adj. posthumous

посмешище /posméshishche/ n. laughing-stock

пособие /posóbie/ n. grant

пособник /posóbnik/ m. accomplice

посол /posól/ m. ambassador

посольство /posól'stvo/ n. embassy

поспевать /pospevát'/ v. ripen; be in time

поспешный /pospéshnyi/ adj. hasty; abrupt

посрамлять /posramliát'/ v. disgrace

посреди(не) /posredí(ne)/ adv. in the middle (of)

посредник /posrédnik/ m. agent; mediator

посредственный /posrédstvennyi/ adj. mediocre; satisfactory

пост /post/ m. post; position; station; fast(ing)

поставка /postávka/ f. delivery, supply

постамент /postamént/ m. pedestal

постановка /postanóvka/ f. production; statement (of question)

постановление /postanovlénie/ n. resolution; decision

постановлять /postanovliát'/ v. resolve; decide

постановщик /postanóvshchik/ m. producer

постель /postél'/ f. bed

постепенный /postepénnyi/ adj. gradual

поститься /postít'sia/ v. fast

постный /póstnyi/ adj. lean; vegetable (oil)

постовой /postovói/ m. militia-man on point-duty

постольку /postól'ku/ conj. in so far as

посторонний /postorónnii/ adj. strange; outside; m. stranger

постоялец /postoiálets/ m. lodger

постоянный /postoiánnyi/ adj. constant; steady

постройка /postróika/ f. building

построчный /postróchnyi/ adj. by the line

постскриптум /postskríptum/ m. postscript

постукивать /postúkivat'/ v. tap, knock

поступательный /postupátel'nyi/ adj. onward; progressive

поступать /postupát'/ v. act; enter; join

поступаться /postupát'sia/ v. give up; п. своим правом /p. svoím právom/ waive one's right

поступок /postúpok/ m. act; action; deed

поступь /póstup'/ f. gait; step

постыдный /postýdnyi/ adj. shameful, disgraceful

посуда /posúda/f. plates and dishes; crockery

посылать /posylát'/ v. send; dispatch

посылка /posýlka/ f. parcel

посыльный /posýl'nyi/ m. messenger

посягать /posiagát'/ v. encroach (upon), infringe (on)

пот /pot/ m. sweat

потайной /potainói/ adj. secret, hidden

потакать /potakát'/ v. coll. indulge

потасовка /potasóvka/ f. coll. brawl

поташ /potásh/ m. potash

по-твоему /po-tvóemu/ adv. in your opinion

потемки /potiómki/ pl. darkness

потенциал /potentsiál/ m. potential

потертый /potiórtyi/ adj. shabby; threadbare

потеря /potéria/ f. loss

потирать /potirát'/ v. rub

потихоньку /potikhón'ku/ adv. slowly; quietly; secretly

потный /pótnyi/ adj. sweaty

поток /potók/ m. stream

потолок /potolók/ m. ceiling

потом /potóm/ adv. afterwards; later on

потомок /potómok/ m. descendant

потомственный /potómstvennyi/ adj. hereditary

потомство /potómstvo/ n. posterity

потому /potomú/ adv. that is why

потребитель /potrebítel'/ m. consumer

потреблять /potrebliát'/ v. consume

потребность /potrébnost'/ f. need; requirement

потрясать /potriasát'/ v. shake; impress

потрясение /potriasénie/ n. shock

потусторонний мир /potustorónnii/mir/ adj. the other world

поучать /pouchát'/ v. lecture (smb.)

похвала /pokhvalá/ f. praise

похвальный /pokhvál'nyi/ adj. approving; laudable

похититель /pokhitítel'/ m. stealer; kidnapper; п. самолетов /p. samoliótov/ hijacker

похищать /pokhishchát'/ v. steal; kidnap

похмелье /pokhmél'e/ n. hangover; morning after

поход /pokhód/ m. march; campaign

походка /pokhódka/ f. walk; gait

похождение /pokhozhdénie/ n. adventure

похожий /pokhózhii/ adj. similar (to)

похолодание /pokholodánie/n. cold snap

похоронный /pokhorónnyi/ adj. funeral

похотливый /pokhotlívyi/ adj. lustful

поцелуй /potselúi/ m. kiss

почасно /pochásno/ adv. by the hour

початок /pochátok/ m. cob

почва /póchva/ f. soil

почему /pochemú/ adv. why

почерк /pócherk/ m. handwriting

почет /pochiót/ m. honour; respect

починка /pochínka/ f. repairing

почитатель /pochitátel'/ m. admirer

почитать /pochitát'/v. read (for a while); respect; revere

почка /póchka/ f. bud; kidney

почта /póchta/ f. post, mail; post-office

почтальон /pochtal'ón/ m. postman

почтамт /pochtámt/ m. post office

почтение /pochténie/ n. respect

почти /pochtí/ adv. almost, nearly

почтовый /pochtóvyi/ adj. postal; п. ящик /p. iashchik/ letter-box

пошатнуть /poshatnút'/ v. shake

пошатываться /poshátyvat'sia/ v. stagger

пошивка /poshívka/ f. sewing

пошлина /póshlina/ f. duty

пошлый /póshlyi/ adj. vulgar, shallow

поштучный /poshtúchnyi/ adj. by the piece

пощада /poshcháda/ f. mercy

пощечина /poshchióchina/ f. box on the ear, slap in the face

поэзия /poéziia/ f. poetry

поэма /poéma/ f. long poem

поэтому /poétomu/ adv. therefore

появление /poiavlénie/ n. emergence

появляться /poiavliát'sia/ v. appear

пояс /póias/ m. belt

пояснение /poiasnénie/ n. explanation

поясница /poiasnítsa/ f. small of the back; loins

пояснять /poiasniát'/ v. explain

прабабушка /prabábushka/ f. great-grandmother

правда /právda/ f. truth

правдивый /pravdívyi/ adj. truthful

праведный /právednyi/ adj. pious; righteous

правило /právilo/ n. rule

правильный /právil'nyi/ adj. true

правитель /pravítel'/ m. ruler

правительство /pravítel'stvo/ n. government

править /právit'/ v. rule, govern; drive; correct

правление /pravlénie/ n. administration; government

право /právo/ n. right

правовой /pravovói/ adj. legal

правомерный /pravomérnyi/ adj. lawful

правомочный /pravomóchnyi/adj. competent

правописание /pravopisánie/ n. spelling

правопорядок /pravoporiádok/ m. law and order

православие /pravoslávie/ n. orthodoxy

правосудие /pravosúdie/ n. justice

правота /pravotá/ f. rightness

правый /právyi/ adj. right

праздник /prázdnik/ m. holiday; festival

праздновать /prázdnovat'/ v. celebrate

практика /práktika/ f. practice

практичный /praktíchnyi/ adj. practical

прах /prakh/ m. dust; remains

прачечная /práchechnaia/ f. laundry; п. самообслуживания /p. samoobslúzhivaniia/ launderette

пребывание /prebyvánie/ n. stay

пребывать /prebyvát'/ v. be

превозмогать /prevozmogát'/ v. overcome

превозносить /prevoznosít'/ v. laud

превосходить /prevoskhodít'/ v. exceed, surpass

превосходный /prevoskhódnyi/ adj. superb

превосходство /prevoskhódstvo/ n. superiority

превратно /prevrátno/ adv. wrongly; понимать п. /ponimát' p./ misunderstand

превращать /prevrashchát'/ v. turn, change

превращение /prevrashchénie/ n. transformation

превышать /prevyshát'/ v. exceed

преграда /pregráda/ f. obstacle

преграждать /pregrazhdát'/ v. bar; block

предавать /predavát'/ v. betray

преданность /prédannost'/ f. devotion

предатель /predátel'/ m. betrayer

предательство /predátel'stvo/ n. treachery

предварительный /predvarítel'nyi/ adj. preliminary

предвестник /predvéstnik/ m. forerunner

предвзятый /predvziátyi/ adj. biased

предвидеть /predvídet'/ v. foresee

предводитель /predvodítel'/ m. leader, chief

предвосхищать /predvoskhishchát'/ v. anticipate

предгорье /predgór'e/ n. foothills

136

преддверие /preddvérie/ n. threshold
предел /predél/ m. limit
предельный /predél'nyi/ adj. maximum, limit
предисловие /predislóvie/ n. preface
предлагать /predlagát'/ v. offer; propose, suggest
предлог /predlóg/ m. pretext; exuse
предложение /predlozhénie/ n. suggestion; offer; sentence
предместье /predmést'e/ n. suburb
предмет /predmét/ m. object; thing; article; subject
предназначать /prednaznachát'/ v. destine; intend
преднамеренный /prednamérennyi/ adj. premeditated
предначертать /prednachertát'/ v. foreordain
предок /prédok/ m. ancestor
предоставлять /predostavliát'/ v. give; allow; grant
предостерегать /predosteregát'/ v. warn
предосторожность /predostorózhnost'/ f. precaution
предосудительный /predosudítel'nyi/ adj. reprehensible
предотвращать /predotvrashchát'/ v. prevent; avert
предотвращение /predotvrashchénie/ n. preventing
предохранение /predokhranénie/ n. protection (against)
предохранитель /predokhranítel'/ m. safety device
предохранять /predokhraniát'/ preserve (from); protect
предписание /predpisánie/ n. order
предписывать /predpísyvat'/ v. order
предплечье /predpléch'e/ n. forearm
предполагать /predpolagát'/ v. assume; suppose
предположительный /predpolozhítel'nyi/ adj. hypothetical

предпоследний /predposlédnii/ adj. last but one
предпосылка /predposýlka/ f. premiss; prerequisite
предпочитать /predpochitát'/ v. prefer
предприниматель /predprinimátel'/ m. employer; businessman
предпринимать /predprinimát'/ v. undertake
предрасполагать /predraspolagát'/ v. predispose (to)
предрассудок /predrassúdok/ m. prejudice
предрекать /predrekát'/ v. foretell
предрешать /predreshát'/ v. predetermine
председатель /predsedátel'/m. chairman
предсказывать /predskázyvat'/v. fortell; predict
представитель /predstavítel'/ m. representative; spokesman
представительство /predstavítel'stvo/n. representation; agency
представление /predstavlénie/ n. presentation; notion; idea; performance
представлять /predstavliát'/ v. present; produce; introduce
предстоять /predstoiát'/ v. lie ahead
предупреждать /preduprezhdát'/v. anticipate warn; give notice (of)
предупреждение /preduprezhdénie/ n. notice
предусматривать /predusmátrivat'/ v. foresee; provide for
предусмотрительный /predusmotrítel'nyi/ adj. prudent
предшественник /predshéstvennik/ m. predecessor; forerunner
предшествовать /predshéstvovat'/ v. precede
предъявитель /pred"iavítel'/ m. bearer (of note cheque)

пред.ъявлять /pred''iavliát'/ v. produce; present

предыдущий /predydúshchii/ adj. previous

преемник /preémnik/ m. successor

преемственность /preémstvennost'/ f. continuity

прежде /prézhde/ adv. formerly

преждевременный /prezhdevrémennyi/ adj. premature, early

прежний /prézhnii/ adj. former

президент //prezidént/ m. president

президиум /prezídium/ m. presidium

презирать /prezirát'/ v. despise

презрение /prezrénie/ n. contempt

презрительный /prezrítel'nyi/ adj. scornful

преимущество /preimúshchestvo/ n. advantage

прейскурант /preiskuránt/ m. price-list

преклонный (возраст) /preklónnyi vózrast/ adj.+m. old age

преклонять /prekloniát'/ v. bend

преклоняться /prekloniát'sia/ v. worship, revere

прекословить /prekoslóvit'/ v. contradict

прекрасный /prekrásnyi/ adj. beautiful, fine, lovely

прекращать /prekrashchát'/ v. stop; cease

прелестный /preléstnyi/ adj. charming

прельщать /prel'shchát'/ v. entice; attract

прелюбодеяние /preliubodeiánie/ n. adultery

прелюдия /preliúdiia/ f. prelude

премия /prémiia/ f. bonus

премудрый /premúdryi/ adj. wise

премьер /prem'ér/ m. prime minister, premier

премьера /prem'éra/ f. first night

пренебрегать /prenebregát'/ v. ignore; neglect

пренебрежительный /prenebrezhítel'nyi/ adj. scornful

прения /préniia/ pl. discussion; debate

преображать /preobrazhát'/ v. transform, transfigure

преодолевать /preodolevát'/ v. overcome, surmount

препарат /preparát/ m. preparation

препинание /prepinánie/ n. punctuation; знаки препинания /znáki prepinániia/ punctuation marks

преподаватель /prepodavátel'/ m. teacher

преподавать /prepodavát'/ v. teach

преподносить /prepodnosít'/ v. present

преподобный /prepodóbnyi/ adj. reverend

препровождать /preprovozhdát'/ v. escort; forward

препятствие /prepiátstvie/ n. obstacle; hindrance

препятствовать /prepiátstvovat'/ v. hinder; prevent

пререкаться /prerekát'sia/ v. altercate

прерывать /preryvát'/ v. interrupt; break

пресекать /presekát'/ v. stop; curb

преследовать /preslédovat'/ v. chase; persecute

пресловутый /preslovútyi/ adj. notorious

пресмыкаться /presmykát'sia/ v. cringe; kowtow

пресмыкающееся /presmykáiushcheesia/ n. reptile

пресноводный /presnovódnyi/ adj. freshwater

пресный /présnyi/ adj. fresh (water); unsalted; insipid

пресс /press/ m. press (tech.)

пресса /préssa/ f. the press

престарелый /prestarélyi/ adj. aged

престиж /prestízh/ m. prestige

престол /prestól/ m. throne

преступление /prestuplénie/ n. crime

преступник /prestúpnik/ m. criminal

пресыщенный /presýshchennyi/ adj. satiated; bloated

претворять /pretvoriát'/ v. convert; п.

планы в жизнь /p. plány v zhizn'/ carry out one's plans

претендент /pretendént/ m. pretender

претензия /preténziia/ f. claim; complaint

претерпевать /preterpevát'/ v. suffer; undergo (changes)

преувеличивать /preuvelíchivat'/ v. exaggerate; overstate

преуменьшать /preumen'shát'/ v. underestimate

преуспевать /preuspevát'/ v. succeed (in); prosper

прецедент /pretsedént/ m. precedent

при /pri/ prep. by; with; при всем том /pri vsióm tom/ for all that

прибавлять /pribabliát'/ v. add; increase

прибавочный /pribávochnyi/ adj. surplus

прибегать /pribegát'/ v. come running; resort (to)

прибежище /pribézhishche/ n. refuge

приберегать /priberegát'/ v. put by; reserve

прибивать /pribivát'/ v. nail

приближать /priblizhát'/ v. bring nearer

приближение /priblizhénie/ n. approach

приблизительный /priblizítel'nyi/ adj. rough

прибой /pribói/ m. surf

прибор /pribór/ m. device

прибрежный /pribrézhnyi/ adj. coastal

прибывать /pribyvát'/ v. arrive

прибыль /príbyl'/ f. profit

прибытие /pribýtie/ n. arrival

привал /privál/ m. halt; stop

приверженец /privérzhenets/ m. adherent

привет /privét/ m. greetings

приветливый /privétlivyi/ adj. amiable

приветственный /privétstvennyi/ adj. salutatory

приветствие /privétstvie/ n. welcoming address

приветствовать /privétstvovat'/ v. greet; welcome; salute

прививать /privivát'/ v. inoculate; implant

прививка /privívka/ f. vaccination

привидение /prividénie/ n. ghost

привилегия /privilégiia/ f. privilege

привинчивать /privínchivat'/ v. screw on (to)

привкус /prívkus/ m. after-taste; flavour

привлекательный /privlekátel'nyi/ adj. attractive

привлекать /privlekát'/ v. attract; draw

привод /privód/ m. drive

приводить /privodít'/ v. bring; lead

привозить /privozít'/ v. bring; import

привозной /privoznói/ adj. imported

привольный /privól'nyi/ adj. open; free

привораживать /privorázhivat'/ v. bewitch

привыкать /privykát'/ v. get accustomed (to)

привычка /privýchka/ f. habit

привычный /privýchnyi/ adj. habitual

привязанность /priviázannost'/ f. attachment

привязывать /priviázyvat'/ v. tie (to); fasten

пригвождать /prigvozhdát'/ v. pin (to)

пригибать /prigibát'/ v. bend down (to)

приглаживать /priglázhivat'/ v. smooth

приглашать /priglashát'/ v. invite

приглашение /priglashénie/ n. invitation

приглушать /priglushát'/ v. muffle; suppress

приговаривать /prigovárivat'/ v. condemn (to); keep on saying

приговор /prigovór/ m. sentence

пригодиться /prigodit''sia/ v. prove useful

пригодный /prigódnyi/ adj. suitable (for); fit

пригород /prígorod/ m. suburb

пригоршня /prígorshnia/ f. handful

пригорюниваться /prigoriúnivat'sia/ v. become sad

приготавливать /prigotávlivat'/ v. prepare; make

пригревать /prigrevát'/ v. warm

придавать /pridavát'/ v. add; give; attach

придавливать /pridávlivat'/ v. press down

приданое /pridánoe/ n. dowry

придача /pridácha/ f. giving adding; в придачу /v pridáchu/ in addition

придвигать /pridvigat'/ v. draw (up), move (up)

придворный /pridvórnyi/ adj. court

приделывать /pridélyvat'/ v. fix (to)

придерживаться /pridérzhivat'sia/ v. hold on; keep to; adhere

придираться /pridirát'sia/ v. find fault (with)

придирка /pridírka/ f. cavil

придорожный /pridorózhnyi/ adj. roadside

придумывать /pridúmyvat'/ v. invent; make up

приезд /priézd/ m. arrival

приезжать /priezzhát'/ v. arrive; come

приезжий /priézzhii/ m. newcomer

прием /priióm/ m. reception; admission; method

приемлемый /priémlemyi/ adj. acceptable

приемная /priiómnaia/ f. reception room

приемный /priiómnyi/ adj. reception; adopted; п. экзамен /p. ekzámen/ entrance examination; п. отец /p. otéts/ foster-father

приживаться /prizhivát'sia/ v. take root; settle down

прижигать /prizhigát'/ v. cauterize

прижимать /prizhimát'/ v. press; restrict; hold tight

приз /priz/ m. prize

приземистый /prizémistyi/ adj. stocky; low-built

приземление /prizemlénie/ n. landing

призма /prízma/ f. prism

признавать /priznavát'/ v. recognize; admit

признаваться /priznavát'sia/ v. confess (to)

признак /príznak/ m. sign

признательный /priznátel'nyi/ adj. grateful, thankful

призрак /prízrak/ m. ghost; spectre

призрачный /prízrachnyi/ adj. illusory; ghostly

призыв /prizýv/ m. call; appeal

призывать /prizyvát'/ v. call; appeal

прииск /priísk/ m. mine

приказ /prikáz/ m. order

приказывать /prikázyvat'/ v. order

прикалывать /prikályvat'/ v. pin; fasten

приканчивать /prikánchivat'/ v. finish off

прикарманивать /prikarmánivat'/ v. pocket

прикасаться /prikasát'sia/ v. touch

прикидывать /prikídyvat'/ v. estimate

приклад /priklád/ m. butt (of rifle)

прикладной /prikladnói/ adj. applied

прикладывать /prikládyvat'/ v. put (to), apply

приклеивать /prikléivat'/ v. stick, paste

приключаться /prikliuchát'sia/ v. occur; happen

приключение /prikliuchénie/ n. adventure

приковывать /prikóvyvat'/ v. chain

прикованный (к постели) /prikóvannyi k postéli/ adj.+prep.+f. bedridden

приколачивать /prikoláchivat'/ v. nail up

прикомандировывать /prikomandiróvyvat'/ v. attach (to)

прикосновение /prikosnovénie/ n. touch

прикрашивать /prikráshivat'/ v. embellish

прикреплять /prikrepliát'/ v. fasten; attach; register

прикрикивать /prikríkivat'/ v. raise one's voice (at)

прикрывать /prikryvát'/ v. cover; screen; half close

прикуривать /prikúrivat'/ v. get a light

прикусывать /prikúsyvat'/ bite; прикусить язык /prikusít' iazýk/ keep one's mouth shut; hold one's tongue

прилавок /prilávok/ m. counter

прилагательное /prilagátel'noe/ n. adjective

прилагать /prilagát'/ v. attach; devote

прилаживать /prilázhivat'/ v. fit

прилежный /prilézhnyi/ adj. diligent

прилеплять /prilepliát'/ v. stick (to)

прилет /priliót/ m. arrival

прилетать /priletát'/ v. arrive (by air); fly (in)

прилив /prilív/ m. rising tide

приливать /prilivát'/ v. flow (to)

приливный /prilívnyi/ adj. tidal

прилипать /prilipát'/ v. stick (to)

приличие /prilíchie/ n. decency

приличный /prilíchnyi/ adj. respectable; decent; passable

приложение /prilozhénie/ n. supplement

приманка /primánka/ f. bait

применение /primenénie/ n. use

применимый /primenímyi/ adj. applicable

применительно /primenítel'no/ adv. in conformity (with)

применять /primeniát'/ v. apply; use

пример /primér/ m. example; instance; model

примерка /primérka/ f. fitting

примерный /primérnyi/ adj. exemplary; approximate

примерять /primeriát'/ v. try on

примета /priméta/ f. sign

приметный /primétnyi/ adj. conspicuous

примечание /primechánie/ n. note

примечательный /primechátel'nyi/ adj. outstanding

примешивать /priméshivat'/ v. add, mix

приминать /priminát'/ trample down

примирение /primirénie/ n. conciliation

примирять /primiriát'/ v. reconcile

примитивный /primitívnyi/ adj. primitive

приморский /primórskii/ adj. seaside; maritime

примочка /primóchka/ f. lotion

примыкать /primykát'/ v. adjoin; border; side (with)

принадлежать /prinadlezhát'/ v. belong (to)

принадлежность /prinadlézhnost'/ f. article; accessory; membership

принижать /prinizhát'/ v. humiliate; belittle

принимать /prinimát'/ v. accept; receive; take over

приносить /prinosít'/ v. bring; carry

принудительный /prinudítel'nyi/ adj. compulsory

принуждать /prinuzhdát'/ v. force; compel

принцип /príntsip/ m. principle

принятие /priniátie/ n. acceptance

принятый /príniatyi/ adj. accepted

приободрять /priobodriát'/ v. hearten; encourage

приобретать /priobretát'/ v. acquire; gain

приодеть /priodét'/ v. smarten up; dress up

приостанавливать /priostanávlivat'/ v. check; hold up; stop

приоткрывать /priotkryvát'/ v. open slightly

припадок /pripádok/ m. fit, attack

припаивать /pripáivat'/ v. solder (to)

припасы /pripásy/ pl. supplies

припев /pripév/ m. refrain

приписывать /pripísyvat'/ v. add; register; ascribe

приплата /pripláta/ f. extra payment

приплывать /priplyvát'/ v. come swimming; sail up

приплясывать /pripliásyvat'/ v. jig up and down

приподнимать /pripodnimát'/ v. raise slightly

приподнятый /pripódniatyi/ elated; elevated

приползать /pripolzát'/ v. come crawling

припоминать /pripominát'/ v. recall

приправа /priprávа/ f. seasoning

приправлять /pripravliát'/ v. flavour, season

припрятывать /pripriátyvat'/ v. hide

припугивать /pripúgivat'/ v. scare

припухлость /pripúkhlost'/ f. swelling

приработок /prírabotok/ m. extra earnings

приравнивать /prirávnivat'/ v. equate (with)

прирезать /prirezát'/ v. cut the throat of; allot

природа /priróda/ f. nature

природный /priródnyi/ adj. natural; innate

прирожденный /prirozhdiónnyi/ adj. innate; born

прирост /priróst/ m. increase

приручать /priruchát'/ v. tame

присаживаться /prisázhivat'sia/ v. take a seat

присваивать /prisváivat'/ v. appropriate; confer

присвистывать /prisvístyvat'/ v. whistle

присвоение /prisvóenie/ n. appropriation; awarding

приседать /prisedát'/ v. squat

прискорбный /priskorbnyi/ adj. sorrowful; п. случай /p. sluchai/ sad occasion

прислонять /prisloniát'/ v. lean, rest (against)

прислуга /prislúga/ f. servant(s)

прислушиваться /prislúshivat'sia/ v. lend an ear (to); listen to

присматривать /prismátrivat'/ v. keep an eye on

присмотр /prismótr/ m. care; surveillance

присоединять /prisoediniát'/ v. joint; add; connect; annex

приспособление /prisposoblénie/ n. adjustment; device

приспособлять /prisposobliát'/ v. adapt

приставать /pristavát'/ v. stick to; pester

приставка /pristávka/ f. prefix

приставлять /pristavliát'/ v. put (against); lean (against)

пристальный /prístal'nyi/ adj. intent; fixed

пристань /prístan'/ f. pier

пристегивать /pristiógivat'/ v. fasten; button

пристойный /pristóinyi/ adj. decent, seemly

пристраивать /pristráivat'/ v.bild on (to)

пристрастие /pristrástie/ n. bent, passion

пристрастный /pristrástnyi/ adj. partial, biased

пристреливать /pristrélivat'/ v. shoot down

пристройка /pristróika/ f. annex; wing

приступ /prístup/ m. storm; attack, fit

приступать /pristupát'/ v. begin; start; approach

присуждать /prisuzhdát'/ v. sentence; award

присутствие /prisútstvie/ n. presence

присутствовать /prisútstvovat'/ v. be present

присущий /prisúshchii/ adj. inherent; intrinsic

присылать /prisylát'/ v. send

присыпка /prisýpka/ f. powder

присяга /prisiága/ f. oath

присягать /prisiagát'/ v. make an oath; swear

притаиться /pritaít'sia/ v. lurk

притворный /pritvórnyi/ adj. feigned

притворство /pritvórstvo/ n. sham

притворщик /pritvórshchik/ m. hypocrite; pretender

притворять /pritvoriát'/ v. shut

притворяться /pritvoriát'sia/ v. feign, simulate; pretend (to be)

притеснять /pritesniát'/ v. oppress

притихать /pritikhat'/ v. grow quiet

приток /pritók/ m. tributary; п. воздуха /p. vózdukha/ (in) flow of air

притолока /prítoloka/ f. lintel

притом /pritóm/ conj. besides

притон /pritón/ m. den

притопывать /pritópyvat'/ v. stamp; tap

притрагиваться /pritrágivat'sia/ v. touch

притуплять /pritupliát'/ v. blunt

притягательный /pritiagátel'nyi/ adj. attractive, magnetic

притягивать /pritiágivat'/ v. attract; pull

притязание /pritiázanie/ n. claim

приумножение /priumnozhénie/ n. increase

приуныть /priunýt'/ v. become sad

приурочивать /priuróchivat'/ v. time (smth.) to coincide; arrange

приучать /priuchát'/ v. accustom; train (to)

прихварывать /prikhváryvat'/ v. feel unwell

прихвостень /príkhvosten'/ m. toady

прихлопывать /prikhlópyvat'/ v. slap; slam; clap

приход /prikhód/ m. arrival; receipts; parish

приходить /prikhodít'/ v. come; arrive

приходовать /prikhódovat'/ v. credit

приходящий /prikhodiáshchii/ adj. nonresident

прихожая /prikhózhaia/ f. entrance hall, anteroom

прихорашивать /prikhoráshivat'/ v. smarten up

прихотливый /prikhotlívyi/ adj. capricious

прихоть /príkhot'/ f. whim, caprice

прихрамывать /prikhrámyvat'/ v. limp

прицеливаться /pritsélivat'sia/ v. take aim

прицеп /pritsép/ m. trailer

прицеплять /pritsepliát'/ v. couple (to); hook (to)

причал /prichál/ m. berth

причаливать /prichálivat'/ v. moor

причастие /prichástie/ n. the eucharist; participle

причастный /prichástnyi/ adj. involved, concerned (in)

причащать /prichashchát'/ v. give communion

причем /prichóm/ conj. moreover

прическа /prichóska/ f. hair-do

причесывать /prichósyvat'/ v. do smb.'s hair

причина /prichína/ f. cause; reason

причинять /prichiniát'/ v. cause; inflict

причислять /prichisliát'/ v. add; rank

причитать /prichitát'/ v. lament (over); moan

причитаться /prichitát'sia/ v. be due

причмокивать /prichmókivat'/ v. smack one's lips

причуда /prichúda/ f. whim; caprice

причудливый /prichúdlivyi/ adj. fanciful; whimsical

пришвартовывать /prishvartóvyvat'/ v. moor, make fast

пришелец /prishélets/ m. newcomer

пришествие /prishéstvie/ n. advent

пришивать /prishivát'/ v. sew (to)

пришлый /príshlyi/ adj. strange

пришпиливать /prishpílivat'/ v. pin

пришпоривать /prishpórivat'/ v. spur on

прищелкивать пальцами /prishchiólkivat' pál'tsami/ v.+pl. snap one's fingers

прищемлять /prishchemliát'/ v. nip; pinch

прищуривать /prishchúrivat'/ v. screw up (eyes)

приютить /priiutít'/ v. shelter

приязнь /priiázn/ f. amity

приятель /priiátel'/ m. friend

приятельский /priiátel'skii/ adj. friendly

приятный /priiátnyi/ adj. pleasant

про /pro/ prep. about

проба /próba/ f. test

пробег /probég/ m. run

пробегать /probegát'/ v. run; race

пробел /probél/ m. gap; blank

пробивать /probivát'/ v. make a hole; pierce

пробиться /probít'sia/ v. force one's way (through)

пробирка /probírka/ f. test-tube

пробка /probka/ f. cork; traffic jam; fuse (elrctr.)

проблема /probléma/ f. problem

пробный /próbnyi/ adj. trial; п. камень /p. kámen'/ touchstone

пробовать /próbovat'/ v. try; taste

пробоина /probóina/ f. hole; gap

пробор /probór/ m. parting (of the hair)

пробуждать /probuzhdát'/ v. (a)rouse; awaken

пробуждение /probuzhdénie/ n. awakening

пробуравливать /proburávlivat'/ v. bore; drill

пробыть /probýt'/ v. stay, be

провал /prován/ m. collapse; failure

проваливать /proválivat'/ v. fail (in exams); ruin; проваливай! /proválivai!/ be off!

проваривать /provárivat'/ v. boil thoroughly

проведывать /provédyvat'/ v. come to see; learn

проверка /provérka/ f. checking; inspection

проверять /proveriát'/ v. check; test; inspect

проветривать /provétrivat'/ v. air

провидение /providénie/ n. Providence

провиниться /provinít'sia/ v. be guilty (of)

провинциальный /provintsiál'nyi/ adj. provincial

провод /próvod/ m. wire; wiring

проводник /provodník/ m. conductor; guide

провожать /provozhát'/ v. see off

провозглашать /provozglashát'/ v. declare; proclaim

провозглашение /provozglashénie/ n. declaration

провозить /provozít'/ v. get through; carry

провокатор /provokátor/ m. agant provocateur

проволока /próvoloka/ f. wire

проворный /provórnyi/ adj. quick, brisk

провоцировать /provotsírovat'/ v. provoke (to)

прогибаться /progibát'sia/ v. sag

проглаживать /proglázhivat'/ v. iron

проглатывать /proglátyvat'/ v. swallow

проглядывать /progliádyvat'/ v. skim (through); break (through)

прогнивать /prognivát'/ v. rot to pieces

прогноз /prognóz/ m. forecast

прогонять /progoniát'/ v. drive away; banish

прогорать /progorát'/ v. burn down; go bankrupt

прогорклый /progórklyi/ adj. rank

программа /prográmma/ f. programme

прогревать /progrevát'/ v. heat; warm up

прогресс /progréss/ m. progress
прогуливать /progúlivat'/ v. miss work
прогуливаться /progúlivat'sia/ v. take a
stroll
прогулка /progúlka/ f. walk
продавать /prodavát'/ v. sell
продавец /prodavéts/ m. salesman
продавщица /prodavshchítsa/ f. sale-
woman
продвигать /prodvigát'/ v. move forward; promote push forward
продвигаться /prodvigát'sia/ v. advance;
get on; make progress
продевать /prodevát'/ v. put through
проделка /prodélka/ f. trick; swindle
продлевать /prodlevát'/ v. prolong
продление /prodlénie/ n. extension; prolongation
продовольствие /prodovól'stvie/n. foodstuffs; provisions
продолжать /prodolzhát'/ v. continue
продолжительный /prodolzhítel'nyi/
adj. long; protracted
продольный /prodól'nyi/ adj. lengthwise
продукт /prodúkt/ m. product; foodstuffs
продуктивный /produktívnyi/ adj. productive
продуктовый (магазин) /produktóvyi
magazín/ adj.+m. groceres
продукция /prodúktsiia/ f. output
проезд Ё/proézd/ m. passage, thoroughfare
проезжать /proezzhát'/ v. pass by; drive;
go through
проект /proékt/ m. project; design
проектировать /proektírovat'/ v. plan;
design
проекционный (аппарат) /proektsión-
nyi apparát/ adj.+m. projector
прожаривать /prozhárivat'/v. roast well;
fry well
прожевывать /prozhióvyvat'/ v. chew
well

прожектер /prozhektiór/ m. schemer
прожектор /prozhéktor/ m. searchlight
проживать /prozhivát'/ v. live; reside;
spend
прожилка /prozhílka/ f. vein
прожорливый /prozhórlivyi/ adj. voracious
проза /próza/ f. prose
прозаик /prozáik/ m. prose-writer
прозвище /prózvishche/ n. nickname
прозевать /prozevát'/ v. miss an opportunity
прозрачный /prozráchnyi/ adj. transparent
прозрение /prozrénie/ n. enlightement
прозябание /proziabánie/ n. vegetation
проигрыватель /proígryvatel'/ m.
record-player
проигрывать /proígryvat'/ v. lose
проигрыш /próigrysh/ m. loss; defeat
произведение /proizvedénie/ n. work
производительность /proizvodítel'-
nost'/ n. productivity
производить /proizvodít'/ v. make
производственный /proizvódstvennyi/
adj. industrial
производство /proizvódstvo/ n. production
произвол /proizvól/ m. tyranny
произвольный /proizvól'nyi/ adj. arbi-
trary
произносить /proiznosít'/ v. pronounce;
say
произношение /proiznoshénie/ n. pronunciation
произрастать /proizrastát'/ v. grow
происки /próiski/ pl. intrigues
проистекать /proistekát'/ v. result
происходить /proiskhodít'/v. occur, happen
происшествие /proisshéstvie/ n. incident; accident

прокаженный /prokazhónnyi/ adj. leprous; m. leper

прокалывать /prokályvat'/ v. pierce

прокапывать /prokápyvat'/ v. dig

прокат /prokát/ m. hire; rolling

прокисать /prokisat'/ v. turn sour

прокладка /prokládka/ f. laying

прокладывать /prokládyvat'/ v. build; lay; проложить себе дорогу /prolozhít' sébe dorógu/ make one's way

прокламация /proklamátsiia/ f. leaflet

проклинать /proklinat'/ v. curse

проклятие /prokliátie/ n. curse; damnation

проклятый /prokliátyi/ adj. accursed; damned

прокол /prokól/ m. puncture

прокрадываться /prokrádyvat'sia/ v. creep in (to)

прокурор /prokurór/ m. public prosecutor

проламывать /prolámyvat'/ v. break through; make a hole

пролегать /prolegát'/ v. pass; run across

пролежень /prólezhen'/ m. bedsore

пролезать /prolezát'/ v. climb through; worm oneself into

пролет /proliót/ m. flight (of stairs); span (of bridge)

пролетариат /proletariát/ m. proletariat

пролетать /proletát'/ v. fly (past); fly by

пролив /prolív/ m. strait(s)

проливать /prolivát'/ v. spill, shed

проливной (дождь) /prolivnói dozhd'/ adj.+m. downpour

пролог /prológ/ m. prologue

пролом /prolóm/ m. break

промасливать /promáslivat'/ v. grease

промах /prómakh/ m. miss

промачивать /promáchivat'/ v. wet; drench

промедление /promédlenie/ n. delay

промежуток /promézhutok/ m. interval

промежуточный /promezhútochnyi/ adj. intermediate

промоина /promóina/ f. hollow

промокательная (бумага) /promokátel'naia bumága/ adj.+f. blotting-paper

промокать /promokát'/ v. get wet

промтовары /promtováry/ pl. manufactured goods

промчаться /promchát'sia/ v. rush past

промывать /promyvát'/ v. wash thoroughly

промысел /prómysel/ m. trade

промышленник /promýshlennik/ m. industrialist

промышленность /promýshlennost'/ f. industry

пронзать /pronzát'/ v. transfix

пронзительный /pronzítel'nyi/ adj. piercing; shrilly

пронизывать /pronízyvat'/ v. pierce; permeate

проникать /pronikát'/ v. penetrate

проницательный /pronitsátel'nyi/ adj. acute; sharp; perspicacious

проносить /pronosit'/ v. carry through

проныра /pronýra/ m. and f. pusher

пронюхивать /proniúkhivat'/ v. nose out

прообраз /proóbraz/ m. prototype

пропаганда /propagánda/ f. propaganda

пропадать /propadát'/ v. be lost; perish; disappear

пропажа /propázha/ f. loss

пропалывать /propályvat'/ v. weed

пропасть /própast'/ f. precipice; f. abyss

пропащий /propáshchii/ adj. hopeless; п. человек /p. chelovék/ lost soul

пропекать /propekát'/ v. bake to a turn

пропивать /propivát'/ v. spend on drink

прописка /propíska/ f. registration; residence permit

прописывать /propísyvat'/ v. register; prescribe

пропитание /propitánie/ n. sustenance

пропитывать /propítyvat'/ v. saturate

пропихивать /propíkhivat'/ v. shove through

проплывать /proplyvát'/ v. swim (sail) past; drift

проповедник /propovédnik/ m. preacher

проповедовать /propovédovat'/ v. preach; expound

проповедь /própoved'/ f. sermon

прополаскивать /propoláskivat'/ v. rinse

проползать /propolzát'/ v. crawl

пропорция /propórtsiia/ f. proportion

пропуск /própusk/ m. pass (document)

пропускать /propuskát'/ v. let through; miss

прорез /proréz/ m. cut

прорезь /prórez'/ f. opening

прореха /prorékha/ f. rent

прорицать /proritsát'/ v. prophesy

пророк /prorók/ m. prophet

проронить /proronít'/ v. utter

пророческий /prorócheskii/ adj. prophetic

пророчество /proróchestvo/ n. prophecy

пророчить /proróchit'/ v. predict

прорубать /prorubát'/ v. cut through

прорубь /prórub'/ f. ice-hole

прорыв /prorýv/ m. breech; breakthrough

прорывать /proryvát'/ v. break through; tear; dig through

просачиваться /prosáchivat'sia/ v. seap out; leak out

просвет /prosvét/ m. opening; gap

просвечивать /prosvéchivat'/ v. X-ray; be transparent

просвещать /prosveshchát'/ v. enlighten; inform

просвещение /prosveshchénie/ n. entightenment; education

проседь /prósed'/ f. grey hair

просеивать /proséivat'/ v. sift

проселок /prosiólok/ m. country track, cart-track

проситель /prosítel'/ m. applicant

просить /prosít'/ v. ask; beg; request

проскакивать /proskákivat'/ v. rush by

прославлять /proslavliát'/ v. glorify

прослеживать /proslézhivat'/ v. trace

прослойка /proslóika/ f. layer

прослушивать /proslúshivat'/ v. listen; hear

просматривать /prosmátrivat'/ v. look through; glance through

просмотр /prosmótr/ m. examination; preview

просо /próso/ n. millet

проспаться /prospát'sia/ v. sleep oneself sober; have a good sleep

проспект /prospékt/ m. avenue; prospectus

просрочивать /prosróchivat'/ v. delay; exceed the time limit of

проставлять /prostavliát'/ v. put down, fill (in, out)

простаивать /prostáivat'/ v. stay; stand idle

простак /prosták/ m. simpleton

простегивать /prostiógivat'/ v. quilt

простенок /prosténok/ m. pier (between windows)

простирать /prostirát'/ v. stretch

простительный /prostítel'nyi/ adj. excusable

простоволосый /prostovolósyi/ adj. bare-headed

простодушие /prostodúshie/ n. simpleheartedness

простодушный /prostodúshnyi/ adj. artless, unsophisticated

простой /prostói/ adj. simple; common

простокваша /prostokvásha/ f. sour clotted milk

просторный /prostórnyi/ adj. spacious, roomy

пространный /prostránnyi/ adj. vast; lengthy

прострел /prostrél/ m. lumbago

простреливать /prostrélivat'/ v. shoot through

простуда /prostúda/ f. chill, cold

простужать /prostuzhát'/ v. let catch cold

проступать /prostupát'/ v. come through

проступок /prostúpok/ m. offence; misdemeanour

простывать /prostyvát'/ v. catch a chill

простыня /prostyniá/ f. sheet

просушивать /prosúshivat'/ v. dry

просчитываться /proschítyvat'sia/ v. miscalculate; blunder

просыпать /prosypát'/ v. spill

просыпаться /prosypát'sia/ v. wake up

просыхать /prosykhát'/ v. dry (up)

просьба /prós'ba/ f. request

проталкивать /protálkivat'/ v. push (through)

протаптывать /protáptyvat'/ v. tread (path)

протаскивать /protáskivat'/ v. pull through

протежировать /protezhírovat'/ v. pull strings for

протез /protéz/ m. artificial limb; зубной п. /zúbnoi p./ denture

протеин /protein/ m. protein

протекать /protekát'/ v. run; come through; leak

протекция /protéktsiia/ f. patronage, influence

протест /protést/ m. protest

протестант /protestánt/ m. Protestant

протестовать /protestovát'/ v. protest (against)

против /prótiv/ prep. opposite; against; contrary to

противиться /protívit'sia/ v. object; oppose

противник /protívnik/ m. opponent; enemy

противный /protívnyi/ adj. contrary; nasty

противозачаточное (средство) /protivozachátochnoe srédstvo/ adj.+n. contraceptive; противозачаточная пилюля /protivozachátochnaia piliúlia/ adj.+f. the pill

противоположность /protivopolózhnost'/ f. contrast; opposite

противоположный /protivopolózhnyi/ adj. opposite; contrary

противоречие /protivoréchie/ n. contradiction

противостоять /protivostoiát'/ v. oppose

противоядие /protivoiádie/ n. antidote

протирать /protirát'/ v. wear out; wipe, clean; rub through

протокол /protokól/ m. protocol

проточный /protóchnyi/ adj. flowing

протрезвляться /protrezvliát'sia/ v. get sober

протухать /protukhát'/ v. become rotten

протыкать /protykát'/ v. pierce

протягивать /protiágivat'/ v. extend; stretch

профан /profán/ m. ignoramus

профессионал /professionál/ m. professional

профессия /proféssiia/ f. profession

профессор /proféssor/ m. professor

профиль /prófil'/ m. profile

профсоюз /profsoiúz/ m. trade union

прохвост /prokhvóst/ m. scoundrel

прохладительный /prokhladítel'nyi/ adj. refreshing; soft (drink)

прохладный /prokhládnyi/ adj. cool; fresh

проход /prokhód/ m. passage

проходимец /prokhodímets/ m. rogue

проходить /prokhodít'/ v. go; pass (through, by)

прохожий /prokhózhii/ m. passer-by

процветать /protsvetát'/ v. flourish

процедура /protsedúra/ f. procedure

процеживать /protsézhivat'/ v. filter

процент /protsént/ m. percentage

процесс /protséss/ m. process; trial

процессия /protséssiia/ f. procession

прочерчивать /prochérchivat'/ v. draw

прочий /próchii/ adj. other

прочитывать /prochítyvat'/ v. read (through)

прочищать /prochishchát'/ v. clear out; clean

прочный /próchnyi/ adj. durable

прочтение /prochténie/ n. reading

прочь /proch/ adv. away; руки п.! /rúki p.!/ hands off!

прошедший /proshédshii/ adj. past; last

прошение /proshénie/ n. petition

прошивать /proshivát'/ v. stitch

прошлое /próshloe/ n. the past

прощай /proshchái/ interj. good-bye

прощальный /proshchál'nyi/ adj. farewell

прощать /proshchát'/ v. forgive

прощаться /proshchát'sia/ v. say goodbye (to)

прощение /proshchénie/ n. forgiveness

прощупывать /proshchúpyvat'/ v. feel; touch

проявлять /proiavliát'/ v. show, display; develop (phot.)

проясняться /proiasniát'sia/ v. clear (up); clarify

пруд /prud/ m. pond

пружина /pruzhína/ f. spring

прут /prut/ m. twig

прыгалка /prýgalka/ f. skipping rope

прыгать /prýgat'/ v. jump, leap; skip

прыскать /prýskat'/ v. sprinkle

прыщ /pryshch/ m. pimple

прядь /priád'/ f. lock (of hair)

пряжа /priázha/ f. yarn

пряжка /priázhka/ f. buckle

прялка /priálka/ f. spinning-wheel

прямо /priámo/ adv. straight

прямой /priámoi/ adj. straight; direct

прямоугольник /priamougól'nik/ m. rectangle

пряник /priánik/ m. gingerbread

пряность /priánost'/ f. spice

прясть /priást'/ v. spin

прятать /priatát'/ v. hide, conceal

прятки /priátki/ pl. hide-and-seek

псалом /psalóm/ m. psalm

псевдоним /psevdoním/ m. pseudonym

психиатр /psikhiátr/ m. psychiatrist

психопат /psikhopát/ m. psychopath

птенец /ptenéts/ m. fledgeling

птица /ptítsa/ f. bird

птицеводство /ptitsevódstvo/ n. poultry farming

публика /públika/ f. public; audience

публиковать /publikovát'/ v. publish

публичный /publíchnyi/ adj. public; п. дом /p. dom/ brothel

пугать /pugát'/ v. frighten, scare; alarm

пугливый /puglívyi/ adj. timorous; nervous

пуговица /púgovitsa/ f. button

пудель /púdel'/ m. poodle

пудинг /púding/ m. pudding

пудра /púdra/ f. powder

пудреница /púdrenitsa/ f. powder-case

пудрить /púdrit'/ v. powder

пузырь /puzýr'/ m. bubble

пук /puk/ m. bunch

пулемет /pulemiót/ m. machine-gun

пульверизатор /pul'verizátor/ m. spray

пульс /pul's/ m. pulse

пульт /pul't/ m. control panel

пуля /puliá/ f. bullet

пункт /punkt/ m. point; spot; item

пунктир /punktír/ m. dotted line

пунцовый /puntsóvyi/ adj. crimson

пунш /punsh/ m. punch

пуп(ок) /pup(ók)/ m. navel

пуповина /pupovína/ f. umbilical cord

пурпурный /purpúrnyi/ adj. purple

пуск /pusk/ m. start

пускать /puskát'/ v. let; set in motion; start

пустовать /pustovát'/ v. be empty

пустыня /pustýnia/ f. desert

пустяк /pustiák/ m. trifle

путаница /pútanitsa/ f. confusion

путать /pútat'/ v. tangle; mix up; confuse

путевка /putióvka/ f. pass

путеводитель /putevodítel'/ m. guide

путевой /putevói/ adj. travelling

путешественник /puteshéstvennik/ m. traveller

путешествие /puteshéstvie/ n. journey, voyage; trip

путешествовать /puteshéstvovat'/ v. travel; voyage; tour

путина /putína/ f. fishing season

путы /púty/ pl. fetters

путь /put'/ m. way; path; route; course

пух /pukh/ m. down

пухлый /púkhlyi/ adj. chubby

пухнуть /púkhnut'/ v. swell

пучеглазый /pucheglázyi/ adj. goggle-eyed

пучок /puchók/ m. bunch

пушистый /pushístyi/ adj. fluffy

пушка /púshka/ f. cannon; gun

пушнина /pushnína/ f. furs

пчела /pchelá/ f. bee

пчеловодство /pchelovódstvo/ n. bee-keeping

пшеница /pshenítsa/ f. wheat

пшено /pshenó/ n. millet

пылать /pylát'/ v. flame; blaze

пылесос /pylesós/ m. vacuum cleaner

пылинка /pýlinka/ f. speck of dust

пылить /pýlit'/ v. raise dust

пылкий /pýlkii/ adj. ardent

пыль /pyl'/ f. dust

пытать /pytát'/ v. torture; torment

пытливый /pýtlivyi/ adj. searching; curious; keen

пыхтеть /pykhtét'/ v. puff

пышка /pýshka/ f. doughnut; bun

пышный /pýshnyi/ adj. fluffy; thick; plump; luxuriant

пьедестал /p'edestál/ m. pedestal

пьеса /p'ésa/ f. play

пьянеть /p'ianét'/ v. be (get) drunk; get tipsy

пьяница /p'iánitsa/ m. and f. drunkard

пьянство /p'iánstvo/ n. drunkenness

пюре /piuré/ n. purée; картофельное п. /kartófel'noe p./ mashed potatoes

пятерка /piatiórka/ f. five; five-rouble note

пятиборье /piatibór'e/ n. fifth anniversary

пятилетие /piatilétie/ n. quinquennium

пятилетка /piatilétka/ f. five-year plan

пятиться /piátit'sia/ v. back away; retreat

пятиугольник /piatiugól'nik/ m. pentagon

пятка /piátka/ f. heel

пятнадцать /piatnádtsat'/ num. fifteen

пятнать /piatnát'/ v. spot

пятница /piátnitsa/ f. Friday

пятно /piatnó/ n. spot, stain; родимое п. /rodímoe p./ birth-mark

пять /piát'/ num. five

пятьдесят /piat'desiát/ num. fifty

пятьсот /piat'sót/ num. five hundred

Р

раб /rab/ m. slave

раболепие /rabolépie/ n. servility

работа /rabóta/ f. work; job

работать /rabótat'/ v. work; operate

работник /rabótnik/ m. worker

работодатель /rabotodátel'/ m. employer

работоспособный /rabotosposóbnyi/ adj. able-bodied

рабочий /rabóchii/ m. worker; adj. worker's, working

раввин /ravvín/ m. rabbi

равенство /rávenstvo/ n. equality

равнение /ravnénie/ n. dressing, alignment

равнина /ravnína/ f. plain

равно /ravnó/ adv. equally, alike; все р. /vsió r./ it's all the same

равновесие /ravnovésie/ n. balance

равнодушие /ravnodúshie/ n. indifference

равноправие /ravnoprávie/ n. equality

равный /rávnyi/ adj. equal

равнять /ravniát'/ v. even

радар /radár/ m. radar

ради /rádi/ prep. for the sake (of)

радиатор /radiátor/ m. radiator

радио /rádio/ n. radio

радиоактивный /radioaktívnyi/ adj. radioactive

радиовещание /radioveshchánie/ n. broadcasting

радиостанция /radiostántsiia/ f. radio station

радист /radíst/ m. wireless operator

радиус /rádius/ m. radius

радовать /rádovat'/ v. make happy

радоваться /rádovat'sia/ v. rejoice (at)

радостный /rádostnyi/ adj. joyful

радость /rádost'/ f. gladness; joy

радуга /ráduga/ f. rainbow

радушный /radúshnyi/ adj. cordial

раз /raz/ m. time; one; один р. /odin r./ once; два раза /dva ráza/ twice

разбавлять /razbavliát'/ v. dilute

разбалтывать /razbáltyvat'/ v. shake up; let out

разбег /razbég/ m. running start

разбегаться /razbegát'sia/ v. scatter; take one's run

разбивать /razbivát'/ v. break; smash; defeat

разбинтовывать /razbintóvyvat'/ v. unbandage

разбирать /razbirát'/ v. take to pieces; sort out; analyse

разбитый /razbítyi/ adj. broken; ruined; beaten

разбойник /razbóinik/ m. robber

разборный /razbórnyi/ adj. sectional (furniture)

разборчивый /razbórchivyi/ adj. legible; exacting; fastidious

разбрасывать /razbrásyvat'/ v. scatter

разброд /razbród/ m. confusion

разбухать /razbukhát'/ v. swell

разбушеваться /razbushevát'sia/ v. rage; get violent

разваливать /razválivat'/ v. pull down; wreck, ruin

разваливаться /razválivat'sia/ v. fall to pieces

развалина /razválina/ f. wreck; ruin

разваривать /razvárivat'/ v. boil soft

разве /rázve/ part. really; perhaps

разведенный /razvediónnyi/ adj. divorced

разведка /razvédka/ f. exploring; intelligence service; reconnaissance

разведчик /razvédchik/ m. secret service man; intelligence officer; explorer

развеивать /razvéivat'/ v. disperse, dispel, scatter

развенчивать /razvénchivat'/ v. destroy smb.'s prestige; deflate

развертывать /razviórtyvat'/ v. unfold; unwrap; display; turn round

развернутый /razviórnutyi/ adj. unfolded; detailed; full-scale

развесистый /razvésistyi/ adj. branchy

развешивать /razvéshivat'/ v. hang (out)

развивать /razvivát'/ v. develop

развинчивать /razvínchivat'/ v. unscrew

развитие /razvítie/ n. development

развитой /razvitói/ adj. developed; intelligent

развлекать /razvlekát'/ v. entertain

развод /razvód/ m. divorce

разводить /razvodít'/ v. part; divorce; dilute; breed

разводной (мост) /razvodnói most/ adj.+m. drawbridge; p. ключ /r.kliúch/ adjustable spanner

развозить /razvozít'/ v. drive; deliver

разворачивать /razvoráchivat'/ v. turn; unfold

разворот /razvorót/ m. turn

развращать /razvrashchát'/ v. corrupt

развязка /razviázka f. outcome

развязывать /razviázyvat'/untie; unleash (a war)

разгадка /razgádka/ f. clue

разгадывать /razgádyvat'/ v. solve

разгар /razgár/ m. peak; height

разгибать /razgibát'/ v. unbend, straighten

разглаживать /razglázhivat'/ v. smooth out; iron out

разглядывать /razgliádyvat'/ v. examine

разговаривать /razgovárivat'/ v. talk; speak

разговор /razgovór/ m. conversation; talk

разговорник /razgovórnik/ m. phrasebook

разговорный /razgovórnyi/ adj. colloquial

разговорчивый /razgovórchivyi/ adj. talkative

разгонять /razgoniát'/ disperse; drive away

разгораживать /razgorázhivat'/ v. partition

разгораться /razgorát'sia/ v. burn up; flare up

разграничивать /razgraníchivat'/ v. delimit; differentiate

разгребать /razgrebát'/ v. rake away

разгром /razgróm/ m. crushing; defeat; devastation

разгружать /razgruzhát'/ v. unload

разгул /razgúl/ m. orgy; debauch

разгуливать /razgúlivat'/ v. stroll about

раздавать /razdavát'/ v. give out

раздавливать /razdávlivat'/ v. crush

раздача /razdácha/ f. distribution

раздвигать /razdvigát'/ v. part; move apart

раздевалка /razdeválka/ f. cloakroom

раздевать /razdevát'/ v. undress; strip

раздел /razdél/ m. division; part

разделывать /razdélyvat'/ v. dress; cut

раздельный /razdél'nyi/ adj. separate

раздор /razdór/ m. discord

раздосадовать /razdosádovat'/ v. vex; annoy

раздражать /razdrazhát'/ v. irritate

раздроблять /razdrobliát'/ v. crush; disunite

раздувать /razduvát'/ v. fan; inflate

раздумывать /razdúmyvat'/ v. ponder; change one's mind

разевать /razevát'/ v. open wide

разжалобить /razzhálobit'/ v. move to pity

разжёвывать /razzhóvyvat'/ v. masticate; /coll./ spoon-feed

разжимать /razzhimát' v. part, unclench

разительный /razítel'nyi/adj. striking

разлагать /razlagát'/ v. decompose; demoralize

разлад /razlád/ m. discord

разламывать /razlámyvat'/ v. break

разлечься /razléch'sia/ v. stretch out

разливать /razlivát'/ v. spill; pour out

разливной /razlivnói/ adj. draught (beer)

разлиновывать /razlinóvyvat'/ v. rule

различать /razlichát'/ v. make out; distinguish

различие /razlíchie/ n. difference; distinction

разложение /razlozhénie/ decomposition; corruption

разлука /razlúka/ f. separation; parting

разлюбить /razliubít'/ v. cease to love (to care for)

размазывать /razmázyvat'/ v. spread

размалывать /razmályvat'/ v. grind
разматывать /razmátyvat'/ v. unwind
размах /razmákh/ m. scope
размахивать /razmákhivat'/ v. brandish;
р. руками /r. rukámi/ wave one's hands
about
размачивать /razmáchivat'/ v. soak
разменивать /razménivat'/ v. change
(money)
размер /razmér/ m. size
размешивать /razméshivat'/ v. stir
размещать /razmeshchát'/ v. accommodate; place
разминать /razminát'/ v. stretch (one's
legs); mash
разминка /razmínka/ f. warming up; workout
разминуться /razminút'sia/ v. miss one
another
размножать /razmnozhát'/ v. make copies; multiply
размножение /razmnozhénie/ n. reproduction
размолвка /razmólvka/ f. misunderstanding
размораживать /razmorázhivat'/ v. defrost
размывать /razmyvát'/ v. wash away
размыкать /razmykát'/ v. open; disconnect
размягчать /razmiagchát'/ v. soften
разнашивать /raznáshivat'/ v. wear in
(make comfortable)
разнимать /raznimát'/ v. part, separate;
disjoint
разниться /raznít'sia/ v. differ
разница /ráznitsa/ f. difference
разногласие /raznoglásie/ n. dissension;
disagreement
разнообразие /raznoobrázie/ n. variety;
diversity
разносить /raznosít'/ v. deliver; scold

разносторонний /raznostorónnii/ adj.
versatile; many-sided
разносчик /raznóschik/ m. hawker
разноцветный /raznotsvétnyi/ adj. variegated; multi-coloured
разнузданный /raznúzdannyi/ adj. unbridled; wild
разный /ráznyi/ adj. different; varied
разнюхивать /razniúkhivat'/ v. smell out
разоблачать /razoblachát'/ v. expose
разобщать /razobshchát'/ v. separate; dissociate
разогревать /razogrevát'/ v. heat up;
warm up
разодеть /razodét'/ v. dress up
разорение /razorénie/ n. ruin; devastation
разоружать /razoruzhát'/ v. disarm
разорять /razoriát'/ v. ravage; ruin
разочаровывать /razocharóvyvat'/ v. disappoint; disillusion
разрабатывать /razrabátyvat'/ v. prepare;
work out; develop
разработка /razrabótka/ f. working out,
elaboration
разражаться /razrazhát'sia/ v. burst (out)
разрез /razréz/ m. cut
разрезать /razrezát'/ v. cut
разрешать /razreshát'/ v. allow; permit;
let
разрешение /razreshénie/ v. permission
разрозненный /razróznennyi/ adj. odd;
isolated
разрубать /razrubát'/ v. split; chop
разруха /razrúkha/ f. disruption
разрушать /razrushát'/ v. destroy; demolish; ruin, wreck
разрыв /razrýv/ m. break; rupture
разрывать /razryvát'/ v. tear up; slit;
break off
разрыдаться /razrydát'sia/ v. burst into
tears
разрыхлять /razrykhliát'/ v. loosen; hoe
разряд /razriád/ m. grade; type; category
разрядка /razriádka/ f. detente

разубеждать /razubezhdát'/ v. dissuade
разувать /razuvát'/ v. remove shoes off
разузнавать /razuznavát'/ v. find out
разукрашивать /razukráshivat'/ v. decorate, embellish
разум /rázum/ m. reason; mind
разучивать /razúchivat'/ v. learn
разъедать /raz''edát'/ v. corrode
разъединять /raz''ediniát'/ v. separate; disconnect
разъезд /raz''ézd/ m. railway siding; departure
разъездной /raz''ezdnói/ adj. travelling
разъярять /raz''iariát'/ v. infuriate
разъяснение /raz''iasnénie/ n. explanation
разъяснять /raz''iasniát'/ v. elucidate; make clear
разыгрывать /razýgryvat'/ v. raffle; play a trick on
разыскивать /razýskivat'/ v. look for; search
рай /rai/ m. paradise
район /raión/ m. region; district; area
райский /ráiskii/ adj. heavenly
райсовет /raisovét/ m. district Soviet
рак /rak/ m. crayfish; cancer
ракета /rakéta/ f. rocket
ракетка /rakétka/ f. racket; bat
раковина /rákovina/ f. shell; sink
ракушка /rákushka/ f. mussel
рамка /rámka/ f. frame; framework
рампа /rámpa/ f. footlights
рана /rána/ f. wound
ранг /rang/ m. rank
ранее /ránee/ adv. earlier
ранец /ránets/ m. haversack; satchel
ранить /ránit'/ v. wound; injure
ранний /ránnii/ adj. early
раньше /rán'she/ adv. earlier
рапира /rapíra/ f. foil
рапортовать /raportovát'/ v. report
раса /rása/ f. race
расизм /rasízm/ m. racism

раскаиваться /raskáivat'sia/ repent
раскалывать /raskályvat'/ v. split
раскапывать /raskápyvat'/ v. excavate
раскачивать /raskáchivat'/ v. rock
раскаяние /raskáianie/ n. repentance
расквитаться /raskvitát'sia/ v. settle accounts (with)
раскладной /raskladnói/ adj. folding
раскладывать /raskládyvat'/ v. lay out
раскол /raskól/ m. split
раскосый /raskósyi/ adj. slanting
раскраивать /raskráivat'/ v. cut out
раскрашивать /raskráshivat'/ v. paint
раскрепощать /raskreposhchát'/ v. emancipate
раскручивать /raskrúchivat'/ v. untwist
раскрывать /raskryvát'/ v. open; expose; reveal
раскупать /raskupát'/ v. buy up
распад /raspád/ m. disintegration; decay
распаковывать /raspakóvyvat'/ v. unpack
распарывать /raspáryvat'/ v. rip
распахивать /raspákhivat'/ v. plough up; throw open
распашонка /raspashónka/ f. baby's vest
распечатывать /raspechátyvat'/ v. unseal
распиливать /raspílivat'/ v. saw up
расписание /raspisánie/ n. time-table
расписка /raspíska/ f. receipt
расписывать /raspísyvat'/ v. decorate; assign
расписываться /raspísyvat'sia/ v. sign; register one's marriage
расплакаться /rasplákat'sia/ v. burst into tears
расплата /respláta/ f. payment; punishment
расплачиваться /raspláchivat'sia/ v. pay
расплетать /raspletát'/ v. untwist; unplait
располагать /raspolagát'/ v. arrange; dispose
располагаться /raspolagát'sia/ v. make oneself comfortable; be situated

распорядитель /rasporiadítel'/ m. manager, organizer

распорядок /rasporiádok/ m. routine; order

распоряжение / rasporiazhénie/ n. instruction; order

расправа /raspráva/ f. reprisals

расправлять /raspravliát'/ v. smooth out; straighten

расправляться /raspravliát'sia/ v. smooth out; deal with

распределение /raspredelénie/ v. distribution; allocation

распределять /raspredeliát'/ v. distribute; allocate; assign

распродавать /rasprodavát'/ v. sell out

распродажа /rasprodázha/ f. sale

распространять /rasprostraniát'/ v. spread, distribute

распрягать /raspriagát'/ v. unharness

распрямлять /raspriamliát'/ v. straighten

распускать /raspuskát'/ v. dissollve; dismiss; undo

распутывать /raspútyvat'/ v. unravel

распылять /raspyliát'/ v. powder; disperse; spray

распятие /raspiátie/ n. crucifix; crucifixion

рассада /rassáda/ v. seedlings

рассадник /rassádnik/ m. breeding-ground

рассаживать /rassázhivat'/ v. seat

рассвет /rassvét/ m. dawn

рассеивать /rasséivat'/ v. scatter; disperse; divert

рассекать /rassekát'/ v. cleave; cut

рассеянный /rasséiannyi/ adj. absent-minded

рассказ /rasskáz/ m. story, tale

рассказчик /rasskázchik/ m. narrator

рассказывать /rasskázyvat'/ v. tell; narrate

расслаблять /rasslabliát'/ v. weaken

расследование /rasslédovanie/ n. inquest

расследовать /rasslédovat'/ v. investigate; inquire

расслышать /rasslýshat'/ v. catch, hear

рассматривать /rassmátrivat'/ v. regard; look at; examine; consider

рассмеяться /rassmeiát'sia/ v. burst out laughing

рассмотрение /rassmotrénie/ n. examination; consideration; scrutiny

рассорить /rassórit'/ v. set at variance

рассортировывать /rassortiróvyvat'/ v. sort out; classify

расспрашивать /rasspráshivat'/ v. question; make enquiries

рассрочка /rassróchka/ f. instalment; купить в рассрочку /kupít' v rassrochku/ buy in instalments

расставаться /rasstavát'sia/ v. part (with); quit

расставлять /rasstavliát'/ v. place; arrange

расстегивать /rasstiógivat'/ v. undo; unfasten

расстилать /rasstilát'/ v. spread

расстояние /rasstoiánie/ n. distance

расстраивать /rasstráivat'/ v. disogranize; upset

расстреливать /rasstrélivat'/ v. shoot

рассудительный /rassuditel'nyi/ adj. sober-minded; rational

рассудить /rassudít'/ v. judge; decide

рассудок /rassúdok/ m. reason

рассуждение /rassuzhdénie/ n. reasoning

рассчитывать /rasschítyvat'/ v. calculate; count (on), plan

рассыльный /rassýl'nyi/ m. errand-boy

рассыпать /rassypát'/ v. spill

расталкивать /rastálkivat'/ v. push apart

растапливать /rastáplivat'/ v. kindle; melt

раствор /rastvór/ m. solution

растворять /rastvoriát'/ v. dissolve; open

растение /rasténie/ n. plant

растерянный /rastériannyi/ adj. bewildered; confused
растерять /rasteriát'/ v. lose
расти /rastí/ v. grow (up); increase
растирать /rastirát'/ v. grind; rub
растительность /rastítel'nost'/ f. vegetation; hair
растительный /rastítel'nyi/ adj. vegetable
растить /rastít'/ v. raise; grow
растлевать /rastlevát'/ v. seduce; corrupt
растолковывать /rastolkóvyvat'/ v. explain
растопыривать /rastopýrivat'/ v. spread wide
расторгать /rastorgát'/ v. cancel
расточать /rastochát'/ v. squander; lavish, shower
расточительный /rastochítel'nyi/ adj. extravagant
растрата /rastráta/ f. embezzlement
растрачивать /rastráchivat'/ v. waste; squander
растрепать /rastrepát'/ v. disarrange; tousle
растрепанный /rastrićpannyi/ adj. tattered
растрескиваться /rastréskivat'sia/ v. crack
растрогать /rastrógat'/ v. touch
растущий /rastúschii/ adj. growing
растягивать /rastiágivat'/ v. stretch; strain
расфасовывать /rasfasóvyvat'/ v. pack
расформировывать /rasformiróvyvat'/ v. disband
расхватывать /raskhvátyvat'/ v. snatch; /coll./ buy up
расхититель /raskhitítel/ m. plunderer
расход /raskhód/ m. expense(s); expenditure; consumption

расходиться /raskhodít'sia/ v. disperse; miss; pass; separate
расцвет /rastsvét'/ m. blooming; flourishing
расцветать /rastsvetát'/ v. bloom; flourish
расценивать /rastsénivat'/ v. estimate; value
расценка /rastsénka/ f. valuation; price
расцеплять /rastseplíat'/ v. unhook
расческа /raschóska/ f. comb.
расчет /raschót/ m. calculation; settling (of bill)
расчетливый /raschótlivyi/ adj. prudnt; thrifty
расчищать /raschishchát'/ v. clear
расшатывать /rasshátyvat'/ shake ; loose; undermine
расшибать /rasshibát'/ v. hurt; smash
расшивать /rasshivát'/ v. unpick; embroider
расширение /rasshirénie/ n. expansion
расширять /rasshiriát'/ v. widen; broaden; expand
расшифровывать /rasshifróvyvat'/ v. decipher
расшнуровывать /rasshnuróvyvat'/ v. unlace
расщепление /rasshcheplénie/ n. disintegration; fission
расщеплять /rasshchepliát'/ v. split
ратификация /ratifikátsiia/ f. ratification
ратифицироватьЁ /ratifitsírovat'/ v. ratify
ратуша /rátusha/ f. town hall
раунд /ráund/ m. round (sport)
рафинад /rafinád/ m. lump sugar
рахит /rakhít/ m. rickets
рационализировать /ratsionalizírovat'/ v. rationalize
рация /rátsiia/ f. portable radio
рвануть /rvanút'/ v. dash
рвота /rvóta/ f. vomiting

реабилитировать /reabilitírovat'/ v. rehabilitate

реагировать /reagírovat'/ react (to); respond

реактивный /reaktívnyi/ adj. jet

реактор /reáktor/ m. reactor

реакционер /reaktsionér/ m. reactionary

реализм /realízm/ m. realism

реальный /reál'nyi/ adj. real; actual

ребёнок /rebiónok/ m. child; baby; infant

ребро /rebró/ n. rib

ребяческий /rebiácheskii/ adj. childish

рев /riov/ m. roar реванш /revánsh/ m. revenge

ревень /revén'/ m. rhubarb

реверанс /reveráns/ m. curtsy

реветь /revét'/ v. roar; howl

ревизионизм /revizionízm/ m. revisionism

ревизия /revíziia/ f. revision

ревизор /revizór/ m. inspector

ревматизм /revmatízm/ m. rheumatism

ревновать /revnovát'/ v. be jealous

револьвер /revol'vér/ m. revolver

революционер /revoliutsionér/ m. revolutionary

регент /régent/ m. regent

регистратура /registratúra/ f. registry

регистрация /registrátsiia/ f. registration

регистрировать /registrírovat'/ v. register; record

регламент /regláment/ m. regulations; time-limie

регулировать /regulírovat'/ v. regulate; control

регулировщик /reguliróvshchik/ m. (traffic) controller

регулярный /reguliárnyi/ adj. regular

редактировать /redaktírovat'/ v. edit

редактор /redáktor/ m. editor

редакция /redáktsiia/ f. editorial office; editorship

редиска /redíska/ f. radish

редкий /rédkii/ adj. thin; rare

редкость /redkóst'/ f. rarity; curiosity

редька /réd'ka/ f. (black) radish

режим /rezhím/ m. regime

режиссер /rezhissiór/ m. producer

резать /rézat'/ v. cut

резвиться /rezvít'sia/ v. frolic; frisk about

резерв /rezérv/ m. reserve(s)

резервуар /rezervuár/ m. reservoir; tank

резец /rézets/ m. cutter

резиденция /rezidéntsia/ f. residence

резина /rezína/ f. rubber

резинка /rezínka/ f. eraser

резкий /rézkii/ adj. sharp; harsh

резной /reznói/ adj. carved

резня /rezniá/ f. carnage; massacre

резолюция /rezoliútsiia/ f. resolution

резонанс /rezonáns/ m. resonance

результат /rezul'tát/ m. result

резчик /rézchik/ m. engraver; carver

резь /rez'/ f. colic

резюмировать /reziumírovat'/ v. sum up

рейд /réid/ m. raid

рейс /réis/ m. trip; voyage

рейсфедер /reisféder/ m. drawing-pen

рейтузы /reitúzy/ (riding) pants

река /reká/ f. river

реклама /rekláma/ f. advertisement

рекламировать /reklamírovat'/ v. advertise

рекомендация /rekomendátsiia/ f. reference

рекомендовать /rekomendovát'/ v. recommend

реконструировать /rekonstruírovat'/ v. reconstruct

рекорд /rekórd/ m. record

рекордсмен /rekordsmén/ m. record-holder

ректор /réktor/ m. rector, chancellor (of university)

религиозный /religióznyi/ adj. religious; pious

религия /relígiia/ f. religion

реликвия /relíkviia/ f. relic
рельеф /rel'éf/ m. relief
ремень /remén'/m.`belt; p. безопасности
/r. bezopásnosti/ lapbelt; safety belt
ремесленник /reméslennik/m. craftsman
ремесло /remesló/ n. trade
ремешок /remeshók/ m. strap
ремонт /remónt/ m. repair(s)
ремонтировать /remontírovat'/ v. repair;
decorate
ремонтная (мастерская) /remóntnaia
masterskáia/ adj. + f. repair shop
рента /rénta/ f. rent; income (from capital)
рентабельный /rentábel'nyi/ adj. paying
рентген /rentgén/ m. X-ray
реорганизовать /reorganizovát'/v. reor-
ganize
репа /répa/ f. turnip
репарация /reparátsiia/ f. reparation
репатриировать /repatriírovat'/ v. repatriate
репертуар /repertuár/ m. repertoire
репетировать /repetírovat'/ v. rehearse
репетиция /repetítsiia/ f. rehearsal
репортер /reportiór/ m. reporter
репрессия /représiia/ f. repression
репродуктор /reprodúktor/ m. loudspeaker
репутация /reputátsiia/ f. reputation
ресница /resnítsa/ f. eyelash
республика /respúblika/ f. republic
республиканец /respublikánets/ m. republican
рессора /ressóra/ f. spring
реставрация /restavrátsiia/ f. restoration
реставрировать /restavrírovat'/v. restore
ресторан /restorán/ m. restaurant
ресурс /resúrs/ m. resource
ретушировать /retushírovat'/ v. retouch
реформа /refórma/ f. reform
реформатор /reformátor/ m. reformer
рефрижератор /refrizherátor/ m. refrigerator

рецензировать /retsenzírovat'/ v. review
рецепт /retsépt/ m. prescription; recipe
речка /réchka/ f. stream
речь /rech/ f. speech; talk
решать /reshát'/ v. decide; resolve
решетка /reshótka/ f. grating; bars
решимость /reshímost'/ f. determination
решительный /reshítel'nyi/ adj. resolute
решка (орел или р.) /oriól íli réshka?/
heads or tails?
ржаветь /rzhavét'/ v. rust
ржаной /rzhanói/ adj. rye
ржать /rzhat'/ v. neigh
риза /ríza/ f. chasuble
ризница /ríznitsa/ f. vestry
римлянин /rímlianin/ m. Roman
римлянка /rímlianka/ f. Roman
римский /rímskii/ adj. Roman
рис /ris/ m. rice
риск /risk/ m. risk;
рискнуть /risknút'/ v. take a risk; venture
рисовальщик / risovál'shchik/ m. designer
рисовать /risovát'/ draw; paint
рисунок /risúnok/ m. drawing
ритм /ritm/ m. rhythm
ритмический /ritmícheskii/ adj. rhyth-
mic(al)
риф /rif/ m. reef
рифма /rífma/ f. rhyme
робеть /robét'/ v. be timid
робкий /róbkii/ adj. shy
ров /rov/ m. ditch
ровесник /rovésnik/ m. person of the same age
ровный /róvnyi/ adj. even; level; smooth;
straight
ровнять /rovniát'/ v. level off
рог /rog/ m. horn
рогатка /rogátka/ f. turnpike; catapult
роговица /rogovítsa/ f. cornea
рогожа /rogózha/ f. bast mat

род /rod/ m. family; kin; gender; p.
человеческий /r. chelovécheskii/ mankind
родильный (дом) /rodíl'nyi dom/ adj. +
m. maternity home
родимый /rodímyi/ adj. (of) birth
родина /ródina/ f. homeland
родинка /ródinka/ f. birthmark
родители /rodíteli/ pl. parents
родить /rodít'/ v. give birth to
родиться /rodít'sia/ v. be born
родник /rodník/ m. spring
родной /rodnói/ adj. native
родня /rodniá/ j. relative(s); relations
родоначальник /rodonachál'nik/ m. forefather
родословная /rodoslóvnaia/f. genealogy; pedigree
родственник /ródstvennik/ m. relative
родственный /ródstvennyi/ adj. related
родство /rodstvó/ n. relationship
роды /ródy/ pl. childbirth; labour
рожать /rozhát'/ v. give birth to
рождаемость /rozhdáemost'/ f. birthrate
рождение /rozhdénie/ n. birth; день
рождения /den' rozhdéniia/ birthday
рождество /rozhdestvó/ n. Christmas
рожь /rozh/ f. rye
роза /róza/ f. rose
розетка /rozétka/ f. electric socket
розничная (торговля) /róznichnaia torgóvlia/ adj. + f. retail trade
розовый /rózovyi/ adj. pink
розыгрыш /rózygrysh/ m. draw
розыск /rózysk/ m. search
ролик /rólik/ m. roller; кататься на
роликах /katát'sia na rólikakh/ go roller-skating
роль /rol'/ f. role; part
ром /rom/ m. rum
роман /román/ m. novel; bove-affair
романист /romaníst/ m. novelist
романс /románs/ m. romance
ромашка /romáshka/ f. camomile

ронять /roniát'/ v. drop
роса /rosá/ f. dew
роскошный /roskóshnyi/ adj. luxurious
российский /rossíiskii/ adj. Russian
рост /rost/ m. growth; height
ростбиф /róstbif/ m. roast beef
ростовщик /rostovshchík/ m. money-lender
росток /rostók/ m. sprout; shoot
рот /rot/ m. mouth
рота /róta/ f. company
роща /róshcha/ f. grove
рояль /roiál'/ m. grand piano
ртуть /rtut'/ f. mercury
рубанок /rubánok/ m. plane
рубашка /rubáshka/ f. shirt
рубеж /rubézh/ m. boundary; за рубежом /za rubezhóm/ abroad
рубец /rubéts/ m. scar
рубин /rubín/ m. ruby
рубить /rubít'/ v. chop; fell
рубка /rúbka/ f. felling; deckcabin
рубленый /rúblenyi/ adj. minced
рубль /rubl'/ m. rouble
ругань /rúgan'/ f. foul language
ругательный /rugátel'nyi/ adj. abusive
ругательство /rugátel'stvo/ n. curse
ругать /rugát'/ v. abuse
руда /rudá/ f. ore
рудник /rudník/ m. mine
ружейный /ruzhéinyi/ adj. rifle
ружье /ruzh'ió/ n. gun
руина /ruína/ f. ruin
рука /ruká/ f. hand; arm
рукав /rukáv/ m. sleeve
рукавица /rukavítsa/ f. mitten
руководитель /rukovodítel'/ m. leader; head
руководить /rukovodít'/ v. lead; direct; head; guide
рукоделие /rukodélie/ n. needlework
рукоятка /rukoiátka/ f. handle
рулет (мясной p.) /miasnói rulét/ adj.+m. beef-roll, meat loaf

рулетка /rulétka/ f. roulette

руль /rul'/ m. steering-wheel

румын /rumýn/ m. Rumanian

румынка /rumýnka/ f. Rumanian

румынский /rumýnskii/ adj. Rumanian

румяна /rumiána/ pl.rouge

румяный /rumiányi/ adj. rosy, ruddy

рупор /rúpor/ m. mouthpiece

русалка /rusálka/ f. mermaid

русский /rússkii/ adj. Russian

русый /rúsyi/ adj. liagt brown

рухлядь /rúkhliad'/ f. junk

ручательство /ruchátel'stvo/ n. guarantee

ручаться /ruchát'sia/ v. answer (for); vouch (for)

ручей /ruchéi/ m. brook

ручка /rúchka/ f. pen

рыба /rýba/ f. fish

рыбак /rybák/ m. fisherman

рыжий /rýzhii/ adj. red, red-haired

рынок /rýnok/ m. market

рысак /rysák/ m. trotter

рысь /rys'/ f. lynx; trot

рытвина /rýtvina/ f. rut

рыть /ryt'/ v. dig

рыхлить /rykhlít'/ v. loosen

рыцарский /rýtsarskii/ adj. chivalrous

рыцарь /rýtsar'/ m. knight

рычаг /rychág/ m. lever

рычать /rychát'/ v. growl

рюкзак /riukzák/ m. rucksack

рюмка /riúmka/ f. wineglass

рябина /riabína/ f. rowan

рябиновка /riabínovka/ rowan-berry brandy

рябой /riabói/ adj. pock-marked

рявкать /riavkat'/ v. bellow

ряд /riad/ m. row; lane

рядовой /riadovói/ adj. ordinary; m. private (soldier)

рядом /riádom/ adv. side by side; close by

ряса /riása/ f. cassock

С

с /s/ prep. with

сабля /sáblia/ f. sabre

саботаж /sabotázh/ m. sabotage

сад /sad/ m. garden

садиться /sadít'sia/ v. sit down

садовник /sadóvnik/ m. gardener

сажа /sázha/ f. soot

сажать /sazhát'/ v. seat; land; put under arrest

саженец /sázhenets/ m. seedling

сазан /sazán/ m. carp

саквояж /sakvoiázh/ m. travelling bag

салазки /salázki/ pl. toboggan

салака /saláka/ f. sprat

саламандра /salamándra/ f. salamander

салат /salát/ m. salad

сало /sálo/ n. fat; lard

салон /salón/ m. saloon

салфетка /salfétka/ f. napkin

салют /saliút/ m. salute

сам /sam/ pron. himself

сама /samá/ pron. herself

сами /sámi/ pron. ourselves, yourselves, themselves

само /samó/ pron. itself

самец /saméts/ m. male

самка /sámka/ f. female

самобытный /samobýtnyi/ adj. original

самовар /samovár/ m. samovar

самовластный /samovlástnyi/ adj. despotic

самовольный /samovól'nyi/ adj. unauthorized

самодвижущийся /samodvízhushchiisia/ adj. self-propelled

самодельный /samodél'nyi/ adj. homemade

самодержавие /samoderzhávie/ n. autocracy

самодовольный /samodovól'nyi/ adj. self-satisfied, complacent самозащита /samozashchíta/ f. self-defence

самозванец /samozvánets/ m. impostor; pretender

самокат /samokát/ m. scooter

самолет /samoliót/ m. aircraft, plane

самолюбивый /samoliubívyi/ adj. proud, touchy

самомнение /samomnénie/ n. self-importance

самонадеянный /samonadéiannyi/ adj. presumptuous

самообладание /samoobladánie/ n. self-control

самообслуживание /samoobslúzhivanie/ n. self-service

самоопределение /samoopredelénie/ n. self-determination

самоотверженный /samootvérzhennyi/ adj. selfless

самопожертвование /samopozhértvovanie/ n. self-sacrifice

самородок /samoródok/ n. nugget

самосвал /samosvál/ m. tip-up lerry

самосохранение /samosokhranénie/ n. self-preservation

самостоятельный /samostoiátel'nyi/ adj. independent

самосуд /samosúd/ m. lynch law

самотек /samotiók/ m. drift; самотеком /samotiókom/ of one' own accord

самоубийство /samoubíistvo/ n. suicide

самоуважение /samouvazhénie/ n. self-respect

самоуверенный /samouvérennyi/ adj. self-confident

самоуправление /samoupravlénie/ n. self-government

самоучитель /samouchítel'/ m. teach-yourself manual

самоцвет /samotsvét/ m. semi-precious stone

самшит /samshít/ m. box

самый /sámyi/ pron. (the) very; (the) same; (the) most

санаторий /sanatórii/ m. sanatorium

сандал /sandál/ m. sandal - wood

сандалии /sandálii/ pl. sandals

сани /sáni/ pl. sledge

санитар /sanitár/ m. medical orderly

санкционировать /sanktsionírovat'/ v. sanction

сантиметр /santimétr/ m. centimetre

сапер /sapiór/ m. sapper

сапог /sapóg/ m. boot; top- boot

сапожник /sapózhnik/ m. shoemaker

сапфир /sapfír/ m. sapphire

сарай /sarái/ m. shed

саранча /saranchá/ f. locust(s)

сарафан /sarafán/ m. sarafan; pinafore dress

сарделька /sardél'ka/ f. small fat sausage; frankfrter

сардина /sardína/ f. sardine

саржа /sárzha/ f. serge

сатана /sataná/ m. satan

сателлит /satellít/ m. satellite

сатин /satín/ m. sateen

сатира /satíra/ f. satire

сафьян /saf'ián/ m. morocco

сахар /sákhar/ m. sugar

сахарин /sakharín/ m. saccharine

сачок /sachók/ m. net; butterfly net

сбербанк /sberbánk/ abbr., m. savings bank

сберегать /sberegát'/ v. save

сближать /sblizhát'/ v. bring together

сбоку /sbóku/ adv. on one side

сболтнуть /sboltnút'/ v. blurt out

сборище /sbórishche/ n. mob

сборка /sbórka/ f. assembling

сборник /sbórnik/ m. collection

сбрасывать /sbrásyvat'/ v. throw down; cast off, shed

сбривать /sbrivát'/ v. shave off

сброд /sbrod/ m. riff-raff

сбруя /sbrúia/ f. harness

сбывать /sbyvát'/ v. sell; market
свадьба /svád'ba/ f. wedding
сваливать /sválivat'/ v. heap up, pile up
свалка /sválka/ f. scrap-heap
сварщик /svárshchik/ m. welder
сват /svat/ m. match-maker
свая /sváia/ f. pile
сведения /svédeniia/ pl. information
свежий /svézhii/ adj. fresh
свекла /sviókla/ f. beet; сахарная с. /sákharnaia s./ sugar-beet
свекор /sviókor/ m. father-in-law (husband's father)
свекровь /svekróv'/ f. mother-in-law; (husband's mother)
свергать /svergát'/ v. overthrow
сверкать /sverkát'/ v. sparkle
сверлить /sverlít'/ v. drill
сверток /sviórtok/ m. bundle
свертывать /sviórtyvat'/ v. roll up
сверх /sverkh/ prep. over; above
сверхзвуковой /sverkhzvukovói/ adj. supersonic
сверхплановый /sverkhplánovyi/ adj. over and above the plan
сверху /svérkhu/ adv. from above
сверхурочный /sverkhuróchnyi/ adj. overtime
сверхчеловек /sverkhchelovék/ m. superman
сверхъестественный /sverkh''estéstvennyi/ adj. supernatural
сверчок /sverchók/ m. cricket
свершаться /svershát'sia/ v. be fulfilled
свершение /svershénie/ n. achievement
свет /svet/ m. light; society, beau monde
светать /svetát'/ v. dawn
светлеть /svetlét'/ v. grow lighter
светлый /svétlyi/ adj. light
светлячок /svetliachók/ m. glow-worm
светофор /svetofór/ m. traffic light(s)
светочувствительный /svetochuvstvítel'nyi/ adj. photosensitive

светский /svétskii/ adj. secular; society; fashionable
свеча /svechá/ f. candle
свешивать /svéshivat'/ v. lower; dangle
свидание /svidánie/ n. meeting; date; до свидания /do svidániia/ good-bye
свидетель /svidétel'/ m. witness
свидетельство /svidétel'stvo/ n. evidence
свинарник /svinárnik/ m. pigsty
свинец /svinéts/ m. lead
свинина /svinína/ f. pork
свинка /svínka/ f. mumps
свинчивать /svínchivat'/ v. screw together
свинья /svin'iá/ f. pig; swine
свирепый /svirépyi/ adj. ferocious
свисать /svisát'/ v. dangle, droop
свистеть /svistét'/ v. whistle
свита /svíta/ f. suite
свитер /svitér/ m. sweater
свихнуться /svikhnút'sia/ v. sl. go mad
свищ /svishch/ m. fistula
свобода /svobóda/ f. freedom, liberty
свободолюбивый /svobodoliubívyi/ adj. freedom-loving
свободомыслие /svobodomýslie/ n. freethinking
свод /svod/ m. arch; code (of laws)
сводить /svodít'/ v. bring together
сводка /svódka/ f. summary
сводник /svodník/ m. pimp
сводный /svódnyi/ adj. composite, combined; step-
своевременный /svoevrémennyi/ adj. timely
своенравный /svoenrávnyi/ adj. wilful
своеобразие /svoeobrázie/ n. originality
своеобразный /svoeobráznyi/ adj. peculiar
свой /svói/ pron. one's own
свойственный /svóistvennyi/ adj. characteristic
свойство /svóistvo/ n. property, attribute
сволочь /svóloch/ f. riff-raff, rascal

свора /svóra/ f. pack

сворачивать /svoráchivat'/ v. roll up; turn aside

свояк /svoiák/ m. brother-in-law (husband of wife's sister)

свояченица /svoiáchenitsa/ f. sister-in-law (wife's sister)

свыкаться /svykát'sia/ v. get used (to)

свысока /svysoká/ adv. haughtily

свыше /svýshe/ adv. from above; over; beyond

связка /sviázka/ f. bunch

связывать /sviázyvat'/ v. tie

связь /sviáz'/ f. communication(s); link; relation

святилище /sviatílishche/ n. sanctuary

святить /sviatít'/ v. sanctify

святки /sviátki/ pl. Christmas-tide

святой /sviatói/ adj. holy; saint

святотатство /sviatotátstvo/ n. sacrilege

священник /sviashchénnik/ m. priest

священный /sviashchénnyi/ adj. sacred

сгибать /sgibát'/ v. bend

сглазить /sglázit'/ v. cast bad luck on a person

сгнивать /sgnivát'/ v. rot

сговариваться /sgovárivat'sia/ v. come to an arrangement

сгонять /sgoniát'/ v. drive away

сгорание /sgoránie/ n. combustion

сгорать /sgorát'/ v. burn down

сгребать /sgrebát'/ v. rake together

сгружать /sgruzhát'/ v. unload

сгущать /sgushchát'/ v. thicken

сгущенное (молоко) /sgushchónnoe molokó/ adj. + n. condensed milk

сдавливать /sdávlivat'/ v. squeeze

сдача /sdácha/ f. surrender; change (money)

сдвигать /sdvigát'/ v. shift, displace

сделка /sdélka/ f. deal

сдельный /sdél'nyi/ adj. piece-work

сдельщина /sdél'shchina/ f. piece-work

сдергивать /sdiórgivat'/ v. pull off

сдерживать /sdérzhivat'/ v. hold back

сдирать /sdirát'/ v. strip off

сдоба /sdóba/ f. fancy bread, bun(s)

сдружиться /sdruzhít'sia/ v. become friends (with)

сдувать /sduvát'/ v. blow off

сдуру /sdúru/ adv. foolishly

сеанс /seáns/ m. show; sitting

себестоимость /sebestóimost'/ f. cost price; prime cost

себя /sebiá/ pron. oneself

себялюбивый /sebia'liubívyi/ adj. selfish, self-loving

сев /sev/ m. sowing

север /séver/ m. north

северо-восток /severo-vostók/ m. north-east

северянин /severiánin/ m. northerner

севрюга /sevriúga/ f. sturgeon

сегодня /sevódnia/ adv. today

седеть /sedét'/ v. go grey

седлать /sedlát'/ v. saddle

седло /sedló/ n. saddle

седой /sedói/ adj. grey

седок /sedók/ m. horseman, rider; passenger

сезон /sezón/ m. season

сейф /séif/ m. safe

сейчас /seichás/ adv. (right) now

секрет /sekrét/ m. secret

секретарь /sekretár'/ m. secretary

секта /sékta/ f. sect

сектант /sektánt/ m. sectarian

сектор /séktor/ m. sector

секунда /sekúnda/ f. second

секундная (стрелка) /sekúndnaia strélka/ adj. + f. second hand

секундомер /sekundomér/ m. stop-watch

секция /séktsiia/ f. herring

селедка /seliódka/ f. herring

селезенка /seliziónka/ f. spleen

селезень /sélezen'/ m. drake

селить /selít'/ v. settle

село /seló/ n. village

сельдерей /sel'deréi/ m. celery
сельский /sél'skii/ adj. rural; сельское
  хозяйство /sél'skoe khoziáistvo/ agriculture
семафор /semafór/ m. semaphore
семга /siómga/ f. salmon
семерка /semiórka/ f. seven
семестр /seméstr/ m. term, semester
семечки /sémechki/ pl. sunflower seeds
семинар /seminár/ m. seminar
семинария /semináriia/ f. seminary
семнадцать /semnádtsat'/ num. seventeen
семь /sem'/ num. seven
семьдесят /sém'desiat/ num. seventy
семьсот /sem'sót/ num. seven hundred
семья /sem'iá/ f. family
семя /sémia/ n. seed; sperm
сенат /sénat/ m. senate
сенатор /senátor/ m. senator
сено /séno/ n. hay
сенсация /sensátsiia/ f. sensation
сентиментальный /sentimentál'nyi/ adj.
  sentimental
сентябрь /sentiábr'/ m. september
сепаратный /separátnyi/ adj. separate
сера /séra/ f. sulphur; ear-wax
серб /serb/ m. Serb
сербка /sérbka/ f. Serbian
сербский /sérbskii/ adj. Serbian
серб(ск)охорватский /serb(sk)okhor-
  vátskii/ adj. Serbo-Croat
сервиз /serviz/ m. service, set
сервировать (стол) /servirovát' stol/ v. +
  m. lay a table
сердечный /serdéchnyi/ adj. heart; car-
  diac; cordial
сердитый /serdítyi/ adj. angry
сердить /serdít'/ v. anger
сердиться /serdít'sia/ v. be angry
сердобольный /serdoból'nyi/ adj. tender-
  hearted
сердце /sérdtse/ n. heart
сердцевина /serdtsevína/ f. core

серебро /serebró/ n. silver
середина /seredína/ f. middle
сержант /serzhánt/ m. sergeant
серийный /seríinyi/ adj. serial
серия /sériia/ f. series
серп /serp/ m. sickle
сертификат /sertifikát/ m. certificate
серый /séryi/ adj. grey
серьга /sér'ga/ f. earring
серьезный /ser'ióznyi/ adj. serious
сессия /séssiia/ f. session
сестра /sestrá/ f. sister
сеть /set'/ f. net
сеять /seiát'/ v. sow
сжалиться /szhálit'sia/ v. take pity (on)
сжигать /szhigát'/ v. burn down
сжимать /szhimát'/ v. squeeze
сжиматься /szhimát'sia/ v. shrink
сзади /szádi/ adv. behind; from behind
сибирский /sibírskii/ adj. Siberian
сигара /sigára/ f. cigar
сигарета /sigaréta/ f. cigarette
сигнал /signál/m. signal
сиделка /sidélka/ f. nurse
сиденье /sidén'e/ n. seat
сидеть /sidét'/ v. sit
сидр /sidr/ m. cider
сидячий /sidiáchii/ adj. sitting
сила /síla/ f. strength; power, force
силач /silách/ m. strong man
силикат /silikát/ m. silicate
силос /sílos/ m. silo
силуэт /siluét/ m. silhouette
сильный /síl'nyi/ adj. strong
символ /símvol/ m. symbol
симметрия /simmétriia/ f. symmetry
симпатизировать /simpatizírovat'/ v.
  sympathize (with)
симулировать /simulírovat'/ v. feign,
  sham
симфонический /simfonícheskii/ adj.
  symphonic
симфония /simfóniia/ f. symphony
синагога /sinagóga/ f. synagogue

синий /sínii/ adj. blue
синить /sinít'/ v. blue
синица /sinítsa/ f. tomtit
синод /sinód/ m. synod
синтетический /sintetícheskii/ adj. synthetic
синяк /siniák/ m. bruise; c. под глазом /s. pod glázom/ black eye
сиплый /síplyi/ adj. hoarse
сирена /siréna/ f. siren
сирень /sirén'/ f. lilac
сириец /siríets/ m. Syrian
сирийка /siríika/ f. Syrian
сирийский /siríiskii/ adj. Syrian
сироп /siróp/ m. syrup
сирота /sirotá/ m. and f. orphan
система /sistéma/ f. system
ситец /sítets/ m. (printed) cotton; chintz
сито /síto/ n. sieve
ситуация /situátsiia/ f. situation
сиять /siiát'/ v. shine
сказка /skázka/ f. fairy-tale
скакать /skakát'/ v. jump; gallop
скала /skalá/ f. rock
скалка /skálka/ f. rolling-pin
скамья /skam'iá/ f. bench
скандал /skandál/ m. scandal
скандинав /skandináv/ m. Scandinavian
скандинавка /skandinávka/ f. Scandinavian
скандинавский /skandinávskii/ adj. Scandinavian
скапливать /skáplivat'/ v. save up
скарлатина /skarlatína/ f. scarlet fever
скатерть /skátert'/ f. table-cloth
скатывать /skátyvat'/ v. roll (up)
скафандр /skafándr/ m. diving-suit; space-suit
скачки /skáchki/ pl. horse-race
скважина /skvázhina/ f. chink; замочная c. /zamóchnaya s./ keyhole
сквер /skver/ m. public garden; park

скверословие /skvernoslóvie/ n. foul language
сквозняк /skvozniák/ m. draught
сквозь /skvoz'/ prep. through
скворец /skvoréts/ m. starling
скелет /skelét/ m. skeleton
скептик /sképtik/ m. sceptic
скидка /skídka/ f. discount
скипетр /skípetr/ m. sceptre
скипидар /skipidár/ m. turpentine
скисать /skisát'/ v. go sour
скитаться /skitát'sia/ v. wander
скиф /skif/ m. Scythian
склад /sklad/ m. warehouse
складной /skladnói/ adj. folding
складывать /skládyvat'/ v. put together, add; fold up
склеивать /skléivat'/ v. stick together
склон /sklon/ m. slope
скоба /skobá/ f. cramp
скобка /skóbka/ f. bracket
сковорода /skovorodá/ f. frying-pan
сколачивать /skoláchivat'/ v. knock together
скользить /skol'zít'/ v. slide
скользкий /skól'zkii/ adj. slippery
сколько /skól'ko/ adv. how much, how many
скорбеть /skorbét'/ v. grieve
скорлупа /skorlupá/ f. shell
скорняк /skorniák/ m. furrier
скоро /skóro/ adv. quickly
скоропортящийся /skoropórtiashchiisia/ adj. perishable
скорость /skórost'/ f. speed
скорый /skóryi/ adj. fast
скот /skot/ m. cattle; beast, swine
скребок /skrebók/ m. scraper
скрепка /skrépka/ f. clip
скреплять /skrepliát'/ v. fasten
скрести /skresti/ v. scratch
скрипеть /skripét'/ v. creak
скрипка /skrípka/ f. violin

скромный /skrómnyi/ adj. modest
скручивать /skrúchivat'/ v. roll; twist
скрывать /skryvát'/ v. conceal
скрываться /skryvát'sia/ v. hide
скряга /skriága/ m. and f. miser
скудный /skúdnyi/ adj. scanty; meagre
скука /skúka/ f. boredom
скула /skulá/ f. cheek-bone
скулить /skulít'/ v. whine
скульптор /skúl'ptor/ m. sculptor
скумбрия /skúmbriia/ f. mackerel
скунс /skuns/ m. skunk
скупать /skupát'/ v. buy up
скупой /skupói/ adj. miserly
скупщик /skúpshchik/ m. buyer (up)
скучать /skuchát'/ v. be bored; miss
скучный /skúchnyi/ adj. tedious; мне
скучно /mne skúchno/ I'm bored
слабеть /slabét'/ v. weaken
слабительное /slabítel'noe/ n. laxative
слабость /slábost'/ f. weakness
слабоумие /slaboúmie/ n. imbecility
слабый /slábyi/ adj. weak
слава /sláva/ f. fame
славист /slavíst/ m. Slavist
славить /slávit'/ v. glorify
славянин /slaviánin/ m. Slav
славянка /slaviánka/ f. Slav
славянофил /slavianofíl/ m. Slavophile
славянский /slaviánskii/ adj. Slav; Slavonic
сладкий /sládkii/ adj. sweet
сладкое /sládkoe/ n. dessert
сладострастие /sladostrástie/ n. voluptuousness
слаженный /slázhennyi/ adj. harmonious
сластена /slastióna/ m. and f. sweet tooth
слать /slat'/ v. send
слева /sléva/ adv. from (the) left
слегка /slegká/ adv. slightly
след /sled/ m. track; footstep; trace
следить /sledít'/ v. watch

следование (поезд дальнего следования) /póezd dál'nevo slédovaniia/ long-distance train
следователь /slédovatel'/ m. investigator
следовать /slédovat'/ v. follow
следующий /sléduiushchii/ adj. following
слежка /slézhka/ f. shadowing
слеза /slezá/ f. tear
слезать /slezát'/ v. climb down
слепень /slepén'/ m. horse-fly
слепой /slepói/ adj. blind
слесарь /slésar'/ m. fitter; locksmith
слет /sliót/ m. gathering
слива /slíva/ f. plum
сливать /slivát'/ v. pour out; pour together; merge
сливки /slívki/ pl. cream
слизистый /slízistyi/ adj. mucous
слипаться /slipát'sia/ v. stick together
слиток /slítok/ m. bar, ingot
слишком /slíshkom/ adv. too; too much
словак /slovák/ m. Slovak
словарь /slovár'/ m. dictionary
словенец /slovénets/ m. Slovene
словно /slóvno/ adv. as if
слово /slóvo/ n. word; address
слог /slog/ m. syllable; style
слоеный /sloiónyi/ adj. puff
сложение /slozhénie/ n. addition; build, constitution
слой /slói/ m. layer
слон /slon/ m. elephant
слоновая (кость) /slonóvaia kost'/ adj. + f. ivory
слуга /slugá/ m. servant
служанка /sluzhánka/ f. maid
служащий /slúzhashchii/ m. employee
служба /slúzhba/ f. service
служить /sluzhít'/ v. serve
слух /slukh/ m. hearing; rumour
случай /slúchai/ m. case; chance; несчастный с. /neschástnyi s./ accident
случаться /sluchát'sia/ v. happen

слушатель /slúshatel'/ m. listener
слушать /slúshat'/ v. listen
слушаться /slúshat'sia/ v. obey
слышать /slýshat'/ v. hear
слюда /sliudá/ f. mica
слюна /sliuná/ f. saliva
слюнявый /sliuniávyi/ adj. dribbling
слякоть /sliákot'/ f. slush
смазка /smázka/ f. lubrication
смазливый /smazlívyi/ adj. pretty
сманивать /smánivat'/ v. entice
сматывать /smátyvat'/ v. wind
смахивать /smákhivat'/ v. brush away
смачивать /smáchivat'/ v. moisten
смелость /smélost'/ f. courage
смелый /smélyi/ adj. bold
смена /sména/ f. change; shift
сменять /smeniát'/ v. replace
смерть /smert'/ f. death
смерч /smerch/ m. sandstorm; tornado
смесь /smes'/ f. mixture
смета /sméta/ f. estimate
сметана /smetána/ f. sour cream
сметать /smetát'/ v. sweep off
сметь /smet'/ v. dare
смех /smekh/ m. laugh; laughter
смехотворный /smekhotvórnyi/ adj. ridiculous
смешанный /sméshannyi/ adj. mixed
смешивать /smeshívat/ v. blend; confuse
смешить /smeshít'/ v. make laugh
смешной /smeshnói/ adj. funny
смещать /smeshchát'/ v. displace
смеяться /smeiát'sia/ v. laugh
смирительная (рубашка) /smirítel'naia rubáshka/ adj. + f. straitjacket
смирный /smírnyi/ adj. quiet; submissive; смирно! /smírno!/ attention
смирять /smiriát'/ v. subdue
смоква /smókva/ f. fig
смокинг /smóking/ m. dinner-jacket
смола /smolá/ f. resin
смолкать /smolkát'/ v. fall silent

сморкаться /smorkát'sia/ v. blow one's nose
смородина /smoródina/ f. currants
сморщенный /smórshchennyi/ adj. wrinkled
смотр /smotr/ m. review
смотреть /smotrét'/ watch; look (at); look (after)
смотритель /smotrítel'/ m. supervisor
смрад /smrad/ m. stench
смрадный /smrádnyi/ adj. stinking
смуглый /smúglyi/ adj. dark-complexioned
смутный /smútnyi/ adj. vague
смутьян /smut'ián/ m. trouble-maker
смущать /smushchát'/ v. embarrass
смывать /smyvát'/ v. wash off
смысл /smysl/ m. sense
смыслить /smýslit'/ v. understand
смычок /smychók/ m. bow
смышленый /smyshliónyi/ adj. intelligent
смягчать /smiagchát'/ v. soften
смятение /smiaténie/ n. confusion
смятый /smiátyi/ adj. rumpled
снабжать /snabzhát'/ v. supply
снайпер /snáiper/ m. sniper
снаружи /snarúzhi/ adv. on the outside
снаряд /snariád/ m. shell
снаряжать /snariazhát'/ v. equip
сначала /snachála/ adv. at first
снег /sneg/ m. snow
снегирь /snegír'/ m. bullfinch
снегоочиститель /snegoochistítel'/ m. snow-plough
снегопад /snegopád/ m. snowfall
снегурочка /snegúrochka/ f. snow-maiden
снежинка /snezhínka/ f. snow-flake
снежок /snezhók/ m. snowball
снижать /snizhát'/ v. reduce; lower
снизу /snízu/ adv. from below
снимать /snimát'/ v. take away; photograph; lease, rent; cut (cards)

снимок /snímok/ m. photograph
снисхождение /sniskhozhdénie/ n. condescension; indulgence
сниться /snít'sia/ v. dream
снова /snóva/ adv. again
сновидение /snovidénie/ n. dream
сноп /snop/ m. sheaf
сноровка /snoróvka/ f. knack
снос /snos/ m. pulling down, demolishing; wear; wearing out
сносить /snosít'/ v. fetch down; wear out
сноска /snóska/ f. footnote
сносный /snósnyi/ adj. tolerable
снотворное /snotvórnoe/ n. sleeping-pills
сноха /snokhá/ f. daughter-in-law
сношение /snoshénie/ n. relation(s); intercourse
снятие /sniátie/ n. removal
снятое (молоко) /sniátoe molokó/ adj. + n. skim milk
собака /sobáka/ f. dog
собирать /sobirát'/ v. collect
собираться /sobirát'sia/ v. gather
соблазн /soblázn/ m. temptation
соблазнитель /soblaznítel'/ m. seducer
соблазнять /soblazniát'/ v. tempt; seduce
соблюдать /sobliudát'/ v. observe
соболезнование /soboleznovánie/ n. condolence
соболь /sóbol'/ m. sable
собор /sóbor/ m. cathedral
собрание /sobránie/ n. meeting
собственник /sóbstvennik/ m. proprietor; owner
собственность /sóbstvennost'/ f. property
событие /sobýtie/ n. event
сова /sová/ f. owl
совать /sovát'/ v. thrust
совершать /sovershát'/ v. perform
совершеннолетие /sovershennolétie/ n. full age; majority
совершеннолетний /sovershennolétnii/ adj. of age

совершенный /sovershénnyi/ adj. perfect
совесть /sóvest'/ f. conscience
совет /sovét/ m. advice; council
советовать /sovétovat'/ v. advise
советоваться /sovétovat'sia/ v. consult
советский /sovétskii/ adj. Soviet
совещание /soveshchánie/ n. conference
совещаться /soveshchát'sia/ v. consult; deliberate
совместимый /sovmestímyi/ adj. compatible
совместный /sovméstnyi/ adj. joint
совмещать /sovmeshchát'/ v. combine
совок /sovók/ m. scoop
совпадать /sovpadát'/ v. coincide
совращать /sovrashchát'/ v. seduce
современный /sovreménnyi/ adj. contemporary
совсем /sovsém/ adv. entirely
согласие /soglásie/ n. agreement
согласно /soglásno/ adv. in accordance (with)
согласовывать /soglasóvyvat'/ v. coordinate
соглашение /soglashénie/ n. agreement; treaty
сограждане /sográzhdane/ pl. fellow citizens
согревать /sogrevát'/ v. warm
сода /sóda/ f. soda
содействовать /sodéistvovat'/ v. assist
содержание /soderzhánie/ n. upkeep; content(s); substance
содрогаться /sodrogát'sia/ v. shudder
содружество /sodrúzhestvo/ n. commonwealth
соединять /soediniát'/ v. connect, join, unite
сожаление /sozhalénie/ n. regret
сожалеть /sozhalét'/ v. regret, deplore
сожжение /sozhzhénie/ n. burning; cremation
созвездие /sozvézdie/ n. constellation

созвучие /sozvúchie/ n. accord; consonance
создавать /sozdavát'/ v. create
создатель /sozdátel'/ m. creator
сознавать /soznavát'/ v. realize
сознательный /soznátel'nyi/ adj. conscious
созревание /sozrevánie/ n. ripening
созревать /sozrevát'/ v. mature
созыв /sozýv/ m. convocation
созывать /sozyvát'/ v. summon; convene
сойка /sóika/ f. jay
сок /sok/ m. juice
сокол /sókol/ m. falcon
сокращать /sokrashchát'/ v. reduce
сокровище /sokróvishche/ n. treasure
сокрушать /sokrushát'/ v. shatter
солдат /soldát/ m. soldier
соленый /soliónyi/ adj. salted, pickled
солидный /solídnyi/ adj. solid; respectable
солист /solíst/ m. soloist
солитер /solitiór/ m. tape-worm
солить /solít'/ v. salt
солнце /sólntse/ n. sun
соло /sólo/ n. solo
соловей /solovéi/ m. nightingale
солод /solód/ m. malt
солома /solóma/ f. straw
солонина /solonína/ f. corned beef
соль /sol'/ f. salt
сомневаться /somnevát'sia/ v. doubt
сон /son/ m. sleep, dream
соната /sonáta/ f. sonata
сонет /sonét/ m. sonnet
соображать /soobrazhát'/ v. consider; understand
сообща /soobshchá/ adv. together
сообщать /soobshchát'/ v. communicate
сообщение /soobshchénie/ n. report

сообщество /soóbshchestvo/ n. association
сообщник /soóbshchnik/ m. accomplice
сооружать /sooruzhát'/ v. build
соотечественник /sootéchestvennik/ m. compatriot
соперник /sopérnik/ m. rival
соперничать /sopérnichat'/ v. compete, vie
сопеть /sopét'/ v. wheeze; snuffle
сопка /sópka/ f. hill
сопливый /soplívyi/ adj. snotty
сопоставлять /sopostavliát'/ v. compare
соприкасаться /soprikasát'sia/ v. adjoin
сопровождать /soprovozhdát'/ v. accompany
сопровождение /soprovozhdénie/ n. escort
сопротивляться /soprotivliát'sia/ v. resist
сопутствовать /sopútstvovat'/ v. accompany
сор /sor/ m. litter
соратник /sorátnik/ m. brother-in-arms
сорванец /sorvanéts/ v. imp
соревнование /sorevnovánie/ n. competition
сорить /sorít'/ v. litter
сорок /sórok/ num. forty
сорока /soróka/ f. magpie
сороконожка /sorokonózhka/ f. centipede
сорт /sort/ m. sort; grade
сосать /sosát'/ v. suck
сосед /soséd/ m. neighbour
сосиска /sosíska/ f. sausage
соска /sóska/ f. (baby's) dummy
соскабливать /soskáblivat'/ v. scrape off
соскакивать /soskákivat'/ v. jump off, jump down
соскальзывать /soskál'zyvat'/ v. slide down
соскучиться /soskúchit'sia/ v. miss; get bored

сословие /soslóvie/ n. estate; class
сослуживец /sosluzhívets/ m. colleague
сосна /sosná/ f. pine
сосок /sosók/ m. nipple
сосредоточенность /sosredotóchen-nost'/ f. concentration
состав /sostáv/ m. composition
составлять /sostavliát'/ v. put together; compile; amount to
состояние /sostoiánie/ n. condition; fortune
состоять /sostoiát'/ v. be; consist (of)
состояться /sostoiát'sia/ v. take place
сострадание /sostradánie/ n. compassion
сострадательный /sostradátel'nyi/ adj. sympathetic
состригать /sostrigát'/ v. cut off
состязание /sostiazánie/ n. contest
состязаться /sostiazát'sia/ v. compete
сосуд /sosúd/ m. vessel
сосулька /sosúl'ka/ f. icicle
сосуществование /sosushchestvovánie/ n. coexistence
сотворение /sotvorénie/ n. creation
сотня /sótnia/ f. hundred
сотрудник /sotrúdnik/ m. staff worker; colleague; employee
сотрудничать /sotrúdnichat'/ v. collaborate
сотрясать /sotriasát'/ v. shake
соты /sóty/ pl. honeycomb
соус /sóus/ m. sauce
соучастник /souchástnik/ m. accomplice
софа /sofá/ sofa
соха /sokhá/ f. (wooden) plough
сохнуть /sókhnut'/ v. dry
сохранение /sokhranénie/ n. preservation
сохранность /sokhránnost'/ f. safety
сохранять /sokhraniát'/ v. preserve
сохраняться /sokhraniát'sia/ v. remain (intact); last out
социализм /sotsializm/ m. socialism
социалист /sotsialist/ m. socialist

социальный /sotsiál'nyi/ adj. social
соцстрах /sotsstrákh/ abbr., m. social insurance
сочельник /sochél'nik/m. Christmas Eve
сочетание /sochetánie/ n. combination
сочинение /sochinénie/ n. composition
сочинитель /sochinítel'/ m. author
сочинять /sochiniát'/ v. write; make up, fabricate
сочный /sóchnyi/ adj. juicy
сочувствовать /sochúvstvovat'/ v. sympathize with
союз /soiúz/ m. union
союзник /soiúznik/ m. ally
спазм /spazm/ m. spasm
спаивать /spáivat'/ v. make drunk
спаять /spaiát'/ v. solder
спальный /spál'nyi/ adj. sleeping; с. вагон /s. vágon/ sleeping-car
спальня /spál'nia/ f. bedroom
спаржа /spárzha/ f. asparagus
спарывать /spáryvat'/ v. rip off
спасательный /spasátel'nyi/ adj. rescue; с. круг /s. krug/ lifebuoy
спасать /spasát'/ v. save
спасаться /spasát'sia/ v. escape
спасибо /spasíbo/ part. thank you
спаситель /spasítel'/ m. saviour
спать /spat'/ v. sleep
спектакль /spektákl'/ m. performance
спектр /spektr/ m. spectrum
спекулировать /spekulírovat'/ v. speculate; profiteer
спелый /spélyi/ adj. ripe
сперва /spervá/ adv. at first
спереди /spéredi/ adv. at the front
спертый /spiórtyi/ adj. stuffy
специалист /spetsialíst/ m. specialist
специальность /spetsiál'nost'/ f. profession
специальный /spetsiál'nyi/ adj. special
спешить /speshít'/ v. hurry
спешка /spéshka/ f. haste
спешный /spéshnyi/ adj. urgent

спина /spiná/ f. back
спираль /spirál'/ f. spiral
спирт /spirt/ m. alcohol, spirit(s)
список /spísok/ m. list
спица /spítsa/ f. knitting-needle; spoke
спичка /spíchka/ f. match
сплачивать /spláchivat'/ v. rally
сплетник /splétnik/ m. gossip
сплетничать /splétnichat'/ v. gossip
сплошной /sploshnói/ adj. solid
сплошь /splosh/ adv. all over; throughout
сплющивать /spliúshchivat'/ v. flatten
сподвижник /spodvízhnik/ m. comrade-in-arms
спокойный /spokóinyi/ adj. calm
сполна /spolná/ adv. in full
спор /spor/ m. argument
спорить /spórit'/ v. dispute
спорт /sport/ m. sport
спортсмен /sportsmén/ m. sportsman
способ /spósob/ m. way
способность /sposóbnost'/ f. ability
способствовать /sposóbstvovat'/ v. assist
спотыкаться /spotykát'sia/ v. stumble
справа /správa/ adv. from the right
справедливость /spravedlívost'/ f. justice
справедливый /spravedlívyi/ adj. fair
справка /správka/ f. information; reference; certificate
справлять /spravliát'/ v. celebrate
справочник /správochnik/ m. reference-book
справочный /správochnyi/ adj. inquiry
спрашивать /spráshivat'/ v. ask
спрос /spros/ m. demand
спросонок /sprosónok/ adv. only half-awake
спрут /sprut/ m. octopus
спрыскивать /sprýskivat'/ v. sprinkle
спрягать /spriagát'/ v. conjugate
спугивать /spúgivat'/ v. frighten away
спуск /spusk/ m. slope
спускать /spuskát'/ v. lower; unleash
спускаться /spuskát'sia/ v. descend

спутник /spútnik/ m. companion; sputnik
спутывать /spútyvat'/ v. confuse
спячка /spiáchka/ f. hibernation
сравнивать /srávnivat'/ v. compare
сражать /srazhát'/ v. strike down
сражаться /srazhát'sia/ v. fight
сражение /srazhénie/ n. battle
сразу /srázu/ adv. at once
среда /sredá/ f. Wednesday; milieu; medium
среди /sredí/ adv. among
средиземноморский /sredizemnomórskii/ adj. Mediterranean
среднеазиатский /sredneaziátskii/ adj. Central Asian
средневековый /srednevekóvyi/ adj. mediaeval
средневековье /srednevekóv'e/ n. the Middle Ages
средний /srédnii/ adj. middle; average
средство /srédstvo/ n. means
срезать /srezát'/ v. cut off
срисовывать /srisóvyvat'/ v. copy
срок /srok/ m. term
срочный /sróchnyi/ adj. urgent
срывать /sryvát'/ v. tear away; raze to the ground
ссадина /ssádina/ f. scratch
ссора /ssóra/ f. quarrel
ссуда /ssúda/ f. loan
ссужать /ssuzhát'/ v. lend
ссылать /ssylát'/ v. exile
стабильный /stabíl'nyi/ adj. stable
ставить /stávit'/ v. stand; place
ставни /stávni/ pl. shutters
стадион /stadión/ m. stadium
стадия /stádiia/ f. stage
стаж /stazh/ m. length of service
стажер /stazhór/ m. probationer
стакан /stakán/ m. glass, tumbler
сталкивать /stálkivat'/ v. push away
стамеска /staméska/ f. chisel
стандарт /standárt/ m. standard
становиться /stanovít'sia/ v. become

станок /stanók/ m. machine (tool)
станция /stántsia/ f. station
старание /staránie/ n. effort
старатель /starátel'/ m. prospector (for gold)
стараться /starát'sia/ v. try
стареть /starét'/ v. grow old
старик /starík/ m. old man
старинный /starínnyi/ adj. antique
старовер /starovér/ m. Old Believer
старожил /starozhíl/ m. old resident
старомодный /staromódnyi/ adj. old-fashioned
старость /stárost'/ f. old age
стартовать /startovát'/ v. start
старуха /starúkha/ f. old woman
старший /stárshii/ adj. elder; older; eldest; oldest
старый /stáryi/ adj. old
стаскивать /stáskivat'/ v. pull down
статистика /statístika/ f. statistics
статуэтка /statuétka/ f. statuette
статуя /státuia/ f. statue
стать /stat'/ v. become
статья /stat'iá/ v. article
стачка /stáchka/ f. strike
стая /stáia/ f. pack; flock; school, shoal
ствол /stvol/ m. trunk; barrel
стебель /stébel'/ m. stem
стеганый /stióganyi/ adj. quilted
стегать /stegát'/ v. quilt; whip
стежок /stezhók/ m. stitch
стекать /stekát'/ v. flow down
стекло /steklо́/ n. glass
стелить /stelít'/ v. spread
стеллаж /stellázh/ m. shelves
стена /stená/ f. wall
стенограмма /stenográmma/ f. shorthand record
стенографистка /stenografístka/ f. stenographer
степень /stépen'/ f. degree; extent
степь /step'/ f. steppe
стеречь /steréch/ v. guard

стержень /stérzhen'/ m. pivot
стерильный /sterílnyi/ adj. sterile
стерлядь /stérliad'/ f. sterlet
стертый /stiórtyi/ adj. worn, effaced
стеснительный /stesnítel'nyi/ adj. shy
стеснять /stesniát'/ v. embarrass
стиль /stil'/ m. style
стимулировать /stimulírovat'/ v. stimulate
стипендия /stipéndiia/ f. grant
стиральный /stirál'nyi/ adj. washing;
стиральная машина /stirál'naia mashína/ washing-machine
стирать /stirát'/ v. wash
стискивать /stískivat'/ v. squeeze
стих /stikh/ m. verse
стихать /stikhát'/ v. calm down
стихийное (бедствие) /stikhíinoe bédstvie/ adj. + n. calamity
стихия /stikhíia/ f. element
стлать /stlat'/ v. spread
сто /sto/ num. hundred
стог /stog/ m. stack
стоимость /stóimost'/ f. cost
стоить /stóit'/ v. cost, be worth
стойка /stóika/ f. bar
стойкий /stóikii/ adj. stable
стойло /stóilo/ n. stall
стол /stol/ m. table; desk
столб /stolb/ m. pole; pillar
столетие /stolétie/ n. century
столица /stolítsa/ f. capital
столкновение /stolknovénie/ n. clash
столовая /stolóvaia/ f. dining-room; canteen
столько /stól'ko/ adv. so much, so many
столяр /stol'ár/ m. joiner
стонать /stonát'/ v. groan
стоп! /stop!/ int. stop!
стоп-кран /stop-kran/ m. emergency brake
сторож /stórozh/m. guard
сторожить /storozhít'/ v. watch over

172

сторона /storoná/ f. side
сторонник /storónnik/ m. supporter
сточный /stóchnyi/ adj. sewage;
стоянка /stoiánka/ f. parking place or lot
стоять /stoiát'/ v. stand
страдать /stradát'/ v. suffer
стража /strázha/ f. guard(s)
страна /straná/ f. country
страница /stranítsa/ f. page
странник /stránnik/ m. wanderer
странный/ stránnyi/ adj. strange
страстной /strastnói/ adj. of Holy Week
страсть /strast'/ f. passion
страус /stráus/ m. ostrich
страх /strakh/ m. fear
страхование /strakhovánie/ n. insurance
страховать /strakhovát'/ v. insure
стрекоза /strekozá/ f. dragonfly
стрекотать /strekotát'/ v. chirr
стрела /strelá/ f. arrow
стрелка /strélka/ f. hand; pointer
стрельба /strel'bá/ f. shooting
стрелять /streliát'/ v. shoot
стремиться /stremít'sia/ v. strive (for)
стремянка /stremiánka/ f. step-ladder
стриж /strizh/ m. sand martin
стрижка /strízhka/ f. hair-cut
стричься /stríchsia/ v. have one's hair cut
строгать /strogát'/ v. plane
строгий /strógii/ adj. strict
строение /stroénie/ n. structure
строитель /stroítel'/ m. builder
строить /stróit'/ v. construct, build
строй /strói/ m. system; order
стройка /stróika/ f. building-site
стройный /stróinyi/ adj. shapely
строка /stroká/ f. line
стронций /stróntsii/ m. strontium
стропило /stropílo/ n. rafter
строфа /strofá/ f. stanza
строчить /strochít'/ v. stitch
стружка /strúzhka/ f. shaving, filing
структура /struktúra/ f. structure
струна /struná/ f. string

стручок /struchók/ m. pod
струя /strúia/ f. stream
стряхивать /striákhivat'/ v. shake off
студент /studént/ m. student
студить /studít'/ v. cool
студия /stúdiia/ f. studio
стужа /stúzha/ f. cold; frost
стук /stuk/ m. knock
стул /stul/ m. chair
ступать /stupát'/ v. step
ступенька /stupén'ka/ f. step
стучать /stuchát'/ v. knock
стыд /styd/ m. shame
стыдить /stydít'/ v. put to shame
стыдливый /stydlívyi/ adj. bashful
стынуть /stýnut'/ v. get cold
стычка /stýchka/ f. skirmish
стюардесса /stiuardéssa/ f. air hostess
стяжатель /stiazhátel'/ m. money-grubber
суббота /subbóta/ f. Saturday
субсидировать /subsidírovat'/ v. subsidize
субтитр /subtítr/ m. sub-title
субъект /sub''ékt/ m. subject
сувенир /suvenír/ m. souvenir
суверенитет /suverenitét/ m. sovereignty
сугроб /sugrób/ m. snowdrift
суд /sud/ m. court; trial
судак /sudák/ m. pike-perch
судебный /sudébnyi/ adj. judicial
судимость /sudímost'/ f. previous convictions
судить /sudít'/ v. judge
судно /súdno/ n. ship
судоверфь /sudovérf'/ f. shipyard
судомойка /sudomóika/ f. scullery maid
судопроизводство /sudoproizvódstvo/ n. legal proceedings
судорога /súdoroga/ f. cramp
судостроение /sudostroénie/ n. shipbuilding

судоходный /sudokhódnyi/ adj. navigable

судьба /sud'bá/ f. fate

судья /sud'iá/ m. , f. judge; referee

суеверие /suevérie/ n. superstition

суета /suetá/ f. fuss

суетиться /suetít'sia/ v. bustle

суждение /suzhdénie/ n. opinion

суживать /súzhivat'/ v. narrow

суживаться /súzhivat'sia/ v. contract

сука /súka/ f. bitch

султан /sultán/ m. sultan

сумасброд /sumasbród/ m. madcap

сумасшедший /sumasshédshij/ adj. mad

суматоха /sumatókha/ f. bustle

сумерки /súmerki/ pl. twilight

суметь /sumét'/ v. manage to

сумка /súmka/ f. bag

сумма /súmma/ f. sum

суммировать /summírovat'/ v. summarize

сумочка /súmochka/ f. handbag; дамская с. /dámskaia s./ purse

сумрачный /súmracnhyi/ adj. gloomy

сундук /sundúk/ m. trunk

суп /sup/ m. soup

супруг /suprúg/ m. husband; spouse

супруга /suprúga/ f. wife; spouse

супружество /suprúzhestvo/ n. matrimony

сургуч /surgúch/ m. sealing-wax

суровый /suróvyi/ adj. severe

сурок /surók/ m. marmot

суррогат /surrogát/ m. substitute

сурьма /súr'ma/ f. antinomy

сустав /sustáv/ m. joint

сутки /sútki/ pl. twenty-four hours

суточный /sútochnyi/ adj. daily

сутулиться /sutúlit'sia/ v. stoop

сутулый /sutúlyi/ adj. round-shouldered

суть /sut'/ f. essence

суфлер /sufliór/ m. prompter

сухарь /sukhár'/ m. cracker; biscuit

сухожилиеcevjxrf /sukhozhílie/ n. sinew

сухой /sukhói/ adj. dry

сухощавый /sukhoshchávyi/ adj. lean

сучок /suchók/ m. twig

суша /súsha/ f. dry land

сушеный /sushónyi/ adj. dried

сушить /sushít'/ v. dry

существенный /sushchéstvennyi/ adj. essential

существительное /sushchestvítel'noe/ n. noun

существо /sushchestvó/ n. being

существовать /sushchestvovát'/ v. exist

сущий /súshchii/ adj. real

сфера /sféra/ f. sphere

сфинкс /sfinks/ m. sphinx

схватка /skhvátka/ f. skirmish; родовые схватки /rodovýe skhvátki/Ё labour

схватывать /skhvátyvat'/ v. grab

схема /skhéma/ f. scheme

сходить /skhodít'/ v. come off; go to fetch

сходни /skhódni/ pl. gangway

схожий /skhózhii/ adj. similar

сцеживать /stsézhivat'/ v. decant

сцена /stséna/ f. stage; scene

сценарий /stsenárii/ m. script

сцеплять /stsepliát'/ v. couple

счастливый /schastlívyi/ adj. happy

счастье /schást'e/ n. happiness

счет /schot/ m. account; score

счетовод /schetovód/ m. accountant

счетчик /schótchik/ m. meter

считать /schitát'/ v. count

счищать /schishchát'/ v. clean off

сшибать /schibát'/ v. knock down

сшивать /schivát'/ v. sew together

съедобный /s''edóbnyi/ adj. edible

съеживаться /s''iózhivat'sia/ v. shrink

съезд /s''ézd/ m. congress

съемка /s''iómka/ f. survey; shooting

съемщик /s''iómshchik/ m. tenant

сын /syn/ m. son

сыпать /sýpat'/ v. pour

сыпной (тиф) /sýpnoi tif/ adj. + m. typhus

сыпь /syp'/ f. rash
сыр /syr/ m. cheese
сырник /sýrnik/ m. cheese pancake
сырой /syrói/ adj. damp
сырье /syr'ió/ n. raw material(s)
сытный /sýtnyi/ adj. satisfying; substantial
сытый /sýtyi/ adj. satisfied
сыщик /sýshchik/ m. detective
сюда /siudá/ adv. here
сюжет /siuzhét/ m. plot
сюита /siuíta/ f. (mus.) suite
сюрприз /siurpríz/ m. surprise

Т

табак /tabák/ m. tobacco
табакерка /tabakérka/ f. snuff-box
таблетка /tablétka/ f. tablet
таблица /tablítsa/ f. table
табор /tábor/ m. gipsy encampment
табун /tabún/ m. herd (of horses)
табурет /taburét/ m. stool
тавро /tavró/ m. brand
таджик /tadzhík/ m. Tajik
таджикский /tadzhíkskii/ adj. Tajik
таджичка /tadzhíchka/ f. Tajik
таз /taz/ m. basin; pelvis
таинственный /tainstvennyi/ adj. mysterious
таинство /táinstvo/ n. sacrament
тайга /taigá/ f. taiga
тайна /táina/ f. mystery
тайник /tainík/ m. hiding place
тайный /táinyi/ adj. secret
тайфун /taifún/ m. typhoon
так /tak/ adv. so; так как /tak kak/ since
такелаж /takelázh/ m. rigging
также /tákzhe/ adv. also
такой /takói/ pron. such

такса /táksa/ f. tariff, fixed price; dachshund
такси /taksí/ n. taxi
тактика /táktika/ f. tactics
тактичный /taktíchnyi/ adj. tactful
талант /talánt/ m. talent
талисман /talismán/ m. talisman, charm
талия /táliia/ f. waist
талон /talón/ m. coupon
тальк /tal'k/ m. talcum powder
там /tam/ adv. there
тамада /tamadá/ m., f. toast-master
таможня /tamózhnia/ f. custom-house
танец /tánets/ m. dance
танк /tank/ m. tank
танкер /tánker/ m. tanker
танцевать /tantsevát'/ v. dance
танцовщик, танцор /tantsóvshchik, tantsór/ m. dancer
тапочка /tápochka/ f. slipper
тара /tára/ f. packing
таракан /tarakán/ m. cockroach
таращить (глаза) /taráshchit' glazá/ v.+pl. goggle
тарелка /tarélka/ f. plate
тариф /taríf/ m. tariff
таскать /taskát'/ v. drag
тасовать /tasovát'/ m. shuffle
ТАСС /tass/ abbr., m. Telegraph Agency of the Soviet Union
татарин /tatárin/ m. Tartar
татарка /tatárka/ f. Tartar
татарский /tatárskii/ adj. Tartar
татуировка /tatuiróvka/ f. tattoo
тафта /taftá/ f. taffeta
тахта /takhtá/ f. ottoman
тачка /táchka/ f. wheelbarrow
тащить /tashchit'/ v. drag
таять /táiat'/ v. melt
твердеть /tverdét'/ v. become hard
твердить /tverdít'/ v. repeat
твердолобый /tverdolóbyi/ adj. diehard
твердость /tveórdost'/ f. firmness
твердый /tveórdyi/ adj. hard; solid

твердыня /tverdýnia/ f. stronghold
твой /tvói/ pron. your(s)
творение /tvorénie/ n. creation
творец /tvoréts/ m. creator
творить /tvorít'/ v. create
творог /tvórog/ m. cottage cheese
творческий /tvórcheskii/ adj. creative
театр /teátr/ m. theatre
тевтон /tevtón/ m. Teuton
тезис /tézis/ m. thesis; proposition
тезка /tiózka/ m. , f. namesake
текст /tekst/ m. text
текстиль /tekstíl'/ m. textiles
текучий /tekúchii/ adj. fluid
текущий /tekúshchii/ adj. current
телевидение /televídenie/ n. television
телевизор /televízor/ m. television set
телега /teléga/ f. waggon, cart
телеграмма /telegrámma/ f. telegram
телеграф /telegráf/ m. telegraph
телеграфировать /telegrafírovat'/ v. cable, wire
телезритель /telezrítel'/ m. (television) viewer
теленок /teliónok/ m. calf
телепатия /telepátiia/ f. telepathy
телепередача /teleperedácha/ f. telecast
телескоп /teleskóp/ m. telescope
телефон /telefón/ m. telephone; т.-автомат /t. avtomát/ public telephone
телец /teléts/ m. Taurus
телиться /telít'sia/ m. calve
телка /tiólka/ f. heifer
тело /télo/ n. body
телогрейка /telogréika/ f. padded jacket
телосложение /teloslozhénie/ n. build
телохранитель /telokhranítel'/ m. bodyguard
телятина /teliátina/ f. veal
тема /téma/ f. theme
тембр /tembr/ m. timbre
темнеть /temnét'/ v. become dark
темнота /temnotá/ f. darkness
темп /temp/ m. tempo

темперамент /temperáment/ m. temperament
температура /temperatúra/ f. temperature
тенденция /tendéntsiia/ f. tendency
тенистый /tenístyi/ adj. shady
теннис /ténnis/ m. tennis
теннисист /tennisíst/ m. tennis-player
тенор /ténor/ m. tenor
тень /ten'/ f. shadow
теология /teológiia/ f. theology
теорема /teoréma/ f. theorem
теория /teóriia/ f. theory
теперь /tepér'/ adv. now
теплеть /teplét'/ v. grow warm
теплица /teplítsa/ f. hothouse
тепловоз /teplovóz/ m. diesel locomotive
тепловой /teplovói/ adj. heat, thermal
теплота /teplotá/ f. heat; warmth
теплотехник /teplotékhnik/ m. heating engineer
теплоход /teplokhód/ m. motor ship
теплый /tióplyi/ adj. warm
терапевт /terapévt/ m. therapeutist
терапия /terapíia/ f. therapy
тереть /terét'/ v. rub
терзать /terzát'/ v. torture; tear to pieces
терка /tiórka/ f. grater
термометр /termómetr/ m. thermometer
термос /térmos/ m. thermos
термостат /termostát/ m. thermostat
термоядерный /termoiáderny/ adj. thermo-nuclear
терновник /ternóvnik/ m. blackthorn
терпеть /terpét'/ v. bear
терпкий /térpkii/ adj. astringent
терраса /terrása/ f. terrace
территория /territóriia/ f. territory
террор /terrór/ m. terror
террорист /terroríst/ m. terrorist
терять /teriát'/ v. lose
тес /tios/ m. boards
тесемка /tesiómka/ f. tape
теснить /tesnít'/ v. squeeze; crowd
тесный /tésnyi/ adj. tight

тесто /tésto/ n. dough

тесть /test'/ m. father-in-law (wife's father)

тетерев /téterev/ m. black grouse

тетрадь /tetrád'/ f. exercise book

тетя /tiótia/ f. aunt

техник /tékhnik/ m. technician

техника /tékhnika/ f. technique; machinery

техникум /tékhnikum/ m. technical college

технология /tekhnológiia/ f. technology

течение /techénie/ n. course

течь /tech/ v. flow; leak

теща /tióshcha/ f. mother-in-law (wife's mother)

тигр /tigr/ m. tiger

тигрица /tigrítsa/ f. tigress

тикать /tíkat'/ v. tick

тина /tína/ f. mud, slime

тип /tip/ m. type

типичный /tipíchnyi/ adj. typical

типография /tipográfiia/ f. printing-house

тир /tir/ m. shooting-range

тираж /tirázh/ m. circulation; edition

тиран /tirán/ m. tyrant

тирания /tiraníia/ f. tyranny

тире /tiré/ n. dash

тис /tis/ m. yew

тискать /tískat'/ v. squeeze

тиски /tiskí/ pl. vice

тиснение /tisnénie/ n. stamping

титул /títul/ m. title

тиф /tif/ m. typhus

тихий /tikhíi/ adj. quiet

тишина /tishína/ f. silence

ткань /tkan'/ f. cloth, fabric

ткать /tkat'/ v. weave

ткач /tkach/ m. weaver

тлеть /tlet'/ v. decay; smoulder

товар /továr/ m. commodity; goods

товарищ /továrishch/ m. comrade

товарообмен /tovaroobmén/ m. barter; commodity exchange

тогда /togdá/ adv. then

тоже /tózhe/ adv. also, too

ток /tok/ m. current

токарь /tókar'/ m. turner

толкать /tolkát'/ v. shove

толкаться /tolkát'sia/ v. jostle

толки /tólki/ pl. gossip

толкучка /tolkúchka/ f. second-hand market

толочь /tolóch/ v. grind

толпа /tolpá/ f. crowd

толстеть /tolstét'/ v. grow fat

толстый /tólstyi/ adj. fat

толчок /tolchók/ m. push; stimulus

толщина /tolshchiná/ f. thickness; fatness

толь /tol'/ m. roofing felt

только /tól'ko/ adv. only

том /tom/ m. volume

томат /tomát/ m. tomato

томатный (сок) /tomátnyi sok/ adj.+m. tomato juice

тон /ton/ m. tone; shade

тональность /tonál'nost'/ f. (mus.) key

тонизировать /tonizírovat'/ v. tone up

тонкий /tónkii/ adj. slim; subtle

тонна /tónna/ f. ton

тоннель /tonnél'/ m. tunnel

тонус (жизненный т.) /zhíznennyi tónus/ adj.+m. vitality

тонуть /tonút'/ v. sink; drown

топать /tópat'/ v. stamp

топить /topít'/ v. light a fire, heat; drown

топливо /tóplivo/ n. fuel

тополь /tópol'/ m. poplar

топор /topór/ m. axe

топот /tópot/ m. tread

топтать /toptát'/ v. trample

топь /top'/ f. marsh, mire

торговать /torgovát'/ v. trade

торговаться /torgovát'sia/ v. bargain

торговец /torgóvets/ m. trader

торжественный /torzhéstvennyi/ adj. solemn

торжество /torzhestvó/ n. ceremony; triumph

торжествовать /torzhestvovát'/ v. exult, triumph

тормоз /tórmoz/ m. brake

тормозить /tormozít'/ v. brake

тормошить /tormoshít'/ v. pester; tousle

торопить /toropít'/ v. hurry

торопливый /toroplívyi/ adj. hasty

торпеда /torpéda/ f. torpedo

торс /tors/ m. torso

торт /tort/ m. pie; fancy cake

торф /torf/ m. peat

торфяной /torfianói/ adj. peat

торчать /torchát'/ v. protrude

тоска /toská/ f. melancholy; т. по родине /t. po ródine/ homesickness

тоскливый /tosklívyi/ adj. dreary

тосковать /toskovát'/ v. pine, long

тост /tost/ m. toast; toasted sandwich

тот /tot/ pron. that

тотчас /tótchas/ adv. immediately

точильщик /tochíl'shchik/ m. (knife-)grinder

точить /tochít'/ v. sharpen

точно /tóchno/ adv. precisely

точность /tóchnost'/ f. exactness

точный /tóchnyi/ adj. accurate

тошнить (меня тошнит) /meniá toshnít/ I feel sick

тощий /tóshchii/ adj. skinny

трава /travá/ f. grass

травить /travít'/ v. poison

травма /trávma/ f. trauma

травянистый /travianístyi/ adj. grassy; tasteless, insipid

трагедия /tragédiia/ f. tragedy

традиция /tradítsiia/ f. tradition

трактор /tráktor/ m. tractor

трамвай /tramvái/ m. tram

трамплин /tramplín/ m. spring-board

транзит /tranzít/ m. transit

трансатлантический /transatlantícheskii/ adj. transatlantic

транслировать /translírovat'/ v. broadcast

транспорт /tránsport/ m. transport

трансформатор /transformátor/ m. transformer

трансформировать /transformírovat'/ v. transform

траншея /transhéiia/ f. trench

трап /trap/ f. ladder

трасса /trássa/ f. route

трата /tráta/ f. expenditure

тратить /trátit'/ v. spend

траур /tráur/ m. mourning

требование /trébovanie/ n. demand

требовать /trébovat'/ v. demand; summon

тревога /trevóga/ f. alarm

тревожить /trevózhit'/ v. worry

трезвенник /trézvennik/ v. teetotaller

трезвый /trézvyi/ adj. sober

трезубец /trezúbets/ m. trident

трель /trel'/ f. trill

тренер /tréner/ m. coach

трение /trénie/ n. friction

тренировать /trenirovát'/ v. train

треножник /trenózhnik/ m. tripod

трепать /trepát'/ v. tousle

трепетать /trepetát'/ v. tremble

треск /tresk/ m. crack

треска /treská/ f. cod

трескаться /tréskat'sia/ v. crack

тресковый (жир) /treskóvyi zhir/ adj.+m. cod-liver oil

трест /trest/ m. trust

третейский (суд) /tretéiskii sud/ adj.+m. arbitration; tribunal

третий /trétii/ num. third

третировать /tretírovat'/ v. slight

треть /tret'/ f. a third

третьесортный /tret'esórtnyi/ adj. third-rate

треугольник /treugól'nik/ m. triangle

треугольный /treugól'nyi/ adj. triangular
трефы /tréfy/ pl. clubs
трещать /treshchát'/ v. crackle
трещина /tréshchina/ f. split
трещотка /treshchótka/ f. rattle
три /tri/ num. three
трибуна /tribúna/ f. rostrum
трибунал /tribunál/ m. tribunal
тригонометрия /trigonométriia/ f. trigonometry
тридцать /trídtsat'/ num. thirty
трижды /trízhdy/ adv. three times, thrice
трико /trikó/ n. tights
трикотаж /trikotázh/ m. knitted fabric
трилистник /trilístnik/ m. shamrock
трилогия /trilógiia/ f. trilogy
тринадцать /trinádtsat'/ num. thirteen
триста /trísta/ num. three hundred
триумф /triúmf/ m. triumph
трогательный /trógatel'nyi/ adj. moving
трогать /trógat'/ v. touch
трое /tróe/ pl. three
троекратный /troekrátnyi/ adj. thrice-repeated
троица /tróitsa/ f. Trinity
тройка /tróika/ f. (figure) three; troika; three-piece suit
тройной /troinói/ adj. treble, triple
тройня /tróinia/ f. triplets
троллейбус /trolléibus/ m. trolley-bus
тромб /tromb/ m. clot
трон /tron/ m. throne
тропик /trópik/ m. tropic
тропинка /tropínka/ f. path
трос /tros/ m. rope
тростник /tróstnik/ m. reed
тротуар /trotuár/ m. pavement
трофей /troféi/ m. trophy
троюродный (брат, сестра) /troiúrodnyi brat, sestrá/ adj.+m., f. second cousin
труба /trubá/ f. chimney; trumpet
трубач /trubách/ m. trumpeter
трубить /trubít'/ v. blow
трубка /trúbka/ f. pipe

труд /trud/ m. labour, work
трудиться /trudít'sia/ v. work
трудность /trúdnost'/ f. difficulty
трудящийся /trudiáshchiisia/ m. worker
труженик /trúzhenik/ m. toiler
труп /trup/ m. corpse
труппа /trúppa/ f. company
трус /trus/ m. coward
трусы /trusý/ pl. shorts; trunks
трутень /trúten'/ m. drone
трущоба /trushchóba/ f. slum
трюк /triuk/ m. trick
трюм /trium/ m. hold
трюмо /triumó/ n. pier-glass
трюфель /triúfel'/ m. truffle
тряпка /triápka/ f. rag
тряпье /triap'ió/ n. rags
трясина /triasína/ f. quagmire
трясти /triastí/ v. shake
трястись /triastís'/ v. tremble
туалет /tualét/ m. dress; toilet; lavatory; cloak-room
туберкулез /tuberkulióz/ m. tuberculosis
тугой /tugói/ adj. tight; taut
туда /tudá/ adv. there
туз /tuz/ m. ace
туземец /tuzémets/ m. native
туловище /túlovishche/ n. trunk; torso
тулуп /tulúp/ m. sheepskin coat
туман /tumán/ m. mist
тумбочка /túmbochka/ f. bedside table
тундра /túndra/ f. tundra
тунец /túnets/ m. tuna
туннель /tunnél'/ m. tunnel
тупик /tupík/ m. blind alley
тупить /tupít'/ v. blunt
тупой /tupói/ adj. blunt; stupid
тур /tur/ m. turn; round
тура /turá/ f. castle, rook
турбаза /turbáza/ f. tourist centre
турбина /turbína/ f. turbine
турецкий /turétskii/ adj. Turkish
турист /turíst/ m. tourist
туркмен /turkmén/ m. Turkmen

туркменка /turkménka/ f. Turkmen
туркменский /turkménskii/ adj. Turkmen
турне /turné/ n. tour
турнепс /turnéps/ m. turnip
турник /turník/ m. horizontal bar
турнир /turnír/ m. tournament
турок /túrok/ m. Turk
турчанка /turchánka/ f. Turk
тут /tut/ adv. here
туфля /túflia/ f. shoe
тухлый /túkhlyi/ adj. rotten, bad
тухнуть /túkhnut'/ v. go out
туча /túcha/ f. cloud
тушеный /tushónyi/ adj. stewed
тушить /tushít'/ v. stew; extinguish
тушь /tush/ f. Indian ink; mascara
тщетный /tshchétnyi/ adj. futile
тщательный /tshchátel'nyi/ adj. thorough, careful
ты /ty/ pron. you
тыква /týkva/ f. pumpkin
тыл /tyl/ m. rear
тысяча /týsiacha/ num. thousand
тысячелетие /tysiachelétie/ n. millennium
тьма /t'ma/ f. darkness; host, multitude
тюбетейка /tiubetéika/ f. embroidered skull-cap
тюбик /tiúbik/ m. tube
тюк /tiúk/ m. bale
тюлень /tiul'en'/ m. seal
тюль /tiúl'/ m. tulle
тюльпан /tiul'pán/ m. tulip
тюрбан /tiurbán/ m. turban
тюркский /tiúrkskii/ adj. Turklic
тюрьма /tiur'má/ f. prison
тюфяк /tiufiák/ m. mattress
тявкать /tiávkat'/ v. yap
тяготение /tiagoténie/ n. gravity
тяжеловес /tiazhelovés/ m. heavy-weight
тяжелый /tiazhólyi/ adj. heavy
тяжкий /tiázhkii/ adj. distressing
тянуть /tianút'/ v. pull

тянучка /tianúchka/ f. toffee

У

у /u/ prep. near, by
убавлять /ubavliát'/ v. reduce
убаюкивать /ubaiúkivat'/ v. lull
убегать /ubegát'/ v. run away
убедительный /ubedítel'nyi/ adj. convincing
убеждать /ubezhdát'/ v. persuade
убеждение /ubezhdénie/ n. conviction
убежище /ubézhishche/ n. shelter
уберегать /uberegát'/ v. protect, keep safe
убивать /ubivát'/ v. kill
убийство /ubíistvo/ n. murder
убийца /ubíitsa/ f. murderer
убирать /ubirát'/ v. remove; tidy up
убожество /ubózhestvo/ n. poverty; mediocrity
убой /ubói/ m. slaughter
убористый /ubóristyi/ adj. small, close (handwriting)
уборка /ubórka/ f. harvesting; tidying up
уборная /ubórnaia/ f. lavatory
уборщица /ubórshchitsa/ f. cleaner
убыток /ubýtok/ m. loss
убыточный /ubýtochnii/ adj. unprofitable
уважать /uvazhát'/ v. respect
уведомление /uvedomlénie/ n. notification
увековечивать /uvekovéchivat'/ v. immortalize
увеличивать /uvelíchivat'/ v. increase
увеличительное (стекло) /uvelichítel'noe stekló/ adj.+n. magnifying glass
увенчивать /uvénchivat'/ v. crown
уверенность /uvérennost'/ f. confidence
увертливый /uviórtlivyi/ adj. evasive
увертюра /uvertiúra/ f. overture
уверять /uveriát'/ v. assure
увеселение /uveselénie/ n. entertaiment

увесистый /uvésistyi/ adj. weighty

увечить /uvéchit'/ v. maim

увиливать /uvílivat'/ v. evade

увлажнять /uvlazhniát'/ v. moisten

увлекательный /uvlekátel'nyi/ adj. fascinating

увлечение /uvlechénie/ n. passion (for), enthusiasm

увозить /uvozít'/ v. take away

увольнять /uvol'niát'/ v. sack

увы /uvý/ int. alas!

увядать /uviadát'/ v. fade

увязывать /uviázyvat'/ v. tie up; coordinate

угадывать /ugádyvat'/ v. guess (right)

угарный (газ) /ugárnyi gaz/ adj.+m. carbon monoxide

угасать /ugasát'/ v. go out; die down

углевод /uglevód/ m. carbohydrate

углублять /uglubliát'/ v. deepen

угнетатель /ugnetátel'/ m. oppressor

угнетать /ugnetát'/ v. depress; oppress

уговаривать /ugovárivat'/ v. persuade

угождать /ugozhdát'/ v. please, oblige

угол /úgol/ m. corner; angle

уголовник /ugolóvnik/ m. criminal

уголовный /ugolóvnyi/ adj. criminal

уголь /úgol'/ m. coal

угомонить /ugomonít'/ v. calm down

угонять /ugoniát'/ v. drive away; steal

угорелый (как у.) /kak ugorélyi/ conj. +adj. like a madman

угорь /úgor'/ m. eel; blackhead

угощать /ugoshchát'/ v. treat

угощение /ugoshchénie/ n. refreshments

угрожать /ugrozhát'/ v. menace

угроза /ugróza/ f. threat

угрызение /ugryzénie/ n. pangs

угрюмый /ugriúmyi/ adj. gloomy

удав /udáv/ m. boa-constrictor

удавка /udávka/ f. running knot

удалой /udalói/ adj. daring

удалять /udaliát'/ v. remove; send away; dismiss

удар /udár/ m. blow; stroke; attack

ударение /udarénie/ n. stress

ударять /udariát'/ v. strike

ударяться /udariát'sia/ v. strike, hit

удача /udácha/ f. good luck

удачный /udáchlyi/ adj. successful

удваивать /udváivat'/ v. double

удел /udél/ m. destiny

уделять /udeliát'/ v. spare, devote

удерживать /udérzhivat'/ v. hold back; hold on to

удешевлять /udeshevliát'/ v. reduce the price of

удивительный /udivítel'nyi/ adj. amazing

удивлять /udivliát'/ v. surprise

удирать /udirát'/ v. run away

удить /udít'/ v. fish

удобный /udóbnyi/ adj. comfortable; convenient

удобрение /udobrenie/ n. fertilizer

удовлетворять /uvodletvoriát'/ v. satisfy

удовольствие /udovól'stvie/ n. pleasure

удой /udói/ m. milk-yield

удойная (корова) /udóinaia korova/ adj.+f. good milker

удорожать /udorozhát'/ v. raise the price of

удостаивать /udostáivat'/ v. honour; confer (on), award

удостоверение /udostoverénie/ n. certificate; у. личности /u. lichnosti/ identity card

удостоверять /udostoveriát'/ v. certify

удостоверяться /udostoveriát'sia/ v. make sure (of)

удочерять /udocheriát'/ v. adopt

удочка /údochka/ f. fishing-rod

уединение /uedinénie/ n. seclusion

уезжать /uezzhát'/ v. go away

уж /uzh/ part. really; to be sure; m. grass-snake

ужас /úzhas/ m. horror

ужасать /uzhasát'/ v. horrify

ужасный /uzhásnyi/ adj. terrible

уже /uzhé/ adv. already, by now

уживчивый /uzhívchivyi/ adj. easy to get on with

ужимка /uzhímka/ f. grimace

ужин /úzhin/ m. supper

узаконивать /uzakónivat'/ v. legalize

узбек /uzbék/ m. Uzbek

узбекский /uzbékskii/ adj. Uzbek

узбечка /uzbéchka/ f. Uzbek

уздечка /uzdéchka/ f. bridle

узел /úzel/ m. knot

узкий /úzkii/ adj. narrow; limited; narrow-minded

узнавать /uznavát'/ v. recognize; find out

узор /uzór/ m. pattern

узурпировать /uzurpírovat'/ v. usurp

узы /úzy/ pl. bonds

уйма /úima/ f. great lot

указ /ukáz/ m. decree

указание /ukazánie/ n. instruction

указатель /ukazátel'/ m. index; directory

указка /ukázka/ f. pointer

указывать /ukázyvat'/ v. show

укалывать /ukályvat'/ v. prick

укладывать / ukládyvat'/ v. lay; pile, stack

уклончивый /uklónchivyi/ adj. evasive

уклоняться /ukloniát'sia/ v. avoid

укол /ukól/ m. injection

укор /ukór/ m. reproach

укорачивать /ukoráchivat'/ v. shorten

украдкой /ukrádkoi/ adv. furtively

украинец /ukráinets/ m. Ukrainian

украинка /ukráinka/ f. Ukrainian

украинский /ukráinskii/ adj. Ukrainian

украшать /ukrashát'/ v. adorn; decorate

украшение /ukrashénie/ n. ornament; decoration

укреплять /ukrepliát'/ v. strengthen

укромный /ukrómnyi/ adj. secluded

укроп /ukróp/ m. dill

укротитель /ukrotítel'/ m. tamer

укрощать /ukroshchát'/ v. tame

укрупнять /ukrupniát'/ v. enlarge

укрывать /ukryvát'/ v. cover; conceal

уксус /úksus/ m. vinegar

укус /ukús/ m. bite, sting

укутывать /ukútyvat'/ v. wrap up

улаживать /ulázhivat'/ v. settle, arange; reconcile

улей /úlei/ m. (bee)hive

улетать /uletát'/ v. fly away

улика /ulíka/ f. evidence

улитка /ulítka/ f. snail

улица /úlitsa/ f. street

улов /ulóv/ m. catch

улучшать /uluchshát'/ v. improve

улыбаться /ulybát'sia/ v. smile

ультиматум /ul'timátum/ m. ultimatum

ультразвуковой /ul'trazvukovói/ adj. supersonic

ультрафиолетовый /ul'trafiolétovyi/ adj. ultra-violet

ум /um/ m. mind, intellect

умалишенный /umalishónnyi/ adj. lunatic

умалчивать /umálchivat'/ v. fail to mention

умелый /umélyi/ adj. skilful

умение /uménie/ n. ability, skill

уменьшать /umen'shát'/ v. decrease

умеренный /umérennyi/ adj. moderate

уместный /uméstnyi/ adj. appropriate

уметь /umét'/ v. know how, be able

умещать /umeshchát'/ v. fit in, find room for

умилять /umiliát'/ v. touch

умиротворять /umirotvoriát'/ v. pacify

умирать /umirát'/ v. die

умножать /umnozhát'/ v. multiply

умный /úmnyi/ adj. clever, intelligent

умолкать /umolkát'/ v. fall silent

умолять /umoliát'/ v. implore

умудряться /umudriát'sia/ v. contrive

умывать /umyvát'/ v. wash

умываться /umyvát'sia/ v. wash (oneself)
умысел /úmysel/ m. design
умышленный /umýshlennyi/ adj. intentional
унавоживать /unavózhivat'/ v. manure
универмаг /univermág/ m. department store
универсальный /univérsal'nyi/ adj. universal
университет /universitét/ m. university
унижать /unizhát'/ v. humiliate
униженный /unízhennyi/ adj. humiliated
уникальный /unikál'nyi/ adj. unique
унитаз /unitáz/ m. lavatory pan
унифицировать /unifitsírovat'/ v. unify
уничтожать /unichtozhát'/ v. destroy
уносить /unosít'/ v. take away
унтер-офицер /unter-ofitsér/ m. noncommissioned officer
унты /únty/ pl. high fur boots
унция /úntsiia/ f. ounce
унылый /unýlyi/ adj. depressed
упадок /upádok/ m. decay
упаковывать /upakóvyvat'/ v. pack
упитанный /upítannyi/ adj. well-fed
уплата /upláta/ f. payment
уплачивать /upláchivat'/ v. pay
уплотнять /uplotniát'/ v. condence
уплывать /uplyvát'/ v. swim away
упоение /upoénie/ n. ecstasy
уползать /upolzát'/ v. crawl away
уполномоченный /upolnomóchennyi/ adj. representative; plenipotentiary
уполномочивать /upolnomóchivat'/ v. authorize
упоминать /upominát'/ v. mention
упор /upór/ m. rest, support
упорный /upórnyi/ adj. stubborn
упорствовать /upórstvovat'/ v. persist
упорядочивать /uporiádochivat'/ v. put in order
употреблять /upotrebliát'/ v. use
управление /upravlénie/ n. administration

управлять /upravliát'/ v. direct
управляющий /upravliáiushchii/ m. manager
упражнение /uprazhnénie/ n. exercise
упражнять /uprazhniát'/ v. exercise
упражняться /uprazhniát'sia/ v. practise
упразднять /uprazdniát'/ v. abolish
упрашивать /upráshivat'/ v. entreat
упрекать /uprekát'/ v. reproach
упрочивать /upróchivat'/ v. strengthen, consolidate
упрощать /uproshchát'/ v. simplify
упругий /uprúgii/ adj. elastic; resilient
упряжь /úpriazh/ f. harness
упрямиться /upriámit'sia/ v. persist
упрямый /upriámiyi/ adj. stubborn
упускать /upuskát'/ v. let slip
упущение /upushchénie/ n. ommission
ура /urá/ int. hurrah
уравнение /uravnénie/ n. equation
уравнивать /urávnivat'/ v. equalize
уравниловка /uravnílovka/ f. wage-levelling
уравновешивать /uravnovéshivat'/ v. balance; neutralize
ураган /uragán/ m. hurricane
уральский /urál'skii/ adj. Ural
уран /urán/ m. uranium
урегулирование /uregulírovanie/ n. settlement
урезать /urezát'/ v. cut off; cut down
урна /úrna/ f. urn; ballot-box; litter-bin
уровень /urovén'/ m. level
урод /uród/ m. freak
уродиться /urodít'sia/ v. ripen, grow
уродливый /uródlivyi/ adj. ugly
уродовать /uródovat'/ v. disfigure
уродство /uródstvo/ n. deformity
урожай /urozhái/ m. harvest
урожайность /urozháinost'/ f. yield
урожденная /urozhdiónnaya/ adj. née
уроженец /urozhénets/ m. native
урок /urók/ m. lesson

урон /urón/ m. loss
усадьба /usád'ba/ f. country estate
усаживать /usázhivat'/ v. seat
усатый /usátyi/ adj. moustached
усваивать /usváivat'/ v. master
усеивать /uséivat'/ v. dot; litter, strew
усердный /usérdnyi/ adj. zealous
усеченный /usechónnyi/ adj. truncated
усидчивый /usídchivyi/ adj. assiduous
усиливать /usílivat'/ v. strengthen
усилие /usílie/ n. effort
усилитель /usílitel'/ m. amplifier
ускользать /uskol'zát'/ v. slip off
ускорять /uskoriát'/ v. spead up
уславливаться /uslávlivat'sia/ v. agree
условие /uslóvie/ n. condition
условленный /uslóvlennyi/ adj. fixed, stipulated
усложнять /uslozhniát'/ v. complicate
услуга /uslúga/ f. service
услужливый /uslúzhlivyi/ adj. obliging
усмехаться /usmekhát'sia/ v. grin
усмирять /usmiriát'/ v. suppress
уснуть /usnút'/ v. go to sleep
усовершенствование /usovershénstvovanie/ n. improvement
успеваемость /uspeváemost'/ f. progress
успевать /uspevát'/ v. have time, succeed
успение /uspénie/ n. Assumption
успех /uspékh/ m. success
успокаивать /uspokáivat'/ v. quiet
успокаиваться /uspokáivat'sia/ v. calm down
устав /ustáv/ m. regulations
уставать /ustavát'/ v. get tired
усталость /ustálost'/ f. tiredness
усталый /ustályi/ adj. weary
устанавливать /ustanávlivat'/ v. install; establish
устарелый /ustarélyi/ adj. obsolete
устилать /ustilát'/ v. cover, lay out (with)

устный /ústnyi/ adj. verbal, oral
устой /ustói/ m. foundation
устойчивый /ustóichivyi/ adj. stable
устоять /ustoiát'/ v. keep one's balance
устраивать /ustráivat'/ v. arrange
устранять /ustraniát'/ v. remove
устрашать /ustrashát'/ v. frighten
устрица /ústritsa/ f. oyster
устройство /ustróistvo/ n. arrangement; construction
уступ /ustúp/ m. ledge
уступать /ustupát'/ v. yield
уступка /ustúpka/ f. concession
устье /úst'e/ n. mouth; estuary
усугублять /usugubliát'/ v. aggravate
усы /úsy/ pl. moustache
усылать /usýlat'/ v. send away
усыновлять /usynovliát'/ v. adopt
усыплять /usypliát'/ v. lull to sleep
усыхать /usykhát'/ v. dry up
утаивать /utáivat'/ v. conceal; keep to oneself
утварь /útvar'/ f. utensils
утвердительный /utverdítel'nyi/ adj. affirmative
утверждать /utverzhdát'/ v. affirm
утверждение /utverzhdénie/ n. assertion
утекать /utekát'/ v. flow away
утенок /utiónok/ m. duckling
утеплять /utepliát'/ v. warm
утерять /uteriát'/ v. lose
утес /utiós/ m. cliff
утечка /utéchka/ f. leakage
утешать /uteshát'/ v. console
утирать /utirát'/ v. wipe
утихать /utakhát'/ v. become calm
утка /útka/ f. duck
утолщать /utolshchát'/ v. make thicker
утолять /utoliát'/ v. quench
утомительный /utomítel'nyi/ adj. tiresome
утомление /utomlénie/ n. weariness
утомлять /utomliát'/ v. fatigue
утончать /utonchát'/ v. make thinner

утопия /utópiia/ f. utopia
уточнять /utochniát'/ v. specify
утраивать /utraivát'/ v. treble
утрата /utráta/ f. loss
утро /útro/ n. morning
утроба /utróba/ f. womb
утюг /utiúg/ m. iron
уха /ukhá/ f. fish soup
ухабистый /ukhábistyi/ adj. bumpy
ухажер /ukhazhór/ m. boy-friend
ухаживать /ukházhivat'/ v. nurse; make
advances to
ухватка /ukhvátka/ f. manner
ухватывать /ukhvátyvat'/ v. seize
ухватываться /ukhvátyvat'sia/ v. catch
hold of
ухитряться /ukhitriát'sia/ v. contrive
ухмыляться /ukhmyliát'sia/ v. smirk
ухо /úkho/ n. ear
уход /ukhód/ m. departure; maintenance
of; nursing
уходить /ukhodít'/ v. go away
ухудшать /ukhudshát'/ v. make worse
ухудшаться /ukhudshát'sia/ v. deteriorate
уцелеть /utselét'/ v. survive
участвовать /uchástvovat'/ v. participate
участник /uchástnik/ m. participant
участок /uchástok/ m. plot; section
участь /úchast'/ f. lot
учащийся /ucháshchiisia/ m. student; pupil
учеба /uchóba/ f. studies
учебник /uchébnik/ m. text-book
учение /uchénie/ n. doctrine
ученый /uchónyi/ m. scholar
учет /uchót/ m. calculation; registration
учетверять /uchetveriát'/ v. quadruple
училище /uchílishche/ n. college
учитель /uchítel'/ m. teacher
учитывать /uchítyvat'/ v. take into account
учить /uchít'/ v. learn; teach
учиться /uchít'sia/ v. learn, study

учредительный /uchredítel'nyi/ adj. constituent
учреждать /uchrezhdát'/ v. institute
учреждение /uchrezhdénie/ n. establishment
учтивый /uchtívyi/ adj. courteous
ушанка /ushánka/ f. fur cap with earflaps
ушиб /ushíb/ m. injury
ушко /ushkó/ n. tab
ущелье /ushchél'e/ n. gorge
ущемлять /ushchemliát'/ v. pinch; encroach on
ущерб /ushchérb/ m. damage
ущипнуть /ushchipnút'/ v. pinch
уэльский /uél'skii/ adj. Welsh
уют /uiút/ m. comfort
уязвимый /uiazvímyi/ adj. vulnerable
уязвлять /uiazvliát'/ v. hurt
уяснять /uiasniát'/ v. comprehend, make
out

Ф

фабрика /fábrika/ f. factory
фабула /fábula/ f. plot
фагот /fagót/ m. bassoon
фаза /fáza/ f. phase
фазан /fazán/ m. pheasant
факел /fákel/ m. torch
факт /fakt/ m. fact
фактический /faktícheskii/ adj. real
фактор /fáktor/ m. factor
факультативный /fakul'tatívnyi/ adj. op-
tional
факультет /fakul'tét/ m. faculty
фальшивый /fal'shívyi/ adj. false
фамилия /famíliia/ f. surname
фанатизм /fanatízm/ m. fanaticism
фанера /fanéra/ f. plywood
фантазер /fantaziór/ m. dreamer
фантазия /fantáziia/ f. fantasy
фара /fára/ f. head light

фарватер /farváter/ m. fairway
фарисей /fariséi/ m. Pharisee
фармацевт /farmatsévt/m. pharmaceutist
фарс /fars/ m. farce
фартук /fartúk/ m. apron
фарфор /farfór/ m. china; porcelain
фарш /farsh/ m. stuffing
фаршировать /farshirovát'/ v. stuff
фасад /fasád/ m. façade
фасовка /fasóvka/ f. package
фасоль /fasól'/ f. bean(s)
фасон /fasón/ m. fashion
фата /fatá/ f. veil
фатальный /fatál'nyi/ adj. fatal
фашизм /fashízm/ m. fascism
фаянс /faiáns/ m. pottery
февраль /fevrál'/ m. February
фейерверк /feiervérk/ m. firework(s)
фельдмаршал /fel'dmárshal/ m. field-marshal
фельдшер /fel'dshér/ m. medical assistant
феномен /fenomén/ m. phenomenon
феодализм /feodalízm/ m. feudalism
феодальный /feodál'nyi/ adj. feudal
ферзь /ferz'/ m. queen
ферма /férma/ f. farm
фермер /fermér/ m. farmer
фестиваль /festivál'/ m. festival
фетр /fetr/ m. felt
фехтовать /fekhtovát'/ v. fence
фея /féia/ f. fairy
фиалка /fiálka/ f. violet
фибра /fíbra/ f. fibre
фига /fíga/ f. fig
фигура /figúra/ f. figure
фигуральный /figurál'nyi/ adj. figurative
фигурист /figuríst/ m. figure-skater
физик /fízik/ m. physicist
физика /fízika/ f. physics
физиолог /fiziólog/ m. physiologist
физиология /fiziológiia/ f. physiology
физиономия /fizionómiia/ f. physiognomy

физкультура /fizkul'túra/ f. gymnastics
фиктивный /fiktívnyi/ adj. fictitious
филантроп /filantróp/ m. philanthropist
филармония /filarmóniia/ f. philharmonic
филателист /filatelíst/ m. philatelist
филе /filé/ n. sirloin; fillet
филиал /filiál/ m. branch
филигрань /filigrán'/ f. filigree
филин /filín/ m. eagle-owl
философ /filosóf/ m. philosopher
философия /filosófiia/ f. philosophy
фильм /fil'm/ m. film
фильтр /fil'tr/ m. filter
фимиам /fimiám/ m. incense
финал /finál/ m. final; finale
финансировать /finansírovat'/ v. finance
финансист /finansíst/ m. financier
финик /fínik/ m. date
финиш /fínish/ m. finish
финн /finn/ m. Finn
финка /fínka/ f. Finn
финскийabprekmnehf /fínskii/ adj. Finnish
фиолетовый /fiolétovyi/ adj. violet
фирма /fírma/ f. firm
фисгармония /fisgarmóniia/ f. harmonium
фитиль /fitíl'/ m. wick
фишка /físhka/ f. chip
флаг /flag/ m. flag
флакон /flakón/ m. (scent-)bottle
фланель /flanél'/ f. flannel
флейта /fléita/ f. flute
флиртовать /flirtovát'/ v. flirt
флот /flot/ m. fleet
флотский /flótskii/ adj. naval
флюгер /fliúger/ m. weathercock
флюс /flius/ m. gumboil
фляга /fliága/ f. flask
фойе /foié/ n. foyer
фокус /fókus/ m. focus; trick
фокусник /fókusnikj/ m. juggler
фольга /fol'gá/ f. foil
фольклор /fol'klór/ m. folklore

фон /fon/ m. background
фонарь /fonár'/ m. lantern
фонд /fond/ m. fund
фонетика /fonétika/ f. phonetics
фонтан /fontán/ m. fountain
форель /forél'/ f. trout
форма /fórma/ f. form; mould; uniform
формальность /formál'nost'/ f. formality
формат /formát/ m. size
формировать /formirovát'/ v. form
формула /fórmula/ f. formula
форсировать /forsírovat'/ v. force; speed up
форсить /forsít'/ v. swagger
форт /fort/ m. fort
фортепьяно /fortep'iáno/ n. piano
форточка /fórtochka/ f. (window-)pane
фосфор /fósfor/ m. phosphorus
фотоаппарат /fotoapparát/ m. camera
фотограф /fotógraf/ m. photographer
фотографировать /fotografírovat'/ v. photograph
фотография /fotográfiia/ f. photograph
фраза /fráza/ f. phrase
фрак /frak/ m. dress coat
фракция /fráktsiia/ f. faction
франкмасон /frankmasón/ m. freemason
франт /frant/ m. dandy
француженка /frantsúzhenka/ f. Frenchwoman
француз /frantsúz/ m. Frenchman
французский /frantsúzskii/ adj. French
фрахт /frakht/ m. freight
фрегат /fregát/ m. frigate
фрезер /frézer/ m. milling cutter
френч /french/ m. service jacket
фреска /fréska/ f. fresco
фронт /front/ m. front
фрукт /frukt/ m. fruit
фуганок /fugánok/ m. plane
фужер /fuzhér/ m. tall wine glass
фундамент /fundáment/ m. foundation
фундаментальный /fundamentál'nyi/ adj. solid

фоникулер /fonikuliór/ m. funicular railway
фунт /funt/ m. pound
фуражка /furázhka/ f. peaked cap
фурор /furór/ m. furore
футбол /futból/ m. football; soccer
фуфайка /fufáika/ f. jersey
фыркать /fýrkat'/ v. snort

X

халат /khalát/ m. dressing-gown
хам /kham/ m. boor
хамелеон /khameleón/ m. chameleon
хан /khan/ m. khan
хандра /khandrá/ f. depression
ханжа /khanzhá/ m., f. hypocrite
хаос /kháós/ m. chaos
характер /kharákter/ m. character
характеристика /kharakterístika/ f. reference; description
хата /kháta/ f. peasant hut
хвалебный /khvalébnyi/ adj. laudatory
хвалить /khvalít'/ v. praise
хвастаться /khvástat'sia/ v. boast
хвастливый /khvastlívyi/ adj. boastful
хвастун /khvastún/ m. braggart
хватать /khvatát'/ v. grasp; be sufficient
хвойный /khvóinyi/ adj. coniferous
хворать /khvorát'/ v. be ill
хворост /khvórost/ m. brushwood
хвоя /khvóiia/ f. (pine-) needles
хижина /khízhina/ f. cabin
хилый /khílyi/ adj. sickly
химик /khímik/ m. chemist
химия /khímiia/ f. chemistry
химчистка /khimchístka/ f. dry cleaning
хинин //khinín/ m. quinine
хирург /khirúrg/ m. surgeon
хирургия /khirurgíia/ f. surgery
хитрить /khitrít'/ v. be cunning
хитрость /khítrost'/ f. cunning
хитрый /khítryi/ adj. sly, crafty

хихикать /khikhíkat'/ v. giggle

хищение /khishchénie/ n. embezzlement

хищник /khíshchnik/ m. beast (bird) of prey

хищный /khíshchnyi/ adj. predatory

хладнокровный /khladnokróvnyi/ adj. cool, self-possessed

хлам /khlam/ m. rubbish

хлеб /khleb/ m. bread

хлебать /khlebát'/ v. gulp down; sip

хлебница /khlébnitsa/ f. bread-basket

хлебозавод /khlebozavód/ m. bakery

хлеборезка /khleborézka/ f. bread-cutter

хлев /khlev/ m. cattle-shed

хлестать /khlestát'/ v. lash

хлопать /khlópat'/ v. bang; clap

хлопкороб /khlopkorób/ m. cotton grower

хлопок /khlópok/ m. cotton

хлопотать /khlopotát'/ v. bustle; petition (for)

хлопотливый /khlopotlívyi/ adj. bustling

хлопоты /khlópoty/ pl. trouble; efforts

хлопушка /khlopúshka/ f. cracker

хлопчатобумажный /khlopchatobumázhnyi/ adj. cotton

хлопья /khlóp'ia/ pl. flakes

хлороформ /khloroфórm/ m. chloroform

хлынуть /khlýnut'/ v. gush

хлыст /khlyst/ m. whip

хлюпать /khliúpat'/ v. squelch

хлястик /khliastík/ m. strap (on dress)

хмель /khmel'/ m. hops

хмельной /khmel'nói/ adj. drunken; intoxicvating

хмуриться /khmúrit'sia/ v. frown

хмурый /khmúryi/ adj. gloomy

хна /khna/ f. henna

хныкать /khnýkat'/ v. whimper

хобот /khóbot/ m. trunk

ход /khod/ m. move; motion; course; entrance

ходатай /khodátai/ m. intercessor

ходатайство /khodátaistvo/ n. application

ходатайствовать /khodátaistvovat'/ v. petition, apply

ходить /khodít'/ v. go, walk

ходули /khodúli/ pl. stilts

ходьба /khod'bá/ f. walking

хозяин /khoziáin/ m. master; host; landlord

хозяйка /khoziáika/ f. proprietress, hostess; landlady

хозяйничать /khoziáinichat'/ v. keep house

хозяйственный /khoziáistvennyi/ adj. economic

хозяйство /khoziáistvo/ n. economy

хоккей /khokkéi/ m. hockey; ice-hockey

холера /kholéra/ m. cholera

холм /kholm/ m. hill

холод /khólod/ m. cold

холодильник /kholodíl'nik/ m. refrigerator

холодныйüjlfnfqcndj /kholódnyi/ adj. cold

холостяк /kholostiák/ m. bachelor

холст /kholst/ m. canvas; linen

хомут /khomút/ m. (hortse-)collar; yoke

хомяк /khomiák/ m. hamster

хор /khor/ m. choir; chorus

хорват /khorvát/ m. Croat

хорватка /khorvátka/ f. Croat

хорватский /khorvátskii/ adj. Croatian

хорек /khoriók/ m. polecat

хоровод /khorovód/ m. round dance

хоронить /khoronít'/ v. bury

хорошенький /khoróshen'kii/ adj. pretty

хорошенько /khoroshén'ko/ adv. thoroughly

хороший /khoróshii/ adj. good

хотеть /khotét'/ v. want

хотя /khotiá/ adv. although

хохол /khohól/ m. tuft

хохот /khókhot/ m. laughter

хохотать /khokhotát'/ v. guffaw

храбрец /khrabréts/ m. brave man

храбрый /khrábryi/ adj. valiant
храм /khram/ m. temple
хранение /khranénie/ n. storage
хранилище /khranílishche/ n. storehouse; depository
хранить /khranít'/ v. preserve; store
храниться /khranít'sia/ v. be kept
храпеть /khrapét'/ n. snore
хребет /khrebét/ m. spinel; (mountain) range; ridge
хрен /khren/ m. horseradish
хрестоматия /khrestomátiia/ f. reader
хризантема /khrizantéma/ f. chrysanthemum
хрипеть /khripét'/ v. hoarse
христианин /khristianín/ m. Christian
христианство /khristiánstvo/ n. Christianity
хром /khrom/ m. chrome leather
хромать /khromát'/ v. limp
хромовый /khrómovyi/ adj. chrome; calfskin
хромой /khromói/ adj. lame
хромота /khromotá/ f. lameness
хроника /khrónika/ f. chronicle
хронология /khronológiia/ f. chronology
хронометр /khronómetr/ m. chronometer
хрупкий /khrúpkii/ adj. fragile
хруст /khrust/ m. crackle
хрусталь /khrustál'/ m. cut glass; crystal
хрустальный /khrustál'nyi/ adj. cut-glass
хрустеть /khrustét'/ v. crunch
хрюкать /khriúkat'/ v. grunt
хряк /khriak/ m. hog
хрящ /khriashch/ m. cartilage
худеть /khudét'/ v. grow thin
художественный /khudózhestvennyi/ adj. artistic
художник /khudózhnik/ m. artist; painter
худощавый /khudoshchávyi/ adj. lean
худший /khúdshii/ adj. worst
хуже /khúzhe/ adv. worse
хулиган /khuligán/ m. hooligan

хулиганство /khuligánstvo/ n. hooliganism

Ц

цапля /tsáplia/ f. heron
царапать /tsarápat'/ v. scratch
царапина /tsarápina/ f. scratch
царевич /tsarévich/ m. prince (son of tsar)
царевна /tsarévna/ f. princess (tsar's daughter)
царизм /tsarízm/ m. tsarism
царить /tsarít'/ v. reign
царица /tsarítsa/ f. tsarina
царский /tsárskii/ adj. tsar's
царство /tsárstvo/ n. tsardom
царствовать /tsárstvovat'/ v. reign
царь /tsar'/ m. tsar
цвести /tsvestí/ v. blossom
цвет /tsvet/ m. colour
цветник /tsvetník/ m. flower-bed
цветной /tsvetnói/ adj. coloured
цветок /tsvetók/ m. flower
цедить /tsedít'/ v. strain
цейлонский /tseilónskii/ adj. Ceylonese
целебный /tselébnyi/ adj. curative, healing
целесообразный /tselesoobráznyi/ adj. expedient
целеустремленный /tseleustremliónnyi/ adj. purposeful
целиком /tselikóm/ adv. entirely; whooly
целина /tseliná/ f. virgin land
целлюлоза /tselliulóza/ f. cellulose
целовать /tselovát'/ v. kiss
целомудренный /tselomúdrennyi/ adj. chaste
целый /tsélyi/ adj. whole; intact
цель /tsel'/ f. aim, target
цемент /tsemént/ m. cement
цементировать /tsementírovat'/ v. cement
цена /tsená/ f. price

ценз /tsenz/ m. qualification
цензор /tsénzor/ m. censor
цензура /tsenzúra/ f. censorship
ценитель /tsenítel'/ m. connoisseur
ценить /tsenít'/ v. value; appreciate
ценный /tsénnyi/ adj. valuable
центр /tsentr/ m. centre
центральный /tsentrál'nyi/ adj. central
цепляться /tsepliát'sia/ v. clutch at
цепочка /tsepóchka/ f. chain
цепь /tsep'/ f. chain; series; circuit
церемониться /tseremónit'sia/ v. stand on ceremony
церемония /tseremóniia/ f. ceremony
церковно-славянский /tserkóvno-slaviánskii/ adj. Church Slavonic
церковный /tserkóvnyi/ adj. Church, ecclesiastical
церковь /tsérkov'/ f. church
цех /tsekh/ m. workshop
цивилизация /tsivilizátsiia/ f. civilization
цигейка /tsigéika/ f. beaver lamb
цикл /tsikl/ m. cycle
циклон /tsiklón/ m. cyclone
цикорий /tsikórii/ m. chicory
цилиндр /tsilíndr/ m. cylinder; top hat
цинга /tsyngá/ f. scurvy
цинизм /tsinízm/ m. cynicism
циник /tsínik/ m. cynic
циничный /tsiníchnyi/ adj. cynical
цинк /tsink/ m. zinc
циновка /tsynóvka/ f. mat
цирк /tsirk/ m. circus
циркулировать /tsirkulírovat'/ v. circulate
циркуль /tsírkul'/ m. (pair of) compasses
цистерна /tsistérna/ f. cistern
цитадель /tsitadél'/ f. stronghold
цитата /tsitáta/ f. quotation
цитировать /tsitírovat'/ v. quote
цитрус /tsítrus/ m. citrus
циферблат /tsiferblát/ m. dial, face
цифра /tsífra/ f. number, figure
цукат /tsukát/ m. candied fruit
ЦУМ /tsum/ abbr., m. Central Department Store

цыган /tsygán/ m. Gypsy
цыганка /tsygánka/ f. Gypsy
цыганский /tsygánskii/ adj. Gypsy
цыпленок /tsypliónok/ m. chicken
цыпочки (на цыпочках) /na tsýpoch-kakh/ prep.+pl. on tiptoe

Ч

чавкать /chávkat'/ v. slurp
чадить /chadít'/ v. smoke
чаевые /chaevýe/ pl. tip
чайка /cháika/ f. gull
чайная /cháinaia/ f. tea-rooom
чайник /cháinik/ m. teapot
чалма /chalmá/ f. turban
чан /chan/ m. vat
чаровать /charovát'/ v. charm
час /chas/ m. hour
часовня /chasovniá/ f. chapel
часовой /chasovói/ m. sentry
часовщик /chasovshchík/ m. watchmaker
частица /chastítsa/ f. particle
частичный /chastíchnyi/ adj. partial
частная (собственность) /chástnaia sóbstvennost'/ adj.+f. private property
частность /chástnost'/ f. detail
частный /chástnyi/ adj. private
часто /chásto/ adv. often
частокол /chastokól/ m. palisade
частота /chastotá/ f. frequency
частый /chástyi/ adj. frequent
часть /chast'/ f. part
часы /chasý/ pl. clock, watch
чахлый /chákhlyi/ adj. stunted; sickly
чахотка /chakhótka/ f. consumption
чаша /chásha/ f. chalice
чашка /cháshka/ f. cup
чаща /cháshcha/ f. thicket
чаще /cháshche/ adv. more often
чаяние /cháianie/ n. hope
чванливый /chvanlívyi/ adj. boastful

чей /chei/ pron. whose
чек /chek/ m. cheque
чеканить /chekánit'/ v. mint
челка /chólka/ f. fringe
челнок /chelnók/ m. shuttle
человек /chelovék/ m. man
человечество /chelovéchestvo/ n. mankind
человечный /chelovéchnyi/ adj. humane
челюсть /chéliust'/ f. jaw
чем /chem/ conj. than
чемодан /chemodán/ m. suitcase
чемпион /chempión/ m. champion
чемпионат /chempionát/ m. championship
чепуха /chepukhá/ f. nonsense
чепчик /chépchik/ m. cap; bonnet
червивый /chervívyi/ adj. worm-eaten
червонец /chervónets/ m. 10 roubles
червонный /chervónnyi/ adj. of hearts; red; червонное золото /chervónnoe zóloto/ pure gold
червы /chérvy/ pl. hearts
червь /cherv'/ m. worm
чердак /cherdák/ m. garret
чередоваться /cheredovát'sia/ v. alternate
через /chérez/ prep. over; through; via
черемуха /cheriómukha/ f. bird cherry
череп /chérep/ m. skull
черепаха /cherepákha/ f. turtle
черепаший /cherepáshii/ adj. tortoise
черепица /cherepítsa/ f. tile
черепок /cherepók/ m. crock
чересчур /chereschúr/ adv. too; too much
черешня /cheréshnia/ f. cherry(-tree)
черкес /cherkés/ m. Circassian
черкесский /cherkésskii/ adj. Circassian
черкешенка /cherkéshenka/ f. Circassian
черника /chernika/ f. bilberry
чернила /chernila/ pl. ink
чернильница /chernil'nitsa/ f. ink-pot
чернобурка /chernobúrka/ f. silver fox
черновик /chernovík/ m. rough copy

черновой /chernovói/ adj. draft
чернозем /chernozióm/ m. black earth
чернокожий /chernokózhii/ adj. Negro, black
чернорабочий /chernorabóchii/ m. unskilled worker
чернослив /chernoslív/ m. prunes
чернота /chernotá/ f. blackness
черный /chiórnyi/ adj. black
черпак /cherpák/ m. scoop
черпать /chérpat'/ v. ladle
черствый /chórstvyi/ adj. stale; callous
черт /chort/ m. devil
черта /chertá/ f. line
чертеж /chertiózh/ m. sketch
чертежник /chertiózhnik/ m. draughtsman
чертежный /chertiózhnyi/ adj. drawing
чертить /chertít'/ v. draw
чесать /chesát'/ v. comb; scratch
чесаться /chesát'sia/ v. itch
чеснок /chesnók/ m. garlic
чесотка /chesótka/ f. itch
честный /chéstnyi/ ajdj. honest
честолюбивый /chestoliubívyi/ adj. ambitious
честь /chest'/ f. honour
чета /chetá/ f. married couple; match
четверг /chetvérg/ m. Thursday
четвереньки (на четвереньках) /na chetverén'kakh/ on all fours
четверка /chetviorka/ f. figure 4; four; good (mark)
четвероногий /chetveronógii/ adj. four-legged
четверть /chétvert'/ f. quarter
четки /chótki/ pl. beards
четкий /chótkii/ adj. clear
четный /chótnyi/ adj. even
четыре /chetýre/ num. four
четырехместный /chetyriokhméstnyi/ adj. four-seater
четырехугольник /chetyriokhugól'nik/ m. quadrangle

чех /chekh/ m. Czech
чехарда /chekhardá/ f. leap-frog
чехол /chekhól/ m. cover
чечевица /chechevítsa/ f. lentil
чечевичная (похлебка) /chechevíchnaia pokhlióbka/ adj.+f. mess of pottage
чешка /chéshka/ f. Czech
чешский /chéshskii/ adj. Czech
чешуя /cheshuiá/ f. scales
чибис /chíbis/ m. lapwing
чиж /chizh/ m. siskin
чин /chin/ m. rank
чинить /chinít'/ v. repair; sharpen
чиновник /chinóvnik/ m. official
чирей /chírei/ m. boil
чирикать /chiríkat'/ v. chirp
численность /chíslennost'/ v. numbers; strength
численный /chíslennyi/ adj. numerical
числитель /chislítel'/ m. numerator
число /chisló/ n. number; date
чистилище /chistílishche/ m. purgatory
чистильщик /chístil'shchik/ m. cleaner; bootblack
чистить /chístit'/ v. clean
чистка /chístka/ f. cleaning; purge
чистовой /chistovói/ adj. fair, clean
чистый /chístyi/ adj. clean
читать /chitát'/ v. read
член /chlen/ m. member; limb
членство /chlénstvo/ n. membership
чокаться /chókat'sia/ v. clink glasses
чопорный /chópornyi/ adj. prim, stiff
чреватый /chrevátyi/ adj. fraught with
чрево /chrévo/ n. womb
чревовещатель /chrevoveshchátel'/ m. ventriloquist
чрезвычайный /chrezvycháinyi/ adj. extraordinary
чрезмерный /chrezmérnyi/ adj. excessive
чтение /chténie/ n. reading
чтец /chtets/ m. reciter
чтить /chtit'/ v. revere

что /chto/ pron. what; conj. that
что-либо, что-нибудь /chto-líbo, chto-nibúd'/ something
чувственный /chúvstvennyi/ adj. sensual
чувствительный /chuvstvítel'nyi/ adj. sensitive
чувство /chúvstvo/ n. feeling
чувствовать /chúvstvovat'/ v. feel
чугун /chúgun/ m. cast iron
чудак /chudák/ m. crank
чудесный /chudésnyi/ adj. wonderful
чудиться /chúdit'sia/ v. seem
чудной /chudnói/ adj. queer, strange
чудо /chúdo/ n. miracle
чудовище /chudóvishche/ n. monster
чудовищный /chudóvishchnyi/ adj. monstrous
чудотворец /chudotvórets/ m. miracle-worker
чужак /chuzhák/ m. stranger
чужбина /chuzhbína/ f. foreign land
чуждый /chúzhdyi/ adj. alien
чужеземец /chuzhezémets/ m. foreigner
чужой /chuzhói/ adj. foreign
чулан /chulán/ m. store-room
чулок /chulók/ m. stocking
чума /chumá/ f. plague
чурбан /churbán/ m. block; blockhead
чуткий /chútkii/ adj. sensitive; tactful
чуть /chut'/ adv. hardly; ч.-чуть /ch.-chut'/ a tiny bit; ч. не /ch. ne/ almost, nearly
чутье /chut'ió/ n. scent; instinct (for)
чучело /chúchelo/ n. stuffed animal or bird
чушь /chush/ f. nonsense
чуять /chúiat'/ v. scent, smell

Ш

шаблон /shablón/ m. pattern
шаблонный /shablónnyi/ adj. trite
шаг /shag/ m. step

шагать /shagát'/ v. step
шагом /shágom/ adv. at walking pace
шайба /sháiba/ f. puck
шайка /sháika/ f. gang; tub
шакал /shakál/ m. jackal
шалаш /shalásh/ m. hut
шалить /shalít'/ v. be naughty
шаловливый /shalovlívyi/ adj. playful
шалость /shálost'/ f. prank
шалун /shalún/ m. naughty child
шалфей /shalféi/ m. sage
шаль /shal'/ f. shawl
шальной /shal'nói/ adj. mad
шамкать /shámkat'/ v. mumble
шампанское /shampánskoe/ n. champagne
шампунь /shampún'/ m. shampoo
шанс /shans/ m. chance
шантаж /shantázh/ m. blackmail
шапка /shápka/ f. hat
шар /shar/ m. ball; воздушный ш. /vozdushnyi sh./ balloon
шарахаться /sharákhat'sia/ v. shy; rush
шарж /sharzh/ m. cartoon
шариковая (ручка) /shárikovaia rúchka/ adj.+f. ball-point pen
шарикоподшипник /sharikopodshípnik/ m. ball-bearing
шарить /shárit'/ v. rummage
шарлатан /sharlatán/ m. charlatan
шарманка /sharmánka/ f. barrel-organ
шарнир /sharnír/ m. joint
шаровары /sharováry/ pl. (wide) trousers
шарф /sharf/ m. scarf
шасси /shássi/ pl. chassis
шатать /shatát'/ v. rock
шататься /shatát'sia/ v. stagger
шатен /shatén/ m. person with dark brown hair
шатер /shatiór/ m. tent
шаткий /shátkii/ adj. unsteady
шафер /sháfer/ m. best man
шафран /shafrán/ m. saffron
шах /shakh/ m. shah; check (chess)

шахматист /shakhmatíst/ m. chess-player
шахматы /shákhmaty/ pl. chess
шахта /shákhta/ f. mine
шахтер /shakhtiór/ m. miner
шашка /sháshka/ f. sabre; draught; pl. draughts
шашлык /shashlýk/ m. shashlik
швартовать /shvartovát'/ v. moor
швед /shved/ m. Swede
шведка /shvédka/ f. Swede
шведский /shvédskii/ adj. Swedish
швейный /shvéinyi/ adj. sewing
швейцар /shveitsár/ m. door-keeper
швейцарец /shveitsárets/ m. Swiss
швейцарка /shveitsárka/ f. Swiss
швейцарский /shveitsárskii/ adj. Swiss
швырять /shvyriát'/ v. fling
шевелить /shevelít'/ v. move, stir
шедевр /shedévr/ m. masterpiece
шелестеть /shelestét'/ v. rustle
шелк /sholk/ m. silk
шелуха /shelukhá/ f. peel; husk
шелушить /shelushít'/ v. peel
шелушиться /shelushít'sia/ v. flake off
шельма /shél'ma/ m. and f. rascal, rogue
шепелявить /shepeliávit'/ v. lisp
шепот /shópot/ m. whisper
шептать /shéptat'/ v. whisper
шеренга /sherénga/ f. rank; column
шероховатый /sherokhovátyi/ adj. rough
шерсть /sherst'/ f. wool
шерстяной /sherstianoi/ adj. wool(len)
шершень /shérshen'/ m. hornet
шест /shest/ m. pole
шествие /shéstvie/ n. procession
шествовать /shéstvovat'/ v. march
шестерня /shesterniá/ f. cogwheel
шестнадцать /shestnádtsat'/ num. sixteen
шесть /shest'/ num. six
шестьдесят /shest'desiát/ num. sixty
шестьсот /shest'sót/ num. six hundred
шеф /shef/ m. chief

шея /sheiá/ f. neck
шик /shik/ m. chic
шикарный /shikárnyi/ adj. smart
шикать /shíkat'/ v. hiss
шило /shílo/ n. awl
шимпанзе /shimpánze/ m. chimpanzee
шина /shína/ f. tyre
шинель /shinél'/ f. greatcoat
шинковать /shinkovát'/ v. shred
шип /ship/ m. thorn
шипеть /shipét'/ v. hiss
шиповник /shipóvnik/ m. dog-rose
шипучий /shipúchii/ adj. sparkling; fizzy
ширина /shiriná/ f. breadth, width
ширма /shírma/ f. screen
широкий /shirókii/ adj. wide
широта /shirotá/ f. latitude
ширпотреб /shirpotréb/ m. consumer goods
шить /shit'/ v. swe
шитье /shit'ió/ n. embrouidery; needle-work
шифер /shífer/ m. slate
шифр /shifr/ m. cipher
шишка /shíshka/ f. bump; cone
шкала /shkalá/ f. scale
шкатулка /shkatúlka/ f. box, casket
шкаф /shkaf/ m. cupboard; wardrobe
школа /shkóla/ f. school
школьник /shkól'nik/ m. schoolboy
школьница /shkól'nitsa/ f. schoolgirl
шкура /shkúra/ f. hide
шлагбаум /shlagbáum/ m. barrier
шлак /shlak/ m. slag
шланг /shlang/ m. hose
шлейф /shléif/ m. train (of dress)
шлем /shlém/ m. helmet
шлепать /shliópat'/ v. smack
шлюз /shliúz/ m. lock
шлюпка /shliúpka/ f. launch, boat
шляпа /shliápa/ f. hat
шмель /shmel'/ m. bumble-bee
шнур /shnur/ m. cord
шнуровать /shnurovát'/ v. lace up

шнурок /shnurók/ m. lace
шов /shov/ m. slitch
шовинизм /shovinízm/ m. chauvinism
шок /shok/ m. shock
шоколад /shokolád/ m. chocolate
шорох /shórokh/ m. rustle
шоры /shóry/ pl. blinkers
шоссе /shossé/ n. highway
шотландец /shotlándets/ m. Scotыman
шотландка /shotlándka/ f. Scotswoman
шотландский /shotlándskii/ adj. Scottish
шофер /shofiór/ m. driver
шпага /shpága/ f. sword
шпагат /shpagát/ m. cord
шпала /shpála/ f. sleeper
шпаргалка /shpargálka/ f. crib
шпиль /shpil'/ m. spire
шпилька /shpíl'ka/ f. hairpin
шпинат /shpinát/ m. spinach
шпингалет /shpingalét/ m. bolt
шпион /shpión/ m. spy
шпионаж /shpionázh/ m. espionage
шпионить /shpiónit'/ v. spy
шпиц /shpits/ m. Pomeranian (dog)
шпора /shpóra/ f. spur
шприц /shprits/ m. syringe
шпрот /shprot/ m. sprat
шрам /shram/ m. scar
шрифт /shrift/ m. print, type
штаб /shtab/ m. staff; headquarters
штабель /shtábel'/ m. stack
штамп /shtamp/ m. punch; cliché
штамповать /shtampovát'/ v. stamp
штангист /shtangíst/ m. weight-lifter
штаны /shtaný/ pl. trousers
штат /shtat/ m. state; staff
штатив /shtatív/ m. tripod
штатный /shtátnyi/ adj. regular
штатский /shtátskii/ adj. civil
штемпелевать /shtempelevát'/ v. stamp
штепсель /shtépsel'/ m. plug
штиль /shtil'/ m. calm
штопать /shtópat'/ v. darn
штопор /shtópor/ v. corkscrew

штора /shtóra/ f. blind
шторм /shtorm/ m. gale
штраф /shtraf/ m. fine
штрафной /shtrafnoi/ adj. penalty
штрафовать /shtrafiovát'/ v. fine
штрейкбрехер /shtreikbrékher/ m. strike-breaker
штрих /shtrikh/ m. trait; hatching
штука /shtúka/ f. piece
штукатур /shtukatúr/ m. plasterer
штукатурить /shtukatúrit'/ v. plaster
штукатурка /shtukatúrka/ f. plaster
штурвал /shturvál/ m. steering wheel
штурм /shturm/ m. storm, assault
штурман /shtúrman/ m. navigator
штурмовать /shturmovát'/ v. assault
штык /shtyk/ m. bayonet
шуба /shúba/ f. fur-coat
шулер /shúler/ m. card-sharper
шум /shum/ m. noise
шуметь /shumét'/ v. make a noise
шурин /shúrin/ m. brother-in-law (wife's brother)
шуршать /shurshát'/ v. rustle
шустрый /shústryi/ adj. smart, sharp
шут /shut/ m. fool; clown
шутить /shutít'/ v. joke
шутка /shútka/ f. joke
шуточный /shútochnyi/ adj. comic
шушукаться /shushúkat'sia/ v. whisper together
шхуна /shkhúna/ f. schooner

Щ

щавель /shchavél'/ m. sorrel
щадить /shchadít'/ v. spare; have mercy on
щебень /shchében'/ m. road-metal
щебетать /shchebetát'/ v. twitter
щегол /shchegól/ m. goldfinch
щеголь /shchógol'/ m. dandy

щедрость /shchédrost'/ f. generosity
щедрый /shchédryi/ adj. generous
щека /shcheká/ f. cheek
щеколда /shchekólda/ f. latch
щекотать /shchekotát'/ v. tickle
щелка /shchólka/ f. chink
щелкать /shchólkat'/ v. click
щелкунчик /shchelkúnchik/ m. nutcracker
щелчок /shchelchók/ m. flick; fillip
щель /shchel'/ f. crack; голосовая щ. /golosováia shch./ glottis
щемить /shchemít'/ v. press; oppress
щенок /shchenók/ m. pup, cub
щепка /shchépka/ f. splinter, chip
щепотка /shchepótka/ f. pinch
щетина /shchetina/ f. bristle
щетка /shchótka/ f. brush
щи /shchi/ pl. cabbage soup
щиколотка /shchíkolotka/ f. ankle
щипать /shchipát'/ v. pinch
щипцы /shchiptsý/ pl. pincers
щипчики /shchípchiki/ pl. tweezers
щит /shchit/ m. shield
щука /shchúka/ f. pike
щупальце /shchúpal'tse/ n. tentacle
щупать /shchúpat'/ v. feel; probe
щуплый /shchúplyi/ adj. puny; frail
щуриться /shchúrit'sia/ v. screw up one's eyes

Э

эвакуация /evakuátsiia/ f. evacuation
эвакуировать /evakuírovat'/ v. evacuate
эвкалипт /evkalípt/ m. eucalyptus
эволюционировать /evoliutsionírovat'/ v. evolve
эволюция /evoliútsiia/ f. evolution
эгоизм /egoízm/ m. egoism
эгоист /egoíst/ m. egoist
экватор /ekvátor/ m. equator
эквивалент /ekvivalént/ m. equivalent

экзамен /ekzámen/ m. exam
экзаменовать /ekzamenovát'/ v. examine
экземпляр /ekzempliár/ m. copy
экзотический /ekzotícheskii/ adj. exotic
экипаж /ekipázh/ m. crew
экономика /ekonómika/ f. economics
экономист /ekonomíst/ m. economist
экономить /ekonómit'/ v. save
экономия /ekonómiia/ f. economy, saving
экономный /ekonómnyi/ adj. thrifty
экран /ekran/ m. screen
экранизировать /ekranizírovat'/ v. make a film of
экскаватор /ekskavátor/ m. excavator
экскурсант /ekskursánt/ m. tourist
экскурсия /ekskúrsiia/ f. excursion
экскурсовод /ekskursovód/ m. tour guide
экспедиция /ekspedítsiia/ f. expedition
эксперимент /eksperimént/ m. experiment
эксперт /ékspert/ m. expert
эксплуатация /ekspluatátsiia/ f. exploitation
эксплуатировать /ekspluatírovat'/ v. exploit
экспонировать /eksponírovat'/ v. exhibit; expose
экспорт /éksport/ m. export
экспортер /exportiór/ m. exporter
экспресс /ekspréss/ m. express
экспромт /eksprómt/ m. impromptu
экстаз /ekstáz/ m. ecstasy
экстренный /ékstrennyi/ adj. extraordinary; emergency
эластичный /elastíchnyi/ adj. elastic
элеватор /elevátor/ m. elevator
элегантный /elegántnyi/ adj. elegant
электрик /eléktrik/ m. electrician
электрический /elektrícheskii/ adj. electric
электричество /electríchestvo/ n. electricity
электричка /elektríchka/ f. electric train

элемент /elemént/ m. element
элементарный /elementárnyi/ adj. elementary
эмалевый /emálevyi/ adj. enamel
эмаль /emál'/ f. enamel
эмансипация /emansipátsiia/ f. emancipation
эмблема /embléma/ f. emblem
эмигрант /emigránt/ m. emigrant
эмиграция /emigrátsiia/ f. emigration
эмигрировать /emigrírovat'/ v. emigrate
эмоциональный /emotsionál'nyi/ adj. emotional
эмоция /emótsiia/ f. emotion
эмульсия /emúl'siia/ f. emulsion
энергичный /energíchnyi/ adj. energetic; vigorous
энергия /enérgiia/ f. energy; power
энтузиазм /entuziázm/ m. enthusiasm
энциклопедия /entsiklopédiia/ f. encyclopaedia
эпиграмма /epigrámma/ f. epigram
эпиграф /epígraf/ m. epigraph
эпидемия /epidémiia/ f. epidemic
эпизод /epizód/ m. episode
эпилепсия /epilépsiia/ f. epilepsy
эпилептик /epiléptik/ m. epileptic
эпилог /epilóg/ m. epilogue
эпитафия /epitáfiia/ f. epitaph
эпитет /epítet/ m. epithet
эпический /epícheskii/ adj. epic
эпос /épos/ m. epic (poem)
эпоха /epókha/ f. epoch
эрудиция /erudítsiia/ f. erudition
эскалатор /eskalátor/ m. escalator
эскиз /eskíz/ m. sketch
эскимос /eskimós/ m. Eskimo
эскимоска /eskimóska/ f. Eskimo
эскимосский /eskimósskii/ adj. Eskimo
эскорт /eskórt/ m. escort
эсминец /esmínets/ m. destroyer
эссенция /esséntsiia/ f. essence
эстакада /estakáda/ f. trestle, platform
эстафета /estaféta/ f. relay race

эстет /estét/ m. aesthete
эстонец /estónets/ m. Estonian
эстонка /estónka/ f. Estonian
эстонский /estónskii/ adj. Estonian
эстрада /estráda/ f. variety
этаж /etázh/ m. storey; floor
этажерка /etazhérka/ f. whatnot; bookshelf
этап /etáp/ m. stage
этика /étika/ f. ethics
этикет /etikét/ m. etiquette
этикетка /etikétka/ f. label
этнический /etnícheskii/ adj. ethnic
этот /étot/ pron. this
этюд /etiúd/ m. study; sketch
эфир /efír/ m. ether; air
эффект /effékt/ m. effect
эхо /ékho/ n. echo
эшафот /eshafót/ m. scaffold
эшелон /eshelón/ m. echelon

Ю

юбилей /iubiléi/ m. jubilee
юбилейный /iubiléinyi/ adj. anniversary
юбка /iúbka/ f. skirt; нижняя ю. /nízhniaia yu./ petticoat
ювелир /iuvelír/ m. jeweller
ювелирный /iuvelírnyi/ adj. jeweller's
юг /iúg/ m. south
юго-восток /iugo-vostók/ m. south-east
южанин /iuzhánin/ m. southerner
южный /iúzhnyi/ adj. south(ern)
юлить /iulít'/ v. fidget
юмор /iúmor/ m. humour
юнга /iúnga/ m. cabin boy
юность /iúnost'/ f. youth
юноша /iúnosha/ m. youth
юношество /iúnoshestvo/ n. young people
юный /iúnyi/ adj. youthful

юридический /iuridícheskii/ adj. legal
юрисконсульт /iuriskónsul't/ m. legal adviser
юриспруденция /iurisprudéntsiia/ f. jurisprudence
юрист /iuríst/ m. lawyer
юстиция /iustítsiia/ f. justice

Я

я /ia/ pron. I
ябеда /iábeda/ m. and f. sneak; informer
яблоко /iábloko/ n. apple
явный /iávnyi/ adj. evident
явственный /iávstvennyi/ adj. clear
явь /iáv'/ f. reality
ягненок /iagniónok/ m. lamb
ягода /iágoda/ f. berry
ягодица /iágoditsa/ f. buttock
ягуар /iaguár/ m. jaguar
яд /iád/ m. poison
ядерный /iádernyi/ adj. nuclear
ядовитый /iadovítyi/ adj. poisonous
ядро /iadró/ n. nucleus; shot
язва /iázva/ f. ulcer
язык /iazýk/ m. tongue; language
язычник /iazýchnik/ m. pagan
яичник /iaíchnik/ m. ovary
яичница /iaíchnitsa/ f. fried eggs
яйцо /iaitsó/ n. egg
якобы /iákoby/ conj. as if
якорь /iákor'/ m. anchor
якут /iakút/ m. Yakut
якутка /iakútka/ f. Yakut
якутский /iakútskii/ adj. Yakut
яма /iáma/ f. pit; hole
ямочка /iámochka/ f. dimple
январь /ianvár'/ m. January
янтарь /iantár'/ m. amber
японец /iapónets/ m. Japanese
японка /iapónka/ f. Japanese
японский /iapónskii/ adj. Japanese
яркий /iárkii/ adj. bright

ярлык /iarlýk/ m. label; tag
ярмарка /iármarka/ f. fair
яровой /iarovói/ adj. spring, spring-sown
ярость /iárost'/ f. fury
ярус /iárus/ m. circle; tier
ярый /iáryi/ adj. vehement, fervent
ясень /iásen'/ mash. (-tree)
ясли /iásli/ pl. manger; creche, day nursery
ясновидец /iasnovídets/ m. clairvoyant
ясный /iásnyi/ adj. clear

ястреб /iástreb/ m. hawk
яхта /iákhta/ f. yacht
ячейка /iachéika/ f. cell
ячмень /iachmén'/ m. barley
яшма /iáshma/ f. jasper
ящерица /iáshcheritsa/ f. lizard
ящик /iáshchik/ m. box; drawer; мусорный я. /músornyi ia./ dustbin
ящур /iáshchur/ m. foot-and-mouth disease

RUSSIAN CUISINE AND MENU TERMS

Ivan says to Masha:
"Our national food is shchi and kasha."
Says Klava to Vlas:
"Our national drink is vodka. And kvas."

A Brief Talk about Russian Cuisine

The traditional Russian cooking has come to us through the depths of history. Since the dimensions of the country are huge indeed, in various areas and districts, nooks and corners there developed different styles of cuisine. Still, despite all shades and tones, the major hors d'oeuvres and snacks, dishes and beverages are basically the same.

Hors d'oeuvres

The main purpose of serving snacks is to arouse appetite. And Russian cuisine has always been rich and abundant in cold and hot hors d'oeuvres. They may be fresh and pickled vegetables and mushrooms; numerous jellies (meat, fish, mushroom, etc.); dried, smoked and salted fish; meat and pork sausage, suckling pigs and stuffed poultry; and a whole gamut of mixed salads (meat, fish, egg) and vinaigrettes.

It should be pointed out that many snacks contain onion and garlic (as well as some soups and main course dishes). An old Russian saying goes: "Garlic and onion will cure all pains and maladies for sure." Also of interest might be the following fact: in the United States and elsewhere in the West only one type of mushrooms is used for cooking—champignons. In Russia dozens of various kinds of mushrooms are fried and boiled, pickled and salted, wrapped in flour and soaked with sour cream. Mushroom hunting is a favorite pastime for the young and the old alike.

I

To top it all, caviar, the Czarina of all the hors d'oeuvres, will be a pride of any table, be it in the Kremlin palace or in a modest home somewhere in the depths of the country. The best black caviar comes from beluga sturgeon, the best red — from fresh-water salmon.

Soups

The common ancestor of all Russian soups is *ukha* — a fish soup. Originally the root of the word comes from ancient Sanskrit and means broth (liquid). Up to the 19th century any soup was called ukha, but then the word got its today's meaning. There might be a single, double or treble ukha — consecutively one, two or more kinds of fish are boiled, the broth is kept and the fish itself thrown away, and only the last which is always the best is used for eating.

Today *shchi* is the most popular soup in Russia (though not so much in the restaurants as in the family cooking). It is a cabbage soup and it may be sour or sweet, depending on whether the major ingredient is sauerkraut or fresh cabbage. There is an old folk tale how a travelling soldier staying overnight at a village house and being hungry told the greedy hostess that he could cook shchi out of an axe. To begin with, he put up fire in the stove and threw the axe into the pot filled with water. When it started boiling he took his spoon, sipped a few drops and said to the greedy woman: "Delicious! I need just a tiny little bit of something." "What is it?" — asked the intrigued woman. "Salt." So she gave him salt. In a minute he said he needed a slice of garlic. So within an hour he got from her about 25 spices, meats and vegetables which are usually used in cooking Russian shchi.

Equally popular, but mostly in the southern regions of Russia, in the Ukraine and Byelorussia and, perhaps, Lithuania is *borshch*. Its basic substance is beet. Otherwise shchi and borshch are more or less alike in all their one hundred odd varieties. Last but not least — they should be thick, so thick that the spoon is to stand in your plate upright as if at the command "Shun!"

Among others, *rassolnik* with salted cucumbers and kidneys as its base *solianka*, also with salted cucumbers and up to twelve different sorts of either meat or fish, *okroshka*, chilled chopped vegetable and sausage soup, *botvinia*, chilled vegetable and fish soup, and *svekolnik*, chilled beetroot soup, should be mentioned. The last three are summer soups and have *kvas* as their stock. Kvas is a fermented beverage made from grain. It is number one nonalcoholic drink of the country. The first mention of it in the ancient chronicles dates as far back as 988. It was then that after the baptism of Rus in Kiev Duke Vladimir "ordered to give to the newly baptized citizens of the city kvas and honey".

Naturally, there is a whole host of foreign soups which came to Russia from abroad. The "invaders" broadly represent two groups — French and Oriental. A bright representative of the first is consomme, and of the second —*harcho*, a Georgian beef, tomato and onion soup-stew.

Main Course

Depending on the place, season and taste non-vegetarian as well as vegetarian dishes can be enjoyed. They may be cooked from meat or pork, chicken or duckling, crawfish or stellate sturgeon, flour or eggs, cottage cheese or vegetables.

Among the meat dishes one will find braised veal with caviar sauce, marinated skewered beef, roast suckling pig, stuffed cabbage rolls, skewered lamb, sauteed beef with mushrooms and onions in sour-cream sauce.

Poultry may be represented by braised chicken with prune

III

sauce, chicken a la mode de Kiev (deep-fried chicken rissoles), roast chicken with walnut sauce, pressed fried chicken (chicken *tabaka*) and chicken and rice pies.

If you are a fish connoisseur, you will be glad to order sturgeon on a spit or sturgeon (or halibut) in tomato and mushroom sauce, carp in sour cream or pike in tomato marinade, fish cakes with mustard sauce or fish baked monastery style, fish balls or pies, trout with pomegranates and grapes or pike-perch fillet in Russian sauce.

Pelmeni, meat-filled dumplings, are a pride of Russian cuisine. They are small balls and to make them well one should have a special talent. Meat is of two kinds, properly ground and mixed (usually pork and beef). The noodle dough must be rolled flat and thin and the best balls are not to exceed a quarter in diameter. Garlic and onion, pepper and salt, milk or broth are added, as well as butter and eggs. Pelmeni bear a distant resemblance to ravioli. But only a distant one. In Siberia they prepare in winter hundreds and thousands of pelmeni and put them in big sacks which are hung in cold sheds or barns. Whenever the guests are coming the hosts are ready to welcome them with pelmeni, a masterpiece of Russian cuisine. Ten minutes of boiling and the delicious meal is ready. And as the saying goes, they jump into your mouth themselves.

Sweet Dishes

Thin jelly (*kisel*) and stewed fruit (*kompot*), tarts and pastry, pies and curd cakes (*vatrushki*), sweet pan-cakes and apples baked with honey, patties and sugared porridges are just a few examples of traditional Russian sweet dishes.

Some very old Russian sweet dishes are not yet forgotten. Cucumbers with honey, sweet omelette (*drachona*), baked turnip stuffed with honey and jam, home-made cake of fruit jelly

IV

(*pastila*), and candied watermelon peels are on the menu of experienced and hospitable housewives.

* * *

To conclude these random notes a few words must be said about Russian vodka. First it appeared in Russia in 15th century. Before that they used to drink various brands of honey. Those were raspberry and strawberry, blackberry and apple and many other brands prepared with hops. Initially vodka was called "grain wine". In 17-19th centuries, landlords had their own breweries. Some of the richer nobles would brew up to two hundred brands of vodka. Also it should be remembered that vodka was distilled three times and was almost as strong as pure spirits. Herbs, berries and fruits would build dozens and dozens of colors and flavors and tastes—bitter, sour or sweet. Now at best one will find 10-12 sorts of vodka — and that too with great difficulty. The only consolation however is that *Stolichnaya* is available at many of the good restaurants. The Russian way to drink vodka is during the meals (with snacks, first and main courses).

* * *

To round off this brief talk about Russian cuisine, we reproduce here the menu of the Golden Hall, a restaurant at the Intourist Hotel in Moscow. We had dinner there with some of our American friends and enjoyed jointly a charming variety show presented by Teatr na Tverskoi — the theater on Tverskaya Street. The unforgettable event took place on February 21, 1992. Below follows the menu.

ФИРМЕННЫЕ БЛЮДА	SPECIALITIES
/fírmennye bliúda/	/спéшиэ́литиз/

Рыбная закуска	"Russian Bouquet"
"Русский букет"	fish hors d'oeuvre
/rýbnaia zakúska	/рашн букéй
rússkii bukét/	фиш одёёвр/

Ассорти мясное	"Cornucopia"
"Изобилие"	assorted meat
/assortí miasnóe	/кóрньюкóупиэ
izobílie/	эсóртыд миит/

| Салат "Интурист" | "Intourist" salad |
| /salát inturíst/ | /интуэ́рист сэ́лэд/ |

Солянка любительская	"Lyubitelskaya" solyanka
с грибами	with mushrooms
/soliánka liubítel'skaia	/люби́тельская
s gribámi/	соля́нка виз мáшрумз/

| Судак "Селигер" | "Seliger" pike-perch |
| /sudák seligér/ | /селигéр пáйкпёрч/ |

Шницель из кур	"Intourist"
"Интурист"	chicken schnitzel
/shnítsel iz kur inturíst/	/интуэ́рист чикин шни́тцел/

| Мороженое "Лада" | "Lada" ice-cream |
| /morózhenoe láda/ | /лáда áйскри́им/ |

| Торт "Интурист" | "Intourist" cake |
| /tort inturíst/ | /интуэ́рист кейк/ |

| ХОЛОДНЫЕ ЗАКУСКИ | COLD HORS D'OEUVRES |
| /kholódnye zakúski/ | /кóулд одёёврз/ |

| Икра зернистая | Granular caviar |

/ikrá zernístaia/

/грэ́ньюлэ кэ́виар/

Шпроты с лимоном
/shpróty s limónom/

Sprats in oil and lemon
/спрэтс ин ойл энд лéмэн/

Осетрина отварная
с хреном
/osetrína otvarnáia
s khrénom/

Boiled sturgeon
with horse-radish
/бойлд стёёджн
виз хóосрэ́диш/

Колбаса с/к
/kolbasá syrokopchónaia/

Uncooked smoked sausage
/анкýкт смóукт сóсидж/

Бок осетра x/к
/bok osetrá/
kholódnovo kopchéniia/

Cold-smoked sturgeon side
/кóулд смоýкт стёёджн сайд/

Сельдь с картофелем
и маслом
/sel'd' s kartófelem
i máslom/

Herring with
potatoes and butter
/хéринг виз пэтэ́йтоуз
энд бáтэ/

Крабы п/м
/kráby pod marinádom/

Crab meat pickled in marinade
/крэб миит пиклд ин
мэ́ринэйд/

Сельдь в сметане
с яблоками
/sel'd' v smetáne
s iáblokami/

Herring in sour
cream and apples
/хéринг ин сáуэ
криим энд эплз/

Ветчина с гарниром
/vetchiná s garnírom/

Ham with side-dish
/хэм виз сáйдиш/

Индейка с солениями
/indéika s soléniiami/

Turkey with pickles
/тёрки виз пиклз/

Масло сливочное
/máslo slívochnoe/

Butter
/бáтэ/

САЛАТЫ И СОЛЕНИЯ
/saláty i soléniia/

SALADS AND PICKLES
/сэ́лэдз энд пиклз/

Салат из осетрины
/salát iz osetríny/

Sturgeon salad
/стёёджн сэ́лэд/

Салат с крабами
/salát s krábami/

Crab meat salad
/крэб миит сэ́лэд/

Салат с крабами
по-итальянски
/salát s krábami
po ital'iánski/

Crab meat salad
a l'italienne
/крэб миит сэ́лэд
а литальйа́н/

Салат по-чешски
/salát po chéshski/

Salad a la tcheque
/сэ́лэд а ля чек/

Салат из свежих
огурцов
/salát iz svézhikh ogurtsóv/

Cucumber salad
/кьюю́окэ́мбэ сэ́лэд/

Салат из свежих помидоров
/salát iz svézhikh pomidórov/

Tomato salad
/тэмáатоу сэ́лэд/

Маслины
/maslíny/

Olives
/óливз/

ГОРЯЧИЕ ЗАКУСКИ
/goriáchie zakúski/

HOT HORS D'OEUVRES
/хот одёёврз/

Кнели из судака
с грибами
/knéli iz sudaká s gribámi/

Pike-perch kneli
with mushrooms
/пáйкпёрч кнéли виз
мáшрумз/

VIII

Жульен мясной /zhul'én miasnói/	Meat Julienne /миит джуулиéн/
СУПЫ /supý/	SOUPS /сууnc/
Бульон с пирожком /bul'ón s pirozhkóm/	Broth and patty /брос энд пэ́ти/
Бульон с яйцом /bul'ón s iaitsóm/	Broth with egg /брос виз эг/
Борщ московский /borshch moskóvskii/	Moscow borsh (beetroot and cabbage soup) /мóскоу борщ (бйитрут энд кэ́бидж сууп)/
Солянка рыбная /soliánka rýbnaia/	Fish solyanka /фиш соля́нка/
Солянка мясная сборная /soliánka miasnáia sbórnaia/	Assorted-meat solyanka /эсóртыд миит соля́нка/
Суп-пюре из кур /sup piuré iz kur/	Chicken cream soup /чи́кин криим сууп/
РЫБНЫЕ ГОРЯЧИЕ БЛЮДА /rýbnye goriáchie bliúda/	HOT FISH DISHES /хот фиш ди́шиз/
Судак отварной — соус польский /sudák otvarnói sóus pól'skii/	Boiled sturgeon, polonaise sauce /бойлд стёёджн полонэ́з сооc/
Судак "фри" /sudák fri/	Fried sturgeon /фрайд стёёджн/

IX

Осетрина припущенная — соус паровой /osetrína pripúshchennaia sóus parovói/	Lightly-stewed sturgeon, fish sauce /ла́йтли стьююд стёёджн фиш соос/
Осетрина, запеченная по-московски /osetrína zapechónnaia po moskóvski/	Sturgeon baked a la mode de Moscou /стёёджн бэйкт а ля мод дэ моску́/
Осетрина на вертеле — соус "Тартар" /osetrína na vertelé sóus tartár/	Sturgeon on a spit, tartare sauce /стёёджн он э спит тарта́р соос/
МЯСНЫЕ ГОРЯЧИЕ БЛЮДА /miasnýe goriáchie bliúda/	HOT MEAT DISHES /хот миит ди́шиз/
Антрекот /antrekót/	Rib roast /риб ро́уст/
Бифштекс по-деревенски /bifshtéks po derevénski/	Beefsteak a la paysanne /би́ифстэ́йк а ля пэйза́н/
Бифштекс с яйцом /bifshtéks s iaitsóm/	Beefsteak with egg /би́ифстэ́йк виз эг/
Лангет в соусе /langét v sóuse/	Long flank steak in sauce /лонг флэнк стейк ин соос/
Филе на вертеле /filé na vertelé/	Fillet on a spit /фи́лит он э спит/
Жаркое по-берлински /zharkóe po berlínski/	Roast meat a la mode de Berlin /ро́уст миит а ля мод дэ берли́н/

X

Бефстроганов /befstróganov/	Beef a la Stroganoff /бииф а ля строганóф/	
Бастурма	Basturma	
Шашлык по-кавказски /shashlýk po kavkázski/	Shashlik (mutton grilled on a spit) a la caucasienne /шашлúк (матн грилд он э спит) а ля коказьáн/	
Люля-кебаб /liuliá kebáb/	Lyulya kebab /люля́ кебáб/	
БЛЮДА ИЗ ПТИЦЫ И ДИЧИ /bliúda iz ptítsy i díchi/	POULTRY AND GAME /пóултри энд гейм/	
Филе куриное паровое /filé kurínoe parovóe/	Steamed chicken fillet /стиимд чúкин фúлит/	
Котлеты по-киевски /kotléty po kíevski/	Rissoles a la mode de Kiev /рúсоулз а ля мод дэ кúев/	
Котлеты пожарские /kotléty pozhárskie/	Rissoles a la Pozharsky /рúсоулз а ля пожáрски/	
Цыплята "Табака" /tsypliáta tabaká/	"Tabaka" chickens /табакá чúкинз/	
Утка с яблоками /útka s iáblokami/	Duck with apples /дак виз эплз/	
Индейка жареная с вареньем /indéika zhárenaia s varén'em/	Roast turkey and jam /рóуст тёрки энд джем/	

Рябчик жареный в сметанном соусе /riábchik zhárenyi v smetánnom sóuse/	Roast hazel grouse in sour cream sauce /póуст хэйзл гра́ус ин са́уэ криим соос/
ЯИЧНЫЕ, ОВОЩНЫЕ, МУЧНЫЕ БЛЮДА /iaíchnye ovoshchnýe muchnýe bliúda/	EGG, VEGETABLE AND FARINACEOUS DISHES /эг ве́джитэбл энд фэ́ринэ́йшес ди́шиз/
Яичница-глазунья натуральная /iaíchnitsa glazún'ia naturál'naia/	Fried eggs /фра́йд эгз/
Омлет с ветчиной /omlét s vetchinói/	Ham omelette /хэм о́млит/
Капуста цветная запеченная — соус голландский /kapústa tsvetnáia zapechónnaia sóus gollándskii/	Baked cauliflower, hollandaise sauce /бэ́йкт ко́лифлауэ холанд́э́з соос/
Морковь, тушенная с яблоками /morkóv' tushónnaia s iáblokami/	Stewed carrots with apples /стьююд ка́рэтс виз эплз/
Блинчики с мясом /blínchiki s miásom/	Small meat pancakes /смоол миит пэ́нкейкс/
Сырники со сметаной /sýrniki so smetánoi/	Curd fritters with sour cream /ке́рд фри́тэз виз са́уэ криим/

XII

СЫРЫ /syrý/	CHEESE /чииз/
Ассорти из русских сыров /assortí iz rússkikh syróv/	Assorted Russian cheese /эсóртыд рашн чииз/
СЛАДКИЕ БЛЮДА /sládkie bliúda/	SWEET DISHES /свиит дúшиз/
Мороженое с наполнителем /morózhenoe с napolnítelem/	Ice-cream with filler /áйскрúим виз фúлэ/
Компот консервированный — ассорти /kompót konservírovannyi assortí/	Assorted canned fruits /эсóртыд кэнд фруутс/
Суфле ванильное /suflé vaníl'noe/	Vanilla soufflé /ванúлэ сýуфлей/
Фрукты со взбитыми сливками /frúkty so vzbítymi slívkami/	Fruits with whipped cream /фруутс виз випт криим/
Кофе гляссе /kófe gliassé/	Ice coffee /айс кóфи/
Кофе гляссе со взбитыми сливками /kófe gliassé so vzbítymi slívkami/	Ice coffee with with whipped cream /айс кóфи виз випт криим/
Какао гляссе /kakáo gliassé/	Ice cocoa /айс кóукоу/

XIII

ГОРЯЧИЕ НАПИТКИ /goriáchie napítki/	HOT DRINKS /хот дринкс/
Чай с лимоном /chái s limónom/	Tea and lemon /тии энд лéмэн/
Чай с молоком /chái s molokóm/	Tea and milk /тии энд милк/
Чай с вареньем /chái s varén'em/	Tea and jam /тии энд джем/
Кофе черный /kófe chórnyi/	Black coffee /блэк кóфи/
Кофе по-восточному /kófe po vostóchnomu/	Oriental coffee /óориéнтл кóфи/
Кофе с молоком /kófe s molokóm/	Coffee and milk /кóфи энд милк/
Кофе со сливками /kófe so slívkami/	Coffee and cream /кóфи энд криим/
Какао /kakáo/	Cocoa /кóукоу/
Шоколад /shokolád/	Hot chocolate /хот чóкэлит/
ФРУКТЫ /frúkty/	FRUITS /фруутс/
Апельсины /apel'síny/	Oranges /óринджиз/
Виноград /vinográd/	Grapes /грэйпс/

XIV

Груши /grúshi/	Pears /пéэз/
Яблоки /iábloki/	Apples /эплз/
КОНДИТЕРСКИЕ ИЗДЕЛИЯ /kondíterskie izdéliia/	CONFECTIONERY /кэнфéкшнэри/
Пирожное ассорти /pirózhnoe assortí/	Assorted pastries /эсóртыд пэ́йстриз/
Торт "Снежинка" /tort snezhínka/	"Snezhinka" cake /снежи́нка кейк/
Пай яблочный /pái iáblochnyi/	Apple pie /эпл пай/
Рулет шоколадный /rulét shokoládnyi/	Chocolate Swiss roll /чóкэлит свис рóул/
Кекс лимонный /keks limónnyi/	Lemon cake /лéмэн кейк/
Печенье берлинское /pechén'e berlínskoe/	Berliner biscuits /бёли́нэ би́скитс/
Конфеты трюфели /konféty triúfeli/	Truffle chocolates /трафл чóкэлитс/
Шоколад /shokolád/	Chocolate /чóкэлит/
ВОДКА /vódka/	VODKAS /вóдкэз/
"Пшеничная"	"Pshenichnaya"

"Столичная"	"Stolichnaya"
"Юбилейная"	"Yubileinaya"
КОНЬЯКИ /kon'iakí/	BRANDIES /брэ́ндиз/
"Юбилейный"	"Yubileiny"
"Отборный"	"Otborny"
"Двин"	"Dvin"
"ОС"	"OS"
ЛИКЕРЫ /likióry/	LIQUEURS /ли́кэз/
"Шартрез"	"Chartreuse"
"Бенедиктин"	"Bénédictine"
"Южный"	"Juzhny"
ВИНА СТОЛОВЫЕ—БЕЛЫЕ /ví na stolóvye bélye/	WHITE TABLE WINES /вайт тэйбл вайнз/
"Цинандали" — сухое грузинское /tsinandáli — sukhóe gruzínskoe/	"Tsinandali", dry wine from Georgia /цинанда́ли драй вайн фром джо́оджье/
"Гурджаани" — сухое грузинское /gurdzhaáni — sukhóe gruzínskoe/	"Gourdgaani", dry wine from Georgia /гурджаа́ни драй вайн фром джо́оджье/
"Фетяска" — сухое	"Fetyaska", dry

молдавское	wine from Moldavia
/fetiáska — sukhóe	/фетя́ска драй
moldávskoe/	вайн фром молдэ́йвье/

"Твиши" — полусладкое	"Tvishi", semisweet
грузинское	wine from Georgia
/tvishí — polusládkoe	/твиши́ сэ́мисвит
gruzínskoe/	вайн фром джо́оджье/

"Рислинг"	"Riesling"

ВИНА СТОЛОВЫЕ—КРАСНЫЕ	RED TABLE WINES
/vína stolóvye krásnye/	/рэд тэйбл вайнз/

"Мукузани" — сухое	"Mukuzani", dry
грузинское	wine from Georgia
/mukuzáni sukhóe	/мукуза́ни драй
gruzínskoe/	вайн фром джо́оджье/

"Напареули" — сухое	"Napareuli", dry
грузинское	wine from Georgia
/napareúli sukhóe	/напареу́ли драй
gruzínskoe/	вайн фром джо́оджье/

"Хванчкара" — полусладкое	"Khvanchkara", semisweet
грузинское	wine from Georgia
/khvanchkára polusládkoe	/хванчка́ра сэ́мисвит
gruzínskoe/	вайн фром джо́оджье/

"Киндзмараули" —	"Kindzmarauli", semisweet
полусладкое грузинское	wine from Georgia
/kindzmaraúli polusládkoe	/киндзмарау́ли сэ́мисвит
gruzínskoe/	вайн фром джо́оджье/

ВИНА ВИНОГРАДНЫЕ—	FORTIFIED TABLE
КРЕПЛЕНЫЕ	WINES
/vína vinográdnye krepliónye/	/фо́ртифайд тэйбл вайнз/

"Мадера"	"Madeira"
"Портвейн 777" /portvéin sem'sót sém'desiat sem'/	"Port 777" /порт сэвн хáндрэд сэ́внти сэвн/
Портвейн "Сурож" /portvéin súrozh/	"Sourozh" port /сýрож порт/
Портвейн "Крымский" /portvéin krýmskii/	"Krymsky" port /крымский порт/
"Мускат" /muskáт/	Muscat /мáскет/
"Фрага"	"Fraga"

СОВЕТСКОЕ ШАМПАНСКОЕ /sovétskoe shampánskoe/	SOVIET SPARKLING WINES /сóувьет спáрклинг вайнз/
Шампанское сухое /shampánskoe sukhóe/	Sec /сэк/
Шампанское полусухое /shampánskoe polusukhóe/	Demi-sec /дéмисэк/
Шампанское сладкое /shampánskoe sládkoe/	Doux /дуу/
Шампанское полусладкое /shampánskoe polusládkoe/	Semisweet /сэ́мисвит/
ПИВО /pívo/	BEERS /бúэз/
"Московское" /moskóvskoe/	"Moskovskoe" (Moscow Beer) /мóскоу бúэ/

XVIII

"Двойное золотое"	"Dvoinoe Zolotoe"
	(The Golden Double)
/dvoinóe zolotóe/	/зэ гóулдн дабл/
ХОЛОДНЫЕ НАПИТКИ,	COLD DRINKS
СОКИ	AND JUICES
/kholódnye napítki sóki/	/кóулд дринкс энд джýусыз/
Квас "Петровский" с хреном	"Petrovsky" kvass with
	horse-radish
/kvas petróvskii s khrénom/	/петрóвский квас виз
	хóосрэ́диш/
Напиток фруктовый	Fruit drink
/napítok fruktóvyi/	/фруут дринк/
Вода минеральная	Mineral water
/vodá minerál'naia/	/мѝнерал вóотэ/
Соки фруктовые	Fruit juices
/sóki fruktóvye/	/фруут джýусыз/
ТАБАЧНЫЕ ИЗДЕЛИЯ	TOBACCO
/tabáchnye izdélia/	/тэбэ́коу/
Сигареты	Cigarettes
/sigaréty/	/сѝгэрэ́тс/
Папиросы	Russian cigarettes
/papirósy/	/рашн сѝгэрэ́тс/

Продажа указанных блюд и напитков производится на
свободно конвертируемую и советскую валюту.
The aforementioned dishes and beverages are on sale for hard
currency and roubles.

XIX

Перед вами не совсем обычный словарь. Он предназначен для тех, кто еще недостаточно хорошо овладел английским языком и испытывает затруднения при чтении транскрипций. Поэтому в этом словаре произношение английских слов дается в русской транслитерации. Задача, стоявшая перед нами, казалась легкой только на первый взгляд. Трудность заключалась в том, что английскому звучанию далеко не всегда можно подобрать точное русское соответствие. Мы постарались с этим справиться и руководствовались при этом здравым смыслом.

Наибольшие затруднения вызвала транслитерация следующих звуков английского языка:

1. Глухой и звонкий межзубные звуки, которые на письме передаются сочетанием букв -th-; в данном словаре они обозначаются русскими буквами з, с, т, ф.

2. Т.н. "нейтральный" звук, который весьма распространен в английском языке, - в большинстве случаев гласный звук, на который не падает ударение - будет звучать нейтрально. У нас в словаре он передан буквами э, е.

3. Долгий "нейтральный" звук, особенно в начале слова - early, urgent и т.п. Для его обозначения в русском языке более всего подходит буква ё. Однако следует помнить, что произно-

сить этот звук надо без напряжения, т.е. как что-то среднее между -о- и -ё-.

Что касается ударений, то в односложных словах они опущены; кроме того, ударение не проставлено в тех случаях, когда оно падает на букву ё. Многие слова имеют два или даже три ударения. Это соответствует английскому произношению, однако в английской транскрипции главное ударение стоит сверху, а второстепенные - снизу. Мы, к сожалению, были вынуждены отказаться от этого принципа в силу причин технического характера.

В английском языке гласные звуки различаются по долготе звучания. Мы пользовались удвоенной буквой для обозначения долгого ударного звука; в безударных слогах долгота не указывается.

Словарь содержит более 18000 слов и словосочетаний, снабженных краткими грамматическими пояснениями, а также небольшое количество наиболее употребительных выражений. В конце приведен список географических названий.

Мы надеемся, что этот словарь поможет вам овладеть английским языком, как устным, так и письменным, и быстрее адаптироваться в новой языковой среде. Желаем успеха!

ENGLISH-RUSSIAN DICTIONARY

Английский алфавит

Aa	Jj	Ss
Bb	Kk	Tt
Cc	Ll	Uu
Dd	Mm	Vv
Ee	Nn	Ww
Ff	Oo	Xx
Gg	Pp	Yy
Hh	Qq	Zz
Ii	Rr	

Русский алфавит

Аа	Кк	Хх
Бб	Лл	Цц
Вв	Мм	Чч
Гг	Нн	Шш
Дд	Оо	Щщ
Ее	Пп	Ъъ
Ёё	Рр	Ыы
Жж	Сс	Ьь
Зз	Тт	Ээ
Ии	Уу	Юю
Йй	Фф	Яя

ав.	авиация	презр.	презрительное употребление
анат.	анатомия		
архит.	архитектура	пренебр.	пренебрежительное выражение
астр.	астрономия		
библ.	библеизм		
биол.	биология	полигр.	полиграфия
бот.	ботаника	радио	радиотехника
бухг.	бухгалтерия	разг.	разговорное слово
воен.	военное дело		
вчт.	вычислительная техника	рел.	религия
		сокр.	сокращение
геогр.	география	спорт.	спортивное выражение
грам.	грамматика		
ед.ч.	единственное число	с.-х.	сельское хозяйство
жарг.	жаргонное слово	театр.	театроведение
ж/д	железная дорога	текст.	текстильное дело
иск.	искусство	тел.	телефония, телеграфия
л.	лицо		
лат.	латинский язык	тех.	техника
		усил.	усилительно
матем.	математика	фин.	финансовый термин
мед.	медицина		
мин.	минералогия	фотогр.	фотография
мн.ч.	множественное число	хим.	химия
		церк.	церковное выражение
мор.	морское дело		
муз.	музыка	шахм.	шахматный термин
образн.	образное употребление	эл.	электротехника
перен.	в переносном значении	юр.	юридический термин

adj - adjective	имя прилага-тельное	n - noun	имя сущест-вительное
adv - adverb	наречие	num - numeral	числительное
aux - auxiliary	вспомога-тельный гла-гол	ord - ordinal	порядковый
		part - particle	частица
cap - capitalized	с заглавной буквы	pl - plural	множествен-ное число
conj - conjunction	союз	possess - possessive	притяжатель-ный
i - intransitive	непереход-ный	predic - predicative	предикатив-ное употреб-ление
imper - imperative	повелитель-ный		
		prep - preposition	предлог
indef - indefinite	неопределен-ный	pron - pronoun	местоимение
		t - transitive	переходный
interj - interjection	междометие	v - verb	глагол

IV

A

A, a /эй/ (муз.) ля; (А) высшая оценка, "отлично"; from A to Z /фром эй ту зэд/ от а до я

a, an /эй, э, эн/ неопределенный артикль (на русский не переводится)

aback /эбэ́к/ adv: taken ~ /тэйкн ~/ застигнутый врасплох

abacus /э́бэкэс/ n счеты

abandon /эбэ́ндэн/ vt оставлять, покидать

abandoned /эбэ́нднд/ adj покинутый

abate /эбэ́йт/ vi стихать, успокаиваться

abbess /э́бис/ n настоятельница монастыря

abbey /э́би/ n аббатство

abbot /э́бэт/ n аббат

abbreviate /эбри́ивиэйт/ vt сокращать

abbreviation /эбри́ивизи́йшн/ n сокращение

abdicate /э́бдикейт/ vti отрекаться (от престола); отказываться

abdomen /э́бдэмен/ n брюшная полость; живот

abdominal /эбдо́минл/ adj брюшной

abduct /эбда́кт/ vt похищать

abhor /эбхо́р/ vt ненавидеть

ability /эби́лити/ n способность

ablaze /эблэ́йз/ predic adj and adv в огне; сверкающий

able /эйбл/ adj способный; be ~ /би ~/ мочь, быть в состоянии

ably /э́йбли/ adj умело

abnormal /эбно́рмл/ adj ненормальный

aboard /эбо́рд/ adv на борту

abolish /эбо́лиш/ vt отменять

abominable /эбо́минэбл/ adj отвратительный

aboriginal /э́бори́джнл/ adj туземный, коренной

abortion /эбо́ршн/ n аборт

abortive /эбо́ртив/ adj неудавшийся

abound /эба́унд/ vi изобиловать

about /эба́ут/ prep о; вокруг; adv приблизительно

above /эба́в/ prep над; более; выше

abreast /эбре́ст/ adv в ряд

abridge /эбри́дж/ vt сокращать

abroad /эбро́од/ adv за границей

abrupt /эбра́пт/ adj отрывистый; крутой; резкий

abscess /э́бсис/ n нарыв

absent /э́бсент/ adj отсутствующий

absent-minded /э́бсентма́йндыд/ adj рассеянный

absinth /э́бсинт/ n абсент

absolute /э́бсэлют/ adj абсолютный

absolutely /э́бсэлютли/ adv совершенно

absolution /э́бсэлю́юшн/ n отпущение грехов

absorb /эбсо́рб/ vt поглощать, впитывать

abstain /эбстэ́йн/ vi воздерживаться

abstainer /эбстэ́йнэ/ n трезвенник

abstract /э́бстрэкт/ adj абстрактный; /эбстрэ́кт/ vt извлекать; резюмировать

absurd /эбсёрд/ adj нелепый

absurdity /эбсёрдити/ n абсурд

abundance /эба́ндэнс/ n изобилие

abundant /эба́ндэнт/ adj обильный; изобильный

abuse /эбью́юс/ n брань; злоупотребление

abusive /эбью́юсив/ adj оскорбительный

abyss /эби́с/ n бездна

acacia /экэ́йше/ n акация

academic /э́кэдэ́мик/ adj академический

academician /экэ́деми́шн/ n академик

academy /экэ́деми/ n академия

accelerate /экса́лерэйт/ vti ускорять (ся)

accelerator /экса́лерэйтэ/ n ускоритель; акселератор

accent /э́ксент/ n ударение; акцент

accept /эксэ́пт/ vt принимать

acceptable /эксэ́птэбл/ adj приемлемый, допустимый

accepted /эксэ́птыд/ adj распространенный

access /э́ксэс/ n доступ
accessible /эксэ́сибл/ adj доступный
accessories /эксэ́сориз/ n pl аксессуары
accessory /эксэ́сори/ n соучастник
accident /э́ксидэнт/ n несчастный случай
accidental /э́ксидэ́нтл/ adj случайный
accidentally /э́ксидэ́нтэли/ adv случайно
acclaim /эклэ́йм/ vt приветствовать
acclimatization /эклá́ймэтайзэ́йшн/ n акклиматизация
acclimatize /эклá́ймэтайз/ vti акклиматизировать (ся)
accommodate /экó́мэдэйт/ vt размещать; вмещать
accommodation /экó́мэдэ́йшн/ n жилье
accompaniment /экá́мпэнимент/ n сопровождение, аккомпанемент
accompanist /экá́мпэнист/ n аккомпаниатор
accompany /экá́мпэни/ vt сопровождать; аккомпанировать
accomplice /экó́мплис/ n соучастник
accomplish /экó́мплиш/ vt завершать; исполнять
accomplished /экó́мплишт/ adj превосходный; законченный
accomplishment /экó́мплишмент/ n достижение; pl достоинства
accord /экó́рд/ n согласие; аккорд; vi гармонировать
according to /экó́рдингтэ/ prep согласно
accordingly /экó́рдингли/ adv соответственно
accordion /экó́рдьен/ n аккордеон
accost /экó́ст/ vt приставать к
account /экá́унт/ n счет; отчет; settle ~s /сэтл ~с/ сводить счеты; take into ~ /тэйк и́нту ~/ принимать во внимание
accountancy /экá́унтэнси/ n бухгалтерское дело
accountant /экá́унтэнт/ n бухгалтер
accredit /экрé́дит/ vt аккредитовывать
accredited /экрé́дитыд/ adj аккредитованный

accumulate /экьюю́юмьюлэйт/ vt накапливать
accumulation /экью́юмьюлэ́йшн/ n накопление; масса, груда
accuracy /э́кьюрэси/ n точность
accurate /э́кьюрит/ adj точный
accursed /экёрсид/ adj проклятый
accusal /экьюю́юзэл/ n обвинение
accusative /экьюю́юзэтив/ n винительный падеж
accuse /экьюю́юз/ vt обвинять
accuser /экьюю́юзэ/ n обвинитель
accustom /экá́стэм/ vt приучать
accustomed /экá́стэмд/ adj привыкший; become ~ /бикá́м ~/ привыкать
ace /эйс/ n (карты) туз; ас
acetylene /эсэ́тилин/ n ацетилен
ache /эйк/ n боль; vi болеть
achieve /эчи́ив/ vt достигать
achievement /эчи́ивмент/ n достижение
acid /э́сид/ adj кислый; n кислота
acknowledge /экнó́лидж/ vt признавать; подтверждать получение (письма)
acknowledgement /экнó́лиджмент/ n признание; подтверждение
acorn /э́йкорн/ n желудь
acoustic /экý́устик/ adj акустический
acoustics /экý́устикс/ n pl акустика
acquaint /эквэ́йнт/ vt знакомить; ~ oneself with /~ вансэ́лф виз/ знакомиться с
acquaintance /эквэ́йнтэнс/ n знакомый; знакомство
acquire /эквá́йе/ vt приобретать, получать
acquit /экви́т/ vt оправдывать
acquittal /экви́тл/ n оправдание
acquittance /экви́тэнс/ n расписка об уплате долга
acre /э́йкэ/ n акр
acrimonious /э́кримó́уньес/ adj язвительный; раздражительный
acrimony /э́кримэни/ n желчность
acrobat /э́крэбэт/ n акробат

across /экро́с/ adv поперек; на той стороне; крест-накрест

act /экт/ n поступок; акт; vti действовать; исполнять (роль)

action /экшн/ n действие

active /э́ктив/ adj активный; энергичный

activity /экти́вити/ n деятельность

actor /э́ктэ/ n актер

actress /э́ктрис/ n актриса

actual /э́кчюэл/ adj действительный

actuality /э́кчюэ́лити/ n реальность

actually /э́кчюэли/ adv на самом деле, фактически

acute /экью́ют/ adj острый; проницательный

adamant /э́дэмэнт/ adj непреклонный

Adam's apple /э́дэмзэ́пл/ n кадык

adapt /эдэ́пт/ vt приспособлять; переделывать

adaptation /э́дэптэ́йшн/ n адаптация

adapter /эдэ́птэ/ n адаптер

add /эд/ vt добавлять; складывать

addendum /эдэ́ндэм/ n приложение (к книге, договору и т.п.)

addict /э́дикт/ n наркоман

addiction /эди́кшн/ n наркомания; пристрастие

addition /эди́шн/ n прибавление; (матем.) сложение

additional /эди́шнл/ adj дополнительный

address /эдрэ́с/ n адрес; обращение; vt адресовать; обращаться к

addressee /э́дрэси́и/ n адресат

adenoids /э́диноидз/ n pl аденоиды

adequacy /э́диквэси/ n адекватность

adequate /э́диквит/ adj соответствующий

adhere /эдхи́э/ vi прилипать; твердо держаться (принципов и т.п.)

adherence /эдхи́эрэнс/ n приверженность

adherent /эдхи́эрэнт/ adj липкий; n приверженец

adhesive /эдхи́исив/ adj клейкий

adjacent /эджэ́йсэнт/ adj смежный

adjective /эджи́ктив/ n (грам.) имя прилагательное

adjourn /эджёрн/ vt отсрочивать; объявлять перерыв (в работе)

adjournment /эджёрнмент/ n перерыв

adjust /эджа́ст/ vt поправлять; регулировать

adjustment /эджа́стмент/ n приспособление

adjutant /э́джютэнт/ n адьютант

administer /эдми́нистэ/ vt управлять; отправлять правосудие; ~ an oath /~ эн о́уф/ приводить к присяге

administration /эдми́нистрэ́йшн/ n управление; администрация; правительство

administrative /эдми́нистрэтив/ adj административный

administrator /эдми́нистрэйтэ/ n администратор

admirable /э́дмэрэбл/ adj восхитительный; похвальный

admiral /э́дмэрл/ n адмирал

Admiralty /э́дмэрлти/ n адмиралтейство; военно-морское министерство (в Англии)

admiration /э́дмэрэ́йшн/ n восхищение

admire /эдма́йе/ vt восхищаться, любоваться

admirer /эдма́йерэ/ n поклонник

admissible /эдми́сэбл/ adj допустимый

admission /эдми́шн/ n признание; вход

admit /эдми́т/ vt впускать; допускать

admonish /эдмо́ниш/ vt убеждать; делать замечание

admonition /э́дмэни́шн/ n выговор; увещевание

ado /эду́у/ n суматоха; хлопоты

adolescence /э́долёснс/ n отрочество

adolescent /э́долёснт/ adj подростковый; n юноша; девушка; подросток

adopt /эдо́пт/ vt усыновлять, удочерять; принимать

adorable /эдо́орэбл/ adj восхитительный

adore /эдо́р/ vt обожать

adorn /эдóрн/ vt украшать

adornment /эдóрнмент/ n украшение

adrift /эдри́фт/ adv по течению; be ~ /би ~/ дрейфовать

adroit /эдрóйт/ adj искусный, ловкий

adult /э́далт/ n, adj взрослый

adulterate /эдáлтэрэйт/ vt ухудшать; подмешивать

adultery /эдáлтэри/ n супружеская измена

advance /эдвáанс/ n наступление; успех; (фин.) аванс; vt продвигать; платить авансом; vi делать успехи

advance-guard /эдвáансгáрд/ n авангард

advanced /эдвáанст/ adj передовой; пожилой; успевающий

advantage /эдвáантыдж/ n преимущество

advantageous /э́двэнтэ́йджес/ adj выгодный

advent /э́двент/ n приход; пришествие

adventure /эдвéнче/ n приключение; авантюра

adventurer /эдвéнчерэ/ n авантюрист

adverb /э́дверб/ n наречие

adversary /э́двесри/ n противник

advertise /э́дветайз/ vt рекламировать

advertisement, сокр. ad /эдвéртисмент, эд/ n реклама

advice /эдвáйс/ n совет

advise /эдвáйз/ vt советовать

adviser /эдвáйзэ/ n советник; консультант

advocate /э́двэкит/ n адвокат; сторонник; /э́двэкейт/ vt защищать; отстаивать

aerial /áэриэл/ adj воздушный; n антенна

aerodrome /э́эрэдроум/ n аэродром

aeroplane /э́эрэплэйн/ n самолет

aesthete /и́истыт/ n эстет

aesthetics /иистэ́тикс/ n эстетика

affable /э́фэбл/ adj приветливый

affair /эфэ́э/ n дело; love ~ /лав ~/ роман, связь

affect /эфéкт/ vt влиять на; затрагивать (интересы)

affected /эфéктыд/ adj жеманный

affection /эфéкшн/ n привязанность

affidavit /э́фидэ́йвит/ n письменное показание под присягой

affiliate /эфи́лиэйт/ vt присоединять в качестве филиала

affinity /эфи́нити/ n родство; сходство

affirm /эфёрм/ vt утверждать

affirmative /эфёрмэтив/ adj утвердительный

affix /эфи́кс/ vt прикреплять; ставить (подпись)

afflict /эфли́кт/ vt огорчать; поражать (о болезни)

affluence /э́флюэнс/ n изобилие

afford /эфóрд/ vt позволять себе

afforest /эфóрист/ vt засаживать лесом

afforestation /эфóристэ́йшн/ n лесонасаждение

affront /эфрáнт/ n оскорбление

Afghan /э́фгэн/ n афганец, афганка; афганский язык; adj афганский

aforesaid /эфóрсэд/ adj вышесказанный

afraid /эфрэ́йд/ pred adj испуганный

after /áафтэ/ prep за; после; adv позади; потом; ~ all /~р оол/ в конце концов

afternoon /áафтэнýун/ n время после полудня

afterwards /áафтэвэдз/ adv потом

again /эгéн/ adv опять

against /эгéйнст/ prep против

agate /áгэт/ n агат

age /эйдж/ n возраст; век

aged /э́йджид/ adj пожилой

agency /э́йдженси/ n агентство

agenda /эджéндэ/ n повестка дня

agent /э́йджент/ n агент

aggravate /э́грэвэйт/ vt ухудшать

aggravation /э́грэвэ́йшн/ n обострение

aggregate /э́григит/ n агрегат; adj совокупный; общий

aggression /эгрéшн/ n агрессия

aggressive /эгрéсив/ adj агрессивный

aggressor /эгрэ́сэ/ n агрессор

agile /э́джайл/ adj проворный, живой

agitate /э́джитэйт/ vt волновать; vi аги-
тировать

ago /эгóу/ adv тому назад; long ~ /лонг
~/ давно

agonize /э́гэнайз/ vt мучить; vi быть в
агонии

agony /э́гэни/ n мука

agrarian /эгрэ́риэн/ adj аграрный

agree /эгри́/ vt согласовывать; vi соглашаться

agreeable /эгри́эбл/ adj согласный; приятный

agreement /эгри́имент/ n договор

agriculture /э́грикалче/ n сельское хозяйство

ahead /эхéд/ adv вперед, впереди

aid /эйд/ n пособие; помощь; помощник;
vt помогать

aide-de-camp /э́йддэкáан/ n адьютант

ail /эйл/ vt причинять боль; vi болеть

ailing /э́йлинг/ adj больной

ailment /э́йлмент/ n болезнь, недуг

aim /эйм/ n цель; take ~ /тэйк ~/ прицеливаться

aimless /э́ймлис/ adj бесцельный

air /ээ/ n воздух; adj воздушный

air-conditioning /э́экэнди́шнинг/ n кондиционирование воздуха

airline /э́элайн/ n авиалиния

airmail /э́эмэйл/ n авиапочта

ajar /эджáр/ adv приоткрыто

akin /эки́н/ adj близкий, родственный

alabaster /э́лэбастэ/ n алебастр

alarm /элáрм/ n тревога

alarm clock /элáрмклок/ n будильник

alas /элáас/ interj увы

albatross /э́лбэтрос/ n альбатрос

albino /элби́иноу/ n альбинос

album /э́лбэм/ n альбом

alchemy /э́лкими/ n алхимия

alcohol /э́лкэхол/ n алкоголь, спирт;
спиртные напитки

alcoholic /э́лкэхóлик/ adj алкогольный;
n алкоголик

alder /óолдэ/ n ольха

alderman /óолдэрмэн/ n олдермен

ale /эйл/ n пиво

alert /элёрт/ adj бдительный; проворный

algebra /э́лджибрэ/ n алгебра

Algerian /элджи́эриэн/ n алжирец, ал-
жирка; adj алжирский

alias /э́йлиэс/ adv иначе (называемый)

alibi /э́либай/ n алиби

alien /э́йльен/ adj иностранный; чуждый; n иностранец, иностранка

alike /элáйк/ adj схожий; adv одинаково

alimony /э́лимэни/ n алименты

alive /элáйв/ adj живой

alkali /э́лкэлай/ n щелочь

alkaline /э́лкэлайн/ adj щелочной

all /оол/ adj весь, все, вся; всякий; ~ the
same /~ зэ сэйм/ все равно; ~ right /~
райт/ хорошо; pron все, всё; not at ~
/нот эт ~/ ничуть, пожалуйста

allege /элéдж/ vt утверждать

allegedly /элéджидли/ adv якобы

allegiance /эли́идженс/ n лояльность

allegory /э́лигэри/ n аллегория

allergic /элёрджик/ adj аллергический;
be ~ to /би ~ ту/ не выносить (чего-л.)

allergy /э́лэджи/ n аллергия

alley /э́ли/ n аллея; переулок

alliance /элáйенс/ n союз

allied /элáйд/ adj союзный

alligator /э́лигейтэ/ n аллигатор

allocate /э́лэкейт/ vt ассигновать

allot /элóт/ vt распределять; отводить

allotment /элóтмент/ n участок земли

allow /элáу/ vt позволять, допускать

allowance /элáуэнс/ n пособие; деньги на
расходы; family ~ /фэ́мили ~/ пособие
многосемейным; travelling ~ /трэ́ве-
линг ~/ командировочные

all-round /óолрáунд/ adj всесторонний

allure /элью́э/ vt пленять

alluring /элью́эринг/ adj соблазнитель-
ный

allusion /элю́южн/ n намек

ally /э́лай/ n союзник

almanac /о́олмэнэк/ n альманах

almighty /оолма́йти/ adj всемогущий

almond /а́амэнд/ n миндаль

almost /о́олмоуст/ adv почти

aloe /э́лоу/ n алоэ

alone /эло́ун/ adj один; adv только

along /эло́нг/ prep вдоль; по; ~ the road /~ зэ ро́уд/ по дороге

aloud /эла́уд/ adv вслух, громко

alphabet /э́лфэбит/ n алфавит, азбука

Alpine /э́лпайн/ adj альпийский

already /олрэ́ди/ adv уже

also /о́олсоу/ adv также, тоже

altar /о́олтэ/ n алтарь

alter /о́олтэ/ vt изменять, переделывать

alternate /олтёрнит/ adj чередующийся; on ~ days /он ~ дэйз/ через день; /о́олтэнэйт/ vti чередовать(ся)

alternative /олтёрнэтив/ adj альтернативный; n альтернатива

although /олзо́у/ conj хотя

altitude /э́лтитьюд/ n высота

altogether /о́олтэгéзэ/ adv в целом; всего

alum /э́лэм/ n квасцы

aluminium /э́льюми́ньем/ n алюминий

always /о́олвэз/ adv всегда

amateur /э́мэтё/ n любитель; adj любительский

amaze /эмэ́йз/ vt изумлять

Amazon /э́мэзэн/ n амазонка

ambassador /эмбэ́сэдэ/ n посол

amber /э́мбэ/ n янтарь

ambiguity /эмбигъю́ити/ n двусмысленность

ambiguous /эмби́гъюэс/ adj двусмысленный

ambition /эмби́шн/ n честолюбие

ambulance /э́мбьюлэнс/ n карета скорой помощи, скорая помощь

ambush /э́мбуш/ n засада

amend /эмéнд/ vt исправлять

amenity /эми́инити/ n любезность; pl удобства

amethyst /э́митист/ n аметист

amiable /э́ймьебл/ adj любезный, дружелюбный

amicably /э́микэбли/ adv дружески

ammonia /эмо́унье/ n аммиак; household ~ /ха́усхоулд ~/ нашатырный спирт

ammunition /э́мьюни́ишн/ n боеприпасы

amnesty /э́мнести/ n амнистия

among /эма́нг/ prep среди; между

amortization /эмо́ртизэ́йшн/ n амортизация

amount /эма́унт/ n сумма; количество

ampere /э́мпеэ/ n ампер

amphibian /эмфи́биэн/ n амфибия

amphibious /эмфи́биэс/ adj земноводный

amphitheatre /э́мфиси́этэ/ n амфитеатр

ample /эмпл/ adj обильный

amplifier /э́мплифайе/ n (радио) усилитель

amplitude /э́мплитьюд/ n амплитуда

amputate /э́мпьютэйт/ vt ампутировать

amputation /э́мпьютэ́йшн/ n ампутация

amulet /э́мьюлит/ n амулет

amuse /эмью́юз/ vt забавлять, развлекать

amusing /эмью́юзинг/ adj забавный

anaemia /эни́имье/ n анемия, малокровие

analogous /энэ́лэгэс/ adj аналогичный

analyse /э́нэлайз/ vt анализировать

analysis /энэ́лэсис/ n анализ

anarchist /э́нэкист/ n анархист

anarchy /э́нэки/ n анархия

anathema /энэ́фимэ/ n анафема

anatomy /энэ́тэми/ n анатомия

ancestor /э́нсистэ/ n предок

ancestral /энсéстрэл/ adj наследственный, родовой

ancestry /э́нсистри/ n происхождение

anchor /э́нкэ/ n якорь

anchovy /э́нчэви/ n анчоус

ancient /эйншнт/ adj древний

and /энд/ conj и

anecdote /э́никдоут/ n анекдот

anemone /энéмэни/ n анемон
angel /э́йнжел/ n ангел
anger /э́нгэ/ n гнев, ярость; vt сердить
angle /энгл/ n угол
angling /э́нглинг/ n рыбная ловля
angry /э́нгри/ adj сердитый; be ~ with /би ~ виз/ сердиться на
aniline /э́нилин/ n анилин
animal /э́нимэл/ n животное
animate /э́нимэйт/ vt оживлять
animated /э́нимэйтыд/ adj оживленный, бодрый; ~ cartoon (s) /~ картýун (з) / мультипликация; мультфильм
animosity /э́нимóсити/ n враждебность
aniseed /э́нисиид/ n анисовое семя
ankle /энкл/ n лодыжка
annals /энлз/ n анналы, летопись
annex /энэ́кс/ vt аннексировать
annexation /э́нексэ́йшн/ n аннексия
anniversary /э́нивёсри/ n годовщина
annotate /э́нотэйт/ vt аннотировать
announce /энáунс/ vt объявлять
announcement /энáунсмент/ n объявление
announcer /энáунсэ/ n диктор (радио)
annoy /энóй/ vt раздражать
annoyance /энóйэнс/ n раздражение
annual /э́ньюэл/ adj ежегодный, годовой
annul /энáл/ vt аннулировать
annulment /энáлмент/ n отмена
Annunciation /энáнсиэ́йшн/ n Благовещение
anode /э́ноуд/ n анод
anodyne /э́нодайн/ n болеутоляющее средство
anoint /энóйнт/ vt смазывать (рану); (церк.) помазывать
anomaly /энóмэли/ n аномалия
anonymous /энóнимэс/ adj анонимный
another /энáзэ/ pron, adj другой, еще один
answer /áансэ/ n ответ; vt отвечать
ant /энт/ n муравей
antagonism /энтэ́гэнизм/ n вражда
antagonist /энтэ́гэнист/ n противник

Antarctic /энтáрктик/ adj антарктический
antelope /э́нтилоуп/ n антилопа
ante meridiem, сокр. a.m. /э́нтимирúдиэм, эй эм/ до полудня
anthem /э́нтэм/ n гимн
anthology /энтóлэджи/ n антология
anthracite /э́нтрэсайт/ n антрацит
anthrax /э́нтрэкс/ n сибирская язва
anthropology /э́нтрэпóлэджи/ n антропология
anti-aircraft /э́нтиэ́экрафт/ adj противовоздушный
antibiotic /э́нтибайóтик/ n антибиотик
Antichrist /э́нтикрайст/ n антихрист
anticipate /энтúсипэйт/ vt предчувствовать
anticipation /энтúсипэ́йшн/ n ожидание, предвкушение
antidote /э́нтидоут/ n противоядие
antifreeze /э́нтифрúиз/ n антифриз
antimony /э́нтимэни/ n сурьма
antipathy /энтúпэфи/ n антипатия
antique /энтúик/ adj старинный; n антикварная вещь
antiquity /энтúквити/ n античность; древность, глубокая старина
antiseptic /э́нтисéптик/ n антисептическое средство; adj антисептический
antithesis /энтúфисис/ n антитеза, противоположность
anus /э́йнэс/ n (анат.) задний проход
anvil /э́нвил/ n наковальня
anxiety /энгзáйети/ n беспокойство
anxious /э́нкшес/ adj озабоченный; be ~ /би ~/ страстно желать
any /э́ни/ adj любой, всякий; pron кто-нибудь, что-нибудь; adv сколько-нибудь, несколько
anybody, anyone /э́нибóди, э́ниван/ pron кто-нибудь, кто-либо
anyhow /э́нихау/ adv как-нибудь; так или иначе
anything /э́нифинг/ pron что-нибудь
anyway /э́нивэй/ adv где-нибудь, где-либо, где/куда угодно

aorta /эйо́ртэ/ n аорта
apart /эпа́рт/ adv отдельно
apartheid /эпа́ртхайд/ n апартеид
apartment /эпа́ртмент/ n квартира
apathy /э́пэфи/ n апатия
ape /эйп/ n обезьяна; vt подражать,
обезьянничать
apex /э́йпекс/ n вершина
aphis /э́йфис/ n тля
aphorism /э́фэризм/ n афоризм
apiary /э́йпьери/ n пасека
apogee /э́поджи/ n апогей
apologize /эпо́лэджайз/ vi извиняться
apology /эпо́лэджи/ n извинение; аполо-
гия
apoplexy /э́пэплекси/ n удар, паралич
apostle /эпо́сл/ n апостол
apostrophe /эпо́стрэфи/ n апостроф
apothecary /эпо́фикэри/ n аптекарь
apotheosis /эпо́фио́усис/ n апофеоз
appal /эпо́ол/ vt ужасать
appalling /эпо́олинг/ adj ужасный
apparatus /э́пэрэ́йтэс/ n аппарат; гимнастический снаряд
apparent /эпэ́рэнт/ adj явный
appeal /эпи́ил/ n призыв; vi обращаться,
взывать; подавать апелляционную
жалобу
appear /эпи́э/ vi появляться; казаться
appearance /эпи́эрэнс/ n появление; вид,
наружность; видимость
appease /эпи́из/ vt умиротворять
appendicitis /эпе́ндиса́йтис/ n аппенди-
цит
appendix /эпе́ндикс/ n аппендикс; приложение
appetite /э́питайт/ n аппетит
appetizer /э́питайзэ/ n закуска
appetizing /э́питайзинг/ adj вкусный,
аппетитный
applaud /эпло́од/ vt аплодировать
applause /эпло́оз/ n аплодисменты;
одобрение
apple /эпл/ n яблоко; ~ of the eye /~ ов зы
ай/ зеница ока

apple-tree /э́плтри/ n яблоня
appliance /эпла́йенс/ n прибор; устройство
applicant /э́пликэнт/ n кандидат; абиту-
риент
application /э́пликэ́йшн/ n заявление; ~
form /~ форм/ анкета
apply /эпла́й/ vt применять; vi ~ to /~ ту/
обращаться к
appoint /эпо́йнт/ vt назначать
appointment /эпо́йнтмент/ n назначение;
должность; встреча; прием (у врача)
appraisal /эпрэ́йзл/ n оценка
appraise /эпрэ́йз/ vt оценивать
appreciable /эпри́ишебл/ adj заметный,
ощутимый
appreciate /эпри́ишиэйт/ vt ценить
appreciation /эпри́ишиэ́йшн/ n призна-
тельность; оценка по достоинству
apprehensive /э́прихе́нсив/ adj полный
страха; опасающийся
apprentice /эпре́нтис/ n подмастерье
approach /эпро́уч/ vi приближаться к;
обращаться к; n подход
appropriate /эпро́уприит/ adj подходящий; /эпро́уприэйт/ vt присваивать,
красть; ассигновывать
approval /эпру́увл/ n одобрение
approve /эпру́ув/ vt одобрять
approximate /эпро́ксимит/ adj приблизительный
approximately /эпро́ксимитли/ adj приблизительно
apricot /э́йприкот/ n абрикос
April /эйпрл/ n апрель
apron /эйпрн/ n передник
apropos /э́прэпоу/ adv кстати
aquafortis /э́квэфо́ртис/ n концентриро-
ванная азотная кислота
aquarium /эквэ́риэм/ n аквариум
aqueduct /э́квидакт/ n акведук
Arab /э́рэб/ n араб, арабка; арабская лошадь; adj арабский
arabesque /э́рэбе́ск/ n арабеска

Arabic /эрэбик/ n арабский язык; adj арабский

arable /э́рэбл/ adj пахотный

arbiter /а́рбитэ/ n арбитр

arbitrate /а́рбитрэйт/ vt решать третейским судом

arbitration /а́рбитрэ́йшн/ n арбитраж

arc /арк/ n дуга

arcade /аркéйд/ n пассаж (с магазинами); аркада

arch /арч/ n арка

archaeology /а́ркио́лэджи/ n археология

archaic /аркéйик/ adj устарелый

archaism /а́ркейизм/ n архаизм

archangel /а́ркéйнджл/ n архангел

archbishop /а́рчбúшэп/ n архиепископ

archdeacon /а́рчдúикэн/ n архидиакон

archduchess /а́рчда́чис/ n эрцгерцогиня

archduke /а́рчдью́юк/ n эрцгерцог

arched /арчт/ adj сводчатый; изогнутый

archer /а́рче/ n стрелок из лука

archery /а́рчери/ n стрельба из лука

archipelago /а́ркипéлигоу/ n архипелаг

architect /а́ркитэкт/ n архитектор

architectural /а́ркитэ́кчерэл/ adj архитектурный

architecture /а́ркитэкче/ n архитектура

archives /а́ркайвз/ n pl архив

archivist /а́ркивист/ n архивариус

Arctic /а́рктик/ adj арктический

ardent /а́рдэнт/ adj горячий, пылкий

ardour /а́рдэ/ n рвение

area /э́эриэ/ n площадь; зона

argue /а́ргью/ vt обсуждать; аргументировать; vi спорить

argument /а́ргьюмент/ n аргумент; спор

argumentation /а́ргьюментэ́йшн/ n аргументация

arid /э́рид/ adj сухой; бесплодный

arise /эрáйз/ vi возникать

aristocrat /э́ристэкрэт/ n аристократ

aristocratic /э́ристэкрэ́тик/ adj аристократический

arithmetic /эри́фметик/ n арифметика

ark /арк/ n ковчег; Noah's ~ /нóэз ~/ Ноев ковчег

arm /арм/ n рука; pl оружие; vti вооружать(ся)

armament /а́рмэмент/ n вооружение

armchair /а́рмчеэ/ n кресло

armpit /а́рмпит/ n подмышка

armistice /а́рмистис/ n перемирие

armour /а́рмэ/ n броня, доспехи

army /а́рми/ n армия; join the ~ /джóйн зы ~/ поступить на военную службу

aroma /эрóумэ/ n аромат

aromatic /э́ромэ́тик/ adj ароматный

around /эрáунд/ prep вокруг; adv всюду; кругом

arrange /эрэ́йндж/ vt устраивать; приводить в порядок; (муз.) аранжировать

arrest /эрéст/ n арест; vt арестовывать

arrival /эрáйвл/ n прибытие

arrive /эрáйв/ vi приезжать

arrogance /э́рэгэнс/ n высокомерие, надменность

arrogant /э́рэгэнт/ adj надменный

arrow /э́роу/ n стрела

arsenal /а́рсинл/ n арсенал

arsenic /арсéник/ n мышьяк

arson /арсн/ n поджог

art /арт/ n искусство

artery /а́ртэри/ n артерия

artesian well /артúизьенвэ́л/ n артезианский колодец

artful /а́ртфул/ adj ловкий

artichoke /а́ртичоук/ n артишок

article /а́ртикл/ n статья; предмет; (грам.) артикль

articulate /артúкьюлит/ adj ясный; /артúкьюлэйт/ vt произносить отчетливо

artificial /а́ртифúшл/ adj искусственный

artillery /артúлери/ n артиллерия

artisan /а́ртизэ́н/ n ремесленник

artist /а́ртист/ n художник

artless /а́ртлис/ adj простодушный, бесхитростный

Aryan /э́эриэн/ n ариец, арийка; adj арийский

as /эз/ adv как, в качестве; ~ a rule /~ э руул/ как правило; ~ if /~ иф/ как будто

asbestos /эзбе́стос/ n асбест

ascend /эсэ́нд/ vi подниматься; vt подниматься на

ascension /эсэ́ншн/ n восхождение; the A. (рел.) Вознесение

ascertain /э́сэтэ́йн/ vt устанавливать, выяснять

ascetic /эсе́тик/ adj аскетический; n аскет

ash (es) /эш (из) / n pl зола, пепел; n ясень

ashamed /эше́ймд/ adj пристыженный; I feel ~ /ай фиил ~/ мне стыдно

ashore /эшо́р/ adv на берег, на берегу

ashtray /э́штрэй/ n пепельница

Asian /эйшн/ n азиат, азиатка; adj азиатский

ask /ааск/ vt спрашивать; просить; ~ a question /~ э квесчн/ задавать вопрос

asleep /эсли́ип/ adj спящий; be ~ /би ~/ спать; fall ~ /фоол ~/ засыпать

asp /эсп/ n гадюка

asparagus /эспэ́рэгэс/ n спаржа

aspect /э́спект/ n аспект; сторона

aspen /э́спен/ n осина

asphalt /э́сфэлт/ n асфальт; vt асфальтировать

aspiration /э́спэрэ́йшн/ n стремление

aspire (to) /эспа́йе ту/ vi стремиться к

aspirin /э́спэрин/ n аспирин

ass /эс/ n осел

assassin /эсэ́син/ n убийца

assassinate /эсэ́синэйт/ vt совершать убийство по политическим мотивам; вероломно убивать

assassination /эсэ́синэ́йшн/ n убийство по политическим мотивам; вероломное убийство

assault /эсо́олт/ n нападение; vt нападать

assemble /эсэ́мбл/ vt собирать; монтировать; vi собираться

assembly /эсэ́мбли/ n собрание; монтаж

assent /эсэ́нт/ n согласие; vi соглашаться

assert /эсе́рт/ vt утверждать

assess /эсэ́с/ vt оценивать; облагать (налогом)

assessment /эсэ́смент/ n оценка; обложение (налогом)

assets /э́сэтс/ n pl (фин.) актив; имущество

assign /эса́йн/ vt назначать; ассигновать

assignment /эса́йнмент/ n назначение; ассигнование

assimilate /эси́милэйт/ vt ассимилировать; усваивать

assist /эси́ст/ vt помогать

assistance /эси́стэнс/ n помощь

assistant /эси́стэнт/ n помощник; ассистент

associate /эсо́ушиит/ n коллега; /эсо́ушиэйт/ vt соединять; vi общаться

association /эсо́усиэ́йшн/ n ассоциация

assort /асо́рт/ vt сортировать

assortment /эсо́ртмент/ n ассортимент

assume /эсъю́юм/ vt брать на себя; присваивать; предполагать; ~d name /~d нэйм/ вымышленное имя

assumption /эса́мпшн/ n предположение; the A. (рел.) Успение

assurance /эшу́эрэнс/ n заверение

assure /эшу́э/ vt уверять

assuredly /эшу́эридли/ adv несомненно

asthma /э́смэ/ n астма

astonish /эсто́ниш/ vt удивлять

astonishment /эсто́нишмент/ n удивление

astrakhan /э́стрэкэ́н/ n каракуль

astray /эстрэ́й/ adv: go ~ /го́у ~/ сбиться с пути

astrologer /эстро́лэдже/ n астролог

astrology /эстро́лэджи/ n астрология

astronomer /эстро́нэмэ/ n астроном

astronomy /эстро́нэми/ n астрономия

asunder /эса́ндэ/ adv порознь

asylum /эса́йлэм/ n приют; психиатрическая больница

at /эе/ в; на; ~ first /~ фёрст/ сначала; ~ home /~ хо́ум/ дома; ~ last /~ лааст/ наконец; ~ least /~ лиист/ по крайней мере; ~ night /~ найт/ ночью; ~ once /~ ванс/ сразу; ~ 5 o'clock /~ файв окло́к/ в пять часов

atheist /э́йфиист/ n атеист

athlete /э́тлиит/ n спортсмен, атлет

atlas /э́тлэс/ n атлас

atmosphere /э́тмэсфиэ/ n атмосфера

atom /э́тэм/ n атом

atomic /это́мик/ adj атомный

atrocious /этро́ушес/ adj свирепый

atrocity /этро́сити/ n зверство

attach /этэ́ч/ vt прикреплять; придавать

attaché /этэ́шей/ n атташе

attachment /этэ́чмент/ n привязанность; прикрепление

attack /этэ́к/ n атака; припадок

attain /этэ́йн/ vt достигать

attainment /этэ́йнмент/ n достижение

attempt /этэ́мпт/ n попытка; покушение; vt пытаться

attend /этэ́нд/ vt посещать (лекции); ухаживать (за больным)

attendance /этэ́ндэнс/ n посещаемость; обслуживание

attention /этэ́ншн/ n внимание

attentive /этэ́нтив/ adj внимательный; заботливый

attic /э́тик/ n чердак

attire /эта́йе/ n наряд; vt наряжать

attitude /э́титьюд/ n отношение

attorney /этёрни/ n поверенный

attract /этрэ́кт/ vt привлекать; пленять

attraction /этрэ́кшн/ n притяжение; привлекательность

attractive /этрэ́ктив/ adj привлекательный

attribute /э́трибьют/ n свойство, атрибут; /этри́бьют/ vt приписывать

auction /о́окшн/ n аукцион; vt продавать с аукциона

auctioneer /о́окшени́э/ n аукционист

audacious /одэ́йшес/ adj смелый; дерзкий

audacity /одэ́сити/ n смелость; дерзость

audible /о́одэбл/ adj слышный, слышимый

audience /о́одьенс/ n публика

audit /о́одит/ n ревизия; vt проверять (счета)

auditor /о́одитэ/ n ревизор

auditorium /о́одито́ориэм/ n аудитория

augment /огмє́нт/ vti увеличивать (ся)

augmentation /о́огментэ́йшн/ n увеличение

August /о́огэст/ n август

aunt /аант/ n тетя

aureole /о́ориоул/ n ореол

auspices /о́осписыз/ n pl покровительство

austere /ости́э/ adj суровый; аскетический

Australian /острэ́йлиэн/ n австралиец, австралийка; adj австралийский

Austrian /о́остриэн/ n австриец, австрийка; adj австрийский

authentic /офє́нтик/ adj подлинный

authenticity /о́офенти́сити/ n достоверность

author /о́осэ/ n автор

authority /осо́рити/ n авторитет; pl власти

authorize /о́осэрайз/ vt уполномочивать

autobiography /о́отобайо́грэфи/ n автобиография

autocracy /ото́крэси/ n самодержавие

autocrat /о́отэкрэт/ n самодержец

autocratic /о́отэкрэ́тик/ adj самодержавный; деспотический

autograph /о́отэграф/ n автограф

automatic /о́отэмэ́тик/ adj автоматический

autonomy /ото́нэми/ n автономия

autopsy /о́отэпси/ n вскрытие трупа

autumn /о́отэм/ n осень

auxiliary /огзи́льери/ adj вспомогательный

avail /эвэ́йл/ vi быть полезным; vt: ~ oneself of /~ вансэ́лф ов/ воспользоваться (чем-л.)

available /эвэ́йлэбл/ adj имеющийся; доступный

avalanche /э́вэланш/ n лавина

avenge /эвéндж/ vt мстить

avenger /эвéндже/ n мститель

avenue /э́винью/ n авеню

average /э́вэридж/ adj средний; n: on ~ /он ~/ в среднем

avert /эвёрт/ vt предотвращать (беду)

aviation /э́йвиэ́йшн/ n авиация

aviator /э́йвиэйтэ/ n летчик

avid /э́вид/ adj жадный

avoid /эвóйд/ vt избегать

await /эвэ́йт/ vt ждать, ожидать

awake /эвэ́йк/ adj бодрствующий; vt будить; vi просыпаться

awaken /эвэ́йкн/ vti пробуждать(ся)

award /эвóрд/ n награда; vt присуждать, награждать

aware /эвэ́э/ adj сознающий; be ~ of /би ~ ов/ сознавать

away /эвэ́й/ adj отсутствующий; adv прочь; far ~ /фар ~/ далеко

awe /oo/ n благоговение

awful /óофул/ adj ужасный

awhile /эвáйл/ adv ненадолго

awkward /óоквэд/ adj неуклюжий; an ~ situation /эн ~ си́тьюэ́йшн/ неловкое положение

awning /óонинг/ n навес

axe /экс/ n топор

axiom /э́ксиэм/ n аксиома

axis /э́ксис/ n ось

B

babble /бэбл/ vti бормотать; журчать

babbler /бэ́блэ/ n болтун

baby /бэ́йби/ n младенец

bachelor /бэ́челэ/ n холостяк

back /бэк/ n спина; спинка; корешок (книги); защитник (футбол); adj задний; запоздалый; отсталый; adv назад; vt поддерживать; отступать

backbone /бэ́кбоун/ n спинной хребет; суть

back door /бэкдóр/ n черный ход

background /бэ́кграунд/ n фон; подготовка, образование; происхождение

backward /бэ́квэд/ adj обратный; отсталый; adv назад; задом наперед

backwardness /бэ́квэднис/ n отсталость

bacon /бэйкн/ n грудинка, бекон

bad /бэд/ adj плохой

badge /бэдж/ n значок; эмблема; знак

badger /бэ́дже/ n барсук

bag /бэг/ n мешок; сумка

baggage /бэ́гидж/ n багаж

bagpipe /бэ́гпайп/ n волынка

bail /бэйл/ n залог, поручительство; vt брать на поруки

bailiff /бэ́йлиф/ n судебный пристав

bait /бэйт/ n приманка; наживка

bake /бэйк/ vt печь

baker /бэ́йкэ/ n пекарь

baker's shop /бэ́йкэшóп/ n булочная

bakery /бэ́йкэри/ n пекарня

balance /бэ́лэнс/ n весы; равновесие; баланс; vt взвешивать; подводить баланс

balanced /бэ́лэнст/ adj уравновешенный

balcony /бэ́лкэни/ n балкон

bald /боолд/ adj лысый

bale /бэйл/ n тюк

ball /боол/ n шар; мяч; бал

ballad /бэ́лэд/ n баллада

ballast /бэ́лэст/ n балласт

ball-bearing /бóолбэ́эринг/ n шарикоподшипник

ballet /бэ́лей/ n балет

balloon /бэлýун/ n воздушный шар

ballot /бэ́лэт/ n баллотировка

ballot-paper /бэ́лэтпэ́йпэ/ n избирательный бюллетень

ball-point pen /бóолпойнтпéн/ n шариковая ручка
balm, balsam /бáам, бóлсэм/ n бальзам
bamboo /бэмбýу/ n бамбук
ban /бэн/ n запрещение; vt запрещать
banal /бэнáал/ adj банальный
banana /бэнáанэ/ n банан
band /бэнд/ n оркестр; банда; лента
bandage /бэ́ндыдж/ n бинт, повязка; vt
бинтовать
bandit /бэ́ндит/ n бандит
bandsman /бэ́ндзмэн/ n оркестрант
bang /бэнг/ n удар; vti ударять(ся)
bangle /бэнгл/ n браслет
banish /бэ́ниш/ vt изгонять
banishment /бэ́нишмент/ n изгнание
banisters /бэ́нистэз/ n pl перила
banjo /бэ́нджоу/ n банджо
bank /бэнк/ n берег; банк
banker /бэ́нкэ/ n банкир
bankrupt /бэ́нкрэпт/ n банкрот; go ~ /гóу
~/ обанкротиться
bankruptcy /бэ́нкрэпси/ n банкротство
banner /бэ́нэ/ n знамя
banquet /бэ́нквит/ n банкет
baptize /бэптáйз/ vt крестить
baptism /бэ́птизм/ n крещение
bar /бар/ n полоска (металла); брусок;
преграда; бар; ~ of chocolate /~ ов чó-
колит/ плитка шоколада; ~ of soap /~
ов сóуп/ кусок мыла; vt преграждать;
запирать на засов
barbarian /бабэ́эриэн/ adj варварский; n
варвар
barbed wire /бáрбдвáйе/ n колючая проволока
barber /бáрбэ/ n парикмахер
barber's shop /бáрбэзшóп/ n парикмахерская
bard /бард/ n бард
bare /бэ́э/ adj голый; vt обнажать
barefoot /бэ́эфут/ adv босиком
bareheaded /бэ́эхéдыд/ adj с непокрытой
головой
barely /бэ́эли/ adv едва

bargain /бáргин/ n сделка; into the ~ /и́н-
ту зэ ~/ к тому же; vi торговаться
barge /бардж/ n баржа
baritone /бэ́ритоун/ n баритон
bark /барк/ n кора (дерева); лай (собаки); vi лаять
barley /бáрли/ n ячмень
barn /барн/ n амбар, сарай
barometer /бэрóмитэ/ n барометр
baron /бэ́рэн/ n барон
barrack /бэ́рэк/ n барак; pl казарма
barrel /бэ́рэл/ n бочка; ~ of gun /~ ов ган/
ствол ружья
barren /бэ́рэн/ adj бесплодный
barricade /бэ́рикéйд/ n баррикада
barrier /бэ́риэ/ n барьер
barrow /бэ́роу/ n тачка
barter /бáртэ/ n меновая торговля; vt обмениваться (товарами)
basalt /бэ́солт/ n базальт
base /бэйс/ n основа; база
baseball /бэ́йсбол/ n бейсбол
baseless /бэ́йслис/ adj необоснованный
basement /бэ́йсмент/ n фундамент; (по-
лу)подвальный этаж
bashful /бэ́шфул/ adj застенчивый
basic /бэ́йсик/ adj основной
basin /бэйсн/ n таз; водоем
basis /бэ́йсис/ n базис, основание; база
basket /бáаскит/ n корзина
Basque /бэск/ n баск; баскский язык; adj
баскский
bas-relief /бэ́срилии́ф/ n барельеф
bass /бэйс/ (муз.) бас
bass /бэс/ n морской окунь
bastard /бэ́стэд/ adj незаконнорожденный; n внебрачный ребенок
bat /бэт/ n (спорт.) бита; летучая мышь
bath /баас/ n ванна; make a ~ /мэйк э ~/
принимать ванну
bathhouse /бáасхаус/ n баня
bathe /бэйз/ n купание; vti купать(ся)
battalion /бэтэ́льен/ n батальон
batter /бэ́тэ/ n взбитое тесто
battery /бэ́тэри/ n батарея; аккумулятор
battle /бэтл/ n битва

battlefield /бэ́тлфилд/е n поле боя

bay /бэй/ n залив

bayonet /бэ́йэнит/ n штык

bazaar /бэза́р/ n базар

be /бии/ vi быть; how are you? /ха́у ар ю/ как вы поживаете?; how much is it? /ха́у мач из ит/ сколько это стоит?; ~ off /~ оф/ уезжать

beach /биич/ n пляж

beacon /биикн/ n маяк

bead /биид/ n бусина; pl бусы; четки

beak /биик/ n клюв

beam /биим/ n балка (дерева); луч (света); vt излучать; vi сиять

bean /биин/ n боб

bear /бээ/ n медведь; Great (Little) ~ /грэйт (литл) ~/ Большая (Малая) Медведица; vt носить; рожать; приносить; терпеть, выносить; vi держаться; опираться; ~ in mind /~ ин майнд/ помнить

bearable /бэ́эрэбл/ adj сносный, терпимый

beard /би́эд/ n борода

bearded /би́эдыд/ adj бородатый; усатый

beardless /би́эдлис/ adj безбородый; безусый

bearer /бэ́эрэ/ n носитель; носильщик; предъявитель

bearing /бэ́эринг/ n поведение; манера держаться; pl направление, ориентация

beast /биист/ n зверь; (перен.) скотина

beastly /би́истли/ adj противный

beat /биит/ n бой (барабана); биение (сердца); vt ударять; выбивать; взбивать; vi биться; the ~en track /зэ ~н трэк/ проторенная дорожка

beautiful /бью́ютэфул/ adj красивый, прекрасный

beauty /бью́юти/ n красота; красавица

beaver /би́ивэ/ n бобр; бобер

because /бико́з/ conj потому что; ~ of /~ ов/ из-за

become /бика́м/ vi становиться; vt: this dress ~s you /зыс дрэс ~з ю/ это платье вам идет

becoming /бика́минг/ adj подобающий; идущий к лицу

bed /бед/ n постель, кровать; клумба; грядка; дно; русло; go to ~ /го́у ту ~/ ложиться спать

bed-clothes /бе́дклоуз/ n pl постельное белье

bedlam /бе́длэм/ n бедлам

bedroom /бе́друм/ n спальня

bedspread /бе́дспрэд/ n покрывало

bee /бии/ n пчела

beech /биич/ n бук

beef /бииф/ n говядина

beefsteak /би́ифстэйк/ n бифштекс

beehive /би́ихайв/ n улей

beekeeping /би́ики́ипинг/ n пчеловодство

beer /би́э/ n пиво

beetle /биитл/ n жук

beetroot /би́итрут/ n свекла

befit /бифи́т/ vt подходить

befitting /бифи́тинг/ adj подходящий

before /бифо́р/ adv раньше; long ~ /лонг ~/ задолго; prep перед; впереди; the day ~ /зэ дэй ~/ позавчера; adv прежде чем

beforehand /бифо́рхэнд/ adv заранее

beg /бег/ vt просить, умолять; ~ pardon /~ пардн/ просить прощения; vi нищенствовать

beggar /бе́гэ/ n нищий

beggary /бэ́гэри/ n нищета

begin /биги́н/ vti начинать(ся)

beginner /бегги́нэ/ n начинающий

beginning /беги́нинг/ n начало

behalf /биха́аф/ n: on ~ of /он ~ ов/ от имени

behave /бихе́йв/ vi вести себя; ~ yourself /~ йосэ́лф/ ведите себя прилично

behaviour /бихе́йвье/ n поведение

behind /биха́йнд/ adv позади; prep за, сзади

being /бѝинг/ n существо; человек; бытие; human ~ /хьюмэн ~/ человек
belfry /бѐлфри/ n колокольня
Belgian /белджн/ n бельгиец, бельгийка; adj бельгийский
belief /билѝиф/ n вера; верование
believe /билѝив/ vt верить; ~ in /~ ин/ верить в
believer /билѝивэ/ n верующий
belittle /билѝтл/ vt умалять
bell /бел/ n колокол; звонок
belligerent /билѝиджерент/ adj воюющий
bellow /бѐлоу/ vi мычать
belly /бѐли/ n брюхо
belong /билѐнг/ vi принадлежать
belongings /билѐнгингз/ n pl пожитки
beloved /билѐвд/ adj, n возлюбленный
below /билѐу/ adv внизу; prep ниже, под
belt /белт/ n пояс; ремень
bench /бенч/ n скамья; место (в парламенте)
bend /бенд/ n изгиб; vt сгибать; гнуть; vi изгибаться
beneath /бинѝис/ adv внизу; prep под, ниже
benediction /бѐнидѝкшн/ n благословение
benefaction /бѐнифѐкшн/ n благодеяние
benefactor /бѐнифѐктэ/ n благодетель
beneficial /бѐнифѝшл/ adj благотворный
benefit /бѐнифит/ n выгода; бенефис
benevolence /бинѐвэлэнс/ n благосклонность
benevolent /бинѐвэлэнт/ adj щедрый; благосклонный
bent /бент/ adj изогнутый; n склонность
bereave /бирѝив/ vt лишать
bereavement /бирѝивмент/ n утрата
beret /бѐрей/ n берет
berry /бѐри/ n ягода
berth /бёрс/ n койка; якорная стоянка
beseech /бисѝич/ vt умолять
beside /бисѐйд/ prep рядом с, около; ~ oneself /~ вансѐлф/ вне себя
besides /бисѐйдз/ adv кроме того

besiege /бисѝидж/ vt осаждать
best /бест/ adj самый лучший; all the ~ /оол зэ ~/ всего хорошего; do one's ~ /ду ванз ~/ делать все от себя зависящее; adv лучше всего
bestial /бѐстьел/ adj скотский
bestiality /бѐстиѐлити/ n зверство
bestseller /бѐстсѐлэ/ n бестселлер
bet /бет/ n пари; make a ~ /мэйк э ~/ заключать пари; vi биться об заклад
betray /битрѐй/ vt выдавать
betrayal /битрѐйел/ n предательство
betrother /битрѐйе/ n изменник
betroth /битрѐуз/ vt обручать
betrothal /битрѐузл/ n обручение
better /бѐтэ/ adj лучший; be ~ off /би ~p оф/ жить лучше; adv лучше, больше; all the ~ /оол зэ ~/ тем лучше; vt улучшать
betterment /бѐтэрмент/ n улучшение
between /битвѝин/ adv между
beverage /бѐвэридж/ n напиток
beware /бивѐѐ/ vi остерегаться; ~ of trains! /~ ов трэйнз/ берегись поезда!
bewitch /бивѝч/ vt заколдовывать
beyond /бийѐнд/ prep по ту сторону; выше; ~ doubt /~ дѐут/ вне сомнения
bias /бѐйес/ n пристрастие; vt оказывать влияние; be ~ed /би ~т/ иметь предубеждение
Bible /бѐйбл/ n библия
biblical /бѝбликл/ adj библейский
bibliography /бѝблиѐгрэфи/ n библиография
bibliophile /бѝблиофайл/ n библиофил
biceps /бѐйсэпс/ n бицепс
bicycle /бѐйсикл/ n велосипед
bicyclist /бѐйсиклист/ n велосипедист
bid /бид/ n заявка; make a ~ /мэйк э ~/ предлагать цену; vt приказывать; ~ farewell /~ фэѐвэл/ прощаться
big /биг/ adj большой; крупный
bigamy /бѝгэми/ n бигамия, двоеженство, двоемужие
bigot /бѝгэт/ n фанатик, изувер
bigotry /бѝгэтри/ n фанатизм

15

bike /байк/ n велосипед
bilberry /би́лбери/ n черника; red ~ /ред
~/ брусника
bile /байл/ n желчь
bilious /би́льес/ adj желчный
bilingual /байли́нгвэл/ adj двуязычный
bill /бил/ n законопроект; счет; афиша;
банкнота; ~ of entry /~ ов э́нтри/ таможенная декларация; 10 dollar ~ /тен
до́лэ ~/ десятидолларовая купюра
billiards /би́льедз/ n бильярд
billion /би́льен/ n миллиард
bin /бин/ n мусорное ведро
bind /байнд/ vt связывать; переплетать;
обязывать
binoculars /бино́кьюлез/ n pl бинокль
biography /байо́грэфи/ n биография
biology /байо́лэджи/ n биология
birch /бёрч/ n береза
bird /бёрд/ n птица
bird's-eye /бёрдзай/ n первоцвет; ~ view
/~ вьюю/ вид с птичьего полета
birth /бёрс/ n рождение; ~ certificate /~
сети́фикит/ метрика; ~ control /~ кэн-
тро́ул/ противозачаточные меры
birthday /бёрсдэй/ n день рождения
biscuit /би́скит/ n печенье
bishop /би́шеп/ n епископ; (шахм.) слон
bismuth /би́змэс/ n висмут
bison /байсн/ n бизон
bit /бит/ n частица; a ~ /э ~/ немного; not
a ~ /нот э ~/ ничуть
bitch /бич/ n сука
bite /байт/ n укус; клев; have a ~ /хэв э
~/ перекусить; vt кусать; жалить; vi
кусаться; клевать
biting /ба́йтинг/ adj острый; едкий; язвительный
bitter /би́тэ/ adj горький; ~enemy /~ эни́-
ми/ злейший враг
bitterness /би́тэнис/ n горечь
bizarre /биза́э/ adj эксцентричный
black /блэк/ adj черный; ~ eye /~ ай/
подбитый глаз, синяк под глазом; ~ list
/~ лист/ черный список; n негр
blackberry /блэ́кбери/ n ежевика
blackboard /блэ́кбод/ n классная доска

blackmail /блэ́кмэйл/ n шантаж
bladder /блэ́дэ/ n мочевой пузырь
blade /блэйд/ n лезвие
blame /блэйм/ n порицание, вина; vt порицать; he is to ~ /хи из ту ~/ он виноват
blanket /блэ́нкит/ n одеяло
blasphemy /блэ́сфими/ n богохульство
blast /блааст/ n взрыв; ~ furnace /~ фёр-
нис/ домна; vt взрывать
blatant /блэ́йтнт/ adj вопиющий
blaze /блэйз/ n пламя; ~ a trail /~ э
трэйл/ vt прокладывать путь
blazer /блэ́йзэ/ n блейзер; куртка
bleach /блиич/ vt белить, отбеливать
bleak /блиик/ adj холодный, унылый
bleat /блиит/ vi блеять
bleed /блиид/ vi кровоточить; my heart ~s
/май харт ~з/ сердце кровью облива-
ется; vt пускать кровь; n кровотечение
blemish /блэ́миш/ n позор; пятно, шрам
blend /бленд/ n смесь; vt смешивать
bless /блес/ vt благословлять
blessed /блест/ adj счастливый, блажен-
ный
blessing /блэ́синг/ n благословение
blind /блайнд/ adj слепой; ~ alley /~
э́ли/ тупик; n штора; vt ослеплять
blindfold /бла́йндфоулд/ adj безрассудный
blindly /бла́йндли/ adv слепо
blindness /бла́йнднис/ n слепота
blink /блинк/ vt мигать; vi мерцать
blinkers /бли́нкэз/ n pl шоры
bliss /блис/ n блаженство
blister /бли́стэ/ n волдырь
blizzard /бли́зэд/ n вьюга
bloc /блок/ n блок, объединение
block /блок/ n квартал; затор (транспорта); vt блокировать
blockade /блокэ́йд/ n блокада
blockhead /бло́кхэд/ n болван
blond(e) /блонд/ n блондин, блондинка
blood /блад/ n кровь; ~ pressure /~ прэ́ше/
кровяное давление
bloodshed /бла́дшед/ n кровопролитие

blood-transfusion /блáдтрансфьюю́южн/ n переливание крови

blood-vessel /блáдвéсл/ n кровеносный сосуд

bloody /блáди/ adj кровавый; проклятый

bloom /блуум/ n цветок; расцвет; vi цвести

blossom /блóсэм/ n цвет; vi расцветать

blot /блот/ n клякса, пятно

blotting paper /блóтингпэ́йпэ/ n промокательная бумага

blouse /блáуз/ n кофточка

blow /блóу/ n удар; дуновение; vt дуть; раздувать; ~ one's nose /~ ванз ноуз/ сморкаться; ~ up /~ ап/ взрывать

blue /блюю/ adj синий, голубой; vt окрашивать в синий цвет; подсинивать

blue-eyed /блю́юáйд/ adj голубоглазый

blueprint /блю́юоприн́т/ n проект

bluff /блаф/ n обрыв; блеф; vt обманывать

bluish /блю́юиш/ adj синеватый, голубоватый

blunder /блáндэ/ n ошибка; vi грубо ошибаться

blunt /блант/ adj тупой; vt притуплять

bluntly /блáнтли/ adv резко

blur /блёр/ n неясное очертание; vt затуманивать

blurt out /блёт áут/ vt сболтнуть

blush /блаш/ n краска стыда; vt краснеть

boar /бор/ n кабан

board /борд/ n доска, правление; on ~ /он ~/ на борту; vt садиться (на самолет и т.д.)

boarding /бóрдинг/ n пансион, интернат

boast /бóуст/ vti хвастаться, гордиться

boaster /бóустэ/ n хвастун

boastful /бóустфул/ adj хвастливый

boat /бóут/ n лодка; судно; пароход

boatman /бóутмэн/ n лодочник

bobbin /бóбин/ n катушка

bobsleigh /бóбслей/ n бобслей

bodice /бóдис/ n лиф

body /бóди/ n тело; корпус; орган, ассоциация

body-guard /бóдигард/ n телохранитель

bog /бог/ n болото

bogus /бóугэс/ adj фиктивный

boil /бойл/ vti кипятить(ся); n кипение; фурункул; пузырь

boiled /бойлд/ adj вареный; кипяченый

boiler /бóйлэ/ n бойлер

boisterous /бóйстрэс/ adj шумливый

bold /бóулд/ adj смелый, наглый; жирный

bold-faced /бóулдфейст/ adj наглый

boldness /бóулднис/ n наглость; смелость

bolt /бóулт/ n болт; удар грома; vt запирать на засов (дверь); скреплять болтами

bomb /бом/ n бомба; atom ~ /э́тэм ~/ атомная бомба; vt бомбить

bombast /бóмбэст/ n напыщенность

bomber /бóмэ/ n бомбардировщик

bombing /бóминг/ n бомбежка

bond /бонд/ n связь; облигация; pl оковы, узы

bondage /бóндидж/ n рабство; зависимость

bone /бóун/ n кость; pl игральные кости

bonfire /бóнфáйер/ n костер

bonnet /бóнит/ n чепчик; капот (автомобиля)

bonus /бóунэс/ n премиальные

booby /бýуби/ n болван

book /бук/ n книга; vt заказывать (билеты и т.п.)

booking /бýкинг/ n заказ

booking-office /бýкингóфис/ n билетная касса

bookkeeper /бýкки́ипэ/ n бухгалтер

booklet /бýклит/ n брошюра

book-worm /бýквёрм/ n буквоед

boom /буум/ n гул; большой спрос

boomerang /бýумерэнг/ n бумеранг

boot /буут/ n ботинок; багажник; high ~ /хай ~/ сапог

booth /бууз/ n кабина

bootlicker /бу́утли́кэ/ n подхалим

booty /бу́ути/ n добыча

booze /бууз/ n выпивка

border /бо́рдэ/ n граница; ~ on /~ он/ vi граничить с

bore /бор/ n нудный человек; vt сверлить; надоедать; I am ~d /ай эм ~д/ мне надоело

boredom /бо́одэм/ n скука

bore-hole /бо́рхо́ул/ n буровая скважина

borer /бо́орэ/ n бур

born /борн/ adj (при)рожденный; be ~ /би ~/ родиться

borrow /бо́роу/ vt брать взаймы, заимствовать

bosom /бу́зэм/ n грудь; ~ friend /~ френд/ закадычный друг

boss /бос/ n хозяин, босс, начальник

bossy /бо́си/ adj властный

botany /бо́тэни/ n ботаника

botch /боч/ n халтура

botcher /бо́че/ n халтурщик

both /бо́ус/ adj, pron оба

bother /бо́зэ/ vt беспокоить, надоедать

bottle /ботл/ n бутылка

bottom /бо́тэм/ n дно; зад; from the ~ of one's heart /фром зэ ~ ов ванз харт/ от всей души

bottomless /бо́тэмлис/ adj бездонный

bounce /ба́унс/ vi подпрыгивать; отскакивать

bound /ба́унд/ n прыжок, скачок; adj связанный, обязанный; vt ограничивать; vi прыгать

boundary /ба́ундэри/ n граница

boundless /ба́ундлис/ adj беспредельный

bountiful /ба́унтифул/ adj обильный

bouquet /бу́кей/ n букет

bow /бо́у/ n лук; смычок; бант

bow /ба́у/ n поклон; vi кланяться

bowels /ба́уэлз/ n pl кишечник

bowl /бо́ул/ n чаша, ваза; шар

bowler /бо́улэ/ n котелок (шляпа)

box /бокс/ n коробка, ящик; ложа; vi боксировать

box-office /бо́ксо́фис/ n театральная касса

boxer /бо́ксэ/ n боксер

boxing /бо́ксинг/ n бокс

boxing-gloves /бо́ксингтла́вз/ n pl боксерские перчатки

boy /бой/ n мальчик

boycott /бо́йкэт/ n бойкот; vt бойкотировать

boyhood /бо́йхуд/ n отрочество

boyish /бо́йиш/ adj мальчишеский

brace /брэйс/ n скрепа; pl подтяжки; vt скреплять

bracelet /брэ́йслит/ n браслет

bracket /брэ́кит/ n скобка; vt ставить в скобки

brag /брэг/ vi хвастаться

braid /брэйд/ n коса (волосы); тесьма; vt заплетать

braille /брэйл/ n азбука для слепых

brain /брэйн/ n мозг; pl умственные способности; мозги (блюдо)

brain-drain /брэ́йндрэйн/ n утечка мозгов

brainless /брэ́йнлис/ adj безмозглый

brainwash /брэ́йнвош/ vt "промывать мозги"

brainy /брэ́йни/ adj умный

brake /брэйк/ n тормоз; vt тормозить

bramble /брэмбл/ n ежевика (кустарник)

branch /браанч/ n ветка; отрасль; филиал

brand /брэнд/ n клеймо, марка, сорт

brandy /брэ́нди/ n коньяк

brass /браас/ n желтая медь, латунь; ~ band /~ бэнд/ духовой оркестр; top ~ /топ ~/ руководящая верхушка

brassiere /брэ́сиэ/ n бюстгальтер

brave /брэйв/ adj храбрый

bravery /брэ́йври/ n мужество

brawl /броол/ n ссора

brazen /брэйзн/ adj медный; наглый

Brazilian /брэзи́льен/ n бразилец, бразильянка; adj бразильский

breach /бриич/ n пролом; нарушение (закона)

bread /брэд/ n хлеб
bread-winner /брэ́двинэ/ n кормилец
breadth /брэдс/ n ширина
break /брэйк/ n поломка; lunch ~ /ланч ~/ перерыв на обед; vt ломать; нарушать; побить (рекорд); ~ down /~ да́ун/ vt разбивать; vi ломаться; потерять самообладание
breakable /брэ́йкэбл/ adj хрупкий
break-down /брэ́йкдаун/ n поломка
breaker /брэ́йкэ/ n нарушитель
breakfast /брэ́кфэст/ n завтрак; have ~ /хэв ~/ завтракать
breast /брэст/ n грудь
breath /брэс/ n дыхание
breathe /брииз/ vi дышать
breathing /бри́изинг/ n дыхание
breathing-space /бри́изингспэ́йс/ n передышка
breathless /брэ́слис/ adj запыхавшийся
breed /бриид/ n порода; vt разводить (животных)
breeding /бри́идинг/ n разведение; cattle ~ /кэтл ~/ животноводство
breeze /брииз/ n легкий ветерок, бриз
brevity /брэ́вити/ n краткость
brew /бруу/ n заварка (чая); vt варить (пиво, кофе)
brewer /бру́э/ n пивовар
brewery /бру́эри/ n пивоваренный завод
bribe /брайб/ n взятка; vt давать взятку
bribery /бра́йбэри/ n взяточничество
brick /брик/ n кирпич
bride /брайд/ n невеста
bridegroom /бра́йдгрум/ n жених
bridge /бридж/ n мост; бридж (карточная игра)
bridge-head /бри́джхед/ n плацдарм
bridle /брайдл/ n узда; vt обуздывать
brief /брииф/ n резюме; adj краткий
brief-case /бри́ифкейс/ n портфель
briefly /бри́ифли/ adv кратко
brigade /бригейд/ n бригада
brigadier /бри́гэди́э/ n бригадный генерал
bright /брайт/ adj яркий
brightness /бра́йтнис/ n яркость

brilliant /бри́льент/ adj блестящий
brim /брим/ n край; pl поля (шляпы); full to the ~ /фул ту зэ ~/ полный до краев
bring /бринг/ vt приносить, привозить; ~ to a close /~ ту э кло́уз/ доводить до конца; ~ to life /~ ту лайф/ приводить в чувство; ~ up /~ ап/ воспитывать
brisk /бриск/ adj оживленный
brisket /бри́скит/ n грудинка
bristle /брисл/ n щетина
British /бри́тиш/ adj британский, английский
Briton /бритн/ n британец
brittle /бритл/ adj хрупкий
broad /броод/ adj широкий; in ~ daylight /ин ~ дэ́йлайт/ среди бела дня
broadcast /бро́одкаст/ vt передавать по радио; n радиопередача
broadly /бро́одли/ adv широко
broad-minded /бро́одма́йндид/ adj с широким кругозором; терпимый
broad-shouldered /бро́одшо́улдэд/ adj широкоплечий
brocade /брэкейд/ n парча
broil /бройл/ vti жарить(ся) (на открытом огне)
broiler /бро́йлэ/ n бройлер
broken /бро́укн/ adj разбитый, сломанный
broker /бро́укэ/ n маклер
brokerage /бро́укэридж/ n комиссионное вознаграждение
bronchitis /бронка́йтис/ n бронхит
bronze /бронз/ n бронза; adj бронзовый
brooch /бро́уч/ n брошь
brood /бруд/ n выводок; vi сидеть на яйцах; (образн.) размышлять
brook /брук/ n ручей
broom /брум/ n метла, веник
broth /брос/ n суп
brothel /бросл/ n публичный дом
brother /бра́зэ/ n брат
brotherhood /бра́зэхуд/ n братство
brother-in-law /бра́зэринлоо/ n зять, шурин, деверь
brotherly /бра́зэли/ adj братский; adv побратски

brow /бра́у/ n бровь

brown /бра́ун/ adj коричневый, карий (о глазах); ~ paper /~ пэ́йпэ/ оберточная бумага; ~ sugar /~ шу́гэ/ жженый сахар; ~ rice /~ райс/ неполированный рис

bruise /брууз/ n синяк; vt ушибать

brunette /брунэ́т/ n брюнетка

brunt /брант/ n главный удар

brush /браш/ n щетка, кисть; vt чистить щеткой; ~ up /~ ап/ освежить (в памяти)

Brussels sprouts /бра́слзспра́утс/ n pl брюссельская капуста

brutal /бруутл/ adj жестокий

brute /бруут/ n животное; жестокий человек

bubble /бабл/ n пузырь

bucket /ба́кит/ n ведро

buckle /бакл/ n пряжка; vt застегивать (пряжкой)

buckwheat /ба́квит/ n гречиха

bud /бад/ n почка

Buddhist /бу́дист/ n буддист

budget /ба́джит/ n бюджет

buffalo /ба́фэлоу/ n буйвол

buffer /ба́фэ/ n буфер

buffet /ба́фит/ n буфет (для посуды)

buffet /бу́фей/ n буфет, буфетная стойка

buffoon /бафу́ун/ n шут

bug /баг/ n клоп; (жарг.) потайной микрофон; big ~ /биг ~/ "шишка"

bugbear /ба́гбээ/ n пугало

bugle /бью́югл/ n горн

bugler /бью́юглэ/ n горнист

build /билд/ n телосложение; vt строить

builder /би́лдэ/ n строитель

building /би́лдинг/ n здание

bulb /балб/ n электрическая лампочка; (бот.) луковица

bulge /балдж/ n выпуклость

bulk /балк/ n бо́льшая часть; sell in ~ /сел ин ~/ продавать оптом

bulky /ба́лки/ adj громоздкий

bull /бул/ n бык

bulldog /бу́лдог/ n бульдог

bullfight /бу́лфайт/ n бой быков

bullet /бу́лит/ n пуля

bullet-proof /бу́литпруф/ adj пуленепробиваемый

bulletin /бу́улитин/ n бюллетень

bullion /бу́льен/ n слиток (золота и т.д.)

bully /бу́ли/ n задира

bulwark /бу́лвэк/ n оплот

bumble-bee /ба́мблбии/ n шмель

bump /бамп/ n глухой удар; шишка; vi стукаться

bumper /ба́мпэ/ n что-то очень крупное; бампер; ~ crop /~ кроп/ небывалый урожай

bun /бан/ n булочка

bunch /банч/ n пучок; пачка; букет; связка (ключей)

bundle /бандл/ n узел; ~ of nerves /~ ов нёёвз/ комок нервов

bungalow /ба́нгэлоу/ n бунгало

bunk /банк/ n койка

bunker /ба́нкэ/ n бункер

buoy /бой/ n буй

buoyant /бо́йэнт/ adj плавучий; жизнерадостный

burden /бёдн/ n бремя; vt обременять

burdensome /бёднсэм/ adj тягостный

bureau /бьюро́у/ n бюро

bureaucracy /бьюро́крэси/ n бюрократизм

bureaucrat /бью́оэрокрэт/ n бюрократ

bureaucratic /бьюоэрокрэ́тик/ adj бюрократический

burglar /бёрглэ/ n взломщик

burglary /бёрглэри/ n кража со взломом

burial /бэриэл/ n погребение

burn /бён/ n ожог; vt жечь; vi гореть; adj горячий, жгучий

burst /бёст/ n взрыв; vi взрываться; ~ into blossom /~ и́нту бло́сэм/ расцветать; ~ open /~ о́упэн/ распахиваться; ~ with envy /~ виз э́нви/ лопаться от зависти

bury /бэ́ри/ vt хоронить

bus /бас/ n автобус

bush /буш/ n куст

bushy /бу́ши/ adj кустистый

business /бизнис/ n дело, коммерческое предприятие; mind your own ~! /майнд йор óун ~/ не ваше дело!

business-like /бизнислайк/ adj деловой

businessman /бизнисмэн/ n бизнесмен

bust /баст/ n бюст, грудь

bustle /басл/ n суета; vi суетиться

busy /бизи/ adj занятой, занятый, оживленный

but /бат/ conj но, a; adv только; all ~ /оол ~/ почти; prep кроме; anything ~ /энифинг ~/ далеко не

butcher /буче/ n мясник; палач

butler /батлэ/ n дворецкий

butt /бат/ n мишень; приклад (оружия); vt бодать; ~ into /~ йнту/ натыкаться

butter /батэ/ n масло

butterfly /батэфлай/ n бабочка

buttock /батэк/ n ягодица

button /батн/ n пуговица; vt застегивать

buttonhole /батнхоул/ n петля (для пуговицы)

buy /бай/ vt покупать

buyer /байе/ n покупатель, покупательница

buzz /баз/ n жужжание; vi жужжать

by /бай/ pron у, около, мимо, посредством; ~ airmail /~ эамэйл/ авиапочтой; ~ law /~ лоо/ по закону; ~ no means /~ нóу миинз/ ни в коем случае; ~ 5 o'clock /~ файв оклóк/ к пяти часам; ~ the way /~ зэ вэй/ между прочим; ~ Jove! /~ джóув/ ей-Богу!; adv близко, рядом, мимо

by-election /байилéкшн/ n дополнительные выборы

by-pass /байпас/ n обход

by-product /байпрóдэкт/ n побочный продукт

byte /байт/ n (вчт.) байт, слог

C

cab /кэб/ n такси

cabaret /кэбэрэй/ n кабаре

cabbage /кэбидж/ n капуста; head of ~ /хед ов ~/ кочан капусты

cabin /кэбин/ n кабина; хижина; каюта

cabinet /кэбинит/ n кабинет, кабинет министров

cable /кейбл/ n кабель, трос; телеграмма; vt телеграфировать

cackle /кэкл/ vi кудахтать

cactus /кэктэс/ n кактус

cafe /кэфей/ n кафе

cage /кейдж/ n клетка

cake /кейк/ n торт, пирожное

calculate /кэлкьюлэйт/ vt вычислять, подсчитывать; рассчитывать

calculation /кэлкьюлэйшн/ n вычисление; расчет

calendar /кэлиндэ/ n календарь

calf /кааф/ n теленок; икра (ноги)

calibre /кэлибэ/ n калибр

call /коол/ n зов, призыв; (телефонный) вызов; визит, остановка (поезда); заход в порт; vt звать, будить; vi заходить; ~ for /~ фо/ требовать;~ off /~ оф/ отзывать; ~ on /~ он/ навещать; ~ up /~ ап/ вызывать по телефону

caller /кóолэ/ n посетитель

callous /кэлэс/ adj мозолистый

calm /каам/ n тишина; adj спокойный; vt успокаивать; ~ down /~ дáун/ утихать, успокаиваться

calmly /кáамли/ adv хладнокровно

calorie /кэлери/ n калория

Calvary /кэлвэри/ n (библ.) Голгофа

cambric /кэймбрик/ n батист

camel /кэмэл/ n верблюд

camellia /кэмиилье/ n камелия

cameo /кэмиоу/ n камея

camera /кэмерэ/ n фотоаппарат

cameraman /кэмерэмэн/ n фоторепортер; кинооператор; телеоператор

camouflage /кэмуфлааж/ n маскировка

camp /кэмп/ n лагерь; vi жить в палатке

campaign /кэмпэйн/ n кампания

camphor /кэмфэ/ n камфара

can /кэн/ n бидон; банка консервная; vt консервировать

can /кэн/ v aux мочь, уметь

Canadian /кэнэ́йдьен/ n канадец, канадка; adj канадский

canal /кэнэ́л/ n канал

canary /кэнэ́эри/ n канарейка

cancel /кэнсл/ vt отменять, аннулировать

cancer /кэ́нсэ/ n рак

candid /кэ́ндид/ adj искренний

candidate /кэ́ндидит/ n кандидат

candidature /кэ́ндидиче/ n кандидатура

candle /кэндл/ n свеча

Candlemas /кэ́ндлмэс/ n праздник Сретения

candlestick /кэ́ндлстик/ n подсвечник

cane /кэйн/ n трость; камыш

cannon /кэ́нэн/ n пушка; ~ fodder /~ фо́дэ/ пушечное мясо

canny /кэ́ни/ adj себе на уме

canoe /кэну́у/ n каноэ

canon /кэ́нэн/ n (церк.) канон; критерий

canteen /кэнти́ин/ n столовая

canvas /кэ́нвэс/ n холст, парусина

canyon /кэ́ньен/ n каньон

cap /кэп/ n шапка, фуражка

capability /кэйпэби́лити/ n способность

capable /кэ́йпэбл/ adj одаренный; ~ of /~ ов/ способный на

capacity /кэпэ́сити/ n емкость; способность; (тех.) мощность

cape /кейп/ n мыс

capital /кэ́питл/ n капитал; столица; adj главный; ~ letter /~ лэ́тэ/ заглавная буква; ~ punishment /~ па́нишмент/ смертная казнь

capitalism /кэ́питэлизм/ n капитализм

capitalist /кэ́питэлист/ n капиталист

caprice /кэпри́ис/ n каприз

capricious /кэпри́шес/ adj капризный

capsize /кэпса́йз/ vti опрокидывать(ся)

captain /кэ́птин/ n капитан

caption /кэпшн/ n подпись под фото; титр; заголовок

captivate /кэ́птивэйт/ vt пленять

captive /кэ́птив/ n пленник

captivity /кэпти́вити/ n плен

capture /кэ́пче/ n захват; vt захватывать (силой)

car /кар/ n автомобиль (легковой); вагон

caravan /кэ́рэвэ́н/ n караван; дом на колесах

carbon /ка́рбэн/ n углевод

carbon paper /ка́рбэнпэ́йпэ/ n копирка

carburettor /ка́рбьюрэтэ/ n карбюратор

card /кард/ n карта; билет (членский, пригласительный)

cardboard /ка́рдбод/ n картон

card-index /ка́рди́ндекс/ n картотека

cardigan /ка́рдиген/ n картиган

cardinal /ка́рдинэл/ n кардинал; adj главный; (грам.) количественный

care /кээ/ n забота, уход, внимание; take ~! /тэйк ~/ берегись!; take ~ of /тэйк ~ ов/ заботиться о; vi заботиться; I don't ~ /ай до́унт ~/ мне все равно

career /кэри́э/ n карьера; быстрый бег

careful /кэ́эфул/ adj заботливый

careless /кэ́элис/ adj беззаботный

carelessness /кэ́элиснис/ n небрежность

caress /кэрэ́с/ n ласка; vt ласкать

cargo /ка́ргоу/ n груз; ~ ship /~ шип/ грузовое судно

caricature /кэ́рикэтьюэ/ n карикатура

carnation /карнэ́йшн/ n гвоздика

carnival /ка́рнивэл/ n карнавал

carol /кэ́рэл/ n гимн (рождественский)

carotid /кэро́тид/ n сонная артерия

carp /карп/ n карп

carpenter /ка́рпинтэ/ n плотник

carpet /ка́рпит/ n ковер

carriage /кэ́ридж/ n повозка; вагон; перевозка

carrier /кэ́риэ/ n носильщик

carrot /кэ́рэт/ n морковь

carry /кэ́ри/ vt везти, нести; ~ on /~ он/ продолжать; ~ out /~ а́ут/ выполнять

cart /карт/ n телега

carter /ка́ртэ/ n возчик

cartoon /кату́ун/ n карикатура; мультфильм

cartoonist /кату́унист/ n карикатурист

cartridge /ка́ртридж/ n патрон

carve /карв/ vt вырезать (по дереву, кости), ваять; разделывать (мясо)

carved /карвд/ adj резной

cascade /кэскéйд/ n каскад

case /кейс/ n случай, (судебное) дело; чемодан; падеж; in any ~ /ин э́ни ~/ во всяком случае

cash /кэш/ n наличные деньги; ~ on delivery /~ он дили́вэри/ наложенным платежом; vt: ~ out the cheque /~ а́ут зэ чек/ получать деньги по чеку

cashier /кэши́э/ n кассир

cashmere /кэшми́э/ n кашемир

casing /кéйсинг/ n обшивка

cask /кааск/ n бочонок

casket /ка́аскит/ n шкатулка

casserole /ка́сэроул/ n кастрюля; запеканка с овощами

cassette /кэсéт/ n кассета; video ~ /ви́деоу ~/ видеокассета

cast /кааст/ n бросок, бросание, метание; форма для отливки; гипсовый слепок, образец; (театр.) состав; ~ in the eye /~ ин зы ай/ небольшое косоглазие; ~ of features /~ ов фи́чез/ выражение лица; ~ of mind /~ ов майнд/ склад ума; vt бросать; распределять (роли); отливать; ~ a vote /~ э вóут/ голосовать; ~ lots /~ лотс/ бросать жребий; ~ the net /~ зэ нет/ закидывать сеть

caste /кааст/ n каста

cast-iron /ка́аста́йен/ n чугун

castle /кáастл/ n зáмок; (шахм.) ладья; vt рокировать

castor oil /ка́астэрóйл/ n касторовое масло

castrate /кэ́стрэйт/ vt кастрировать

casual /кэ́жьюэл/ adj случайный; небрежный

casualty /кэ́жьюэлти/ n несчастный случай; pl потери

cat /кэт/ n кот, кошка

catalogue /кэ́тэлог/ n каталог

catapult /кэ́тэпалт/ n катапульта; рогатка

cataract /кэ́тэрэкт/ n водопад; (мед.) катаракта

catarrh /кэтáр/ n катар, простуда

catastrophe /кэтэ́стрэфи/ n катастрофа

catch /кэч/ n улов (рыбы), добыча; vt ловить; vi цепляться; ~ cold /~ кóулд/ простужаться; ~ up /~ ап/ подхватывать; догонять

categorical /кэ́тигóрикэл/ adj категорический

category /кэ́тигэри/ n категория

cater /кéйтэ/ vi обслуживать

caterer /кéйтэрэ/ n поставщик

caterpillar /кэ́тэпилэ/ n гусеница

cathedral /кэфи́идрэл/ n собор

Catholic /кэ́фэлик/ adj католический; n католик

Catholicism /кефóлисизм/ n католицизм

cattle /кэтл/ n скот

cauliflower /кóлифлáуэ/ n цветная капуста

cause /кооз/ n причина; ~ of peace /~ ов пиис/ дело мира; vt причинять

caustic /кóостик/ adj каустический; язвительный

caution /коошн/ n осторожность; vt предостерегать

cautious /кóошес/ adj осторожный

cavalry /кэвэлри/ n кавалерия

cave /кэйв/ n пещера

caviar /кэ́виа/ n икра

cavity /кэ́вити/ n полость; дупло (в зубе)

cease /сиис/ vti прекращать(ся)

ceaseless /си́ислис/ adj непрестанный

cedar /си́идэ/ n кедр

cede /сиид/ vt уступать

ceiling /си́илинг/ n потолок

celebrate /сэ́либрэйт/ vt праздновать

celebrated /сэ́либрэйтыд/ adj прославленный

celebration /сэ́либрэ́йшн/ n празднование

celebrity /силе́брити/ n знаменитость

celery /сэ́лери/ n сельдерей

celestial /силе́стиэл/ adj небесный, божественный

cell /сел/ n тюремная камера; (биол.) клетка

cellar /сэ́лэ/ n подвал; wine ~ /вайн ~/ винный погреб

cellist /че́лист/ n виолончелист

cello /че́лоу/ n виолончель

Celt /келт/ n кельт

Celtic /ке́лтик/ adj кельтский

cement /симе́нт/ n цемент; vt цементировать

cemetery /сэ́митри/ n кладбище

censor /сэ́нсэ/ n цензор; vt подвергать цензуре

censorship /сэ́нсэшип/ n цензура

census /сэ́нсэс/ n перепись

cent /сэнт/ n цент; per ~ /пер ~/ процент

centenary /сэнти́инэри/ n столетняя годовщина

central /сэ́нтрэл/ adj центральный

centre /сэ́нтэ/ n центр

century /сэ́нчури/ n столетие, век

cereal /си́эриэл/ adj зерновой; n крупа, овсянка

ceremonial /сэ́римо́уньел/ adj строго официальный; торжественный

ceremonially /сэ́римо́уньели/ adv формально

ceremony /сэ́римэни/ n церемония

certain /сётн/ adj определенный; некий; несомненный; for ~ /фо ~/ наверняка; I'm ~ /айм ~/ я уверен(а)

certainly /сётнли/ adv непременно

certificate /сэти́фикит/ n удостоверение; ~ of health /~ ов хелф/ справка о состоянии здоровья

certify /сёти́фай/ vt удостоверять

cessation /сэсе́йшн/ n прекращение

chaff /чааф/ n мякина

chaffinch /чэ́финч/ n зяблик

chain /чейн/ n цепь; pl оковы; ~ of stores /~ ов сторэ/ цепь магазинов

chair /чээ/ n стул; кафедра; take the ~ /тэйк зэ ~/ председательствовать

chairman /чэ́эмэн/ n председатель

chalk /чоок/ n мел

challenge /чэ́линдж/ n вызов; vt вызывать

challenger /чэ́линже/ n претендент

chamber /че́ймбэ/ n комната; ~ of commerce /~ ов ко́мес/ торговая палата; (тех.) камера; ~ music /~ мьюю́зик/ камерная музыка

chambermaid /че́ймбэмэйд/ n горничная

chameleon /кэми́ильен/ n хамелеон

chamois /шэ́муа/ n серна

chamois-leather /шэ́милэ́зэ/ n замша

champagne /шэмпе́йн/ n шампанское

champion /чэ́мпиэн/ n чемпион; ~ of human rights /~ ов хьюю́мэн райтс/ борец за права человека

championship /чэ́мпьеншип/ n первенство

chance /чаанс/ adj случайный; n случайность, шанс; by ~ /бай ~/ случайно; take a ~ /тэйк э ~/ рисковать

chandelier /шэ́ндилиэ́/ n люстра

change /чейндж/ n перемена, изменение; here's your ~ /хи́эз йо ~/ вот ваша сдача; for a ~ /фор э ~/ для разнообразия; vt менять, заменять; делать пересадку; ~ clothes /~ кло́увз/ переодеваться; ~ one's mind /~ ванз майнд/ передумывать changeable /чéйнжебл/ adj непостоянный

changeless /чéйнжлис/ adj постоянный

channel /чэнл/ n пролив; канал (телевизионный)

chaos /кéйос/ n хаос

chap /чэп/ n парень

chapel /чэ́пэл/ n часовня

chaplain /чэ́плин/ n капеллан

chapter /чэ́птэ/ n глава (книги)

character /кэ́риктэ/ n характер; буква; персонаж

characteristic /кэ́риктэри́стик/ adj типичный

characterize /кэ́риктэрайз/ vt характеризовать

charcoal /чá́ркоул/ n древесный уголь

charge /чардж/ n заряд; обвинение; поручение; цена; pl расходы; be in ~ of /би ин ~ ов/ возглавлять; vt заряжать; поручать; обвинять

chariot /чэ́риэт/ n колесница

charitable /чэ́ритэбл/ adj милосердный

charity /чэ́рити/ n благотворительность; ~ bazaar /~ бэзáр/ благотворительный базар

charlatan /шáалэтн/ n шарлатан

charm /чарм/ n очарование; pl амулет; vt очаровывать

charming /чáрминг/ adj прелестный

chart /чарт/ n карта (морская)

charter /чáртэ/ n устав; vt фрахтовать (судно, самолет)

chase /чейс/ n погоня; vt гнаться за, охотиться на

chassis /шэ́си/ n шасси

chaste /чейст/ adj целомудренный

chastity /чэ́стити/ n чистота, добродетельность

chat /чэт/ n беседа; vt дружески беседовать

chatter /чэ́тэ/ vi болтать

chatterbox /чэ́тэбокс/ n пустомеля

chatty /чэ́ти/ adj болтливый

chauffeur /шóуфэ/ n шофер

cheap /чиип/ adj дешевый

cheat /чиит/ n обман, мошенник; vi мошенничать

check /чек/ n задержка; проверка; (багажная) квитанция; номерок (в раздевалке); (шахм.) шах; vt проверять; сдерживать

checked /чект/ adj в клетку

checking /чéкинг/ n контроль

checkmate /чéкмэ́йт/ n (шахм.) шах и мат

cheek /чиик/ n щека; наглость

cheek-bone /чи́икбоун/ n скула

cheeky /чи́ики/ adj дерзкий

cheer /чи́э/ n веселье; ура; pl аплодисменты; за здоровье!; vt ободрять; ~ up /~ ап/ не унывай!

cheerful /чи́эфл/ adj веселый

cheerio /чи́эриоу/ interj (разг.) ваше здоровье!; всего хорошего!

cheerless /чи́элис/ adj унылый

cheese /чииз/ n сыр; ~ dairy /~ дэ́эри/ сыроварня

chemical /кéмикл/ adj химический

chemise /шими́из/ n женская сорочка

chemist /кéмист/ n химик, аптекарь; ~'s shop /~с шоп/ аптека

chemistry /кéмистри/ n химия

cheque /чек/ n чек

check book /чéкбук/ n чековая книжка

cherish /чéриш/ vt лелеять

cherry /чéри/ n вишня

cherry-stone /чéристоун/ n вишневая косточка

chess /чес/ n шахматы

chessman /чéсмэн/ n шахматная фигура

chest /чéст/ n сундук; (анат.) грудная клетка; ~ of drawers /~ ов дрооз/ комод

chestnut /чéстнат/ adj каштановый; n каштан

chevron /шеврн/ n шеврон

chew /чуу/ vt жевать

chewing gum /чу́ингам/ n жевательная резинка

chic /шиик/ adj нарядный; n шик

chick /чик/ n цыпленок

chicken /чи́кин/ n курица

chicken-pox /чи́кинпокс/ n ветрянка

chicory /чи́кери/ n цикорий

chief /чииф/ adj главный; n глава; ~ of
staff /~ оф стааф/ начальник штаба

chiefly /чи́ифли/ adv главным образом

chieftain /чи́ифтэн/ n вождь

chiffon /ши́фон/ n шифон

child /чайлд/ n ребенок

child-birth /ча́йлдбёс/ n роды

childhood /ча́йлдхуд/ n детство

childish /ча́йлдиш/ adj детский

childless /ча́йлдлис/ adj бездетный

children /чи́лдрн/ n pl дети

Chilean /чи́лиэн/ n чилиец, чилийка;
adj чилийский

chill /чил/ adj холодный; n холод, озноб;
catch a ~ /кэч э ~/ простудиться; vt
охлаждать

chili   /чи́ли/ n красный острый
перец

chilly /чи́ли/ adj зябкий, холодный; сухой, чопорный

chime /чайм/ n бой часов; vi звонить (в
колокола)

chimney /чи́мни/ n труба

chimney-sweep /чи́мнисвип/ n трубочист

chin /чин/ n подбородок

china (-ware) /ча́йнэ(вээ) / n фарфор,
фарфоровое изделие

Chinese /чайни́из/ n китаец, китаянка;
adj китайский

chip /чип/ n щепка; осколок (стекла);
фишка (в играх); pl жареная картошка

chiropodist /киро́педист/ n педикюрша

chiropody /киро́педи/ n педикюр

chirp /чёрп/ vi чирикать, щебетать

chisel /чизл/ n резец; vt ваять, долбить
долотом

chit-chat /чи́тчэт/ n болтовня

chivalrous /ши́вэлрэс/ adj рыцарский

chocolate /чо́кэлит/ n шоколад

choice /чойс/ adj отборный; n выбор,
альтернатива

choir /ква́йе/ n хор

choir-master /ква́йема́астэ/ n хормейстер

choke /чо́ук/ vt душить; vi задыхаться,
давиться

choose /чууз/ vt выбирать

chop /чоп/ n удар; отбивная котлета; vt
рубить, крошить

chord /корд/ n струна; (муз.) аккорд

chorus /ко́орэс/ n хор; in ~ /ин ~/ хором;
~ girl /~ гёрл/ хористка; ~ singer /~
си́нгэ/ хорист

Christ /крайст/ n Христос

christen /крисн/ vt крестить

christening /кри́снинг/ n крещение

Christian /кри́стьен/ adj христианский;
n христианин, христианка; ~ name /~
нэйм/ имя

Christianity /кристиэ́нити/ n христианство

Christianize /кри́стьенайз/ vt обращать в
христианство

Christmas /крисмс/ n Рождество; Father
С. /фа́азэ ~/ Дед Мороз; Merry С.! /ме́-
ри ~/ с Рождеством!; С. Eve /~ иив/
сочельник; С. tree /~ трии/ рождественская елка

chrome /кро́ум/ n хром

chrome-plated /кро́умпле́йтыд/ adj хро-
мированный

chronic /кро́ник/ adj хронический

chronicle /кро́никл/ n хроника

chronicle- /кро́никлэ/ n хроникер; лето-
писец

chum /чам/ n приятель

chunk /чанк/ n кусок, ломоть

church /чёрч/ n церковь; ~ services
/~ сёрвисыз/ богослужение; ~ yard
/~ ярд/ погост

churn /чёрн/ n маслобойка; vt сбивать
(масло)

cider /са́йдэ/ n сидр

cigar /сига́р/ n сигара

cigarette /сигэре́т/ n сигарета, папироса;
~ end /~ энд/ окурок
cigarette case /си́гэре́ткейс/ n портсигар
cigarette holder /си́гэре́тхо́улдэ/ n мунд-
штук
cigarette lighter /си́гэре́тла́йтэ/n зажигалка
Cinderella /си́ндэрэ́лэ/ n Золушка
cinema /си́нимэ/ n кино
cinema-goer /си́нимэго́уэ/ n кинозритель
cinnamon /си́нэмэн/ n корица
cipher /са́йфэ/ n шифр; цифра; нуль
circle /сёркл/ n круг, (театр.) ярус; vt
кружиться вокруг; окружать
circuit /сёркит/ n объезд; (эл.) цепь
circular /сёркьюлэ/ adj круговой; ~
railway /~ рэ́йлвэй/окружная железная дорога; n циркуляр
circulate /сёркьюлэйт/ vt распространять; vi циркулировать
circulation /сёркьюлэ́йшн/ n тираж; (денежное) обращение
circumcise /сёркемсайз/ vt совершать об-
резание
circumstance /сёркемстэнс/ n обстоятельство
circus /сёркес/ n цирк
cistern /си́стен/ n цистерна
citadel /си́тэдл/ n крепость, оплот
citation /сайтэ́йшн/ n цитата
cite /сайт/ vt цитировать
citizen /си́тизн/ n гражданин
citizenship /си́тизншип/ n подданство
citric /си́трик/ adj лимонный
citron /си́трэн/ n цитрон
city /си́ти/ n (большой) город; adj городской
civil /сивл/ adj гражданский; вежливый
civilian /сиви́льен/ adj штатский
civilization /си́вилайзэ́йшн/ n цивилизация
civilize /си́вилайз/ vt цивилизовать
civilized /си́вилайзд/ adj цивилизован-
ный
clad /клэд/ adj одетый
claim /клэйм/ n претензия; (юр.) иск; vt
требовать; (юр.) возбуждать иск о

claimant /кле́ймент/ n (юр.) истец
clairvoyance /клээво́йенс/ n ясновидение
clamber /кла́мбэ/ vi карабкаться
clamorous /кла́мэрэс/ adj крикливый,
шумный
clamour /кла́мэ/ n шум, крики; vt кричать; ~ for /~ фо/ шумно требовать
clamp /клэмп/ n скоба; vt скреплять
clan /клэн/ n клан, клика
clandestine /клэндестин/ adj тайный
clang, clank /клэнг, клэнк/ n лязг; vi ля́з-
гать
clap /клэп/ vti хлопать (в ладоши); n pl
аплодисменты
clapping /кла́пинг/ n аплодисменты
clarification /кла́рификейшн/ n выясне-
ние
clarify /кла́рифай/ vt вносить ясность в
clarinet /кла́ринет/ n кларнет
clarity /кла́рити/ n ясность
clash /клэш/ n столкновение; vi сталкиваться
clasp /клаасп/ n застежка; vt застегивать; пожимать (руки)
class /клаас/ n класс; сорт
classic /кла́сик/ n классик; классическое
произведение
classical /кла́сикл/ adj классический
classify /кла́сифай/ vt классифицировать
classmate /кла́асмэйт/ n одноклассник
clatter /кла́тэ/ n грохот; vi греметь
clause /клооз/ n статья; (грам.) предложение
claw /клоо/ n коготь
clay /клэй/ n глина
clean /клиин/ adj чистый; vt чистить; ~
up /~ ап/ прибирать
cleaner /кли́инэ/ n уборщик, уборщица
cleanliness /кле́нлинис/ n чистота
cleanse /кленз/ vt почистить
clear /кли́э/ adj ясный, светлый; четкий;
vt очищать; vi проясняться
clearance /кли́эренс/ n очистка (в т.ч. от
пошлин)
clear-sighted /кли́эса́йтыд/ adj проницательный

clench /кленч/ vt сжимать (кулак); сти-
    скивать (зубы)
clergy /клёрджи/ n духовенство
clergyman /клёрджимэн/ n священник
clerk /клаак/ n клерк
clever /клэ́вэ/ adj умный, искусный
cleverness /клэ́вэнис/ n одаренность; ис-
    кусность
cliche /кли́ишей/ n штамп
client /кла́йент/ n клиент, покупатель
clientele /кли́иантэ́йл/ n клиентура
cliff /клиф/ n утес
climate /кла́ймит/ n климат
climatic /клайма́тик/ adj климатический
climax /кла́ймэкс/ n высшая точка
climb /клайм/ n подъем, восхождение; vt
    взбираться на; ~ down /~ да́ун/ спу-
    скаться
climber /кла́ймэ/ n альпинист
cling /клинг/ vi льнуть
clinic /кли́ник/ n клиника
clip /клип/ n приколка (для волос);
    скрепка (канцелярская); video ~ /ви́-
    деоу ~/ видеоклип; vt стричь (овец)
clipping /кли́пинг/ n вырезка из газеты
clique /клиик/ n клика
cloak /кло́ук/ n плащ, покров
cloak-room /кло́укрум/ n раздевалка
clock /клок/ n часы; at five o'~ /эт файв
    окло́к/ в пять часов

clockwork /кло́к вёрк/ n часовой меха-
    низм
cloister /кло́йстэ/ n монастырь
close /кло́ус/ adj тесный; близкий; при-
    стальный (взгляд); точный (перевод);
    сжатый (почерк); n окончание; /кло́-
    уз/ vti закрывать(ся), заканчивать(ся)
closely /кло́усли/ adv близко; тесно; вни-
    мательно
closeness /кло́уснис/ n близость
closet /кло́зит/ n чулан; уборная
close-up /кло́усап/ n крупный план (фо-
    то)
clot /клот/ n сгусток; vi запекаться
cloth /клоф/ n ткань, сукно
clothe /кло́уз/ vt одевать

clothes /кло́увз/ n pl одежда
cloud /кла́уд/ n облако; be up in the ~s /би
    ап ин зэ ~з/ витать в облаках
cloudless /кла́удлис/ adj безоблачный
cloudy /кла́уди/ adj облачный
clove /кло́ув/ n гвоздика (пряность);
    долька (чеснока)
clown /кла́ун/ n клоун
club /клаб/ n дубинка; (спорт.) клюшка;
    клуб; pl трефы (карты) ; vt ~ together
    /~ тэгэ́зэ/ собираться вскладчину;
    "сброситься"
clue /клуу/ n ключ (к разгадке)
clumsiness /кла́мзинис/ n неуклюжесть
clumsy /кла́мзи/ adj неуклюжий
cluster /кла́стэ/ n гроздь; пучок
clutch /клач/ n зажим; fall into the ~es
    /фоол и́нту зэ ~из/ попасть в когти; vt
    зажимать
coach /ко́уч/ n карета; (ж/д) вагон; ав-
    тобус; тренер; vt тренировать
coal /ко́ул/ n уголь
coal-mine /ко́улмайн/ n угольная шахта
coarse /коос/ adj грубый
coast /ко́уст/ n побережье
coat /ко́ут/ n пальто; пиджак; ~ of arms
    /~ ов армз/ герб
coating /ко́утинг/ n слой (краски); об-
    шивка
coax /ко́укс/ vt упрашивать; выманивать
cob /коб/ n кукурузный початок
cobble /кобл/ n булыжник
cobbler /ко́блэ/ n сапожник
cobweb /ко́бвэб/ n паутина
cocaine /кэкейн/ n кокаин
cock /кок/ n петух, курок (пистолета);
    ~-a-doodle-doo /ко́кэдуудлду́у/ кука-
    реку
cockchafer /ко́кчейфэ/ n майский жук
cockpit /ко́кпит/ n кабина (пилота)
cockroach /ко́кроуч/ n таракан
cocktail /ко́ктэйл/ n коктейль
cocoa /ко́укоу/ n какао
coconut /ко́укэнат/ n кокосовый орех
cod /код/ n треска; ~-liver oil /ко́дливер-
    ойл/ рыбий жир
code /ко́уд/ n кодекс; код

coeducation /ко́уэ́дьюкéйшн/ n совмест-
    ное обучение
coefficient /ко́уифи́шент/ n коэффициент
coerce /коёрс/ vt принуждать
coercion /коуёршн/ n насилие
co-exist /ко́уигзи́ст/ vi сосуществовать
co-existence /ко́игзи́стэнс/ n сосущест-
    вование
coffee /ко́фи/ n кофе; ~ bean /~ биин/
    кофейное зерно
coffee-grounds /ко́фиграундз/ n pl ко-
    фейная гуща
coffee-mill /ко́фимил/ n кофемолка
coffee-pot /ко́фипот/ n кофейник
coffin /ко́фин/ n гроб
cog /ког/ n зубец
cog-wheel /ко́гвил/ n зубчатое колесо
cognition /когни́шн/ n познание
coil /койл/ n кольцо, (эл.) катушка; vt
    свертывать спиралью, наматывать; ~
    up /~ ап/ извиваться
coin /койн/ n монета; vt чеканить
coinage /ко́йнидж/ n чеканка
coincide /ко́уинса́йд/ vi совпадать
coincidence /коуи́нсидэнс/ n совпадение
coke /ко́ук/ n кокс; кока-кола
colander /ка́лэндэ/ n дуршлаг
cold /ко́улд/ adj холодный; I am ~ /ай эм
    ~/ мне холодно; in ~ blood /ин ~ блад/
    хладнокровно; n холод, простуда
coldness /ко́улднис/ n холодность
colic /ко́лик/ n колика, резкая боль
collaborate /кэлэ́бэрэйт/ vi сотрудничать
collaboration /кэлэ́бэрэ́йшн/ n сотрудни-
    чество
collapse /кэлэ́пс/ n обвал; крах (надежд,
    планов); упадок сил; vi терпеть крах;
    терять сознание
collapsible /кэлэ́псэбл/ adj складной
collar /ко́лэ/ n воротник; ошейник (соба-
    ки)
collar-bone /ко́лэбоун/ n ключица
colleague /ко́лииг/ n коллега, сослужи-
    вец
collect /кэлéкт/ vt собирать
collection /кэлéкшн/ n коллекция; сбор
    (налогов)

collective /кэлéктив/ adj коллективный;
    ~ farm /~ фарм/ колхоз
collector /кэлéктэ/ n сборщик; коллек-
    ционер
college /ко́лидж/ n колледж, универси-
    тет
collegiate /кэли́иджиит/ adj универси-
    тетский; коллегиальный
collide /кэлáйд/ vi сталкиваться
collier /ко́лиэ/ n шахтер
collision /кэли́жн/ n столкновение
colloquial /кэло́уквиэл/ adj разговорный
colloquialism /кэло́уквиэлизм/ n разго-
    ворное выражение
colon /ко́улэн/ n двоеточие
colonel /кёнэл/ n полковник
colonial /кело́униэл/ adj колониальный
colonist /ко́лэнист/ n колонист, поселе-
    нец
colony /ко́лэни/ n колония
colossal /кэло́сл/ adj колоссальный
colossus /кэло́сэс/ n колосс
color /ка́лэ/ n цвет, краска; колорит; ~
    prejudice /~ прэ́джудис/ расовая дис-
    криминация; vt раскрашивать
color blindness   /ка́лэбла́йнднис/ n
    дальтонизм
colored /ка́лэд/ adj цветной
colorful /ка́лэфул/ adj красочный
colorless /ка́лэлис/ adj бесцветный
colors /ка́лэз/ n pl знамя
colt /ко́улт/ n жеребенок
column /ко́лэм/ n колонна; столб; стол-
    бец (газеты); графа
columnist /ко́лэмнист/ n фельетонист
comb /ко́ум/ n расческа, гребень; vt че-
    сать, расчесывать
combat /ко́мбэт/ n бой; vt сражаться
combatant /ко́мбэтэнт/ n боец
combination /ко́мбинэ́йшн/ n сочетание,
    комбинация
combine /ко́мбайн/ n комбайн; объеди-
    нение; /кэмбáйн/ vt объединять; vi
    смешиваться
combustible /кэмбáстэбл/ adj горючий

come /кам/ vi приходить, приезжать; ~ about /~ эба́ут/ случаться; ~ back /~ бэк/ возвращаться; ~ in! /~ ин/ войди(те)!; ~ to /~ ту/ приходить в себя; ~ to light /~ ту лайт/ обнаруживаться; ~ what may /~ вот мэй/ будь что будет!

comedian /кэми́идьен/ n комик

comedy /ко́миди/ n комедия

comely /ка́мли/ adj миловидный

comet /ко́мит/ n комета

comfort /ка́мфэт/ n утешение; комфорт; vt утешать

comfortable /ка́мфэтэбл/ adj удобный

comic /ко́мик/ adj комический; n pl комиксы

coming /ка́минг/ adj наступающий

comma /ко́мэ/ n запятая; inverted ~s /инве́ртыд ~з/ кавычки

command /кэма́анд/ n приказ; vt приказывать, командовать

commandant /ко́мэнда́нт/ n комендант

commander /кэма́андэ/ n командир; ~-in-chief /~-ин-чииф/ главнокомандующий

commandment /кэма́андмент/ n приказ; заповедь

commemorate /кэме́мэрэйт/ vt праздновать, отмечать (годовщину)

commend /кэме́нд/ vt хвалить

commendable /кэме́ндэбл/ adj похвальный

comment /ко́мент/ vi комментировать

commentary /ко́ментэри/ n комментарий

commentator /ко́ментэйтэ/ n комментатор

commerce /ко́мес/ n торговля

commercial /кеме́ршэл/ adj коммерческий

commission /кэми́шн/ n поручение; комиссия; комиссионное вознаграждение; vt уполномочивать; назначать на должность

commissioner /кэми́шнэ/ n комиссар; член комиссии

commit /кэми́т/ vt совершать (преступление, самоубийство); предавать (огню, суду); ~ oneself /~ вансэ́лф/ обязаться

commitment /кэми́тмент/ n обязательство

committee /кэми́ти/ n комитет

commodity /кэмо́дити/ n товар; hard-to-get ~ /хард ту гет ~/ дефицит

common /ко́мэн/ adj общий; обыкновенный; ~ sense /~ сэнс/ здравый смысл; have nothing in ~ /хэв на́финг ин ~/ не иметь ничего общего

commonplace /ко́мэнплэйс/ n банальность

commonwealth /кома́нвэлф/ n государство; the British C. /зэ бри́тиш ~/ Британское Содружество Наций

commotion /кэмо́ушн/ n смятение

commune /ко́мьюн/ n коммуна

communicate /кэмью́юникейт/ vti сообщать, сообщаться

communication /кэмью́юникейшн/ n связь; means of ~ /миинз ов ~/ средства связи

communion /кэмью́юньен/ n общение; C. (церк.) причастие

communism /ко́мьюнизм/ n коммунизм

communist /ко́мьюнист/ adj коммунистический; n коммунист

community /кэмью́юнити/ n община; общность

compact /ко́мпэкт/ adj компактный

companion /кэмпэ́ньен/ n товарищ; компаньон(ка)

company /ка́мпэни/ n компания; рота; труппа

comparable /ко́мпэрэбл/ adj сравнимый

comparative /кэмпэ́рэтив/ adj сравнительный

compare /кэмпэ́э/ vt сравнивать

comparison /кэмпэ́рисн/ n сравнение

compartment /кэмпа́ртмент/ n отделение; купе

compass /ка́мпэс/ n компас; pl циркуль

compassion /кэмпэ́шн/ n сострадание

compatibility /кэмпэтэби́лити/ n совместимость

compatible /кэмпэ́тэбл/ adj совместимый

compatriot /кэмпэ́триэт/ n соотечественник

compel /кэмпе́л/ vt вынуждать, заставлять

compensate /ко́мпенсэйт/ vt возмещать (убытки), компенсировать compete /кэмпи́ит/ vi конкурировать, соревноваться

competence /ко́мпитэнс/ n компетентность

competent /ко́мпитэнт/ adj компетентный

competition /ко́мпити́шн/ n конкуренция; соревнование; конкурс

competitive /кэмпе́титив/ adj конкурирующий

competitor /кэмпе́титэ/ n конкурент

compile /кэмпа́йл/ vt составлять

complain /кэмпплэ́йн/ vi жаловаться

complaint /кэмпплэ́йнт/ n жалоба

complement /ко́мплимент/ n дополнение

complete /кэмпли́ит/ adj полный, законченный; vt завершать

completely /кэмпли́итли/ adv совершенно

completion /кэмпли́ишн/ n окончание

complex /ко́мплекс/ adj сложный; n комплекс

complexion /кэмпле́кшн/ n цвет лица

complexity /кэмпле́ксити/ n сложность

compliant /кэмпла́йент/ adj уступчивый

complicate /ко́мпликейт/ vt усложнять

complicated /ко́мпликейтыд/ adj сложный

complication /ко́мпликейшн/ n усложнение

complicity /кэмпли́сити/ n соучастие (в преступлении)

compliment /ко́мплимент/ n комплимент; pl поздравление

complimentary /ко́мплиме́нтэри/ adj приветственный;~ ticket /~ ти́кит/ бесплатный билет

comply /кэмпла́й/ vi уступать; ~ with /~ виз/ соглашаться с

component /кэмпо́унент/ adj составной; n компонент

compose /кэмпо́уз/ vti составлять; сочинять (музыку)

composed /кэмпо́узд/ adj спокойный, сдержанный

composer /кэмпо́узэ/ n композитор

composition /ко́мпэзи́шн/ n состав; сочинение (школьное); произведение (литературное, музыкальное)

compositor /кэмпо́зитэ/ n наборщик

composure /кэмпо́уже/ n спокойствие

compound /ко́мпаунд/ adj составной, сложный

comprehend /ко́мприхе́нд/ vt постигать

comprehension /ко́мприхе́ншн/ n понимание; beyond one's ~ /бийо́нд ванз ~/ выше чьего-л. понимания

comprehensive /ко́мприхе́нсив/ adj исчерпывающий

compress /ко́мпрес/ n компресс; /кэмпре́с/ vt сжимать

comprise /кэ́мпрайз/ vt заключать в себе

compromise /ко́мпрэмайз/ n компромисс; vt компрометировать; vi идти на компромисс

compulsion /кэмпа́лшн/ n принуждение; under ~ /а́ндэ ~/ вынужденный

compulsory /кэмпа́лсэри/ adj обязательный

compute /кэмпью́ют/ v вычислять

computer /кэмпью́ютэ/ n компьютер

comrade /ко́мрид/ n товарищ

concave /ко́нкэйв/ adj вогнутый

conceal /кэнси́ил/ vt скрывать

concealment /кэнси́илмент/ n утаивание; тайное убежище

concede /кэнси́ид/ vt уступать; допускать

conceit /кэнси́ит/ n тщеславие

conceited /кэнси́итыд/ adj чванливый

conceivable /кэнси́ивэбл/ adj мыслимый

conceive /кэнси́ив/ vt задумывать; (физиол.) зачать

concentrate /ко́нсентрэйт/ vti сосредоточивать(ся)

concentration /ко́нсэнтрэ́йшн/ n концентрация; сосредоточенность; ~ camp /~ кэмп/ концлагерь

concept /ко́нсэпт/ n понятие

conception /кэнсэ́пшн/ n концепция; (физиол.) зачатие

concern /кэнсёрн/ n интерес; беспокойство; концерн; it is no ~ of mine /ит из но́у ~ ов майн/ это меня не касается; vt касаться; ~ oneself /~ вансэ́лф/ интересоваться concerned /кэнсёрнд/ adj заинтересованный; as far as I am ~ /эз фар эз ай эм ~/ что касается меня

concerning /кэнсёрнинг/ prep относительно

concert /кóнсэт/ n концерт

concerted /консёртыд/ adj согласованный

concession /кэнсэ́шн/ n уступка; концессия

conciliate /кэнси́лиэйт/ vt примирять

concise /кэнсáйс/ adj краткий

conclude /кэнклу́уд/ vti заканчивать(ся)

conclusion /кэнклу́ужн/ n вывод

concoct /кэнкóкт/ vt состряпать небылицу; готовить

concord /кóнкод/ n согласие; договор

concrete /кóнкриит/ adj конкретный; бетонный; n бетон

concussion /кэнкáшн/ n контузия; brain ~ /брэйн ~/ сотрясение мозга

condemn /кэндэ́м/ vt осуждать

condemnation /кóндэмнэ́йшн/ n осуждение, приговор

condense /кэндэ́нс/ vt конденсировать; condensed milk /кэндэ́нст милк/ сгущенное молоко

condenser /кэндэ́нсэ/ n конденсатор

condition /кэнди́шн/ n условие, состояние; pl обязательства; on ~ that /он ~ зэт/ при условии, что

conditional /кэнди́шнл/ adj условный

condole /кэндóул/ vi сочувствовать

condolence /кэндóулэнс/ n соболезнование

condone /кэндóун/ vt отпускать (грехи)

conduct /кóндэкт/ n поведение; /кэндáкт/ vt руководить; вести; дирижировать

conductor /кэндáктэ/ n дирижер; кондуктор (автобуса); проводник

cone /кóун/ n конус; шишка; мороженое в стаканчике

confection /кэнфéкшн/ n кондитерское изделие

confectioner /кэнфéкшнэ/ n кондитер; ~'s shop /~з шоп/ кондитерская

confederacy /кэнфéдэрэси/ n конфедерация, союз государств

confederate /кэнфéдрит/ adj союзный, федеративный; n член конфедерации, союзник; /кэнфéдэрэйт/ vi вступать в союз, составлять федерацию

confer /кэнфёр/ vt присуждать (звание, степень); присваивать (титул); vi совещаться

conference /кóнференс/ n конференция

confess /кэнфéс/ vti признавать(ся); исповедовать(ся)

confession /кэнфéшн/ n исповедальня

confessor /кэнфéсэ/ n духовник

confidence /кóнфидэнс/ n доверие

confident /кóнфидэнт/ adj уверенный

confidential /кóнфидэ́ншл/ adj конфиденциальный

confidentially /кóнфидэ́ншели/ adv по секрету

confine /кэнфáйн/ vt ограничивать; be confined /би кэнфáйнд/ рожать; be confined to bed /би кэнфáйнд ту бед/ быть прикованным к постели

confinement /кэнфáйнмент/ n тюремное заключение

confirm /кэнфёрм/ vt подтверждать

confirmation /кóнфемéйшн/ n подтверждение; (церк.) конфирмация

confiscate /кóнфискейт/ vt конфисковать

confiscation /кóнфискéйшн/ n конфискация

conflict /кóнфликт/ n конфликт

conflicting /кэнфли́ктинг/ adj противоречивый

conform /кэнфóрм/ vt сообразовать; vi подчиняться (правилам)

conformity /кэнфóрмити/ n соответствие; in ~ with /ин ~ виз/ в соответствии с

confound /кэнфáунд/ vt спутывать

confront /кэнфрáнт/ vt стоять лицом к лицу с

confuse /кэнфью́юз/ vt спутывать; смущать

confused /кэнфью́юзд/ adj перепутанный

confusion /кэнфью́южн/ n беспорядок

congested /кэнджéстид/ adj переполненный

congratulate /кэнгрэ́тьюлейт/ vt поздравлять

congratulation /кэнгрэ́тьюлéйшн/ n поздравление

congratulatory /кэнгрэ́тьюлейтэри/ adj поздравительный

congress /кóнгрес/ n конгресс, съезд

Congressman /кóнгрэсмэн/ n член конгресса США

conjecture /кэнджэ́кче/ n предположение

conjugate /кóнджугейт/ vt спрягать

conjunction /кэнджáнкшн/ n соединение; (грам.) союз

conjuncture /кэнджáнкче/ n конъюнктура

conjure /кáндже/ vt заклинать; vi колдовать; показывать фокусы; ~ up /~ ап/ вызывать (дух)

conjurer /кáнджерэ/ n волшебник, фокусник

connect /кэнэ́кт/ vti соединять(ся), связывать(ся)

connection, connexion /кэнэ́кшн/ n связь; родство; have good ~s /хэв гуд ~з/ иметь хорошие связи

connive /кэнáйв/ vi смотреть сквозь пальцы

connoisseur /кóнисё/ n знаток

conquer /кóнкэ/ vt завоёвывать

conqueror /кóнкэрэ/ n завоеватель

conquest /кóнквест/ n победа

conscience /кóншенс/ n совесть

conscientious /кóншиéншес/ adj добросовестный

conscious /кóншес/ adj сознательный

consciously /кóншесли/ adv сознательно

consciousness /кóншеснис/ n сознательность

conscript /кóнскрипт/ n новобранец; /кэнскри́пт/ vt призывать на военную службу

conscription /кэнскри́пшн/ n воинская повинность

consecrate /кóнсикрэйт/ vt посвящать; освящать

consecutive /кэнсéкъютив/ adj последовательный

consensus /кэнсэ́нсэс/ n единодушие

consent /кэнсэ́нт/ n согласие; by common ~ /бай кóмэн ~/ с общего согласия; vi соглашаться

consequence /кóнсиквенс/ n последствие; важность

consequently /кóнсиквентли/ adv поэтому

conservation /кóнсёвéйшн/ n сохранение

conservative /кэнсёветив/ n консерватор

conservatory /кэнсёветри/ n консерватория

conserve /кэнсёв/ vt консервировать

consider /кэнси́дэ/ vt рассматривать, обдумывать; vi полагать

considerable /кóнси́дэрэбл/ adj значительный

considerate /кэнси́дэрит/ adj чуткий

consideration /кэнси́дэрэ́йшн/ n рассмотрение, соображение; take into ~ /тэйк и́нту ~/ принимать во внимание; under ~ /áндэ ~/ рассматриваемый

consign /кэнсáйн/ vt отправлять (товары)

consignee /кóнсайни́и/ n грузополучатель

consignment /кэнсáйнмент/ n груз; ~ note /~ нóут/ накладная

consist (of) /кэнси́ст ов/ vi состоять из

consistency /кэнси́стэнси/ n последовательность

consistent /кэнси́стэнт/ adj последовательный

consolation /кóнсэлэ́йшн/ n утешение; ~ prize /~ прайз/ утешительный приз

console /кэнсóул/ vt утешать

consolidate /кэнсóлидэйт/ vt укреплять

consolidation /кэнсóлидэ́йшн/ n консолидация

consonant /кóнсэнэнт/ n согласный звук

conspicuous /кэнспи́кьюэс/ adj видный; бросающийся в глаза

conspiracy /кэнспи́рэси/ n заговор

conspirator /кэнспи́рэтэ/ n заговорщик

constant /ко́нстэнт/ adj постоянный

constellation /ко́нстэлэ́йшн/ n созвездие

constipation /ко́нстипэ́йшн/ n (мед.) запор

constituency /кэнсти́тьюэнси/ n избирательный округ

constituent /кэнсти́тьюэнт/ adj составной; избирающий

constitution /ко́нституью́юшн/ n конституция

constrain /кэнстрэ́йн/ vt принуждать

constraint /кэнстрэ́йнт/ n принуждение

construct /кэнстра́кт/ vt строить

construction /кэнстра́кшен/ n строительство

constructive /кэнстра́ктив/ adj конструктивный

constructor /кэнстра́ктэ/ n конструктор; строитель

consul /ко́нсл/ n консул

consular /ко́нсъюлэ/ adj консульский

consulate /ко́нсъюлит/ n консульство

consult /кэнса́лт/ vt советоваться с; справляться (по книге)

consultation /ко́нсэлтэ́йшн/ n консультация; (мед.) консилиум

consume /кэнсъю́юм/ vt потреблять

consumer /кэнсъю́юмэ/ n потребитель; ~ goods /~ гудз/ ширпотреб

consumption /кэнса́мпшн/ n потребление; (мед.) чахотка

contact /ко́нтэкт/ n соприкосновение, контакт; /кэнтэ́кт/ vt устанавливать контакт

contagion /кэнтэ́йджен/ n зараза

contagious /кэнтэ́йджес/ adj инфекционный

contain /кэнтэ́йн/ vt содержать, вмещать

container /кэнтэ́йнэ/ n контейнер

contaminate /кэнтэ́минэйт/ vt загрязнять; заражать

contamination /кэнтэ́минэ́йшн/ n загрязнение; заражение

contemn /кэнтэ́м/ vt презирать

contemplate /ко́нтэмплейт/ vti созерцать

contemplation /ко́нтэмплэ́йшн/ n созерцание, размышление

contemporary /кэнтэ́мпэрэри/ adj современный; n современник

contempt /кэнтэ́мпт/ n презрение; ~ of court /~ ов корт/ неуважение к суду

contemptible /кэнтэ́мптэбл/ adj презренный

contemptuous /кэнтэ́мптьюэс/ adj презрительный

content /кэнтэ́нт/ adj довольный; vt удовлетворять; ~ oneself with /~ вансэ́лф виз/ довольствоваться; n удовлетворение

contents /ко́нтэнтс/ n pl содержимое; table of ~s /тэ́йбл ов ~/ оглавление

contentious /кэнтэ́ншес/ adj придирчивый

contest /ко́нтэст/ n соревнование, состязание, конкурс

continence /ко́нтиненс/ n сдержанность

continent /ко́нтинент/ adj целомудренный; n материк

continental /ко́нтинэ́нтл/ adj континентальный

contingent /кэнти́нджент/ adj случайный; n контингент

continuation /кэнти́ньюэ́йшн/ n продолжение

continue /кэнти́нью/ vt продолжать

continuity /ко́нтиньюю́ити/ n непрерывность

continuous /конти́ньюэс/ adj непрерывный

contraband /ко́нтрэбэнд/ n контрабанда; adj контрабандный

contrabandist /ко́нтрэбэндист/ n контрабандист

contraceptive /ко́нтрэсэ́птив/ n противозачаточное средство

contract /ко́нтрэкт/ n контракт; /кэнтрэ́кт/ vt заключать договор; сжимать

contracting parties /контрэ́ктинг па́ртиз/ договаривающиеся стороны

contractor /кэнтрэ́ктэ/ n подрядчик

contradict /ко́нтрэди́кт/ vt противоречить

contradiction /ко́нтрэди́кшн/ n противоречие

contradictory /ко́нтрэди́ктри/ adj противоречивый

contrary /ко́нтрэри/ adj противоположный; противный (ветер); on the ~ /он зэ ~/ наоборот; ~ to /~ ту/ вопреки

contrast /ко́нтрэст/ n контраст, противоположность

contribute /кэнтри́бьют/ vt способствовать; жертвовать (деньги); ~ to /~ ту/ вносить вклад (в науку); сотрудничать (в газете)

contribution /ко́нтрибью́юшн/ n содействие; вклад; статья; взнос; контрибуция

contrition /кэнтри́шн/ n раскаяние

contrivance /кэнтра́йвэнс/ n изобретение

contrive /кэнтра́йв/ vt придумывать; ~ to /~ ту/ ухитряться

control /кэнтро́ул/ n контроль, проверка; under ~ /а́ндэ ~/ в подчинении; vt управлять; сдерживать (чувства)

controller /кэнтро́улэ/ n инспектор

controversial /ко́нтрэвёшл/ adj спорный

controversy /ко́нтрэвёси/ n полемика

convalesce /ко́нвэлéс/ vi выздоравливать

convalescence /ко́нвэлéснс/ n выздоровление

convalescent /ко́нвэлéснт/ adj выздоравливающий

convene /конви́ин/ vt созывать

convenience /кэнви́иньенс/ n удобство; at your earliest ~ /эт йор ёрлиэст ~/ когда вам будет удобно

convenient /кэнви́иньент/ adj удобный

convent /ко́нвент/ n монастырь (женский)

convention /кэнвéншн/ n съезд; договор; конвенция

conventional /кэнвéншенл/ adj общепринятый

converge /кэнвёрдж/ vi сходиться в одной точке

convergence /кэнвёрджнс/ n конвергенция

conversation /ко́нвесэ́йшн/ n разговор

conversation /ко́нвесэ́йшэнл/ adj разговорный

converse /ко́нвéс/ vi разговаривать

conversion /кэнвёшн/ n превращение; обращение (в другую веру)

convert /ко́нвёт/ n новообращенный; /кэнвёрт/ vt превращать, обращать

convertible /кэнвёртэбл/ adj откидной; ~ car /~ кар/ автомобиль с убирающейся крышей; обратимый; ~ currency /~ кá-рэнси/ конвертируемая валюта

convey /кэнвéй/ vt перевозить; сообщать; выражать (идею); передавать (собственность)

conveyance /кэнвéйенс/ n доставка

conveyer /кэнвéйе/ n конвейер

convict /ко́нвикт/ n осужденный; /кэнви́кт/ vt (юр.) осуждать

conviction /кэнви́кшн/ n убеждение; (юр.) осуждение

convince /кэнви́нс/ vt убеждать

convincing /кэнви́нсинг/ adj убедительный

convocation /ко́нвэкéйшн/ n созыв, собрание

convoke /кэнвóук/ vt созывать

convoy /ко́нвой/ n конвой; vt сопровождать, конвоировать

cook /кук/ n повар; vt готовить; vi вариться

cookbook /кýкбук/ n поваренная книга

cool /куул/ adj прохладный; vti охлаждать(ся); ~ down /~ дáун/ успокаиваться

coolness /кýулнис/ n хладнокровие

cooper /кýупэ/ n бондарь

cooperate /кóоперэйт/ vi сотрудничать

cooperation /кóоперэ́йшн/ n сотрудничество

cooperative /кóоперэтив/ adj кооперативный; ~ society /~ сэсáйети/ кооператив

cope /кóуп/ n риза; vt покрывать; ~ with /~ виз/ справляться с

copeck /кóупек/ n копейка

copper /ко́пэ/ n медь; медная монета
coppice, copse /ко́пис, копс/ n роща, под-
лесок
copulate /ко́пьюлэйт/ vt спариваться
copulation /ко́пьюлэ́йшн/ n копуляция;
спаривание
copy /ко́пи/ n копия, экземпляр; rough ~
/раф ~/ черновик; vt копировать, спи-
сывать, подражать

copyright /ко́пирайт/ n авторское право
coquet /коке́т/ vi кокетничать
coquette /коке́т/ n кокетка
coquettish /коке́тиш/ adj кокетливый
coral /ко́рэл/ n коралл; ~ reef /~ рииф/
коралловый риф
cord /корд/ n веревка; шнур; струна;
vocal ~s /во́укэл ~з/ голосовые связки
cordial /ко́рдьел/ adj сердечный
cordiality /ко́рдиэ́лити/ n радушие
corduroy /ко́рдерой/ n вельвет
core /кор/ n сердцевина
cork /корк/ n пробка, поплавок; vt закупоривать
corkscrew /ко́ркскру/ n штопор
corn /корн/ n кукуруза; мозоль (на ноге)
corn-flour /ко́рнфла́уэ/ n кукурузная
мука
corned beef /ко́рндби́иф/ n солонина
corner /ко́рнэ/ n угол; (спорт.) корнер; vt
загонять в угол; ~ the market /~ зэ ма́р-
кит/ овладеть рынком
corner-stone /ко́рнэстоун/ n краеугольный камень
cornice /ко́рнис/ n карниз
coronation /ко́рэнэ́йшн/ n коронация
corporal /коопрл/ adj телесный; ~
punishment /~ па́нишмент/ телесное
наказание; n капрал
corporation /ко́рпэрэ́йшн/ n корпорация
corps /кор/ n (воен.) корпус
corpulent /ко́рпьюлент/ adj дородный
correct /кэре́кт/ adj правильный; vt исправлять, поправлять
correction /кэре́кшн/ n исправление,
(по)правка

corrective /кэре́ктив/ adj исправительный
correctness /кэре́ктнис/ n правильность
correspond /ко́риспо́нд/ vi соответствовать; переписываться
correspondence /ко́риспо́ндэнс/ n соответствие; переписка; ~ courses /~ ко́р-
сыз/ заочные курсы
correspondent /ко́риспо́ндэнт/ n корреспондент
corridor /ко́ридор/ n коридор
corrosion /кэро́ужен/ n коррозия
corrupt /кэра́пт/ adj продажный; vt развращать
corruption /кэра́пшн/ n коррупция
cosmetic /козме́тик/ adj косметический;
n pl косметика
cosmic /ко́змик/ adj космический
cosmonaut /ко́змэноот/ n космонавт
cosmopolitan /ко́змэпо́литн/ n космополит
Cossack /ко́сэк/ n казак
cost /кост/ n стоимость; pl издержки; ~
of living /~ ов ли́винг/ стоимость жизни; ~ price /~ прайс/ себестоимость; at
all ~s /эт оол ~с/ любой ценой; vi стоить
costly /ко́стли/ adj дорогой, ценный
costume /ко́стьюм/ n костюм
cosy /ко́узи/ adj уютный
cot /кот/ n детская кроватка; койка в
больнице
cottage /ко́тыдж/ n коттедж; summer ~
/са́мэ ~/ дача
cotton /котн/ n хлопок; ~ cloth /~ клоф/
хлопчатобумажная ткань; ~ wool /~
вул/ вата
couch /ка́уч/ n кушетка; лечение психо-
анализом
cough /коф/ n кашель; vi кашлять
council /ка́унсл/ n совет
councillor /ка́унсилэ/ n советник
counsel /ка́унсэл/ n совет, адвокат; take
~ /тэйк ~/ совещаться; vt советовать
counsellor /ка́унсэлэ/ n консультант; адвокат

count /ка́унт/ n счет; граф; vt считать; ~
on /~ он/ рассчитывать на; that does not
~ /зэт даз нот ~/ это не считается
countenance /ка́унтинэнс/ n лицо; самообладание
counter /ка́унтэ/ n прилавок; счетчик;
adv напротив; run ~ to /ран ~ ту/ идти
наперекор
counteract /ка́унтэрэ́кт/ vt противодей-
ствовать
counter-attack /ка́унтэрэтэ́к/ n контратака
counterbalance /ка́унтэбэ́лэнс/ n проти-
вовес
counter-claim /ка́унтэклэ́йм/ n встреч-
ный иск
counterfeit /ка́унтэфит/ adj поддельный;
n подделка, подлог; vt подделывать
counterfeiter /ка́унтэфитэ/ n фальшивомонетчик
counterrevolution /ка́унтэрэ́револю́юшн/
n контрреволюция
countess /ка́унтис/ n графиня
countless /ка́унтлис/ adj бесчисленный
country /ка́нтри/ n страна; родина; the ~
/зэ ~/ сельская местность; ~ town /~
та́ун/ провинциальный город
countryman /ка́нтримэн/ n соотечественник; сельский житель
countrywoman /ка́нтриву́мэн/ n соотече-
ственница; сельская жительница
county /ка́унти/ n графство (в Англии);
округ (в США)
couple /капл/ n пара; married ~ /мэ́рид
~/ супруги; vt соединять
couplet /ка́плит/ n куплет
coupling /ка́плинг/ n сцепление
courage /ка́ридж/ n мужество
courageous /кэрéйджес/ adj храбрый
courier /ку́риэ/ n курьер
course /корс/ n курс; ход (событий); течение (времени); in due ~ /ин дью ~/ в
свое время; of ~ /ов ~/ конечно; take its
~ /тэйк итс ~/ идти своим чередом

court /корт/ n двор; суд; (спорт.) корт; vt
ухаживать за
courteous /кётьес/ adj вежливый
courtesy /кётси/ n вежливость
court-martial /ко́ртма́ршл/ n военный
суд
courtship /ко́ртшип/ n ухаживание
cousin /казн/ n двоюродный брат; двоюродная сестра
cover /ка́вэ/ n покрывало; укрытие;
предлог; under ~ /а́ндэ ~/ под защи-
той; vt покрывать; прикрывать
coverage /ка́вэридж/ n освещение в пе-
чати
covering /ка́вринг/ n укрытие; обшивка
covert /ка́вет/ adj тайный
covet /ка́вит/ vt жаждать, домогаться
covetous /ка́витэс/ adj алчный, завистливый
cow /ка́у/ n корова
coward /ка́уэд/ n трус
cowardice /ка́уэдис/ n трусость
cowardly /ка́уэдли/ adj малодушный
cowboy /ка́убой/ n ковбой
cower /ка́уэ/ vi сжиматься (от холода, от
страха)
cowshed /ка́ушед/ n хлев, коровник
coy /кой/ adj застенчивый
crab /крэб/ n краб; Рак (созвездие, знак
зодиака)
crack /крэк/ n трещина, треск; adj первоклассный; vt щелкать (хлыстом);
колоть (орехи); vi раскалываться
crack-brained /крэ́кбрэ́йнд/ adj слабоумный
cracked /крэкт/ adj пошатнувшийся (о
репутации)
cracker /крэ́кэ/ n хлопушка; крекер;
щипцы для орехов
crackle /крэкл/ n треск; vi хрустеть
cradle /крэйдл/ n колыбель; vt убаюкивать
craft /краафт/ n ремесло, искусность
craftily /кра́афтили/ adv хитро

craftsman /кра́афтсмэн/ n мастер; ремесленник

cram /крэм/ vt пичкать; наполнять; зубрить

cramp /крэмп/ n судорога; (тех.) скоба

cranberry /крэ́нбери/ n клюква

crane /крэйн/ n журавль; (тех.) кран

crank /крэнк/ n рукоятка; (тех.) кривошип; чудак

crash /крэш/ n грохот; крах; авария; vi падать с грохотом; терпеть аварию, крах

crate /крэйт/ n упаковочный ящик

crater /крэ́йтэ/ n кратер

cravat /крэвэ́т/ n галстук

craving /крэ́йвинг/ n страстное желание, стремление

crawl /кроол/ vi ползать, ползти; ~ with /~ виз/ кишеть

crayfish /крэ́йфиш/ n речной рак

crayon /крэ́йен/ n цветной карандаш, мелок

crazy /крэ́йзи/ adj сумасшедший, помешанный; drive ~ /драйв ~/ сводить с ума

creak /криик/ n скрип; vi скрипеть

cream /криим/ n сливки, крем

cream-cheese /кри́имчйиз/ n плавленый сыр

crease /криис/ n складка; vt мять, загибать

create /криэ́йт/ vt творить, создавать

creation /криэ́йшн/ n создание; произведение (искусства)

creative /криэ́йтив/ adj творческий

creator /криэ́йтэ/ n творец, создатель

creature /кри́иче/ n живое существо; домашнее животное

crèche /крейш/ n детские ясли

credence /кри́идэнс/ n доверие; letter of ~ /лэ́тэ ов ~/ рекомендательное письмо

credentials /кридэ́ншлз/ n pl верительные грамоты

credit /кре́дит/ n доверие, кредит; do ~ to /ду ~ ту/ делать честь; on ~ /он ~/ в долг

creditor /кре́дитэ/ n кредитор

credulous /кре́дьюлэс/ adj легковерный

creed /криид/ n вероучение; кредо

creek /криик/ n бухта

creep /криип/ vi ползать; виться (о растении)

creeper /кри́ипэ/ n ползучее растение; пресмыкающееся животное

Creole /кри́иоул/ n креол(ка)

crescent /креснт/ n полумесяц

crest /крест/ n гребешок (петушиный); грива (конская); гребень (волны); конек (крыши)

crevice /кре́вис/ n расщелина

crew /круу/ n экипаж (судна), команда

crib /криб/ n детская кроватка; кормушка; шпаргалка

cricket /кри́кит/ n сверчок; (спорт.) крикет; ~ bat /~ бэт/ бита

crime /крайм/ n преступление

criminal /кри́минл/ adj преступный; n преступник

crimson /кримзн/ adj малиновый; n румянец

cripple /крипл/ n калека; vt калечить

crisis /кра́йсис/ n кризис

crisp /крисп/ adj хрустящий; живительный (воздух); кудрявый (о волосах)

crisps /криспс/ n pl хрустящий картофель

criterion /крайти́эриэн/ n критерий

critic /кри́тик/ n критик

critical /кри́тикэл/ adj критический

criticism /кри́тисизм/ n критика

criticize /кри́тисайз/ vt критиковать

critique /крити́ик/ n рецензия

croak /кро́ук/ vi каркать; квакать

crochet /кро́ушей/ n вязальный крючок; vi вязать крючком

crockery /кро́кэри/ n посуда

crocodile /кро́кэдайл/ n крокодил

crony /кро́уни/ n дружище

crook /крук/ n крюк; мошенник; vt сгибать

crooked /крýкид/ adj кривой; нечестный

crop /кроп/ n урожай, жатва; зоб (птицы); стрижка; pl посевы; vt собирать урожай с; подстригать

cross /крос/ n крест; vt пересекать; vi скрещиваться; ~ out /~ áут/ вычеркивать; ~ oneself /~ вансэ́лф/ креститься; it ~ed my mind /ит ~т май майнд/ мне пришло в голову; be ~ed with /би ~ виз/ сердиться на

cross-bones /крóсбоунз/ n pl череп и кости

cross-examination /крóсигзэ́минэ́йшн/ n перекрестный допрос

cross-eyed /крóсайд/ adj косоглазый

crossing /крóсинг/ n переход

crossroad /крóсроуд/ n перекресток

crosswise /крóсвайз/ adv крест-накрест

crossword (puzzle) /крóсвёд (пазл)/ n кроссворд

crow /крóу/ n ворона, пение петуха; ~'s feet /~з фиит/ морщинки у глаз

crowd /крáуд/ n толпа; vi толпиться

crowded /крáудыд/ adj набитый битком

crown /крáун/ n корона; крона; коронка (зубная); ~ prince /~ принс/ наследник престола; vt короновать

crucial /крýушьел/ adj решающий

crucifix /крýусификс/ n распятие

crucify /крýусифай/ vt распинать

crude /крууд/ adj сырой; грубый

crudeness /крýуднис/ n необработанность; грубость

cruel /крýэл/ adj жестокий

cruelty /крýэлти/ n жестокость

cruise /круз/ n плавание, круиз; vi совершать рейс; ~missile /~ мúсайл/ крылатая ракета

cruiser /крýузэ/ n крейсер

crumb /крам/ n крошка, крупица

crumble /крамбл/ vt крошить, толочь; vi разрушаться

crumple /крампл/ vt мять, комкать

crunch /кранч/ vt грызть; vi хрустеть

crusade /крусэ́йд/ n крестовый поход

crusader /крусэ́йдэ/ n крестоносец

crush /краш/ vt давить, сокрушать

crushing /крáшинг/ adj сокрушительный

crust /краст/ n корка; земная кора

crusty /крáсти/ adj сварливый

crutch /крач/ n костыль

crux /кракс/ n трудный вопрос; the C. (астр.) Южный Крест

cry /край/ n крик, плач; vi кричать, плакать; ~ down /~ дáун/ заглушать криками

crystal /кристл/ adj хрустальный; чистый; n хрусталь

crystallize /крúстэлайз/ vti кристаллизовать(ся)

cub /каб/ n детеныш

cube /кьююб/ n куб; ~ sugar /~ шýгэ/ пиленый сахар

cubic /кьюóбик/ adj кубический

cubism /кьюóюбизм/ n (иск.) кубизм

cuckoo /кýкуу/ n кукушка; "тронутый", сумасшедший

cucumber /кьюóюкэмбэ/ n огурец

cuddle /кадл/ n объятие; vi ласково прижиматься

cue /кьюю/ n намек; (театр.) реплика; кий (бильярдный)

cuff /каф/ n манжета

cuff-links /кáфлинкс/ n pl запонки

culinary /кáлинэри/ adj кулинарный

culmination /кáлминэ́йшн/ n кульминация

culprit /кáлприт/ n преступник

cult /калт/ n культ

cultivate /кáлтивэйт/ vt возделывать, культивировать; развивать (таланты)

cultivation /кáлтивэ́йшн/ n обработка; культура (растений)

cultivator /кáлтивэйтэ/ n земледелец

culture /кáлче/ n культура

cultured /кáлчед/ adj культурный

cumbrous /кáмбрэс/ adj затруднительный; громоздкий

cumulative /кьюóюмьюлэтив/ adj накопленный

cunning /кáнинг/ adj коварный

cup /кап/ n чашка, кубок; vt (мед.) ставить банки

cupboard /ка́бэд/ n шкаф, буфет

cupola /кью́юпэлэ́/ n купол

curable /кью́эрэбл/ adj излечимый

curative /кью́эрэтив/ adj целебный

curator /кьюрэ́йтэ/ n хранитель (музея, библиотеки)

curb /кёрб/ n узда; край (тротуара); vt обуздывать

curd /кёрд/ n творог

curdle /кёрдл/ vi свертываться (о молоке, крови)

cure /кью́э/ n лечение; vt исцелять

curfew /кёрфью/ n комендантский час

curing /кью́эринг/ n лечение, исцеление

curiosity /кью́эрио́сити/ n любопытство; редкость; ~ shop /~ шоп/ антикварный магазин

curious /кью́эриэс/ adj любопытный

curl /кёрл/ n локон; кольцо (дыма); pl кудри; vt завивать; кривить (губы); vi виться (о волосах)

curly /кёрли/ adj кудрявый

currant /карнт/ n; black (red) ~ /блэк (ред) ~/ черная (красная) смородина

currency /ка́рнси/ n валюта

current /карнт/ adj текущий (о времени, событии), общепринятый; ~ affairs /~ эфэ́эз/ текущие события; n поток; (эл.) ток; alternating ~/о́олтэнэйтинг ~/ переменный ток; direct ~ /дире́кт ~/ постоянный ток

curriculum /кэри́кьюлэм/ n учебная программа

curse /кёрс/ n проклятие; vt проклинать; vi ругаться

cursed /кёрсид/ adj проклятый

cursory /кёсри/ adj беглый, поверхностный

curt /кёрт/ adj краткий

curtail /кёртэ́йл/ vt сокращать

curtain /кёртн/ n занавеска, штора; (театр.) занавес; ~ rings and rod /~ рингз энд род/ кольца и штанга для штор; drop the ~ /дроп зэ ~/ опускать занавес; raise the ~ / рэйз зэ ~/ поднимать занавес

curtsy /кёртси/ n реверанс, приседание

curve /кёрв/ n кривая линия, изгиб; vt гнуть; vi изгибаться

curved /кёрвд/ adj кривой, изогнутый

cushion /кушн/ n подушка (диванная)

cushion-cover /ку́шнкавэ/ n чехол для подушки

custodian /касто́удьен/ n страж; хранитель (музея); опекун

custody /ка́стэди/ n охрана; in ~ /ин ~/ под охраной

custom /ка́стэм/ n обычай; привычка

customary /ка́стэмри/ adj обычный, привычный

customer /ка́стэмэ/ n покупатель

customs /ка́стэмз/ n pl таможня; ~ officer /~ о́фисэ/ таможенник

cut /кат/ n разрез, порез; покрой (платья); снижение (цен); гравюра (на дереве); vt резать; стричь; рубить (дерево); прорезываться (о зубах); сокращать (дорогу, расходы); выключать (воду, электричество); ~ in /~ ин/ вмешиваться (в разговор), ~ short /~ шорт/ прерывать

cute /кьюют/ adj умный; прелестный

cutler /ка́тлэ/ n ножовщик

cutlery /ка́тлэри/ n котлета; ножевые изделия

cutlet /ка́тлит/ n отбивная котлета

cutter /ка́тэ/ n резец; резчик (по дереву/камню); закройщик; (мор.) катер

cut-throat /ка́тсроут/ n убийца

cutting /ка́тинг/ adj режущий; резкий; язвительный (о реплике, замечании); n резка; газетная вырезка; кройка (одежды)

cuttle-fish /ка́тлфиш/ n каракатица

cybernetics /са́йбэнэ́тикс/ n кибернетика

cycle /сайкл/ n цикл; велосипед; vi ездить на велосипеде

cycling /са́йклинг/ n езда на велосипеде

cyclist /са́йклист/ n велосипедист

cyclone /са́йклоун/ n циклон

cylinder /си́линдэ/ n цилиндр

cymbals /симблз/ n pl (муз.) тарелки

cynic /синик/ n циник

cynical /синикл/ adj циничный

cynicism /синисизм/ n цинизм

Cynosure /синэзьюэ/ n созвездие Малой Медведицы; Полярная звезда

cypress /сайприс/ n кипарис

cyst /сист/ n киста

czar /зар/ n царь

Czech /чек/ n чех, чешка; чешский язык; adj чешский

Czechoslovak /чéкослóувэк/ adj чехословацкий

D

dab /дэб/ n мазок (кистью)

dabble /дэбл/ vi плескаться; ~ in politics /~ ин пóлитикс/ политиканствовать

dabbler /дэблэ/ n дилетант

dad(dy) /дэд(и)/ n папа, папочка

daffodil /дэфэдил/ n желтый нарцисс

dagger /дэгэ/ n кинжал

dahlia /дэйлье/ n георгин

daily /дэйли/ adj ежедневный; adv ежедневно; n ежедневная газета

dainty /дэйнти/ adj утонченный, изящный; n лакомство, деликатес

dairy /дээри/ n молочная, маслодельня

daisy /дэйзи/ n маргаритка

Dalmatian /дэлмэйшьен/ n далматский; n далматский дог

dam /дэм/ n дамба, плотина; vt запруживать

damage /дэмидж/ n повреждение, ущерб; vt повреждать, наносить ущерб

damn /дэм/ n проклятие; vt проклинать

damp /дэмп/ adj сырой; n сырость

dampness /дэмпнис/ n сырость, влажность

dance /даанс/ n танец; танцевальный вечер; vi танцевать, плясать

dancer /дáансэ/ n танцовщик, танцовщица

dandruff /дэндрэф/ n перхоть

dandy /дэнди/ n денди, франт

Dane /дэйн/ n датчанин, датчанка; great ~ /грэйт ~/ датский дог

danger /дэйндже/ n опасность

dangerous /дэйнджрес/ adj опасный

dangle /дэнгл/ vt покачивать; vi свисать, болтаться

Danish /дэйниш/ n датский язык

dare /дээ/ vi сметь, отважиться; n смельчак

daring /дээринг/ adj отважный; n бесстрашие

dark /дарк/ adj темный; it is getting ~ /ит из гéтинг ~/ темнеет; n темнота; in the ~ /ин зэ ~/ впотьмах

darkness /дáркнис/ n темнота, мрак

darling /дáрлинг/ adj дорогой, милый, любимый; n голубчик

darn /дарн/ vt штопать

dart /дарт/ n дротик; pl игра "метание стрелок"; vi мчаться стрелой; vt метать; бросать (взгляд)

dash /дэш/ n стремительное движение, порыв; тире; примесь; vodka with a ~ of lemon /вóдка виз э ~ ов лéмэн/ водка с кусочком лимона; cut a ~ /кат э ~/ рисоваться; vt швырять; брызгать; разбивать; vi мчаться

dashing /дэшинг/ adj стремительный

dastardly /дэстэдли/ adj подлый

data /дэйтэ/ n pl данные, факты

date /дэйт/ n дата; свидание; out of ~ /áут ов ~/ устаревший; up to ~ /ап ту ~/ современный; vt датировать; назначать свидание; ~ back to /~ бэк ту/ вести начало от

dative /дэйтив/ n дательный падеж

daub /дооб/ n мазня, пачкотня

daughter /дóотэ/ n дочь

daughter-in-law /дóотэринлоо/ n невестка; сноха

daughterly /дóотэли/ adj дочерний

daunt /доонт/ vt устрашать

dauntless /дóонтлис/ adj бесстрашный

daw /доо/ n галка

dawn /доон/ n рассвет, заря; vi (рас)светать

day /дэй/ n день; all ~ long /оол ~ лонг/ весь день; by ~ /бай ~/ днем; ~ by ~ /~ бай ~/ день за днем; ~ off /~ оф/ выходной день; good ~! /гуд ~/ добрый день! всего хорошего!; the ~ after tomorrow /зэ ~ áафтэ тумóроу/ послезавтра; the ~ before /зэ ~ бифóр/ накануне; the ~ before yesterday /зэ ~ бифóр йéстэди/ позавчера; one ~ /ван ~/ однажды; some ~ /сам ~/ когда-нибудь; the other ~ /зы áзэ ~/ на днях

daylight /дэ́йлайт/ n дневной свет; in broad ~ /ин броод ~/ средь бела дня

daze /дэйз/ vt ошеломлять

deacon /диикн/ n дьякон

dead /дэд/ adj мертвый; ~ drunk /~ дранк/ мертвецки пьян; ~ tired /~ тáйед/ смертельно усталый

dead-end /дэ́дэ́нд/ n тупик

dead-lock /дэ́длок/ n тупик

deadly /дэ́дли/ adj смертельный; ~ sin /~ син/ смертный грех

deaf /дэф/ adj глухой

deafen /дэфн/ vt оглушать

deafening /дэ́фнинг/ adj оглушительный

deafness /дэ́фнис/ n глухота

deal /диил/ n количество; доля; сделка; соглашение; сдача (в картах); a good ~ /э гуд ~/ много; make a ~ with /мэйк э ~ виз/ заключать сделку с; vt сдавать (карты); наносить (удар); ~ with /~ виз/ поступать с, иметь дело с; ~ in /~ ин/ торговать

dealer /ди́илэ/ n торговец

dealings /ди́илингз/ n pl (торговые) дела; сделки

dean /диин/ n декан; настоятель собора

dear /ди́э/ adj дорогой, милый; ~ me! /~ ми/ боже мой! D~ Sir /~ сёр/ уважаемый господин (в письмах)

dearness /ди́энис/ n дороговизна

dearth /дёс/ n голод, нехватка продуктов

death /дес/ n смерть; put to ~ /пут ту ~/ казнить

deathless /дéслис/ adj бессмертный

deathly /дéсли/ adv смертельный; ~ silence /~ сáйлэнс/ гробовое молчание

death rate /дéсрейт/ n смертность

death roll /дéсроул/ n список убитых

debatable /дибэ́йтэбл/ adj спорный

debate /дибэ́йт/ n дебаты; vi дискутировать

debit /дéбит/ n (бухг.) дебет

debris /дéбри/ n осколки, развалины

debt /дет/ n долг; run into ~ /ран и́нту ~/ влезать в долг

debtor /дéтэ/ n должник

début /дэ́йбю/ n дебют

decade /дэ́кейд/ n десятилетие

decadence /дéкэднс/ n упадок

decadent /дéкэднт/ adj упадочный; n декадент

decanter /дикэ́нтэ/ n графин

decay /дикэ́й/ vi гнить, разлагаться; приходить в упадок; n разложение, упадок

deceit /диси́ит/ n обман

deceitful /диси́итфул/ adj обманчивый, лживый

deceive /диси́ив/ vt обманывать

deceiver /диси́ивэ/ n лгун

December /дисэ́мбэ/ n декабрь

decency /ди́иснси/ n порядочность

decent /ди́иснт/ adj приличный

decentralize /дисэ́нтрэлайз/ vt децентрализовать

deception /дисэ́пшн/ n обман

decide /дисáйд/ vti решать

decidedly /дисáйдидли/ adv несомненно

decimal /дэ́симл/ adj десятичный; ~ fraction /~ фрэкшн/ десятичная дробь

decimate /дэ́симейт/ vt казнить каждого десятого

decipher /дисáйфэ/ vt расшифровывать

decision /диси́жн/ n решение; решимость

decisive /дисáйсив/ adj решающий; решительный

deck /дэк/ n палуба; колода (карт.)

declamation /дэ́клэмэ́йшн/ n декламация, торжественная речь

declaration /дэ́клэрэ́йшн/ n заявление; объявление (войны)

declare /диклэ́э/ vt объявлять, заявлять; предъявлять (вещи, облагаемые пошлиной на таможне)

decline /дикла́йн/ n упадок; vt отклонять, отказываться от; (грам.) склонять

decompose /ди́икэмпо́уз/ vi разлагаться, гнить

decomposition /ди́икэмпэзи́шн/ n распад

decorate /дэ́кэрэйт/ vt украшать; награждать

decoration /дэ́кэрэ́йшн/ n украшение; награда

decorative /дэ́крэтив/ adj декоративный

decorator /дэ́кэрэйтэ/ n декоратор; маляр

decorum /дико́орэм/ n приличие

decoy /дико́й/ n западня, приманка; vt заманивать в ловушку

decrease /ди́икрис/ n уменьшение; /дикри́ис/ vt уменьшать

decree /дикри́и/ n декрет, указ; vt постановлять

dedicate /дэ́дикейт/ vt посвящать

dedication /дэ́дикейшн/ n посвящение

deduce /дидью́юс/ vt делать вывод о

deduct /дида́кт/ vt вычитать

deduction /дида́кшн/ n вычет; вывод

deed /диид/ n дело; подвиг; (юр.) акт

deep /диип/ adj глубокий; густой (цвет); низкий (звук); n пучина

deepen /диипн/ vti углублять(ся)

deeply /ди́ипли/ adv глубоко

deepness /ди́ипнис/ n глубина

deer /ди́э/ n олень

defamation /дэ́фэмэ́йшн/ n клевета

default /дифо́олт/ n неплатеж; неявка в суд

defeat /дифи́ит/ n поражение; vt побеждать

defeatism /дифи́итизм/ n пораженчество

defect /дифе́кт/ n недостаток, дефект; vi изменять, дезертировать

defection /дифе́кшн/ n отступничество

defence /дифе́нс/ n оборона, защита

defenceless /дифе́нслис/ adj беззащитный

defend /дифе́нд/ vt защищать

defendant /дифе́ндэнт/ n (юр.) обвиняемый

defender /дифе́ндэ/ n защитник

defer /дифёр/ vt отсрочивать

deferment /дифёрмент/ n отсрочка

defiance /дифа́йенс/ n вызов

defiant /дифа́йент/ adj вызывающий

deficiency /дифи́шнси/ n недостаток

deficient /дифи́шнт/ adj недостаточный

deficit /дэ́фисит/ n дефицит

define /дифа́йн/ vt определять

definite /дэ́финит/ adj определенный

definitely /дэ́финитли/ adv определенно

definition /дэ́фини́шн/ n определение

deflate /дифлэ́йт/ vt выкачивать, выпускать воздух из; сокращать выпуск денежных знаков

deflation /дифлэ́йшн/ n выкачивание, выпускание; дефляция

deflect /дифле́кт/ vti отклонять(ся), преломлять(ся)

deflection /дифле́кшн/ n отклонение, преломление

defloration /ди́ифлорэ́йшн/ n лишение девственности

deflower /дэфла́уэ/ vi лишать девственности, насиловать

deforest /дифо́рист/ vt вырубать леса, обезлесить

deform /дифо́рм/ vt деформировать

deformation /ди́ифомэ́йшн/ n уродование

defy /дифа́й/ vt вызывать (на спор, борьбу); не поддаваться

degenerate /дидже́нерэйт/ vi вырождаться, ухудшаться

degeneration /дидженерэйшн/ n упадок, дегенерация

degrade /дигрэйд/ vt ухудшать, портить

degree /дигрии/ n степень, градус; take a ~ /тэйк э ~/ получать ученую степень

deign /дейн/ vi соизволять

deity /диити/ n божество

deject /диджект/ vt удручать

dejection /диджекшн/ n уныние

delay /дилэй/ n задержка; vt задерживать, отсрочивать

delegate /делигит/ n делегат; /делигейт/ vt делегировать

delegation /делигейшн/ n делегация

delete /дилиит/ vt вычеркивать

deliberate /дилибрит/ adj (пред)намеренный, неторопливый; /дэлиберэйт/ vt обдумывать

deliberately /дилибритли/ adv умышленно

deliberation /дилиберэйшн/ n обдумывание; pl обсуждение

delicacy /дэликэси/ n деликатность, нежность; лакомство

delicate /деликит/ adj щекотливый (о сиуации); слабый (о здоровье)

delicious /дилишес/ adj вкусный

delight /дилайт/ n восторг, наслаждение; vt приводить в восторг; ~ed to meet you /~ыд ту миит ююэ/ очень рад познакомиться с вами

delightful /дилайтфул/ adj очаровательный

delinquency /дилинквенси/ n правонарушение; juvenile ~ /джуувинайл ~/ подростковая преступность

delinquent /дилинквент/ n правонарушитель

delirious /дилириэс/ adj бредящий; be ~ /би ~/ бредить

delirium /дилириэм/ n бред; ~ tremens /~ триименз/ белая горячка

deliver /диливэ/ vt доставлять, разносить (письма); произносить (речь); (мед.) be ~ed /би ~д/ рожать

deliverance /диливрэнс/ n освобождение

delivery /диливэри/ n доставка, вручение; роды

deluge /дельююж/ n потоп

demagogue /демэгог/ n демагог

demand /димаанд/ n требование; great ~ for /грэйт ~ фор/ большой спрос на; vt требовать

demeanor /димиинэ/ n манера держаться

demobilize /димоубилайз/ vt демобилизовывать

democracy /димокрэси/ n демократия

democrat /демэкрэт/ n демократ

democratic /демэкрэтик/ adj демократический

demolish /димолиш/ vt разрушать

demolition /демэлишн/ n разрушение

demon /диимэн/ n демон

demonstrate /дэмэнстрэйт/ vt демонстрировать; доказывать

demonstration /дэмэнстрэйшн/ n демонстрация; доказательство

demonstrative /димонстрэтив/ adj демонстративный

demonstrator /дэмэнстрэйтэ/ n демонстрант

demoralize /диморэлайз/ vt деморализовать

demur /димёр/ vi возражать; n колебание

demure /димьюэ/ adj сдержанный

den /дэн/ n логовище; thieves' ~ /сиивз ~/ притон, "малина"

denial /динайел/ n отрицание, отказ

denim /деним/ n джинсовая ткань

denomination /диноминэйшн/ n название; вероисповедание; достоинство (денежных знаков)

denote /диноут/ vt означать

denounce /динаунс/ vt разоблачать; доносить на; денонсировать (договор)

dense /денс/ adj плотный, густой; глупый

dent /дент/ n выбоина, впадина

dental /дентл/ adj зубной

dentist /дéнтист/ n зубной врач

denunciation /динáнсиэ́йшн/ n разоблачение; денонсирование (договора); донос

deny /динáй/ vt отрицать; отказывать в

depart /дипáрт/ vi уезжать, отправляться

department /дипáртмент/ n министерство; департамент; факультет; ~ store /~ стор/ универмаг

departmental /дúипатмéнтл/ adj ведомственный

departure /дипáрче/ n отъезд, отправление

depend /дипéнд/ vi зависеть; it ~s /ит ~з/ смотря по обстоятельствам

dependable /дипéндэбл/ adj надежный

dependant /дипéндэнт/ n иждивенец, иждивенка

dependence /дипéндэнс/ n зависимость

dependent /дипéндэнт/ adj зависимый, подчиненный; be ~ on /би ~ он/ зависеть от

depict /дипúкт/ vt изображать

deplete /диплúит/ vt истощать

deplorable /диплóорэбл/ adj плачевный, прискорбный

deplore /диплóр/ vt сожалеть о

deport /дипóрт/ vt ссылать

deportation /дúипотэ́йшн/ n высылка

depose /дипóуз/ vt смещать, свергать; vi (юр.) свидетельствовать

deposit /дипóзит/ n вклад в банке; задаток; месторождение; vt класть в банк; давать задаток

depositor /дипóзитэ/ n вкладчик

depository /дипóзитри/ n хранилище

depot /дéпоу/ n депо, склад

depreciate /диприúишиэйт/ vti обесценивать(ся)

depreciation /диприúишиэ́йшн/ n обесценение

depress /дипрéс/ vt подавлять; снижать (цену)

depressed /дипрéст/ adj удрученный

depressing /дипрéсинг/ adj тягостный

depression /дипрéшн/ n депрессия; (экон.) застой

deprive /дипрáйв/ vt лишать

depth /депс/ n глубина; in the ~ of winter /ин зэ ~ ов вúнтэ/ в разгар зимы

deputy /дéпьюти/ n депутат, заместитель

deride /дирáйд/ vt высмеивать

derider /дирáйдэ/ n насмешник

derision /дирúжн/ n осмеяние

derivative /дирúвэтив/ adj производный; n (грам.) производное слово

derive /дирáйв/ vt извлекать

derogatory /дирóгэтри/ adj унизительный

descend /дисэ́нд/ vt спускаться с; vi происходить

descendant /дисэ́ндэнт/ n потомок

descent /дисэ́нт/ n происхождение; десант; спуск

describe /дискрáйб/ vt описывать

description /дискрúпшн/ n описание

descriptive /дискрúптив/ adj описательный

desecrate /дéсикрэйт/ vt осквернять

desert /дéзет/ adj необитаемый; n пустыня; /дизéрт/ vi дезертировать

deserted /дизéртыд/ adj покинутый

deserter /дизéртэ/ n дезертир

desertion /дизéршн/ n дезертирство

deserts /дизéртс/ n pl заслуги

deserve /дизéрв/ vt заслуживать

deservedly /дизéрвидли/ adv заслуженно

deserving /дизéрвинг/ adj достойный

design /дизáйн/ n замысел, проект; узор; vt замышлять; проектировать; делать эскизы (костюмов и т.д.)

designate /дéзигнэйт/ vt (пред)назначать; обозначать

designation /дéзигнэ́йшн/ n назначение на должность; знак, обозначение

designer /дизáйнэ/ n конструктор, дизайнер

desirable /дизáйерэбл/ adj желательный

desire /дизáйе/ n желание; желать

desk /деск/ n письменный стол

desolate /дéсэлит/ adj заброшенный; /дэ́сэлэйт/ vt опустошать

desolation /дéсэлэ́йшн/ n запустение

despair /диспэ́э/ n отчаяние; vi отчаиваться

despatch /диспэ́ч/ n депеша; vt посылать

desperate /дéспэрит/ adj отчаянный

desperately /дéспэритли/ adv в отчаянии

despite /диспáйт/ prep вопреки

despot /дéспот/ n деспот

despotic /деспóтик/ adj деспотический

despotism /дéспэтизм/ n деспотизм

dessert /дизёрт/ n десерт

destination /дéстинэ́йшн/ n предназначение, место назначения

destine /дéстин/ vt предопределять

destiny /дéстини/ n судьба

destitute /дéститьют/ adj неимущий

destitution /дéститьюошн/ n нищета

destroy /дистрóй/ vt разрушать

destroyer /дистрóйе/ n эсминец

destruction /дистрáкшн/ n разрушение

destructive /дистрáктив/ adj разрушительный

detach /дитэ́ч/ vt отделять; (воен.) отряжать

detachable /дитэ́чебл/ adj съемный

detached /дитэ́чт/ adj обособленный; semi- ~ house /сэ́ми ~ хáус/ один из двух особняков, имеющих общую стену

detachment /дитэ́чмент/ n (воен.) отряд

detail /дúитэйл/ n подробность; in ~ /ин ~/ подробно

detailed /дúитэйлд/ adj детальный

detain /дитэ́йн/ vt задерживать; арестовывать

detect /дитéкт/ vt обнаруживать

detective /дитéктив/ n сыщик; adj детективный; ~ story /~ стóори/ детектив

deter /дитёр/ vt отпугивать; удерживать

deteriorate /дитúэриэрэ́йт/ vti ухудшать(ся)

deterioration /дитúэриэрэ́йшн/ n порча

determination /дитёрминэ́йшн/ n решительность

determine /дитёрмин/ vt определять

determined /дитёрминд/ adj решительный

deterrent /дитёрнт/ n средство устрашения; сдерживающее средство

detest /дитéст/ vt ненавидеть

detestable /дитéстэбл/ adj отвратительный

dethrone /дисрóун/ vt свергать с престола

detonate /дéтонэйт/ vi взрывать

detour /дитýэ/ n объезд

detriment /дéтримент/ n вред, ущерб

detrimental /дéтримéнтл/ adj вредный

devaluation /дúивэльюэ́йшн/ n девальвация

devalue /дúивэ́лью/ vt обесценивать

devastate /дéвэстэйт/ vt опустошать, разорять

devastation /дéвэстэ́йшн/ n опустошение, разорение

develop /дивéлоп/ vt развивать; (фотогр.) проявлять; vi развиваться

developer /дивéлэпэ/ n (фотогр.) проявитель

development /дивéлэпмент/ n развитие; разработка (полезных ископаемых); (фотогр.) проявление

deviate /дúивиэйт/ vi отклоняться

device /дивáйс/ n приспособление

devil /девл/ n дьявол; lucky ~ /лáки ~/ счастливец; poor ~ /пýэ ~/ бедняга

devilish /дéвлиш/ adj адский

devise /дивáйз/ vt изобретать; (юр.) завещать недвижимость

devisee /дéвизúи/ n наследник недвижимости по завещанию

deviser /дивáйзэ/ n изобретатель

devoid (of) /дивóйд ов/ adj лишенный (чего-л.); свободный (от чего-л.)

devote /дивóут/ vt посвящать

devoted /дивóутыд/ adj преданный

devotee /девóтии/ n ревностный поклонник; приверженец

devotion /дивóушн/ n преданность

devotional /дивóушенл/ adj набожный

devour /дивáуэ/ vt пожирать

devout /дивáут/ adj преданный

dew /дьюю/ n роса; honey ~ /хáни ~/ "медвяная роса" (сорт дыни)

dexterity /декстéрити/ n ловкость

dexterous /дéкстерес/ adj проворный

diabetes /дáйэбúитиз/ n сахарный диабет

diabetic /дáйэбéтик/ adj диабетический

diagnose /дáйэгноуз/ vt ставить диагноз

diagnosis /дáйэгнóусис/ n диагноз

diagonal /дайэ́гэнл/ n диагональ

diagram /дáйэгрэм/ n диаграмма

dial /дáйэл/ n диск набора (тел.); циферблат; vt набирать (номер)

dialect /дáйэлект/ n диалект, говор

dialogue /дáйэлог/ n диалог, разговор

diameter /дайэ́митэ/ n диаметр

diamond /дáйэмэнд/ n алмаз, бриллиант; pl бубны (карты)

diapason /дáйэпéйсн/ n диапазон

diaphragm /дáйэфрэм/ n диафрагма

diarrhoea /дáйэрúэ/ n понос

diary /дáйэри/ n дневник

dice /дайс/ n pl игральные кости

dictaphone /дúктэфоун/ n диктофон

dictate /диктэ́йт/ vt диктовать; /дúктэйт/ n диктат

dictation /диктэ́йшн/ n диктант

dictator /диктэ́йтэ/ n диктатор

dictatorship /диктэ́йтэшип/ n диктатура

dictionary /дúкшэнри/ n словарь

didactic /дидэ́ктик/ adj дидактический

die /дай/ vi умирать; очень хотеть, жаждать

die /дай/ n игральная кость; the ~ is cast /зэ ~ из каст/ жребий брошен

diehard /дáйхард/ n твердолобый

diet /дáйэт/ n диета, пища

differ /дúфэ/ vi различаться

difference /дúфрэнс/ n разница; (матем.) разность

different /дúфрэнт/ adj различный, иной

differentiate /дифирéншиэйт/ vti дифференцировать (ся)

differently /дúфрентли/ adv иначе

difficult /дúфикэлт/ adj трудный

difficulty /дúфикэлти/ n затруднение

dig /диг/ vti копать, рыть, вонзаться

digest /дáйджест/ n обзор, дайджест; /диджéст/ vti переваривать (пищу)

digestion /диджéсчн/ n пищеварение

digger /дúгэ/ n землекоп

dignified /дúгнифайд/ adj величавый, важный

dignitary /дúгнитэри/ n сановник

dignity /дúгнити/ n достоинство, сан

digress /дайгрэ́с/ vi отклоняться

dike /дайк/ n дамба, плотина

dilapidated /дилэ́пидэйтыд/ adj ветхий, полуразвалившийся, разоренный

dilemma /дилéмэ/ n дилемма

dilettante /дúлитэ́нти/ n дилетант

diligent /дúлиджент/ adj прилежный

dill /дил/ n укроп

dilute /дайльюют/ vt разбавлять

dim /дим/ adj тусклый, смутный

dimension /димéншн/ n измерение; pl размеры

diminish /димúниш/ vti уменьшать (ся)

diminutive /димúньютив/ adj миниатюрный; (грам.) уменьшительный

dimple /димпл/ n ямочка (на щеке)

din /дин/ n грохот, шум

dine /дайн/ vi обедать

diner /дáйнэ/ n обедающий; вагон-ресторан

dining-car /дáйнингкар/ n вагон-ресторан

dinner /дúнэ/ n обед

dinner-jacket /дúнэджэ́кит/ n смокинг

dinner-party /дúнэпáрти/ n званый обед

dip /дип/ n погружение, макание; take a ~ /тэйк э ~/ искупаться; vti погружать (ся) diphtheria /дифти́эриэ/ n дифтерия

diploma /дипло́умэ/ n диплом

diplomacy /дипло́умэси/

diplomat /ди́плэмэт/ n дипломат

diplomatic /ди́плэмэ́тик/ adj дипломатический

direct /дире́кт/ adj прямой; (эл.) постоянный; vt направлять, руководить; дирижировать

direction /дире́кшн/ n направление, управление

directly /дире́ктли/ adv прямо, немедленно

director /дире́ктэ/ n директор; режиссер

directorate /дире́ктэрит/ n дирекция, правление

directory /дире́ктэри/ n адресная (телефонная) книга

dirt /дёрт/ n грязь

dirty /дёрти/ adj грязный; неприличный

disabled /дисэ́йблд/ adj нетрудоспособный

disadvantage /ди́сэдва́нтидж/ n невыгодное положение, ущерб, вред

disadvantageous /ди́сэдвантэ́йджес/ adj невыгодный; неблагоприятный

disagree /ди́сэгрии/ vi не соглашаться; быть вредным

disagreeable /ди́сэгрие́бл/ adj неприятный

disagreement /ди́сэгри́имент/ n разногласие

disappear /ди́сэпи́э/ vi исчезать

disappearance /ди́сэпи́эрэнс/ n исчезновение

disappoint /ди́сэпо́йнт/ vt разочаровывать

disappointing /ди́сэпо́йнтинг/ adj разочаровывающий

disappointment /ди́сэпо́йнтмент/ n разочарование

disapproval /ди́сэпру́увл/ n неодобрение

disapprove /ди́сэпру́ув/ vt не одобрять

disarm /диса́рм/ vt обезоруживать; vi разоружаться

disarmament /диса́рмэмент/ n разоружение

disarray /ди́сэрэ́й/ n смятение

disaster /диза́астэ/ n бедствие

disastrous /диза́астрэс/ adj катастрофический

disband /дисбэ́нд/ vt распускать, расформировывать

disbelief /ди́сбили́иф/ n неверие

disbelieve /ди́сбили́ив/ vt не верить

discard /диска́рд/ vt отбрасывать; сбрасывать (карты)

discern /дисёрн/ vt распознавать

discernible /дисёрнибл/ adj различимый

discerning /дисёрнинг/ adj проницательный

discharge /дисча́рдж/ n разгрузка; исполнение; vt разгружать; выстрелить; освобождать (от обязанностей)

disciple /диса́йпл/ n последователь; апостол

discipline /ди́сиплин/ n дисциплина; vt дисциплинировать; наказывать

disclose /дискло́уз/ vt раскрывать, разоблачать

disclosure /дискло́уже/ n раскрытие; разоблачение

discomfort /диска́мфэт/ n неудобство

disconnect /ди́скэнэ́кт/ vt разъединить; (эл.) выключать

discontent /ди́скэнте́нт/ n недовольство

discontented /ди́скэнте́нтыд/ adj недовольный

discord /диско́рд/ n разногласие; (муз.) диссонанс

discount /диска́унт/ n скидка; vt учитывать векселя; снижать; сбавлять; не принимать в расчет

discourage /диска́ридж/ vt обескураживать

discover /диска́вэ/ vt делать открытие, обнаруживать

discovery /диска́вери/ n открытие

discredit /дискре́дит/ n дискредитация; vt позорить; не доверять

discreet /дискри́ит/ adj осмотри́тель-
ный, сде́ржанный

discretion /дискре́шн/ n благоразу́мие; at
your ~ /эт йо ~/ на ва́ше усмотре́ние

discrimination /дискри́мине́йшн/ n дискриминация

discus /ди́скэс/ n диск

discuss /диска́с/ vt обсужда́ть

discussion /диска́шн/ n дискуссия

disdain /дисдэ́йн/ n презре́ние; vt пре-
небрега́ть

disdainful /дисдэ́йнфул/ adj презри́тель-
ный

disease /дизи́из/ n боле́знь

diseased /дизи́изд/ adj больно́й

disembark /ди́симба́рк/ vti выгру-
жа́ть(ся)

disensage /ди́сингéйдж/ vt освобожда́ть

disengaged /ди́сингéйджд/ adj свобо́д-
ный, незанятый

disentagle /ди́синтэ́нгл/ vt распутывать;
~ oneself /~ вансэ́лф/ выпутываться

disfavor /дисфэ́йвэ/ n неми́лость

disfigure /дисфи́гэ/ vt обезобра́живать

disfranchise /ди́сфрэ́нчайз/ vt лиша́ть
гражда́нских или избира́тельных прав

disgrace /дисгрэ́йс/ n позо́р, неми́лость;
vt позо́рить

disgraceful /дисгрэ́йсфул/ adj посты́д-
ный

disguise /дисга́йз/ n маскиро́вка; vt мас-
кирова́ть

disgust /дисга́ст/ n омерзе́ние; vt вну-
ша́ть отвраще́ние

dish /диш/ n блю́до

dishwasher /ди́шво́ше/ n маши́на для
мытья́ посу́ды

dishearten /дисха́ртн/ vt обескура́живать

dishonest /дисо́нист/ adj нече́стный

dishonesty /дисо́нисти/ n нече́стность

dishonor /дисо́нэ/ n бесче́стие; vt позо́-
рить; ~ed bill /~д бил/ просро́ченный
ве́ксель

dishonorable /дисо́нэрэбл/ adj позо́р-
ный, по́длый

disillusion /ди́силю́южн/ vt разочаро́вы-
вать

diusillusionment /ди́силю́оюженмент/ n
разочарова́ние

disinfect /ди́синфéкт/ vt дезинфици́ро-
вать

disinherit /ди́синхéрит/ vt лиша́ть на-
сле́дства

disintegrate /диси́нтегрэ́йт/ vti разла-
га́ть(ся)

disinterested /диси́нтристыд/ adj беско-
ры́стный; незаинтересо́ванный

disk /диск/ n магни́тный диск, диске́та

dislike /дисла́йк/ n неприя́знь; vt не лю-
би́ть

dislocate /ди́слэкейт/ vt вы́вихнуть; вно-
си́ть беспоря́док

dislodge /дисло́дж/ vt вытесня́ть, сме-
ща́ть

disloyal /дисло́йел/ adj вероло́мный

dismal /ди́змэл/ adj мра́чный, уны́лый

dismantle /дисмэ́нтл/ vt демонти́ровать

dismiss /дисми́с/ vt увольня́ть; распу-
ска́ть

dismissal /дисми́сл/ n увольне́ние; роспуск

dismount /дисма́унт/ vt демонти́ровать;
vi спе́шиваться

disobedience /ди́сэби́идьенс/ n непови-
нове́ние

disobedient /ди́сэби́идьент/ adj непо-
слу́шный

disobey /ди́сэбéй/ vt ослу́шаться

disorder /дисо́рдэ/ n беспоря́док; рас-
стро́йство, боле́знь; vt приводи́ть в бес-
поря́док

disorderly /дисо́рдэли/ adj беспоря́доч-
ный

disorganize /дисо́ргэнайз/ vt дезоргани-
зо́вывать

disparity /диспэ́рити/ n нера́венство

dispassionate /дисп́ашнит/ adj бесстра́ст-
ный

dispel /диспéл/ vt разгоня́ть

dispense /диспéнс/ vt раздавать; ~ with /~ виз/ обходиться без

disperse /диспёрс/ vt разгонять; vi рассеиваться

displace /дисплэ́йс/ vt перемещать, смещать; ~ed person /~т пёрсн/ перемещенное лицо

displacement /дисплэ́йсмент/ n смещение, перемещение; водоизмещение

display /дисплэ́й/ n выставка; проявление; дисплей; vt выставлять; проявлять

displease /дисплии́з/ vt вызывать недовольство, не нравиться

displeasing /дисплии́зинг/ adj неприятный

displeasure /дисплéже/ n недовольство

disposable /диспóузэбл/ adj могущий быть использованным

disposal /диспóузл/ n расположение, размещение; at your ~ /эт йо ~/ в вашем распоряжении

dispose /диспóуз/ vt располагать, размещать; ~ of /~ ов/ распоряжаться; избавляться от

disposed /диспóузд/ adj склонный

disposition /ди́спэзи́шн/ n расположение, размещение; характер, нрав

dispute /диспью́ют/ n диспут, спор; vt оспаривать; обсуждать

disqualify /дисквóлифай/ vt дисквалифицировать

disquiet /дисквá́йэт/ n беспокойство; vt тревожить

disregard /ди́сригáрд/ vt игнорировать, пренебрегать

disrepute /ди́срипью́ют/ n дурная слава

disrespect /ди́сриспéкт/ n неуважение

dissatisfaction /ди́ссэ́тисфэ́кшн/ n недовольство

disseminate /дисéминэйт/ vt распространять

dissension /дисéншн/ n раздор

dissent /дисéнт/ n разногласие; (церк.) раскол

dissenter /дисéнтэ/ n раскольник, диссидент

dissertation /ди́сэтэ́йшн/ n диссертация

dissipate /ди́сипейт/ vt рассеивать, проматывать (деньги)

dissipation /ди́сипéйшн/ n беспутство

dissolution /ди́сэлю́юшн/ n растворение; роспуск, закрытие

disolvable /дизóлвэбл/ adj растворимый

dissolve /дизóлв/ vt расторгать, распускать; vi растворяться

dissonance /ди́сэнэнс/ n диссонанс

dissuade /дисвэ́йд/ vt разубеждать

distance /ди́стэнс/ n расстояние, дистанция; at a ~ /эт э ~/ вдали

distant /ди́стэнт/ adj дальний, далекий

distemper /дистэ́мпэ/ n плохое настроение; темпера; чумка

distil /дисти́л/ vt дистиллировать; перегонять (спирт)

distillery /дисти́лэри/ n винный завод

distinct /дисти́нкт/ adj отчетливый; особый

distinction /дисти́нкшн/ n отличие

dictinstive /дисти́нктив/ adj отличительный

distinctly /дисти́нктли/ adv отчетливо

distinguish /дисти́нгвиш/ vt различать; ~ oneself /~ вансэ́лф/ отличаться

distinguished /дисти́нгвишт/ adj выдающийся, известный

distort /дистóрт/ vt искажать

distortion /дистóршн/ n искажение, искривление

distract /дистрэ́кт/ vt отвлекать

distrain /дистрэ́йн/ vt описывать (имущество)

distress /дистрéс/ n беда, бедствие; vt огорчать

distressed /дистрéст/ adj терпящий бедствие, бедствующий

distribute /дистри́бьют/ vt распределять, раздавать

distribution /ди́стрибью́юшн/ n распределение, раздача

district /ди́стрикт/ n район, округ

distrust /дистра́ст/ n недоверие; vt не доверять

disturb /дистёрб/ vt беспокоить, нарушать (покой)

disturbance /дистёрбэнс/ n волнение; pl беспорядки

disunite /ди́съюна́йт/ vt разделять

ditch /дич/ n канава, ров

diuretic /да́йуэрéтик/ adj мочегонный

divan /дивэ́н/ n диван

dive /дайв/ n прыжок (в воду); пикирование; vt нырять; пикировать

diver /да́йвэ/ n водолаз; гагара

diverge /дайвёрдж/ vi расходиться; отклоняться

diverse /дайвёрс/ adj разнообразный

diversion /дайвёршн/ n отклонение; развлечение; отвлекающий удар

diversity /дайвёрсити/ n разнообразие

divert /дайвёрт/ vt отвлекать; развлекать

divide /дива́йд/ vti разделять (ся)

dividend /ди́виденд/ n делимое; дивиденд

dividers /дива́йдэз/ n pl циркуль

divine /дива́йн/ adj божественный; n богослов; vt пророчествовать

diviner /дива́йнэ/ n предсказатель

diving /да́йвинг/ n прыжки в воду

divinity /диви́нити/ n божество; богословие

division /диви́жн/ n деление; отдел; дивизия

divorce /диво́рс/ n развод; vt разводиться с

dizzy /ди́зи/ adj головокружительный; I feel ~ /ай фиил ~/ у меня кружится голова

do /ду/ vt поступать, делать; ~ a room /~ э руум/ убирать комнату; that will ~! /зэт вил ~/ довольно; ~ away with /~ эвэ́й виз/ покончить с; ~ without /~ виза́ут/ обходиться без; how do you~? /ха́у ду ю ~ / здравствуйте; ~ well /~ вэл/ процветать; well-to-~ /вэл ту ~/ зажиточный

docile /до́усайл/ adj послушный

dock /док/ n док; скамья подсудимых; щавель

docket /до́кит/ n ярлык, этикетка

docking /до́кинг/ n стыковка (космических кораблей)

dockyard /до́къярд/ n верфь

doctor /до́ктэ/ n врач, доктор

doctorate /до́кторит/ n докторская степень

doctrine /до́ктрин/ n учение, доктрина

document /до́кьюмент/ n документ

documentary /до́кьюмéнтэри/ n документальный фильм

dodge /додж/ n увертка; vt избегать

dodger /до́джэ/ n хитрец

doer /ду́э/ n деятель, созидатель

dog /дог/ n собака; ~ in the manger /~ ин зэ мэ́нгэ/ собака на сене

dog collar /до́гко́лэ/ n ошейник

dogged /до́гид/ adj настойчивый

dogma /до́гмэ/ n догма

doings /ду́ингз/ n pl действия

doleful /до́улфул/ adj скорбный

doll /дол/ n кукла

dollar /до́лэ/ n доллар

dolly /до́ли/ n куколка

dolphin /до́лфин/ n дельфин

dolt /до́улт/ n болван

domain /дэмэ́йн/ n владение; (образн.) область

dome /до́ум/ n купол

domestic /дэмéстик/ adj домашний; внутренний; ручной

domesticate /дэмéстикэйт/ vt приручать

dominate /до́минэйт/ vt господствовать над; vi доминировать

domination /до́минэ́йшн/ n господство

dominion /дэми́ньен/ n владычество; доминион

domino(es) /до́миноу (з) / n домино

donate /донэ́йт/ vt передавать в дар

donation /донэ́йшн/ n денежное пожертвование

done /дан/ adj сделанный

donkey /до́нки/ n осел

donor /дóунэ/ n донор

doom /дуум/ n рок; гибель; vt обрекать

doomsday /дýумздэй/ n судный день

door /дор/ n дверь

doorbell /дóрбел/ n дверной звонок

doorkeeper /дóркипэ/ n швейцар

doorway /дóрвэй/ n дверной проем

dope /дóуп/ n (разг.) наркотик

dormitory /дóрмитри/ n общая спальня

dose /дóус/ n доза

dot /дот/ n точка; vt ставить точки; ~ the i's / ~ зы айз/ ставить точки над i; dotted line /дóтыд лайн/ пунктирная линия

dote /дóут/ vi впадать в детство; ~ on /~ он/ любить до безумия

double /дабл/ adj двойной; ~ bed /~ бед/ двуспальная кровать; ~ chin /~ чин/ двойной подбородок; ~ room /~ руум/ номер на двоих; adv вдвойне, вдвое; n двойник, дубликат; vti удваивать(ся)

double-dealing /дáблдѝилинг/ n двурушничество

doubt /дáут/ n сомнение; vt сомневаться в

doubtful /дáутфул/ adj сомневающийся, сомнительный

doubtless /дáутлис/ adv несомненно

douche /дууш/ n душ, промывание; vt поливать (из душа), обливать водой

dough /дóу/ n тесто

doughnut /дóунат/ n пончик

dove /дав/ n голубь

down /дáун/ n спуск, падение; pron вниз; adv внизу; ~ with /~ виз/ долой!; vt опускать; сбивать

down /дáун/ n пух; пальто на пуху

downfall /дáунфол/ n падение, гибель

downhill /дáунхѝл/ adv под гору

downpour /дáунпо/ n ливень

downright /дáунрайт/ adv совершенно

downstairs /дáунстэ́эз/ adv внизу

dowry /дáури/ n приданое

doze /дóуз/ vi дремать

dozen /дазн/ n дюжина; baker's ~ /бэ́йкез ~/ чертова дюжина

draft /драфт/ n черновик, набросок; чек; (воен.) набор; vt набрасывать черновик

drag /дрэг/ n драга; обуза; vti тащить(ся), тянуть(ся)

dragon /дрэгн/ n дракон

dragonfly /дрэ́гнфлай/ n стрекоза

drain /дрэйн/ n дренажная канава; vt дренировать, осушать (почву)

drainage /дрэ́йнидж/ n дренаж

draining /дрэ́йнинг/ n осушение

drainpipe /дрэ́йнпайп/ n водосточная труба

drake /дрэйк/ n селезень

drama /дрáамэ/ n драма

dramatic /дрэмэ́тик/ adj драматический

dramatist /дрэ́метист/ n драматург

drape /дрэйп/ vt драпировать

drapery /дрэ́йпери/ n драпировка; магазин тканей

drastic /дрэ́стик/ adj суровый, крутой; радикальный

draught /драафт/ n тяга, сквозняк; pl шашки

draughtsman /дрáафтсмэн/ n чертежник

draw /дроо/ n жеребьевка; ничья (в игре); in a ~ /ин э ~/ вничью; vt тянуть; рисовать; выписывать (чек); выводить (заключение); задергивать (занавеску); кончать (игру) вничью; привлекать (внимание)

drawback /дрóобэк/ n недостаток

drawbridge /дрóобридж/ n разводной мост

drawer /дроо/ n (выдвижной) ящик; pl кальсоны

drawing /дрóоинг/ n рисунок, чертеж

drawing room /дрóоингрум/ n гостинная

dread /дред/ n страх; vt бояться

dreadful /дрéдфул/ adj ужасный

dream /дриим/ n сон; мечта; vt видеть во сне; мечтать о

dreamer /дрѝимэ/ n фантазер

dreamy /дрѝими/ adj мечтательный

dreary /дрѝэри/ adj мрачный

dredge /дредж/ n драга, землечерпалка

dregs /дрегз/ n pl отбросы; ~ of society /~ ов сэсáйети/ подонки общества

drench /дренч/ vt промачивать; ~ed to the skin /~т ту зэ скин/ вымокший до нитки

dress /дресс/ n платье, одежда; vt одевать; перевязывать (рану); приправлять (салат); vi одеваться; (воен.) выравниваться

dress-circle /дрéссёркл/ n бельэтаж

dress clothes /дрéсклóуз/ n фрак

dresser /дрéсэ/ n кухонный шкаф

dressing /дрéсинг/ n одевание; перевязка; приправа, соус

dressing-gown /дрéсингтáун/ n халат

dressing room /дрéсингрум/ n артистическая комната

dressing table /дрéсингтэ́йбл/ n туалетный столик

dressmaker /дрéсмэ́йкэ/ n портниха

dress rehearsal /дрéсрихёёсл/ n генеральная репетиция

dribble /дрибл/ vi капать

dried /драйд/ adj сушеный

drift /дрифт/ n течение; сугроб (снега); дрейф; vi дрейфовать

drill /дрил/ n муштра; сверло; vi сверлить

drilling /дри́линг/ n строевая подготовка

drink /дринк/ n напиток; hard ~s /хард ~с/ спиртные напитки; soft ~s /софт ~с/ безалкогольные напитки; have a ~ /хэв э ~/ выпить; vt пить; vi пьянствовать; ~ his health /~ хиз хелс/ пить за его здоровье

drinker /дри́нкэ/ n пьяница

drinking /дри́нкинг/ n пьянство

drinking-bout /дри́нкингбáут/ n запой

drinking-water /дри́нкингвóотэ/ n питьевая вода

drip /дрип/ n капля; vi капать

dripping /дри́пинг/ n капанье

drive /драйв/ n поездка; (тех.) привод; vt гнать; вбивать (гвоздь); водить (автомобиль); ~ into a corner /~ и́нту э кóрнэ/ загонять в угол

driver /дрáйвэ/ n шофер

driving /дрáйвинг/ n вождение (автомобиля); ~ licence /~ лáйсенс/ водительские права

drizzle /дризл/ n мелкий дождь; vi моросить

drone /дрóун/ n трутень; vi жужжать, гудеть, бубнить

droop /друуп/ vi поникать

drooping /дрýупинг/ adj понурый

drop /дроп/ n капля; pl (мед.) капли; vt ронять; подвозить (до дома); сбрасывать (с самолета); vi падать

drought /дрáут/ n засуха

drown /дрáун/ vt топить; vi тонуть

drowsy /дрáузи/ adj сонный, дремотный

drug /драг/ n лекарство; наркотик; ~ addict /~ э́дикт/ наркоман; vt подмешивать наркотики

druggist /дрáгист/ n аптекарь

drugstore /дрáгстор/ n аптека

drum /драм/ n барабан; vi барабанить

drumhead /дрáмхед/ n барабанная перепонка

drummer /дрáмэ/ n барабанщик

drumstick /дрáмстик/ n барабанная палочка

drunk /дранк/ adj пьяный; get ~ /гет ~/ напиться

drunkard /дрáнкэд/ n пьяница

drunkenness /дрáнкеннис/ n пьянство

dry /драй/ adj сухой; vti сушить(ся)

dry-cleaning /дрáйкли́нинг/ n химчистка

dryness /дрáйнис/ n сушь

dual /дью́юэл/ adj двойственный

dub /даб/ vt дублировать (фильм)

dubious /дью́юбьес/ adj сомнительный

duchess /дáчис/ n герцогиня

duck /дак/ n утка; vi окунаться

duckling /дáклинг/ n утенок

dud /дад/ adj бесполезный; негодный

due /дьюю/ adj должный, надлежащий; ~ to /~ ту/ благодаря; in ~ time /ин ~ тайм/ в свое время; ~ west /~ вест/ прямо на запад; n должное; pl сборы, пошлины, членские взносы; give smb. his ~ /гив са́мбэди хиз ~/ отдавать кому-либо должное

duel /дью́эл/ n дуэль

duelist /дюэ́лист/ n дуэлянт

duet /дью́эт/ n дуэт

dug-out /да́гаут/ n землянка

duke /дьюю́к/ n герцог

dull /дал/ adj тупой, скучный; пасмурный

duly /дью́юли/ adv должным образом; своевременно

dumb /дам/ adj немой; deaf and ~ /дэф энд ~/ глухонемой; ~ show /~ шо́у/ пантомима

dumbness /да́мнис/ n немота

dummy /да́ми/ adj подставной; учебный; n манекен; макет

dump /дамп/ n свалка; vt сваливать

dumping /да́мпинг/ n демпинг

dunce /данс/ n тупица

dunderhead /данд́эхед/ n болван

dune /дью́юн/ n дюна

dung /данг/ n навоз

dungeon /да́нджен/ n темница

dupe /дью́юп/ n простофиля; vt надувать

duplicate /дью́юпликит/ n дубликат, копия; in ~ /ин ~/ в двух экземплярах; /дью́юпликейт/ vt копировать

duplicator /дью́юпликейтэ/ n копировальная машина

durable /дью́эрэбл/ adj прочный; длительного пользования

duration /дьюрэ́йшн/ n продолжительность

during /дью́эринг/ prep в течение

dusk /даск/ n сумерки

dusky /да́ски/ adj сумеречный

dust /даст/ n пыль

dustbin /да́стбин/ n мусорный ящик

duster /да́стэ/ n тряпка (щетка) для вытирания пыли

dustman /да́стмэн/ n мусорщик

dustpan /да́стпэн/ n совок для мусора

dusty /да́сти/ adj пыльный

Dutch /дач/ adj голландский; n голландский язык

Dutchman /да́чмэн/ n голландец

Dutchwoman /да́чву́мэн/ n голландка

duty /дью́юти/ n долг, обязанность; пошлина; be on ~ /би он ~/ дежурить; ~-free /~ фрии/ не подлежащий обложению пошлиной; do one's ~ /ду ванз ~/ исполнять долг

dwarf /дворф/ n карлик

dwell /двел/ vi жить, обитать

dweller /дв́елэ/ n житель

dwelling /дв́елинг/ n жилище; ~ house /~ ха́ус/ жилой дом

dye /дай/ n краска, краситель; vt красить

dyer /да́йе/ n красильщик

dynamic /дайн́эмик/ adj динамический

dynamics /дайн́эмикс/ n динамика

dynamite /да́йнэмайт/ n динамит

dynamo /да́йнэмоу/ n динамо

dynasty /ди́нэсти/ n династия

dysentery /ди́снтри/ n дизентерия

dyspepsia /дисп́епсиэ/ n расстройство пищеварения

E

each /иич/ adj, pron каждый; ~ other /~ а́зэ/ друг друга

eager /и́игэ/ adj страстно стремящийся; be ~ to /би ~ ту/ жаждать

eagerly /и́игэли/ adv охотно

eagerness /и́игэнис/ n усердие

eagle /иигл/ n орел

ear /и́э/ n ухо; колос; be all ~s /би оол ~з/ превращаться в слух

earl /эрл/ n граф

early /ёрли/ adj ранний; adv рано

earn /ёрн/ vt зарабатывать; заслуживать

earnest /ёрнист/ adj серьезный; искренний; in ~ /ин ~/ всерьез earnings /ёрнингз/ n pl заработок

earring /йэринг/ n серьга

earth /ёрс/ n земля, земной шар; vt (эл.) заземлять

earthen /ёрсн/ adj земляной

earthenware /ёрснвээ/ n глиняная посуда

earthly /ёрсли/ adj земной

earthquake /ёрсквэйк/ n землетрясение

ease /ииз/ n покой; with ~ /виз ~/ с легкостью; at~ /эт~/ вольно!; vt облегчать

easily /йизили/ adv свободно

easiness /йизинис/ n легкость

Easter /йистэ/ n пасха

eastern /йистэн/ adj восточный

easy /йизи/ adj легкий, непринужденный

easy chair /йизичээ/ n кресло

easy-going /йизигоуинг/ adj добродушный, покладистый

eat /иит/ vt есть

eatable /йитэбл/ adj съедобный

eatables /йитэблз/ n pl съестное

eau-de-Cologne /оудэкэлоун/ n одеколон

eaves /иивз/ n pl карниз

eavesdrop /йивздроп/ vi подслушивать

ebb /эб/ n отлив

ebony /эбэни/ n черное дерево

eccentric /иксентрик/ adj эксцентричный; n чудак

eccentricity /эксэктрисити/ n эксцентричность

ecclesiastical /иклийизиэстикл/ adj церковный, духовный

echo /экоу/ n эхо; vt вторить; vi отражаться

eclipse /иклипс/ n упадок; ~ of the moon (sun) /~ ов зэ муун (сан) / лунное (солнечное) затмение

economic /йикэномик/ adj экономический

economical /йикэномикл/ adj бережливый

economics /йикэномикс/ n экономика; народное хозяйство

economist /иконэмист/ n экономист

economize /иконэмайз/ vi экономить

economy /иконэми/ n хозяйство

ecstasy /экстэси/ n экстаз

eczema /экзимэ/ n экзема

eddy /эди/ n водоворот

edelweiss /эйдлвайс/ n эдельвейс

Eden /иидн/ n Эдем, рай

edge /эдж/ n край; лезвие; опушка (леса)

edging /эджинг/ n кайма

edible /эдибл/ adj съедобный

edict /йидикт/ n эдикт, указ

edification /эдификейшн/ n назидание

edifice /эдифис/ n здание

edify /эдифай/ vt поучать

edit /эдит/ vt редактировать; монтировать (фильм)

editing /эдитинг/ n редактирование

edition /идишн/ n издание

editor /эдитэ/ n редактор

editorial /эдиториэл/ adj редакционный; n передовица

educate /эдьюкейт/ vt давать образование; воспитывать

education /эдьюкейшн/ n образование

educational /эдьюкейшенл/ adj образовательный

educator /эдьюкейтэ/ n педагог

eel /иил/ n угорь

efface /ифэйс/ vt изглаживать

effect /ифект/ n действие; эффект; pl имущество; take ~ /тэйк ~/ дать (желаемый) результат

effective /ифектив/ adj эффективный

effeminate /ифеминит/ adj женоподобный

efficacious /эфикейшес/ adj эффективный

efficiency /ифишенси/ adj умелость, работоспособность

efficient /ифишент/ adj умелый, эффективный

e.g. /йиджи/ abbr например

egg /эг/ n яйцо; fried ~s /фрайд ~з/ глазунья; scrambled ~s /скрэмблд ~з/ яичница

eggshell /эгшел/ n яичная скорлупа

ego /э́гоу/ n я (сам); эго
egoism /э́гоизм/ n эгоизм
egoist /э́гоист/ n эгоист
Egyptian /иджи́пшен/ n египтянин,
    египтянка; adj египетский
eight /эйт/ num восемь
eighteen /эйти́ин/ num восемнадцать
eighteenth /эйти́инс/ ord num восемна-
    дцатый
eighth /эйтс/ ord num восьмой
eightieth /э́йтис/ ord num восьмидесятый
eighty /э́йти/ num восемьдесят
either /а́йзэ/ adj один из двух; тот или
    другой; любой; ~ ... or ... /~ ... op .../
    или... или...; ~ way /~ вэй/ и так и этак
ejaculate /иджэ́кьюлейт/ vt восклицать
ejaculation /иджэ́кьюлэ́йшн/ n изверже-
    ние
eject /иджéкт/ vt выселять; выбрасывать
elaborate /илэ́брит/ adj подробный; vt
    /илэ́бэрэйт/ тщательно разрабатывать
elapse /илэ́пс/ vt истекать
elastic /илэ́стик/ adj эластичный, упру-
    гий; n резинка
elate /илэ́йт/ vt поднимать настроение
elation /илэ́йшн/ n восторг
elbow /э́лбоу/ n локоть; vt толкать локтя-
    ми; ~ one's way /~ ванз вэй/ проталки-
    ваться
elder /э́лдэ/ adj старший; n старец; бузина
elderly /э́лдэли/ adj пожилой
eldest /э́лдист/ adj самый старший
elect /илéкт/ adj избранный; n избран-
    ник; vi избирать, выбирать
election /илéкшн/ n выборы
elector /илéктэ/ n избиратель, выборщик
electoral /илéктэрл/ adj избирательный
electric /илéктрик/ adj электрический
electrician /илектри́шн/ n электротехник
electricity /илектри́сити/ n электричество
electrify /илéктрифай/ vt электрифици-
    ровать
electrocute /илéктрэкьют/ vt убивать
    электрическим током; казнить на
    электрическом стуле

elegant /э́лигэнт/ adj элегантный, изящ-
    ный
element /э́лимент/ n элемент; стихия
elementary /э́лимéнтэри/ adj элементар-
    ный
elephant /э́лифэнт/ n слон
elevate /э́ливэйт/ vt поднимать
elevated /э́ливэйтыд/ adj возвышенный
elevation /э́ливэ́йшн/ n возвышенность
elevator /э́ливэйтэ/ n лифт
eleven /илéвн/ num одиннадцать
eleventh /илéвнс/ ord num одиннадцатый
eliminate /или́мэнейт/ vt ликвидировать
elimination /или́минéйшн/ n устранение
elite /эйли́ит/ n элита
elixir /или́ксэ/ n эликсир
elk /элк/ n лось
elm /элм/ n вяз
eloquence /э́локвэнс/ n красноречие
eloquent /э́локвэнт/ adj красноречивый
else /элс/ adv еще; кроме; what ~ /вот ~/
    что еще?; nobody ~ /но́убэди ~/ боль-
    ше никто; or ~ /ор ~/ а то; somebody ~
    /са́мбэди ~/ кто-нибудь другой
elusive /илю́юсив/ adj уклончивый
emancipate /имэ́нсипейт/ vt освобождать
emancipation /имэ́нсипéйшн/ n эманси-
    пация
embalm /имба́ам/ vt бальзамировать
embankment /имбэ́нкмент/ n набереж-
    ная
embargo /эмба́ргоу/ n эмбарго
embark /имба́рк/ vti грузить(ся); ~ upon
    /~ эпо́н/ браться (за что-л.)
embarkation /э́мбакéйшн/ n посадка, по-
    грузка
embarrass /имбэ́рэс/ vt смущать; затруд-
    нять
embarrassment /имбэ́рэсмент/ n смуще-
    ние; затруднение
embassy /э́мбэси/ n посольство
embezzle /имбéзл/ vt растрачивать
embezzlement /имбéзлмент/ n растрата
embitter /имби́тэ/ vt озлоблять

emblem /э́мблем/ n эмблема

embodiment /имбо́димент/ n воплощение

embody /имбо́ди/ vt воплощать

emboss /имбо́с/ vt выбивать, чеканить

embrace /имбре́йс/ n объятия; vt обнимать; охватывать

embroider /имбро́йдэ/ vt вышивать

embroidery /имбро́йдэри/ n вышивка

embryo /э́мбрио/ n зародыш

emerald /э́мерлд/ n изумруд

emerge /имёёдж/ vi всплывать, возникать

emergency /имёёдженси/ n крайность; in case of ~ /ин кейс ов ~/ при крайней необходимости; ~ brake /~ брейк/ запасной тормоз; ~ exit /~ э́ксит/ запасный выход; ~ landing /~ лэ́ндинг/ вынужденная посадка; ~ store /~ стор/ неприкосновенный запас; ~ powers /~ па́уэз/ чрезвычайные полномочия

emery /э́мери/ n наждак

emery paper /э́мерипэ́йпэ/ n наждачная бумага

emigrant /э́мигрэнт/ n эмигрант

emigrate /э́мигрэйт/ vi эмигрировать

emigration /э́мигрэ́йшн/ n эмиграция

eminence /э́миненс/ n возвышенность; высокое положение; высокопреосвященство

eminent /э́минент/ adj выдающийся

emission /ими́шн/ n эмиссия

emit /ими́т/ vt испускать; выпускать (деньги)

emotion /имо́ушн/ n волнение

emotional /имо́ушенл/ adj эмоциональный

emperor /э́мперэ/ n император

emphasis /э́мфэсис/ n ударение

emphasize /э́мфэсайз/ vt подчеркивать

emphatic /имфэ́тик/ adj выразительный

empire /э́мпайе/ n империя

employ /импло́й/ n служба; vt нанимать; применять; be ~ed by /би ~д бай/ работать у

employee /э́мплойи́и/ n служащий

employer /импло́йе/ n наниматель

employment /импло́ймент/ n служба; использование; full ~ /фул ~/ полная занятость

emporium /эмпо́ориэм/ n большой магазин

empower /импа́уэ/ vt уполномочивать

empress /э́мприс/ n императрица

emptiness /э́мтинис/ n пустота

empty /э́мти/ adj пустой; vt опорожнять

emulate /э́мьюлейт/ vt соперничать с

emulsion /има́лшн/ n эмульсия

enable /инэ́йбл/ vt давать возможность

enact /инэ́кт/ vt постановлять; ставить на сцене

enactment /инэ́ктмент/ n постановление; принятие закона

enamel /инэ́мл/ n эмаль

encamp /инкэ́мп/ vi располагаться лагерем

encampment /инкэ́мпмент/ n лагерь

encase /инкэ́йс/ vt упаковывать в ящик

enchain /инчэ́йн/ vt заковывать

enchant /инча́ант/ vt очаровывать

enchanter /инча́антэ/ n чародей

enchanting /инча́антинг/ adj прелестный

enchantment /инча́антмент/ n очарование

encircle /инсёёкл/ vt окружать

enclose /инкло́уз/ vt огораживать; прилагать (к письму, документу)

enclosure /инкло́уже/ n ограда; приложение (к письму, документу)

encore /онко́р/ interj бис!

encounter /инка́унтэ/ n (неожиданная) встреча; vt наталкиваться на

encourage /инка́ридж/ vt ободрять

encouragement /инка́риджмент/ n поощрение

encroach on /инкро́уч он/ vi покушаться на

encroachment /инкро́учмент/ n вторжение

encrust /инкра́ст/ vt инкрустировать

encumber /инка́мбэ/ vt обременять

encumbrance /инка́мбрэнс/ n затруднение

encyclopedia /энса́йклопи́идье/ n энциклопедия

end /энд/ n конец; in the /ин зы ~/ в конце концов; make both ~s meet /мэйк бо́ус ~з миит/ сводить концы с концами; vti конча́ть(ся)

endanger /индэ́йнжэ/ vt подвергать опасности

endeavour /индэ́ве/ n (энергичная) попытка, усилие; vi пытаться

ending /э́ндинг/ n окончание

endless /э́ндлис/ adj бесконечный

endorse /индо́рс/ vt подписывать; одобрять

endurance /индью́оэрэнс/ n выносливость; прочность

endure /индью́оэ/ vt выдерживать

enema /э́нимэ/ n клизма

enemy /э́ними/ n враг; adj вражеский

energetic /энэджэ́тик/ adj энергичный

energy /э́нэджи/ n энергия

enforce /инфо́рс/ vt проводить в жизнь

enforcement /инфо́рсмент/ n принуждение

engage /ингэ́йдж/ vt нанимать; обязывать; be ~d /би ~д/ быть занятым; обручиться

engaged /ингэ́йджд/ adj занятый; помолвленный

engagement /ингэ́йджмент/ n обязательство; помолвка; (воен.) стычка; ~ ring /~ ринг/ обручальное кольцо

engender /индже́ндэ/ vt порождать

engine /э́нджин/ n мотор, двигатель; паровоз

engine driver /э́нджиндра́йвэ/ n машинист

engineer /э́нджини́э/ n инженер

English /и́нглиш/ n английский язык; adj английский; the ~ /зы ~/ n pl англичане

Englishman /и́нглишмэн/ n англичанин

Englishwoman /и́нглишву́мэн/ n англичанка

engrave /ингрэ́йв/ vt гравировать

engraver /ингрэ́йвэ/ n гравер

engraving /ингрэ́йвинг/ n гравюра

engross /ингро́ус/ vt завладевать (вниманием); be ~ ed in (by) /би ~т ин (бай)/ быть поглощенным чем-то

engulf /инга́лф/ vt поглощать

enhance /инха́анс/ vt повышать

enjoy /инджо́й/ vt наслаждаться; I ~ed talking to her /ай ~д то́окинг ту хё/ мне разговор с ней понравился

enjoyable /инджо́йэбл/ adj приятный

enjoyment /инджо́ймент/ n удовольствие

enlarge /инла́рдж/ vti увеличивать(ся)

enlargement /инла́рджмент/ n увеличение

enlighten /инла́йтн/ vt просвещать

enlightened /инла́йтнд/ adj просвещенный

enlightenment /инла́йтнмент/ n просвещение

enlist /инли́ст/ vi поступать на военную службу

enliven /инла́йвн/ vt оживлять

enmity /э́нмити/ n вражда

ennoble /ино́убл/ vt облагораживать

enormous /ино́рмэс/ adj громадный

enough /ина́ф/ adj достаточный; adv довольно; ~ and to spare /~ энд ту спээ/ более чем достаточно

enquire /инква́йе/ vi спрашивать, узнавать

enquiry /инква́йери/ n наведение справок; расследование; ~ office /~ о́фис/ справочное бюро

enrage /инрэ́йдж/ vt бесить

enrapture /инрэ́пче/ vt восхищать

enrich /инри́ч/ vt обогащать; удобрять

enrol(l) /инро́ул/ vt вербовать; вносить в список

ensign /э́нсайн/ n флаг; младший лейтенант (в.-м. флота)

enslave /инслэ́йв/ vt порабощать

enslavement /инслэ́йвмент/ n порабощение

ensue /инсью́ю/ vi следовать; получаться в результате

ensure /иншуэ́/ vt обеспечивать

entail /интэ́йл/ vt влечь за собой

entangle /интэ́нгл/ vt запутывать

entanglement /интэ́нглмент/ n затруднение

enter /э́нтэ/ vti входить (в); поступать (в институт); вносить (в книгу)

enterprize /э́нтэпрайз/ n предприятие; предпринимательство

enterprizing /э́нтэпрайзинг/ adj предприимчивый

entertain /э́нтэтэ́йн/ vt развлекать; принимать (гостей)

entertaining /э́нтэтэ́йнинг/ adj занимательный

entertainment /э́нтэтэ́йнмент/ n развлечение; прием (гостей); банкет

enthusiasm /инфью́юзиэзм/ n энтузиазм

enthusiast /инфью́юзиэст/ n энтузиаст

enthusiastic /инфью́юзиэ́стик/ adj восторженный

entice /интáйс/ vt увлекать, соблазнять

enticement /интáйсмент/ n соблазн

entire /интáйе/ adj полный, весь

entirely /интáйели/ adv полностью

entitle /интáйтл/ vt озаглавливать; be ~d to /би ~д ту/ иметь право на

entrails /э́нтрэйлз/ n pl внутренности

entrance /э́нтрэнс/ n вход; ~ exam /~ игзэ́м/ вступительный экзамен; ~ hall /~ хоол/ вестибюль

entreat /интри́ит/ vt умолять

entreaty /интри́ити/ n мольба

entrust /интрáст/ vt поручать

entry /э́нтри/ n вход; запись; no ~ /нóу ~/ проезда нет; ~ permit /~ пёрмит/ разрешение на въезд

enumerate /иньюю́мерейт/ vt перечислять

enumeration /иньюю́мерéйшн/ n перечисление; перечень

envelop /инвéлэп/ vt заворачивать

envelope /э́нвилоуп/ n конверт

enviable /э́нвиэбл/ adj завидный

envious /э́нвиэс/ adj завистливый

environment /инвáйерэнмент/ n среда, окружение

environs /э́нвирэнз/ n окрестности

envisage /инви́зидж/ vt предусматривать

envoy /э́нвой/ n посланник

envy /э́нви/ n зависть; vt завидовать

epic /э́пик/ adj эпический; n поэма

epicure /э́пикьюэ/ n эпикуреец

epidemic /э́пидéмик/ adj эпидемический; n эпидемия

epigram /э́пигрэм/ n эпиграмма

epilepsy /э́пилепси/ n эпилепсия

epilogue /э́пилог/ n эпилог

Epiphany /ипи́фэни/ n богоявление; крещение (праздник)

episode /э́писоуд/ n эпизод

epithet /э́пифет/ n эпитет

epitome /ипи́тэми/ n конспект; олицетворение

epoch /и́ипок/ n эпоха

equal /и́иквэл/ adj равный; n ровня; vt равняться

equality /иквóлити/ n равенство

equalize /и́иквэлайз/ vt уравнивать

equally /и́иквэли/ adv поровну

equation /иквэ́йшн/ n уравнение

equator /иквэ́йтэ/ n экватор

equilibrium /и́иквили́бриэм/ n равновесие

equinox /и́иквинокс/ n равноденствие

equip /икви́п/ vt снаряжать; оборудовать; вооружать (знаниями)

equipment /икви́пмент/ n оборудование

equivalence /икви́вэлэнс/ n равноценность

equivalent /икви́вэлэнт/ adj равносильный; n эквивалент

equivocal /икви́вэкл/ adj двусмысленный

era /и́эрэ/ n эра

eradicate /ирэ́дикейт/ vt искоренять

erase /ирэ́йз/ vt стирать

eraser /ирэ́йзэ/ n ластик

erect /ирэ́кт/ adj прямой, поднятый; vt воздвигать

ermine /ёрмин/ n горностай
erode /ироуд/ vt разъедать
erosion /ироужн/ n эрозия
erotic /иротик/ adj эротический
err /ёр/ vi ошибаться
errand /эрэнд/ n поручение
errand boy /эрэндбой/ n рассыльный
erratum /эраатэм/ n опечатка
erroneous /ироуньес/ adj ошибочный
error /эрэ/ n ошибка
erudite /эрудайт/ n эрудит
erudition /эрудишн/ n эрудиция
erupt /ирапт/ vi извергаться
eruption /ирапшн/ n извержение; сыпь
escalator /эскэлэйтэ/ n эскалатор
escape /искейп/ n побег; vt избегать, из-
    бавляться от; vi бежать (из тюрьмы)
escort /эскорт/ n эскорт; /искорт/ vt со-
    провождать
Eskimo /эскимоу/ n эскимос; эскимоска
especial /испешл/ adj специальный
especially /испешели/ adv особенно
espionage /эспиэнааж/ n шпионаж
essay /эсэй/ n очерк
essence /эснс/ n сущность; эссенция
essential /иснншл/ adj существенный
establish /истэблиш/ vt устанавливать;
    учреждать
established /истэблишт/ adj установлен-
    ный; упрочившийся
establishment /истэблишмент/ n учреж-
    дение; the ~ /зы ~/ правящие круги
estate /истэйт/ n имение; имущество;
    personal ~ /пёрснл ~/ движимость; real
    ~ /риэл ~/ недвижимость
esteem /истиим/ n уважение; vt уважать
estimate /эстимит/ n оценка, смета; /эс-
    тимэйт/ vt оценивать
Estonian /эстоуньен/ n эстонец; эстонка;
    эстонский язык; adj эстонский
estrange /истрэйнж/ vt отдалять, делать
    чуждым
estuary /эстьюэри/ n устье реки
etcetera, etc. /итсэтрэ/ и так далее (и т.д.)
etch /этч/ vt гравировать
etcher /эче/ n гравер

etching /эчинг/ n гравюра
eternal /итёрнл/ adj вечный
eternity /итёрнити/ n вечность
ether /ийфэ/ n эфир
ethereal /ифиэриэл/ adj эфирный
ethics /этикс/ n этика
Ethiopian /ийфиоупьен/ n эфиоп; adj
    эфиопский
etiquette /этикет/ n этикет
ethnic /этник/ adj этнический
ethnographer /этнографэ/ n этнограф
ethnologist /этнолэджист/ n этнолог
ethyl /эфил/ n этил; ~ alcohol /~ /элкэ-
    хол/ винный спирт
Etruscan /итраскэн/ n этруск; этрусский
    язык; adj этрусский
etymologist /этимолэджист/ n этимолог
eucalyptus /ююкэлиптэс/ n эвкалипт
Eucharist /ююкэрист/ n причастие
eulogy /ююлэджи/ n панегирик
eunuch /ююнэк/ n евнух
European /юэрэпиэн/ n европеец; adj
    европейский
evacuate /ивэкьюэйт/ vt эвакуировать
evacuation /ивэкьюэйшн/ n эвакуация
evade /ивэйд/ vt уклоняться от; обходить
    (закон)
evaluate /ивэльюэйт/ vt оценивать
evaluation /ивэльюэйшн/ n оценка
evangelical /ивэнджеликл/ adj еван-
    гельский; протестантский
evangelist /ивэнжилист/ n евангелист
evaporate /ивэпэрэйт/ vi испаряться
evaporation /ивэпэрэйшн/ n испарение
evasion /ивэйжн/ n уклонение
evasive /ивэйсив/ adj уклончивый
eve /иив/ n канун; on the ~ /он зы ~/
    накануне; Christmas ~ /крисмэс ~/ со-
    чельник
even /ийвэн/ adj ровный; одинаковый;
    четный (число); be ~ with /би ~ виз/
    сводить счеты с; adv даже; vt выравни-
    вать
evening /ийвнинг/ n вечер; good ~! /гуд
    ~/ добрый вечер!; ~ party /~ парти/
    вечеринка

evenly /и́ивенли/ adv равномерно
event /иве́нт/ n событие; случай; at all ~s /эт оол ~с/ во всяком случае
eventful /иве́нтфул/ adj полный событий
eventual /иве́нчюэл/ adj возможный; окончательный
ever /э́вэ/ adv когда-либо; ~ since /~ синс/ с тех пор; for ~ /фор ~/ навсегда; hardly ~ / ха́адли ~/ очень редко
evergreen /э́вэгриин/ adj вечнозеленый
everlasting /э́вэла́астинг/ adj вечный
every /э́ври/ adj каждый; ~ now and then /~ на́у энд зэн/ то и дело; ~ other day /~ а́зэ дэй/ через день
everybody /э́врибоди/ pron каждый, всякий; все
everything /э́врисинг/ pron все
everywhere /э́вривээ/ adv повсюду, везде
evict /иви́кт/ vt выселять
eviction /иви́кшн/ n выселение
evidence /э́видэнс/ n свидетельство; улика
evident /э́видэнт/ adj очевидный
evidently /э́видэнтли/ adv ясно
evil /иивл/ adj злой, дурной; ~ doer /~ ду́э/ злодей; n зло
evolution /и́ивэлю́юшн/ n эволюция
evolutionary /и́ивэлю́юшнэри/ adj эволюционный
evolve /иво́лв/ vti развивать(ся)
ewe /юю/ n овца
exact /игзэ́кт/ adj точный; vt взыскивать
exacting /игзэ́ктинг/ adj взыскательный
exactly /игзэ́ктли/ adv точно
exactness /игзэ́ктнис/ n точность
exaggerate /игзэ́джерейт/ vt преувеличивать
exaggeration /игзэ́джере́йшн/ n преувеличение
exalt /игзо́олт/ vt превозносить
exaltation /э́гзолтэ́йшн/ n возвеличение; экзальтация
examination /игзэ́мине́йшн/ n экзамен; осмотр
examine /игзэ́мин/ vt исследовать; экзаменовать

example /игза́ампл/ n пример; for ~ /фор ~/ например
excavator /э́кскэвэйтэ/ n экскаватор
exceed /икси́ид/ vt превышать
exceeding /икси́идинг/ adj чрезмерный
excel /иксэ́л/ vt превосходить; vi отличаться
excellence /э́ксленс/ adj превосходство; выдающееся мастерство
Excellency /э́ксленси/ n превосходительство
excellent /э́ксленнт/ adj превосходный, отличный
except /иксэ́пт/ prep за исключением; кроме; vt исключать
exception /иксэ́пшн/ n исключение
exceptional /иксэ́пшнл/ adj исключительный
excerpt /э́ксэрпт/ n отрывок
excess /иксэ́с/ n излишек; эксцесс; ~ luggage /~ ла́гидж/ багаж выше нормы; ~ fare /~ фээ/ доплата; to ~ /ту ~/ до крайности
excessive /иксэ́сив/ adj чрезмерный
exchange /иксче́йндж/ n обмен; биржа; bill of ~ /бил ов ~/ вексель; ~ rate /~ рэйт/ валютный курс; vt обменивать
excite /икса́йт/ vt возбуждать
excitement /икса́йтмент/ n возбуждение
exciting /икса́йтинг/ adj захватывающий
exclaim /икскла́йм/ vi восклицать
exclamation /э́ксклэмэ́йшн/ n восклицание
exclude /икскл́ууд/ vt исключать
exclusion /икскл́ужн/ n исключение
exclusive /икскл́уусив/ adj исключительный
excursion /икскёршн/ n экскурсия
excusable /икскь́юзэбл/ adj простительный
excuse /икскь́юс/ n извинение; отговорка; /икскь́юз/ vt прощать; ~ me! /~ ми/ извините!

execute /э́ксикьют/ vt исполнять; казнить
execution /э́ксикью́юшн/ n исполнение; казнь
executioner /э́ксикью́юшнэ/ n палач
executive /игзэ́кьютив/ n исполнительная власть; adj исполнительный
executor /игзэ́кьютэ/ n душеприказчик
exemplary /игзэ́мплэри/ adj образцовый
exemplify /игзэ́мплифай/ vt подтверждать примером
exempt /игзэ́мт/ adj освобожденный; tax ~ /тэкс ~/ освбожденный от налогов; vt освобождать (от обязанности и т.п.)
exemption /игзэ́мшн/ n освобождение
exercise /э́ксэсайз/ n упражнение; vti упражнять(ся)
exert /игзёрт/ vt напрягать; ~ oneself /~ вансэ́лф/ напрягаться
exertion /игзёшн/ n усилие
exhalation /э́ксэлэ́йшн/ n выдох
exhale /эксхе́йл/ vt выдыхать
exhaust /игзо́ост/ n выхлоп; vt истощать; исчерпывать
exhausted /игзо́остыд/ adj изнуренный
exhaustion /игзо́осчн/ n изнеможение
exhaustive /игзо́остив/ adj исчерпывающий
exhaust pipe /игзо́остпайп/ n выхлопная труба
exhibit /игзи́бит/ n экспонат; vt выставлять
exhibition /э́ксиби́шн/ n выставка
exile /экса́йл/ n ссылка; изгнанник; vt ссылать
exist /игзи́ст/ vi существовать
existence /игзи́стэнс/ n существование
existent /игзи́стэнт/, existing /игзи́стинг/ adj существующий
exit /э́ксит/ n выход; ~ visa /~ ви́изэ/ выездная виза
exodus /э́ксэдэс/ n массовый отъезд; (библ.) исход
exorcism /э́ксосизм/ n изгнание духов

exotic /эгзо́тик/ adj экзотический
expand /икспэ́нд/ vti расширять(ся)
expanse /икспэ́нс/ n пространство
expansion /икспэ́ншн/ n расширение; экспансия
expect /икспе́кт/ vt ожидать
expectancy /икспе́ктэнси/ n ожидание
expectant /икспе́ктэнт/ adj ожидающий; ~ mother /~ ма́ззэ/ беременная женщина
expectation /э́кспектэ́йшн/ n ожидание
expedient /икспи́идьент/ adj целесообразный; n средство для достижения цели
expedite /э́кспидайт/ vt ускорять
expedition /э́кспиди́шн/ n экспедиция; посылка, отправка
expel /икспе́л/ vt исключать
expend /икспе́нд/ vt тратить
expenditure /икспе́ндиче/ n расходование; трата
expense /икспе́нс/ n расход; at our ~ /эт а́уэ ~/ за наш счет
expensive /икспе́нсив/ adj дорогой
experience /икспи́эриэнс/ n (жизненный) опыт, переживание; vt переживать
experiment /икспе́римент/ n эксперимент; vi производить опыты
experimental /экспе́риме́нтл/ adj экспериментальный
expert /э́кспёт/ adj опытный; n эксперт
expire /икспа́йе/ vi истекать (о сроке)
explain /иксплэ́йн/ vt объяснять
explanation /э́ксплэнэ́йшн/ n объяснение
explanatory /иксплэ́нэтри/ adj объяснительный
explode /иксплóуд/ vt взрывать; vi взрываться, разражаться (смехом и т.п.)
exploit /э́ксплойт/ n подвиг; /иксплó йт/ vt эксплуатировать
exploitation /э́ксплойтэ́йшн/ n эксплуатация
exploration /э́ксплорэ́йшн/ n исследование

explore /иксплóр/ vt исследовать

explorer /иксплóорэ/ n исследователь

explosion /иксплóужн/ n взрыв

explosive /иксплóусив/ adj взрывчатый; n взрывчатка

export /э́кспорт/ n экспорт; /экспóрт/ vt экспортировать

exporter /экспóртэ/ n экспортер

expose /икспóуз/ vt выставлять; подвергать; разоблачать; давать выдержку

exposition /э́кспэзи́шн/ n выставка; изложение; (фото) экспозиция

exposure /икспóуже/ n разоблачение; (фото) выдержка

express /икспрэ́с/ n ж.-д. экспресс; federal ~ /фéдэрэл ~/ срочная почта; adj срочный; недвусмысленный; vt выражать

expression /икспрэ́шн/ n выражение

expressive /икспрэ́сив/ adj выразительный

expulsion /икспáлшн/ n изгнание

exquisite /э́ксквизит/ adj изысканный, прелестный

extant /экстáнт/ adj сохранившийся, дошедший до нас

extempore /экстэ́мпэри/ adj импровизированный; adv экспромтом

extend /икстэ́нд/ vt протягивать; продлевать; vi простираться

extension /икстэ́ншн/ n протяжение; продление; пристройка; добавочный номер (телефона)

extensive /икстэ́нсив/ adj обширный

extent /икстэ́нт/ n протяжение; to what ~ /ту вот ~/ до какой степени

exterior /эксти́эриэ/ adj внешний; n внешность; экстерьер

exterminate /экстэ́рминэйт/ vt истреблять

extermination /экстёрминэ́йшн/ n уничтожение

external /экстэ́рнл/ adj внешний; ~ trade /~ трэйд/ внешняя торговля

extinct /икстúнкт/ adj исчезнувший

extinguish /икстú́нгвиш/ vt тушить; уничтожать

extinguisher /икстú́нгвишэ/ n огнетушитель

extirpate /э́кстёрпейт/ vt искоренять; вырывать с корнем; истреблять

extirpation /э́кстёрпейшн/ n искоренение; истребление

extol /икстóл/ vt превозносить

extort /икстóрт/ vt вымогать (деньги); выпытывать (секрет)

extortion /икстóршн/ n вымогательство; назначение грабительских цен

extortionate /икстóошнит/ adj вымогательский; грабительский (о ценах)

extortioner /икстóошнэ/ n вымогатель; спекулянт

extra /э́кстрэ/ adj добавочный; особый; ~ charge /~ чардж/ доплата; adv дополнительно; n экстренный выпуск (газеты)

extract /э́кстрэкт/ n отрывок; экстракт; /икстрэ́кт/ vt удалять (зуб); вырывать (согласие); (мат.) извлекать

extradition /э́кстрэди́шн/ n выдача (преступника)

extraordinary /икстрóоднри/ adj чрезвычайный, внеочередной; необычный

extravagance /икстрэ́вигэнс/ n расточительство; сумасбродство

extravagant /икстрэ́вигент/ adj расточительный; экстравагантный

extreme /икстри́им/ adj крайний; n крайность

extremely /икстри́имли/ adv чрезвычайно

extremist /икстри́имист/ n экстремист

extremity /икстрэ́мити/ n край; крайность; pl конечности

extricate /э́кстрикейт/ vt выпутывать; ~ oneself /~ вансэ́лф/ выпутываться

exult /игзáлт/ vi ликовать

exultation /э́гзалтэ́йшн/ n ликование

eye /ай/ n глаз; глазок (в двери); ушко (иглы); keep an ~ on /киип эн ~ он/ следить за; vt рассматривать

eyeball /а́йбол/ n глазное яблоко

eyebrow /а́йбрау/ n бровь

eyelash /а́йлэш/ n ресница

eyelid /а́йлид/ n веко

eyesight /а́йсайт/ n зрение

eyewitness /а́йви́тнис/ n очевидец

F

fable /фэйбл/ n басня

fabric /фэ́брик/ n ткань; структура

fabricate /фэ́брикейт/ vt фабриковать

fabrication /фэ́брике́йшн/ n подделка

fabulous /фэ́бьюлэс/ adj баснословный

face /фэйс/ n лицо; внешний вид; лицевая сторона; фасад; циферблат; наглость; ~ cream /~ криим/ крем для лица; make ~s /мэйк ~ыз/ гримасничать; ~ value /~ вэ́лью/ номинальная стоимость; vt стоять лицом к, смело встречать; ~ the facts /~ зэ фэктс/ смотреть правде в глаза

facet /фэ́сит/ n грань; аспект

facial /фэйшл/ adj лицевой

facilitate /фэси́литэйт/ vt содействовать

facility /фэси́лити/ n легкость; pl удобства

facing /фэ́йсинг/ n (лицевая) отделка

facsimile /фэкси́мили/ n факсимиле

fact /фэкт/ n факт; in ~ /ин ~/ на самом же деле...

faction /фэкшн/ n фракция; клика

factor /фэ́ктэ/ n фактор

factory /фэ́ктэри/ n фабрика, завод

factual /фэ́ктьюел/ adj действительный

faculty /фэ́кэлти/ n способность; факультет

fade /фэйд/ vi увядать; постепенно исчезать

fading /фэ́йдинг/ n затухание

fail /фэйл/ vt обманывать ожидания, подводить; vi потерпеть неудачу; проваливаться (на экзаменах); n: without ~ /виза́ут ~/ непременно

failure /фэ́йлье/ n неудача, провал; неудачник

faint /фэйнт/ adj слабый, тусклый; n потеря сознания; vi падать в обморок

fair /фэə/ adj красивый; справедливый; белокурый; ~ copy /~ ко́пи/ чистовик; play ~ /плэй ~/ играть честно; n ярмарка

fairly /фэ́эли/ adv справедливо; довольно

fairy /фэ́эри/ n фея; adj волшебный; ~ tale /~ тэйл/ сказка

faith /фэйф/ n вера, доверие; in good ~ /ин гуд ~/ честно

faithful /фэ́йсфул/ adj преданный

faithfully /фэ́йсфули/ adv честно; yours ~ /йооз ~/ с искренним уважением (в конце письма)

faithless /фэ́йслис/ adj вероломный

fake /фэйк/ n фальшивка; vt подделывать

falcon /фоолкн/ n сокол

fall /фоол/ n падение; осень; водопад; vi падать, понижаться; ~ asleep /~ эсли́ип/ засыпать; ~ behind /~ биха́йнд/ отставать; ~ in love with /~ ин лав виз/ влюбляться в; ~ sick /~ сик/ заболевать

fallen /фоолн/ adj падший

fall-out /фо́олаут/ n радиоактивные осадки

false /фоолс/ n ложный; ошибочный; фальшивый; поддельный; искусственный

falsehood /фо́олсхуд/ n ложь; фальшь

falsify /фо́олсифай/ vt фальсифицировать

falter /фо́олтэ/ vi спотыкаться; запинаться

fame /фэйм/ n слава

famed /фэймд/ adj знаменитый

familiar /фэми́лье/ adj знакомый; близкий; фамильярный

familiarity /фэми́лиэ́рити/ n знакомство; фамильярность; осведомленность

familiarize /фэми́льерайз/ vt ознакомить

family /фэ́мили/ n семья; adj семейный; ~ man /~ мэн/ семьянин; ~ tree /~ трии/ родословная

famine /фэ́мин/ n голод

famous /фэ́ймэс/ adj знаменитый

fan /фэн/ n веер; вентилятор; поклонник, болельщик; vt: ~ the flame /~ зэ флэйм/ разжигать страсти

fanatic /фэнэ́тик/ n фанатик

fancied /фэ́нсид/ adj воображаемый

fanciful /фэ́нсифул/ adj причудливый

fancy /фэ́нси/ adj модный; ~-dress ball /~ дрэс боол/ маскарад; n воображение, фантазия; каприз; take a ~ to /тэйк э ~ ту/ увлекаться

fang /фэнг/ n клык; ядовитый зуб

fantastic /фэнтэ́стик/ adj фантастический

fantasy /фэ́нтэси/ n фантазия

far /фар/ adj далекий; adv далеко; by ~ /бай ~/ намного; ~ better /~ бе́тэ/ гораздо лучше; ~ from it /~ фром ит/ отнюдь нет; in so ~ as /ин со́у ~ эз/ поскольку; go too ~ /го́у туу ~/ заходить слишком далеко

farce /фарс/ n фарс

fare /фээ/ n плата за проезд; bill of ~ /бил ов ~/ меню

farewell /фээвэл/ n прощание; say ~ /сэй ~/ прощаться; interj прощай(те)!; adj прощальный

farm /фарм/ n ферма, хутор; collective ~ /кэле́ктив ~/ колхоз

farmer /фа́рмэ/ n фермер

farmhand /фа́рмхэнд/ n сельскохозяйственный рабочий

farming /фа́рминг/ n сельское хозяйство

farther /фа́азэ/ adj более отдаленный; дальнейший; adv дальше

farthest /фа́азист/ adj самый дальний; adv дальше всего (всех)

fascinate /фэ́синэйт/ vt очаровывать

fascinating /фэ́синэйтинг/ adj очаровательный

fascination /фэсинэйшн/ n очарование

fascism /фэ́шизм/ n фашизм

fascist /фэ́шист/ n фашист

fashion /фэшн/ n мода; образ; манера; out of ~ /а́ут ов ~/ старомодный

fashionable /фэ́шнэбл/ adj модный

fast /фааст/ adj быстрый, скорый; adv крепко, прочно; be ~ asleep /би ~ эсли́-ип/ крепко спать; vt поститься; n пост; break one's ~ /брэйк ванз ~/ разговляться

fasten /фаасн/ vt прикреплять; застегивать

fastener /фа́аснэ/ n задвижка; застежка

fastidious /фэсти́диэс/ adj привередливый

fat /фэт/ adj жирный, толстый; n жир

fatal /фэйтл/ adj роковой, фатальный

fatalist /фэ́йтэлист/ n фаталист

fatality /фэтэ́лити/ n несчастный случай, смерть

fate /фэйт/ n судьба, рок

fateful /фэ́йтфул/ adj роковой; важный

father /фа́азэ/ n отец; vt быть автором

father-in-law /фа́азэринло/ n свекор; тесть

fatherland /фа́азэлэнд/ n отчизна

fatherly /фа́азэли/ adj отеческий

fatigue /фэти́иг/ n утомление; vt изнурять

fatness /фэ́тнис/ n тучность

fatten /фэтн/ vt откармливать (на убой); vi толстеть

fatty /фэ́ти/ n толстяк

fault /фоолт/ n недостаток; ошибка; вина; (эл.) замыкание; (тех.) повреждение; be at ~ /би эт ~/ быть виновным

fault-finder /фо́олтфа́йндэ/ n придира

faultless /фо́олтлис/ adj безупречный

faulty /фо́олти/ adj порочный

fauna /фо́онэ/ n фауна

favor /фэ́йвэ/ n расположение, милость; in ~ of /ин ~ ов/ в пользу; vt покровительствовать; предпочитать

favorable /фэ́йвэрэбл/ adj благоприятный

favorite /фэ́йвэрит/ adj излюбленный; n фаворит

fear /фиэ/ n страх; for ~ of /фо ~ ов/ из боязни; vt бояться

fearful /фиэфул/ adj страшный; испуганный

fearless /фиэлис/ adj неустрашимый

fearsome /фиэсэм/ adj грозный

feasibility /фиизэбилити/ n возможность; осуществимость

feasible /фиизэбл/ adj выполнимый

feast /фиист/ n пир, праздник; vi пировать, наслаждаться

feat /фиит/ n подвиг

feather /фёзэ/ n перо; birds of a ~ /бёрдз ов э ~/ одного поля ягоды

featherbed /фёзэбед/ n перина

featherweight /фёзэвэйт/ n полулегкий вес, "вес пера"

feathery /фёзэри/ adj пернатый; перистый

feature /фииче/ n особенность, черта; pl черты лица; ~film /~ филм/ художественный фильм; vt изображать; vi участвовать

February /фёбруэри/ n февраль

federal /фёдэрл/ adj федеральный

federation /фёдэрэйшн/ n федерация

fee /фии/ n гонорар; членский взнос; плата (за учение)

feeble /фиибл/ adj хилый

feebleminded/фииблмайндыд/ adj слабоумный

feeble-mindedness /фииблмайндыднис/ n слабоумие

feed /фиид/ n питание, корм; (тех.) подача материала; vt питать, кормить; vi питаться; I am fed up /ай эм фед ап/ надоело

feeder /фиидэ/ n едок

feel /фиил/ n чутье, ощущение; vt чувствовать, ощущать; vi чувствовать себя; I ~ cold /ай ~ коулд/ мне холодно; I ~ like sleeping /ай ~ лайк слиипинг/ мне хочется спать

feeling /фиилинг/ n чувство

feign /фейн/ vt выдумывать; ~ an excuse /~ эн икскьююс/ придумывать оправдание; vi притворяться, симулировать

feint /фейнт/ n притворство

felicitation /филиситэйшн/ n поздравление

felicitous /филиситэс/ adj удачный; уместный

felicity /филисити/ n блаженство

fell /фел/ vt рубить

fellow /фёлоу/ n товарищ; собрат; парень; nice ~ /найс ~/ славный малый

fellow-countryman /фёлоукантримэн/ n соотечественник

fellow-traveller /фёлоутрэвлэ/ n попутчик

fellowship /фёлоушип/ n братство; стипендия

felon /фёлэн/ n уголовный преступник

felony /фёлэни/ n уголовное преступление

felt /фелт/ n фетр

female /фиимэйл/ adj женский; n женщина; (зоол.) самка

feminine /фёминин/ adj женский; женственный

femur /фиимэ/ n бедро

fence /фенс/ n забор, изгородь; vt огораживать; vi фехтовать

fencer /фёнсэ/ n фехтовальщик

fencing /фёнсинг/ n фехтование; изгородь

fender /фёндэ/ n решетка; крыло (автомобиля)

fennel /фенл/ n укроп

ferment /фёрмент/ n брожение; /фемёнт/ vt вызывать брожение в; (образн.) возбуждать; vi бродить, (образн.) быть в возбуждении

fermentation /фёрментэйшн/ n брожение

fern /фёрн/ n папоротник

ferocious /фероушес/ adj свирепый

ferocity /феросити/ n дикость, лютость

ferry /фёри/ n паром; vt переправлять

fertile /фёртайл/ adj плодородный

fertility /фети́лити/ n плодородие

fertilize /фёртилайз/ vt удобрять; (биол.) оплодотворять

fertilizer /фёртилайзэ/ n удобрение

fervent /фёрвент/ adj пылкий

fervour /фёрвэ/ n усердие

festival /фе́стивл/ n фестиваль

festive /фе́стив/ adj праздничный

festivity /фести́вити/ n веселье, праздничность; pl торжества

festoon /фесту́ун/ n гирлянда

fetch /феч/ vt принести, сходить за

fetish /фи́итиш/ n фетиш

fetter /фе́тэ/ vt заковывать

fetters /фе́тэз/ n оковы; (образн.) путы

feud /фьююд/ n междоусобица

feudal /фьюю́дл/ adj феодальный

feudalism /фью́юдэлизм/ n феодализм

fever /фи́ивэ/ n лихорадка

feverish /фи́ивэриш/ adj лихорадочный

few /фьюю/ adj немногие, мало; a ~ /э ~/ немного; quite a ~ /квайт э ~/ много

fiancé /фиа́ансэй/ n жених

fiancée /фиа́ансэй/ n невеста

fibber /фи́бэ/ n враль

fibre /фа́йбэ/ n волокно

fibrous /фа́йбрэс/ adj волокнистый

fiction /фикшн/ n вымысел; беллетристика

fictitious /фикти́шес/ adj фиктивный; воображаемый

fiddle /фидл/ n скрипка; interj вздор!

fiddler /фи́длэ/ n скрипач

fidelity /фиде́лити/ n верность; точность, правильность

fidget /фи́джит/ n непоседа; vi ерзать

fidgety /фи́джити/ adj беспокойный

field /фиилд/ n поле; область, сфера деятельности

field-marshal /фи́илдма́ршл/ n фельдмаршал

fiend /фиинд/ n дьявол

fierce /фи́эс/ adj свирепый; неистовый, сильный

fiery /фа́йери/ adj огненный; пламенный

fifteen /фифти́ин/ num пятнадцать

fifteenth /фифти́инс/ ord num пятнадцатый

fifth /фифс/ ord num пятый

fiftieth /фифти́с/ ord num пятидесятый

fifty /фи́фти/ num пятьдесят; ~ fifty /~ фи́фти/ пополам

fig /фиг/ n инжир, фига

fight /файт/ n бой, драка; (образн.) борьба; vt драться, сражаться, бороться с

fighter /фа́йтэ/ n борец; боец; (авиа) истребитель

fig-leaf /фи́глиф/ n фиговый лист

figurative /фи́гъюрэтив/ adj фигуральный; изобразительный; пластический

figure /фи́гэ/ n фигура; цифра; рисунок

filament /фи́лэмент/ n (эл.) нить накала

file /файл/ n напильник; папка; подшивка (газет); картотека; дело; досье; ряд; шеренга; (вчт.) файл; vt подпиливать; подшивать; vi идти гуськом

fill /фил/ vt заполнять; пломбировать (зуб); занимать (должность); vi наполняться; ~ in /~ ин/ заполнять (бланк)

fillet /фи́лит/ n филе

filling /фи́линг/ n пломба; начинка, фарш

film /филм/ n фильм; (фото)пленка; ~ star /~ стар/ кинозвезда; vt производить киносъемку; экранизировать

filter /фи́лтэ/ n фильтр

filth /филф/ n грязь; сквернословие

filthy /фи́лфи/ adj грязный; непристойный

fin /фин/ n плавник

final /файнл/ adj финальный; окончательный; n (спорт.) финал

finally /фа́йнэли/ adv окончательно; в конце концов

finance /файнэ́нс/ n финансы; vt финансировать

finch /финч/ n зяблик

find /файнд/ n находка; vt находить; ~ out /~ а́ут/ разузнать

fine /файн/ adj превосходный; тонкий; изящный; мелкий; ~ arts /~ артс/ изящные искусства; that's ~! /зэтс ~/ прекрасно!; n штраф; vt штрафовать

finger /фи́нгэ/ n палец; index/middle/fourth ~ /и́ндэкс, мидл, форс ~/ указательный/средний/безымянный палец; little ~ /литл ~/ мизинец

finish /фи́ниш/ n конец; (спорт.) финиш; отделка; vt кончать;

finishing touch /фи́нишингта́ч/ последний штрих

Finn /фин/ n финн, финка

Finnish /фи́ниш/ n финский язык; adj финский

fir /фёр/ n пихта; ель

fir-cone /фёркоун/ n еловая шишка

fire /фа́йе/ n огонь, пожар; set ~ to /сэт ~ ту/ поджигать; vt зажигать; увольнять; стрелять из; vi стрелять

fire alarm /фа́йерэла́рм/ n пожарная тревога

firearms /фа́йеа́рмз/ n pl огнестрельное оружие

fire brigade /фа́йебригейд/ n пожарная команда

fire escape /фа́йерискейп/ n пожарная лестница

fire extinguisher /фа́йерикстингвише/ n огнетушитель

fireplace /фа́йеплэйс/ n камин

fireproof /фа́йепрууф/ adj огнеупорный

fireworks /фа́йевёркс/ n фейерверк

firing /фа́йеринг/ n стрельба

firm /фёрм/ adj твердый; прочный; n фирма

first /фёрст/ adj первый; adv сначала; ~ of all /~ ов оол/ прежде всего

first aid /фёрстэйд/ n скорая помощь

firstborn /фёрстборн/ n первенец

first floor /фёрстфлор/ n второй этаж

first-hand /фёрстхэнд/ adj из первых рук

firstly /фёрстли/ adv во-первых

first night /фёрстнайт/ n премьера

first-rate /фёрстрэйт/ adj первоклассный

fiscal /фи́скэл/ adj финансовый

fish /фиш/ n рыба; vi ловить рыбу

fisherman /фи́шемэн/ n рыбак, рыболов

fishing /фи́шинг/ n рыбная ловля; ~ line /~ лайн/ леска; ~ rod /~ род/ удочка

fishy /фи́ши/ adj (образн.) подозрительный; there's something ~ /зэээ са́мфинг ~/ здесь что-то не так

fist /фист/ n кулак

fit /фит/ adj годный, подходящий; ~ to drink /~ ту дринк/ годный для питья; n припадок; a ~ of coughing /э ~ ов ко́финг/ приступ кашля; vt прилаживать; vi годиться; ~ in /~ ин/ приспосабливать (ся)

fitness /фи́тнис/ n (при) годность; хорошая форма (у спортсмена)

fitter /фи́тэ/ n монтер

fitting /фи́тинг/ adj подходящий; n примерка; сборка; pl принадлежности

fitting-room /фи́тингрум/ n примерочная

five /файв/ num пять; n пятерка

fix /фикс/ n дилемма, затруднительное положение; vt прикреплять; устанавливать; чинить

fixed /фикст/ adj неподвижный; постоянный; установленный

flabbergast /флэ́бегаст/ vt ошеломлять

flabby /флэ́би/ adj вялый

flag /флэг/ n флаг; lower the ~ /ло́уэ зэ ~/ сдаваться

flagon /флэ́гэн/ n графин

flagrant /флэ́йгрэнт/ adj вопиющий

flail /флэйл/ n цеп

flake /флэйк/ n снежинка; pl хлопья

flame /флэйм/ n пламя

flank /флэнк/ n бок; (воен.) фланг

flannel /флэнл/ n фланель

flap /флэп/ n взмах; клапан; отворот; шлепок; хлопок

flare /флээ/ n вспышка; vi ярко гореть

flash /флэш/ n вспышка; in a ~ /ин э ~/
в мгновение ока; ~ of wit /~ ов вит/
блеск остроумия; vi сверкать
flashlight /флэ́шлайт/ n (фото) вспышка
магния
flask /флааск/ n фляжка
flat /флэт/ adj плоский; ровный; ~ denial
/~ дина́йел/ категорический отказ; n
квартира; равнина; (муз.) бемоль
flatly /флэ́тли/ adv решительно
flatten /флэтн/ vt сплющивать; выравнивать
flatter /флэ́тэ/ vt льстить; ~ oneself /~
вансэ́лф/ тешить себя
flatterer /флэ́тэрэ/ n льстец
flattery /флэ́тэри/ n лесть
flavour /флэ́йвэ/ n привкус, аромат; vt
приправлять
flavouring /флэ́йвэринг/ n приправа
flaw /флоо/ n изъян; трещина
flawless /фло́олис/ adj безукоризненный
flax /флэкс/ n лен
flaxen /флэ́ксн/ adj льняной
flay /флэй/ vt сдирать кожу с
flea /флии/ n блоха
fledgeling /фле́джлинг/ n оперившийся
птенец
flee /флии/ vti бежать, спасаться бег-
ством
fleece /флиис/ n руно
fleet /флиит/ n флот
fleeting /фли́итинг/ adj мимолетный
flesh /флеш/ n мясо; плоть; мякоть
fleshy /фле́ши/ adj мясистый
flexible /фле́ксэбл/ adj гибкий
flicker /фли́кэ/ vi мерцать, колыхаться
flickering /фли́керинг/ adj мерцающий
flight /флайт/ n полет; стая (птиц); пролет (ступеней); бегство
flimsy /фли́мзи/ adj непрочный, хрупкий
fling /флинг/ vt швырять; n бросок
flint /флинт/ n кремень
flirt /флёрт/ n кокетка; vi флиртовать

flirtation /флёрэ́йшн/ n флирт
float /фло́ут/ n поплавок; плот; vi плавать, плыть
floating /фло́утинг/ adj плавучий
flock /флок/ n стадо (овец); стая (птиц);
vi держаться вместе
flog /флог/ vt пороть, сечь
flood /флад/ n наводнение; прилив; vt
наводнять
floodgate /фла́дгейт/ n шлюз
floor /флор/ n пол; этаж; ground ~ /гра́-
унд ~/ первый этаж; take the ~ /тэйк зэ
~/ брать слово
flop /флоп/ n (разг.) провал, фиаско
flora /фло́орэ/ n флора
florist /фло́рист/ n торговец цветами;
цветовод
flounder /фла́ундэ/ n камбала
flour /фла́уэ/ n мука
flourish /фла́риш/ n росчерк; vi процветать; vt размахивать
flourishing /фла́ришинг/ adj процветающий
flout /фла́ут/ vt пренебрегать, попирать
flow /фло́у/ n течение, поток, прилив; vi
течь
flower /фла́уэ/ n цветок; vi цвести
flower bed /фла́уэб
flower girl /фла́уэгёрл/ n цветочница
flowery /фла́уэри/ adj цветистый
flowing /фло́уинг/ adj текущий, текучий; плавный (о стиле)
fluctuate /фла́ктьюэйт/ vi колебаться
fluent /флю́энт/ adj беглый, плавный; he
speaks ~ Russian /хи спиикс ~ рашн/
он бегло говорит по-русски
fluently /флю́энтли/ adv бегло
fluff /флаф/ n пух
fluffy /фла́фи/ adj пушистый
fluid /флю́ид/ adj жидкий; n жидкость
fluorescent /флюэрэ́снт/ adj флюоресци-
рующий; ~ lamp /~ лэмп/ лампа днев-
ного света
flush /флаш/ vi вспыхнуть, покраснеть

flute /флююот/ n флейта

flutter /фла́тэ/ vi махать крыльями; порхать; трепетать; развеваться (флаг)

fly /флай/ n муха; ширинка (в брюках); vi летать; vt управлять самолетом; ~ a kite /~ э кайт/ запускать змея; ~ into a rage /~ и́нту э рэйдж/ впадать в ярость

flying /фла́йинг/ adj летающий; летная (погода); ~ visit /~ ви́зит/ краткий визит

foam /фо́ум/ n пена; vi пениться

focus /фо́укэс/ n фокус; in the ~ of attention /ин зэ ~ ов этэ́ншн/ в центре внимания

fodder /фо́дэ/ n корм

foe /фо́э/ n враг

fog /фог/ n туман; vt окутывать туманом

foggy /фо́ги/ adj туманный

foil /фойл/ n фольга; (спорт.) рапира; vt срывать планы

fold /фо́улд/ n складка, сгиб; vt складывать, сгибать

folder /фо́улдэ/ n папка; брошюра

folding /фо́улдинг/ adj складной; ~ bed /~ бед/ раскладушка

foliage /фо́улидж/ n листва

folk /фо́ук/ n народ; own ~(s) /о́ун ~(c)/ родня

folklore /фо́уклор/ n фольклор

follow /фо́лоу/ vt следовать, идти за; провожать (взглядом); vi следовать; as ~s /эз ~з/ как следует ниже

follower /фо́лоуэ/ n последователь

following /фо́лоуинг/ adj следующий

folly /фо́ли/ n безрассудство; глупость; безумие, каприз

fond /фонд/ adj любящий; be ~ of /би ~ ов/ любить

fondle /фондл/ vt ласкать

fondly /фо́ндли/ adv нежно

food /фууд/ n пища, съестное

foodstuffs /фу́удстафс/ n pl еда, продукты

fool /фуул/ n дурак, глупец; шут; play the ~ /плэй зэ ~/ валять дурака; vt дурачить

foolish /фу́улиш/ adj глупый

foolishness /фу́улишнис/ n глупость

foolproof /фу́улпруф/ adj несложный; (тех.) не требующий квалифицированного обслуживания

foot /фут/ n нога; фут (мера); подножие холма; from head to ~ /фром хед ту ~/ с головы до ног; by ~ /бай ~/ пешком; set on ~ /сэт он ~/ пускать в ход; trample under ~ /трэмпл а́ндэ ~/ попирать

football /фу́тбол/ n футбол

footing /фу́тинг/ n фундамент; be on equal ~ /би он и́иквэл ~/ быть на равной ноге

footnote /фу́тноут/ n примечание, сноска

footstep /фу́тстэп/ n след

footwear /фу́твээ/ n обувь

for /фор/ prep для, за, к, вместо; as ~ me /эз ~ ми/ что касается меня; ~ good /~ гуд/ навсегда; what ~? /вот ~/ зачем?; conj ибо

forbear /фобэ́э/ vi воздерживаться

forbid /фэби́д/ vt запрещать; God ~! /год ~/ избави Боже!

force /форс/ n сила; pl (воен.) вооруженные силы; by ~ of circumstances /бай ~ ов сёркемстэ́нсыз/ в силу обстоятельств; vt заставлять, принуждать; форсировать; ~ one's way /~ ванз вэй/ прокладывать себе дорогу

forced /форст/ adj вынужденный; ~ labour /~ лэ́йбэ/ принудительный труд; ~ landing /~ лэ́ндинг/ вынужденная посадка

forceful /фо́рсфул/ adj сильный, мощный; убедительный

forcible /фо́рсэбл/ adj насильственный

ford /форд/ n брод; vt переходить вброд

fore /фор/ adj передний; adv впереди

forearm /фо́раам/ n предплечье

forebode /фобо́уд/ vt предвещать

foreboding /фобо́удинг/ n предчувствие

forecast /фо́ркаст/ n прогноз; weather ~ /вэ́зэ ~/ прогноз погоды; /фэка́аст/ vt предсказывать forefather /фо́рфа́азэ/ n праотец

forefinger /фо́рфи́нгэ/ n указательный палец

foregound /фо́рграунд/ n передний план

forehead /фо́рид/ n лоб

foreign /фо́рин/ adj иностранный, чужой; ~ policy /~ по́лиси/ внешняя политика; ~ trade /~ трэйд/ внешняя торговля

foreigner /фо́ринэ/ n иностранец

foreman /фо́рмэн/ n старшина (присяжных); десятник; прораб

foremost /фо́рмоуст/ adj главный

foresee /фоси́и/ vt предвидеть

forest /фо́рист/ n лес

forester /фо́ристэ/ n лесник

foretell /фотэ́л/ vt предсказывать

forethought /фо́осот/ n предусмотрительность

foreword /фо́рвёд/ n предисловие

forfeit /фо́рфит/ n штраф; pl игра в фанты; vt терять право на

forge /фордж/ n кузница; vt ковать; подделывать (деньги); ~ ahead /~ эхе́д/ продвигаться вперед

forger /фо́рдже/ n фальшивомонетчик

forgery /фо́рджери/ n подделка; подлог

forget /фэге́т/ vt забывать

forgetful /фэге́тфул/ adj забывчивый

forget-me-not /фэге́тминот/ n незабудка

forgive /фэги́в/ vt прощать

forgiveness /фэги́внис/ n прощение

forgiving /фэги́винг/ adj всепрощающий

forgo /фогбу/ vt отказываться от, воздерживаться от

fork /форк/ n вилка; вилы; развилка; vi разветвляться

form /форм/ n форма; бланк; класс (в школе); in ~ /ин ~/ в ударе; vt формировать, образовывать

formal /фо́рмэл/ adj формальный; ~ visit /~ ви́зит/ официальный визит

formality /фомэ́лити/ n формальность

formally /фо́рмэли/ adv формально

formation /фоме́йшн/ n образование; формирование

former /фо́рмэ/ adj прежний; the ~ /зэ ~/ первый (из двух)

formerly /фо́рмэли/ adv раньше

formidable /фо́рмидэбл/ adj громадный; устрашающий

formula /фо́рмьюлэ/ n формула

formulate /фо́рмьюлэйт/ vt формулировать

fornication /фо́рникéйшн/ n блуд

forsake /фэсэ́йк/ vt покидать

fort /форт/ n форт

forth /форс/ adv вперед; and so ~ /энд со́у ~/ и так далее

forthcoming /фоска́минг/ adj грядущий

fortieth /фо́ртис/ ord num сороковой

fortification /фо́ртификéйшн/ n укрепление

fortify /фо́ртифай/ vt укреплять

fortitude /фо́ртитьюд/ n стойкость

fortnight /фо́ртнайт/ n две недели

fortnightly /фо́ртнáйтли/ adj двухнедельный

fortress /фо́ртрис/ n крепость

fortunate /фо́рчнит/ adj счастливый, удачный

fortunately /фо́рчнитли/ adv к счастью

fortune /фо́рчен/ n счастье, удача; судьба; состояние; tell ~s /тэл ~з/ гадать; make a ~ /мэйк э ~/ разбогатеть

forty /фо́рти/ num сорок

forum /фо́орэм/ n форум

forward /фо́рвэд/ adj передовой; adv вперед; vt пересылать; способствовать, ускорять

forward-looking /фо́рвэдлу́кинг/ adj дальновидный

foster /фо́стэ/ vt воспитывать, лелеять

foster-mother /фо́стэма́зэ/ n приемная мать

foster-sister /фо́стэси́стэ/ n молочная сестра

foul /фа́ул/ adj скверный, непристойный; ~ language /~ ла́нгвидж/ сквернословие; ~ play /~ плэй/ нечестная игра; n (спорт.) нарушение правил

found /фа́унд/ vt основывать; плавить, выплавлять

foundation /фаундэ́йшн/ n основание, фундамент

foundry /фа́ундри/ n литейный завод

fountain /фа́унтин/ n фонтан

fountain-pen /фа́унтинпен/ n авторучка

four /фор/ num четыре; on all ~s /он оол ~з/ на четвереньках

fourteen /фо́ртин/ num четырнадцать

fourteenth /фо́ртиинс/ ord num четырнадцатый

fourth /форс/ ord num четвертый

fowl /фа́ул/ n домашняя птица; дичь

fowling /фа́улинг/ n охота за дичью

fox /фокс/ n лиса, лисица

foxy /фо́кси/ adj хитрый; рыжий, красно-бурый

foyer /фо́йей/ n фойе

fraction /фрэкшн/ n дробь; частица

fracture /фрэ́кче/ n перелом; vt ломать

fragile /фрэ́джайл/ adj хрупкий

fragment /фрэ́гмент/ n осколок; фрагмент

fragrance /фрэ́йгрэнс/ n аромат

fragrant /фрэ́йгрэнт/ adj благоухающий

frail /фрэйл/ adj хрупкий, тщедушный

frailty /фрэ́йлти/ n хрупкость

frame /фрэйм/ n рама; остов; телосложение; ~ of mind /~ ов майнд/ настроение; vt обрамлять; строить

framework /фрэ́ймвёк/ n структура; рамки

franchise /фрэ́нчайз/ n право участия в выборах

frank /фрэнк/ adj откровенный

frantic /фрэ́нтик/ adj неистовый

fraternal /фрэтёрнл/ adj братский

fraternity /фрэтёрнити/ n братство

fraud /фроод/ n обман; обманщик

fraudulent /фро́одьюлэнт/ adj мошеннический

freckle /фрекл/ n веснушка

free /фрии/ adj свободный; бесплатный; ~ city /~ си́ти/ вольный город; ~ trade /~ трэйд/ беспошлинная торговля; of one's own ~ will /ов ванз бун ~ вил/ добровольно; vt освобождать

freedom /фрии́дэм/ n свобода; ~ of worship /~ ов вёршип/ свобода вероисповедания

freelance /фрии́ила́анс/ adj работающий внештатно; vi работать внештатно

freely /фрии́или/ adv свободно

freemason /фрии́имэйсн/ n масон

freeze /фрииз/ vt замораживать; ~ wages /~ вэ́йджиз/ замораживать заработную плату; vi замерзать, мерзнуть

freezer /фрии́изэ/ n морозильник

freezing /фрии́изинг/ adj леденящий; ~ point /~ пойнт/ точка замерзания

freight /фрэйт/ n груз; ~ train /~ трэйн/ товарный поезд

freighter /фрэ́йтэ/ n грузовое судно

French /фрэнч/ n французский язык; adj французский

Frenchman /фрэ́нчмэн/ n француз

Frenchwoman /фрэ́нчву́мэн/ n француженка

frenzy /фрэ́нзи/ n бешенство, неистовство

frequency /фрии́иквэнси/ n частота

frequent /фрии́иквэнт/ adj частый

frequenter /фриквэ́нтэ/ n завсегдатай

frequently /фрии́иквэнтли/ adv часто

fresco /фрэ́скоу/ n фреска

fresh /фреш/ adj свежий; ~ water /~ во́отэ/ пресная вода

freshness /фрэ́шнис/ n свежесть, прохлада

friction /фрикшн/ n трение; (образн.) трения

Friday /фра́йди/ n пятница

friend /френд/ n друг; girl ~ /гёрл ~/ подруга

friendliness /фрэ́ндлинис/ n дружелюбие

friendly /фрэ́ндли/ adj дружественный

friendship /фре́ндшип/ n дружба

frieze /фрииз/ n (текст.) бобрик; ворс; (архит.) фриз; бордюр

fright /фрайт/ n испуг

frighten /фрайтн/ vt пугать

frightful /фра́йтфул/ adj страшный

frigid /фри́джид/ adj холодный

frill /фрил/ vt гофрировать

fringe /фриндж/ n бахрома, челка; ~ benefits /~ бе́нифитс/ дополнительные льготы

frippery /фри́пери/ n мишура

frisk /фриск/ vi резвиться

frisky /фри́ски/ adj игривый

frivolous /фри́вэлэс/ adj легкомысленный; пустячный

fro /фро́у/ adv: to and ~ /ту энд ~/ взад и вперед

frock /фрок/ n платье; ряса

frog /фрог/ n лягушка

frolic /фро́лик/ n шалость

from /фром/ prep от, из, с; ~ above /~ эба́в/ сверху; ~ afar /~ эфа́р/ издали; ~ behind /~ биха́йнд/ из-за; ~ now on /~ на́у он/ отныне; ~ under /~ а́ндэ/ из-под

front /франт/ n передняя сторона, фасад; (воен.) фронт; in ~ of /ин ~ ов/ перед; adj передний; ~ door /~ дор/ парадный вход; ~ page /~ пейдж/ первая полоса (газеты); титульный лист

frontier /фра́нтье/ n граница

frost /фрост/ n мороз; Father F. /фа́азэ ~/ дед Мороз; ~-bitten /~ битн/ обмороженный; ~ed glass /~ ыд глаас/ матовое стекло

frosty /фро́сти/ adj морозный; (образн.) холодный

froth /фроф/ n пена; vi пениться

frown /фра́ун/ n хмурый взгляд; vi хмуриться

frozen /фро́узн/ adj замороженный; замерзший

frugal /фруугл/ adj скудный

fruit /фруут/ n плод, фрукт(ы); tinned ~ /тинд ~/ консервированные фрукты

fruitful /фру́утфул/ adj плодородный; плодотворный

fruitless /фру́утлис/ adj бесплодный

fruity /фру́ути/ adj фруктовый; сочный, смачный

frustrate /фрастрэ́йт/ vt расстраивать; срывать

frustration /фрастрэ́йшн/ n срыв; крах; разочарование

fry /фрай/ n мелкая рыбешка; vti жарить(ся)

frying pan /фра́йингпэн/ n сковорода с ручкой

fuddle /фадл/ vt спаивать

fudge /фадж/ n помадка

fuel /фью́эл/ n топливо, горючее

fugitive /фью́юджитив/ adj беглый; n беглец

fulfil /фулфи́л/ vt выполнять, осуществлять

fulfilment /фулфи́лмент/ n исполнение

full /фул/ adj полный; сытый; целый

full-blooded /фу́лбла́дыд/ adj полнокровный

full dress /фу́лдрэ́с/ n парадная форма

fullness /фу́лнис/ n полнота

full stop /фу́лстоп/ n точка

full time /фу́лта́йм/ n полный рабочий день

fully /фу́ли/ adv вполне, полностью

fulsome /фу́лсэм/ adj раболепный; ~ praise /~ прэйз/ грубая лесть

fumble /фамбл/ vi идти ощупью, шарить

fume /фьююм/ n дым; pl испарения

fuming /фью́юминг/ adj дымящийся; кипящий от злости

fun /фан/ n потеха, забава; have ~ /хэв ~/ веселиться; for ~ /фо ~/ в шутку; make ~ of /мэйк ~ ов/ высмеивать

function /фанкшн/ n функция; торжество; vi функционировать

functionary /фа́нкшнэри/ n должностное лицо

fund /фанд/ n фонд; pl денежные средства

fundamental /фа́ндэмéнтл/ adj основной

funeral /фью́юнэрл/ n похороны; ~ service /~ сёрвис/ панихида

fungus /фáнгэс/ n грибок

funk /фанк/ vt (разг.) трусить

funnel /фанл/ n дымоход; воронка

funny /фáни/ adj забавный, чудной

fur /фёр/ n мех; налет (на языке); накипь (в чайнике); ~ coat /~ кóут/ шуба

furious /фью́эриэс/ adj взбешенный, яростный

furnace /фёрнис/ n печь, горн; blast ~ /бласт ~/ домна

furnish /фёрниш/ vt снабжать; меблировать

furnished /фёрништ/ adj меблированный

furniture /фёрниче/ n мебель

furrier /фáриэ/ n скорняк, меховщик

furrow /фáроу/ n борозда; глубокая морщина; vt бороздить

further /фёрзэ/ adj дальнейший; adv далее, затем; vt продвигать

furthermore /фёрзэмóр/ adv кроме того

furtive /фёртив/ adj скрытый

furtively /фёртивли/ adv украдкой

fury /фью́эри/ n ярость

fuse /фью́юз/ n взрыватель; (эл.) предохранитель; time ~ /тайм ~/ дистанционный взрыватель; vt плавить; vi соединяться; перегорать; the bulb is ~d /зэ балб из ~д/ лампочка перегорела

fusion /фью́южн/ n плавка; сплав; слияние

fuss /фас/ n суета; make a ~ (about) /мэйк э ~ (эбáут)/ поднимать шум (вокруг)

fussy /фáси/ adj суетливый

futile /фью́ютайл/ adj тщетный

futility /фьюти́лити/ n тщетность

future /фью́юче/ adj будущий; n будущее; in ~ /ин ~/ в будущем

fuzzy /фáзи/ adj курчавый

G

gable /гейбл/ n (архит.) фронтон

gadfly /гáдфлай/ n овод

gadget /гáджит/ n приспособление

gag /гэг/ n кляп; (театр.) отсебятина; vt затыкать рот кляпом; vi отпускать шутки

gaiety /гэ́йети/ n веселость, веселье

gaily /гэ́йли/ adv весело; ярко

gain /гейн/ n прибыль, выигрыш; pl доходы; vt выигрывать, достигать; ~ time /~ тайм/ выигрывать время

gait /гейт/ n походка

gala /гáалэ/ n празднество

galaxy /гáлэкси/ n галактика

gale /гейл/ n шторм, буря

gall /гоол/ n желчь; желчный пузырь

gallant /гáлэнт/ adj храбрый; галантный

gallantry /гáлэнтри/ n храбрость; галантность

gallery /гáлери/ n галерея; (театр.) галерка

galley proof /гáлипру́уф/ n гранка

gallon /гáлэн/ n галлон

gallop /гáлэп/ n галоп; vi нестись галопом

gallows /гáлоуз/ n pl виселица

galvanize /гáлвэнайз/ vt гальванизировать

gamble /гэмбл/ n азартная игра, рискованное дело; vi играть (в азартные игры)

gambler /гáмблэ/ n игрок

game /рейм/ n игра; дичь; play the ~ /плэй зэ ~/ играть честно

gander /гáндэ/ n гусак

gang /гэнг/ n банда

gangster /гáнгстэ/ n гангстер

gangway /гáнгвэй/ n сходни

gap /гэп/ n брешь; пробел (в знаниях)

gape /гейп/ vi зевать; зиять; ~ at /~ эт/ глазеть на

garage /гэрáж/ n гараж

garbage /гáрбидж/ n мусор

garble /гарбл/ vt искажать, фальсифицировать

garden /гардн/ n сад; kitchen ~ /кичин ~/ огород; nursery ~ /нёёсри ~/ питомник

gardner /гáрднэ/ n садовник

gargle /гаргл/ vi полоскать горло

garland /гáрлэнд/ n гирлянда

garlic /гáрлик/ n чеснок

garment /гáрмент/ n одеяние

garnet /гáрнит/ n (мин.) гранат

garnish /гáрниш/ n гарнир

garret /гэ́рет/ n чердак

garrison /гэ́рисн/ n гарнизон

garter /гáртэ/ n подвязка

gas /гэс/ n газ; (US) бензин; vt отравлять газом

gas cooker /гэ́ску́кэ/ n газовая плита

gas-mask /гэ́смаск/ n противогаз

gas-meter /гэ́сми́итэ/ n газовый счетчик

gasolene /гэ́сэлин/ n газолин; (US) бензин

gasp /гаасп/ n удушье; vi задыхаться; ~ out /~ áут/ говорить задыхаясь; ~ for breath /~ фо брес/ ловить ртом воздух

gastric /гэ́стрик/ adj желудочный

gastritis /гэстрáйтис/ n гастрит

gastronomy /гэстрóнэми/ n гастрономия

gate /гейт/ n ворота; застава

gatekeeper /гéйтки́ипэ/ n привратник

gather /гэ́зэ/ vt собирать; ~ strength /~ стренгс/ копить силы; vi собираться

gathering /гэ́зэринг/ n собрание (людей); (мед.) нагноение

gauge /гейдж/ n измерительный прибор; vt измерять

gaunt /гоонт/ adj сухопарый; костлявый

gauntlet /гóонтлит/ n рукавица

gauze /гооз/ n газ, марля

gay /гэй/ adj веселый; (разг.) гомосексуальный

gaze /гейз/ n пристальный взгляд; vi смотреть

gear /гиэ/ n прибор; передача; ~ box /~ бокс/ коробка скоростей; change ~ /чейндж ~/ переключать передачу

gelatine /джéлэти́ин/ n желатин

gem /джем/ n драгоценный камень; (образн.) драгоценность

Gemini /джéмини/ n pl Близнецы (созвездие и знак зодиака)

gender /джéндэ/ n (грам.) род

genealogy /джи́иниэ́лэджи/ n генеалогия

general /джéнэрэл/ adj общий, всеобщий; обычный; G. Assembly /~ эсэ́мбли/ Генеральная Ассамблея; ~ election /~ илéкшн/ всеобщие выборы; in ~ /ин ~/ вообще; n генерал

generalissimo /джéнэрэли́симоу/ n генералиссимус

generalize /джéнэрэлайз/ vt обобщать

generally /джéнэрэли/ adv вообще; обычно

generate /джéнэрэйт/ vt порождать

generation /джéнэрэ́йшн/ n поколение

generator /джéнэрэйтэ/ n генератор

generosity /джéнэрóсити/ n щедрость

generous /джéнэрэс/ adj щедрый, великодушный

genial /джи́иньел/ adj приветливый; мягкий

genital /джéнитл/ adj (анат.) половой

genitals /джéнитлз/ n pl половые органы

genitive case /джéнитив кейс/ n родительный падеж

genius /джи́иньес/ n гений

gentle /джентл/ adj мягкий, нежный, кроткий

gentleman /джéнтлмэн/ n джентльмен

gentleness /джéнтлнис/ n мягкость

gently /джéнтли/ adv осторожно; мягко

genuine /джéньюин/ adj подлинный, настоящий; искренний

geography /джиóгрэфи/ n география

geology /джиóлэджи/ n геология

geometry /джиóмитри/ n геометрия

Georgian /джóрджьен/ n грузин(ка); грузинский язык; уроженец штата Джорджия; adj грузинский

germ /джёрм/ n микроб; зародыш

German /джёрмэн/ n немец, немка; немецкий язык; adj немецкий, германский gesture /джéсче/ n жест

get /гет/ vt получать; доставлять; достигать; добиваться; понимать; vi: ~ better /~ бéтэ/ поправляться; ~ down to /~ дáун тэ/ приниматься за; ~ marrried /~ мэ́рид/ жениться; выйти замуж; ~ on /~ он/ преуспевать; ~ out of order /~ áут ов óрдэ/ портиться; ~ ready /~ рéди/ готовить(ся); ~ rid of /~ рид ов/ избавляться от; ~ up /~ ап/ вставать

gherkin /гéркин/ n корнишон

ghost /гóуст/ n привидение, призрак, дух

ghostly /гóустли/ n прозрачный

giant /джáйент/ n великан, гигант

gibe /джайб/ n насмешка; vi: ~ at /~ эт/ насмехаться над

giddiness /гúдинис/ n головокружение

giddy /гúди/ adj головокружительный; легкомысленный, ветреный; I feel ~ /ай фиил ~/ у меня кружится голова

gift /гифт/ n подарок, дар; талант

gifted /гúфтыд/ adj даровитый

gigantic /джайгэ́нтик/ adj гигантский

giggle /гигл/ n хихиканье; vi хихикать

gild /гилд/ vt золотить

gill /гил/ n жабра

gilt /гилт/ adj золоченый; n позолота

gimmick /гúмик/ n трюк

gin /джин/ n джин

ginger /джúнже/ n имбирь; ~ bread /~ брэд/ имбирный пряник

gingery /джúнжери/ adj имбирный; рыжеватый

gipsy /джúпси/ цыган(ка); adj цыганский

giraffe /джирáаф/ n жираф

gird /гёрд/ vt опоясывать

girdle /гёрдл/ n пояс

girl /гёрл/ n девочка, девушка

girlhood /гёрлхуд/ n девичество

girlish /гёрлиш/ adj девический

gist /джист/ n суть

give /гив/ vt давать; ~ away /~ эвэ́й/ выдавать; ~ birth to /~ бёрф ту/ родить; ~ in /~ ин/ уступать; ~ up /~ ап/ отдавать, отказываться от, бросать; ~ oneself up /~ вансэ́лф ап/ сдаваться

glacial /глэ́йсьел/ adj ледниковый

glacier /глэ́сье/ n ледник

glad /глэд/ adj довольный, радостный; I am ~ /ай эм ~ / я рад(а)

gladiator /глэ́диэйтэ/ n гладиатор

gladiolus /глэ́диóулэс/ n гладиолус

gladly /глэ́дли/ adv с удовольствием

gladness /глэ́днис/ n радость

glamorous /глэ́мэрэс/ adj шикарный

glamour /глэ́мэ/ n очарование

glance /глаанс/ n (быстрый) взгляд; at first ~ /эт фёрст ~/ с первого взгляда; vi взглянуть; ~ through /~ фру/ бегло просматривать

gland /глэнд/ n железа

glass /глаас/ adj стеклянный; n стекло; стакан; рюмка; зеркало; pl очки

glaze /глэйз/ n глазурь; vt застеклять; покрывать глазурью

glazed /глэйзд/ adj застекленный

glazier /глэ́йзье/ n стекольщик

gleam /глиим/ n слабый свет, проблеск; vi светиться

gleamy /глúими/ adj мерцающий

glean /глиин/ vi подбирать колосья; vt (образн.) собирать факты, сведения

glide /глайд/ n скольжение; (авиа) планирование; vi скользить; планировать

glider /глáйдэ/ n планер

glimmer /глúмэ/ n мерцание, тусклый свет; vi мерцать

glimmering /глúмеринг/ adj мерцающий

glimpse /глимпс/ n быстрый взгляд; мерцание; vt видеть мельком

glisten /глисн/ vi блестеть

glitter /глúтэ/ vi сверкать

globe /глóуб/ n земной шар; глобус

gloom /глуум/ n мрачность

gloomy /глýуми/ adj угрюмый

glorify /глóрифай/ vt прославлять

glorious /глóориэс/ adj славный

glory /глóори/ n слава

gloss /глос/ n лоск, глянец

glossary /глóсэри/ n словарь

glossy /глóси/ adj глянцевитый

glove /глав/ n перчатка

glow /глóу/ n заря; румянец; свечение; vi сиять, пылать

glow-worm /глóувёрм/ n светлячок

glowing /глóуинг/ adj раскаленный докрасна; ярко светящийся; ~ with health /~ виз хелф/ пышущий здоровьем

glue /глюю/ n клей; vt приклеивать

gluey /глюúи/ adj липкий

glutton /глатн/ n обжора

gnat /нэт/ n комар

gnaw /ноо/ vt глодать

gnome /нóум/ n гном

go /гóу/ vi идти, ходить, ехать, ездить; ~ ahead /~ эхéд/ двигаться вперед; ~ away /~ эвэй/ уходить, уезжать; ~ back /~ бэк/ возвращаться; ~ by /~ бай/ проходить мимо; ~ in for an exam /~ ин фор эн игзэм/ сдавать экзамен; ~ on /~ он/ продолжать; let ~ /лет ~/ освобождать; n попытка; have a ~ at /хэв э ~ эт/ попытаться

go-ahead /гóуэхед/ adj (разг.) предприимчивый

goal /гóул/ n цель; (спорт.) гол; ворота; score a ~ /скор э ~/ забивать гол

goal-keeper /гóулкúипэ/ n вратарь

goat /гóут/ n коза, козел

goatee /гоутúи/ n козлиная бородка

go-between /гóубитвúин/ n посредник

goblet /гóблит/ n бокал

goblin /гóблин/ n домовой

god /год/ n бог; my G.! /май ~/ боже мой!; thank G.! /сэнк ~/ слава Богу!

godchild /гóдчайлд/ n крестник, крестница

goddess /гóдыс/ n богиня

godfather /гóдфáазэ/ n крестный отец

godless /гóдлис/ adj безбожный

godly /гóдли/ adj набожный

godmother /гóдмáзэ/ n крестная мать

gold /гóулд/ n золото

golden /гóулдэн/ adj золотой

goldfield /гóулдфилд/ n золотой прииск

goldfish /гóулдфиш/ n золотая рыбка

goldsmith /гóулдсмит/ n ювелир

golf /голф/ n гольф

good /гуд/ adj хороший, добрый; ~ morning /~ мóрнинг/ доброе утро!; ~ night /~ найт/ спокойной ночи; ~ afternoon (evening)! /~ áафтэнýун (úивнинг)/ добрый день (вечер)!; ~ bye /~ бай/ до свидания!; say ~-bye /сэй ~ бай/ прощаться; a ~ deal /э ~ диил/ много; ~ Friday /~ фрáйди/ страстная пятница; ~ heavens! /~ хéвенз/ господи!; for ~ /фо ~/ навсегда; n благо, польза; it is no ~ /ит из нóу ~/ бесполезно

goodies /гýдиз/ n pl сладости

goods /гудз/ n pl товары

goose /гуус/ n гусь, гусыня

gooseflesh /гýусфлеш/ n гусиная кожа

gooseberry /гýзбэри/ n крыжовник

gorge /гордж/ n глотка; ущелье

gorgeous /гóрджес/ adj великолепный

gospel /госпл/ n евангелие; ~ truth /~ труус/ истинная правда

gossip /гóсип/ n сплетня; сплетник, сплетница: vi сплетничать

Goth /гот/ n гот

Gothic /гóтик/ adj готический

gourmet /гýэмэй/ n гурман

gout /гáут/ n подагра

govern /гавн/ vt управлять, править

governess /гáвэнис/ n гувернантка

government /гáвэнмент/ n правительство; правление

governmental /гáвэнмéнтл/ adj правительственный

governor /гáвэнэ/ n губернатор

gown /рáун/ n платье (женское); мантия; morning ~ /мóрнинг ~/ халат

grab /грэб/ vt хватать, захватывать

grace /грэйс/ n грация; милосердие; милость

graceful /грэйсфул/ adj грациозный, изящный

gracious /грэйшес/ adj милосердный; good ~ /гуд ~/ боже мой!

graciously /грэйшесли/ adv милостиво; благосклонно

grade /грэйд/ n степень; сорт; класс; vt располагать по степеням, классам

gradual /грэдьюэл/ adj постепенный

graduate /грэдьюит/ n выпускник; /грэдьюэйт/ vt оканчивать университет

graft /граафт/ n взятка; черенок; прививка; vt прививать (растение); пересаживать (ткань)

grain /грэйн/ n зерно; against the ~ /эгэйнст зэ ~/ против шерсти

grammar /грэмэ/ n грамматика

grammatical /грэмэтикл/ adj грамматический

gram(me) /грэм/ n грамм

gramophone /грэмэфоун/ n граммофон, патефон

granary /грэнэри/ n зернохранилище

grand /грэнд/ adj величественный

grandchild /грэндчайлд/ n внук, внучка

granddaughter /грэндоотэ/ n внучка

grandeur /грэндже/ n величие

grandfather /грэнфаазэ/ n дедушка

grandiose /грэндиоус/ adj грандиозный

grand master /грэнмаастэ/ n гроссмейстер

grandmother /грэнмазэ/ n бабушка

grand piano /грэндпьэноу/ n рояль

granite /грэнит/ n гранит

granny /грэни/ n бабушка

grant /граант/ n субсидия; стипендия; vt дарить; предоставлять; допускать; take for ~ed /тэйк фо ~ыд/ считать само собой разумеющимся

granulate /грэньюлэйт/ vt дробить; ~d sugar /~ыд шугэ/ сахарный песок

grape /грэйп/ n виноград

grapefruit /грэйпфрут/ n грейпфрут

graph /грэф/ n график

graphic /грэфик/ adj наглядный

grasp /граасп/ n хватка; понимание; beyond one's ~ /бийонд ванз ~/ выше чьего-либо понимания; vt схватывать; понимать

grass /граас/ n трава

grasshopper /граасхопэ/ n кузнечик

grassplot /граасплот/ n лужайка

grass widow /граасвидоу/ n соломенная вдова

grassy /грааси/ adj травянистый

grateful /грэйтфул/ adj благодарный

grater /грэйтэ/ n терка

grating /грэйтинг/ n решетка

gratis /грэйтис/ adv бесплатно

gratitude /грэтитьюд/ n благодарность

gratuity /грэтьюити/ n денежное пособие; чаевые

grave /грэйв/ adj серьезный, важный; n могила

gravestone /грэйвстоун/ n надгробие

gravel /грэвл/ n гравий

graver /грэйвэ/ n гравер

gravitate /грэвитэйт/ vi тяготеть

gravitation /грэвитэйшн/ n гравитация; тяготение

gravity /грэвити/ n серьезность; сила тяжести; specific ~ /спесифик ~/ удельный вес

gravy /грэйви/ n подливка

graze /грэйз/ n царапина; vti пасти(сь)

grease /гриис/ n жир, смазка; /грииз/ vt смазывать

greasy /гриизи/ adj сальный, скользкий

great /грэйт/ adj великий, большой; a ~ many /э ~ мэни/ множество

greatcoat /грэйткоут/ n пальто (мужское)

great-grandchild /грэйтгрэнчайлд/ n правнук, правнучка

greatly /грэйтли/ adv очень

greatness /грэйтнис/ n величие

greed, greediness /гриид, гриидинис/ n жадность

greedy /гри́иди/ adj алчный

Greek /гриик/ n грек, гречанка; греческий язык; adj греческий

green /гриин/ adj зеленый

green-eyed /гри́инайд/ adj зеленоглазый; завистливый

greengrocer /гри́ингро́усэ/ n зеленщик

greenish /гри́иниш/ adj зеленоватый

greet /гриит/ vt приветствовать; кланяться

greeting /гри́итинг/ n приветствие

Gregorian /григо́ориэн/ adj грегорианский

grenade /грине́йд/ n граната

grey /грэй/ adj серый; седой

grief /грииф/ n горе

grievance /гри́ивэнс/ n обида; жалоба

grieve /гриив/ vt огорчать; vi горевать

grill /грил/ n решетка, гриль; рашпер; a mixed ~ /э микст ~/ ассорти из жареного мяса; vti жарить (ся)

grim /грим/ adj угрюмый; жестокий

grimace /гриме́йс/ n гримаса; vi гримасничать

grin /грин/ n ухмылка; vi ухмыляться

grind /грайнд/ vt молоть; скрежетать (зубами); точить

grindstone /гра́йнстоун/ n жернов, точильный станок

grip /грип/ n хватка; сжатие; рукоятка; vt схватывать

grit /грит/ n крупный песок, гравий

grits /гритс/ n pl овсяная крупа

groan /гро́ун/ n стон; vi стонать

grocer /гро́усэ/ n бакалейщик

grocery /гро́усэри/ n бакалея

groin /гройн/ n пах

groom /груум/ n конюх; жених; vt ухаживать за лошадью

groove /груув/ n желоб, паз

grope /гро́уп/ vi идти ощупью; ~ for /~ фо/ искать (ощупью)

gross /грос/ adj грубый; крупный; валовой; ~ income /~ и́нкэм/ валовой доход; ~ weight /~ вэйт/ вес брутто

ground /гра́унд/ n земля; почва; причина, мотив; gain ~ /гэйн ~/ делать успехи; on the ~s of /он зэ ~з ов/ на основании; vt обосновывать

ground floor /гра́ундфло́р/ n первый этаж

groundwork /гра́ундвёрк/ n подготовительная работа

group /грууп/ n группа; vti группировать (ся)

grouse /гра́ус/ n (шотландская) куропатка; тетерев

grove /гро́ув/ n роща

grow /гро́у/ vt выращивать, отращивать; vi расти, становиться; ~ little /~ литл/ уменьшаться; ~ old /~ óулд/ стареть

growing /гро́уинг/ adj растущий

growl /гра́ул/ vi ворчать; рычать

grown-up /гро́унап/ n, adj взрослый

growth /гро́ус/ n рост

grudge /градж/ n злоба, зависть; vt неохотно давать, жалеть; завидовать

grudgingly /гра́джингли/ adv неохотно

gruff /граф/ adj грубоватый

grumble /грамбл/ n ворчание; vi ворчать

grumbler /гра́мблэ/ n ворчун

grumpy /гра́мпи/ adj сварливый

grunt /грант/ n хрюканье; vi хрюкать

guarantee /гэ́рэнти́и/ n гарантия; vt гарантировать

guarantor /гэ́рэнто́р/ n поручитель, гарант

guard /гард/ n охрана; стража, караул; часовой; гвардия; advance ~ /эдва́анс ~/ авангард; be on ~ /би он ~/ быть начеку; vt охранять

guardian /га́рдьен/ n опекун

guerilla /гери́лэ/ n партизан; ~ warfare /~ во́рфээ/ партизанская война

guess /гес/ n догадка; vt отгадывать

guest /гест/ n гость, гостья

guidance /га́йдэнс/ n руководство

guide /гайд/ n гид, проводник; vt руководить

guile /гайл/ n хитрость, коварство

guilt /гилт/ n вина
guiltless /гилтлис/ adj невиновный
guilty /гилти/ adj виновный
guise /гайз/ n вид, личина, маска; предлог; under the ~ of /а́ндэ зэ ~ ов/ под видом
guitar /гита́р/ n гитара
guitarist /гита́арист/ n гитарист
gulf /галф/ n залив
gull /гал/ n чайка
gulp /галп/ n глоток; at one ~ /эт ван ~/ залпом; vt глотать с жадностью или поспешностью
gum /гам/ n десна; камедь; клей; vt склеивать
gumboil /ра́мбойл/ n флюс
gun /ган/ n ружье, винтовка; орудие; пушка; револьвер; double-barrelled ~ /да́блбэ́рэлд ~/ двустволка
gunpowder /ра́нпа́удэ/ n порох
gunner /ра́нэ/ n артиллерист
gurgle /гёргл/ n бульканье; vi булькать
gush /гаш/ n сильный поток; vi хлынуть
gust /гаст/ n порыв (ветра)
gut /гат/ n кишка; pl внутренности
gutter /ра́тэ/ n сточная канава
guy /гай/ n парень
gymnasium /джимнэ́йзьем/ n гимнастический зал; гимназия
gymnast /джи́мнэст/ n гимнаст
gymnastic /джимнэ́стик/ adj гимнастический
gymnastics /джимнэ́стикс/ n гимнастика
gynecologist /ра́йнико́лэджист/ n гинеколог

H

haberdasher /хэ́бэдэ́ше/ n галантерейщик
haberdashery /хэ́бэдэ́шери/ n галантерея
habit /хэ́бит/ n привычка; обычай
habitation /хэ́битэ́йшн/ n жилье
habitual /хэби́чьюэл/ adj обычный, привычный

hack /хэк/ vt рубить
hackneyed /хэ́книд/ adj банальный, избитый
hemorrage /хэ́мэридж/ n кровотечение
hemorrhoids /хэ́мэройдз/ n pl геморрой
hag /хэг/ n ведьма
haggard /хэ́гэд/ adj изможденный
hail /хэйл/ n град; приветствие; vt приветствовать; it is hailing /ит из ~инг/ идет град
hair /хээ/ n волос(ы); шерсть (животного)
haircut /хэ́экат/ n стрижка
hairdo /хэ́эду/ n прическа
hairdresser /хэ́эдрэ́сэ/ n парикмахер
hair-drier /хэ́эдра́йе/ n сушилка для волос
hairless /хэ́элис/ adj безволосый
hairy /хэ́эри/ adj волосатый
half /хааф/ n половина; one's better ~ /ванз бэ́тэ ~/ "лучшая половина", жена; adj половинный; adv наполовину, полу-; go halves /ро́у хаавз/ делить пополам; ~ an hour /~ эн а́уэ/ полчаса; ~ pay /~ пэй/ половинный оклад; at ~ price /эт ~ прайс/ за полцены
half-back /ха́афбэ́к/ n полузащитник
half-mast /ха́афма́аст/ adv в приспущенном положении
halfway /ха́афвэй/ adj лежащий на полпути, компромиссный; adv на полпути; meet smb. ~ /миит са́мбэди ~/ идти на компромисс
half-witted /ха́афви́тыд/ adj слабоумный
hall /хоол/ n зал, холл

hallow /хэ́лоу/ vt освящать
halo /хэ́йлоу/ n ореол, нимб
halt /хоолт/ n остановка, привал; interj стой!
halve /хаав/ vt делить пополам
ham /хэм/ n ветчина, окорок
hamlet /хэ́млит/ n деревушка
hammer /хэ́мэ/ n молот(ок); курок; vt вбивать, забивать молотком

hammock /хэ́мэк/ n гамак

hamper /хэ́мпэ/ vt мешать, затруднять

hamster /хэ́мстэ/ n хомяк

hand /хэнд/ n рука, кисть руки; стрелка (часов); работник; at ~ /эт ~/ наготове; by ~ /бай ~/ от руки; ~ in ~ /~ ин ~/ рука об руку; on ~ /он ~/ в наличии; ~s off! /~з оф/ руки прочь!; ~s up! /~з ап/ руки вверх!; get the upper ~ /гет зы а́пэ ~/ брать верх; vt передавать, вручать

handbag /хэ́ндбэг/ n сумка

handbook /хэ́ндбук/ n справочник

handcart /хэ́ндкарт/ n ручная тележка

handcuffs /хэ́ндкафс/ n pl наручники

handful /хэ́ндфул/ n горсть

handicap /хэ́ндикэп/ n гандикап, помеха

handicraft /хэ́ндикрафт/ n ремесло; ручная работа; ~ industry /~ и́ндэстри/ кустарное производство

handicraftsman /хэ́ндикра́афтсмэн/ n ремесленник

handkerchief /хэ́нкэчиф/ n носовой платок; косынка

handle /хэ́ндл/ n рукоятка; vt трогать рукой; обращаться с; иметь дело с

handmade /хэ́ндмэйд/ adj ручной работы

handshake /хэ́ндшейк/ n рукопожатие

handsome /хэ́нсэм/ adj красивый

handwriting /хэ́ндра́йтинг/ n почерк

handy /хэ́нди/ adj удобный, (имеющийся) под рукой; come in ~ /кам ин ~/ пригодиться

hang /хэнг/ vt вешать; vi висеть; ~ down /~ да́ун/ свисать; ~ in the balance /~ ин зэ бэ́лэнс/ колебаться, сомневаться; ~ on /~ он/ упорствовать

hangar /хэ́нгэ/ n ангар

hanger /хэ́нгэ/ n вешалка

hanging /хэ́нгинг/ adj висячий; подвесной; n повешение

hangman /хэ́нгмэн/ n палач

haphazard /хэ́пхэ́ззд/ adj случайный; adv случайно; at ~ /эт ~/ наудачу

happen /хэпн/ vi случаться; whatever ~s /вотэ́вэ ~з/ чтобы ни случилось

happening /хэ́пнинг/ n случай, событие

happily /хэ́пили/ adv счастливо; к счастью

happiness /хэ́пинис/ n счастье

happy /хэ́пи/ adj счастливый; удачный

happy-go-lucky /хэ́пигоула́ки/ adj беспечный

harass /хэ́рэс/ vt беспокоить; изматывать

harbinger /ха́рбиндже/ n предвестник

harbour /ха́рбэ/ n гавань

hard /хард/ adj твердый; жесткий; тяжелый; трудный; ~ cash /~ кэш/ наличные деньги; adv твердо; крепко; упорно; drink ~ /дринк ~/ сильно пить; work ~ /вёрк ~/ много работать

hard-boiled /ха́рдбо́йлд/ adj сваренный вкрутую (о яйце)

harden /ха́рдэн/ vt делать твердым; закаливать (металл); vi твердеть

hardly /ха́рдли/ adv едва, едва ли

hardware /ха́рдвээ/ n металлические изделия; (вчт.) аппаратное обеспечение (в отличие от программного)

hare /хээ/ n заяц

hare-lip /хэ́элип/ n заячья губа

harlot /ха́рлэт/ n шлюха

harm /харм/ n вред; vt вредить; обижать

harmful /ха́рмфул/ adj вредный

harmless /ха́рмлис/ adj безвредный

harmonic /хармо́ник/ adj гармонический

harmonica /хармо́никэ/ n губная гармоника

harmonious /хармо́уньес/ adj гармонический, гармоничный

harmonize /ха́рмэнайз/ vi гармонировать

harmony /ха́рмэни/ n гармония

harness /ха́рнис/ n упряжь; vt запрягать

harp /харп/ n арфа

harpist /ха́рпист/ n арфист(ка)

harrow /хэ́роу/ n борона; vt боронить

harsh /харш/ adj суровый; грубый; шероховатый

harvest /ха́рвист/ n урожай; vt собирать урожай

harvester /ха́рвистэ/ n уборочная машина

haste /хейст/ n спешка, торопливость

hasten /хейсн/ vti торопить(ся)

hastily /хе́йстили/ adv поспешно

hasty /хе́йсти/ adj поспешный, опрометчивый

hat /хэт/ adj шляпа, шапка

hatch /хэч/ n выводок; люк; vt высиживать; vi вылупливаться (из яйца)

hatchet /хэ́чит/ n топорик; bury the ~ /бе́ри зэ ~/ заключать мир

hate /хейт/ vt ненавидеть

hateful /хе́йтфул/ adj ненавистный; злобный

hatred /хе́йтрид/ n ненависть

haughty /хо́оти/ adj надменный

haul /хоол/ n вытаскивание; перевозка; улов; vt тянуть

haunch /хоонч/ n ляжка, бедро

haunt /хоонт/ vt являться (как призрак), преследовать; ~ed house /~ыд ха́ус/ дом с привидениями

have /хэв/ vt иметь; I ~ /ай ~/ у меня есть...; I ~ not /ай ~ нот/ у меня нет...; I ~ to /ай ~ ту/ я должен...; you had better... /ю хэд бе́тэ / вам лучше бы...

haven /хейвн/ n гавань; убежище

hawk /хоок/ n ястреб; (перен.) хищник; vt торговать в разнос

hawker /хо́окэ/ n уличный торговец

hay /хэй/ n сено

hay-fever /хэ́йфи́ивэ/ n сенная лихорадка

haymaking /хэ́ймэ́йкинг/ n сенокос

haystack /хэ́йстэк/ n стог сена

hazard /хэ́ззэд/ n риск, опасность; vt рисковать

hazardous /хэ́ззэдэс/ adj рискованный

haze /хейз/ n дымка

hazel /хейзл/ adj карий; ореховый; n фундук

he /хи/ pron он; n мужчина; самец

head /хед/ n голова; верхняя часть; руководитель; hit the nail on the ~ /хит зэ нэйл он зэ ~/ попадать в точку; ~s or tails /~з о тэйлз/ орел или решка; vt возглавлять; озаглавливать

headache /хе́дэйк/ n головная боль

head-dress /хе́ддрэс/ n головной убор

heading /хе́динг/ n заглавие

head-light /хе́длайт/ n фара

headline /хе́длайн/ n заголовок

headphones /хе́дфоунз/ n pl наушники

headquarters /хе́дквбо́тэз/ n pl штаб

headstone /хе́дстоун/ n надгробная плита

heal /хиил/ vt излечивать; vi заживать

healer /хи́илэ/ n целитель

healing /хи́илинг/ adj целебный

health /хелф/ n здоровье

health-resort /хе́лфризо́рт/ n курорт

healthy /хе́лфи/ adj здоровый

heap /хиип/ n куча; vt нагромождать

hear /хи́э/ vt слышать; слушать; ~ of /~ов/ узнавать о; ~ from /~ фром/ получать известия от

hearing /хи́эринг/ n слух; (юр.) слушание дела

hearsay /хи́эсэй/ n молва

heart /харт/ n сердце; сущность; pl (карты) черви; by ~ /бай ~/ наизусть; ~ and soul of the party /~ энд со́ул ов зэ па́рти/ душа общества; take to ~ /тэйк ту ~/ принимать близко к сердцу

heartburn /ха́ртбёрн/ n изжога

hearten /хартн/ vt ободрять

heartfelt /ха́ртфелт/ adj искренний

hearth /харс/ n очаг; домашний очаг

hearty /ха́рти/ adj сердечный; обильный (о еде)

heat /хиит/ n жара; пыл; период течки; vti нагревать(ся), топить(ся)

heater /хи́итэ/ n печь; обогреватель

heath /хииф/ n пустошь

heathen /хиизн/ n язычник, язычница; adj языческий

heating /хи́итинг/ n отопление

heat-stroke /хи́итстроук/ n тепловой удар

heave /хиив/ vi вздыматься (волны и т.п.); vt поднимать

heaven /хевн/ n небо; рай

---

heavenly /хе́внли/ adj небесный, божественный

heaviness /хе́винис/ n тяжесть

heavy /хе́ви/ adj тяжелый; сильный
(дождь); бурный (о море); мрачный (о
небе); ~ traffic /~ трэ́фик/ сильное
движение

heavy-weight /хе́вивэйт/ n тяжеловес

hectic /хе́ктик/ adj лихорадочный

hedge /хедж/ n живая изгородь

hedgehog /хе́джхог/ n еж

heed /хиид/ n внимание; vt обращать
внимание на

heedful /хи́идфул/ adj внимательный

heedless /хи́идлис/ adj небрежный

heel /хиил/ n пятка; каблук

hefty /хе́фти/ adj дюжий

heifer /хе́фэ/ n телка

height /хайт/ n высота; рост; возвышенность

heighten /хайтн/ vti усиливать (ся)

heir /ээ/ n наследник

heiress /э́эрис/n наследница

helicopter /хе́ликоптэ/ n вертолет

hell /хел/ n ад

hello /хело́у/ interj алло!; здравствуйте!

helm /хелм/ n руль; бразды правления

helmet /хе́лмит/ n шлем

helmsman /хе́лмзмэн/ n рулевой

help /хелп/ n помощь; vt помогать; ~
yourself /~ йосэ́лф/ угощайтесь; I can't
~ it /ай кант ~ ит/ я ничего не могу
поделать

helper /хе́лпэ/ n помощник

helping /хе́лпинг/ n порция

helpless /хе́лплис/ adj беспомощный

hem /хем/ n подрубочный шов; кайма

hemisphere /хе́мисфиэ/ n полушарие

hemp /хемп/ n конопля; пенька

hen /хен/ n курица

hence /хенс/ adv отсюда, следовательно

henceforth /хе́нсфорс/ adv впредь

henna /хе́нэ/ n хна

hen-pecked /хе́нпект/ adj под башмаком
у жены

her /хё/ pron ee, ей

herald /хе́рэлд/ n вестник; vt возвещать;
предвещать

herb /хёрб/ n трава; целебное растение

herd /хёрд/ n стадо, табун

herdsman /хёрдзмэн/ n пастух

here /хи́э/ adv здесь, тут, сюда, вот; ~
goes /~ го́уз/ начнем!; ~'s to you! /~з ту
ю/ ваше здоровье!; look ~ /лук ~/ по-
слушай (те)!

hereabouts /хи́эрэба́утс/ adv поблизости

hereafter /хи́эрэа́афтэ/ adv в дальнейшем

hereby /хи́эбай/ adv таким образом,
этим, настоящим

hereditary /хире́дитэри/ adj наследственный

heredity /хире́дити/ n наследственность

heresy /хе́рэси/ n ересь

heretic /хе́рэтик/ n еретик

herewith /хи́эви́з/ adv настоящим, при
сем

heritage /хе́ритэдж/ n наследство

hermetic /хёме́тик/ adj герметический

hermit /хёрмит/ n отшельник

hernia /хёрнье/ n грыжа

hero /хи́эроу/ n герой

heroic /хиро́ик/ adj героический

heroine /хе́роин/ n героиня

heroism /хе́роизм/ n героизм

heron /хе́рэн/ n цапля

herring /хе́ринг/ n сельдь

hers /хёрз/ pron ee, принадлежащий ей;
this book is ~ /зыс бук из ~/ эта книга
принадлежит ей

herself /хёсэ́лф/ pron себя, себе, собой

hesitate /хе́зитэйт/ vi колебаться

hesitation /хе́зитэ́йшн/ n нерешитель-
ность

hew /хьюю/ vt рубить

heyday /хе́йдэй/ n расцвет

hi /хай/ interj эй!, привет!

hiccup /хи́кап/ n икота; vi икать

hide /хайд/ n шкура; vti прятать (ся)

hide-and-seek /ха́йдэнси́ик/ (игра в)
прятки

hide-out /хáйдáут/ n убежище

hieroglyph /хáйэрэглиф/ n иероглиф

high /хай/ adj высокий, высший; сильный (ветер); испорченный (о мясе); большой (о скорости); H. Command /~ кэмáанд/ верховное командование; ~ jump /~ джамп/ прыжок в высоту; ~ school /~ скуул/ средняя школа; ~ sea /~ сии/ открытое море; ~ tide /~ тайд/ прилив; adv высоко

high-brow /хáйбрау/ adj (презр.) ученый; n интеллектуал

highly /хáйли/ adv очень; весьма; чрезвычайно

highness /хáйнис/ n высота; высочество (титул)

high-spirited /хáйспúритыд/ adj отважный; пылкий

highway /хáйвэй/ n шоссе

hijack /хáйджек/ vt угонять (самолет)

hijacker /хáйджéкэ/ n угонщик самолета

hill /хил/ n холм

hilly /хúли/ adj холмистый

hilt /хилт/ n рукоятка

him /хим/ pron его, ему

himself /химсэ́лф/ pron себя, себе, собой

hind /хайнд/ adj задний

hind /хайнд/ n самка благородного оленя

hinder /хúндэ/ vt мешать

hindrance /хúндрэнс/ n препятствие, помеха

Hindu /хúндýу/ n индус, индуска; adj индусский

hinge /хиндж/ n петля, шарнир; vt прикреплять на петлях

hint /хинт/ n намек; vt: ~ at /~ эт/ намекать на

hip /хип/ n бедро

hip-pocket /хúппóкит/ n задний карман (брюк)

hippodrome /хúпэдроум/ n ипподром

hippopotamus /хúпэпóтэмэс/ n гиппопотам

hire /хáйе/ n наем; прокат; vt нанимать; брать напрокат; снимать

hireling /хáйелинг/ n наемник

hire-purchase /хáйепéчес/ n покупка в рассрочку

hirer /хáйерэ/ n наниматель

his /хиз/ pron его, свой

hiss /хис/ vt освистывать; vi шипеть

historian /хистóриэн/ n историк

historic(al) /хистóрик(л)/ adj исторический

history /хúстэри/ n история

hit /хит/ n удар; попадание; успех; гвоздь сезона, популярная песня, пластинка; make a ~ /мэйк э ~/ производить сенсацию; vt ударять, попадать в цель

hitch /хич/ n помеха; without a ~ /визáут э ~/ как по маслу; vti зацеплять(ся)

hitch-hike /хúчхайк/ vt "голосовать" на дороге

hither /хúзэ/ adv сюда

hithermost /хúзэмоуст/ adj ближайший

hitherto /хúзэтýу/ adv до сих пор

hive /хайв/ n улей

hoard /хорд/ n запас; vt запасать

hoarfrost /хóорфрóст/ n иней

hoarse /хоорс/ adj хриплый

hoary /хóори/ adj седой, древний

hoax /хóукс/ n злая шутка, обман; vt мистифицировать

hobby /хóби/ n любимое занятие, конек

hockey /хóки/ n хоккей

hockey-stick /хóкистык/ n (хоккейная) клюшка

hocus-pocus /хóукэс-пóукэс/ n фокус

hoe /хóу/ n мотыга; vt мотыжить

hog /хог/ n свинья, боров

hoist /хойст/ n подъем; подъемник; vt поднимать

hold /хóулд/ n захват; трюм; vt держать; владеть; вмещать; занимать; проводить; ~ on /~ он/ подожди!; ~ one's tongue /~ ванз танг/ держать язык за зубами; ~ up /~ ап/ задерживать

holder /хóулдэ/ n владелец, держатель

holding /хóулдинг/ n владение

hole /хо́ул/ n дыра, нора

holiday /хо́лидэй/ n праздник; отпуск; выходной день; pl каникулы

holiness /хо́улинис/ n святость; your ~ /йо ~/ ваше святейшество

hollow /хо́лоу/ adj пустотелый, полый; впалый (о щеках); ~ tree /~ трии/ дуплистое дерево; vt: ~ out /~ а́ут/ выдалбливать

holster /хо́улстэ/ n кобура

holy /хо́ули/ adj священный, святой; H. spirit /~ спи́рит/ Святой дух; ~ Week /~ виик/ страстная неделя; ~ Writ /~ рит/ Священное писание

homage /хо́мидж/ n почтение; pay ~ /пэй ~/ отдавать должное

home /хо́ум/ n дом, жилище; родина; at ~ /эт ~/ дома; adj домашний; родной (город и т.п.); внутренний (торговля и т.п.); adv домой; make yourself at ~ /мэйк йосэ́лф эт ~/ будьте как дома!

homeless /хо́умлис/ adj бездомный

homework /хо́умвёк/ n домашняя работа

homicide /хо́мисайд/ n убийство; убийца

homeopath /хо́умьепэт/ n гомеопат

honest /о́нист/ adj честный

honestly /о́нистли/ adv честно

honesty /о́нисти/ n честность

honey /ха́ни/ n мед; (разг.) дорогой, голубчик, милый

honeycomb /ха́никоум/ n медовый сот

honeymoon /ха́нимун/ n медовый месяц

honorary /о́нэрэри/ adj почетный

honor /о́нэ/ n честь; pl почести; on my ~ /он май ~/ честное слово; your ~ /йо ~/ ваша честь; vt почитать

honorable /о́нэрэбл/ adj почтенный; честный; благородный

hood /худ/ n капюшон, капор; капот

hoof /хуув/ n копыто

hook /хук/ n крючок, крюк; by ~ or by crook /бай ~ о бай крук/ не мытьем, так катаньем

hookah /ху́кэ/ n кальян

hooked /хукт/ adj крючковатый (нос)

hooligan /ху́улигэн/ n хулиган

hoop /хууп/ n обруч

hooper /ху́упэ/ n бондарь

hop /хоп/ n хмель

hop /хоп/ vi скакать; n прыжок

hope /хо́уп/ n надежда; vi надеяться

hopeful /хо́упфул/ adj надеющийся; подающий надежды

hopeless /хо́уплис/ adj безнадежный

horde /хорд/ n орда

horizon /хэра́йзн/ n горизонт

horizontal /хо́ризо́нтл/ adj горизонтальный

horn /хорн/ n рог, гудок, рожок; ~ of plenty /~ ов пле́нти/ рог изобилия

horned /хорнд/ adj рогатый

horoscope /хо́рэскоуп/ n гороскоп

horrible /хо́рэбл/ adj ужасный

horribly /хо́рэбли/ adv страшно

horrid /хо́рид/ adj противный; отвратительный

horror /хо́рэ/ n ужас

horse /хоос/ n лошадь, конь

horseback /хо́осбэк/ n спина лошади; on ~ /он ~/ верхом

horse-collar /хо́оско́лэ/ n хомут

horseflesh /хо́осфлеш/ n конина

horsefly /хо́осфлай/ n слепень

horseman /хо́осмэн/ n всадник

horsepower /хо́оспа́уэ/ n (тех.) лошадиная сила

horse-race /хо́осрэйс/ n скачки, бега

horse-radish /хо́оср᷷диш/ n хрен

horseshoe /хо́ошшу/ n подкова

horticultural /хо́ртика́лчерэл/ adj садовый

horticulture /хо́ртикалче/ n садоводство

horticulturist /хо́ртика́лчерист/ n садовод

hose /хо́уз/ n шланг; чулки

hosier /хо́уже/ n торговец трикотажем

hosiery /хо́ужери/ n чулочные изделия, трикотажное белье

hospitable /хо́спитэбл/ adj гостеприимный

hospitably /хо́спитэбли/ adv радушно

hospital /хóспитл/ n больница
hospitality /хóспитэ́лити/ n гостеприимство
host /хóуст/ n хозяин (дома)
hostage /хóстыдж/ n заложник
hostel /хостл/ n общежитие
hostess /хóустыс/ n хозяйка (дома)
hostile /хóстайл/ adj враждебный
hostility /хости́лити/ n враждебность; pl
военные действия
hot /хот/ adj горячий, острый
hotel /хоутэ́л/ n гостиница
hotbed /хóтбэд/ n парник; рассадник, очаг
hot-headed /хóтхéдыд/ adj вспыльчивый
hot-house /хóтхаус/ n оранжерея
hot-water bottle /хóтвóотэботл/ n грелка
hound /хáунд/ n гончая
hour /áуэ/ n час
hourglass /áуэглас/ n песочные часы
hourly /áуэли/ adj ежечасный; adv еже-
часно
house /хáус/ n дом, династия; full ~ /фул
~/ (театр.) полный сбор; H. of
Commons /~ ов кóмэнз/ палата общин;
H. of Lords /~ ов лордз/ палата лордов;
vt обеспечивать жильем
household /хáусхóулд/ n домочадцы; домашнее хозяйство
householder /хáусхóулдэ/ n домовладелец; квартиросъемщик
housewarming /хáусвóрминг/ n новоселье
housewife /хáусвайф/ n домашняя хозяйка
housing /хáузинг/ n жилищное строительство; ~ problem /~ прóблем/ жи-
лищная проблема
hover /хóвэ/ vi пари́ть
how /хáу/ adv как, каким образом; ~ far
/~ фар/ как далеко; ~ long /~ лонг/ как
долго; ~ much (many)? /~ мач (мэ́ни)/
сколько?; ~ do you do? /~ ду ю ду/
здравствуйте!
however /хáуэ́вэ/ adv как бы ни; conj однако

howl /хáул/ n вой, рев; vi выть
hue /хьюю/ n оттенок
hug /хаг/ n объятие; vt обнимать
huge /хьююдж/ adj громадный
hull /хал/ n кожура; корпус (корабля);
vt шелушить
hullabaloo /хáлэбэлýу/ n шумиха
hum /хам/ n жужжание; vi жужжать
human /хьююмэн/ adj человеческий
humane /хьюмэ́йн/ adj гуманный
humanism /хьюю́мэнизм/ n гуманизм
humanity /хьюмэ́нити/ n человечество
humble /хамбл/ adj смиренный, покорный; vt смирять (гордыню)
humbleness /хáмблнис/ n покорность
humbly /хáмбли/ adv покорно
humdrum /хáмдрам/ adj банальный
humid /хьюю́мид/ adj влажный
humidity /хьюми́дити/ n сырость
humiliate /хьюми́лиэйт/ vt унижать
humiliating /хьюми́лиэйтинг/ adj унизительный
humiliation /хьюми́лиэ́йшн/ n унижение
humorist /хьюю́мэрист/ n юморист
humorous /хьюю́мэрэс/ adj юмористи-
ческий, забавный
humor /хьюю́мэ/ n юмор; настроение
hump /хамп/ n горб
humpback /хáмпбэк/ n горбун
hump-backed /хáмпбэ́кт/ adj горбатый
hundred /хáндрэд/ n сто
hundredth /хáндредф/ ord num сотый
hundredweight /хáндредвэйт/ n центнер
Hungarian /хангэ́риэн/ n венгр, венгерка; венгерский язык; adj венгерский
hunger /хáнгэ/ n голод
hunger strike /хáнгэстрайк/ n голодовка
hungrily /хáнгрили/ adv жадно
hungry /хáнгри/ adj голодный
hunt /хант/ n охота; vt охотиться на; ~ for
/~ фо/ искать
hunter /хáнтэ/ n охотник
hunting /хáнтинг/ n охота; ~ lodge /~
лодж/ охотничий домик
hurdle /хёрдл/ n барьер

hurdle-race /хёрдлрэйс/ n барьерный
бег, скачки с препятствиями
hurl /хёрл/ vt швырять
hurrah /хурáа/ interj ура!
hurricane /хáрикэн/ n ураган
hurry /хáри/ n спешка; in a ~ /ин э ~/
второпях; vti торопить(ся); ~ up /~ ап/
скорее!
hurt /хёрт/ n вред; боль; vt ушибать; vi
болеть
husband /хáзбэнд/ n муж
husbandry /хáзбэндри/ n земледелие
hush /хаш/ n тишина; vti успокаи-
вать(ся); ~ up /~ ап/ замалчивать;
interj тише!
husk /хаск/ n шелуха, оболочка; vt очищать (от шелухи)
husky /хáски/ adj хриплый
hussar /хузáар/ n гусар
hussy /хáси/ n нахальная девка
hustle /хасл/ vti толкать(ся), тес-
нить(ся), торопить(ся)
hut /хат/ n хижина
hyacinth /хáйэсинт/ n гиацинт
hybrid /хáйбрид/ n гибрид
hydrant /хáйдрэнт/ n водоразборный
кран
hydraulic /хайдрóолик/ adj гидравличе-
ский
hydrogen /хáйдрэджен/ n водород; ~
bomb /~ бом/ водородная бомба
hyena /хайúинэ/ n гиена
hygiene /хáйджин/ n гигиена
hymn /хим/ n гимн (церковный)
hyphen /хайфн/ n дефис
hypnotic /хипнóтик/ adj гипнотический
hypocrisy /хипóкрэси/ n лицемерие
hypocrite /хúпокрит/ n лицемер
hypodermic /хáйпэдёрмик/ adj подкожный; ~ syringe /~ сирúндж/ шприц
hypothesis /хайпóтысис/ n гипотеза
hypothetical /хáйпотéтикл/ adj гипоте-
тический
hysteria /хистúэриэ/ n истерия
hysterical /хистéрикл/ adj истерический
hysterics /хистéрикс/ n истерика

I

I /ай/ pron я
Iberian /айбúэриэн/ n ибер; язык древ-
них иберов; adj иберийский
ice /айс/ n лед; мороженое
ice-age /áйсэ́йдж/ n ледниковый период
iceberg /áйсбёг/ n айсберг
icebound /áйсбаунд/ adj скованный
льдом (о реке)
icebreaker /áйсбрэ́йкэ/ n ледоход
ice cream /áйскрúим/ n мороженое
ice hockey /áйсхóки/ n хоккей (на льду)
Icelandic /айслэ́ндик/ n исландский
язык; adj исландский
icicle /áйсикл/ n сосулька
icon /áйкон/ n икона
icy /áйси/ adj ледяной
idea /айдúэ/ n идея, мысль, понятие;
bright ~ /брайт ~/ блестящая идея
ideal /айдúэл/ adj идеальный; n идеал
idealism /айдúэлизм/ n идеализм
idealist /айдúэлист/ n идеалист
idealize /айдиэ́лайз/ vt идеализировать
identical /айдэ́нтикл/ adj тождествен-
ный
identification /айдэ́нтификéйшн/ n опоз-
нание; ~ card /~ кард/ удостоверение
личности
identify /айдэ́нтифай/ vt отождествлять
identity /айдэ́нтити/ n тождество; иден-
тичность; подлинность
ideology /áйдиóлэджи/ n идеология
idiocy /úдиэси/ n идиотизм, идиотство,
глупость
idiom /úдиэм/ n идиома; диалект, говор
idiot /úдиэт/ n идиот
idle /айдл/ adj праздный, ленивый;
тщетный, пустой; ~ time /~ тайм/ простой (машины); vi бездельничать
idleness /áйдлнис/ n праздность; беспо-
лезность
idler /áйдлэ/ n лентяй
idly /áйдли/ adv лениво; тщетно
idol /áйдл/ n кумир

idolize /а́йдэлайз/ vt боготворить

idyll /и́дил/ n идиллия

if /иф/ conj если, если бы, ли; as ~ /эз ~/ как будто; even ~ /иивн ~/ если даже

ignition /игни́шн/ n зажигание

ignoble /игно́убл/ adj подлый

ignominious /и́гнэми́ниэс/ adj бесчестный

ignoramus /и́гнэрэ́ймэс/ n невежда

ignorance /и́гнэрэнс/ n невежество

ignorant /и́гнэрэнт/ adj несведущий; be ~ of /би ~ ов/ не знать

ignore /игно́р/ vt игнорировать

ill /ил/ adj больной; дурной; ~ feeling /~ фи́илинг/ неприязнь; n зло, вред; fall ~ /фоол ~/ заболевать

ill-bred /и́лбрэ́д/ adj невоспитанный

ill-disposed /и́лдиспо́узд/ adj не в духе

illegal /или́игл/ adj незаконный

illegible /иле́джебл/ adj неразборчивый

illegitimate /и́лиджи́тимит/ adj незаконный

ill-founded /и́лфа́ундыд/ adj необоснованный

illicit /или́сит/ adj запрещенный

illiterate /или́тэрит/ adj неграмотный

illness /и́лнис/ n болезнь

ill-tempered /и́лтэ́мпэд/ adj раздражительный

ill-timed /и́лта́ймд/ adj несвоевременный

illuminate /илью́юминэйт/ vt освещать

illumination /илью́юминэ́йшн/ n освещение, иллюминация

illusion /илю́южн/ n иллюзия

illustrate /и́лэстрэйт/ vt иллюстрировать

illustration /и́лэстрэ́йшн/ n иллюстрация

illustrious /ила́стриэс/ adj знаменитый

ill-will /и́лви́л/ n недоброжелательство

image /и́мидж/ n образ, подобие

imaginable /имэ́джинэбл/ adj воображимый

imaginary /имэ́джинэри/ adj воображаемый

imagination /имэ́джинэ́йшн/ n воображение

imagine /имэ́джин/ vt воображать, представлять себе

imbecile /и́мбисил/ n, adj слабоумный

imitate /и́митэйт/ vt подражать, имитировать

imitation /и́митэ́йшн/ n подражание, имитация

immaculate /имэ́кьюлит/ adj безупречный

immature /и́мэтью́э/ adj незрелый

immediate /ими́идьет/ adj непосредственный, немедленный

immemorial /и́мимо́ориэл/ adj древний; from times ~ /фром таймз ~/ с незапамятных времен

immense /име́нс/ adj безмерный, необъятный

immerse /име́рс/ vt погружать

immigrant /и́мигрэнт/ n иммигрант

immigrate /и́мигрэйт/ vi иммигрировать

immigration /и́мигрэ́йшн/ n иммиграция

imminent /и́минэнт/ adj неминуемый

immobile /имо́убайл/ adj неподвижный

immoderate /имо́дэрит/ adj неумеренный

immodest /имо́дыст/ adj наглый

immoral /имо́рл/ adj безнравственный

immortal /имо́ртл/ adj бессмертный

immortality /и́мортэ́лити/ n бессмертие

immovable /иму́увэбл/ adj неподвижный; n pl недвижимость

immunity /имью́юнити/ n иммунитет

impact /и́мпэкт/ n удар, влияние

impair /импэ́э/ vt повреждать

impalpable /импэ́лпэбл/ adj неосязаемый

impart /импа́рт/ vt наделять, сообщать

impartial /импа́ршл/ adj беспристрастный

impassable /импа́асэбл/ adj непроходимый

impassive /импэ́сив/ adj безразличный; безмятежный

impassioned /импэ́шнд/ adj страстный

impatience /и́мпэ́йшнс/ n нетерпение

impatient /импэ́йшнт/ adj нетерпеливый

impeach /импи́ич/ vt сомневаться

impeachment /impи́ичмент/ n привлечение к суду; импичмент

impeccable /импе́кэбл/ adj безупречный

impede /импи́ид/ vt препятствовать

impel /импе́л/ vt побуждать, приводить в движение

impending /импе́ндинг/ adj предстоящий, надвигающийся

impenetrable /импе́нитрэбл/ adj непроходимый; непроницаемый

imperative /импе́рэтив/ adj повелительный

imperfect /импёрфикт/ adj несовершенный

imperfection /имперфе́кшн/ n несовершенство

imperial /импи́эриэл/ adj имперский; императорский

imperialism /импи́эриэлизм/ n империализм

imperialist /импи́эриэлист/ n империалист

imperious /импи́эриэс/ adj властный

imperishable /импе́ришебл/ adj непортящийся; бессмертный

impersonal /импёрснл/ adj безличный

impersonate /импёрсэнэйт/ vt олицетворять

impertinent /импёртинент/ adj дерзкий

imperturbable /и́мпетёбэбл/ adj невозмутимый

impetuous /импе́тьюэс/ adj стремительный

impetus /и́мпитэс/ n импульс

implant /импла́ант/ vt внедрять; пересаживать (сердце и т.п.)

implement /и́мплимент/ n орудие; vt выполнять, осуществлять

implicate /и́мпликэйт/ vt впутывать

implicit /импли́сит/ adj подразумеваемый; безоговорочный

implore /импло́р/ vt умолять

imply /импла́й/ vt подразумевать

impolite /и́мпэла́йт/ adj невежливый

import /импо́рт/ vt ввозить, импортировать; /и́мпорт/ n ввоз, импорт; ~ duty /~ дью́юти/ ввозная пошлина

importance /импо́ртэнс/ n важность

important /импо́ртэнт/ adj значительный

importer /импо́ртэ/ n импортер

impose /импо́уз/ vt налагать; навязывать

imposing /импо́узинг/ adj внушительный

impossibility /импо́сэби́лити/ n невозможность

impossible /импо́сэбл/ adj невозможный

impostor /импо́стэ/ n самозванец

impotence /и́мпэтэнс/ n бессилие; импотенция

impotent /и́мпэтэнт/ adj бессильный

impoverish /импо́вериш/ vt доводить до нищеты

impress /импре́с/ vt производить впечатление; /и́мпрес/ n отпечаток

impression /импре́шн/ n впечатление; переиздание

impressionable /импре́шнэбл/ adj впечатлительный

impressive /импре́сив/ adj внушительный, производящий впечатление

imprint /и́мпринт/ n отпечаток, след; printer's ~ /при́нтэз ~/ выходные данные

imprison /импри́зн/ vt заключать в тюрьму

imprisonment /импри́знмент/ n тюремное заключение

improbability /импро́бэби́лити/ n невероятность, неправдоподобие

improbable /импро́бэбл/ adj невероятный

impromptu /импро́мтью/ adj импровизированный; adv экспромтом

improper /импро́пэ/ adj неприличный; неподходящий

improve /импру́ув/ vti улучшать(ся)

improvement /импру́увмент/ n улучшение

improvise /и́мпрэвайз/ vt импровизировать

imprudence /импру́уденс/ n неосторожность

imprudent /импру́удент/ adj неблагоразумный, неосторожный

impudence /и́мпьюденс/ n бесстыдство

impudent /и́мпьюдент/ adj дерзкий

impulse /и́мпалс/ n побуждение, импульс

impulsive /импа́лсив/ adj импульсивный

impunity /импью́юнити/ n безнаказанность; with ~ /виз ~/ безнаказанно

impure /импью́э/ adj нечистый; непристойный

impurity /импью́эрити/ n нечистота; непристойность

in /ин/ prep в, на, во время, через; ~ all /~ оол/ всего; ~ a week /~ э виик/ за неделю; ~ due course /~ дью корс/ в свое время; ~ the morning /~ зэ мо́рнинг/ утром; ~ my opinion /~ май эпи́ньен/ по моему мнению; ~ the sun /~ зэ сан/ на солнце; ~ time /~ тайм/ вовремя; ~ writing /~ ра́йтинг/ в письменной форме; adv внутри, внутрь

inability /и́нэби́лити/ n неспособность

inaccessible /и́нэксе́сэбл/ adj недоступный

inaccurate /инэ́кьюрит/ adj неточный

inactive /инэ́ктив/ adj инертный

inadequate /инэ́диквит/ adj недостаточный

inadmissible /и́нэдми́сэбл/ adj недопустимый

inalienable /инэ́йльенэбл/ adj неотъемлемый

inappropriate /и́нэпро́уприит/ adj неуместный

inapt /инэ́пт/ adj неподходящий; неискусный

inarticulate /и́нэти́кьюлит/ adj невнятный

inasmuch as /и́нэзма́чэз/ conj поскольку

inattentive /и́нэте́нтив/ adj невнимательный

inaudible /ино́одэбл/ adj неслышный

inaugurate /ино́огъюрэйт/ vt ознаменовать; торжественно открывать

inauguration /ино́огъюрэ́йшн/ n торжественное вступление в должность

inborn /и́нбо́рн/ adj врожденный

incalculable /инкэ́лкьюлэбл/ adj неисчислимый

incapable /инке́йпэбл/ adj неспособный

incarnation /и́нкарнэ́йшн/ n воплощение

incendiary /инсэ́ндиэри/ adj зажигательный; n поджигатель

incense /и́нсенс/ n ладан

incentive /инсе́нтив/ n побуждение, стимул

incessant /инсе́снт/ adj непрерывный

incest /инсе́ст/ n кровосмешение

inch /инч/ n дюйм

incident /и́нсидент/ n происшествие, инцидент

incidental /и́нсиде́нтл/ adj случайный; n pl непредвиденные расходы

incinerate /инси́нэрэйт/ vt сжигать дотла; кремировать

incinerator /инси́нэрэйтэ/ n мусоросжигательная печь/станция

incipient /инси́пиэнт/ adj начинающийся, зарождающийся

incite /инса́йт/ vt подстрекать; стимулировать

incitement /инса́йтмент/ n подстрекательство; побуждение

inclination /и́нклинэ́йшн/ n склонность

incline /инкла́йн/ vti склонять(ся)

inclined /инкла́йнд/ adj склонный

include /инклю́юд/ vt включать

including /инклю́юдинг/ prep в том числе

incoherent /и́нкоухи́эрент/ adj бессвязный

income /и́нкэм/ n доход; ~ tax /~ тэкс/ подоходный налог

incoming /и́нка́минг/ adj прибывающий

incommunicative /и́нкэмью́юникэтив/ adj необщительный

incomparable /инко́мпэрэбл/ adj несравнимый

incompatible /и́нкэмпэ́тэбл/ adj несовместимый

incompetent /инко́мпитент/ adj неспособный, некомпетентный

incomplete /и́нкэмпли́ит/ adj неполный, незавершенный

incomprehensible /инко́мприхе́нсэбл/ adj непостижимый

inconceivable /и́нкэнси́ивэбл/ adj необразимый; непонятный

inconsiderate /и́нкэнси́дерит/ adj невнимательный; неосмотрительный

inconsistency /и́нкэнси́стенси/ n непоследовательность

inconsistent /и́нкэнси́стент/ adj непоследовательный

incontestable /и́нкэнтэ́стэбл/ adj неоспоримый

inconvenience /и́нкэнви́иньенс/ n неудобство

inconvenient /и́нкэнви́иньент/ adj неудобный

incorporate /инко́рпэрэйт/ vti соединить(ся)

incorporation /инко́рпэрэ́йшн/ n корпорация

incorrect /и́нкэре́кт/ adj неправильный

incorrigible /инко́риджебл/ adj неисправимый

incorruptible /и́нкэра́птэбл/ adj неподкупный

increase /и́нкрис/ n увеличение; /инкри́ис/ vt увеличивать

incredible /инкре́дэбл/ adj невероятный

incredulous /инкре́дьюлэс/ adj недоверчивый

increment /и́нкримент/ n прибавка; увеличение

incriminate /инкри́минэйт/ vt вменять в вину

incubation /и́нкьюбэ́йшн/ n инкубация

incur /инкёр/ vt навлекать на себя, подвергаться; ~ losses /~ ло́сыз/ терпеть убытки, нести потери

incurable /инкью́оэрэбл/ adj неизлечимый

indebted /индэ́тыд/ adj находящийся в долгу, обязанный

indecent /инди́иснт/ adj неприличный

indecisive /и́ндиса́йсив/ adj нерешительный

indeed /инди́ид/ adv в самом деле, действительно

indefatigable /и́ндифэ́тигэбл/ adj неутомимый

indefensible /и́ндифе́нсэбл/ adj неудобный для обороны; недоказуемый

indefinite /инде́финит/ adj неопределенный

indelible /инде́либл/ adj неизгладимый

indelicate /инде́ликит/ adj бестактный

indemnity /индэ́мнити/ n компенсация

indenture /индэ́нче/ n контракт

independence /и́ндипе́ндэнс/ n независимость

independent /и́ндипе́ндэнт/ adj независимый

indescribable /и́ндискра́йбэбл/ adj неописуемый

indestructible /и́ндистра́ктэбл/ adj неразрушимый

index /и́ндэкс/ n указатель; показатель; card ~ /кард ~/ картотека; ~ finger /~ фи́нгэ/ указательный палец

Indian /и́ндьен/ n индиец, индеец, индианка; adj индийский, индейский; ~ summer /~ са́мэ/ бабье лето

indicate /и́ндикейт/ vt указывать

indication /и́ндике́йшн/ n указание; симптом

indicator /и́ндикейтэ/ n индикатор

indict /инда́йт/ vt обвинять

indictment /инда́йтмент/ n обвинительный акт

indifference /инди́фрэнс/ n равнодушие

indifferent /инди́фрэнт/ adj безразличный

indigenous /инди́джинэс/ adj туземный, местный

indigestion /и́ндидже́счн/ n расстройство желудка

indignant /инди́гнэнт/ n возмущение
indirect /и́ндире́кт/ adj косвенный, непрямой
indiscipline /инди́сиплин/ n недисциплинированность
indiscreet /и́ндискри́ит/ adj нескромный; неосторожный
indispensable /и́ндиспе́нсэбл/ adj незаменимый
indisposition /и́ндиспэзи́шн/ n недомогание
indisputable /и́ндиспью́ютэбл/ adj неоспоримый
indistinct /и́ндисти́нкт/ adj неясный
indistinguishable /и́ндисти́нгвишебл/ adj неразличимый
individual /и́ндиви́дьюэл/ adj личный; n индивидуум, человек
individuality /и́ндиви́дьюэ́лити/ n индивидуальность
indivisible /и́ндиви́зэбл/ adj неделимый
indoctrinate /индо́ктринэйт/ vt знакомить с теорией, учением
Indo-European /и́ндою́эрэпи́эн/ adj индоевропейский
indolent /и́ндэлэнт/ adj ленивый
indoor /и́ндоо/ adj внутри дома, комнатный
indoors /и́ндо́рз/ adv в помещении
induce /индью́юс/ vt побуждать
inducement /индью́юсмент/ n побуждение
indulge /инда́лдж/ vt баловать, потакать; ~ in /~ ин/ предаваться
indulgence /инда́лдженс/ n потакание
indulgent /инда́лджент/ adj снисходительный
industrial /инда́стриэл/ adj промышленный
industrious /инда́стриэс/ adj трудолюбивый
industry /и́ндэстри/ n промышленность
inedible /инэ́дибл/ adj несъедобный
inefficient /и́ныфи́шнт/ adj неспособный; неэффективный

inelegant /инэ́лигэнт/ adj безвкусный, неизящный
inequality /и́ныкво́лити/ n неравенство
inert /ине́рт/ adj вялый
inertia /ине́ршиэ/ n инерция
inestimable /инэ́стимэбл/ adj неоценимый
inevitable /инэ́витэбл/ adj неизбежный
inexact /и́ныгзэ́кт/ adj неточный
inexcusable /и́ныкскью́юзэбл/ adj непростительный
inexhaustible /и́ныгзо́остэбл/ adj неистощимый
inexpensive /и́ныкспе́нсив/ adj недорогой
inexperience /и́ныкспи́эриэнс/ n неопытность
inexperienced /и́ныкспи́эриэнст/ adj неопытный
inexpert /и́нэкспе́рт/ adj неумелый
inexplicable /инэ́кспликэбл/ adj необъяснимый
inexpressive /и́ныкспре́сив/ adj невыразительный
inextinguishable /и́ныксты́нгвишебл/ adj неугасимый
infallible /инфэ́лэбл/ adj непогрешимый
infamous /и́нфэмэс/ adj позорный; бесславный
infamy /и́нфэми/ n бесчестие
infancy /и́нфэнси/ n младенчество
infant /и́нфэнт/ n младенец
infantry /и́нфэнтри/ n пехота
infatuation /инфэ́тью́эйшн/ n страстное увлечение
infect /инфе́кт/ vt заражать
infection /инфе́кшн/ n инфекция
infectious /инфе́кшес/ adj заразный; заразительный
infer /инфе́р/ vt заключать, делать вывод
inference /и́нферэнс/ n вывод
inferior /инфи́эриэ/ adj низший, худший; n подчиненный
inferiority /инфи́эрио́рити/ n неполноценность; ~ complex /~ ко́мплекс/ комплекс неполноценности

infernal /инфёрнл/ adj адский

infertile /инфёртайл/ adj бесплодный

infidel /ѝнфидэл/ adj неверующий; n неверующий, язычник

infidelity /ѝнфидэ́лити/ n неверность; неверие

infiltrate /ѝнфилтрэйт/ vti проникать

infinite /ѝнфинит/ adj бесконечный

infinity /ѝнфинити/ n бесконечность

infirm /инфёрм/ adj дряхлый, немощный

inflame /инфлэ́йм/ vt воспламенять

inflammation /ѝнфлэмэ́йшн/ n воспламенение; воспаление

inflate /инфлэ́йт/ vt надувать; вздувать (цены)

inflation /инфлэ́йшн/ n надувание; инфляция

inflexible /инфле́ксэбл/ adj негибкий; непреклонный

inflict /инфлѝкт/ vt наносить, причинять (боль)

influence /ѝнфлуэнс/ n влияние; vt влиять на

influential /ѝнфлуэ́ншл/ adj влиятельный

influenza /ѝнфлуэ́нзэ/ n грипп

inform /инфо́рм/ vt сообщать; ~ against /~ эге́йнст/ доносить на

informal /инфо́рмл/ adj неофициальный

information /ѝнфэмэ́йшн/ n информация, сведения

informative /инфо́рмэтив/ adj поучительный

informed /инфо́рмд/ adj осведомленный

informer /инфо́рмэ/ n осведомитель

infringe /инфрѝндж/ vt нарушать

infringement /инфрѝнджмент/ n нарушение

infuriate /инфью́эриэйт/ vt разъярять

ingenious /инджѝиньес/ adj изобретательный

ingenuity /ѝнджинью́юити/ n изобретательность

inglorious /ингло́ориэс/ adj бесславный

ingot /ѝнгэт/ n слиток

ingratitute /ингрэ́титьюд/ n неблагодарность

ingredient /ингрѝидьент/ n составная часть

inhabit /инхэ́бит/ vt населять

inhabitant /инхэ́битэнт/ n житель

inhale /инхэ́йл/ vt вдыхать

inhaler /инхэ́йлэ/ n ингалятор

inherent /инхѝэрэнт/ adj присущий

inherit /инхе́рит/ vt наследовать

inheritance /инхе́ритэнс/ n наследство

inhospitable /инхо́спитэбл/ adj негостеприимный

inhuman /инхью́юмэн/ adj бесчеловечный

inimitable /инѝмитэбл/ adj неподражаемый

initial /инѝшел/ adj первоначальный; n начальная буква; pl инициалы; vt ставить инициалы

initiate /инѝшиит/ vt положить начало; посвящать (в тайну)

initiative /инѝшиэтив/ n инициатива

initiator /инѝшиэйтэ/ n инициатор

inject /индже́кт/ vt впрыскивать

injection /индже́кшн/ n укол

injunction /инджа́нкшэн/ n (юр.) постановление суда

injure /ѝндже/ vt ушибать; ранить

injury /ѝнджери/ n ранение

injustice /инджа́стис/ n несправедливость

ink /инк/ n чернила; printer's ~ /прѝнтэз ~/ типографская краска

ink-pot /ѝнкпот/ n чернильница

inkling /ѝнклинг/ n намек; слабое подозрение

inland /ѝнлэнд/ adv внутрь/внутри страны

inlet /ѝнлет/ n залив, бухточка

inmate /ѝнмэйт/ n жилец; заключенный (в тюрьме)

inmost /ѝнмоуст/ adj сокровенный

inn /ин/ n гостиница

inner /и́нэ/ adj внутренний

innocence /и́нэснс/ n невиновность

innovation /и́нов́эйшн/ n нововведение

innovator /и́нов́эйтэ/ n новатор

innuendo /и́нуэ́ндоу/ n инсинуация

innumerable /инъю́юмэрэбл/ adj бесчисленный

inoculate /ино́кьюлэйт/ vt делать прививку

inoffensive /и́нэфе́нсив/ adj безобидный

inoperative /ино́прэтив/ adj недействующий

inopportune /ино́пэтьюн/ adj несвоевременный

in-patient /инп́эйшнт/ n стационарный больной

inquest /и́нквэст/ n (юр.) следствие

inquisitive /инкви́зитив/ adj любознательный

insane /инс́эйн/ adj душевнобольной

insanity /инс́энити/ n умопомешательство

insatiable /инс́эйшьебл/ adj ненасытный

inscription /инскри́пшн/ n надпись; посвящение

inscrutable /инскру́утэбл/ adj загадочный

insect /и́нсект/ n насекомое

insecure /и́нсикью́ё/ adj небезопасный

insemination /инсе́мин́эйшн/ n оплодотворение; artificial ~ /́артифи́шл ~/ искусственное осеменение

insensible /инс́энсэбл/ adj нечувствительный; потерявший сознание

inseparable /инс́эпрэбл/ adj неотделимый

insert /инсёрт/ vt вставлять; помещать (в газете)

insertion /инсёршн/ n вставка; объявление

inset /и́нсэт/ n вкладка

inside /и́нс́айд/ adj внутренний; n внутренняя часть; adv внутри, внутрь; ~ out /~ ́аут/ наизнанку; prep внутри, в

insidious /инси́диэс/ adj коварный

insight /и́нсайт/ n прозорливость

insignia /инси́гниэ/ n pl знаки отличия

insincere /и́нсинси́э/ adj неискренний

insinuation /инси́ньюз́эйшн/ n инсинуация

insipid /инси́пид/ adj безвкусный

insist /инси́ст/ vi настаивать

insistence /инси́стэнс/ n настойчивость

insolence /и́нсэлэнс/ n наглость

insoluble /инсо́льюбл/ adj неразрешимый

insolvent /инсо́лвент/ adj несостоятельный; become ~ /биќам ~/ обанкротиться

insomnia /инсо́мниэ/ n бессонница

inspect /инспе́кт/ vt осматривать, инспектировать

inspection /инспе́кшн/ n осмотр, инспекция

inspector /инспе́ктэ/ n инспектор

inspiration /и́нспэр́эйшн/ n вдохновение

inspire /инсп́айе/ vt вдохновлять

instability /и́нстэби́лити/ n неустойчивость

install /инсто́ол/ vt водворять; устанавливать; (эл.) проводить

installation /и́нстэл́эйшн/ n монтаж; pl сооружения

instalment /инсто́олмент/ n очередной взнос; pay by ~s /пэй бай ~с/ выплачивать в рассрочку; очередной выпуск

instance /и́нстэнс/ n пример; for ~ /фор ~/ например

instant /и́нстэнт/ adj немедленный; n мгновение

instantaneous /и́нстэнт́эйньес/ adj мгновенный

instantly /и́нстэнтли/ adv немедленно

instead /инст́эд/ adv вместо; вместо того, чтобы

instigate /и́нстигейт/ vt подстрекать

instigator /и́нстигейтэ/ n подстрекатель

instinct /и́нстинкт/ n инстинкт

instinctive /инсти́нктив/ adj инстинктивный

institute /и́нститьют/ n институт; vt учреждать, устанавливать institution /и́нститьюˊюшн/ n учреждение

instruct /инстра́кт/ vt обучать

instruction /инстра́кшн/ n обучение; pl указания

instructive /инстра́ктив/ adj поучительный

instructor /инстра́ктэ/ n инструктор, учитель

instrument /и́нструмент/ n инструмент, прибор, орудие (также образн.)

instrumental /и́нструме́нтл/ adj полезный, определяющий; be ~ in /би ~ ин/ способствовать

insubordination /и́нсэбо́рдинэ́йшн/ n неповиновение

insufferable /инса́фрэбл/ adj невыносимый

insufficient /и́нсэфи́шент/ adj недостаточный

insular /и́нсьюлэ/ adj островной

insulate /и́нсьюлэйт/ vt изолировать

insulin /и́нсьюлин/ n инсулин

insult /и́нсалт/ n оскорбление; /инса́лт/ vt оскорблять

insurance /иншу́эрэнс/ n страхование; fire ~ /фа́йе ~/ страхование от пожара; ~ policy /~ по́лиси/ страховой полис; ~ premium /~ при́имьем/ страховая премия

insure /иншу́э/ vt страховать

insured /иншу́эд/ adj застрахованный

insurer /иншу́эрэ/ n страховое общество; страховщик

insurgent /инсёрджент/ n повстанец

insurmountable /и́нсэма́унтэбл/ adj непреодолимый

insurrection /и́нсэрэ́кшэн/ n восстание

intact /инта́кт/ adj нетронутый, неповрежденный

integral /и́нтигрл/ adj неотъемлемый; цельный; (матем.) интегральный

integrate /и́нтигрэйт/ vt объединять

integration /и́нтигрэ́йшн/ n слияние

integrity /интэ́грити/ n честность; целостность

intellect /и́нтилект/ n интеллект, ум

intellectual /и́нтиле́ктьюэл/ adj умственный; n интеллигент; pl интеллигенция

intelligence /интэ́лидженс/ n ум; понятливость (животных); разведка

intelligent /интэ́лиджент/ adj умный, разумный

intend /интэ́нд/ vt намереваться

intended /интэ́ндыд/ adj предназначенный

intense /интэ́нс/ adj напряженный, сильный

intensify /интэ́нсифай/ vti усиливать (ся)

intensity /интэ́нсити/ n интенсивность, сила

intensive /интэ́нсив/ adj интенсивный

intent /интэ́нт/ adj внимательный

intention /интэ́ншн/ n намерение

intentional /интэ́ншенл/ adj умышленный

intentionally /интэ́ншенли/ adv намеренно

intercept /и́нтэсе́пт/ vt перехватывать

intercession /и́нтэсэ́шэн/ n заступничество

intercessor /и́нтэсэ́сэ/ n ходатай

interchange /и́нтэчэ́йндж/ n обмен

interchangeable /и́нтэчэ́йнджебл/ adj взаимозаменяемый

intercourse /и́нтэко́ос/ n общение; сношения

interdependence /и́нтэдипэ́ндэнс/ n взаимозависимость

interest /и́нтрист/ n интерес; процент; bear ~ /бээ ~/ приносить прибыль; in your ~ /ин йо ~/ в ваших интересах; rate of ~ /рэйт ов ~/ норма процента; vt интересовать

interested /и́нтристыд/ adj заинтересованный; корыстный

interesting /и́нтристинг/ adj интересный

interfere /и́нтэфи́э/ vi вмешиваться; ~ with /~ виз/ мешать

interference /и́нтэфи́эрэнс/ n вмешательство; (радио) помехи interior /интиэриэ/ adj внутренний; n внутренность; интерьер; внутренние дела

interject /интэджéкт/ vt вставлять

interjection /интэджéкшн/ n восклицание

interlocutor /интэлóкьютэ/ n собеседник

intermarriage /интэмэ́ридж/ n брак между людьми разных рас; брак между родственниками

intermediary /интэми́дьери/ adj промежуточный; n посредник

intermingle /интэми́нгл/ vti перемешивать(ся), смешивать(ся)

intermission /интэми́шн/ n (театр.) антракт

intermittent /интэми́тент/ adj прерывистый

intern /интёрн/ vt интернировать

internal /интёрнл/ adj внутренний

internally /интёрнэли/ adv внутренне

international /интэнэ́шнл/ adj международный

internationalism /интэнэ́шнелизм/ n интернационализм

interplay /интэпплэ́й/ n взаимодействие

interpret /интёрприт/ vt переводить (устно)

interpretation /интёрпритэ́йшн/ n перевод

interpreter /интёрпритэ/ n переводчик (устный)

interrogate /интэ́рэгэйт/ vt допрашивать

interrogation /интэ́рэгэ́йшн/ n допрос

interrogator /интэ́рэгэйтэ/ n следователь

interrupt /интэрá́пт/ vt прерывать

interruption /интэрá́пшн/ n перерыв

intersect /интэсéкт/ vti пересекать(ся)

interval /интэвл/ n перерыв; (театр.) антракт; перемена (между уроками)

intervention /интэвéншн/ n интервенция; вмешательство

interview /интэвьюю/ n беседа, интервью; vt интервьюировать

intestine /интэ́стин/ n кишечник

intimacy /интимэси/ n близость; интимность

intimate /интимит/ adj близкий; интимный

intimately /интимитли/ adv близко; интимно

intimidate /интимидэйт/ vt запугивать

intimidation /интимидэ́йшн/ n запугивание

into /инту/ prep в, во, на; ~ the bargain /~ зэ бáргин/ в придачу

intolerable /интóлэрэбл/ adj невыносимый

intolerance /интóлэрэнс/ n нетерпимость

intolerant /интóлэрэнт/ adj нетерпимый

intoxicate /интóксикейт/ vt опьянять

intransigent /интрэ́нсиджент/ adj непримиримый

intrepid /интрéпид/ adj неустрашимый

intricacy /интрикэси/ n сложность

intricate /интрикит/ adj запутанный

intrigue /интри́иг/ n интрига; vti интриговать, заинтриговывать

introduce /интрэдьююс/ vt представлять; вводить; ~ oneself /~ вансэ́лф/ представиться

introduction /интрэдáкшн/ n представление; предисловие

intrude /интрýуд/ vi вторгаться; vt навязывать

intrusion /интрýужн/ n вторжение

intuition /интьюи́шн/ n интуиция

inundation /инандэ́йшн/ n наводнение

invade /инвэ́йд/ vt вторгаться

invader /инвэ́йдэ/ n захватчик

invalid /инвэлид/ adj больной; n инвалид

invalid /инвэ́лид/ adj несостоятельный; недействительный

invalidate /инвэ́лидэйт/ vt делать недействительным

invaluable /инвэ́льюэбл/ adj бесценный

invariable /инвэ́эриэбл/ adj неизменный

invasion /инвэ́йжн/ n нашествие

invent /инвéнт/ vt изобретать

invention /инвéншен/ n изобретение

inventive /инве́нтив/ adj изобретательный

inventor /инве́нтэ/ n изобретатель

inventory /и́нвентри/ n инвентаризация, опись имущества

invest /инве́ст/ vt вкладывать, помещать (капитал)

investigation /инве́стигэ́йшн/ n (юр.) следствие; исследование

investment /инве́стмент/ n капиталовложение

investor /инве́стэ/ n вкладчик

invigorate /инви́гэрэйт/ vt придавать силы

invincible /инви́нсэбл/ adj непобедимый

invisible /инви́зэбл/ adj невидимый; ~ ink /~ инк/ симпатические чернила

invitation /инвитэ́йшн/ n приглашение

invite /инва́йт/ vt приглашать

invoice /и́нвойс/ n накладная

invoke /инво́ук/ vt взывать, заклинать

involuntarily /инво́лэнтрили/ adv нечаянно

involuntary /инво́лэнтри/ adj невольный

involve /инво́лв/ vt вовлекать, запутывать; включать в себя

invulnerable /инва́лнэрэбл/ adj неуязвимый

inward /и́нвэд/ adj внутренний

inwardly /и́нвэдли/ adv в душе

iodine /а́йэдин/ n йод

I.O.U. /а́йойу́/ n долговая расписка

Iraqi /ира́аки/ n житель Ирака; adj иракский

irate /айрэ́йт/ adj гневный

iris /а́йэрис/ n радужная оболочка (глаза); (бот.) ирис

Irish /а́йэриш/ n ирландский язык; adj ирландский

Irishman /а́йэришмэн/ n ирландец

Irishwoman /а́йеришву́мэн/ n ирландка

irk /ёрк/ vt раздражать

iron /а́йёрн/ n железо, утюг; pl кандалы; adj железный; ~ rations /~ рэшнз/ неприкосновенный запас; vt гладить

ironic(al) /айро́ник(л)/ adj иронический

ironing /а́йэнинг/ n утюжка; ~ board /~ борд/ гладильная доска

iron-ore /а́йеноо/ n железная руда

irony /а́йерэни/ n ирония

irrational /ирэ́шенл/ adj нерациональный

irreconcilable /ирэ́кэнсайлэбл/ adj непримиримый

irrefutable /ирэ́фьютэбл/ adj неопровержимый

irregular /ирэ́гьюлэ/ adj нерегулярный; неправильный

irregularity /ирэ́гьюлэ́рити/ n нерегулярность; неправильность

irrelevant /ирэ́ливэнт/ adj неуместный; несоответствующий

irreparable /ирэ́пэрэбл/ adj непоправимый

irreproachable /и́рипро́учебл/ adj безупречный

irrespective /и́риспэ́ктив/ adj не зависимый, безотносительный

irresponsible /и́риспо́нсэбл/ adj безответственный

irretrievable /и́ритри́ивэбл/ adj невозместимый

irrevocable /ирэ́вэкэбл/ adj безвозвратный

irrigate /и́ригэйт/ vt орошать

irrigation /и́ригэ́йшн/ n ирригация

irritable /и́ритэбл/ adj раздражительный

irritation /и́ритэ́йшн/ n раздражение

Islam /и́злаам/ n ислам

island /а́йлэнд/ n остров

islander /а́йлэндэ/ n островитянин

islet /а́йлит/ n островок

isolate /а́йсэлэйт/ vt изолировать

isolated /а́йсэлэ́тыд/ adj изолированный

isolation /а́йсэлэ́йшн/ n изоляция

Israeli(te) /и́зриэлайт/ n израильтянин, израильтянка; adj израильский

issue /и́сью/ n выпуск; предмет обсуждения; vi выходить; vt выпускать

isthmus /и́смэс/ n перешеек

it /ит/ pron он, она, оно; what is ~ /вот из ~/ что это?; ~ rains /~ рэйнз/ идет дождь

Italian /итэ́льен/ n итальянец, итальянка; итальянский язык; adj итальянский

italics /итэ́ликс/ n pl курсив

itch /ич/ n зуд; vi зудеть

item /а́йтэм/ n пункт; статья; предмет

itinerary /айти́нрэри/ n маршрут

its /итс/ poss pron его, ее, свой

itself /итсэ́лф/ pron себя, сам, сама, само; she is virtue ~ /ши из вёртью ~/ она сама добродетель

ivory /а́йври/ n слоновая кость

ivy /а́йви/ n плющ

J

jab /джэб/ n толчок, удар; vt толкать, пихать

jack /джэк/ n (тех.) домкрат; (карты) валет; ~ of all trades /~ ов оол трэйдз/ мастер на все руки

jackal /джэ́кол/ n шакал

jackass /джэ́кэс/ n осел

jacket /джэ́кит/ n жакет, куртка, пиджак; суперобложка (книги)

jade /джейд/ n (мин.) нефрит; шлюха

jagged /джэ́гид/ adj зубчатый

jaguar /джэ́гьюэ/ n ягуар

jail /джейл/ n тюрьма

jailer /джéйлэ/ n тюремщик

jam /джэм/ n джем; traffic ~ /трэ́фик ~/ затор; vt загромождать; (радио) заглушать; vi останавливаться, заедать

janitor /джэ́нитэ/ n дворник

January /джэ́ньюэри/ n январь

Japanese /джэ́пэни́из/ n японец, японка; японский язык; adj японский

jar /джар/ n банка, кувшин; шок, потрясение; vi дребезжать

jarring /джаа́ринг/ adj раздражающий

jasmine /джэ́смин/ n жасмин

jasper /джэ́спэ/ n яшма

jaundice /джо́ондис/ n желтуха; зависть

javelin /джэ́влин/ n копье

jaw /джоо/ n челюсть

jazz /джэз/ n джаз

jealous /джéлэс/ adj ревнивый

jealousy /джéлэси/ n ревность

jean /джиин/ n бумажная ткань; pl. джинсы

jeer /джи́э/ vti высмеивать

jelly /джéли/ n желе

jelly-fish /джéлифиш/ n медуза

jemmy /джéми/ n отмычка

jeopardize /джéпэдайз/ vt подвергать опасности

jerk /джёрк/ n толчок, подергивание

jerry-built /джéрибилт/ adj построенный на скорую руку

jersey /джёёзи/ n свитер; ~ dress /~ дрэс/ вязаное платье

jest /джест/ n шутка, острота; vi шутить, острить

jester /джéстэ/ n шут

Jesuit /джéзьюит/ n иезуит

Jesuitic(al) /джéзьюи́тик(эл)/ adj иезуитский; (образн.) коварный

Jesus /джи́изэс/ n Иисус

jet /джет/ n струя; (мин.) агат, жиклёр; ~ plane /~ плэйн/ реактивный самолет

Jew /джуу/ n еврей

jewel /джу́уэл/ n драгоценный камень

jeweller /джу́уэлэ/ n ювелир

jewellery /джу́уэлри/ n ювелирные изделия

Jewess /джу́уис/ n еврейка

Jewish /джу́уиш/ adj еврейский

Jewry /джу́эри/ n еврейство

jig /джиг/ n джига (танец)

jigsaw puzzle /джи́гсопазл/ n составная картинка-загадка

jingle /джингл/ n звяканье; vi звякать

jingo /джи́нгоу/ n шовинист

jingoism /джи́нгоизм/ n шовинизм

job /джоб/ n работа

job-work /джóбвёрк/ n сдельная работа

jockey /джóки/ n жокей

jocose, jocular /джекóус, джóкьюлэ/ adj шутливый

jog /джог/ vt подталкивать; vi бежать мелкой рысцой; ~ along /~ элóнг/ двигаться вперед; n толчок jogging /джо́гинг/ n бег трусцой

jog-trot /джо́гтрот/ n мелкая рысца

join /джойн/ vt соединять; вступать; ~ the army /~ зы а́рми/ вступать в армию; vi соединяться

joiner /джо́йнэ/ n столяр

joint /джойнт/ n сустав; часть разрубленной туши; out of ~ /а́ут ов ~/ вывихнутый; adj совместный; ~ account /~ эка́унт/ общий счет;

jointly /джо́йнтли/ adv совместно

joint-stock /джо́йнсток/ n акционерный капитал; ~ company /~ ка́мпэни/ акционерное общество

joke /джо́ук/ n шутка, анекдот; practical ~ /пра́ктикэл ~/ грубая шутка; vi шутить

joker /джо́укэ/ n шутник; джокер

jokingly /джо́укингли/ adv в шутку

jolly /джо́ли/ adj веселый

jolt /джо́улт/ vt трясти

jolting /джо́ултинг/ n тряска

jot /джот/ n йота; not a ~ /нот э ~/ ни на йоту; ~ down /~ да́ун/ vt быстро записывать

journal /джёрнел/ n журнал, дневник

journalism /джёрнэлизм/ n журналистика

journalist /джёрнэлист/ n журналист

journey /джёрни/ n путешествие, поездка

jovial /джо́увьел/ adj общительный, веселый

joy /джой/ n радость

joyful /джо́йфул/ adj радостный

joyless /джо́йлис/ adj безрадостный

jubilant /джу́убилент/ adj ликующий

jubilee /джу́убили/ n юбилей, годовщина

Judaic /джудэ́йик/ adj иудейский, еврейский

judge /джадж/ n судья, ценитель; vti судить, решать

judg(e)ment /джа́джмент/ n решение суда; суждение, мнение; day of ~ /дэй ов ~/ день страшного суда

jug /джаг/ n кувшин; vt тушить (мясо)

juggle /джагл/ vi жонглировать

juggler /джа́глэ/ n жонглер

juice /джуус/ n сок

juicy /джу́уси/ adj сочный; пикантный

July /джула́й/ n июль; adj июльский

jump /джамп/ n прыжок; vti прыгать; ~ the rails /~ зэ рэйлз/ сходить с рельсов

jumper /джа́мпэ/ n прыгун; джемпер

junction /джанкшн/ n соединение; (ж/д) узел

June /джуун/ n июнь

jungle /джангл/ n джунгли

junior /джу́унье/ n, adj младший

junk /джанк/ n джонка; хлам, утильсырье

junk-shop /джа́нкшоп/ n лавка старьевщика

juridical /джери́дикл/ adj юридический

jurisdiction /джу́ерисди́кшн/ n юрисдикция

jurisprudence /джу́ериспру́уденс/ n юриспруденция

jurist /джу́ерист/ n юрист

juror /джу́ерэ/ n присяжный; член жюри

jury /джу́ери/ n суд присяжных; жюри

just /джаст/ adj справедливый; adv точно, как раз, только что; ~ in case /~ ин кэйс/ на всякий случай

justice /джа́стис/ n справедливость; do ~ to /ду ~ ту/ отдавать должное

justifiable /джа́стифайебл/ adj простительный; законный, позволительный

justification /джа́стифике́йшн/ n оправдание

justify /джа́стифай/ vt оправдывать

justly /джа́стли/ adv справедливо

jut /джат/ vi выступать, торчать

jute /джуут/ n джут

juvenile /джу́увинайл/ adj юный; n подросток

juxtapose /джа́кстэпо́уз/ vt сопоставлять

K

kaleidoscope /кэла́йдэскоуп/ n калейдоскоп

kangaroo /кэ́нгэру́у/ n кенгуру

keel /киил/ n киль

keen /киин/ adj острый, проницательный; be ~ on /би ~ он/ страстно увлекаться

keep /киип/ vti держать; хранить; соблюдать (правило); содержать; ~ smiling /~ сма́йлинг/ не переставая улыбаться; ~ silence /~ са́йленс/ молчать; ~ them waiting /~ зэм вэ́йтинг/ заставлять их ждать; ~ a secret /~ э си́икрит/ хранить тайну; ~ up /~ ап/ поддерживать; ~ well /~ вэл/ обладать хорошим здоровьем; ~ one's word /~ ванз вёрд/ держать слово

keg /кег/ n бочонок

kennel /кенл/ n конура; pl собачий питомник

kerb /кёрб/ n край тротуара, обочина

kerchief /кёрчиф/ n платок, косынка

kernel /кёрнл/ n зерно; ядро

kerosene /ке́рэсиин/ n керосин

kettle /кетл/ n чайник

key /кии/ n ключ (также образн.); клавиша

keyboard /ки́иборд/ n клавиатура

keyhole /ки́ихоул/ n замочная скважина

keystone /ки́истоун/ n краеугольный камень

kick /кик/ n удар ногой, пинок, брыканье; vt ударять ногой, пинать, лягать; vi брыкаться; ~ off /~ оф/ начинать игру (в футбол); free ~ /фрии ~/ штрафной удар

kid /кид/ n козленок; ребенок

kidnap /ки́днэп/ vt похищать (людей)

kidnapper /ки́днэпэ/ n похититель

kidnapping /ки́днэпинг/ n похищение

kidney /ки́дни/ n (мед.) почка; ~ beans /~ биинз/ фасоль; ~ machine /~ мэши́ин/ искусственная почка

kill /кил/ vti убивать; резать (скот)

killer /ки́лэ/ n убийца

killjoy /ки́лджой/ n брюзга

kilogram /ки́лэгрэм/ n килограмм

kilometre /ки́лэми́итэ/ n километр

kilowatt /ки́лэвот/ n киловатт

kilt /килт/ n юбка (шотландка)

kin /кин/ n родственники; next of ~ /нэкст ов ~/ ближайший родственник

kind /кайнд/ adj добрый, любезный; how ~ of you /ха́у ~ ов ю/ как мило с вашей стороны!; ~ regards /~ рига́адз/ сердечный привет; n сорт; порода; in ~ /ин ~/ натурой

kindergarten /ки́ндэга́ртн/ n детский сад

kindle /киндл/ vt зажигать; vi загораться

kindness /ка́йнднис/ n доброта

king /кинг/ n король; дамка (в шашках)

kingdom /ки́нгдэм/ n королевство

kingly /ки́нгли/ adj величественный

kiosk /кио́ск/ n киоск

kiss /кис/ n поцелуй; vt целовать

kit /кит/ n комплект инструментов

kit-bag /ки́тбэг/ n вещевой мешок

kitchen /ки́чин/ n кухня; ~ unit /~ ю́нит/ набор кухонной мебели

kitchenette /ки́чине́т/ n маленькая кухня/ниша, используемая в качестве кухни

kite /кайт/ n воздушный змей; коршун

kitten /китн/ n котенок

knack /нэк/ n сноровка

knapsack /нэ́псэк/ n рюкзак

knave /нэйв/ n мошенник; (карты) валет

knead /ниид/ vt месить

knee /нии/ n колено; vi становиться на колени

knee-cap /ни́икэп/ n коленная чашечка

knee-deep /ни́идиип/ adj по колено

knife /найф/ n нож; vt ударять ножом

knight /найт/ n рыцарь; (шахм.) конь

knit /нит/ vti вязать

knitted /ни́тыд/ adj вязаный

knitting /ни́тинг/ n вязание; ~ needle /~ ниидл/ вязальная игла

knitwear /ни́твээ/ n трикотажные изделия

knob /ноб/ n круглая ручка (двери)

knock /нок/ n стук, удар; vt бить, ударять; vi стучаться; ~ down /~ да́ун/ сбивать; ~ out /~ а́ут/ (спорт.) нокаутировать; ~ together /~ тэге́зэ/ сколачивать

knocker /но́кэ/ n дверной молоток; дверное кольцо

knot /нот/ n узел; бант; сучок (в древесине)

know /но́у/ vt знать; n знание; be in the ~ /би ин зэ ~/ быть в курсе дела

know-how /но́уха́у/ n умение; "ноу-хау", научная или техническая информация

knowledge /но́лидж/ n знание; to my ~ /ту май ~/ насколько мне известно

knowledgeable /но́лиджебл/ adj хорошо осведомленный

known /но́ун/ adj известный

knuckle /накл/ n сустав (пальца)

knuckle-duster /на́клда́стэ/ n кастет

kopeck /ко́упек/ n копейка

Koran /кора́ан/ n Коран

kosher /ко́ушe/ n кошер; ~ food /~ фууд/ кошерная пища

Kremlin /кре́млин/ n кремль

L

label /лэ́йбл/ n ярлык; vt наклеивать ярлык

laboratory /лэбо́рэтри/ n лаборатория

labor /лэ́йбэ/ n труд, работа; ~ pains /~ пэйнз/ родовые схватки; L. Party /~ па́рти/ лейбористская партия; vi трудиться

laborer /лэ́йбэрэ/ n рабочий

Labrador /лэ́брэдоо/ n лабрадор (порода собак)

labyrinth /лэ́беринф/ n лабиринт

lac /лэк/ n лак

lace /лэйс/ n кружево; шнурок (ботинок); vt шнуровать

lacerate /лэ́серэйт/ vt раздирать; ~d wound /~ыд вуунд/ рваная рана

lack /лэк/ n недостаток, отсутствие; vti нуждаться в; he ~s courage /хи ~с ка́ридж/ ему недостает смелости

lackey /лэ́ки/ n лакей

laconic /лэко́ник/ adj лаконичный

lacquer /лэ́кэ/ n лак

lad /лэд/ n парень

ladder /лэ́дэ/ n (приставная) лестница

lading /лэ́йдинг/ n фрахт; bill of ~ /бил ов ~/ накладная, коносамент

lady /лэ́йди/ n дама, леди; young ~ /янг ~/ девушка; Our L. /а́уэ ~/ Богоматерь

lady-bird /лэ́йдибёд/ n божья коровка

lag /лэг/ n отставание; vi отставать

laggard /лэ́гэд/ adj медлительный

lagoon /лэгу́ун/ n лагуна

lake /лэйк/ n озеро

lamb /лэм/ n ягненок

lame /лэйм/ adj хромой

lameness /лэ́ймнис/ n хромота

lament /лэме́нт/ n жалоба; vti оплакивать

lamentable /лэ́ментэбл/ adj печальный

lamentation /лэменте́йшн/ n плач

lamp /лэмп/ n лампа, фонарь; фара

lampoon /лэмпу́ун/ n пасквиль

lamprey /лэ́мпри/ n минога

lamp-shade /лэ́мпшейд/ n абажур

lance /лаанс/ n пика

lancet /ла́ансит/ n ланцет

land /лэнд/ n земля; страна; by ~ /бай ~/ по суше; vi высаживаться на берег, приземляться

landing /лэ́ндинг/ n приземление, (авиа) посадка; лестничная площадка

landlady /лэ́нлэйди/ n домовладелица, сдающая квартиры; хозяйка гостиницы

landlord /лэ́ндлорд/ n домовладелец, сдающий квартиры; хозяин гостиницы

landmark /лэ́нмарк/ n поворотный пункт; ориентир

landscape /лэ́нскэйп/ n пландшафт; пейзаж

lane /лэйн/ n тропинка; переулок; проход

language /лэ́нгвидж/ n язык

languish /лэ́нгвиш/ vi томиться

lanky /лэ́нки/ adj долговязый

lantern /лэ́нтэн/ n фонарь

lap /лэп/ n пола; колени; (спорт.) круг; vt ласкать; vi плескаться (о волнах)

lap-dog /лэ́пдог/ n комнатная собачка

lapel /лэпе́л/ n лацкан

lapse /лэпс/ n недосмотр, ляпсус; vi истекать, проходить

lard /лард/ n смалец; vt шпиговать

large /лардж/ adj большой, крупный; at ~ /эт ~/ на свободе; подробно; в целом

largely /ла́рджли/ adv в значительной степени

lark /ларк/ n жаворонок

larva /ла́рвэ/ n личинка

larynx /лэ́ринкс/ n гортань

laser /лэ́йзэ/ n лазер

lash /лэш/ n бич, плеть; vi хлестать; (образн.) бичевать

lass /лэс/ n девушка

lasso /лэ́соу/ n аркан

last /лааст/ adj последний; прошлый; ~ but one /~ бат ван/ предпоследний; ~ night /~ найт/ вчера вечером/ночью; ~ week /~ виик/ на прошлой неделе; at ~ /эт ~/ наконец; vi длиться

lasting /ла́астинг/ adj прочный

latch /лэч/ n задвижка; vt запирать

late /лэйт/ adj поздний; покойный; it is ~ /ит из ~/ поздно; be ~ for a train /би ~ фор э трэйн/ опаздывать на поезд

lately /лэ́йтли/ adv недавно

later /лэ́йтэ/ adj более поздний; adv позднее

latest /лэ́йтист/ adj самый последний

lateral /лэ́тэрл/ adj боковой

lather /ла́азэ/ n (мыльная) пена; vt намыливать

Latin /лэ́тин/ n латинский язык, латынь; adj латинский, романский

latitude /лэ́титьюд/ n (геогр.) широта

latter /лэ́тэ/ adj последний

lattice /лэ́тис/ n решетка

Latvian /лэ́твиэн/ n латыш, латышка; латышский язык; adj латвийский, латышский

laud /лоод/ vt хвалить

laudable /ло́одэбл/ adj похвальный

laugh /лааф/ n смех; vi смеяться; burst out ~ing /бёрст а́ут ~инг/ расхохотаться; ~ing stock /~инг сток/ посмешище

laughter /ла́афтэ/ n смех

launch /лоонч/ n запуск; спуск (на воду); vt запускать (ракету); vti начинать

laundry /ло́ондри/ n прачечная

laurel /ло́рэл/ n лавр; rest on one's ~s /рэст он ванз ~з/ почивать на лаврах

lava /ла́авэ/ n лава

lavatory /лэ́ветри/ n уборная

lavender /лэ́виндэ/ n лаванда

lavish /лэ́виш/ adj щедрый, обильный; vt расточать

law /лоо/ n закон, право; by ~ /бай ~/ по закону; go to ~ /го́у ту ~/ подавать в суд

law-court /ло́окот/ n суд

lawful /ло́офул/ adj законный

lawless /ло́олис/ adj беззаконный

lawn /лоон/ n газон

lawn mower /ло́онмо́э/ n газонокосилка

lawsuit /ло́осьют/ n процесс, тяжба

lawyer /ло́ойе/ n адвокат; юрист

lay /лэй/ vt класть, закладывать (основание, фундамент); накрывать (на стол); vi нестись (о курице); ~ aside /~ эса́йд/ откладывать; ~ by /~ бай/ запасать; ~ off /~ оф/ увольнять; откладывать

layer /лэ́йе/ n слой

layette /лэйе́т/ n приданое новорожденного

layman /лэ́ймэн/ n непрофессионал; мирянин

layout /лэ́йаут/ n планировка; макет (книги и т.п.)

laziness /лэ́йзинис/ n лень

lazy /лэ́йзи/ adj ленивый

lazy-bones /лэ́йзибоунз/ n лентяй

lead /лиид/ n руководство; пример; главная роль; первое место; vt вести, водить; ~ a good life /~ э гуд лайф/ вести хорошую жизнь leader /ли́идэ/ n вождь; передовая статья

leadership /ли́идэшип/ n руководство

leaf /лииф/ n лист

leaflet /ли́ифлит/ n листовка

league /лииг/ n лига, союз

leak /лиик/ n течь; vi давать течь; ~ out /~ а́ут/ просачиваться

leakage /ли́икэдж/ n утечка (также образн.)

lean /лиин/ adj тощий; постный (о мясе); vti наклонять(ся), прислонять(ся)

lean-to /ли́инту/ n пристройка

leap /лиип/ n прыжок; vi прыгать

leap year /ли́ипйе/ n високосный год

learn /лёрн/ vt учить, узнавать; vi учиться

learned /лёрнид/ adj ученый, эрудированный

lease /лиис/ n аренда; vt сдавать, брать в аренду

leaseholder /ли́исхо́улдэ/ n арендатор

leash /лииш/ n поводок; on the ~ /он зэ ~/ на поводке

least /лиист/ adj наименьший; adv менее всего; at ~ /эт ~/ по крайней мере

leather /ле́зэ/ n кожа

leave /лиив/ n разрешение; отпуск; on ~ /он ~/ в отпуске; take one's ~ /тэйк ванз ~/ прощаться; vt оставлять; vi уходить, уезжать

leaven /левн/ n закваска

lechery /ле́чери/ n разврат

lectern /ле́ктёрн/ n аналой

lecture /ле́кче/ n лекция; vi читать лекцию; преподавать; vt читать нотацию

lecturer /ле́кчерэ/ n преподаватель; лектор

ledge /ледж/ n выступ

lee /лии/ n подветренная сторона

leech /лиич/ n пиявка

left /лефт/ adj левый; n левая сторона; on the ~ /он зэ ~/ налево; to the ~ /ту зэ ~/ слева

left-hander /ле́фтхэ́ндыд/ n левша

left-overs /ле́фто́увэз/ n pl остатки

leg /лег/ n нога; ножка (стула и т.п.)

legacy /ле́гэси/ n наследство

legal /лиигл/ adj законный, юридический, правовой; ~ adviser /~ эдва́йзэ/ юрисконсульт; take ~ action /тэйк ~ экшн/ возбуждать судебное дело

legend /ле́дженд/ n легенда

leggings /ле́гингз/ n pl ползунки (для ребенка)

legion /ли́иджен/ n легион

legislate /ле́джислэйт/ vi издавать законы

legislation /ле́джислэ́йшн/ n законодательство

legislative /ле́джислэтив/ adj законодательный

legislator /ле́джислэйтэ/ n законодатель

legitimate /лиджи́тимит/ adj законный

legitimize /лиджи́тимайз/ vt узаконивать

leisure /ле́же/ n досуг; at ~ /эт ~/ на досуге

lemon /ле́мэн/ n лимон

lemonade /ле́мэнэ́йд/ n лимонад

lend /ленд/ vt давать взаймы; одалживать

length /ленгс/ n длина, долгота; at ~ /эт ~/ подробно

lengthen /ле́нгсен/ vti удлинять(ся)

lenient /ли́иньент/ adj снисходительный

lens /ленз/ n линза; contact ~ /ко́нтэкт ~/ контактная линза

Lent /лент/ n Великий пост

leopard /ле́пэд/ n леопард

leprosy /ле́прэси/ n проказа

less /лес/ adj меньший; adv меньше; more or ~ /мо́ро ~/ более или менее

lessen /лесн/ vti уменьшать(ся)

lesson /лесн/ n урок

let /лет/ vt позволять, пускать; сдавать внаем; ~ him talk /~ хим тоок/ пусть говорит!; house to ~ /ха́ус тэ ~/ дом сдается; ~ down /~ да́ун/ подводить; ~ go /~ го́у/ освобождать; ~ out /~ а́ут/ выпускать

lethargy /ле́сэджи/ n летаргия

letter /ле́тэ/ n буква, письмо; ~ of credit /~ ов кре́дит/ аккредитив lettuce /ле́тис/ n салат

level /левл/ adj ровный; n уровень; vt выравнивать

lever /ли́ивэ/ n рычаг

levy /ле́ви/ n взимание; vt взимать (налог)

liability /ла́йеби́лити/ n ответственность, обязательство

liable /ла́йебл/ adj ответственный; подверженный; подлежащий

liaison /лиэ́йзон/ n связь

liar /ла́йе/ n лгун

libel /ла́йбл/ n клевета; vt клеветать

libeller /ла́йблэ/ n клеветник

libellous /ла́йблэс/ adj клеветнический

liberal /ли́берэл/ adj либеральный; щедрый; n либерал

liberate /ли́берэйт/ vt освобождать

liberation /либеро́йшн/ n освобождение

liberty /ли́бети/ n свобода, вольность; at ~ /эт ~/ на свободе

librarian /лайбрэ́эриэн/ n библиотекарь

library /ла́йбрэри/ n библиотека

Libyan /ли́биэн/ n ливиец, ливийка; adj ливийский

licence /ла́йснс/ n лицензия; driving ~ /дра́йвинг ~/ водительские права

lichen /ла́йкэн/ n лишай

lick /лик/ vt лизать

lid /лид/ n крышка

lie /лай/ vi лежать; ~ down /~ да́ун/ ложиться; ~ in wait /~ ин вэйт/ подстерегать

lieutenant /лефтэ́нент/ n лейтенант

life /лайф/ n жизнь; from ~ /фром ~/ с натуры

life-annuity /ла́йфэнью́ити/ n пожизненная рента

lifeboat /ла́йфбоут/ n спасательная шлюпка

life insurance /ла́йфиншу́эрнс/ n страхование жизни

lifeless /ла́йфлис/ adj безжизненный

lifelong /ла́йфлонг/ adj пожизненный

life-size /ла́йфсайз/ adj в натуральную величину

lifetime /ла́йфтайм/ n продолжительность жизни

lift /лифт/ n подъем; give a ~ to /гив э ~ ту/ подвозить; vt поднимать

light /лайт/ n свет, освещение; pl светофор; throw ~ on /сро́у ~ он/ проливать свет на; adj светлый, легкий; vti освещать(ся), зажигать(ся); please, give me a ~ /плииз гив ми э ~/ разрешите прикурить

lighten /ла́йтн/ vt облегчать, смягчать; vi сверкать; it ~s /ит ~с/ сверкает молния

lighter /ла́йтэ/ n зажигалка

lightheaded /ла́йтхе́дыд/ adj бездумный, легкомысленный

lighthearted /ла́йтха́ртыд/ adj беспечный

lighthouse /ла́йтхаус/ n маяк

lighting /ла́йтинг/ n освещение

lightly /ла́йтли/ adv слегка

lightness /ла́йтнис/ n легкость

lightning /ла́йтнинг/ n молния; ~ conductor /~ кэнда́ктэ/ громоотвод

lights /лайтс/ n pl легкие (животных)

lightweight /ла́йтвэйт/ n (спорт.) боксер легкого веса

like /лайк/ adj похожий, подобный; adv как; be ~ /би ~/ быть похожим на; vt любить; as you ~/эз ю ~/ как вам угодно; I should ~ /ай шуд ~/ я хотел бы

likeable /ла́йкэбл/ adj симпатичный

likelihood /ла́йклихуд/ n вероятность

likely /ла́йкли/ adj вероятный; adv вероятно

liken /ла́йкн/ vt уподоблять

likeness /ла́йкнис/ n сходство, подобие

likes /лайкс/ n pl: ~ and dislikes /~ энд ди́слайкс/ симпатии и антипатии

likewise /ла́йквайз/ adv подобно

liking /ла́йкинг/ n вкус, любовь

lilac /ла́йлэк/ n сирень; adj сиреневый

lilliputian /ли́липью́юшн/ adj крошечный

lily /ли́ли/ n лилия; ~ of the valley /~ ов зэ вэ́ли/ ландыш

limb /лим/ n конечность

lime /лайм/ n известь; лимон

limelight /ла́ймлайт/ n свет рампы; in the ~ /ин зэ ~/ в центре внимания

limestone /ла́ймстоун/ n известняк

limit /ли́мит/ n граница, предел; vt ограничивать

limitation /лимитэ́йшн/ n ограничение

limited /ли́митыд/ adj ограниченный; ~ company /~ ка́мпэни/ акционерная компания с ограниченной ответственностью

limitless /ли́митлис/ adj беспредельный

limousine /ли́музин/ n лимузин

limp /лимп/ adj безвольный; vi хромать

line /лайн/ n линия; строка; леска (удочки); очередь; vt линовать; ставить подкладку; ~ up /~ ап/ занимать очередь

linen /ли́нин/ n полотно; белье

liner /ла́йнэ/ n рейсовый пароход/самолет

linger /ли́нгэ/ vi мешкать, задерживаться

liniment /ли́нимент/ n жидкая мазь

lining /ла́йнинг/ n подкладка

link /линк/ n звено, pl узы; vt соединять; связывать

link-up /ли́нкап/ n стыковка (космических кораблей)

linoleum /лино́ульем/ n линолеум

linseed-oil /ли́нсидо́йл// n льняное масло

lion(ess) /ла́йен(ис)/ n лев (львица); ~'s share /~з шээ/ львиная доля

lip /лип/ n губа; край

lipstick /ли́пстык/ n губная помада

liqueur /ликьё́э/ n ликер

liquid /ли́квид/ adj жидкий; n жидкость

liquor /ли́кэ/ n (спиртной) напиток, выпивка; hard ~ /хард ~/ крепкий напиток

list /лист/ n список; vt вносить в список

listen /лисн/ vi слушать; ~ in /~ ин/ слушать радио

listener /ли́снэ/ n слушатель

litre /ли́итэ/ n литр

literal /ли́тэрэл/ adj буквальный

literally /ли́тэрэли/ adv дословно

literary /ли́тэрэри/ adj литературный

literate /ли́тэрит/ adj грамотный

literature /ли́триче/ n литература

Lithuanian /ли́съюзэ́йньен/ n литовец, литовка; литовский язык; adj литовский

litmus /ли́тмэс/ n лакмус

litter /ли́тэ/ n мусор; подстилка; помет (свиньи, собаки); vt сорить; подстилать

little /литл/ adj маленький; ~ finger /~ фи́нгэ/ мизинец; adv мало

live /лайв/ adj живой

live /лив/ vi жить

livelihood /ла́йвлихуд/ n средства к существованию

liveliness /ла́йвлинис/ n живость

lively /ла́йвли/ adj живой, оживленный

liver /ли́вэ/ n печень; печенка

livery /ли́вэри/ n ливрея

livestock /ла́йвсток/ n скот

living /ли́винг/ adj живой; современный; n образ жизни; earn a ~ /ёрн э ~/ зарабатывать на жизнь

living room /ли́вингрум/ n столовая, гостиная

lizard /ли́зэд/ n ящерица

load /ло́уд/ n груз; vt грузить; заряжать (оружие)

loaf /ло́уф/ n каравай, буханка хлеба; vi слоняться

loafer /ло́уфэ/ n бездельник

loan /ло́ун/ n заем; vt давать взаймы

loath /ло́ус/ adj неохотный; be ~ to /би ту/ не хотеть

loathe /ло́уз/ vt чувствовать отвращение

loathing /ло́узинг/ n ненависть

loathsome /ло́узсэм/ adj противный

lobby /ло́би/ n вестибюль; кулуары; лобби

lobbying /ло́биинг/ n воздействие на членов (конгресса и т.п.)

lobster /ло́бстэ/ n омар

local /ло́укл/ adj местный; ~ train /~ трэйн/ пригородный поезд

locality /лоукэ́лити/ n местность

locate /ло́укэйт/ vt обнаруживать

location /лоукэ́йшн/ n местожительство; on ~ /он ~/ (кино) на натуре

lock /лок/ n локон (волос); замок; шлюз; under ~ and key /а́ндэ ~ энд кии/ под замком; vt запирать на замок; ~ out /~ а́ут/ объявлять локаут

locker /ло́кэ/ n шкафчик, ящик (с замком)

locket /ло́кит/ n медальон

locksmith /ло́ксмит/ n слесарь

lock-up /ло́кап/ n тюрьма

locomotive /ло́укэмо́утив/ n локомотив

locust /ло́укэст/ n саранча

lodge /лодж/ n сторожка; ложа (масонская); vt временно поселять; давать на хранение; vi снимать квартиру

lodger /ло́дже/ n квартирант(ка)

lodging /ло́джинг/ n жилье; board and ~ /борд энд ~/ пансион

loft /лофт/ n чердак, сеновал

lofty /ло́фти/ adj высокий, возвышенный

log /лог/ n бревно

log cabin /ло́гкэ́бин/ n бревенчатый дом

logic /ло́джик/ n логика

logical /ло́джикл/ adj логичный

loin /лойн/ n филейная часть; pl поясница

loiter /ло́йтэ/ vi медлить, слоняться

lollipop /ло́липоп/ n леденец

Londoner /ла́ндэнэ/ n лондонец

loneliness /ло́унлинис/ n одиночество

lonely /ло́унли/ adj одинокий

long /лонг/ adj длинный; долгий; three miles ~ /срии майлз ~/ длиной в три мили; in the ~ run /ин зэ ~ ран/ в конце концов; one day and night ~ /ван дэй энд найт ~/ односуточный; adv долго; ~ ago /~ эго́у/ давно; all day ~ /оол дэй ~/ целый день; vi: ~ for /~ фо/ страстно желать

long-distance /ло́нгди́стнс/ adj дальний; ~ call /~ коол/ междугородный/международный телефонный разговор

longevity /лонджэ́вити/ n долговечность; долголетие

longing /ло́нгинг/ n страстное желание

longitude /ло́нджитьюд/ n долгота

long-legged /ло́нглегд/ adj длинноногий

long-lived /ло́нгливд/ adj долговечный

long-playing /ло́нгплэ́йинг/ adj долгоиграющий

longshoreman /ло́нгшо́мэн/ n портовый грузчик

long-sighted /ло́нгса́йтыд/ adj дальнозоркий

long-term /ло́нгтём/ adj долгосрочный

look /лук/ vi смотреть; выглядеть; ~ after /~ а́афтэ/ заботиться о; ~ for /~ фо/ искать; ~ here! /~ хи́э/ послушай(те)!; ~ like /~ лайк/ быть похожим на; ~ out /~ а́ут/ разыскивать; ~ out! /~ а́ут/ берегись!; ~ round /~ ра́унд/ оглядываться; ~ through /~ сруу/ просматривать; ~ well /~ вэл/ выглядеть хорошо; n взгляд, вид, внешность; good ~s /гуд ~с/ красота; take a ~ at /тэйк э ~ эт/ посмотреть на

looking glass /лу́кинглас/ n зеркало

look-out /лу́каут/ n бдительность; наблюдение; перспективы; be on the ~ /би он зэ ~/ быть настороже

loom /луум/ n ткацкий станок

loom /луум/ vi маячить

loop /лууп/ n петля; (ав.) мертвая петля

loophole /лу́упхоул/ n лазейка

loose /луус/ adj свободный, просторный; неприкрепленный; распущенный

loosen /луусн/ vt развязывать

loot /луут/ n добыча; vt грабить

lord /лорд/ n лорд, господин; the Lord (God) /зэ лорд (год)/ Господь Бог; the L.'s Prayer /зэ ~з прэ́йе/ Отче наш

lordly /ло́рдли/ adj барский

lorry /ло́ри/ n грузовик

lose /лууз/ vt терять; проигрывать; ~ heart /~ харт/ падать духом; ~ one's way /~ ванз вэй/ заблудиться

loser /лу́узэ/ n проигравший

loss /лос/ n потеря; проигрыш; at a ~ /эт э ~/ в затруднении

lost /лост/ adj утраченный; ~ and found /~ энд фáунд/ бюро находок

lot /лот/ n жребий; судьба; участок; вещи (на аукционе); a ~ of /э ~ ов/ много

lotion /лóушн/ n лосьон

lottery /лóтэри/ n лотерея

lotus /лóутэс/ n лотос

loud /лáуд/ adj громкий; кричащий (о цвете)

loudness /лáуднис/ n громкость

loudspeaker /лáудспúикэ/ n громкоговоритель

louse /лáус/ n (pl lice) вошь

lousy /лáузи/ adj вшивый; мерзкий

love /лав/ n любовь; возлюбленный, возлюбленная; (спорт.) нуль; fall in ~ /фоол ин ~/ влюбляться в; ~ affair /~ эфэ́э/ роман; vt любить

loveliness /лáвлинис/ n прелесть

lovely /лáвли/ adj прелестный; вкусный

love-making /лáвмэ́йкинг/ n физическая близость

lover /лáвэ/ n любовник; любитель

loving /лáвинг/ adj любящий

low /лóу/ adj низкий (также образн.); тихий; adv низко; ~ neck /~ нэк/ глубокий вырез; ~ pressure /~ прэ́ше/ низкое давление; ~ water /~ вóотэ/ отлив

lower /лóуэ/ adv ниже; vt снижать; спускать (флаг)

lowland /лóулэнд/ n низменность

loyal /лóйел/ adj верный, лояльный

loyalty /лóйелти/ n верность, лояльность

lubricant /лью́юбрикент/ n смазочное средство

lubricate /лью́юбрикейт/ vt смазывать

luck /лак/ n счастье, удача; good ~! /гуд ~/ в добрый путь!; try one's ~ /трай ванз ~/ попытать счастья

lucky /лáки/ adj счастливый; удачный

ludicrous /лью́юдикрэс/ adj смешной

luggage /лáгидж/ n багаж; excess ~ /иксэ́с ~/ багаж выше нормы

lukewarm /лью́юоквёрм/ adj тепловатый

lull /лал/ vt убаюкивать

lullaby /лáлэбай/ n колыбельная

lumbago /ламбэ́йгоу/ n прострел

lumber /лáмбэ/ n хлам, лесоматериалы

lumberjack /лáмбэджэк/ n лесоруб

luminous /лью́юминэс/ adj светящийся

lump /ламп/ n кусок; глыба; опухоль; ~ sum /~ сам/ крупная сумма

lunatic /лýунэтик/ n, adj сумасшедший; ~ asylum /~ эсáйлэм/ психиатрическая больница

lunch, luncheon /ланч, ланчн/ n ленч, второй завтрак; vi обедать

lung /ланг/ n легкое

lure /лью́э/ n приманка; vt завлекать

lurk /лёрк/ vi таиться в засаде

luscious /лáшес/ adj сочный, сладкий

lush /лаш/ adj сочный, пышный

lust /ласт/ n вожделение, похоть; vi: ~ after /~ áафтэ/ страстно желать, испытывать физическое влечение к

lustful /лáстфул/ adj похотливый

lustre /лáстэ/ n глянец, блеск; люстра

Lutheran /лью́юсэрэн/ n лютеранин, лютеранка; adj лютеранский

luxurious /лагзью́эриэс/ adj роскошный

lying-in /лáйингúин/ n роды

lymph /лимф/ n лимфа

lymphatic /лимфэ́тик/ adj лимфатический

lynch /линч/ vt линчевать

lynx /линкс/ n рысь

lyre /лáйе/ n лира

lyric(al) /лúрик(л)/ adj лирический

lyric /лúрик/ n лирическое стихотворение

M

macaroni /мэ́кэрóуни/ n макароны

mace /мэйс/ n жезл

machine /мэшúин/ n машина; adding ~ /э́динг ~/ счетная машина

machine-gun /мэшúинган/ n пулемет

machinery /мэши́инэри/ n машины, машинное оборудование

mad /мэд/ adj сумасшедший; бешеный (о собаке); go ~ /го́у ~/ сходить с ума

madden /мэдн/ vt сводить с ума, бесить

made /мэйд/ adj сделанный; ~ in USA (Japan) /~ ин ю́юз́сэ́й (джепэ́н)/ изготовлено в США (Японии); ~ to order /~ ту о́рдэ/ сделанный на заказ

madeira /мэди́эрэ/ n мадера

made-up /мэ́йда́п/ adj составной; вымышленный

madhouse /мэ́дхаус/ n сумасшедший дом

madly /мэ́дли/ adv безумно

madness /мэ́днис/ n сумасшествие

magazine /мэ́гэзи́ин/ n журнал

maggot /мэ́гэт/ n личинка

magic /мэ́джик/ adj волшебный; ~ wand /~ вонд/ волшебная палочка; n волшебство; as if by ~ /эз иф бай ~/ как по волшебству

magical /мэ́джикл/ adj волшебный, магический

magician /мэджи́шн/ n волшебник

magistrate /мэ́джистрит/ n судья

magnanimous /мэгнэ́нимэс/ adj великодушный

magnet /мэ́гнит/ n магнит

magnetic /мэгнэ́тик/ adj магнитный

magnetism /мэ́гнитизм/ n магнетизм

magnificence /мэгни́фиснс/ n великолепие

magnificent /мэгни́фиснт/ adj великолепный

magnify /мэ́гнифай/ vt увеличивать

magnitude /мэ́гнитьюд/ n величина

magpie /мэ́гпай/ n сорока

magus /мэ́йгэс/ n маг

mahogany /мэхо́гэни/ n красное дерево

maid /мэйд/ n девица; служанка

maiden /мэйдн/ adj девственный; первый; ~ name /~ нэйм/ девичья фамилия

mail /мэйл/ n почта; кольчуга; vt посылать почтой

mailbox /мэ́йлбокс/ n почтовый ящик

mailman /мэ́йлмэн/ n почтальон

main /мэйн/ adj главный; ~ road /~ ро́уд/ шоссе; ~ street /~ стриит/ главная улица; the ~ thing /зэ ~ синг/ главное; in the ~ /ин зэ ~/ в основном

mainland /мэ́йнлэнд/ материк

mainly /мэ́йнли/ adv главным образом

maintain /мэнтэ́йн/ vt поддерживать; содержать

maintenance /мэ́йнтинэнс/ n содержание; (тех.) ремонт

maize /мэйз/ n кукуруза, маис

majestic /меджéстик/ n величественный

majesty /мэ́джисти/ n: Your M. /йо ~/ ваше величество

major /мэ́йдже/ adj больший, главный; n майор

major-general /мэ́йджеджéнерэл/ n генерал-майор

majority /мэджо́рити/ n большинство

make /мэйк/ n производство; модель; тип; vt делать, производить; ~ a bed /~ э бед/ стелить постель; ~ faces /~ фэ́йсыз/ гримасничать; ~ fun of /~ фан ов/ высмеивать; ~ haste /~ хэйст/ спешить; ~ enquiries /~ инквáйериз/ наводить справки; ~ money /~ мáни/ "делать" деньги; ~ up one's mind /~ ап ванз майнд/ решать(ся); ~ use of /~ ю́юс ов/ использовать

maker /мэ́йкэ/ n создатель

make-up /мэ́йкап/ n грим

making /мэ́йкинг/ n создание; становление; pl задатки

malaria /мэлэ́эриэ/ n малярия

Malay (an) /мэлэ́й (ен) / n малаец, малайка; малайский язык; adj малайский

male /мэйл/ adj мужской; n мужчина

malice /мэ́лис/ n злоба

malicious /мэли́шес/ adj злобный

malign /мэлáйн/ n пагубный

malignant /мэли́гнент/ adj злокачественный

malnutrition /мэ́лньютри́шн/ n недоедание

malt /моолт/ n солод

Maltese /мо́олти́из/ n мальтиец, мальтийка; adj мальтийский

mammal /мэ́мл/ n млекопитающее

mammoth /мэ́мэс/ n мамонт; adj гигантский

man /мэн/ n человек, мужчина; ~ and wife /~ энд вайф/ муж и жена; ~ in the street /~ ин зэ стриит/ рядовой человек

manage /мэ́нидж/ vt управлять; vi справляться с

manageable /мэ́нидже́бл/ adj послушный

management /мэ́ниджмент/ n управление; администрация

manager /мэ́нидже/ n управляющий

manageress /мэ́ниджерис/ n управляющая

mandarin /мэ́ндэрин/ n мандарин

mandate /мэ́ндэйт/ n мандат

mandatory /мэ́ндэтри/ adj обязательный

mane /мэйн/ n грива

manhood /мэ́нхуд/ n мужество; зрелость

mania /мэ́йнье/ n мания

maniac /мэ́йниэк/ n маньяк

manicure /мэ́никьюэ/ n маникюр

manicurist /мэ́никьюэрист/ n маникюрша

manifest /мэ́нифест/ adj явный; vt проявлять

manifestation /мэ́нифестэ́йшн/ n проявление

manifesto /мэ́нифе́стоу/ n манифест

manifold /мэ́нифо́улд/ adj разнообразный

manipulate /мэни́пьюлэйт/ vt манипулировать

mankind /мэнка́йнд/ n человечество

manly /мэ́нли/ adj мужественный

manna /мэ́нэ/ n (библ.) манна небесная

mannequin /мэ́никин/ n манекен; манекенщица

manner /мэ́нэ/ n способ, образ; pl манеры; where are your ~s? /вэ́эра йо ~з/ веди себя прилично!

mannered /мэ́нэд/ adj манерный

manoeuvre /мэну́увэ/ n маневр; vi маневрировать

manor /мэ́нэ/ n поместье

mansion /мэншн/ n большой особняк

manslaughter /мэ́нсло́отэ/ n (юр.) непредумышленное убийство

mantle /мэнтл/ n мантия; (образн.) покров

manual /мэ́ньюэл/ adj ручной; n справочник

manufacture /мэ́ньюфэ́кче/ n производство; изделие; vt производить

manufacturer /мэ́ньюфэ́кчерэ/ n фабрикант; изготовитель

manure /мэнью́э/ n навоз, удобрение; vt удобрять

manuscript /мэ́ньюскрипт/ n рукопись

many /мэ́ни/ adj много, многие; how ~? /ха́у ~/ сколько?

map /мэп/ n карта, план

maple /мейпл/ n клен

mar /мар/ vt портить

marble /марбл/ n мрамор

March /марч/ n март

march /марч/ n марш; quick ~ /квик ~/ скорый шаг; vi маршировать; ~ past /~ пааст/ проходить мимо

marching /ма́рчинг/ n маршировка

mare /мээ/ n кобыла

margarine /ма́рджери́ин/ n маргарин

margin /ма́рджин/ n край; грань; запас; ~ of safety /~ ов сэ́йфти/ запас прочности

marine /мэри́ин/ adj морской; n флот; морской пехотинец

mariner /мэ́ринэ/ n моряк, матрос

marital /мэра́йтл/ adj брачный

maritime /мэ́ритайм/ adj приморский

mark /марк/ n знак; метка; след; балл; марка (монета); up to the ~ /ап ту зэ ~/ на должной высоте; vt отмечать, метить; ставить балл

marked /маркт/ adj отмеченный; заметный

market /ма́ркит/ n рынок; сбыт; adj рыночный; money ~ /ма́ни ~/ денежный рынок; vt продавать на рынке, сбывать

marketable /ма́ркитэбл/ adj ходкий

marketing /ма́ркитинг/ n маркетинг

marksman /ма́рксмэн/ n (меткий) стрелок

marmalade /ма́рмелэйд/ n апельсинный или лимонный джем

marriage /мэ́ридж/ n брак, свадьба; ~ licence /~ ла́йсэнс/ свидетельство о браке

married /мэ́рид/ adj женатый, замужняя; ~ couple /~ капл/ супружеская чета; newly-~ couple /нью́юли ~ капл/ чета новобрачных; get ~ (to) /гет ~ ту/ жениться на, выйти замуж за

marry /мэ́ри/ vt женить, выдавать замуж; жениться на, выходить замуж за

Mars /марз/ n Марс

marsh /марш/ n болото

marshal /ма́ршел/ n маршал

mart /март/ n торговый центр

marten /ма́ртин/ n куница

martial /ма́ршел/ adj военный; ~ law /~ лоо/ военное положение

Martian /ма́ршьен/ n марсианин

martyr /ма́ртэ/ n мученик, мученица

martyrdom /ма́ртэдэм/ n мученичество

marvel /ма́рвел/ n диво; vi: ~ at /~ эт/ восхищаться

marvellous /ма́рвилэс/ adj чудесный

Marxist /ма́рксист/ adj марксистский; n марксист

mascot /мэ́скет/ n талисман

masculine /ма́аскьюлин/ adj мужской

mash /мэш/ n пюре; vt разминать; ~ed potatoes /~т пэтэ́йтоуз/ картофельное пюре

mask /мааск/ n маска; vt маскировать; ~ed ball /~т боол/ бал-маскарад

mason /мэйсн/ n каменщик; масон

masonic /мэсо́ник/ adj масонский; ~ lodge /~ лодж/ масонская ложа

masquerade /мэ́скерэ́йд/ n маскарад

mass /мэс/ n масса; месса, обедня; ~ production /~ прэда́кшн/ серийное производство

massacre /мэ́сэкэ/ n резня, бойня

massage /мэса́аж/ n массаж; vt массировать

masseur /мэсёр/ n массажист

masseuze /мэсёёз/ n массажистка

massive /мэ́сив/ adj массивный, крупный

mast /мааст/ n мачта

master /ма́астэ/ n хозяин; мастер; учитель; M. of Arts /~ ов артс/ магистр гуманитарных наук; ~ of ceremonies /~ ов сэ́римениз/ конферансье; vt овладевать, справляться с

masterful /ма́астэфул/ adj властный

master key /ма́астэки/ n отмычка

masterly /ма́астэли/ adj мастерский

mastermind /ма́астэмайнд/ n руководитель; вдохновитель

masterpiece /ма́астэпис/ n шедевр

mastiff /мэ́стиф/ n мастиф (порода собак)

mastodon /мэ́стэдон/ n мастодонт

mat /мэт/ n мат, циновка; подстилка (под блюдо)

match /мэч/ n спичка; ровня; матч; a good ~ /э гуд ~/ хорошая партия; vt подбирать под пару, гармонировать с; состязаться с

match-box /мэ́чбокс/ n спичечная коробка

matchless /мэ́члис/ adj несравненный

matchmaker /мэ́чмэ́йкэ/ n сват, сваха

mate /мэйт/ n товарищ; супруг, супруга; самец, самка (у животных); помощник; (шахм.) мат; vti спаривать(ся)

material /мэти́эриэл/ n материал, материя; adj существенный

materialism /мэти́эриэлизм/ n материализм

materialist /мэти́эриэлист/ n материалист

maternity /мэтёрнити/ n материнство; ~ home /~ хо́ум/ родильный дом

mathematics /мэ́симэтикс/ n математика

matinee /мэ́тиней/ n дневной спек-
такль/концерт/сеанс

matins /мэ́тинз/ n pl заутреня

matrimony /мэ́тримени/ n супружество

matter /мэ́тэ/ n вещество; дело; what's the
~ with you? /вотс зэ ~ виз ю/ что с
вами?; as a ~ of fact /эз э ~ офэ́кт/
фактически; it's a ~ of taste /итс э ~ ов
тэйст/ это дело вкуса; vi иметь значение; it doesn't ~ /ит дазнт ~/ неважно
matter-of-course /мэ́тэрэвко́ос/ adj само
собой разумеющийся

matting /мэ́тинг/ n рогожа, циновка

mattress /мэ́трис/ n матрац

mature /мэтью́оэ/ adj зрелый, созревший;
vi созревать

maturity /мэтью́оэрити/ n зрелость

maul /моол/ vt увечить

Maundy Thursday /мо́ондисёёзди/ n Великий четверг

mausoleum /мо́сэли́иэм/ n мавзолей

maximum /мэ́ксимэм/ n максимум; adj
максимальный

May /мэй/ n май

may /мэй/ v aux мочь, иметь возможность; ~ I say /~ ай сэй/ могу я сказать...; I ~ come /ай ~ кам/ может быть
я приду; ~ I come in? /~ ай кам ин/
можно войти?

maybe /мэ́йби/ adv может быть

mayonnaise /мэ́энэ́йз/ n майонез

mayor /мээ/ n мэр

mayoress /мэ́эрис/ n жена мэра; женщи-
на-мэр

maze /мэйз/ n лабиринт

me /мии/ pron меня, мне и т.д.

meadow /мэ́доу/ n луг

meagre /ми́игрэ/ adj тощий, скудный

meal /миил/ n еда

mealtime /ми́илта́йм/ n время еды

mean /миин/ adj подлый; средний; n середина; vt подразумевать

means /миинз/ n способ, средства; by all
~ /бай оол ~/ конечно; by ~ of /бай ~
ов/ при помощи; by ~ /бай но́у ~/ ни-
коим образом

meaning /ми́ининг/ n значение; double ~
/дабл ~/ двоякий смысл

meantime, meanwhile /ми́инта́йм, ми́ин-
ва́йл/ adv тем временем

measles /ми́излз/ n корь

measure /ме́же/ n мера, мерка, критерий; beyond ~ /бийо́нд ~/ чрезмерно;
made to ~ /мэйд ту ~/ сделанный на
заказ; take ~s /тэйк ~з/ принимать меры; vt мерить, измерять; ~ out /~ а́ут/
отмерять

measured /ме́жед/ adj измеренный

measurement /ме́жемент/ n измерение;
pl размеры

meat /миит/ n мясо; adj мясной

meatballs /ми́итбо́олз/ n pl тефтели; кот-
леты

mechanic /микэ́ник/ n механик

mechanical /микэ́никл/ adj механический

mechanics /микэ́никс/ n механика

medal /медл/ n медаль

meddle /медл/ vi вмешиваться

mediaeval /ме́ди́ивл/ adj средневековый

mediator /ми́идиэ́йтэ/ n посредник

medical /ме́дикл/ adj медицинский, врачебный; ~ examination /~ игзэ́ми-
нэ́йшн/ медицинский осмотр

medicinal /меди́синл/ adj лекарствен-
ный, целебный

medicine /медсн/ n медицина; лекарство; ~-chest /~ чест/ домашняя аптечка

mediocrity /ми́идио́крити/ n посредст-
венность

meditate /ме́дитэйт/ vi размышлять

meditation /ме́дитэ́йшн/ n размышление

Mediterranean /ме́дитэрэ́йньен/ adj средиземноморский

medium /ми́идьем/ n средство; среда; adj
средний; умеренный

medium-sized /ми́идьемса́йзд/ adj среднего размера

meek /миик/ adj кроткий, смиренный

meet /миит/ vt встречать; знакомиться с;
удовлетворять (желания); vi встречаться

meeting /ми́итинг/ n встреча, собрание;
hold a ~ /хо́улд э ~/ проводить собрание

melancholy /ме́лэнкэ́ли/ adj грустный; n
грусть

mellow /ме́лоу/ adj спелый; добродушный

melody /ме́лэди/ n мелодия

melon /ме́лэн/ n дыня

melt /мелт/ vt плавить, растворять; vi таять, плавиться; ~ with love /~ виз лав/
таять от любви

member /мэ́мбэ/ n член; full ~ /фул ~/
полноправный член

membership /мэ́мбэшип/ n членство; ~
card /~ кард/ членский билет

membrane /ме́мбрэйн/ n перепонка;
мембрана

memoirs /ме́мвааз/ n pl мемуары

memorable /ме́мрэбл/ adj памятный

memorial /мимбо́риэл/ n памятник

memorize /ме́мэрайз/ vt запоминать

memory /ме́мэри/ n память

menace /ме́нэс/ n угроза; vt угрожать

mend /менд/ vt чинить, штопать; vi поправляться

mending /ме́ндинг/ n починка, штопка

mental /ментл/ adj умственный; ~ patient
/~ пэйшнт/ душевнобольной

mentality /менте́лити/ n склад ума

mentally /ме́нтэли/ adv мысленно

mention /ме́ншен/ n упоминание; vt упоминать; don't ~ it /до́унт ~ ит/ не стоит
благодарности

mentor /ме́нтор/ n наставник

menu /ме́нььюю/ n меню

mercenary /мёёсинри/ n наемник

merchandise /мёёчендайз/ n товары

merchant /мёёчент/ n купец; adj торговый

merciful /мёрсифул/ adj милосердный

merciless /мёрсилис/ adj беспощадный

mercury /мёёкьюри/ n ртуть

mercy /мёрси/ n милосердие, пощада;
beg for ~ /бег фо ~/ просить пощады

mere /ми́э/ adj простой

merely /ми́эли/ adv только

merge /мёрдж/ vti сливать (ся)

merger /мёрдже/ n объединение

meridian /мери́диэн/ n меридиан

merit /ме́рит/ n заслуга; vt заслуживать

mermaid /мёрмэйд/ n русалка

merriment /ме́римент/ n веселье

merry /ме́ри/ adj веселый

merry-go-round /ме́ригоура́унд/ n карусель

mesh /меш/ n петля; сеть

mess /мес/ n беспорядок, путаница; столовая (в учебном заведении)

message /ме́сидж/ n сообщение

messenger /ме́синдже/ n посыльный,
курьер

Messiah /миса́йе/ n мессия

metal /метл/ n металл; щебень; adj металлический

metalic /мите́лик/ adj металлический

metallurgy /мете́лёджи/ n металлургия

meteor /ми́итье/ n метеор

meteorology /ми́итьеро́лэджи/ n метеорология

meter /ми́итэ/ n счетчик

method /ме́сэд/ n метод, способ

meticulous /мити́кьюлэс/ adj дотошный

metre /ми́итэ/ n метр

metropolis /митро́пэлис/ n столица

metropolitan /ме́трэпо́литн/ adj столич-
ный

mew /мьюю/ n мяуканье; vi мяукать

Mexican /ме́ксикэн/ n мексиканец, мек-
сиканка; adj мексиканский

mezzanine /ме́зэни́ин/ n антресоли

Michaelmas /ми́кэлмэс/ n Михайлов
день

microbe /ма́йкроуб/ n микроб

microphone /ма́йкрэфоун/ n микрофон

microscope /ма́йкрэскоуп/ n микроскоп

mid /мид/ adj средний; in ~ winter /ин ~
ви́нтэ/ в середине зимы

midday /ми́ддэй/ n полдень

middle /мидл/ n середина; adj средний

middle-aged /ми́дле́йджд/ adj средних лет

Middle Ages /ми́длэ́йджис/ n pl средние
века

middle-sized /ми́длса́йзд/ adj среднего
размера

midge /мидж/ n мошка

midget /ми́джит/ n карлик, лилипут

midnight /ми́днайт/ n полночь

midriff /ми́дриф/ n диафрагма

midsummer /ми́дса́мэ/ n середина лета;
M. Day /~ дэй/ Иванов день

midway /ми́двэ́й/ adv на полпути

midwife /ми́двайф/ n акушерка

might /майт/ n могущество, мощь

mighty /ма́йти/ adj могучий, мощный;
adv чрезвычайно

migrate /майгрэ́йт/ vi совершать перелет; переселяться

migration /майгрэ́йшн/ n миграция, пе-
реселение

mild /майлд/ adj мягкий, слабый (на
вкус)

mildness /ма́йлднис/ n мягкость, нежность

mile /майл/ n миля

milestone /ма́йлсто́ун/ n веха

militant /ми́литнт/ adj воинствующий

military /ми́литри/ adj военный, воинский; the ~ /зэ ~/ военные

militia /мили́ше/ n милиция

militiaman /мили́шемэн/ n милиционер

milk /милк/ n молоко; vt доить

milkmaid /ми́лкмэйд/ n доярка, молочница

Milky Way /ми́лкивэ́й/ n Млечный Путь

mill /мил/ n мельница; завод

millstone /ми́лстоун/ n жернов

millet /ми́лит/ n просо

milliard /ми́льярд/ n миллиард; (амер.)
биллион

million /ми́льен/ n миллион

millionaire /ми́льенэ́э/ n миллионер

millionth /ми́льенс/ ord num миллион-
ный

mime /майм/ n мим; vi исполнять роль
без слов; vt имитировать

mimicry /ми́микри/ n мимика; (биол.)
мимикрия

mimosa /мимо́узэ/ n мимоза

minaret /ми́нэрет/ n минарет

mince /минс/ n фарш; vt крошить; ~d
meat /~т миит/ мясной фарш

mind /майнд/ n ум; мнение; bear in ~
/бээр ин ~/ иметь в виду; change one's
~ /чейндж ванз ~/ передумать; keep in
~ /киип ин ~/ помнить; of sound ~ /ов
са́унд ~/ здравомыслящий; vt возражать; I don't ~ /ай до́унт ~/ я не против; never ~ /нэ́вэ ~/ не беспокойтесь!

mindful /ма́йндфул/ adj заботливый

mine /майн/ poss pron мой, моя, мое,
мои; this car is ~ /зыс кар из ~/ это мой
автомобиль; a friend of ~ /э фрэнд ов ~/
мой друг

mine /майн/ n шахта; (воен.) мина; vt
добывать; минировать

miner /ма́йнэ/ n шахтер

mineral /ми́нерэл/ n минерал; adj мине-
ральный

miniature /ми́ньече/ n миниатюра; adj
маленький

minister /ми́нистэ/ n министр; посланник; священник

ministry /ми́нистри/ n министерство; духовенство

mink /минк/ n норка; норковый мех

minor /ма́йнэ/ adj меньший; незначительный; n несовершеннолетний

minority /майно́рити/ n меньшинство

mint /минт/ n монетный двор; мята; a ~
of money /э ~ ов ма́ни/ куча денег; vt
чеканить

minus /ма́йнэс/ n минус

minute /ми́нит/ n минута; pl протокол;
adj крошечный; подробный

minute-hand /ми́нитхэнд/ n минутная
стрелка

miracle /ми́рэкл/ n чудо

miraculous /мирэ́кьюлэс/ adj сверхъестественный, чудесный

mirage /мира́аж/ n мираж

mire /ма́йе/ n грязь

mirror /ми́рэ/ n зеркало; vt отражать

misalliance /ми́сэла́йенс/ n неравный брак

miscarriage /миска́ридж/ n выкидыш

mischief /ми́счиф/ n озорство, шалость

mischievous /ми́счивэс/ adj озорной

misconduct /миско́ндэкт/ n дурное поведение

miser /ма́йзэ/ n скряга

miserable /ми́зэрбл/ adj несчастный, убогий

misery /ми́зэри/ n нищета

misfortune /мисфо́рчен/ n несчастье, неудача

misgiving /мисги́винг/ n опасение

mishap /ми́схэп/ n неудача

misjudge /ми́сджа́дж/ vt недооценивать

mislead /мисли́ид/ vt вводить в заблуждение

misprint /ми́спри́нт/ n опечатка

miss /мис/ n мисс, девушка

miss /мис/ vi промахнуться; vt упускать, опаздывать на; избегать; скучать по; be ~ing /би ~инг/ отсутствовать, недоставать; n промах

missile /ми́сайл/ n ракета; guided ~ /га́йдыд ~/ управляемый реактивный снаряд

missing /ми́синг/ adj отсутствующий, недостающий; без вести пропавший

mission /ми́шен/ n миссия, поручение

missionary /ми́шнэри/ n миссионер

mist /мист/ n туман, дымка

mistake /мисте́йк/ n ошибка

mistaken /мисте́йкен/ adj ошибочный; be ~ /би ~/ ошибаться

mister /ми́стэ/ n мистер, господин

mistress /ми́стрис/ n хозяйка (дома); учительница; любовница; миссис, госпожа

mistrust /мистра́ст/ n недоверие; vt не доверять

misty /ми́сти/ adj туманный

misunderstand /ми́сандэстэ́нд/ vt неправильно понимать

misunderstanding /ми́сандэстэ́ндинг/ n недоразумение

misuse /ми́съю́юс/ n злоупотребление; /ми́съю́юз/ vt злоупотреблять

mitten /митн/ n рукавица

mix /микс/ vt смешивать; ~ up /~ ап/ путать

moan /мо́ун/ n стон; vi стонать

moat /мо́ут/ n ров

mob /моб/ n сборище; ~ law /~ лоо/ самосуд

mobile /мо́убайл/ adj передвижной; подвижный

mobility /моби́лити/ n подвижность

mobilization /мо́билизэ́йшн/ n мобилизация

mock /мок/ vt высмеивать, издеваться над

mockery /мо́кери/ n издевательство, насмешка

mocking /мо́кинг/ adj насмешливый

mocking-bird /мо́кингбёд/ n пересмешник

mode /мо́уд/ n способ; мода, обычай

model /модл/ adj образцовый; n модель, образец; натурщик, натурщица; vt моделировать

moderate /мо́дрит/ adj умеренный; /мо́дэрэйт/ vt умерять

moderation /мо́дэрэ́йшн/ n умеренность

modern /мо́дэн/ adj современный; ~ languages /~ лэ́нгвиджиз/ новые языки

modernist /мо́дэнист/ n модернист

modest /мо́дист/ adj скромный

modesty /мо́дисти/ n скромность

modification /мо́дификэ́йшн/ n (видо)изменение

modify /мо́дифай/ vt (видо)изменять

mohair /мо́ухээ/ n ангорская шерсть, мохер

Mohammedan /моухэ́мидн/ n магометанин, магометанка; adj магометанский

moist /мойст/ adj влажный

moisture /мо́йсче/ n влага

molar /мо́улэ/ n коренной зуб

molasses /мелэ́сиз/ n патока

mole /мо́ул/ n (зоол.) крот; родинка; мол

molest /моулест/ vt приставать (к)

moment /мо́умент/ n миг, момент

momentous /моуме́нтэс/ adj важный

monarch /мо́нэк/ n монарх, монархиня

monarchy /мо́нэки/ n монархия

monastery /мо́нэстри/ n монастырь (мужской)

Monday /ма́нди/ n понедельник

money /ма́ни/ n деньги

money-changer /ма́ничейндже/ n меняла

money order /ма́ниордэ/ n денежный перевод

Mongol /мо́нгол/ n монгол(ка); монгольский язык; adj монгольский

mongoose /мо́нгус/ n мангуста

mongrel /ма́нгрэл/ n помесь, дворняжка

monk /манк/ n монах

monkey /ма́нки/ n обезьяна

monogram /мо́нэгрэм/ n монограмма

monopoly /мэно́пэли/ n монополия

monotonous /мэно́тнэс/ adj однообразный

monotony /мэно́тни/ n монотонность

monster /мо́нстэ/ n чудовище

monstrous /мо́нстрэс/ adj чудовищный

month /манс/ n месяц

monthly /ма́нсли/ adj ежемесячный; n ежемесячник

monument /мо́ньюмент/ n памятник

monumental /мо́ньюме́нтл/ adj монументальный

moo /муу/ n мычание; vi мычать

mood /мууд/ n настроение; (грам.) наклонение

moon /муун/ n луна, месяц

moonlight /му́унлайт/ n лунный свет

moonshine /му́уншайн/ n чепуха, чушь; самогон

moor /му́э/ n моховое болото

moor /му́э/ vt причаливать

moose /муус/ n американский лось

moot /муут/ adj спорный

mop /моп/ n швабра; vt мыть шваброй

moral /морл/ adj моральный, нравственный; n мораль; pl нравственность

morale /мора́ал/ n моральное состояние; боевой дух

Moravian /мэрэ́йвьен/ n житель Моравии; adj моравский

morbid /мо́рбид/ adj болезненный

more /мор/ adv больше, еще; once ~ /ванс ~/ еще раз

moreover /мооро́увэ/ adv кроме того

morning /мо́рнинг/ n утро; good ~ /гуд ~/ доброе утро!

morsel /мо́рсэл/ n кусочек

mortal /мортл/ adj смертный; смертельный

mortality /мотэ́лити/ n смертность

mortar /мо́ртэ/ n ступка; (воен.) миномет

mortgage /мо́огидж/ n закладная; vt закладывать

Moslem /мо́злем/ n мусульманин, мусульманка; adj мусульманский

mosque /моск/ n мечеть

mosquito /мэски́итоу/ n комар, москит

mosquito-net /мэски́итоунет/ n сетка от комаров

moss /мос/ n мох

mossy /мо́си/ adj мшистый

most /мо́уст/ adj наибольший; ~ people /~ пиипл/ большинство людей; adv больше всего; at the ~ /эт зэ ~/ самое большее

mostly /мо́устли/ adv главным образом

motel /мо́утэл/ n мотель

moth /мос/ n моль, мотылек

mother /ма́зэ/ n мать; ~'s day /~з дэй/ (амер.) День матери; ~ tongue /~ танг/ родной язык

motherhood /ма́зэхуд/ n материнство

mother-in-law /ма́зэринло́о/ n теща, свекровь

motherland /ма́зэлэнд/ n родина

motherly /ма́зэли/ adj материнский

mother-of-pearl /ма́зэрэвпёл/ n перламутр

motion /мо́ушн/ n движение; предложение; ~ picture /~ пи́кче/ кинофильм motionless /мо́ушенлис/ adj неподвижный

motive /мо́утив/ n мотив, повод

motley /мо́тли/ adj пестрый

motor /мо́утэ/ n мотор, двигатель; ~ car /~ кар/ автомобиль

motor-cycle /мо́утэса́йкл/ n мотоцикл

motorist /мо́утэрист/ n автомобилист

mottled /мотлд/ adj испещренный

motto /мо́тоу/ n девиз

mould /мо́улд/ n плесень; литейная форма

mound /ма́унд/ n насыпь, холм

mount /ма́унт/ n холм, гора; верховая лошадь; vt монтировать; вставлять в оправу

mountain /ма́унтин/ n гора

mountaineer /ма́унтини́э/ n альпинист; горец

mountainous /ма́унтинэс/ adj гористый

mourn /морн/ vt скорбеть; vi носить траур

mournful /мо́рнфул/ adj траурный

mourning /мо́рнинг/ n траур

mouse /ма́ус/ n (pl mice) мышь

mousetrap /ма́устрэп/ n мышеловка

moustache /мэста́аш/ n усы

mouth /ма́ус/ n рот; устье (реки)

mouthpiece /ма́успиис/ n рупор

movables /му́увэблз/ n pl движимость

move /муув/ n движение; ход (в игре); (образн.) шаг; whose ~ is it? /хууз ~ из ит/ чей ход?; vt двигать; трогать, волновать; vi двигаться

movement /му́увмент/ n движение; (тех.) ход

movies /му́увиз/ n pl кино

moving /му́увинг/ adj движущийся; трогательный

mow /мо́у/ vt косить

mower /мо́уэ/ n косилка

Mrs. /ми́сиз/ госпожа

much /мач/ adj много; adv очень; how ~ ? /ха́у ~/ сколько?; too ~ /туу ~/ слишком много

mud /мад/ n грязь

muddle /мадл/ n путаница; vt спутывать

muddle-headed /ма́длхе́дыд/ adj бестолковый

muddy /ма́ди/ adj грязный

muff /маф/ n муфта

muffle /мафл/ vt запутывать

muffler /ма́флэ/ n кашне; (тех.) глушитель

mug /маг/ n кружка

mule /мьююл/ n мул

multicoloured /ма́лтика́лэд/ adj цветной

multi-millionaire /ма́лтими́льенээ/ n мультимиллионер

multiple /ма́лтипл/ adj многочисленный; составной; n кратное число

multiplication /ма́лтиплике́йшн/ n умножение

multiply /ма́лтиплай/ vt умножать

multitude /ма́лтитьюд/ n множество

mum /мам/ n (разг.) мама, мамочка; молчание; keep ~ /киип ~/ помалкивать

mumble /мамбл/ vi бормотать

mummy /ма́ми/ n мумия

mumps /мампс/ n свинка

munch /манч/ vt жевать

municipal /мьюни́сипл/ adj городской, муниципальный

munitions /мьюни́шенз/ n pl военное снаряжение

mural /мьюэ́рэл/ n стенная живопись, фреска

murder /мёрдэ/ n убийство; vt убивать

murderer /мёрдэрэ/ n убийца

murky /мёрки/ adj пасмурный

murmur /мёрмэ/ vi журчать, шептать

muscat /ма́скет/ n мускат

muscle /масл/ n мускул, мышца

muscular /ма́скьюлэ/ adj мускульный, мускулистый

Muscovite /ма́скэвайт/ n москвич(ка); adj московский

muse /мьюю́з/ n муза

muse /мьюю́з/ vi размышлять

museum /мьюзи́эм/ n музей

mushroom /ма́шрум/ n гриб

music /мьюю́зик/ n музыка; ноты

musical /мьюю́зикл/ adj музыкальный; ~ comedy /~ ко́миди/ оперетта; n мью́зикл

music-hall /мьюю́зикхол/ n мюзик-холл

musician /мьюзи́шен/ n музыкант

musk /маск/ n мускус

must /маст/ v aux должен, должна и т.д.; I ~ /ай ~/ я должен; he ~ have gone /хи ~ хэв гон/ должно быть, он ушел

mustard /ма́стэд/ n горчица; ~ plaster /~ пла́астэ/ горчичник

musty /ма́сти/ adj затхлый

mute /мьюют/ adj немой, безмолвный; n немой; (муз.) сурдинка

muted /мьюю́тыд/ adj приглушенный

mutilate /мьюю́тилэйт/ vt увечить

mutineer /мьюю́ютини́э/ n мятежник

mutiny /мьюю́тини/ n мятеж; vti восставать

mutter /ма́тэ/ vti бормотать

mutton /матн/ n баранина

mutton-chop /ма́тнчоп/ n баранья котлета

mutual /мьюю́ютьюэл/ adj взаимный; ~ relations /~ рилэ́йшнз/ взаимоотношения

mutually /мьюю́ютьюэли/ adv взаимно

muzzle /мазл/ n морда; дуло (пистолета); vt надевать намордник на

my /май/ poss adj мой, моя, мое, мои

myself /майсэ́лф/ pron себя, себе, сам, сама

mysterious /мисти́эриэс/ adj таинственный

mystery /ми́стэри/ n тайна

mystic /ми́стик/ n мистик

mystify /ми́стифай/ vt мистифицировать

myth /мис/ n миф

mythical /ми́сикл/ adj мифический

mythology /мисо́лэджи/ n мифология

N

nag /нэг/ vt придираться к; don't ~ /до́ унт ~/ не ворчи!

naiad /на́йед/ n наяда

nail /нэйл/ n ноготь; коготь; гвоздь; hit the ~ on the head /хит зэ ~ он зэ хед/ попадать в точку; vt прибивать, пригвождать

naive /найи́в/ adj наивный

naked /нэ́йкид/ adj голый, нагой; ~ eye /~ ай/ невооруженный глаз; ~ wire /~ ва́йе/ голый провод

nakedness /нэ́йкиднис/ n нагота

name /нэйм/ n имя, фамилия; название; репутация; in God's ~ /ин годз ~/ ради бога!; call ~s /коол ~з/ обзывать; vt называть

nameless /нэ́ймлис/ adj безымянный

namely /нэ́ймли/ adv именно

namesake /нэ́ймсэйк/ n тезка

nanny /нэ́ни/ n няня

nap /нэп/ n короткий сон; have a ~ /хэв э ~/ вздремнуть

napkin /нэ́пкин/ n салфетка; пеленка

narcissus /нарси́сэс/ n нарцисс

narcotic /нарко́тик/ n наркотик

narrate /нэрэ́йт/ vt рассказывать

narrative /нэ́рэтив/ adj повествовательный; n повествование

narrow /нэ́роу/ adj узкий

narrowness /нэ́роунис/ n узость, ограниченность

nasal /нэйзл/ adj носовой; гнусавый

nasturtium /нэстёшем/ n настурция

nasty /на́асти/ adj гадкий, отвратительный

nation /нэйшн/ n нация, народ; государство

national /нэ́шенл/ n подданный; adj национальный; ~ anthem /~ э́нсэм/ государственный гимн; ~ economy /~ ико́нэми/ народное хозяйство

nationalism /нэ́шнэлизм/ n национализм

nationalist /нэ́шнэлист/ n националист

nationality /нэ́шенэ́лити/ n национальность; подданство

nationalize /нэ́шнэлайз/ vt национализировать

native /нэ́йтив/ adj родной; местный; ~ tongue /~ танг/ родной язык; n туземец, уроженец

natural /нэчрл/ adj естественный

naturalist /нэ́чрэлист/ n натуралист

naturalization /нэ́чрэлизэ́йшн/ n натурализация

naturally /нэ́чрэли/ adv конечно

nature /нэ́йче/ n природа; характер

naught /ноот/ n ничто; ноль

naughty /нóоти/ adj непослушный, шаловливый

nautical /нóотикл/ adj мореходный; ~ mile /~ майл/ морская миля

naval /нэ́йвл/ adj военно-морской

navel /нэ́йвл/ n пупок

navel-cord /нэ́йвлкорд/ n пуповина

navigate /нэ́вигейт/ vt управлять (судном, самолетом); vi плавать

navigation /нэ́вигéйшн/ n навигация

navigator /нэ́вигейтэ/ n штурман

navy /нэ́йви/ n военно-морской флот; ~ blue /~ блюю/ темно-синий

Nazi /нáаци/ n нацист

near /нúэ/ adj близкий; adv близко; prep возле, около, у, близко от

nearly /нúэли/ adv почти

near-sighted /нúэсáйтыд/ adj близорукий

neat /ниит/ adj опрятный

neatness /нúитнис/ n опрятность; четкость

necessary /нéсисри/ adj необходимый; n (самое) необходимое

necessity /нисэ́сити/ n необходимость; предмет первой необходимости

neck /нек/ n шея; горлышко (бутылки)

necklace /нéклис/ n ожерелье

need /ниид/ n нужда, надобность, потребность; if ~ be /иф ~ би/ в случае нужды; vt нуждаться в; vi: it ~s to be done /ит ~з ту би дан/ надо это сделать

needle /ниидл/ n игла, иголка; спица (вязальная); стрелка (компаса)

needless /нúидлис/ adj ненужный

needy /нúиди/ n нуждающийся

negate /нигéйт/ vt отрицать

negative /нéгэтив/ adj отрицательный

neglect /ниглéкт/ n пренебрежение, заброшенность; vt пренебрегать, запускать; ~ one's duties /~ ванз дью́ютиз/ не выполнять своих обязанностей

negligent /нéглиджент/ adj небрежный

negotiable /нигóушьебл/ adj реализуемый; ~ copy /~ кóпи/ действительный экземпляр

negotiate /нигóушиэйт/ vt договариваться о; vi вести переговоры

negotiation /нигóушиэ́йшн/ n переговоры; enter into ~ /э́нтэ и́нту ~/ вступать в переговоры

negotiator /нигóушиэйтэ/ n участник переговоров

neigh /нэй/ n ржание; vi ржать

neighbour /нэ́йбэ/ n сосед(ка); love one's ~ /лав ванз ~/ любить ближнего своего

neighborhood /нэ́йбэхуд/ n округа, район

neighboring /нэ́йбринг/ adj соседний

neighborly /нэ́йбэли/ adj добрососедский

neither /нáйзэ/ adj, pron никакой; ни тот, ни другой; ~ of us /~ ов ас/ никто из нас

Nemesis /нéмисис/ n Немезида

neo- /нúио/ prefix нео-

nephew /нéвью/ n племянник

nepotism /нéпэтизм/ n кумовство

nerve /нёрв/ n нерв, хладнокровие; (разг.) нахальство

nervous /нёрвэс/ adj нервный; be ~ about /би ~ эбáут/ волноваться о

nest /нест/ n гнездо; vi гнездиться

net /нет/ n сеть; adj нетто; ~ cost /~ кост/ себестоимость; ~ profit /~ прóфит/ чистый доход; ~ weight /~ вейт/ вес нетто; vi ловить сетью; получать чистый доход

Netherlander /нэ́злэндэ/ n голландец

Netherlandish /нэ́злэндиш/ adj нидерландский, голландский

netting /нэ́тинг/ n сеть, сетка

nettle /нетл/ n крапива

network /нэ́твёрк/ n сеть (железнодорожная, телевизионная и т.д.)

neurotic /ньюэро́тик/ adj нервный

neuter /нью́ютэ/ adj (грам.) среднего рода

neutral /нью́ютрэл/ adj нейтральный

neutrality /ньютрэ́лити/ n нейтралитет

neutralize /нью́ютрэлайз/ vt нейтрализовать

never /нэ́вэ/ adv никогда; ~ mind /~ майнд/ ничего, неважно

never-ending /нэ́вэрэ́ндинг/ adj бесконечный

nevertheless /нэ́вэззэлес/ adv тем не менее

new /нью́ю/ adj новый; свежий

new-born /нью́юборн/ adj новорожденный

newcomer /нью́юка́мэ/ n приезжий, новичок

newly /нью́юли/ adv вновь, недавно

newly-wed /нью́юливэд/ n новобрачный(ая)

news /нью́юз/ n новость, известие

newspaper /нью́юспэ́йпэ/ n газета

news-stand /нью́юзстэнд/ n газетный киоск

next /нэкст/ adj следующий, ближайший; ~ month /~ манс/ в следующе месяце; adv после; what ~? /вот ~/ что же дальше?

next-door /нэ́кстдо́ор/ adj соседний

nice /найс/ adj хороший, приятный, милый, деликатный

niche /нич, нииш/ n ниша

nickel /никл/ n никель; монета в 5 центов

nickname /ни́кнэйм/ n прозвище

niece /ниис/ n племянница

night /найт/ n ночь; вечер; good ~! /гуд ~/ спокойной ночи!; last ~ /лааст ~/ вчера вечером

nightingale /на́йтингейл/ n соловей

nil /нил/ n ноль, ничего

nimble /нимбл/ adj проворный

nimbus /ни́мбэс/ n нимб

nincompoop /ни́нкэмпуп/ n простофиля

nine /найн/ num девять

nineteen /на́йнти́ин/ num девятнадцать

nineteenth /на́йнти́инс/ ord num девятнадцатый

ninetieth /на́йнтис/ ord num девяностый

ninety /на́йнти/ num девяносто

ninny /ни́ни/ n простофиля

ninth /найнс/ ord num девятый

nip /нип/ n щипок; vt щипать; ~ in the bud /~ ин зэ бад/ пресекать в корне

nipple /нипл/ n сосок; (тех.) ниппель

nitrate /на́йтрэйт/ n нитрат

nitrogen /на́йтриджен/ n азот

no /но́у/ adv нет; adj никакой; ~ admittance /~ эдми́тнс/ вход воспрещен; ~ doubt /~ да́ут/ несомненно; ~ matter /~ мэ́тэ/ неважно; ~ one /~ ван/ никто; ~ smoking /~ смо́укинг/ курить воспрещается

Noah's Ark /но́уэза́рк/ n Ноев ковчег

nobility /ноби́лити/ n дворянство, знать

noble /но́убл/ adj благородный, знатный

nobody /но́убоди/ pron никто

nocturnal /ноктёрнл/ adj ночной

nod /нод/ n кивок; vi кивать

noise /нойз/ n шум; make a ~ /мэйк э ~/ шуметь

noiseless /но́йзлис/ adj бесшумный

noisy /но́йзи/ adj шумный

nolens volens /но́улензво́уленз/ (лат.) волей-неволей

nomad /но́мэд/ n кочевник

nomadic /ноумэ́дик/ adj кочевой

no man's land /но́умэ́нзлэ́нд/ n ничейная полоса

nomenclature /номе́нклэче/ n номенклатура

nominal /но́минл/ adj номинальный; ~ sentence /~ сэ́нтэнс/ условный приговор

nominate /но́минэйт/ vt выставлять кандидатом; назначать

nomination /нóминэ́йшн/ n выставление
кандидатуры; назначение
nominee /нóминйи/ n кандидат
non- /нон/ prefix не-, без-
nonalcoholic /нóнэлкэхóлик/ adj безалкогольный
nonattendance /нóнэтэ́ндэнс/ n непосе-
щение занятий, прогул
noncommissioned officer /нóнкэмúшенд-
óфисэ/ n унтер-офицер
nonconformist /нóнкэнфóрмист/ adj ина-
комыслящий
nondescript /нóндискрипт/ adj неопределенный
none /нан/ pron никто, ничто; ~ of that!
/~ов зэт/ хватит!; adv нисколько
nonetheless /нóнзэлес/ adv тем не менее,
все же
non-existent /нóнигзúстнт/ adj несуще-
ствующий
no-nonsense /нóунóнсэнс/ adj серьезный, деловой
non-payment /нóнпэ́ймент/ n неплатеж
nonsense /нóнсэнс/ n вздор, глупости
non-stop /нóнстóп/ adj (ав.) беспосадочный
noodle /нуудл/ n глупец, балда; pl лапша
nook /нук/ n укромный уголок
noon /нуун/ n полдень; adj полуденный
noose /нуус/ n петля, ловушка
nor /нор/ conj и не, также не, ни
Nordic /нóрдик/ adj скандинавский;
нордический
norm /норм/ n норма
normal /нормл/ adj нормальный
north /норс/ n север; adv на север; adj
северный
northern /нóрзэн/ adj северный; ~ lights
/~ лайтс/ северное сияние
northerner /нóрзнэ/ n северянин
northwards /нóрсвэдз/ adv на север, к се-
веру
northwest /нóрсвэст/ n северо-запад

Norwegian /новúиджн/ n норвежец, норвежка; норвежский язык; adj норвежский
nose /нóуз/ n нос; have a good ~ for /хэв
э гуд ~ фо/ иметь чутье на; vt: ~ out /~
áут/ разнюхивать
nostril /нóстрил/ n ноздря
not /нот/ adv не, ни; ~ at all /~ эт оол/ не
стоит (благодарности), нисколько; it's
~ bad /итс ~ бэд/ неплохо
notary /нóутэри/ n нотариус
notation /нотэ́йшн/ n система обозначе-
ний; (муз.) нотное письмо
notch /ноч/ n зарубка
note /нóут/ n записка, заметка; нота
notebook /нóутбук/ n записная книжка
noted /нóутыд/ adj знаменитый
noteworthy /нóутвёзи/ adj достоприме-
чательный
nothing /нáсинг/ pron ничто, ничего; for
~ /фо ~/ зря; даром
notice /нóутис/ n объявление; внимание;
give ~ /гив ~/ предупреждать (об
увольнении); vt замечать
noticeable /нóутисэбл/ adj заметный
notice-board /нóутисбóд/ n доска для
объявлений
notification /нóутификéйшн/ n извещение
notify /нóутифай/ vt уведомлять
notion /нóушн/ n понятие
notorious /нотóориэс/ adj пресловутый
notwithstanding /нóтвисстэ́ндинг/ prep
несмотря на; adv тем не менее; conj
хотя
nought /ноот/ n ноль
noun /нáун/ n имя существительное
nourish /нáриш/ vt питать
nourishing /нáришинг/ adj питательный
nourishment /нáришмент/ n питание,
пища
novel /новл/ n роман; adj новый, необычный
novelette /нóвелéт/ n новелла
novelist /нóвелист/ n романист

novelty /но́влти/ n новизна

November /новэ́мбэ/ n ноябрь

novice /но́вис/ n новичок

now /на́у/ adv теперь; just ~ /джаст ~/
только что; ~ and then /~ энд зен/ иногда; from ~ on /фром ~ он/ впредь

nowadays /на́уэдэйз/ adv нынче

nowhere /но́увээ/ adv никогда; никуда

nuclear /нью́юклиэ/ adj ядерный

nucleus /нью́юклиэс/ n ядро

nude /ньююд/ adj нагой; n обнаженная
фигура

nugget /на́гит/ n самородок

nuisance /нью́юснс/ n неприятность; надоедливый человек; what a ~! /вот э ~/
какая досада!

null /нал/ adj недействительный; ~ and
void /~ энд войд/ не имеющий законной силы

nullify /на́лифай/ vt аннулировать

numb /нам/ adj онемелый; окоченелый
(от холода)

number /на́мбэ/ n число, номер; ~ plate
/~ плэйт/ номерной знак; a ~ of /э ~
ов/ ряд; quite a ~ /квайт э ~/ много; vt
нумеровать; насчитывать

numbering /на́мбринг/ n нумерация

numberless /на́мбэлис/ adj бесчисленный

numeral /нью́юмрэл/ adj цифровой; n
имя числительное

numerous /нью́юмрэс/ adj многочисленный

nun /нан/ n монахиня

nunnery /на́нэри/ n женский монастырь

nuptial /на́пшел/ adj свадебный

nurse /нёёс/ n медицинская сестра, сиделка; няня; vt ухаживать за; нянчить,
лелеять

nursery /нёёсри/ n детская, ясли, питомник; ~ school /~ скуул/ детский сад

nursing /нёёсинг/ n уход, выкармливание;
~ home /~ хо́ум/ частная лечебница

nurture /нёёче/ vt выращивать; вынашивать (план и т.п.)

nut /нат/ n орех; гайка

nutcracker /на́ткрэ́кэ/ n шипцы для орехов, щелкунчик

nutmeg /на́тмег/ n мускатный орех

nutrition /нью́трӣшн/ n питание; диететика

nylon /на́йлэн/ n нейлон

nymph /нимф/ n нимфа

O

O! /oy/ interj o!; ~ my! /~ май/ Боже мой!

oak /о́ук/ n дуб

oar /oop/ n весло

oasis /оэ́йсис/ n оазис

oath /о́ус/ n клятва; присяга; take an ~
/тэйк эн ~/ давать клятву

oats /о́утс/ n pl овес

oatmeal /о́утмил/ n овсянка

obedience /эби́идьенс/ n послушание,
повинование

obedient /эби́идьент/ adj послушный

obey /эбэ́й/ vt слушаться, повиноваться

obituary /эби́тьюэри/ n некролог

object /о́бджикт/ n предмет; цель; (грам.)
дополнение; /эбджект/ vi возражать

objection /эбджекшн/ n возражение; I
have no ~ /ай хэв но́у ~/ я не против

objective /обджектив/ adj объективный;
n цель

obligate /о́блигэйт/ vt обязывать

obligation /облиге́йшн/ n обязательство

obligatory /обли́гэтри/ adj обязательный

oblige /эбла́йдж/ vt обязывать

obliging /эбла́йджинг/ adj услужливый

oblique /эбли́ик/ adj косой; (грам.) косвенный

oblivion /эбли́виэн/ n забвение

oblong /о́блонг/ adj продолговатый

obscene /обси́ин/ adj непристойный

obscenity /обси́инити/ n непристойность

obscure /эбскью́оэ/ adj темный, смутный,
неясный; vt затемнять, делать неясным

observance /эбзёёвнс/ n ритуал

observation /о́бзэвэ́йшн/ n замечание

observatory /эбзёёветри/ n обсерватория

observe /эбзёёв/ vt наблюдать

observer /эбзёёвэ/ n наблюдатель

obsess /эбсэ́с/ vt преследовать (об идее, страхе и т.п.); obsessed by /~т бай/ одержимый

obsession /эбсэ́шн/ n навязчивая идея

obsolete /о́бсэлит/ adj устарелый

obstacle /о́бстэкл/ n препятствие

obstinacy /о́бстинэси/ n упрямство

obstinate /о́бстинит/ adj упрямый

obstruct /эбстра́кт/ vt препятствовать

obstruction /эбстра́кшн/ n заграждение, препятствие

obtain /эбтэ́йн/ vt получать

obvious /о́бвиэс/ adj очевидный, явный

occasion /экэ́йжн/ n случай (удобный), повод; festive ~ /фэ́стив ~/ праздник

occasional /экэ́йжнл/ adj случайный

occupation /о́кьюпэ́йшн/ n профессия; оккупация

occupy /о́кьюпай/ vt занимать; оккупировать

occur /экёё/ vi происходить; it ~red to me that /ит ~д ту ми зэт/ мне пришло в голову, что

occurrence /эка́рнс/ n происшествие

ocean /о́ушн/ n океан

o'clock /экло́к/: at one ~ /эт ван ~/ в час

October /экто́убэ/ n октябрь

octopus /о́ктэпэс/ n осьминог

odd /од/ adj нечетный; странный; ~ job /~ джоб/ случайная работа

oddity /о́дити/ n странность; чудак; ~ sale /~ сэйл/ распродажа разрозненных товаров

odds /одз/ n pl шансы; ~ and ends /~ энд эндз/ остатки; be at ~ /би эт ~/ быть в ссоре

odious /о́удьес/ adj отвратительный

odour /о́удэ/ n запах

of /ов/ prep: ~ course /~ корс/ конечно; one ~ them /ван ~ зэм/ один из них; think ~ /синк ~/ думать о; be proud ~ /би пра́уд ~/ гордиться; a piece ~ bread /э пиис ~ брэд/ кусок хлеба

off /оф/ adj дальний; незанятый; adv: be ~ /би ~/ уходить; hands ~ /хэндз ~/ руки прочь (от); a mile ~ /э майл ~/ в одной миле от; ~ and on /~ энд он/ время от времени; wash ~ /вош ~/ отмывать; prep c, от

offence /эфе́нс/ n преступление; обида

offend /эфе́нд/ vt обижать

offender /эфе́ндэ/ n правонарушитель; обидчик

offensive /эфе́нсив/ n наступление; adj наступательный; оскорбительный

offer /о́фэ/ n предложение; vt предлагать

offering /о́фринг/ n пожертвование; предложение

office /о́фис/ n контора, ведомство; good ~s /гуд ~ыз/ услуги; ~ hours /~ а́уэз/ служебные часы

officer /о́фисэ/ n офицер

official /эфи́шл/ adj официальный; ~ duties /~ дьюютиз/ служебные обязанности; n чиновник

offspring /о́фспринг/ n отпрыск

often /офн/ adv часто

oil /ойл/ n масло; нефть; pl масляные краски; ~ cloth /~ клос/ клеенка; ~ well /~ вэл/ нефтяная скважина; vt смазывать

oil-field /о́йлфилд/ n месторождение нефти

oily /о́йли/ adj маслянистый; елейный

ointment /о́йнтмент/ n мазь

O.K. /о́укей/ n одобрение; разрешение; interj хорошо! ладно!

old /о́улд/ adj старый; how ~ are you? /ха́у ~ а ю/ сколько вам лет?; ~ maid /~ мэйд/ старая дева; ~ man /~ мэн/ старик; O. Testament /~ тэ́стэмент/ Ветхий Завет; ~ woman /~ ву́мэн/ старуха

old-age /о́улдэ́йдж/ adj старческий; ~ pension /~ пеншн/ пенсия по старости

old-fashioned /о́улдфэ́шнд/ adj старомодный

old-timer /о́улдта́ймэ/ n старожил, ветеран

olive /о́лив/ n маслина; ~ oil /~ ойл/ оливковое масло

Olympic games /оли́мпикге́ймз/ n pl Олимпийские игры

omelet(te) /о́млит/ n омлет, яичница

omission /оми́шн/ n пропуск, упущение

omit /оми́т/ vt пропускать

omnipotent /омни́пэтнт/ adj всемогущий

on /он/ prep на, в, о; ~ Monday /~ ма́нди/ в понедельник; ~ sale /~ сэйл/ в продаже; go ~ /го́у ~/ продолжайте!

once /ванс/ adv раз; ~ more /~ мор/ еще раз; at ~ /эт ~/ сейчас же; ~ upon a time /~ эпо́н э тайм/ давным давно

one /ван/ num один; ~ another /~ эна́зэ/ друг друга; ~ day /~ дэй/ однажды; ~ of us /~ эв ас/ один из нас; no ~ /но́у ~/ никто

oneself /вансэ́лф/ pron себя; be ~ /би ~/ быть самим собой

one-way /ва́нвэ́й/ adj односторонний; ~ street /~ стриит/ улица с односторонним движением

only /о́унли/ adv только; adj единственный

ooze /ууз/ vi просачиваться; n тина

opaque /опе́йк/ adj темный, непрозрачный

open /о́упн/ vti открывать(ся); adj открытый, откровенный; ~ question /~ квесчн/ открытый вопрос; ~ secret /~ си́икрит/ секрет полишинеля

opener /о́упэнэ/ n открывалка

opening /о́упэнинг/ n отверстие; вакансия

opera /о́перэ/ n опера; ~ house /~ ха́ус/ оперный театр

operate /о́перэйт/ vt управлять; vi действовать; делать операцию

operation /о́перэ́йшн/ n действие; операция (также хирург.)

opinion /эпи́ньен/ n мнение; in her ~ /ин хёр ~/ по ее мнению

opium /о́упьем/ n опиум

opponent /эпо́унент/ n противник, оппонент; adj противоположный

opportunity /о́пэтью́юнити/ n удобный случай

oppose /эпо́уз/ vt быть против

opposed /эпо́узд/ adj враждебный

opposite /о́пэзит/ adj противоположный; prep против; adv напротив

opposition /о́пэзи́шн/ n сопротивление; оппозиция

oppress /эпре́с/ vt притеснять

oppression /эпре́шн/ n гнет

oppressive /эпре́сив/ adj гнетущий

oppressor /эпре́сэ/ n угнетатель

optic /о́птик/ adj глазной

optician /опти́шн/ n оптик

optics /о́птикс/ n оптика

optimism /о́птимизм/ n оптимизм

optimist /о́птимист/ n оптимист

optimistic /о́птими́стик/ adj оптимистический

option /опшн/ n выбор

or /ор/ conj или; ~ else /~ элс/ иначе

oral /оорл/ adj устный; ~ test /~ тест/ устный экзамен

orange /о́ринж/ n апельсин; adj оранжевый

orator /о́рэтэ/ n оратор

orbit /о́рбит/ n орбита; глазная впадина

orchard /о́рчед/ n фруктовый сад

orchestra /о́ркистрэ/ n оркестр

orchid /о́ркид/ n орхидея

ordain /одэ́йн/ vt предопределять; (церк.) посвящать в сан

ordeal /оди́ил/ n тяжелое испытание

order /о́рдэ/ n порядок; приказ; заказ; орден (награда, религиозный и т.п.); money ~ /ма́ни ~/ денежный перевод; out of ~ /а́ут ов ~/ неисправный; ~ form /~ форм/ бланк заказа; vt приказывать; заказывать

orderly /о́рдэли/ adj опрятный; n ординарец; санитар

ordinal /о́рдинл/ adj порядковый

ordinance /о́рдинэнс/ n декрет, указ

ordnance /о́рднэнс/ n артиллерия

ore /ор/ n руда

organ /óогэн/ n орган; (муз.) оргáн

organdie /óргэнди/ n кисея, органди

organic /огэ́ник/ adj органический

organism /óргэнизм/ n организм

organization /óргэнизэ́йшн/ n организация

organize /óргэнайз/ vt организовывать

organizer /óргэнайзэ/ n организатор

orgasm /óргэзм/ n оргазм

orgy /óрджи/ n оргия

Orient /óориент/ n Восток

orient /óориент/ vti ориентировать (ся)

oriental /óориéнтл/ adj восточный

orientation /óориентэ́йшн/ n ориентация

origin /óриджин/ n происхождение

original /эри́джинл/ adj первоначальный; оригинальный; n подлинник

originate /эри́джинэйт/ vi происходить

ornament /óрнэмент/ n украшение; vt украшать

ornamental /óрнамéнтл/ adj декоративный

orphan /орфн/ n сирота

orphanage /óрфэнидж/ n сиротский приют

orthodox /óрсэдокс/ adj ортодоксальный; O. (церк.) православный

orthopaedy /óрсопи́ди/ n ортопедия

ostentatious /óстэнтэ́йшес/ adj показной

ostrich /óстрич/ n страус

other /áзэ/ adj другой, иной; every ~ day /э́ври ~ дэй/ через день; the ~ day /зэ ~ дэй/ на днях

otherwise /áзэвайз/ adv иначе

otter /óтэ/ n выдра

ought /оот/ v aux должен, следовало бы; you ~ to go /ю ~ ту гóу/ вам следовало бы уйти

ounce /áунс/ n унция (=28,35 г)

our, ours /áуэ, áуэз/ poss pron наша, наш и т.д.; свой, своя и т.д.

ourselves /áуэсэ́лвз/ pron себя; сами

oust /áуст/ vt вытеснять

out /áут/ adv наружу, из; go ~ /гóу ~/ выходить; she is ~ /ши из ~/ ее нет дома; get ~ /гет ~/ убирайтесь вон!

outbalance /áутбэ́лэнс/ vt перевешивать

outbreak /áутбрэйк/ n взрыв, вспышка

outcast /áуткаст/ n изгнанник

outcome /áуткам/ n исход, результат

outcry /áуткрай/ n протест

outdistance /аутди́стэнс/ vt обгонять

outdo /аутдý у/ vt превосходить

outdoor /áутдо/ adj на открытом воздухе

outer /áутэ/ adj наружный

outfit /áутфит/ n снаряжение; компания

outgoing /áутгóуинг/ adj уходящий

outing /áутинг/ n прогулка

outlaw /áутло/ n бандит; vt объявлять вне закона

outlay /áутлэй/ n издержки, расходы

outlet /áутлет/ n выпускное отверстие; отдушина

outline /áутлайн/ n очертание, набросок; vt описывать в общих чертах

outlook /áутлук/ n вид; перспектива; точка зрения; world ~ /вёрлд ~/ мировоззрение

outlying /áутлáйинг/ adj отдаленный

outnumber /аутнáмбэ/ vt превосходить численно

out of /áут ов/ prep из, вне, за; ~ date /~ дэйт/ устаревший; ~ envy /~ э́нви/ из зависти; ~ favour /~ фэ́йвэ/ в немилости; ~ place /~ плэйс/ неуместный; ~ town /~ тáун/ за город(ом); ~ work /~ вёрк/ безработный

out-patient /áутпэ́йшнт/ n амбулаторный больной

output /áутпут/ n выпуск; продукция

outrage /áутрэйдж/ n насилие

outrageous /аутрэ́йджес/ adj неистовый; оскорбительный

outright /áутрайт/ adj прямой; adv сразу

outrival /аутрáйвл/ vt превосходить

outset /áутсет/ n начало

outshine /аутшáйн/ vt затмевать

outside /áутсáйд/ adj наружный, крайний; prep вне, за

outsider /áутсáйдэ/ n посторонний; аутсайдер

outskirts /áутскётс/ n pl окраина

outspoken /аутспóукн/ adj откровенный

outstanding /аутстэ́ндинг/ adj выдающийся; неуплаченный

outstretched /áутстретчт/ adj растянув-
шийся

outstrip /аутстрúп/ vt превосходить

outward /áутвэд/ adj внешний

outwardly /áутвэдли/ adv внешне

outwit /аутвúт/ vt перехитрить

oven /авн/ n печь, духовка

over /óувэ/ prep над, через, по, за, более,
свыше; adv сверх; all ~ /оол ~/ повсюду; it is all ~ /ит из оол ~/ все кончено;
~ and ~ again /~ энд ~ эгэ́йн/ вновь и
вновь

overact /óуверэ́кт/ vt переигрывать

overall /óуверол/ adj общий; n pl комбинезон

overboard /óувэбóрд/ adv за борт; man ~
/мэн ~/ человек за бортом

overburden /óувэбёёдн/ vt отягощать

overcast /óувэкаст/ adj покрытый обла-
ками; угрюмый

overcharge /óувэчадж/ vt дорого запрашивать

overcoat /óувэкоут/ n пальто, шинель

overcome /óувэкáм/ vt преодолевать

overcrowded /óувэкрáудыд/ adj переполненный

overdo /óувэдýу/ vt утрировать; пережа-
ривать

overdraw /óувэдрóо/ vt превышать кредит (в банке)

overdrive /óувэдрáйв/ n ускоряющая передача

overdue /óувэдьюю/ adj запоздалый;
просроченный

overestimate /óувэрэ́стимейт/ vt переоценивать

overexposure /óуврикспóуже/ n (фото)
передержка

overextend /óуврикстэ́нд/ vt перенапрягать

overfeed /óувэфúид/ vt перекармливать

overflow /óувэфлоу/ n разлив; избыток;
vt переливаться через край

overgrown /óувэгрóун/ adj заросший; пе-
реросший

overhaul /óувэхóол/ vt капитально ремонтировать; тщательно осматривать

overhead /óувэхед/ adj верхний; ~
charges /~ чáрджиз/ накладные расходы; adv наверху

overhear /óувэхúэ/ vt подслушивать

overheat /óувэхúит/ vti перегревать(ся)

overjoyed /óувэджóйд/ adj вне себя от
радости

overland /óувэлэнд/ adj сухопутный; adv
по суше, на суше

overlap /óувэлэ́п/ vt перекрывать

overleaf /óувэлúиф/ adv на обратной
стороне

overload /óувэлоуд/ vt перегружать

overlook /óувэлýк/ vt не замечать, про-
глядеть; выходить на (об окнах)

overnight /óувэнáйт/ adv накануне вечером; вдруг; stay ~ /стэй ~/ ночевать

overpay /óувэпэ́й/ vt переплачивать

overpower /óувэпáуэ/ vt превосходить

overproduction /óувэпрэдáкшн/ n перепроизводство

overrate /óувэрэ́йт/ vt переоценивать

overripe /óувэрáйп/ adj перезрелый

overrule /óувэрýул/ vt отменять

overseas /óувэсúиз/ adj заморский; adv
за морем

oversee /óувэсúи/ vt надзирать, наблюдать за

overseer /óувэсиэ/ n надзиратель; мастер; контролер

overshadow /óувэшэ́доу/ vt затмевать

overshoe /óувэшуу/ n галоша

oversight /óувэсайт/ n недосмотр

oversleep /óувэслúип/ vi просыпáть

overstate /óувэстэ́йт/ vt преувеличивать

overstrain /óувэстрэ́йн/ vt переутомлять

overtake /óувэтэ́йк/ vt догонять; застиг-
нуть (врасплох)

overthrow /óувэсрóу/ vt свергать

overtime /óувэтайм/ adv сверхурочно; work ~ /вёрк ~/ работать сверхурочно

overture /óувэтьюэ/ n зондаж; увертюра

overturn /óувэтёрн/ vti опрокидывать (ся)

overweight /óувэвéйт/ adj тяжелее обычного; ~ luggage /~ лáгидж/ оплачиваемый излишек багажа; n излишек веса

overwhelm /óувэвéлм/ vt сокрушать; ошеломлять

overwork /óувэвёрк/ vti переутомлять (ся)

owe /óу/ vt быть должным, быть обязанным; I ~ him 5 dollars /ай ~ хим файв дóларз/ я должен ему пять долларов; I ~ him everything /ай ~ хим эврифинг/ я всем обязан ему

owl /áул/ n сова

own /óун/ adj собственный; vt владеть

owner /óунэ/ n владелец

ownership /óунэшип/ n собственность, владение; право собственности

ox /окс/ n вол

oxygen /óксиджен/ n кислород

oyster /óйстэ/ n устрица

P

pace /пэйс/ n темп; шаг; keep ~ with /киип ~ виз/ идти наравне с; vi шагать; vt измерять шагами

pacific /пэсúфик/ adj мирный

pacifist /пэ́сифист/ n пацифист

pacify /пэ́сифай/ vt умиротворять

pack /пэк/ n тюк; палка; свора (собак), стая (волков); колода (карт); ~ of lies /~ ов лайз/ сплошная ложь; vt упаковывать; vi: ~ up /~ ап/ укладываться

package /пэ́кидж/ n пакет; посылка; ~ deal /~ диил/ комплексная сделка

packed /пэкт/ adj набитый

packer /пэ́кэ/ n упаковщик

packet /пэ́кит/ n пакет, пачка (сигарет)

packing /пэ́кинг/ n упаковка

packing-case /пэ́кингкейс/ n ящик для упаковки

pact /пэкт/ n пакт

pad /пэд/ n мягкая прокладка; блокнот; vt подбивать

padding /пэ́динг/ n набивка

paddle /пэдл/ n (короткое) весло; лопасть (гребного колеса)

paddle-steamer /пэ́длстúимэ/ n колесный пароход

paddock /пэ́дэк/ n загон

padlock /пэ́длок/ n висячий замóк

pagan /пэ́йгэн/ adj языческий; n язычник

page /пэйдж/ n страница; паж

pail /пэйл/ n ведро

pain /пэйн/ n боль; vt причинять боль

painful /пэ́йнфул/ adj болезненный

painstaking /пэ́йнзтэ́йкинг/ adj старательный

paint /пэйнт/ n краска; vt красить

painter /пэ́йнтэ/ n художник

painting /пэ́йнтинг/ n живопись; картина

pair /пээ/ n пара; ~ of scales /~ ов скэйлз/ весы; vti соединять (ся) по двое

pajamas /пэджáамез/ n pl пижама

pal /пэл/ n приятель

palace /пэ́лис/ n дворец

palate /пэ́лит/ n нёбо; вкус

pale /пэйл/ adj бледный; grow ~ /грóу ~/ бледнеть

pale /пэйл/ n кол, свая; граница, предел

pallid /пэ́лид/ adj бледный

pallor /пэ́лэ/ n бледность

palm /паам/ n пальма; ладонь (руки); P. Sunday /~ сáнди/ Вербное воскресенье

palmistry /пáамистри/ n хиромантия

paltry /пóолтри/ adj ничтожный

pamper /пэ́мпэ/ vt баловать

pamphlet /пэ́мфлит/ n брошюра

pan /пэн/ n сковорода

panacea /пэнэсиэ/ n панацея

panama (hat) /пэнэмáа(хэт)/ n панама

Pan-American /пэ́нэмэ́рикэн/ adj пан-американский

pancake /пэ́нкейк/ n блин

pane /пэйн/ n оконное стекло

panel /пэнл/ n панель; жюри

pang /пэнг/ n острая боль; ~s of conscience /~з ов кóншенс/ угрызения совести

panic /пэник/ n паника

panic-monger /пэникмáнгэ/ n паникер

pansy /пэнзи/ n (бот.) анютины глазки

panther /пэнсэ/ n пантера

panting /пэнтинг/ adj пыхтящий

pants /пэнтс/ n pl штаны; трусы

papa /пэпáа/ n папа

paper /пэйпэ/ n бумага; газета; документ; adj бумажный; ~ money /~ мáни/ ассигнации

paperback /пэйпэбэк/ n книга в бумажной обложке

par /пар/ n равенство; at ~ /эт ~/ по номинальной стоимости; on a ~ /он э ~/ на паритетных началах

parable /пэрэбл/ n притча

parachute /пэрэшуут/ n парашют

parachutist /пэрэшутист/ n парашютист

parade /пэрэйд/ n парад; vt выставлять напоказ

paradise /пэрэдайз/ n рай

paradox /пэрэдокс/ n парадокс

paragraph /пэрэграф/ n параграф, абзац

Paraguayan /пэрэгвáйен/ n парагваец, парагвайка; adj парагвайский

parallel /пэрэлэл/ adj параллельный; n параллель; without ~ /визáут ~/ бесподобный

paralyze /пэрэлайз/ vt парализовать

paralysis /пэрэлисис/ n паралич

paramount /пэрэмаунт/ adj первостепенный; высший

paraphrase /пэрэфрэйз/ vt парафразировать

parasite /пэрэсайт/ n паразит

parcel /пáрсэл/ n пакет; посылка; участок

pardon /пардн/ n прощение; (юр.) помилование; I beg your ~! /ай бег йо ~/ извините!; ~? что вы сказали?; general ~ /джéнэрэл ~/ амнистия; vt извинять, прощать; (юр.) помиловать

pardonable /пáрднэбл/ adj простительный

pare /пээ/ vt срезать

parent /пэрэнт/ n родитель

parentage /пэрэнтидж/ n родословная

parental /пэрэнтл/ adj родительский

parenthesis /пэрэнфисис/ n круглая скобка

parish /пэриш/ n церковный приход; ~ register /~ рéджистэ/ метрическая книга

parishioner /пэришенэ/ n прихожанин, прихожанка

parity /пэрити/ n равенство

park /парк/ n парк; vt ставить (машину)

parking /пáркинг/ n стоянка; no ~ any time /нóу ~ эни тайм/ стоянка категорически запрещена

parliament /пáрлэмент/ n парламент

parliamentary /пáрлэмéнтри/ adj парламентский

parlor /пáрлэ/ n гостиная, приемная

parrot /пэрэт/ n попугай

parsley /пáрсли/ n петрушка

parson /парсн/ n священник

part /парт/ n часть; (театр.) роль; vti разделять (ся), разлучать (ся)

partial /пáршел/ adj частичный; пристрастный

partiality /пáршиэлити/ n пристрастие

participate /патисипейт/ vi участвовать

participation /патисипейшн/ n участие

participator /патисипéйтэ/ n участник, участница

participle /пáатсипл/ n (грам.) причастие

particle /пáртикл/ n частица

particular /пэтикьюлэ/ adj особенный, определенный; in ~ /ин ~/ в особенности; n pl обстоятельства

particularly /пэтикьюлэли/ adv в частности

parting /пáртинг/ n расставание; пробор (в волосах)

partisan /пáртизэн/ n партизан, сторонник

partition /пати́шн/ n раздел, перегородка; vt разделять

partner /па́ртнэ/ n партнер(ша), супруг(а)

part-owner /па́рто́унэ/ n совладелец

partridge /па́ртридж/ n куропатка

part-timer /па́ртта́ймэ/ n рабочий, занятый неполный рабочий день

party /па́рти/ n партия; группа; вечеринка; (юр.) сторона; interested ~ /и́нтристыд ~/ заинтересованная сторона; ~ member /~ мэ́мбэ/ член партии

pass /паас/ vt передавать; выносить (решение); принимать (закон); выдерживать (экзамен); проводить (время); проходить/проезжать мимо; переходить через; обгонять; n пропуск; разрешение; make a ~ at /мэйк э ~ эт/ приставать к

passable /па́асэбл/ adj проходимый; сносный

passage /па́сидж/ n проход, проезд; отрывок

passenger /па́синдже/ n пассажир

passer-by /па́асэбай/ n прохожий

passing /па́асинг/ adj мимолетный; in ~ /ин ~/ мимоходом; ~ fancy /~ фэ́нси/ мимолетное увлечение

passion /па́шен/ n страсть

passionate /па́шенит/ adj пылкий

passionately /па́шенитли/ adv горячо

passive /па́сив/ adj пассивный; ~ voice /~ войс/ страдательный залог

passkey /па́аски/ n отмычка

passport /па́аспорт/ n паспорт

password /па́асвёрд/ n пароль

past /паст/ adj прошлый; (грам.) прошедший; n прошлое; (грам.) прошедшее время; adv мимо; half ~ one /хааф ~ ван/ половина второго

paste /пэйст/ n паста; тесто; клейстер; vt наклеивать

pastime /па́астайм/ n времяпрепровождение

pastor /па́астэ/ n пастырь; пастор

pastry /пэ́йстри/ n печенье, пирожное

pastry-shop /пэ́йстришо́п/ n кондитерская

pasture /па́асче/ n пастбище; vt пасти

pat /пэт/ n хлопок; vt похлопывать

pat /пэт/ adv кстати, своевременно

patch /пэч/ n заплата; участок земли; vt латать; ~ up /~ ап/ улаживать (ссору)

patchwork quilt /пэ́чвёккви́лт/ n стеганое одеяло из лоскутов

pâté /паатэ́й/ n паштет

patent /пэ́йтент/ adj явный; патентованный; ~ medicine /~ медсн/ патентованное лекарство; n патент; ~ office /~ о́фис/ бюро патентов

paternal /пэтёрнл/ adj отеческий

path /паф/ n тропинка, дорожка

pathos /пэ́йфос/ n чувство, воодушевление

patience /пэ́йшенс/ n терпение

patient /пэ́йшент/ adj терпеливый; n пациент

patina /пэ́тинэ/ n патина

patriarch /пэ́йтриарк/ n патриарх

patriot /пэ́йтриэт/ n патриот

patriotic /пэ́трио́тик/ adj патриотический

patriotism /пэ́триэтизм/ n патриотизм

patrol /пэтро́ул/ n патруль, дозор; vt патрулировать

patron /пэ́йтрэн/ n покровитель, патрон

patronize /пэ́трэнайз/ vt покровительствовать

patronymic /пэ́трэни́мик/ n отчество

patter /пэ́тэ/ vt барабанить, постукивать

pattern /пэ́тэн/ n образец; выкройка; узор

patty /пэ́ти/ n пирожок

pauper /по́опэ/ n нищий

pause /пооз/ n пауза; vi делать паузу/перерыв

pave /пэйв/ vt мостить; ~ the way for /~ зэ вэй фо/ прокладывать путь для

pavement /пэ́йвмент/ n тротуар, мостовая

paving stone /пэ́йвингсто́ун/ n брусчатка

paw /поо/ n лапа

pawn /поон/ n (шахм.) пешка; заклад; ростовщик; vt закладывать

pawnshop /пооншоп/ n ломбард

pay /пэй/ n плата; зарплата, жалованье; vt платить, оплачивать; vi приносить доход; ~ attention /~ этэ́ншн/ обращать внимание; ~ back /~ бэк/ отплачивать; ~ in cash /~ ин кэш/ платить наличными; ~ a visit /~ э ви́зит/ наносить визит

payday /пэ́йдэй/ n день зарплаты

payer /пэ́йе/ n плательщик

payment /пэ́ймент/ n уплата, платеж; ~ in advance /~ ин эдва́анс/ плата вперед

pay-office /пэ́йо́фис/ n касса

pay-roll /пэ́йроул/ n платежная ведомость

pea /пии/ n горошина; pl горох

peace /пиис/ n мир

peaceable, peaceful /пи́исэбл, пи́исфул/ adj мирный

peach /пиич/ n персик

peacock /пи́икок/ n павлин

peak /пиик/ n пик; козырек (кепки, фуражки); высшая точка

peal /пиил/ n трезвон; ~ of laughter /~ ов ла́афтэ/ взрыв смеха; vi трезвонить, грохотать

peanut /пи́инат/ n арахис, земляной орех

pear /пээ/ n груша

pearl /пёрл/ n жемчуг, жемчужина, перл

pearl-barley /пёрлба́рли/ n перловая крупа

peasant /пезнт/ n крестьянин

peat /пиит/ n торф

pebble /пебл/ n галька

peck /пек/ n клевок; vt клевать

peculiar /пикью́юлье/ adj особенный; странный

peculiarity /пикью́юлиэ́рити/ n особенность, странность

pedal /педл/ n педаль

peddle /педл/ vt торговать вразнос

pedestal /пе́дистл/ n пьедестал

pedestrian /пиде́стриан/ n пешеход

pedigree /пе́дигрии/ n родословная

pedlar /пе́длэ/ n уличный торговец

peel /пиил/ n кожица, кожура; vt чистить, шелушить

peels /пиилз/ n pl очистки

peep /пиип/ n взгляд украдкой; vi подглядывать; пищать

peer /пи́э/ n ровня; пэр

peer /пи́э/ vi всматриваться

peerless /пи́элис/ adj бесподобный

peg /пег/ n колышек

peg-top /пе́гтоп/ n волчок

Pekinese /пи́икини́из/ n китайский мопс

pelvis /пе́лвис/ n (анат.) таз

pen /пен/ n перо, ручка; загон; vt загонять

penal /пиинл/ adj уголовный; каторжный

penalize /пи́инэлайз/ vt наказывать

penalty /пе́нлти/ n штраф (также спорт.)

pencil /пенсл/ n карандаш

pendant /пе́ндэнт/ n кулон

pendulum /пе́ндьюлэм/ n маятник

penetrate /пе́нитрэйт/ vt пронизывать, проникать

penetration /пе́нитрэ́йшн/ n проникновение; проницательность

penguin /пе́нгвин/ n пингвин

penicillin /пе́ниси́лин/ n пенициллин

peninsula /пени́нсьюлэ/ n полуостров

penitence /пе́нитенс/ n покаяние

penitent /пе́нитент/ adj раскаивающийся

penitentiary /пе́ните́ншери/ n исправительный дом

pen-name /пе́ннэйм/ n литературный псевдоним

pennant /пе́нэнт/ n вымпел, знамя; подвеска

penniless /пе́нилис/ adj без гроша

penny /пе́ни/ n пенни

pension /пеншн/ n пенсия, пансион

pensioner /пе́ншенэ/ n пенсионер

pensive /пе́нсив/ adj задумчивый

pentagon /пе́нтэгэн/ n пятиугольник; the P. /зэ ~/ Пентагон

Pentecost /пе́нтикост/ n пятидесятница

penthouse /пе́нтхаус/ n роскошная квартира на верхнем этаже, выходящая окнами на крышу

peony /пи́эни/ n пион

people /пиипл/ n народ, люди; young ~ /янг ~/ молодежь; vt населять

pepper /пе́пэ/ n перец; мятная лепешка; vt перчить

per /пё/ prep в, на, по; ~ annum /~ э́нэм/ в год; ~ cent /~ сент/ процент

perambulator /прэ́мбьюлэйтэ/ n детская коляска

perceive /песи́ив/ vt воспринимать

percentage /песе́нтидж/ n процентное соотношение

perception /песе́пшн/ n восприятие

perch /пёрч/ n окунь; насест

percolator /пёркэлэ́йтэ/ n ситечко

perfect /пёрфикт/ adj совершенный; /пефе́кт/ vt совершенствовать

perfection /пефе́кшн/ n совершенство

perfectly /пёрфиктли/ adv вполне; превосходно

perfidy /пёрфиди/ n вероломство

perform /пефо́рм/ vt выполнять (обязанности); исполнять (роль)

performance /пефо́рмэнс/ n выполнение; (театр.) представление

performer /пефо́рмэ/ n исполнитель

perfume /пёрфьюм/ n духи

perhaps /пехэ́пс, прэпс/ adv может быть

peril /пе́рил/ n опасность

perilous /пе́рилэс/ adj опасный

period /пи́эриэд/ n период; точка

periodical /пи́эрио́дикл/ n журнал, периодическое издание

perish /пе́риш/ vi погибать

perishable /пе́ришебл/ adj скоропортящийся

perjury /пёрджери/ n лжесвидетельство, клятвопреступление

permanent /пёрмэнент/ adj постоянный

permission /пеми́шн/ n разрешение

permit /пёрмит/ n пропуск, разрешение; /пеми́т/ vt разрешать, позволять

pernicious /пени́шес/ adj пагубный

perpetual /пепе́тьюэл/ adj вечный, бесконечный

perpetuate /пепе́тьюэйт/ vt увековечивать

perplex /пепле́кс/ vt озадачить, запутать

perplexed /пепле́кст/ vt сбитый с толку

perquisite /пёрквизит/ n приработок

persecute /пёрсикьют/ vt преследовать

persecution /пёрсикью́юшн/ n гонение

perservance /пёрсиви́эрэнс/ n упорство

Persian /пёршен/ n перс(иянка); adj персидский

persist /песи́ст/ vi упорствовать

persistence /песи́стэнс/ n настойчивость

persistent /песи́стэнт/ adj упорный, настойчивый

person /пёрсн/ n человек; лицо, особа; in ~ /ин ~/ лично

personage /пёрснидж/ n выдающаяся личность; персонаж

personal /пёрснл/ adj личный

personality /пёрсенэ́лити/ n личность

personally /пёрснэли/ adv лично

personification /пёсо́нификейшн/ n олицетворение

personnel /пёрсенэ́л/ n личный состав

perspective /песпе́ктив/ n перспектива; adj перспективный

perspiration /пёрсперэ́йшн/ n пот

perspire /песпа́йе/ vi потеть

persuade /песвэ́йд/ vt убеждать

persuasion /песвэ́йжн/ n убеждение

persuasive /песвэ́йсив/ adj убедительный

pertinent /пёртинент/ adj уместный

Peruvian /перу́увьен/ n перуанец, перуанка; adj перуанский

perverse /певе́рс/ adj порочный

perversion /певёршн/ n извращение

perversed /певёрст/ adj развратный

pessimist /пе́симист/ n пессимист

pest /пест/ n язва; вредитель, паразит

pester /пéстэ/ vt докучать

pestilence /пéстиленс/ n чума; эпидемия

pestle /пестл/ n пестик; vt толочь

pet /пет/ n любимое животное; баловень, любимец; ~ name /~ нэйм/ ласкательное имя; vt ласкать, баловать

petal /петл/ n лепесток

petition /питúшн/ n петиция, ходатайство; vt подавать прошение

petitioner /питúшнэ/ n проситель

petrol /пéтрэл/ n бензин; ~ tank /~ тэнк/ бензобак

petroleum /питрóульем/ n нефть

petticoat /пéтикоут/ n нижняя юбка

pettifogging /пéтифогинг/ adj кляузный

petty /пéти/ adj мелкий; мелочный; маловажный

pew /пьюю/ n церковная скамья

pewter /пьюютэ/ n олово

phantom /фэ́нтэм/ n призрак

pharisee /фэ́рисии/ n фарисей, ханжа

pharmacy /фáрмэси/ n аптека

phase /фэйз/ n фаза

pheasant /фезнт/ n фазан

phenomenal /финóминл/ adj феноменальный

phenomenon /финóминэн/ n явление, феномен

philanthropist /филэ́нсрэпист/ n филантроп

philatelist /филэ́тэлист/ n филателист

Philippine /фúлипиин/ n филиппинец, филиппинка; adj филиппинский

philistine /фúлистайн/ n филистер, обыватель

philology /филóлэджи/ n филология

philosopher /филóсэфэ/ n философ

philosophy /филóсэфи/ n философия

philtre /фúлтэ/ n любовный напиток, зелье

phlegm /флем/ n мокрота; флегма

phoenix /фúиникс/ n феникс

phosphorus /фóсфэрэс/ n фосфор

photograph /фóутэграф/ n фотография; vt фотографировать

photographer /фэтóгрэфэ/ n фотограф

phrase /фрэйз/ n фраза (также муз.)

physic /фúзик/ n лекарство

physical /фúзикл/ adj физический

physician /физúшн/ n врач

physicist /фúзисист/ n физик

physics /фúзикс/ n физика

physique /физúик/ n телосложение

pianist /пьэ́нист/ n пианист

piano /пьэ́ноу/ n рояль; upright ~ /áпрайт ~/ пианино

pick /пик/ n выбор; лучшая часть; кирка; vt выбирать; рвать; собирать; ~ up /~ ап/ поднимать; выздоравливать

picked /пикт/ adj отборный

picket /пúкит/ n пикет; vt пикетировать

pickle /пикл/ n рассол; vt мариновать

pickpocket /пúкпóкит/ n карманный вор

picture /пúкче/ n картина; фильм

picturesque /пúкчерэск/ adj живописный

pie /пай/ n пирог; apple ~ /эпл ~/ яблочный пирог

piece /пиис/ n кусок, часть; штука; ~ of ground /~ ов грáунд/ участок земли

piecework /пúисвёрк/ n сдельная работа

pier /пúэ/ n мол, пристань

pierce /пúэс/ vt пронзать, прокалывать

piety /пáйети/ n набожность

pig /пиг/ n свинья

pigeon /пúджин/ n голубь

pig-iron /пúгáйэн/ n чугун

pike /пайк/ n щука

pile /пайл/ n куча, груда, кипа (бумаги); atomic ~ /этóмик ~/ ядерный реактор; vt: ~ up /~ ап/ нагромождать; накоплять

pilgrim /пúлгрим/ n паломник

pilgrimage /пúлгримидж/ n паломничество

pill /пил/ n пилюля, таблетка

pillage /пúлидж/ n грабеж; vt грабить

pillar /пúлэ/ n столб; столп

pillar box /пúлэбокс/ n почтовый ящик

pillow /пи́лоу/ n подушка

pillow-case /пи́лоукейс/ n наволочка

pilot /па́йлэт/ n (авиа)пилот, летчик; (мор.) лоцман; vt вести, пилотировать

pimp /пимп/ n сутенер

pimple /пимпл/ n прыщик

pin /пин/ n булавка, шпилька; vt прикалывать булавкой

pincers /пи́нсэз/ n pl щипцы, клещи

pinch /пинч/ n щипок; щепотка (соли и т.п.); vt щипать; жать (об обуви); красть

pine /пайн/ n сосна

pine /пайн/ vi чахнуть

pineapple /па́йнэпл/ n ананас

pinecone /па́йнко́ун/ n сосновая шишка

pink /пинк/ adj розовый; n гвоздика

pinnacle /пи́нэкл/ n остроконечная скала; пик; the ~ of fame /зэ ~ ов фэйм/ вершина славы

pint /пайнт/ n пинта (= 0,57 литра)

pioneer /па́йени́э/ n пионер

pious /па́йес/ adj набожный

pipe /пайп/ n труба; (курительная) трубка; дудка, свирель; pl (муз.) волынка

pipe-line /па́йплайн/ n трубопровод

piquant /пи́икэнт/ adj пикантный

piracy /па́йерэси/ n пиратство

pirate /па́йерит/ n пират

pistol /пистл/ n пистолет

pit /пит/ n яма; шахта; партер

pitch /пич/ n смола; высота (звука); степень; килевая качка (лодки); ~ darkness /~ да́ркнис/ тьма кромешная; vt смолить; (спорт.) подавать

pitcher /пи́че/ n кувшин

pitching /пи́чинг/ n (мор.) килевая качка; (спорт.) подача

pitfall /пи́тфол/ n западня

pitiable, pitiful /пи́тиэбл, пи́тифул/ adj жалкий; жалостливый

pitiless /пи́тилис/ adj безжалостный

pitted /пи́тыд/ adj рябой (о лице)

pity /пи́ти/ n жалость; for ~'s sake! /фо ~з сэйк/ ради Бога!; what a ~! /вот э ~/ как жалко!; vt жалеть

pivot /пи́вэт/ n стержень; (образн.) центр

placard /пла́экард/ n плакат, афиша

place /плэйс/ n место, положение; take ~ /тэйк ~/ состояться; out of ~ /а́ут ов ~/ неуместный; vt класть, ставить

placid /пла́эсид/ adj спокойный

plagiarism /пла́эйджеризм/ n плагиат

plague /плэйг/ n чума, мор

plaid /плэд/ n плед

plain /плэйн/ adj простой, ясный; некрасивый; одноцветный; ~ clothes /~ кло́увз/ штатское платье; in ~ English /ин ~ и́нглиш/ без обиняков; n равнина

plaint /плэйнт/ n иск

plaintiff /пла́эйнтиф/ n истец

plaintive /пла́эйнтив/ adj жалобный

plait /плэт/ n коса; vt заплетать

plan /плэн/ n план, проект; rough ~ /раф ~/ набросок; vt планировать

plane /плэйн/ n плоскость; самолет; (тех.) рубанок; vt строгать

planet /пла́энит/ n планета

plane-tree /пла́эйнтрии/ n платан

plank /плэнк/ n доска, планка; vt выстилать досками

planking /пла́энкинг/ n настил

plant /плаант/ n (бот.) растение; завод; vt сажать; (образн.) насаждать

plantain /пла́энтин/ n подорожник

plantation /плэнтэ́йшн/ n плантация

planter /пла́антэ/ n плантатор

plaster /пла́эастэ/ n (мед.) пластырь; (строит.) штукатурка; ~ of Paris /~ ов пэ́рис/ гипс, алебастр

plastic /пла́эстик/ adj пластический; пластмассовый

plate /плэйт/ n тарелка; (фото) пластинка; vt: ~ with gold /~ виз го́улд/ золотить

plateau /пла́это́у/ n плоскогорье

plate-rack /пла́эйтрэк/ n сушилка для посуды

platform /пла́этформ/ n платформа; помост

platinum /пла́этинэм/ n платина

platoon /плэту́ун/ n взвод

plausible /пло́озэбл/ adj правдоподобный

play /плэй/ n игра; пьеса; vt играть

player /плэ́йе/ n актер; игрок

playful /плэ́йфул/ adj игривый

playgoer /плэ́йго́уэ/ n театрал

plaything /плэ́йфинг/ n игрушка

playwright /плэ́йрайт/ n драматург

plea /плии/ n мольба

plead /плиид/ vi умолять; ~ not guilty /~ нот гу́лти/ не признавать себя виновным; vt: ~ a case /~ э кейс/ защищать дело

pleasant /плезнт/ adj приятный

please /плииз/ vi хотеть, изволить; ~! пожалуйста!; vt нравиться

pleased /плиизд/ adj довольный; ~ to meet you /~ ту миит ю/ приятно познакомиться

pleasure /пле́же/ n удовольствие

pleat /плиит/ n складка; ~ed skirt /~ыд скёрт/ юбка в складку

pledge /пледж/ n залог, обет; vt: ~ one's word /~ ванз вёрд/ давать слово

plentiful /пле́нтифул/ adj обильный

plenty /пле́нти/ n изобилие; ~ of /~ ов/ много

plenum /плии́инэм/ n пленум

pliers /пла́йез/ n щипцы, плоскогубцы

plight /плайт/ n тяжелое положение

plinth /плинф/ n плинтус

plot /плот/ n заговор; фабула; участок земли; vi устраивать заговор

plotter /пло́тэ/ n заговорщик

plough /пла́у/ n плуг; vt пахать

ploughman /пла́умэн/ n пахарь

ploughshare /пла́ушээ/ n плужный лемех

pluck /плак/ n мужество; ливер; vt рвать; ощипывать (птицу); ~ up courage /~ ап ка́ридж/ собираться с духом

plug /плаг/ n затычка; (эл.) штепсель; vt затыкать

plum /плам/ n слива

plumage /плю́юмидж/ n оперение

plumb /плам/ n отвес; лот

plumber /пла́мэ/ n водопроводчик

plump /пламп/ adj полный, пухлый

plunder /пла́ндэ/ n грабеж

plunge /пландж/ n погружение; vi погружаться

plural /плю́оэрл/ adj множественный

plus /плас/ prep плюс

plush /плаш/ n плюш; adj плюшевый

ply /плай/ n сгиб; vi курсировать

plywood /пла́йвуд/ n фанера

pneumatic /ньюмэ́тик/ adj пневматический

pneumonia /ньюмо́унье/ n воспаление легких

poach /по́уч/ vt варить яйцо-пашот; vi браконьерствовать

poacher /по́уче/ n браконьер

pocket /по́кит/ n карман; (авиа) воздушная яма; луза (бильярдного стола); vt класть в карман, прикарманивать

pocket money /по́китма́ни/ n карманные деньги

pod /под/ n стручок

poem /по́уим/ n поэма

poet /по́уит/ n поэт

poetess /по́уитис/ n поэтесса

poetic /поэ́тик/ adj поэтический

poetry /по́уитри/ n поэзия

point /пойнт/ n точка; пункт; острие; очко; ~ of view /~ ов вьюю/ точка зрения; come to the ~ /кам ту зэ ~/ доходить до сути дела; vt направлять; указывать

pointer /по́йнтэ/ n указатель; пойнтер (порода охотничьих собак)

point-blank /по́йнтблэ́нк/ adj прямой, решительный

pointless /по́йнтлис/ adj бессмысленный

poison /пойзн/ n яд; vt отравлять

poisoning /по́йзнинг/ n отравление

poisonous /по́йзнэс/ adj ядовитый

poke /по́ук/ vt тыкать; ~ one's nose in /~ ванз но́уз ин/ совать нос в чужие дела

poker /по́укэ/ n кочерга; покер (карточная игра)

polar /пóулэ/ adj полярный; ~ bear /~ бэ́э/ белый медведь

polarize /пóулэрайз/ vt поляризовать

pole /пóул/ n столб; шест; (геогр., эл.) полюс

pole-cat /пóулкэт/ n хорек

pole star /пóулстар/ n Полярная звезда

pole-vault /пóулвóолт/ n прыжок с шестом

Pole /пóул/ n поляк, полька

police /пэли́ис/ n полиция; ~ station /~ стэ́йшн/ полицейский участок

policeman /пэли́исмэн/ n полицейский

policy /пóлиси/ n политика; страховой полис

Polish /пóулиш/ adj польский

polish /пóлиш/ n политура; крем для обуви; vt полировать; чистить (обувь)

polished /пóлишт/ adj изысканный

polite /пэлáйт/ adj вежливый

politely /пэлáйтли/ adv вежливо

politeness /пэлáйтнис/ n вежливость

politic /пóлитик/ adj благоразумный; расчетливый

political /пэли́тикл/ adj политический

politician /пóлити́ишн/ n политик

politics /пóлитикс/ n политика

poll /пóул/ n баллотировка; опрос населения; vi голосовать; vt получать голоса

polling-booth /пóулингбýус/ n кабина для голосования

polling-station /пóулингстэ́йшн/ n избирательный пункт

pollute /пэльýют/ vt загрязнять

pomegranate /пóмгрэ́нит/ n (бот.) гранат

pomp /помп/ n помпа, пышность

pompous /пóмпэс/ adj напыщенный

pond /понд/ n пруд

ponder /пóндэ/ vt обдумывать; vi размышлять

pontiff /пóнтиф/ n папа римский; архиерей

pontoon /понтýун/ n понтон; (карты) двадцать одно

pontoon-bridge /понтýунбри́дж/ n понтонный мост

pony /пóуни/ n пони

poodle /пýудл/ n пудель (порода собак)

pooh /пýу/ interj тьфу

pool /пýул/ n лужа; бассейн; фонд

poor /пýэ/ adj бедный, плохой; ~ thing /~ синг/ бедняжка; the ~ /зэ ~/ беднота

pop /поп/ n отрывистый звук; ~ art /~ арт/ поп-арт; ~ music /~ мьýюзик/ поп-музыка; vti хлопать

popcorn /пóпкорн/ n кукурузные хлопья

Pope /пóуп/ n папа римский

poppy /пóпи/ n мак

popular /пóпьюлэ/ adj популярный, народный

popularity /пóпьюлэ́рити/ n популярность

popularize /пóпьюлэрайз/ vt популяризировать

populate /пóпьюлэйт/ vt заселять

population /пóпьюлэ́йшн/ n население

porcelain /пóослин/ n фарфор

porch /порч/ n крыльцо

porcupine /пóркьюпайн/ n дикобраз

pore /поор/ n пóра; vi: ~ over /~ óувэ/ размышлять над

pork /порк/ n свинина

porous /пóорэс/ adj пористый

porphyry /пóрфири/ n порфир

porridge /пóридж/ n каша

port /порт/ n порт; портвейн

portable /пóртэбл/ adj портативный

porter /пóртэ/ n швейцар; носильщик; портер (черное пиво)

portfolio /потфóульоу/ n портфель, папка

portion /поршн/ n часть, доля, порция; vt делить на части, разделять

portly /пóртли/ adj осанистый

portrait /пóртрит/ n портрет

Portuguese /пóртьюгиз/ n португалец, португалка; португальский язык; adj португальский

pose /пóуз/ n поза; vi позировать; ~ as /~ эз/ выдавать себя за

position /пэзи́ишн/ n позиция; должность

positive /пóзетив/ adj положительный

possess /пэзéс/ vt владеть, обладать

possessed /пэзéст/ adj одержимый

possession /пэзéшн/ n владение, обладание; pl имущество

possessor /пэзéсэ/ n владелец

possibility /пóсэбѝлити/ n возможность

possible /пóсэбл/ adj возможный

post /пóуст/ n почта; должность; (воен.) пост; столб; ~ office /~ óфис/ почта, почтамт

postage /пóустыдж/ n почтовые расходы

postal /пóустэл/ adj почтовый; ~ order /~ óрдэ/ почтовый перевод

postcard /пóусткард/ n открытка

poste restante /пóустрéстаант/ adv до востребования

poster /пóустэ/ n афиша, плакат

posterior /постѝэриэ/ adj задний; последующий

posterity /постéрити/ n потомство, потомки

postgraduate /пóустгрэ́дьюит/ n аспирант

posthumous /пóстьюмэс/ adj посмертный

postman /пóустмэн/ n почтальон

post meridiem, p.m. /пóустмерѝдиэм, пѝиэ́м/ adv после полудня

postpone /пóустпóун/ vt откладывать

postponement /пóустпóунмент/ n отсрочка

postscript /пóусскрипт/ n постскриптум

postwar /пóуствóр/ adj послевоенный

pot /пот/ n горшок

potato /пэтéйтоу/ n картофелина; pl картофель

potency /пóутэнси/ n сила

potent /пóутэнт/ adj сильный

potential /пэтéншл/ adj потенциальный; n потенциал

potion /пóушн/ n микстура

potter /пóтэ/ n гончар

pottery /пóтэри/ n керамика

pouch /пáуч/ n сумка; мешок (под глазами)

poultry /пóултри/ n домашняя птица

pounce /пáунс/ vi набрасываться

pound /пáунд/ n фунт

pound /пáунд/ vti колотить(ся)

pour /поор/ vti лить(ся), сыпать(ся); it's ~ing /итс ~инг/ идет проливной дождь

pout /пáут/ vi надувать губы

poverty /пóвэти/ n бедность

powder /пáудэ/ n порох; порошок; пудра; vt пудрить

powder-room /пáудэрýум/ n дамская туалетная комната

powdered milk /пáудэдмѝлк/ n порошковое молоко

power /пáуэ/ n сила, мощность; власть; держава; purchasing ~ /пéрчесинг ~/ покупательная способность; ~ house /~ хáус/ электростанция

powerful /пáуэфул/ adj сильный, могущественный

powerless /пáуэлис/ adj бессильный

practicable /прэ́ктикэбл/ adj осуществимый

practical /прэ́ктикл/ adj практический; ~ joke /~ джóук/ грубая шутка

practically /прэ́ктикэли/ adv практически; фактически

practice /прэ́ктис/ n практика; in ~ /ин ~/ на деле; put into ~ /пут ѝнту ~/ осуществлять

practise /прэ́ктис/ vt практиковать

practitioner /прэктѝшнэ/ n практикующий врач/юрист

praise /прэйз/ n похвала; vt хвалить

praiseworthy /прэ́йзвёзи/ adj похвальный

pram /прэм/ n детская коляска

prance /праанс/ vi гарцевать

prank /прэнк/ n шалость

prawn /проон/ n креветка

pray /прэй/ vi молиться

prayer /прэ́йе/ n молитва

preach /приич/ vti проповедовать

preacher /прѝиче/ n проповедник

precarious /прикэ́эриэс/ adj опасный

precaution /прикóошн/ n предосторожность

precautionary /прико́ошнэри/ adj принимаемый для предосторожности

precede /приси́ид/ vt предшествовать

precedent /пре́сидент/ n прецедент

precept /при́исепт/ n наставление

preceptor /присе́пто/ n наставник

precinct /при́исинкт/ n избирательный/полицейский участок

precious /прэ́шес/ adj драгоценный

precipice /пре́сипис/ n пропасть

precipitate /приси́питэйт/ vt низвергать; ускорять

precise /приса́йс/ adj точный

precisely /приса́йсли/ adv точно

precision /приси́жн/ n точность

precocious /прико́ушес/ adj скороспелый

preconceived /при́икэнси́ивд/ adj предвзятый

predatory /пре́дэтри/ adj хищный

predecessor /при́идисэсэ/ n предшественник

predestine /придэ́стин/ vt предопределять

predetermine /при́идитёрмин/ vt предрешать

predicament /приди́кэмент/ n затруднительное положение

predict /приди́кт/ vt предсказывать

prediction /приди́кшн/ n предсказание

predominant /придо́минэнт/ adj преобладающий

preface /пре́фис/ n предисловие

prefer /прифёр/ vt предпочитать

preferable /пре́фрэбл/ adj предпочтительный

preference /пре́ферэнс/ n предпочтение

pregnancy /пре́гнэнси/ n беременность

pregnant /пре́гнэнт/ adj беременная

prehistoric /при́ихисто́рик/ adj доисторический

prejudice /пре́джудис/ n предрассудок, предубеждение; vt наносить ущерб

preliminary /прили́минэри/ adj предварительный

prelude /пре́льюд/ n прелюдия

premature /пре́мэтьюэ/ adj преждевременный

premeditation /приме́дитэ́йшн/ n преднамеренность

premier /пре́мье/ n премьер-министр

première /премьэ́э/ n премьера

premise /пре́мис/ n (пред)посылка; pl помещение

premium /при́имьем/ n награда, премия

premonition /при́имэни́йшн/ n предчувствие

preoccupation /прио́кьюпэ́йшн/ n озабоченность

preordain /при́иодэ́йн/ vt предопределять

preparation /пре́пэрэ́йшн/ n приготовление

preparatory /припэ́рэтри/ adj подготовительный

prepare /припэ́э/ vti готовить(ся)

prepay /при́ипэ́й/ vt платить вперед

preponderant /припо́ндэрнт/ adj преобладающий

preposition /пре́пэзи́йшн/ n (грам.) предлог

preposterous /припо́стрэс/ adj абсурдный, нелепый

presage /пре́сидж/ n предзнаменование; /присэ́йдж/ vt предсказывать

Presbyterian /пре́збити́эриэн/ n пресвитерианин, пресвитерианка; adj пресвитерианский

prescription /прискри́пшн/ n предписание; (мед.) рецепт

presence /презнс/ n присутствие, наличие; ~ of mind /~ ов майнд/ присутствие духа

present /презнт/ adj присутствующий; нынешний; at ~ /эт ~/ в настоящее время; n подарок; настоящее время (также грам.); /призе́нт/ vt дарить; подавать (петицию)

presentation /пре́зэнтэ́йшн/ n представление (также театр.)

presently /пре́знтли/ adv сейчас

preservative /призёрвэтив/ n предохра-
няющее средство
preserve /призёрв/ vt сохранять; консервировать; n заповедник
preside /призáйд/ vi председательствовать
president /прézидент/ n президент
presidential /прézидéншл/ adj президент-
ский
press /прес/ n (тех.) пресс; печать; пресса; типография; ~ conference /~ кóн-
ферэнс/ пресс-конференция; vt жать,
нажимать, давить
pressing /прéсинг/ adj настоятельный
pressman /прéсмэн/ n журналист
pressure /прéше/ n давление, нажим
prestige /прести́иж/ n престиж
presumably /призью́юмэбли/ adv пред-
положительно
presume /призью́юм/ vt предполагать;
осмеливаться
presumption /призáмшн/ n предположение
presumptuous /призáмтьюэс/ adj самонадеянный
presuppose/при́исэпóуз/ vt предполагать
pretence /притэ́нс/ n притворство
pretend /притэ́нд/ vi притворяться; ~ to
/~ ту/ претендовать на
pretender /притэ́ндэ/ n претендент
pretentious /притэ́ншес/ adj претенциоз-
ный
pretext /при́итэкст/ n предлог, отговорка
pretty /при́ти/ adj хорошенький; adv довольно
prevail /привэ́йл/ vi преобладать; ~ over
/~ óувэ/ побеждать
prevailing /привэ́йлинг/ adj господствующий
prevent /привэ́нт/ vt предотвращать,
препятствовать
prevention /привэ́ншн/ n предотвращение
preventive /привэ́нтив/ adj предупреди-
тельный; профилактический

previous /при́ивьес/ adj предыдущий
previously /при́ивьесли/ adv предвари-
тельно
prey /прей/ n добыча; beast of ~ /биист
ов ~/ хищное животное; vt грабить
price /прайс/ n цена; vt назначать цену
priceless /прáйслис/ adj бесценный
price list /прáйслист/ n прейскурант
prick /прик/ n укол; шип; vt колоть
pride /прайд/ n гордость
priest /приист/ n священник
prim /прим/ adj чопорный
primary /прáймэри/ adj первичный;
(перво)начальный; ~ school /~ скуул/
начальная школа
prime /прайм/ adj главный; ~ minister /~
ми́нистэ/ премьер-министр
primer /прáймэ/ n букварь
primeval /прайми́ивл/ adj первобытный
primitive /при́митив/ adj первобытный;
примитивный
primrose /при́мроуз/ n примула
prince /принс/ n принц, князь
princely /при́нсли/ adj царственный
princess /принсэ́с/ n принцесса
principal /при́нсэпл/ adj главный; n глава
principally /при́нсэпэли/ adv главным
образом
principle /при́нсэпл/ n принцип
print /принт/ n отпечаток; шрифт; печать; in ~ /ин ~/ в продаже; out of ~
/áут ов ~/ распроданный; vt печатать
printed /при́нтыд/ adj печатный; набивной
printer /при́нтэ/ n печатник
printing /при́нтинг/ n печатание; тираж;
(текст.) набивка; ~ office /~ óфис/ типография
prior /прáйе/ adj предшествующий
priority /прайóрити/ n приоритет, сроч-
ность
prism /призм/ n призма
prison /призн/ n тюрьма
prisoner /при́знэ/ n пленный; заключенный

privacy /пра́йвэси/ n уединение

private /пра́йвит/ adj частный; ~ secretary /~ се́кретри/ личный секретарь; n рядовой; ~s /~ c/ наружные половые органы; in ~ /ин ~/ по секрету

privation /прайвэ́йшн/ n лишение

privilege /при́вилидж/ n привилегия

prize /прайз/ n приз; award a ~ /эво́рд э ~/ присуждать премию; vt высоко ценить

probability /про́бэби́лити/ n вероятность

probable /про́бэбл/ adj вероятный

probably /про́бэбли/ adv вероятно

probation /прэбэ́йшн/ n испытание, стажировка

probationary /прэбэ́йшнэри/ adj испытательный; ~ sentence /~ се́нтэнс/ условный приговор

probationer /прэбэ́йшнэ/ n стажер; послушник

probe /про́уб/ n зонд; vt зондировать

problem /про́блем/ n проблема, задача

procedure /прэси́идже/ n процедура

proceed /прэси́ид/ vi продолжать

proceeding /прэси́идинг/ n поступок; судебная процедура; pl протокол

proceeds /про́усидз/ n pl выручка

process /про́усэс/ n процесс

procession /прэсэ́шн/ n процессия

proclaim /прэклэ́йм/ vt провозглашать

proclamation /про́клэмэ́йшн/ n провозглашение

procure /прэкьюэ́/ vt доставать

prodigal /про́дигл/ adj расточительный; ~ son /~ сан/ блудный сын; n мот

prodigious /прэди́джес/ adj изумительный; громадный

prodigy /про́диджи/ n чудо; infant ~ /и́нфэнт ~/ вундеркинд

produce /про́дьюс/ n продукция; /прэдь-ю́юс/ vt производить; ставить (пьесу, кинокартину)

producer /прэдью́юсэ/ n производитель; продюсер

product /про́дэкт/ n продукт

production /прэда́кшн/ n производство

productive /прэда́ктив/ adj производительный

productivity /про́дакти́вити/ n производительность

profess /прэфе́с/ vt исповедовать; заниматься (деятельностью)

profession /прэфе́шн/ n профессия

professional /прэфе́шенл/ adj профессиональный; n профессионал

proficient /прэфи́шент/ adj умелый

profile /про́уфил/ n профиль

profit /про́фит/ n прибыль, доход; vi приносить пользу

profitable /про́фитэбл/ adj прибыльный

profiteer /про́фити́э/ n спекулянт

profound /прэфа́унд/ adj глубокий

profuse /прэфью́юс/ adj обильный

program /про́угрэм/ n программа

progress /про́угрэс/ n прогресс; make ~ /мэйк ~/ делать успехи; /прэгре́с/vi продвигаться

progressive /прэгре́сив/ adj прогрессивный; поступательный

prohibit /прэхи́бит/ vt запрещать

prohibition /про́иби́шн/ n запрещение; "сухой закон"

project /про́джект/ n проект; /прэджёкт/ vt проектировать; vi выдаваться

proletarian /про́улетэ́эриэн/ adj пролетарский; n пролетарий

prolific /прэли́фик/ adj плодородный; плодовитый

prologue /про́улог/ n пролог

prolong /прэло́нг/ vt продлевать

prolongation /про́улонге́йшн/ n продление

prominent /про́минэнт/ adj выдающийся

promiscuous /прэми́скьюэс/ adj разнородный; неразборчивый

promise /про́мис/ n обещание; vt обещать; ~d land /~т лэнд/ земля обетованная

promising /про́мисинг/ adj многообещающий

promote /прэмо́ут/ vt повышать в чине или звании; содействовать

promoter /прэмо́утэ/ n покровитель

promotion /прэмо́ушн/ n повышение

prompt /промт/ adj немедленный; ~ payment /~ пэ́ймент/ наличный расчет; n подсказка; vt побуждать

prompter /про́мтэ/ n суфлер

promptly /про́мтли/ adv быстро

pronoun /про́унаун/ n местоимение

pronounce /прэна́унс/ vt провозглашать; произносить

pronunciation /прэна́нсиэ́йшн/ n произношение

proof /прууф/ n доказательство; испытание; корректура

prop /проп/ n подпорка, опора; vt подпирать

propaganda /про́пэгэ́ндэ/ n пропаганда

propel /прэпе́л/ vt приводить в движение

propeller /прэпе́лэ/ n пропеллер, винт

propensity /прэпе́нсити/ n склонность, пристрастие

proper /про́пэ/ adj пристойный, правильный; (грам.) собственный

properly /про́пэли/ adv должным образом

property /про́пэти/ n собственность, имущество; man of ~ /мэн ов ~/ собственник

prophecy /про́фиси/ n пророчество

prophesy /про́фисай/ vt пророчить

prophet /про́фит/ n пророк

prophylaxis /про́филэ́ксис/ n профилактика

proportion /прэпо́ршн/ n пропорция; in ~ to /ин ~ ту/ соразмерно с

proportional /прэпо́ршнл/ adj пропорциональный

proposal /прэпо́узл/ n предложение

propose /прэпо́уз/ vt предлагать; vi делать предложение (о браке)

proposition /про́пэзи́шн/ n предложение; заявление

proprietor /прэпра́йетэ/ n собственник

propulsion /прэпа́лшн/ n движение (вперед)

prose /про́уз/ n проза; ~ writer /~ ра́йтэ/ прозаик

prosecute /про́сикьют/ vt преследовать судебным порядком

prosecutor /про́сикьютэ/ n обвинитель; public ~ /па́блик ~/ прокурор

prospect /про́спект/ n перспектива, вид; pl виды на будущее

prosper /про́спэ/ vi процветать

prosperity /просспе́рити/ n благосостояние

prosperous /про́сперэс/ adj процветающий

prostitute /про́ститьют/ n проститутка; vt проституировать

prostitution /про́ститьюю́шн/ n проституция

protect /прэте́кт/ vt защищать, охранять; покровительствовать

protection /прэте́кшн/ n защита

protective /прэте́ктив/ adj защитный

protector /прэте́ктэ/ n защитник

protest /про́утест/ n протест; /прэте́ст/ vi протестовать

Protestant /про́тистэнт/ n протестант(ка); adj протестантский

protocol /про́утэкол/ n протокол

prototype /про́утэтайп/ n прототип

protrude /прэтру́уд/ vti высовывать(ся)

protrusion /прэтру́ужн/ n выступ

proud /пра́уд/ adj гордый

prove /прууv/ vt доказывать; vi оказываться

proverb /про́вэб/ n пословица

provide /прэва́йд/ vt снабжать; ~ for /~ фо/ обеспечивать

providence /про́видэнс/ n предусмотрительность; P. провидение

provident /про́видэнт/ adj предусмотрительный

province /про́винс/ n провинция, область

provision /прэви́жн/ n обеспечение; условие; pl запасы, провизия; vt снабжать продовольствием

provisional /прэви́жнл/ adj временный;
~ government /~ га́венмент/ временное
правительство
provocation /про́вэкейшн/ n провокация
provoke /прэво́ук/ vt провоцировать
prowess /пра́уис/ n доблесть
proxy /про́кси/ n полномочие, доверенность; by ~ /бай ~/ по доверенности
prudence /пру́удэнс/ n благоразумие
prudent /пру́удэнт/ adj благоразумный
prudery /пру́удэри/ n напускная скромность, притворная стыдливость
prudish /пру́удиш/ adj излишне скромный, жеманный
prurient /пру́эриэнт/ adj похотливый
psalm /саам/ n псалом
pseudo- /съю́юдоу/ prefix псевдо-
pseudonym /съю́юдэним/ n псевдоним
psychiatrist /сайка́йетрист/ n психиатр
psychiatry /сайка́йетри/ n психиатрия
psychic /са́йкик/ adj психический
psychoanalysis /са́йкоэнэ́лэсис/ n пси-
хоанализ
psychological /са́йкэло́джикл/ adj пси-
хологический
psychologist /сайко́лэджист/ n психолог
psychology /сайко́лэджи/ n психология
pub /паб/ n пивная
public /па́блик/ adj общественный; общедоступный; государственный; национальный; ~ health /~ хелс/
здравоохранение; ~ service /~ сёрвис/
коммунальное обслуживание; make ~
/мэйк ~/ предать гласности; n публика, общественность; in ~ /ин ~/ пуб-
лично
publication /па́бликейшн/ n опубликование; издание
publicity /пабли́сити/ n гласность, реклама
publicize /па́блисайз/ vt рекламировать
publish /па́блиш/ vt издавать, опублико-
вывать
publisher /па́блише/ n издатель

publishing /па́блишинг/ n издательское
дело; adj издательский; ~ house
/~ ха́ус/ издательство
puck /пак/ n эльф; (спорт.) шайба
pudding /пу́динг/ n пудинг
puff /паф/ n дуновение (ветра); пуховка
(для пудры); vi пыхтеть; дымить; дуть
порывами
pug /паг/ n мопс (порода собак)
pugnacious /пагнэ́йшес/ adj драчливый
pull /пул/ n тяга, рывок; vt тянуть; грести; ~ strings /~ стрингз/ пускать в ход
связи; ~ oneself together /~ вансэ́лф тэ-
ге́зэ/ брать себя в руки
pulley /пу́ли/ n блок; шкив
pulp /палп/ n мякоть; древесная масса,
целлюлоза
pulse /палс/ n пульс, биение
pump /памп/ n насос; vt накачивать
pumpkin /па́мкин/ n тыква
pun /пан/ n каламбур
punch /панч/ n удар кулаком; компо-
стер; пунш; vt ударять кулаком; ком-
постировать
Punch /панч/ n Панч, Петрушка
punctual /па́нктьюэл/ adj пунктуальный
punctuality /па́нктьюэ́лити/ n пункту-
альность
punctuation /па́нктьюэ́йшн/ n пунктуа-
ция; ~ marks /~ маркс/ знаки препинания
puncture /па́нкче/ n прокол; vt прокалывать (шины)
punish /па́ниш/ vt наказывать
punishable /па́нишебл/ adj наказуемый
punishment /па́нишмент/ n наказание
punitive /пью́юнитив/ adj карательный
pupil /пью́юпл/ n ученик; зрачок
puppet /па́пит/ n марионетка; ~ show /~
шо́у/ кукольный театр
puppy /па́пи/ n щенок
purchase /пёрчес/ n покупка; vt покупать
purchaser /пёрчесэ/ n покупатель
pure /пью́э/ n чистый
purgatory /пёргэтри/ n чистилище
purge /пёрдж/ n чистка; слабительное
purify /пью́эрифай/ vt очищать

Puritan /пьюэритэн/ n пуританин

purity /пьюэрити/ n чистота

purl /пёрл/ vi журчать

purple /пёрпл/ adj пурпурный, фиолетовый, лиловый

purpose /пёрпэс/ n цель; on ~ /он ~/ нарочно

purposeful /пёрпэсфул/ adj целенаправленный; преднамеренный

purr /пёр/ vi мурлыкать

purse /пёрс/ n кошелек; дамская сумочка; the public ~ /зэ паблик ~/ казна

pursue /пэсъюю/ n гнаться за, преследовать; проводить (политику)

pursuit /пэсъюют/ n погоня; занятие

purvey /пэвэй/ vt поставлять продовольствие

push /пуш/ n толчок; vt толкать

pusher /пуше/ n (разг.) торговец наркотиками

puss(y) /пус(и)/ n кошечка, киска

put /пут/ vt класть, ставить; задавать (вопросы); излагать, формулировать; ~ by /~ бай/ откладывать (на черный день); ~ down /~ даун/ подавлять; записывать; снижать; ~ off /~ оф/ отсрочивать: ~ on /~ он/ надевать; ~ out /~ аут/ высовывать, выпячивать; тушить, гасить; ~ through /~ сруу/ соединять (по телефону); ~ a stop to /~ э стоп ту/ прекращать; ~ to a vote /~ ту э воут/ ставить на голосование; ~ together /~ тэгезе/ соединять; ~ up /~ ап/ поднимать; приютить

putty /пати/ n замазка, шпаклевка

puzzle /пазл/ n загадка; vt ставить в тупик

pygmy /пигми/ n пигмей

pyjamas /пэджаамэз/ n pl пижама

pyramid /пирэмид/ n пирамида

Q

quack /квэк/ n кряканье; знахарь; шарлатан; vi крякать; заниматься знахарством

quadrangle /кводрэнгл/ n четырехугольник

quadrille /квэдрил/ n кадриль

quail /квэйл/ n перепел; vi трусить

quaint /квэйнт/ adj причудливый, странный

quake /квэйк/ vi дрожать, трястись

Quaker /квэйкэ/ n квакер

qualification /кволификейшн/ n квалификация; оговорка; ограничение

qualify /кволифай/ vi квалифицировать

quality /кволити/ n качество

quantity /квонтити/ n количество

quarantine /кворэнтин/ n карантин

quarrel /кворл/ n ссора; vi ссориться

quarrelsome /кворлсэм/ adj вздорный

quarry /квори/ n каменоломня

quart /кворт/ n кварта (в Англии = 1,14 л; в Америке = 0,95 л)

quarter /квортэ/ n четверть; квартал; a ~ past five /э ~ пааст файв/ четверть шестого

quarterly /квортэли/ adj трехмесячный; adv раз в квартал

quartet(te) /квортет/ n квартет

quaver /квэйвэ/ vi дрожать

quay /кии/ n набережная

queen /квиин/ n королева; (карты) дама; (шахм.) ферзь

queer /квиэ/ adj странный

quench /квенч/ vt утолять (жажду); тушить

query /квиэри/ n вопрос

quest /квест/ n поиски

question /квесчн/ n вопрос; beyond ~ /бийонд ~/ вне сомнения; vt спрашивать, (д)опрашивать; сомневаться в

questionable /квесченэбл/ adj сомнительный

questionaire /квестиэнээ/ n анкета

question mark /квесчнмарк/ n вопросительный знак

queue /кьюю/ n очередь; jump the ~ /джамп зэ ~/ пролезть без очереди; vi стоять в очереди quick /квик/ adj быстрый, проворный; be ~! /би ~/ живее!

quicken /квикен/ vti ускорять(ся)

quickly /квикли/ adv быстро

quickness /квикнис/ n быстрота

quicksilver /квиксилвэ/ n ртуть

quick-tempered /квиктэмпэд/ adj вспыльчивый

quick-witted /квиквитьид/ adj остроумный

quiet /квайет/ adj тихий; interj тише!; keep smth ~ /киип самсинг ~/ утаивать (что-л.)

quietly /квайетли/ adv тихо

quilt /квилт/ n стеганое одеяло

quince /квинс/ n айва

quinine /квиниин/ n хинин

quinsy /квинзи/ n ангина

quintessence /квинтэснс/ n квинтэссенция

quintet(te) /квинтет/ n квинтет

quit /квит/ vt покидать; ~ the job /~ зэ джоб/ уйти с работы; predic adj: be ~s with /би ~с виз/ быть в расчете с

quite /квайт/ adv совсем, вполне; ~ so /~ соу/ именно так

quiver /квивэ/ n трепет; vi дрожать

quixotic /квиксотик/ adj донкихотский

quiz /квиз/ n опрос; викторина

quorum /квоорэм/ n кворум

quota /квоутэ/ n квота

quotation /квотэйшн/ n цитата

quotation-marks /квотэйшнмаркс/ n pl кавычки

quote /квоут/ vt цитировать; назначать цену

R

rabbi /рэбай/ n раввин

rabbit /рэбит/ n кролик

rabble /рэбл/ n сброд

rabid /рэбид/ adj бешеный

rabies /рэйбиз/ n бешенство

race /рэйс/ n раса, гонка; pl бега, скачки; arms ~ /армз ~/ гонка вооружений; vi состязаться в скорости, мчаться

race-course /рэйскос/ n ипподром

racial /рэйшл/ adj расовый

rack /рэк/ n вешалка; vt мучить, пытать; ~ one's brains /~ ванз брэйнз/ ломать себе голову

racket /рэкит/ n шум; вымогательство, рэкет; ракетка

racoon /рэкуун/ n енот

radar /рэйдэ/ n радар

radiance /рэйдьенс/ n сияние

radiant /рэйдьент/ adj лучистый

radiate /рэйдиэйт/ vt излучать

radiation /рэйдиэйшн/ n радиация

radiator /рэйдиэйтэ/ n радиатор

radical /рэдикэл/ adj коренной; радикальный

radically /рэдикэли/ adv полностью; коренным образом

radio /рэйдиоу/ n радио

radioactive /рэйдиоэктив/ adj радиоактивный

radiolocation /рэйдиолокэйшн/ n радиолокация

radish /рэдиш/ n редиска

radium /рэйдьем/ n радий

radius /рэйдьес/ n радиус

raffle /рэфл/ n лотерея

raft /раафт/ n плот

rag /рэг/ n тряпка

rage /рэйдж/ n гнев, ярость; vi беситься; свирепствовать (об эпидемии и т.п.)

ragged /рэгид/ adj оборванный; неровный

raging /рэйджинг/ adj яростный, бушующий

raglan /рэглэн/ n пальто-реглан

raid /рэйд/ n облава; рейд; vt делать налет на

rail /рэйл/ n перила; рельс; by ~ /бай ~/ по железнодорожной дороге

railway /рэ́йлвэй/ n железная дорога; ~ timetable /~ та́ймтэйбл/ расписание поездов; cable ~ /кейбл ~/ канатная дорога; ~ car /~ кар/ вагон; ~ station /~ стэ́йшн/ вокзал

rain /рэйн/ n дождь; vti лить (ся); it is ~ing cats and dogs /ит из ~инг кэтс энд догз/ дождь льет как из ведра

rainbow /рэ́йнбоу/ n радуга

rainy /рэ́йни/ adj дождливый

raise /рэйз/ vt поднимать; воспитывать (детей); выращивать (растения); повышать (плату)

raisin /рэ́йзн/ adj изюмина; pl изюм

rake /рэйк/ n грабли; vt сгребать

rally /рэ́ли/ n слет; ралли; vti сплачивать (ся)

ram /рэм/ n баран; таран; vt таранить

ramble /рэмбл/ n прогулка; vi бродить

rampart /рэ́мпат/ n вал; (перен.) оплот

ranch /раанч/ n ранчо, ферма

random /рэ́ндэм/ adj случайный; n: at ~ /эт ~/ наугад

range /рэйндж/ n ряд; размах; цепь (гор); полигон; ~ of vision /~ ов вижн/ поле зрения; vt выстраивать в ряд; vi простираться

rank /рэнк/ n ряд; шеренга; чин; ~ and file /~ энд файл/ рядовой состав; vt классифицировать

ransom /рэ́нсэм/ n выкуп

rape /рэйп/ n изнасилование; vt насиловать

rapid /рэ́пид/ adj быстрый; n pl пороги (реки)

rapt /рэпт/ adj восхищенный

rapture /рэ́пче/ n восторг

rare /рээ/ adj редкий; недожаренный

rarity /рэ́эрити/ n редкость, раритет

rascal /ра́аскэл/ n негодяй

rash /рэш/ adj опрометчивый; n сыпь

rasp /раасп/ n рашпиль; терка

raspberry /ра́азбери/ n малина

rat /рэт/ n крыса; ~ race /~ рэйс/ n бесполезная деятельность, бешеная погоня за богатством

rate /рэйт/ n ставка, норма; ~ of exchange /~ ов иксче́йндж/ валютный курс; at any ~ /эт э́ни ~/ во всяком случае; vt оценивать

rather /ра́азэ/ adv скорее; довольно; лучше; interj еще бы!; конечно, да!

ratification /рэ́тификэ́йшн/ n ратификация

ratify /рэ́тифай/ vt ратифицировать

ratio /рэ́йшиоу/ n соотношение, коэффициент

ration /рэшн/ n паек, рацион; ~ card /~ кард/ продовольственная карточка; vt нормировать

rational /рэ́шенл/ adj рациональный

rattle /рэтл/ n грохот; трещотка; vi трещать, дребезжать

rattlesnake /рэ́тлснэйк/ n гремучая змея

rat-trap /рэ́ттрэп/ n крысоловка

ravage /рэ́видж/ vt опустошать

rave /рэйв/ vt бредить; неистовствовать

raven /рэйвн/ n ворон

ravine /рэви́ин/ n ущелье

raw /роо/ adj сырой; ~ material /~ мэти́риэл/ сырье

ray /рэй/ n луч

rayon /рэ́йон/ n искусственный шелк; район, радиус

raze /рэйз/ vt разрушать до основания; вычеркивать

razor /рэ́йзэ/ n бритва

reach /риич/ n предел досягаемости; охват; протяжение; out of ~ /а́ут ов ~/ вне досягаемости; vti протягивать (ся); дотягиваться до, доходить до

react /риэ́кт/ vi реагировать

reaction /риэ́кшн/ n реакция

reactionary /риэ́кшнэри/ adj реакционный; n реакционер

read /риид/ vt читать

readable /ри́идэбл/ adj удобочитаемый, хорошо написанный

reader /ри́идэ/ n читатель

readily /рэ́дили/ adv охотно

readiness /рэ́динис/ n готовность

reading /ри́идинг/ n чтение; ~ room /~ руум/ читальный зал

ready /ре́ди/ adj готовый

real /ри́эл/ adj настоящий, действительный; подлинный; недвижимый (о собственности)

realistic /риэли́стик/ adj реалистический

reality /риэ́лити/ n действительность

realization /ри́элизэ́йшн/ n осуществление

realize /ри́элайз/ vt осуществлять; понимать

really /ри́эли/ adv действительно

realm /релм/ n королевство

reanimate /ри́иэ́нимэйт/ vt оживлять

reap /риип/ vt жать, пожинать

reaper /ри́ипэ/ n жнец

rear /ри́э/ n тыл; задняя сторона; in the ~ /ин зэ ~/ в тылу; adj задний

reason /ри́изн/ n разум; причина; vi рассуждать

reasonable /ри́изнэбл/ adj (благо) разумный

reassure /ри́иэшю́э/ vt успокаивать, заверять

rebate /ри́ибэйт/ n скидка

rebel /ребл/ n бунтовщик; /рибе́л/ vt бунтовать

rebellion /рибе́льен/ n мятеж

rebellious /рибе́льес/ adj мятежный

rebuff /риба́ф/ n отпор; vt давать отпор

rebuke /рибью́юк/ n упрек; vt упрекать

rebut /риба́т/ vt провергать

rebuttal /риба́тл/ n опровержение

recall /рико́ол/ n отзыв (депутата и т.п.); vt вспоминать; отзывать; отменять

recant /рикэ́нт/ vi отрекаться

recantation /ри́икэнтэ́йшн/ n отречение

recede /риси́ид/ vi отступать

receipt /риси́ит/ n квитанция; расписка; получение; pl денежные поступления; выручка

receive /риси́ив/ vt получать, принимать

receiver /риси́ивэ/ n получатель; телефонная трубка; радиоприемник

recent /риисснт/ adj недавний

recently /ри́исснтли/ adv недавно

reception /рисэ́пшн/ n прием; восприятие; ~ room /~ руум/ приемная

recess /рисэ́с/ n перерыв; ниша; in the secret ~es /ин зэ си́икрэт ~ыз/ в тайниках

recipe /ре́сипи/ n рецепт

recipient /риси́пиэнт/ n получатель

reciprocal /риси́прэкл/ adj взаимный

reciprocate /риси́прэкэйт/ vt отвечать взаимностью

reciprocity /ре́сипро́сити/ n взаимность

recite /риса́йт/ vt декламировать

reckless /ре́клис/ adj безрассудный; ~ driving /~ дра́йвинг/ лихачество

reckon /рекн/ vi думать; считать, подсчитывать; ~ with /~ виз/ считаться с

reclaim /рикле́йм/ vt требовать обратно; осваивать (заброшенные земли)

recline /рикла́йн/ vi полулежать

recognition /ре́кэгни́шн/ n узнавание; признание

recognize /ре́кэгнайз/ vt узнавать; признавать

recoil /рико́йл/ n отдача (о ружье); отдавать (о ружье); отпрянуть

recollect /ре́кэле́кт/ vt вспоминать

recollection /ре́кэле́кшн/ n воспоминание

recommend /ре́кэме́нд/ vt рекомендовать

recommendation /ре́кэмендэ́йшн/ n рекомендация

recompense /ре́кэмпенс/ n вознаграждение; vt вознаграждать

reconcile /ре́кэнсайл/ vt примирять

reconciliation /ре́кэнсилиэ́йшн/ n примирение

reconnaissance /рико́нисэнс/ n разведка

reconnoitre /ре́коно́йтэ/ vt разведывать

reconsider /ри́икэнси́дэ/ vt пересматривать

reconstruct /ри́икэнстра́кт/ vt перестраивать

reconstruction /ри́икэнстра́кшн/ n перестройка, реконструкция record /ре́код/ n запись; протокол; (граммофонная) пластинка; репутация; личное дело; (спорт.) рекорд; off the ~ /оф зэ ~/ неофициально; ~ player /~ плэ́йе/ проигрыватель; /рико́рд/ vt записывать; регистрировать

recount /рика́унт/ vt пересказывать; /ри́ика́унт/ пересчитывать

recover /рика́вэ/ vt получать обратно; vi выздоравливать

recovery /рика́вэри/ n возмещение; выздоровление

recreation /ре́криэ́йшн/ n отдых

recruit /рикру́ут/ n новобранец; vt вербовать

recruitment /рикру́утмент/ n вербовка

rectangle /ре́ктэ́нгл/ n прямоугольник

rectify /ре́ктифай/ vt исправлять

rectum /ре́ктэм/ n прямая кишка

recuperate /рикью́юпрэ́йт/ vti выздоравливать; поправить (здоровье)

red /ред/ adj красный; turn ~ /тёрн ~/ краснеть; R. Cross /~ крос/ Красный крест

redeem /риди́им/ vt выкупать, избавлять

redemption /ридэ́мшн/ n выкуп, искупление

red-haired /ре́дхе́эд/ adj рыжеволосый

red-handed /ре́дхэ́ндыд/ adj пойманный с поличным

red-letter day /ре́длэтэдэ́й/ n праздник

red-tape /ре́дтэ́йп/ n бюрократизм

reduce /ридью́юс/ vt снижать (цену); сокращать

reduction /рида́кшн/ n снижение; сокращение

redundant /рида́ндэнт/ adj излишний, лишний, ненужный

reed /риид/ n тростник

reef /рииф/ n риф

reel /риил/ n катушка, шпулька; vi кружиться; пошатываться

refectory /рифе́ктэри/ n трапезная (в монастыре)

refer /рифёр/ vt отсылать, направлять; ~ to /~ ту/ ссылаться на

referee /ре́фэри́и/ n судья

reference /ре́фрэнс/ n ссылка, упоминание; рекомендация

refine /рифа́йн/ vt рафинировать

refined /рифа́йнд/ adj очищенный; утонченный

refinement /рифа́йнмент/ n изысканность

refinery /рифа́йнэри/ n нефтеочистительный завод

reflect /рифле́кт/ vt отражать; vi размышлять

reflection /рифле́кшн/ n отражение; размышление

reform /рифо́рм/ n реформа; vti исправлять (ся)

reformer /рифо́рмэ/ n преобразователь, реформатор

refrain /рифрэ́йн/ n припев; vi воздерживаться; vt сдерживать

refresh /рифре́ш/ vt освежать, подкреплять

refreshment /рифре́шмент/ n отдых; pl закуски

refrigerator /рифри́джерэ́йтэ/ n холодильник

refuge /ре́фьюдж/ n убежище

refugee /ре́фьюджи́и/ n беженец

refund /рифа́нд/ vt возмещать

refusal /рифью́юзл/ n отказ

refuse /рифью́юз/ vt отвергать, отказываться от; /ре́фьюс/ n отбросы, мусор

refutation /ре́фьютэ́йшн/ n опровержение

refute /рифью́ют/ vt опровергать

regal /риигл/ adj царственный, королевский

regard /рига́рд/ n уважение; отношение; pl привет; with ~ to /виз ~ ту/ относительно; vt рассматривать, считать; as ~ /эз ~з/ что касается

regenerate /риджене́рэйт/ vt возрождать, восстанавливать; регенерировать

regime /режи́им/ n режим

regiment /ре́джимент/ n полк

region /рииджн/ n область, район

register /ре́джистэ/ n журнал; список; vt регистрировать, записывать; vi регистрироваться

registered /ре́джистэд/ adj зарегистрированный; ~ letter /~ ле́тэ/ заказное письмо

registration /ре́джистрэ́йшн/ n регистрация

regret /ригре́т/ n сожаление; vt сожалеть

regular /ре́гьюлэ/ adj регулярный; правильный

regularity /ре́гьюлэ́рити/ n регулярность

regulate /ре́гьюлэйт/ vt регулировать

regulation /ре́гьюлэ́йшн/ n регулирование; правило; pl устав

rehabilitation /ри́иэби́литэ́йшн/ n реабилитация

rehearsal /рихёёсл/ n репетиция; dress ~ /дрэс ~/ генеральная репетиция

rehearse /рихёёс/ vt репетировать

reign /рейн/ n царствование; vi царствовать

reimburse /ри́имбёрс/ vt возмещать

rein /рейн/ n повод, вожжа

reindeer /ре́йндиэ/ n северный олень

reinforce /ри́инфо́рс/ vt усиливать; ~d concrete /~т ко́нкрит/ железобетон

reinforcement /ри́инфо́рсмент/ n усиление, подкрепление

reject /риджéкт/ vt отвергать

rejection /риджéкшн/ n отказ, отклонение

rejoice /риджо́йс/ vti радовать(ся)

rejuvenate /риджю́ювинэйт/ vt омолаживать

relapse /рилэ́пс/ n рецидив

relate /рилэ́йт/ vt рассказывать; vi относиться к

relation /рилэ́йшн/ n родственник, родственница; отношение, связь

relationship /рилэ́йшншип/ n родство; взаимоотношение

relative /ре́лэтив/ adj относительный; n родственник, родственница

relax /рилэ́кс/ vti расслаблять(ся)

relaxation /ри́илэксэ́йшн/ n расслабление, отдых

relay /рилэ́й/ n смена; (спорт.) эстафета; vt сменять; транслировать

release /рили́ис/ vt освобождать; выпускать (фильм и т.п.)

relent /риле́нт/ vi смягчаться

relevant /ре́ливэнт/ adj уместный, относящийся к делу

reliability /рилэ́йеби́лити/ n надежность

reliable /рилэ́йебл/ adj надежный

relic /ре́лик/ n остаток; pl останки; реликвии

relief /рили́иф/ n облегчение; пособие; помощь; смена (дежурных); рельеф

relieve /рили́ив/ vt облегчать; сменять

religion /рили́джн/ n религия

religious /рили́джес/ adj религиозный

relish /ре́лиш/ n наслаждение, вкус

reluctant /рилэ́ктэнт/ adj неохотный

rely on /рилэ́й он/ vi полагаться на

remain /римэ́йн/ vi оставаться

remainder /римэ́йндэ/ n остаток

remains /римэ́йнз/ n pl остатки; останки; руины

remark /рима́рк/ n замечание; vt замечать

remarkable /рима́ркэбл/ adj замечательный

remedy /ре́миди/ n средство, лекарство; vt исправлять; вылечивать

remember /римэ́мбэ/ vt помнить, вспоминать

remembrance /римэ́мбрэнс/ n воспоминание

remind /рима́йнд/ vt напоминать

reminder /рима́йндэ/ n напоминание

remittance /реми́тэнс/ n денежный перевод

remnant /ре́мнэнт/ n остаток

remodel /рими́одл/ vt переделывать

remorse /римо́рс/ n угрызения совести

remote /римо́ут/ adj отдаленный

removal /риму́увл/ n перемещение, переезд; ~ van /~ вэн/ фургон для перевозки мебели remove /римуúв/ vt перемещать; удалять; устранять; vi переезжать

remunerate /римьюóюнэрэйт/ vt вознаграждать

renaissance /рэнэ́йсэнс/ n возрождение

render /рéндэ/ vt воздавать; оказывать (помощь); приводить в какое-либо состояние; ~ an account /~ эн экáунт/ представлять счет

renew /риньюю/ vt возобновлять, продлевать

renewal /риньюэл/ n обновление; возобновление

renown /ринáун/ n слава

renowned /ринáунд/ adj знаменитый

rent /рент/ n квартирная плата; vt нанимать; сдавать в аренду; брать напрокат

rental /рентл/ n арендная плата

rep /реп/ n репс

repair /рипэ́э/ n починка, ремонт; vt чинить, ремонтировать

reparation /рéпэрэйшн/ n репарация, возмещение

repatriate /рипэ́триэйт/ vt репатриировать

repay /рипэ́й/ vt отплачивать, возмещать

repayment /рипэ́ймент/ n выплата (долга), возмещение

repeal /рипиил/ n отмена; vt отменять

repeat /рипиит/ vti повторять (ся)

repeatedly /рипииытыдли/ adv неоднократно

repel /рипéл/ vt отталкивать, отражать

repent /рипéнт/ vt раскаиваться

repetition /рéпитиишн/ n повторение

replace /рипплэ́йс/ vt заменять, пополнять

replacement /рипплэ́йсмент/ n замена

replica /рéпликэ/ n реплика, точная копия

reply /рипплáй/ n ответ; ~ paid /~ пэйд/ с оплаченным ответом; vt отвечать

report /рипóрт/ n доклад; vt докладывать, сообщать; vi являться

reporter /рипóртэ/ n докладчик; репортер

represent /рéпризéнт/ vt представлять, изображать

representative /рéпризéнтэтив/ n представитель; adj характерный

repress /рипрéс/ vt подавлять

reprimand /рéприманд/ n выговор; vt делать выговор

reproach /рипрóуч/ n укор; vt упрекать

reproachful /рипрóучфул/ adj укоризненный

reproduce /рíипрэдьююс/ vt воспроизводить

reproduction /рíипрэдáкшн/ n воспроизведение; репродукция

reproof /рипруýф/ n выговор

reprove /рипруýв/ vt порицать

reptile /рéптайл/ n пресмыкающееся

republic /рипáблик/ n республика

republican /рипáбликэн/ adj республиканский

repudiation /рипьюóюдиэ́йшн/ n отречение; отрицание

repulse /рипáлс/ n отпор; vt отражать

repulsive /рипáлсив/ adj отталкивающий

reputation /рéпьютэ́йшн/ n репутация

request /риквéст/ n просьба; vt просить

require /риквáйе/ vt требовать

requirement /риквáйемент/ n требование

rescue /рéскью/ n спасение; vt спасать

research /рисёрч/ n исследование; ~ worker /~ вёркэ/ научный работник

resemblance /ризэ́мблэнс/ n сходство

resemble /ризэ́мбл/ vt походить на

resent /ризэ́нт/ vt обижаться на

resentment /ризэ́нтмент/ n негодование, обида

reservation /рéзэвэ́йшн/ n оговорка; предварительный заказ; резервация (для индейцев)

reserve /ризéрв/ n резерв; заповедник; скрытность; in ~ /ин ~/ в запасе; with ~ /виз ~/ с оговоркой; vt сберегать; бронировать; ~ the right /~ зэ райт/ сохранять право

reserved /ризёёвд/ adj сдержанный; за-
казанный заранее
reside /ризайд/ vi проживать
residence /рéзидэнс/ n местожительство
resident/рéзидэнт/ n постоянный житель
resign /ризáйн/ vi уходить в отставку
resignation /рéзигнэ́йшн/ n отставка;
смирение, покорность
resilient /ризи́лиэнт/ adj упругий; неу-
нывающий
resin /рéзин/ n смола
resist /ризи́ст/ vt сопротивляться
resistance /ризи́стэнс/ n сопротивление
resolute /рéзэлют/ adj решительный
resolution /рéзэлю́юшн/ n решение; резолюция; решительность
resolve /ризóлв/ n решимость; vt решать
resort /ризóрт/ n прибежище; курорт;
last ~ /лааст ~/ последнее средство; vi:
~ to прибегать к
resound /ризáунд/ vi звучать, отдаваться
эхом
resource /рисóрс/ n ресурс; средство
resourceful /рисóрсфул/ adj находчивый
respect /риспéкт/ n уважение; in all ~s
/ин оол ~с/ во всех отношениях; vt уважать
respectable /риспéктэбл/ adj почтенный,
порядочный
respectful /риспéктфул/ adj почтитель-
ный
respective /риспéктив/ adj соответствен-
ный
respectively /риспéктивли/ adv соответственно
respiration /рéспэрэ́йшн/ n дыхание
respite /рéспайт/ n передышка, отсрочка
respond /риспóнд/ vi отвечать; отзываться
respondent /риспóндэнт/ n ответчик
response /риспóнс/ n ответ; отклик
responsibility /риспóнсэби́лити/ n ответственность
responsible /риспóнсэбл/ adj ответственный

responsive /риспóнсив/ adj отзывчивый
rest /рест/ n отдых; покой; остаток; ос-
тальные; vi отдыхать; vt опираться (рукой); прислонять
restaurant /рéстэрон/ n ресторан
restitution /рéститью́юшн/ n возмещение
(убытка)
restoration /рéстэрэ́йшн/ n реставрация,
восстановление
restore /ристóр/ vt реставрировать, восстанавливать
restorer /ристóорэ/ n реставратор
restrain /ристрэ́йн/ vt сдерживать, обуздывать
restraint /ристрэ́йнт/ n сдержанность
restrict /ристри́кт/ vt ограничивать
restriction /ристри́кшн/ n ограничение
result /ризáлт/ n результат; vi: ~ in /~ ин/
vi приводить к; ~ from /~ фром/ происходить из-за
resume /ризью́юм/ vt возобновлять
resurrect /рéзэрéкт/ vt воскрешать
resurrection /рéзэрéкшн/ n воскресение;
воскрешение
retail /ри́итэйл/ n розничная продажа; ~
price /~ прайс/ розничная цена; vt
/ритэ́йл/ продавать в розницу
retailer /ритэ́йлэ/ n розничный торговец
retain /ритэ́йн/ vt сохранять, удерживать
retaliate /ритэ́лиэйт/ vi отплачивать тем
же
retaliation /ритэ́лиэ́йшн/ n отплата, возмездие
retard /ритáрд/ vt задерживать
reticent /рéтисэнт/ adj сдержанный,
скрытный
retire /ритáйе/ vt уходить в отставку;
уединяться
retirement /ритáйемент/ n отставка
retort /ритóрт/ n возражение, резкий ответ
retreat /ритри́ит/ n отступление; vi отступать

return /ритёрн/ n возвращение; прибыль; in ~ /ин ~/ в обмен; tax ~ /тэкс
~/ налоговая декларация; many happy
~s /мэни хэпи ~з/ с днем рождения; ~
ticket /~ тикит/ обратный билет, билет
в оба конца; vti возвращать(ся)
reunion /рииюньен/ n воссоединение;
примирение
reunite /рииюнайт/ vti воссоединять(ся)
reveal /ривиил/ vt обнаруживать
revel /ревл/ vi пировать
revelation /ревилэйшн/ n откровение;
раскрытие; the R. /зэ ~/ Апокалипсис
revenge /ривендж/ n месть; vt мстить
revengeful /ривенджфул/ adj мститель-
ный
revenue /ревинью/ n (государственный)
доход; pl доходные статьи; tax ~ /тэкс
~/ доход от налогов
revere /ривиэ/ vt благоговеть перед
reverence /ревэрэнс/ n благоговение
reverse /риверс/ n обратная сторона; неудача; задний ход; quite the ~ /квайт зэ
~/ совсем наоборот; vt менять (на противоположный); (юр.) отменять, давать задний ход
review /ривьюю/ n обзор, обозрение; рецензия; (юр.) пересмотр; vt рецензировать;   проверять;   (юр.)
пересматривать
revision /ривижн/ n пересмотр
revisionism /ривижензим/ n ревизионизм
revival /ривайвэл/ n возрождение; ожив-
ление
revive /ривайв/ vt приводить в чувство,
оживлять; vi приходить в чувство
revoke /ривоук/ vt отменять
revolt /риво́улт/ n восстание; vi восставать
revolting /риво́ултинг/ adj отвратительный
revolution /ревэлююшн/ n революция;
вращение; оборот
revolutionary /ревэлююшнэри/ n революционер; adj революционный

revolve /риволв/ vti вращать(ся)
revolver /риволвэ/ n револьвер
revolving /риволвинг/ adj вращающийся
reward /риворд/ n награда; vt награждать
rheumatism /руумэтизм/ n ревматизм
rhinoceros /райносрэс/ n носорог
rhubarb /руубаб/ n ревень
rhyme /райм/ n рифма; without ~ or reason
/визаут ~ о риизн/ ни складу, ни ладу
rhythm /ризм/ n ритм
rib /риб/ n ребро
ribbon /рибэн/ n лента, тесьма
rice /райс/ n рис
rich /рич/ adj богатый
riches /ричиз/ n pl богатство
rid /рид/ vt избавлять; get ~ of /гет ~ ов/
отделываться от
riddance /ридэнс/ n избавление
riddle /ридл/ n загадка
ride /райд/ n прогулка; go for a ~ /го́у
фор э ~/ выйти или выехать на прогул-
ку; vt ехать верхом на
rider /райдэ/ n всадник
ridge /ридж/ n горный хребет
ridicule /ридикьюл/ n осмеяние; vt осмеивать
ridiculous /ридикьюлэс/ adj смехотворный
riff-raff /рифрэф/ n подонки общества;
мусор
rifle /райфл/ n винтовка
rifleman /райфлмэн/ n стрелок
rift /рифт/ n трещина; (образн.) разрыв
rig /риг/ n оснастка; vt оснащать; ~ out
/~ аут/ снаряжать
right /райт/ n право; справедливость; правая сторона; the R. /зэ ~/ правые силы,
консерваторы; civil ~s /сивил ~с/ граж-
данские права; human ~s /хьюумэн ~с/
права человека; ~s and duties /~с энд
дьюютиз/ права и обязанности; adj правый;   справедливый;   правильный;   ~
angle /~энгл/ прямой угол; adv правильно; направо; all ~ /ол ~/ ладно; ~ away
/~ эвэй/ немедленно; interj хорошо!

righteous /ра́йчес/ adj праведный; справедливый

rightful /ра́йтфул/ adj законный

right-hand man /ра́йтхэндмэ́н/ n "правая рука", хороший помощник

rightly /ра́йтли/ adv правильно; справедливо

rigid /ри́джид/ adj жесткий, непреклонный

rigorous /ри́гэрэс/ adj суровый

rim /рим/ n обод(ок); оправа (очков)

rind /райнд/ n кора, корка; кожура

ring /ринг/ n круг; кольцо; ринг; клика; шайка; звон; звонок; vt звонить в; vi звучать; ~ true /~ труу/ звучать искренне; ~ up /~ ап/ звонить по телефону

ring-finger /ри́нгфи́нгэ/ n безымянный палец

rink /ринк/ n каток

rinse /ринс/ vt полоскать

riot /ра́йет/ n бунт; vi бунтовать

rioter /ра́йетэ/ n бунтовщик

riotous /ра́йетэс/ adj буйный

rip /рип/ n разрыв, разрез; vt рвать, разрезать; ~ off /~ оф/ сдирать

ripe /райп/ adj зрелый, спелый

ripen /райпн/ vi зреть

ripple /рипл/ n рябь; журчание; vi рябить; журчать

rise /райз/ n подъем, повышение; восход (солнца); vi подниматься; повышаться, вставать

risk /риск/ n риск; vt рисковать

risky /ри́ски/ adj рискованный

rite /райт/ n обряд

rival /ра́йвл/ n соперник; vt соперничать

rivalry /ра́йвэлри/ n соперничество, конкуренция

river /ри́вэ/ n река

rivet /ри́вит/ n заклепка; vt клепать

road /ро́уд/ n дорога, путь; ~ sign /~ сайн/ дорожный знак

road-map /ро́удмэп/ n карта автомобильных дорог

roadside /ро́удсайд/ n обочина

roadway /ро́удвэй/ n проезжая часть дороги

roam /ро́ум/ vi бродить

roar /poop/ n рев; ~ of laughter /~ ов ла́афтэ/ взрыв хохота; vi реветь, грохотать

roaring /ро́оринг/ adj ревущий; бурный; грохочущий

roast /ро́уст/ n жаркое; vti жарить(ся)

roaster /ро́устэ/ n жаровня

rob /роб/ vt грабить

robber /ро́бэ/ n грабитель

robbery /ро́бэри/ n грабеж

robe /ро́уб/ n мантия, халат

robin /ро́бин/ n малиновка

robust /рэба́ст/ adj крепкий; здравый, ясный

rock /рок/ n скала, утес; vti качать(ся), трясти(сь)

rocket /ро́кит/ n ракета

rocking /ро́кинг/ adj качающийся

rocking-chair /ро́кингчéэ/ n кресло-качалка

rocky /ро́ки/ adj скалистый

rod /род/ n прут; удочка

rogue /ро́уг/ n жулик, мошенник

role /ро́ул/ n роль

roll /ро́ул/ n рулон; булочка; качка; раскат (грома); ~ of honour /~ ов о́онэ/ список убитых на войне; vt катить, прокатывать (метал); вращать (глазами); vi катиться; вращаться; ~ up /~ ап/ свертывать(ся); ~ed gold /~д го́улд/ позолота

roll-call /ро́улкол/ n перекличка

roller /ро́улэ/ n (тех.) каток

roller-skates /ро́улэскэ́йтс/ n pl роликовые коньки

Roman /ро́умэн/ n римлянин; adj римский; католический; латинский; ~ Catholic /~ кэ́сэлик/ католик

romance /рэмэ́нс/ n любовная история, роман; романс

Romanian /румэ́йньен/ n румын(ка); румынский язык; adj румынский

romantic /рэмэ́нтик/ adj романтический

romp /ромп/ n шумная игра, возня

roof /рууф/ n крыша; (образн.) кров; ~ of the mouth /~ ов зэ маус/ нёбо

rook /рук/ n грач; (шахм.) ладья

room /руум/ n комната; номер (гостиничный); место, пространство; make ~ for /мэйк ~ фо/ освобождать место

roomy /рууми/ adj просторный

roost /рууст/ n насест

rooster /руустэ/ n петух

root /руут/ n корень; take ~ /тэйк ~/ пускать корни; vi укореняться; ~ out /~ аут/ искоренять

rooted /руутыд/ adj укоренившийся

rope /роуп/ n веревка, канат

rose /роуз/ n роза

rosin /розин/ n канифоль

rostrum /рострэм/ n трибуна; from the UN ~ /фром зы ю эн ~/ с трибуны ООН

rosy /роузи/ adj розовый; румяный

rot /рот/ n гниение; vi гнить

rota /роутэ/ n расписание дежурств

rotary /роутэри/ adj ротационный; R. Club /~ клаб/ клуб "Ротари", клуб деловых людей

rotation /роутэйшн/ n вращение; in ~ /ин ~/ по очереди

rotten /ротн/ adj гнилой; дрянной

rouge /рууж/ n румяна; vti румянить(ся)

rough /раф/ adj грубый; шершавый; бурный (о море); неотделанный; приблизительный (подсчет); ~ copy /~ копи/ черновик

roughly /рафли/ adv грубо; приблизительно

roulette /рулет/ n рулетка

round /раунд/ n круг; шар; обход; (спорт.) раунд; тур; выстрел; adj круглый; ~ sum /~ сам/ кругленькая сумма; adv вокруг; the whole year ~ /зэ хоул йее ~/ круглый год; ~ off /~ оф/ vt округлять

rouse /рауз/ vt будить; возбуждать

rout /раут/ n разгром

route /руут/ n маршрут, путь; en ~ /ан ~/ по пути

routine /рутиин/ n рутина

rove /роув/ vt скитаться

row /роу/ n ряд; vt грести

row /рау/ n (разг.) ссора, скандал; vi скандалить

rowboat /роубоут/ n гребная лодка

rowdy /рауди/ adj шумный, буйный

royal /ройл/ adj королевский

royalty /ройлти/ n авторский гонорар

rub /раб/ vt тереть, натирать; ~ off /~ оф/ счищать

rubber /рабэ/ n каучук; резина; ластик; ~ stamp /~ стэмп/ штамп

rubbish /рабиш/ n мусор, хлам; вздор

rubble /рабл/ n бут, булыжник

rudder /радэ/ n руль

rude /рууд/ adj грубый

rudeness /рууднис/ n грубость

ruffian /рафьен/ n головорез

ruffle /рафл/ vt ерошить (волосы); рябить (воду)

rug /раг/ n коврик, плед

ruin /руин/ n гибель; pl руины; vt губить, разрушать

rule /руул/ n правило; господство, правление; as a ~ /эз э ~/ как правило; vt править, управлять; линовать; vi постановлять; ~ out /~ аут/ исключать

ruler /руулэ/ n правитель; линейка

ruling /руулинг/ n постановление; adj господствующий

rum /рам/ n ром

rumble /рамбл/ n громыханье; vi грохотать

rummage /рамидж/ vi рыться, обыскивать

rumour /руумэ/ n молва, слух; ~ has it that /~ хэз ит зэт/ ходят слухи, что

run /ран/ n бег; пробег; петля на чулке; ход; ряд; in the long ~ /ин зэ лонг ~/ в конечном счете; vt управлять, вести (дела); гнать; vi бегать; бежать; течь; курсировать; работать (о машине); идти (о пьесе); ~ away /~ эвэй/ убегать; ~ out /~ аут/ выбегать; кончаться; ~ over /~ оувэ/ переливаться через край; давить; ~ through /~ сруу/ бегло просматривать; ~ up againt /~апэгэйнст/ натыкаться на; ~ away /~ эвэй/ n убегать runner /ра́нэ/ n бегун

running /ра́нинг/ adj бегущий; текущий; ~ water /~ во́отэ/ проточная вода; three days ~ /срии дэйз ~/ три дня подряд

runway /ра́нвэй/ n взлетно-посадочная полоса

rural /ру́эрэл/ adj сельский

rush /раш/ n наплыв; натиск; ~ hour /~ а́уэ/ час "пик"; ~ order /~ о́рдэ/ срочный заказ; vt торопить; vi мчаться, бросаться

Russian /рашн/ n русский, русская; русский язык; adj русский

rust /раст/ n ржавчина; vi ржаветь

rustic /ра́стик/ adj деревенский

rustle /расл/ n шелест, шорох; vi шелестеть

rusty /ра́сти/ adj ржавый; запущенный; her French is ~ /хё френч из ~/ она подзабыла французский

rut /рат/ n колея

ruthless /ру́услис/ adj безжалостный

rye /рай/ n рожь

rye-bread /ра́йбрэд/ n ржаной хлеб

S

Sabbath /са́бэт/ n (религ.) священный день отдохновения

sable /сэйбл/ n соболь; соболий мех

sabotage /са́бэтаж/ n саботаж; vt саботировать

sabre /сэ́йбэ/ n сабля

sack /сэк/ n мешок; get the ~ /гет зэ ~/ быть уволенным

sacrament /са́крэмент/ n причастие, таинство

sacred /сэ́йкрид/ adj святой, священный

sacrifice /са́крифайс/ n жертва; vt жертвовать

sacrilege /са́крилидж/ n святотатство

sacrilegious /са́крили́джес/ adj кощунственный

sad /сэд/ adj грустный, печальный; be ~ /би ~/ грустить

sadden /сэдн/ vt печалить

saddle /сэдл/ n седло; vt седлать

sadness /са́днис/ n грусть, печаль

safe /сэйф/ adj невредимый; безопасный; надежный; ~ arrival /~ эра́йвл/ благополучное прибытие; ~ and sound /~ энд са́унд/ цел(ый) и невредим(ый); n сейф

safeguard /сэ́йфгард/ n гарантия; охрана; vt гарантировать; охранять

safely /сэ́йфли/ adv благополучно, безопасно

safety /сэ́йфти/ n безопасность

safety pin /сэ́йфтипин/ n английская булавка

safety razor /сэ́йфтирэ́йзэ/ n безопасная бритва

safety valve /сэ́йфтивэлв/ n предохранительный клапан

saffron /са́фрэн/ n шафран

sag /сэг/ vi обвисать; оседать

sagacious /сэга́йшес/ adj прозорливый

sage /сэйдж/ adj мудрый; n мудрец

said /сэд/ adj: the ~ /зэ ~/ вышеупомянутый

sail /сэйл/ n парус; плавание; set ~ /сет ~/ отправляться в плавание; vi поднять паруса

sailing /сэ́йлинг/ n плавание; plain ~ /плэйн ~/ (образн.) легкий путь

sailor /сэ́йлэ/ n матрос, моряк

saint /сэйнт/ n святой

sake /сэйк/ n: for God's ~ /фо годз ~/ ради Бога; for the ~ of /фо зэ ~ ов/ ради (кого-л., чего-л.)

salad /са́лэд/ n салат; ~ bowl /~ ба́ул/ салатница; ~ dressing /~ дре́синг/ заправка к салату

salary /са́лэри/ n жалованье, оклад

sale /сэйл/ n продажа; clearance ~ /кли́-эрэнс ~/ распродажа; be for ~ /би фо ~/ продаваться; bill of ~ /бил ов ~/ закладная, купчая

salesgirl /сэ́йлзгёрл/ n продавщица

salesman /сэ́йлзсмэн/ n продавец

saliva /сэлáйвэ/ n слюна

sally /сэ́ли/ n вылазка

salmon /сэ́мэн/ n лосось; семга

saloon /сэлу́ун/ n салон (автобуса, троллейбуса, самолета); бар, пивная

salt /соолт/ n соль; vt солить

salt cellar /сóолтсéлэ/ n солонка

salty /сóолти/ adj соленый

salute /сэлю́ют/ n приветствие; салют; vt приветствовать; салютовать, отдавать честь

salvage /сэ́лвидж/ n спасение имущества; vt спасать

salvation /сэлвэ́йшн/ n спасение; S. Army /~ áрми/ Армия спасения

salvo /сэ́лвоу/ n залп

same /сэйм/ adj тот же (самый), такой же; the ~ thing /зэ ~ синг/ одно и то же; all the ~ /оол зэ ~/ все равно

sample /сааmпл/ n образец; vt пробовать

sanatorium /сэнэтóориэм/ n санаторий

sanctify /сэ́нктифай/ vt освящать

sanction /сэнкшн/ n санкция; vt санкционировать

sanctuary /сэ́нкчьюэри/ n святилище; убежище

sanctum /сэ́нктэм/ n святилище; рака

sand /сэнд/ n песок; pl пляж

sand paper /сэ́ндпэ́йпэ/ n наждачная бумага

sandwich /сэ́нвидж/ n сандвич, бутерброд

sandy /сэ́нди/ adj песчаный; рыжеватый

sanitary /сэ́нитэри/ adj санитарный

sanitation /сэнитэ́йшн/ n оздоровление; санитарная профилактика

sanity /сэ́нити/ n здравомыслие; нормальная психика

Santa Claus /сэ́нтэклóоз/ n Дед Мороз

sap /сэп/ n сок; жизненные силы

sapling /сэ́плинг/ n молодое дерево

sapphire /сэ́файе/ n сапфир

sarcasm /сáркэзм/ n сарказм

sardine /сарди́ин/ n сардин(к)а

sash /сэш/ n кушак; оконная рама

sash window /сэ́швиндоу/ n подъемное окно

Satan /сэйтн/ n сатана

satchel /сэ́чел/ n ранец

sateen /сэти́ин/ n сатин

satellite /сэ́тэлайт/ n спутник; сателлит

satin /сэ́тин/ n атлас; ~ cloth /~ клос/ блестящий шерстяной материал

satire /сэ́тайе/ n сатира

satisfaction /сэ́тисфэ́кшн/ n удовлетворение

satisfactory /сэ́тисфэ́ктэри/ adj удовлетворительный

satisfy /сэ́тисфай/ vt удовлетворять

saturate /сэ́черэйт/ vt насыщать; пропитывать

Saturday /сэ́тэди/ n суббота

sauce /соос/ n соус; (разг.) нахальство

sauce-boat /сóосбóут/ n соусник

saucepan /сóоспэн/ n кастрюля

saucer /сóосэ/ n блюдце

sausage /сóсидж/ n колбаса; сосиски

savage /сэ́видж/ adj дикий; n дикарь

savagery /сэ́виджри/ n дикость, первобытность; жестокость

save /сэйв/ vt спасать, сберегать; prep кроме

savings /сэ́йвингз/ n pl сбережения; ~ bank /~ бэнк/ сберегательный банк

saviour /сэ́йвье/ n спаситель

savour /сэ́йвэ/ n вкус; привкус; аромат; vt смаковать

savoury /сэ́йвэри/ adj вкусный

saw /соо/ n пила; vt пилить

sawdust /сóодаст/ n опилки

say /сэй/ vt говорить; that is to ~ /зэт из ту ~/ то есть; I ~! /ай ~/ послушайте!; to ~ nothing of /ту ~ нáсинг ов/ не говоря уже о

saying /сэ́йинг/ n поговорка; it goes without ~ /ит гóуз визáут ~/ само собой разумеется

scabbard /скэ́бэд/ n ножны

scaffold /скэ́фэлд/ n эшафот

scaffolding /скэ́фэлдинг/ n леса

scald /скоолд/ n ожог; vt обваривать

scale /скэйл/ n масштаб, шкала; чешуя (рыбы); (муз.) гамма; pl весы; on a large ~ /он э лардж ~/ в большом масштабе; vt чистить

scalp /скэлп/ n скальп

scan /скэн/ vt бегло просматривать

scandal /скэндл/ n скандал; позор; злословие

scandalous /скэндэлос/ adj скандальный; позорный

Scandinavian /скэндинэйвьен/ n скандинав(ка); adj скандинавский

scant(y) /скэнт(и)/ adj скудный

scapegoat /скейпгоут/ n козел отпущения

scar /скар/ n рубец, шрам

scarce /скеэс/ adj редкий; скудный; дефицитный

scarcely /скеэсли/ adv едва

scarcity /скеэсити/ n нехватка; редкость

scare /скеэ/ n испуг, паника; vt пугать; ~ away /~ эвэй/ отпугивать

scarecrow /скеэкроу/ n пугало

scarf /скарф/ n шарф

scarlet /скарлит/ adj алый

scarlet fever /скарлитфийивэ/ n скарлатина

scatter /скэтэ/ vt разбрасывать; рассеивать; vi рассеиваться; расходиться

scenario /синаариоу/ n сценарий

scene /сиин/ n место действия; (театр.) сцена; зрелище; behind the ~s /бихайнд зэ ~з/ за кулисами; make a ~ /мэйк э ~/ устраивать сцену

scenery /сиинэри/ n декорации; пейзаж

scent /сент/ n запах; след; нюх; духи

sceptical /скептикл/ adj скептический

scepticism /скептисизм/ n скептицизм

sceptre /септэ/ n скипетр

schedule /шэдьюл/ n расписание; vt составлять расписание

scheme /скиим/ n схема; план; интрига; vi интриговать

schemer /скиимэ/ n интриган

schism /сизм/ n (религ.) раскол

scholar /сколэ/ n ученый

scholarship /сколэшип/ n эрудиция; стипендия

school /скуул/ n школа

school-book /скуулбук/ n учебник

schoolboy /скуулбой/ n школьник

schoolgirl /скуулгёрл/ n школьница

schoolteacher /скуултийиче/ n учитель(ница)

sciatic /сайэтик/ adj седалищный

sciatica /сайэтикэ/ n ишиас

science /сайенс/ n наука

scientific /сайентификфик/ adj научный

scientist /сайентист/ n ученый

scissors /сызэз/ n pl ножницы

sclerosis /склироусис/ n склероз

scold /сколд/ vt бранить

scoop /скууп/ n ковш, черпак; совок; vt вычерпывать

scooter /скуутэ/ n мотороллер

scope /скоуп/ n пределы; сфера; кругозор

scorch /скорч/ vt обжигать, выжигать

scorching /скорчинг/ adj палящий, знойный

score /скор/ n счет; зарубка; метка; два десятка; pl множество; settle old ~s /сетл оулд ~з/ сводить старые счеты; vi вести счет; забивать (гол)

scorn /скорн/ vt презирать

scornful /скорнфул/ adj презрительный

Scot /скот/ n шотландец, шотландка

Scotch /скоч/ adj шотландский; n (разг.) шотландское виски; ~ tape /~ тэйп/ "скотч" (склеивающая лента)

scoundrel /скаундрэл/ n негодяй, подлец

scourage /скёрдж/ n бич; vt бичевать

scout /скаут/ n разведчик; бойскаут

scowl /скаул/ n хмурый взгляд; vi хмуриться

scramble /скрэмбл/ n драка, схватка; vi карабкаться; ~d eggs /~д эгз/ яичница-болтунья

scrap /скрэп/ n клочок; металлический лом; vt отдавать в утиль; vi драться scrape /скрэйп/ vt скоблить, скрести

scrap-iron /скрэ́пáйен/ n лом черных металлов

scratch /скрэч/ n царапина; vt царапать; чесать

scream /скрим/ n вопль; vi вопить

screen /скриин/n экран; ширма; vt загораживать; демонстрировать на экране; тщательно проверять

screw /скруу/ n винт; vt завинчивать

screwdriver /скру́удрáйвэ/ n отвертка

screw nut /скру́унат/ n гайка

scribble /скрибл/ n каракули; vt писать каракулями, небрежно

script /скрипт/ n сценарий

Scripture /скри́пче/ n священное писание

scriptwriter /скри́птрайтэ/ n сценарист

scroll /скро́ул/ n свиток

scrub /скраб/ n кустарник; vt чистить щеткой

scruff /скраф/ n: take by the ~ of the neck /тэйк бай зэ ~ ов зэ нэк/ брать за шиворот

scrupulous /скру́упьюлэс/ adj скрупулезный, добросовестный

scrutinize /скру́утинайз/ vt тщательно рассматривать; проверять

scull /скал/ vi грести парными веслами

sculptor /скáлптэ/ n скульптор

sculpture /скáлпче/ n скульптура; vt ваять

scum /скам/ n пена; (образн.) негодяй

scurvy /скéрви/ n цинга; adj гнусный

scythe /сайз/ n коса; vt косить

sea /сии/ n море; be at ~ /би эт ~/ быть в полном неведении; by ~ /бай ~/ морем

sea-dog /си́идог/ n "морской волк"

seagull /си́игал/ n чайка

seal /сиил/ n печать; пломба; тюлень; морской котик; vt запечатывать, скреплять печатью

sealing wax /си́илингвэкс/ n сургуч

seam /сиим/ n шов; шрам

seaman /си́имэн/ n моряк

seamless /си́имлис/ adj без шва

search /сёрч/ n поиски, обыск; vt обыскивать; ~ for /~ фо/ искать

searchlight /сёрчлайт/ n прожектор

search warrant /сёрчвóрэнт/ n ордер на обыск

seashore /си́ишор/ n морской берег

seasick /си́исик/ adj: I always get ~ /ай óолвэз гет ~/ меня на море всегда укачивает

season /сиизн/ n время года, сезон; ~ ticket /~ ти́кит/ сезонный билет; vt приправлять (пищу)

seasoning /си́изнинг/ n приправа

seat /сиит/ n сиденье, место; стул; take a ~ /тэйк э ~/ садиться; vt усаживать

secede /сиси́ид/ vi отделяться

seclusion /сиклю́южн/ n уединение

second /сэ́кэнд/ adj второй; ~ to none /~ ту нан/ непревзойденный; n секунда; vt выступать в поддержку, голосовать за

secondary /сэ́кэндэри/ n вторичный; ~ school /~ скуул/ средняя школа

second-hand /сэ́кэндхэ́нд/ adj подержанный

secondly /сэ́кэндли/ adv во-вторых

second-rate /сэ́кэндрэ́йт/ adj второразрядный

secrecy /си́икриси/ n секретность

secret /си́икрит/ n секрет; тайна

secretary /сéкретри/ n секретарь, секретарша, министр; S. ~ of State /~ ов стэйт/ госсекретарь (США)

secretion /сикри́ишн/ n выделение, секреция

secretive /сикри́итив/ adj скрытный

sect /сект/ n секта

section /секшн/ n отдел; секция; купе

secular /сéкьюлэ/ adj мирской, светский

secure /сикью́оэ/ adj безопасный; уверенный; vt доставать, обеспечивать

security /сикью́оэрити/ n безопасность; social ~ /сóушл ~/ социальное обеспечение; pl ценные бумаги

sedative /сéдэтив/ n успокаивающее средство

seduce /сидью́юс/ vt обольщать

seducer /сидью́юсэ/ n соблазнитель

see /сии/ vt видеть; понимать; ~ into /~ и́нту/ изучать, разбираться; ~ off /~ оф/ провожать; ~ you later! /~ ю лэ́йтэ/ до встречи!; I ~ /ай ~/ понятно; let me ~ /лет ми ~/ дай(те) подумать

seed /сиид/ n семя, зерно; vt сеять; (спорт.) отбирать более сильных участников соревнования

seedling /си́идлинг/ n сеянец

seek /сиик/ vt искать; добиваться

seem /сиим/ vt казаться; it ~s he is right /ит ~з хи из райт/ похоже, что он прав

seemingly /си́имингли/ adv по-видимому

segment /сэ́гмент/ n отрезок, часть

segregation /сэ́григе́йшн/ n сегрегация

seize /сииз/ vt хватать, схватывать

seldom /сэ́лдэм/ adv редко

select /силе́кт/ adj избранный; vt отбирать

selection /силе́кшн/ n выбор; natural ~ /нэ́чрэл ~/ естественный отбор

self /сэлф/ n сущность (человека); be one's own ~ /би ванз о́ун ~/ быть самим собой; ~ comes first /~ камз фёрст/ своя рубашка ближе к телу; pron сам; себя; свое

self-confidence /сэ́лфко́нфидэнс/ n самоуверенность

self-control /сэ́лфкэнтро́ул/ n самообладание

self-defence /сэ́лфдифе́нс/ n самооборона

self-denial /сэ́лфдина́йл/ n самоотречение

self-esteem /сэ́лфисти́им/ n чувство собственного достоинства

self-government /сэ́лфга́внмент/ n самоуправление

selfish /сэ́лфиш/ adj эгоистичный

self-made /сэ́лфмэ́йд/ adj обязанный всем самому себе

self-portrait /сэ́лфпо́отрит/ n автопортрет

self-service /сэ́лфсёрвис/ n самообслуживание

self-willed /сэ́лфви́лд/ adj своевольный

sell /сэл/ vti продавать(ся); ~ off /~ оф/ распродавать (со скидкой)

seller /сэ́лэ/ n продавец

semblance /сэ́мблэнс/ n вид, видимость

semester /симе́стэ/ n семестр

semi- /сэ́ми/ prefix полу-, наполовину

semicircle /сэ́мисёркл/ n полукруг

semicolon /сэ́мико́улэн/ n точка с запятой

semi-conductor /сэ́микэнда́ктэ/ n полупроводник

semolina /сэ́мэли́инэ/ n манная крупа

senate /сэ́нит/ n сенат

senator /сэ́нэтэ/ n сенатор

send /сенд/ vt посылать, отправлять

sender /сэ́ндэ/ n отправитель

senile /си́инайл/ adj старческий

senior /си́инье/ adj старший; John Brown ~ /джон бра́ун ~/ Джон Браун старший; n пожилой человек; вышестоящий; студент старшего курса

sensation /сенсэ́йшн/ n ощущение; сенсация

sensational /сенсэ́йшнл/ adj сенсационный

sense /сенс/ n ощущение; чувство; смысл; in a ~ /ин э ~/ в известном смысле; talk ~ /тоок ~/ говорить дело; vt ощущать

senseless /сэ́нслис/ adj бессмысленный, бесчувственный

sensible /сэ́нсибл/ adj (благо)разумный

sensitive /сэ́нситив/ adj чувствительный; чуткий

sensual /сэ́нсьюэл/ adj чувственный; плотский

sentence /сэ́нтэнс/ n приговор; (грам.) предложение; vt приговаривать

sentiment /сэ́нтимент/ n чувство

sentimental /сэ́нтиме́нтл/ adj сентиментальный

sentinel, sentry /сэ́нтинл, сэ́нтри/ n часовой

separate /сэ́прит/ adj отдельный; уединенный; /сэ́пэрэйт/ vt отделять; разлучать; vi расходиться separately /сéпритли/ adv отдельно

separation /сéпэрэйшн/ n отделение

September /септэ́мбэ/ n сентябрь

sequel /сийквэл/ n продолжение (книги, фильма); последствие

sequence /сийквэнс/ n последовательность, порядок следования

Serb /сёрб/ n серб, сербка

Serbian /сёрбьен/ n серб, сербка; сербский язык; adj сербский

serene /сирийин/ adj спокойный, ясный

serf /сёрф/ n крепостной

serfdom /сёрфдэм/ n крепостное право

serge /сёрдж/ n саржа

sergeant /са́рджент/ n сержант

serial /сийэриэл/ adj серийный; n роман, фильм в нескольких частях

series /сийэриз/ n серия, ряд

serious /сийэриэс/ adj серьезный

seriously /сийэриэсли/ adv серьезно

sermon /сёрмэн/ n проповедь

serpent /сёрпент/ n змея

servant /сёрвэнт/ n слуга, прислуга; civil~ /сивил ~/ государственный служащий

serve /сёрв/ vt служить; подавать (еду); отбывать срок (службы, наказания); vi подавать мяч; it~s him right! /ит~з хим райт/ так ему и надо!

service /сёрвис/ n служба; обслуживание; сервиз; подача; active /э́ктив ~/ действительная военная служба; at your ~ /эт йо ~/ к вашим услугам

serviceman /сёрвисмэн/ n военнослужащий

serviette /сёрвиэ́т/ n салфетка

session /сэшн/ n сессия; заседание

set /сэт/ n комплект; декорация; сет; сервиз; аппарат; vt ставить; вставлять в оправу; (полигр.) набирать; vi садиться (о солнце); ~ aside /~ эсáйд/ откладывать; ~ forth /~ форс/ излагать; ~ out /~ áут/ отправляться; ~ right /~ райт/ исправлять; ~ up /~ ап/ учреждать

settle /сэтл/ vt поселять; решать; улаживать; оплачивать (счета); ~ down /~ дáун/ поселяться

settlement /сэ́тлмент/ n поселение; расчет

settler /сэ́тлэ/ n поселенец

seven /сэвн/ num семь; n семерка

seventeen /сэ́внтийин/ num семнадцать

seventeenth /сэ́внтийинс/ ord num семнадцатый

seventh /сэвнс/ ord num седьмой; n седьмая часть

seventieth /сэ́внтис/ ord num семидесятый

seventy /сэ́внти/ num семьдесят

several /сэврл/ adj несколько

severe /сивиэ́/ adj строгий, суровый

sew /сóу/ vt шить; ~ on /~ он/ пришивать

sewer /съюэ́/ n канализационная труба

sewerage /съюэридж/ n канализация

sewing /сóуинг/ n шитье

sewing machine /сóуингмэшúин/ n швейная машина

sex /сэкс/ n пол, секс; the fair ~ /зэ фээ ~/ прекрасный пол

sexual /сэ́кшюэл/ adj половой, сексуальный

shabby /шэ́би/ adj потрепанный, оборванный, жалкий

shack /шэк/ n лачуга

shackles /шэклз/ n pl кандалы

shade /шэйд/ n тень; оттенок; абажур; vt заслонять (от света), затенять

shadow /шэ́доу/ n тень, сумерки; vt затенять, выслеживать

shadowy /шэ́доуи/ adj тенистый

shady /шэ́йди/ adj тенистый; (образн.) сомнительный

shaft /шаафт/ n древко (копья); оглобля; (тех.) вал

shag /шэг/ n (грубый) ворс; махорка

shaggy /шэ́ги/ adj лохматый; грубый, невежливый

shake /шэйк/ vt трясти; vi сотрясаться, дрожать; vt: ~ hands /~ хэндз/ пожимать руки

shall /шэл/ v: I (we) ~ go /ай (ви) ~ róy/
я (мы) пойду (пойдем); you (he, she,
you, they) ~ go /ю (хи, ши, ю, зэй) ~
róy/ ты (он, она, вы, они) должен
(должен, должна, должны) пойти
shallow /шэ́лоу/ adj мелкий; поверхностный, пустой
shallow(s) /шэ́лоу(з)/ n мель, отмель
sham /шэм/ n подделка; притворство; adj
притворный; vi притворяться
shame /шэйм/ n стыд, позор; ~ on you! /~
он ю/ стыдно!; what a ~ /вот э ~/ какая
досада; vt стыдить
shamefaced /шэ́ймфейст/ adj стыдливый
shameful /шэ́ймфул/ adj постыдный
shameless /шэ́ймлис/ adj бесстыдный
shampoo /шэмпу́у/ n шампунь; vt мыть
голову
shape /шэйп/ n форма; очертание; облик; vt придавать форму
shapeless /шэ́йплис/ adj бесформенный
shapely /шэ́йпли/ adj хорошо сложенный
share /шээ/ n доля; акция; пай; лемех; vt
делить; совместно владеть; ~ a room /~
э руум/ жить в одной комнате
shareholder /шэ́эхо́улдэ/ n акционер
shark /шарк/ n акула
sharp /шарп/ adj острый; крутой (поворот); резкий (боль); колкий (замечание); adv точно; four o'clock ~ /фор о
клок ~/ ровно четыре часа
sharpen /ша́рпэн/ vt точить
shatter /шэ́тэ/ vti разбивать(ся) вдребезги
shave /шэйв/ vti брить(ся)
shaver /шэ́йвэ/ n бритва
shawl /шоол/ n шаль
she /ши/ pron она; n женщина; самка
sheaf /шииф/ n сноп; связка, пачка
shear /шиэ/ vt стричь
shears /шииэз/ n pl ножницы
sheath /шииф/ n ножны; футляр
she-bear /шии́бе́э/ n медведица
shed /шед/ n сарай, навес; vt ронять (ли-
стья); проливать (слезы); сбрасывать
(одежду)

sheep /шиип/ n овца
sheep-dog /ши́ипдо́г/ n овчарка
sheepish /ши́ипиш/ adj застенчивый
sheepskin /ши́ипскин/ n дубленка
sheer /шиэ́/ adj отвесный; абсолютный;
сущий; by ~ force /бай ~ форс/ одной
только силой
sheet /шиит/ n простыня; лист (бумаги,
металла)
sheet-lightning /ши́итла́йтнинг/ n зарница
shelf /шелф/ n полка; шельф, отмель
shell /шел/ n раковина; скорлупа (оре-
ха); снаряд; vt чистить, снимать скор-
лупу
shellfish /ше́лфиш/ n моллюск
shelter /ше́лтэ/ n приют, убежище, укрытие; vt приютить, служить убежи-
щем
shelve /шелв/ vt ставить на полку; откладывать в долгий ящик
shepherd /ше́пед/ n пастух
sheriff /ше́риф/ n шериф
sherry /ше́ри/ n херес
shield /шиилд/ n щит; vt защищать
shift /шифт/ n изменение, смена; vti пе-
ремещать(ся); ~ the blame on to /~ зэ
блэйм он ту/ сваливать вину на
shilling /ши́линг/ n шиллинг
shin /шин/ n голень
shine /шайн/ n свет; сияние; блеск; vi
блестеть, светить(ся), сиять
shingle /шингл/ n кровельная дранка
shiny /ша́йни/ adj блестящий; лосня-
щийся
ship /шип/ n корабль, судно
ship boy /ши́пбой/ n юнга
shipment /ши́пмент/ n груз, партия (от-
правленного товара, погрузка, отправка)
shipper /ши́пэ/ n грузоотправитель
shipshape /ши́пшэйп/ adj аккуратный,
опрятный
shipwreck /ши́прек/ n кораблекрушение; suffer ~ /са́фэ ~/ потерпеть кораблекрушение

shipyard /ши́пъярд/ n верфь

shirt /шёрт/ n рубашка

shiver /ши́вэ/ n дрожь; vi дрожать

shock /шок/ n потрясение, шок; удар; vt потрясать, шокировать

shoe /шуу/ n ботинок; туфля; подкова; vt обувать, подковывать

shoeblack /шу́ублэк/ n чистильщик сапог

shoehorn /шу́ухорн/ n рожок для обуви

shoelace /шу́улэйс/ n шнурок для ботинок

shoemaker /шу́умэ́йкэ/ n сапожник

shoe polish/шу́упо́лиш/ n крем для чистки обуви

shoot /шуут/ n росток; состязание в стрельбе; vt стрелять; расстреливать; снимать (фильм); ~ down /~ да́ун/ сбивать

shooter /шу́утэ/ n стрелок

shop /шоп/ n магазин, лавка; цех; vi делать покупки

shop-assistant /шо́пэси́стэнт/ n продавец, продавщица

shopkeeper /шо́пки́ипэ/ n лавочник

shoplifting /шо́пли́фтинг/ n мелкое воровство в магазине

shopper /шо́пэ/ n покупатель

shopping /шо́пинг/ n закупка продуктов; go ~ /го́у ~/ делать покупки

shop window/шо́пви́ндоу/ n витрина

shore /шор/ n берег

short /шорт/ adj короткий; низкого роста; cut ~ /кат ~/ прерывать; fall ~ /фоол ~/ не хватать; I am ~ of money /ай эм ~ ов ма́ни/ у меня не хватает денег; in ~ /ин ~/ вкратце

shortage /шо́ртыдж/ n нехватка, дефицит

shortbread /шо́ртбрэ́д/ n песочное печенье

short-circuit /шо́ртсёркит/ n короткое замыкание

shortcoming /шотка́минг/ n недостаток

shorten /шортн/ vti укорачивать(ся), сокращать(ся)

shorthand /шо́ртхэнд/ n стенография; ~ typist /~ та́йпист/ машинистка-стенографистка

shortly /шо́ртли/ adv вскоре

shorts /шортс/ n pl шорты

shortsighted /шо́ртса́йтыд/ adj близорукий; недальновидный

short story /шо́ртсто́ри/ n рассказ

shot /шот/ n выстрел; удар; бросок; стрелок; ядро

shot silk /шо́тси́лк/ n переливчатый шелк

should /шюд/ v aux: I ~ go /ай ~ го́у/ я должен идти; it ~ be fun /ит ~ би фан/ это должно быть забавно

shoulder /шо́улдэ/ n плечо

shoulder-blade /шо́улдэблэ́йд/ n (анат.) лопатка

shout /ша́ут/ n крик; vi кричать

shove /шав/ vt толкать

shovel /шавл/ n лопата, совок; vt копать, сгребать

show /шо́у/ n показ; зрелище; киносеанс; спектакль; выставка; good ~! /гуд ~/ здорово!; vt показывать; ~ off /~ оф/ щеголять

showcase /шо́укейс/ n витрина

shower /ша́уэ/ n ливень; град; душ; vt лить; осыпать; vi литься; сыпаться

shred /шред/ n клочок, лоскуток; vt кромсать

shrew /шруу/ n сварливая женщина

shrewd /шрууд/ adj проницательный

shriek /шриик/ n пронзительный крик; vi пронзительно кричать, визжать

shrill /шрил/ adj пронзительный

shrimp /шримп/ n креветка

shrine /шрайн/ n святыня

shrink /шринк/ vi садиться (об одежде); уменьшаться

shrivel /шривл/ vi съеживаться

Shrovetide /шро́увтайд/ n масленица

shrub /шраб/ n куст

shrubbery /шра́бери/ n кустарник

shrug /шраг/ vt: ~ one's shoulders /~ ванз шо́улдэз/ пожимать плечами

shudder /ша́дэ/ n содрогание; vi содрогаться
shuffle /шафл/ vt тасовать (карты); шар-
кать (ногами)
shun /шан/ vt избегать
shut /шат/ vti закрывать (ся), затворять (ся); ~ off /~ оф/ выключать (воду
и т.д.); ~ up! /~ ап/ заткнись!
shutter /ша́тэ/ n ставень; задвижка; (фото) затвор объектива
shuttle /шатл/ n челнок; воздушный автобус; космический корабль многора-
зового использования
shy /шай/ adj застенчивый, робкий
shyness /ша́йнис/ n застенчивость
Siberian /сайби́эриэн/ n сибиряк, сиби-
рячка; adj сибирский
Sicilian /сиси́льен/ n житель Сицилии;
adj сицилийский
sick /сик/ adj больной; I feel ~ /ай фиил
~/ меня тошнит; I am ~ of it /ай эм ~ ов
ит/ мне это надоело
sicken /сикн/ vt вызывать тошноту
sickening /си́книнг/ adj тошнотворный
sickle /сикл/ n серп
sick leave /си́клиив/ n отпуск по болезни
sickly /си́кли/ adj болезненный; тошнотворный
sickness /си́книс/ n болезнь, тошнота
side /сайд/ n сторона; бок; борт; ~ by ~
/~ бай ~/ бок о бок; on all ~s /он оол ~з/
со всех сторон; vi: ~ with /~ виз/ быть
на стороне
side-track /са́йдтрэк/ n запасной путь
side-view /са́йдвью/ n профиль
siege /сиидж/ n осада
sieve /сив/ n решето, сито
sift /сифт/ vt просеивать
sigh /сай/ n вздох; vi вздыхать
sight /сайт/ n зрение; вид; зрелище; at the
~ of /эт зэ ~ ов/ при виде; at first ~ /эт
фёрст ~/ с первого взгляда; in ~ /ин ~/ в
поле зрения; know by ~ /но́у бай ~/ знать
в лицо; loose ~ of /лууз ~ ов/ терять из
виду; see the ~s /сии зэ ~с/ осматривать
достопримечательности; vt увидеть

sign /сайн/ n знак; признак; символ, значение; vti подписывать (ся)
signal /си́гнл/ n сигнал; vti сигнализиро-
вать
signature /си́гниче/ n подпись; (полигр.)
печатный лист
sign-board /са́йнборд/ n вывеска
significance /сигни́фикэнс/ n важность,
значение
sign-post /са́йнпоуст/ n указательный
столб
significant /сигни́фикэнт/ adj значительный
silence /са́йлэнс/ n молчание, тишина;
interj тише!; vt заставить замолчать
silencer /са́йлэнсэ/ n глушитель
silent /са́йлэнт/ adj молчаливый; тихий;
~ film /~ филм/ немой фильм; be
(keep) ~ /би (киип) ~/ молчать
silk /силк/ n шелк; adj шелковый
silky /си́лки/ adj шелковистый
sill /сил/ n подоконник; порог (двери)
silliness /си́линис/ n глупость
silly /си́ли/ adj глупый
silver /си́лвэ/ n серебро; vt серебрить; adj
серебряный
silver fox /си́лвэфокс/ n чернобурая лисица
silverware /си́лвэвэ́э/ n столовое серебро
similar /си́милэ/ adj подобный, сходный
similarity /си́миля́рити/ n сходство
similarly /си́милэли/ adv так же
simmer /си́мэ/ vi закипать; кипеть (на
медленном огне)
simple /симпл/ adj простой
simplicity /симпли́сити/ n простота
simplify /си́мплифай/ vt упрощать
simply /си́мпли/ adv просто
simulate /си́мьюлэйт/ vt симулировать
simultaneous /си́млтэ́йньес/ adj одновременный
sin /син/ n грех; vi грешить
since /синс/ adv с тех пор, тому назад; с
тех пор как; так как; long ~ /лонг ~/
давно

sincere /синси́э/ adj искренний

sincerity /синсэ́рити/ n искренность

sinew /си́нью/ n сухожилие

sing /синг/ vti петь; ~ of /~ ов/ воспевать; ~ out of tune /~ áут ов тьююн/ фальши́вить

singe /синж/ n ожог

singer /си́нгэ/ n певец, певица

singing /си́нгинг/ n пение; ~ bird /~ бёрд/ певчая птица

single /сингл/ adj один, единственный; отдельный; холостой; ~ bed /~ бед/ односпальная кровать; ~-breasted /~ брéстыд/ однобортный; ~ room /~ рум/ комната на одного человека; ~-ticket /~ ти́кит/ билет в один конец; vt: ~ out /~ áут/ выделять

singleness /си́нглнис/ n: ~ of purpose /~ ов пёрпэс/ целеустремленность

singlet /си́нглит/ n фуфайка

singly /си́нгли/ adv отдельно, поодиночке

singular /си́нгъюлэ/ n (грам.) единственное число; adj необыкновенный, странный

sinister /си́нистэ/ adj зловещий

sink /синк/ n (кухонная) раковина; vt топить (корабль); vi погружаться, заходить (о солнце)

sinner /си́нэ/ n грешник

sip /сип/ n маленький глоток; vt пить маленькими глотками, потягивать

sir /сёр/ n сэр, господин, сударь

siren /сáйерин/ n сирена (также миф.)

sirloin /сёрлойн/ n филей

sister /си́стэ/ n сестра

sister-in-law /си́стэринлóо/ n невестка, золовка, свояченица

sit /сит/ vi сидеть; ~ down /~ дáун/ садиться

site /сайт/ n местоположение; участок; строительная площадка

sitting /си́тинг/ n заседание

situated /си́тьюэ́йтыд/ adj расположенный

situation /си́тьюэ́йшн/ n ситуация; место (работы); расположение

six /сикс/ num шесть

sixteen /си́ксти́ин/ num шестнадцать

sixteenth /си́ксти́инс/ ord num шестнадцатый

sixth /сикс/ ord num шестой; n шестая часть

sixtieth /си́кстис/ ord num шестидесятый

sixty /си́ксти/ num шестьдесят

size /сайз/ n размер, величина; объем; формат; номер (перчаток и т.п.)

skate /скейт/ n конек; vi кататься на коньках

skater /скéйтэ/ n конькобежец

skating rink /скéйтингринк/ n каток

skeleton /скéлитн/ n скелет; остов; каркас

sketch /скетч/ n набросок; эскиз; (театр.) скетч

ski /скии/ n лыжа; vi ходить на лыжах

skier /скии́э/ n лыжник

skid /скид/ vi буксовать, скользить; the car ~ed /зэ кар ~ыд/ машину занесло

skilful /ски́лфул/ adj умелый

skill /скил/ n мастерство, умение

skilled /скилд/ adj квалифицированный

skim /ским/ vt снимать (пенки, сливки с молока)

skin /скин/ n кожа; шкура (животного); кожура (фрукта); vt сдирать кожу, шкуру, кожуру

skinner /ски́нэ/ n скорняк

skinny /ски́ни/ adj тощий

skip /скип/ n прыжок; vi скакать; vt пропускать

skipper /ски́пэ/ n шкипер, капитан

skipping rope /ски́пингрóуп/ n скакалка

skirmish /скéрмиш/ n стычка

skirt /скёрт/ n юбка

skull /скал/ n череп

skunk /сканк/ n скунс; (перен.) подлец

sky /скай/ n небо

skylark /скáйлак/ n жаворонок

skyline /скáйлайн/ n горизонт

skyscraper /скáйскрэ́йпэ/ n небоскреб

slab /слэб/ n кусок; плита

slack /слэк/ adj замедленный; слабый; вялый; небрежный

slacks /слэкс/ n pl брюки

slam /слэм/ vt хлопать (дверью)

slander /сла́андэ/ n клевета; vt клеветать

slang /слэнг/ n жаргон

slant /слаант/ n склон, уклон

slanting /сла́антинг/ adj наклонный, косой

slap /слэп/ n шлепок; ~ in the face /~ ин зэ фейс/ пощечина; vt шлепать

slash /слэш/ n удар сплеча, разрез; vt хлестать

slate /слэйт/ n шифер; vt крыть шифером; дать нагоняй

slaughter /сло́отэ/ n резня; убой (скота); vt резать, убивать

slaughter-house /сло́отэха́ус/ n бойня

Slav /слаав/ n славянин, славянка; adj славянский

slave /слэйв/ n раб

slavery /слэ́йвэри/ n рабство

Slavonic /слэво́ник/ adj славянский

slay /слэй/ vt убивать

sledge /следж/ n сани, санки

sleek /слиик/ adj гладкий, прилизанный

sleep /слиип/ n сон; ~ walker /~ во́окэ/ лунатик; go to ~ /го́у ту ~/ засыпать; vi спать; ~ like a dog /~ лайк э дог/ спать как убитый

sleeper /сли́ипэ/ n спальный вагон

sleeping /сли́ипинг/ adj спящий

sleeping-draught /сли́ипингдрафт/ n снотворное

sleeping pills /сли́ипингпилз/ n снотворные таблетки

sleepless /сли́иплис/ adj бессонный

sleeplessness /сли́иплиснис/ n бессоница

sleepy /сли́ипи/ adj сонный

sleet /слиит/ n дождь со снегом

sleeve /слиив/ n рукав

sleigh /слей/ n сани; ~ bell /~ бел/ бубенчик

slender /сле́ндэ/ adj стройный; скудный

slice /слайс/ n ломтик, ломоть; vt резать ломтиками; (спорт.) среза́ть (мяч)

slide /слайд/ n слайд; скольжение; ледяная дорожка; vi скользить; кататься с горки

sliding /сла́йдинг/ adj скользящий; ~ door /~ доор/ раздвижная дверь

slight /слайт/ adj легкий, незначительный; тонкий; vt третировать, обижать

slightly /сла́йтли/ adv слегка

slim /слим/ adj стройный; vi худеть

slime /слайм/ n тина, слизь

sling /слинг/ n канат; строп; рогатка; vt метать, швырять

slip /слип/ n скольжение; ошибка; лифчик; длинная узкая полоска; ~ of the pen /~ ов зэ пен/ описка; ~ of the tongue /~ ов зэ танг/ оговорка; vi скользить; ~ away /~ эвэ́й/ ускользать

slipper /сли́пэ/ n комнатная туфля

slippery /сли́пэри/ adj скользкий

slit /слит/ n щель; (продольный) разрез

slogan /сло́угэн/ n лозунг

slope /сло́уп/ n наклон; косогор; откос; vt наклонить; vi иметь наклон

sloping /сло́упинг/ adj отлогий

sloppy /сло́пи/ adj мокрый; грязный; неряшливый

slot /слот/ n прорез, щель

slot machine /сло́тмэши́ин/ n торговый автомат

Slovak /сло́увэк/ n словак, словачка; adj словацкий

sloven /славн/ n неряха; adj необразованный

slow /сло́у/ adj медленный; тупой; the watch is ~ /зэ вотч из ~/ часы отстают; vti ~ down /~ да́ун/ замедлять (ся)

slowly /сло́ули/ adv медленно

sluice /слуус/ n шлюз

slum /слам/ n трущоба

slump /сламп/ n резкое падение (цен и т.п.)

slush /слаш/ n слякоть

slushy /сла́ши/ adj слякотный

sly /слай/ adj лукавый; хитрый; on the ~ /он зэ ~/ тайком

smack /смэк/ n шлепок; чмоканье; привкус

small /смоол/ adj маленький; look ~ /лук ~/ иметь глупый вид

small change /смо́олчейндж/ n мелочь

small fry /смо́олфра́й/ n мальки; мелюзга; (пренебр.) мелкая сошка

smallpox /смо́олпокс/ n оспа

smart /смарт/ adj модный; быстрый; остроумный; n резкая боль; vi вызывать жгучую боль

smartness /сма́ртнис/ n нарядность; изящество; ловкость; остроумие

smash /смэш/ vt разбить вдребезги, разгромить

smashing /смэ́шинг/ adj сокрушительный; (разг.) сногсшибательный; решительный; отличный; потрясающий

smear /сми́э/ n пятно; клевета; vt мазать, пачкать; (разг.) порочить

smell /смел/ n запах; обоняние; нюх; vt нюхать, почуять; vi пахнуть

smile /смайл/ n улыбка; vi улыбаться

smith /смис/ n кузнец

smithy /сми́зи/ n кузница

smoke /смо́ук/ n дым; vt курить; коптить; vi дымить (ся)

smoker /смо́укэ/ n курящий; вагон для курящих

smoking /смо́укинг/ n курение; no ~ /но́у ~/ курить воспрещается

smooth /смууз/ adj гладкий, ровный, плавный; vt приглаживать, делать ровным

smoothly /сму́узли/ adv гладко, плавно

smother /сма́зэ/ vt душить, подавлять

smoulder /смо́улдэ/ vi тлеть

smuggle /смагл/ vt заниматься контрабандой

smuggler /сма́глэ/ n контрабандист

snack /снэк/ n закуска; ~ bar /~ бар/ закусочная, буфет

snail /снэйл/ n улитка

snake /снэйк/ n змея

snap /снэп/ n щелканье, треск; щеколда; cold ~ /ко́улд ~/ резкое похолодание; vt хватать, кусать; щелкать, защелкивать, снимать; ~ at /~ эт/ огрызаться на

snapdragon /снэ́пдрэ́гэн/ n львиный зев

snapshot /снэ́пшот/ n моментальный снимок

snare /снэ́э/ n ловушка; vt поймать в ловушку

snarl /снарл/ n рычание; vi рычать

snatch /снэтч/ vt хватать, схватывать

sneak /сниик/ n подлец; воришка; vi красться; ябедничать; ~ away /~ эвэ́й/ ускользать

sneakers /сни́икэз/ n pl тапочки

sneer /сни́э/ n усмешка; насмешка; vi насмехаться

sneeze /снииз/ n чиханье; vi чихать

snooze /снууз/ vi вздремнуть

snore /снор/ n храп; vi храпеть

snort /снорт/ n фырканье; vi фыркать

snout /сна́ут/ n рыло, морда

snow /сно́у/ n снег; vi: it ~s /ит ~з/ идет снег

snowball /сно́убол/ n снежок

snowdrop /сно́удроп/ n подснежник

snowfall /сно́уфол/ n снегопад

snowflake /сно́уфлэйк/ n снежинка

snowman /сно́умэн/ n снежная баба

snow-plough /сно́уплау/ n снегоочиститель

snowstorm /сно́усторм/ n вьюга, буран

snowy /сно́уи/ adj снежный

snug /снаг/ adj уютный

so /со́у/ adv так, таким образом; настолько; итак; conj поэтому; ~-called /~ коолд/ так называемый; ~ long! /~ лонг/ пока!; and ~ on /энд ~ он/ и так далее; if ~ /иф ~/ в таком случае; ~ and ~ /~ энд ~/ такой-то; ~~ так себе; a month or ~ /э манс о ~/ около месяца

soak /со́ук/ vt намачивать, промачивать; vi пропитываться; I am ~ing wet /ай эм ~инг вет/ я промок до нитки

soap /со́уп/ n мыло; vt намыливать

soar /сор/ vi парить; взмывать; планировать

sob /соб/ n рыдание; vi рыдать

sober /со́убэ/ adj трезвый; vti отрезвлять(ся)

soccer /со́кэ/ n футбол

sociable /со́ушебл/ adj общительный

social /со́ушл/ adj общественный, социальный; n вечеринка

socialism /со́ушелизм/ n социализм

society /сэса́йети/ n общество; светское общество; ассоциация

sock /сок/ n носок

socket /со́кит/ n углубление; гнездо; (глазная) впадина; патрон (лампочки); (штепсельная) розетка

sod /сод/ n дерн

soda /со́удэ/ n сода; ~ water /~ во́отэ/ содовая вода

sofa /со́уфэ/ n диван, софа

soft /софт/ adj мягкий, тихий (звук); ~ drinks /~ дринкс/ безалкогольные напитки

soften /софн/ vti смягчать(ся)

softness /со́фтнис/ n мягкость

soil /сойл/ n почва; native /нэ́йтив ~/ родина

sojourn /со́джёрн/ n временное пребывание

solar /со́улэ/ adj солнечный

solder /со́лдэ/ vt паять

soldier /со́улдже/ n солдат

sole /со́ул/ adj единственный; n подошва, подметка (ботинка)

solely /со́ули/ adv исключительно

solemn /со́лэм/ adj торжественный

solemnity /сэле́мнити/ n торжество

solicit /сэли́сит/ vt выпрашивать; ходатайствовать о; приставать к; no ~ing /но́у ~инг/ не попрошайничать

solicitation /сэлиситэ́йшн/ n ходатайство, приставание

solicitor /сэли́ситэ/ n адвокат, стряпчий

solid /со́лид/ adj твердый; солидный; сплошной

solidarity /со́лидэ́рити/ n солидарность

solidity /сэли́дити/ n твердость; плотность

solitary /со́литри/ adj одинокий; ~ confinement /~ кэнфа́йнмент/ одиночное заключение

solitude /со́литьюд/ n одиночество

solo /со́улоу/ n соло

soloist /со́улоист/ n солист

soluble /со́льюбл/ adj растворимый; разрешимый

solution /сэлю́юшн/ n раствор; решение

solve /солв/ vt решать

solvent /солвнт/ adj платежеспособный; n растворитель

somber /со́мбэ/ adj мрачный

some /сам/ adj какой-либо, какой-нибудь, какой-то, несколько; indef pron некоторые; одни, другие; ~ of them /~ ов зэм/ некоторые из них; ~ time ago /~ тайм эго́у/ недавно; ~ two thousand men /~ туу са́узэнд мен/ около двух тысяч человек

somebody (someone) /са́мбэди (са́мван)/ indef pron кто-нибудь, кто-то; be ~ /би ~/ быть важной персоной

somehow /са́мхау/ adv как-нибудь, как-то; почему-то

somersault /са́мэсолт/ vi кувыркаться

something /са́мсинг/ indef pron что-либо, что-нибудь, что-то; нечто; кое-что; else /~ элс/ что-то другое

sometime /са́мтайм/ adv когда-нибудь, когда-то, некогда

sometimes /са́мтаймз/ adv иногда

somewhat /са́мвот/ adv слегка, немного

somewhere /са́мвээ/ adv где-нибудь, где-то; куда-нибудь, куда-то; ~ else /~ элс/ где-то в другом месте

son /сан/ n сын

song /сонг/ n песня

son-in-law /са́нинло́о/ n зять

soon /суун/ adv вскоре, скоро; рано; as ~ as /эз ~ эз/ как только; as ~ as possible /эз ~ эз по́сэбл/ как можно скорее; ~er or later /~э о лэ́йтэ/ рано или поздно soot /сут/ n сажа, копоть

soothe /сууз/ vt успокаивать

soothsayer /су́уссэ́йе/ n прорицатель

sophisticated /сэфи́стикейтыд/ adj утонченный; умудренный опытом

sorcerer /со́осрэ/ n колдун

sorceress /со́осрис/ n колдунья

sorcery /со́осри/ n колдовство

sore /сор/ adj больной; I've got a ~ throat
/айв гот э ~ сро́ут/ у меня болит горло;
~ spot /~ спот/ болевая точка

sorrow /со́роу/ n горе, печаль, скорбь; vi
горевать

sorrowful /со́рэфул/ adj печальный

sorry /со́ри/ adj сожалеющий; ~ sight /~
сайт/ жалкое зрелище; be ~ /би ~/
(со)жалеть; I am so ~ for them /ай эм
со́у ~ фо зэм/ мне так их жаль; I am ~!
/ай эм ~/ простите!, виноват!

sort /сорт/ n сорт; вид; род; ~ of /~ ов/
как будто; vt сортировать

sot /сот/ n горький пьяница

sought-after /со́отáфтэ/ adj популярный

soul /со́ул/ n душа; upon my ~ /эпо́н май
~/ честное слово

soulless /со́улис/ adj бездушный

sound /са́унд/ n звук; (мор.) узкий залив; (мед.) зонд; adj здоровый, крепкий, прочный; ~ barrier /~ бэ́риэ/
звуковой барьер; safe and ~ /сэйф энд
~/ цел и невридим; vi звучать; выслушивать, зондировать (также перен.)

soup /сууп/ n суп; in the ~ /ин зэ ~/ в
пиковом положении

soup-plate /су́упплэйт/ n глубокая тарелка

sour /са́уэ/ adj кислый (также перен.);
turn ~ /тёрн ~/ прокисать; ~ milk /~
милк/ простокваша

source /соос/ n источник (также перен.)

south /са́ус/ n юг; adj южный; ~-east /~
иист/ юго-восток; ~-west /~ вэст/ юго-
запад

southerly /са́зэли/, southern /са́зэн/ adj
южный

southerner /са́зэнэ/ n южанин, южанка

southward /са́усвэд/ adv к югу, на юг

souvenir /су́увниэ/ n сувенир

sovereign /со́врин/ adj монарх; соверен
(монета); adj суверенный

sovereignty /со́вренти/ n суверенитет

Soviet /со́вьет/ adj советский; n совет

sow /са́у/ n свинья

sow /со́у/ vt сеять, засевать

soybean /со́йбин/ n соя; соевый боб

spa /спаа/ n курорт

space /спейс/ n пространство; космос;
расстояние; промежуток (также о времени); adj космический; ~ rocket /~
ро́кит/ космическая ракета

spacious /спэ́йшес/ adj просторный

spade /спейд/ n лопата; pl (карты) пики;
call a ~ a ~ /коол э ~ э ~/ называть вещи
своими именами

span /спэн/ n расстояние; промежуток;
пролет (моста)

Spaniard /спэ́ньед/ n испанец, испанка

Spanish /спэ́ниш/ n испанский язык; adj
испанский

spank /спэнк/ vt шлепать; n шлепок

sparse /спарс/ adj редкий, неплотный

spare /спээ/ adj запасной, резервный; ~
time /~ тайм/ свободное время; ~ wheel
/~ виил/ запасное колесо; vt щадить;
уделять (время); enough and to ~
/ина́ф энд ту ~/ более, чем достаточно

spark /спарк/ n искра; vi искриться; ~ing
plug /~ инг плаг/ запальная свеча

sparkle /спаркл/ vi сверкать

sparrow /спэ́роу/ n воробей

spasm /спэзм/ n спазм

spatter /спэ́тэ/ vt брызгать

speak /спиик/ vti говорить; so to ~ /со́у ту
~/ так сказать

speaker /спи́икэ/ n оратор; диктор (радио)

spear /спи́э/ n копье

special /спешл/ adj специальный; особенный; экстренный; ~ delivery /~ ди-
ли́ври/ срочная доставка

specialist /спе́шелист/ n специалист

speciality /спе́шиэ́лити/ n специальность

specialize /спе́шелайз/ vi специализироваться

specially /спе́шели/ adv специально

specific /списи́фик/ adj специфический

specification /спе́сификейшн/ n спецификация

specify /спе́сифай/ vt определять

specimen /спе́симин/ n образец

speck /спек/ n крапинка, пятнышко

spectacle /спекткл/ n зрелище; pl очки

spectacular /спектэ́кьюлэ/ adj эффектный

spectator /спектэ́йтэ/ n зритель

spectre /спе́ктэ/ n призрак

speculate /спе́кьюлэйт/ vi размышлять; спекулировать

speculation /спе́кьюлэ́йшн/ n размышление; спекуляция

speech /спиич/ n речь; make a ~ /мэйк э ~/ произносить речь

speechless /спи́ичлис/ adj безмолвный

speed /спиид/ n скорость; at full ~ /эт фул ~/ на полной скорости; vt ускорять; vi спешить; ~ limit /~ ли́мит/ дозволенная скорость

speeding /спи́идинг/ n превышение скорости

speedometer /спидо́митэ/ n спидометр

speedy /спи́иди/ adj быстрый

spell /спел/ n чары; under a ~ /а́ндэр э ~/ зачарованный; short ~ /шорт ~/ короткий период; vt произносить по буквам

spelling /спе́линг/ n правописание

spend /спенд/ vt тратить; проводить (время)

sphere /сфи́э/ n шар; сфера

spice /спайс/ n пряность

spicy /спа́йси/ adj пряный

spider /спа́йдэ/ n паук; ~'s web /~'з вэб/ паутина

spike /спайк/ n гвоздь, шип

spill /спил/ vti проливать(ся)

spin /спин/ vti вращать(ся), крутить(ся); прясть

spinach /спи́нидж/ n шпинат

spine /спайн/ n спинной хребет; корешок (книги)

spineless /спа́йнлис/ adj (образн.) мягкотелый

spinning /спи́нинг/ n прядение; ~ top /~ топ/ волчок

spinster /спи́нстэ/ n старая дева

spiral /спа́йерл/ adj спиральный; n спираль; ~ staircase /~ стэ́экейс/ винтовая лестница

spire /спа́йе/ n шпиль

spirit /спи́рит/ n дух, привидение; pl спиртные напитки; high ~s /хай ~с/ приподнятое настроение

spiritual /спи́ритьюэл/ adj духовный

spit /спит/ vi плевать; ~ poison /~ пойзн/ исходить ядом

spite /спайт/ n злоба; in ~ of /ин ~ ов/ вопреки; vt досаждать

spiteful /спа́йтфул/ adj злорадный

spittle /спитл/ n плевок; слюна

splash /сплэш/ n плеск, брызги; vi брызгаться, плескаться

spleen /сплиин/ n (мед.) селезенка; хандра

splendid /спле́ндид/ adj великолепный

splendor /спле́ндэ/ n великолепие

splint /сплинт/ n лыко, лубок; (мед.) шина

splinter /спли́нтэ/ n осколок; щепка; заноза; vti расщеплять(ся)

split /сплит/ n расщелина; раскол; vt раскалывать; расщеплять; ~ing headache /~инг хе́дэйк/ дикая головная боль

spoil /спойл/ n военная добыча; vt портить; баловать (ребенка)

spoke /спо́ук/ n спица (колеса); put a ~ in his wheel /пут э ~ ин хиз виил/ ставить ему палки в колеса

spokesman /спо́уксмэн/ n представитель

sponge /спандж/ n губка; vt мыть губкой; vi жить за чужой счет sponger /спа́ндже/ n паразит

sponsor /спо́нсэ/ n поручатель, спонсор; vt поддерживать, субсидировать

spontaneous /спонтэ́йньес/ adj самопроизвольный, спонтанный

spook /спуук/ n привидение

spool /спуул/ n катушка, шпулька

spoon /спуун/ n ложка

sport /спорт/ n спорт; (разг.) славный малый

sporting /спо́ртинг/ adj спортивный; охотничий

sportsman /спо́ртсмэн/ n спортсмен

sportswoman /спо́ртсву́мэн/ n спортсменка

spot /спот/ n пятно; on the ~ /он зэ ~/ на месте; vt пятнать; замечать

spotless /спо́тлис/ adj безупречный

spotlight /спо́тлайт/ n прожектор; vt ставить в центр внимания

spouse /спа́уз/ n супруг, супруга

sprain /спрэйн/ vt растянуть связки

sprawl /спроол/ vi растягиваться; сидеть развалясь

spray /спрэй/ n брызги; vt обрызгивать

sprayer /спрэ́йе/ n пульверизатор

spread /спред/ vti развертывать(ся); распространять(ся); расстилать(ся); намазывать

spring /спринг/ n весна; прыжок; пружина; рессора; источник; adj весенний; vi прыгать, пружинить

spring-board /спри́нгборд/ n трамплин

sprinkle /спринкл/ vt брызгать, обрызгивать

sprinkler /спри́нклэ/ n опрыскиватель

sprinkling /спри́нклинг/ n поливка

sprint /спринт/ n бег на короткую дистанцию

sprinter /спри́нтэ/ n спринтер

sprouts /спра́утс/ n pl брюссельская капуста

spur /спёр/ n шпора; vt пришпоривать

spurious /спью́эриэс/ adj поддельный

spurt /спёрт/ n струя; (спорт.) спурт; vi бить струей

spy /спай/ n шпион; vi шпионить

squabble /сквобл/ n ссора; vi ссориться

squad /сквод/ n группа; (воен.) отряд

squadron /скводрн/ n (ав.) эскадрилья; (мор.) эскадра; эскадрон

squander /скво́ндэ/ vt растрачивать, проматывать

square /сквээ/ n квадрат; площадь; клетка; adj квадратный; плотный (о еде); честный; ~ foot /~ фут/ квадратный фут

square-built /сквээби́лт/ adj коренастый

squarely /сквээ́ли/ adv прямо, честно

squash /сквош/ n давка; сок; игра в мяч (вроде тенниса); vt раздавливать

squat /сквот/ vi сидеть на корточках

squeak /сквиик/ n писк, скрип; vi пищать, скрипеть

squeeze /сквииз/ vt сжимать, пожимать (руку); ~ in /~ ин/ втискивать; ~ out /~ а́ут/ выжимать; ~ through /~ сруу/ протискивать(ся)

squint /сквинт/ n косоглазие; ~-eyed /~ айд/ косой; vi косить, смотреть искоса

squirrel /сквирл/ n белка

stab /стэб/ n удар (ножом); vt колоть, ударять (ножом)

stability /стэби́лити/ n устойчивость

stable /стэйбл/ adj прочный; стабильный; постоянный; n конюшня, хлев

stack /стэк/ n скирда, стог (сена); куча; vt складывать в стог

stadium /стэ́йдьем/ n стадион

staff /стааф/ n штат, персонал; (воен.) штаб; посох, жезл; on the ~ /он зэ ~/ в штате

stage /стэйдж/ n сцена; стадия, этап; vt инсценировать, ставить

stagger /стэ́гэ/ vi шататься; vt ошеломлять

staggering /стэ́гэринг/ adj шатающийся; потрясающий

stagnate /стэ́гнэйт/ vi загнивать

stagnation /стэгнэ́йшн/ n застой; (образн.) косность

stain /стэйн/ n пятно (также образн.); vt пятнать (также образн.); ~ed glass /~д глаас/ цветное стекло

stainless /стэ́йнлис/ adj незапятнанный; ~ steel /~ стиил/ нержавеющая сталь

stair /стээ/ n ступенька; pl лестница

staircase /стэ́экейс/ n лестница

stake /стэйк/ n кол; ставка (в игре); (коммерч.) доля капитала; pl приз; be at ~ /би эт ~/ быть поставленным на карту

stale /стэйл/ adj черствый (хлеб); несвежий; избитый (о шутке)

stalemate /стэ́йлмейт/ n (шахм.) пат; (образн.) тупик

stalk /стоок/ n стебель; vt подкрадываться к

stall /стоол/ n стойло; ларек; (театр.) кресло в партере

stallion /стэ́льен/ n жеребец

stammer /стэ́мэ/ n заикание; vi заикаться

stammerer /стэ́мэрэ/ n заика

stamp /стэмп/ n (почтовая) марка; штемпель; топот; vt ставить печать

stampede /стэ́мпиид/ n паническое бегство

stand /стэнд/ n позиция; стоянка; стойка; киоск; остановка; vt ставить; терпеть; vi стоять, находиться; ~ by /~ бай/ быть наготове; ~ in the way of /~ ин зэ вэй ов/ мешать; ~ out /~ а́ут/ выделяться; ~ up /~ ап/ вставать

standard /стэ́ндэд/ n стандарт; норма; образец; знамя; ~ of living /~ ов ли́ винг/ жизненный уровень; ~ size /~ сайз/ стандартный размер

standardize /стэ́ндэдайз/ vt стандартизировать

standing /стэ́ндинг/ n положение, репутация; adj постоянный; ~ committee /~ кэми́ти/ постоянный комитет

standpoint /стэ́ндпойнт/ n точка зрения

staple /стэ́йпл/ adj главный, основной

star /стар/ n звезда

starch /старч/ n крахмал; vt крахмалить

stare /стээ/ n пристальный взгляд; vi уставиться

start /старт/ n начало; отправление; старт; at the ~ /эт зэ ~/ в начале; vt начинать; vi начинаться; отправляться; стартовать; вздрагивать

starter /ста́ртэ/ n стартер

startle /стартл/ vt пугать; vi вздрагивать

starvation /ставэ́йшн/ n голод; голодание

starve /старв/ vi голодать

starving /ста́рвинг/ adj голодающий

state /стэйт/ n государство; штат; состояние; adj государственный; S. Department /~ дипа́ртмент/ Государственный департамент (США); vt заявлять; излагать; констатировать

statement /стэ́йтмент/ n заявление

statesmen /стэ́йтсмэн/ n государственный деятель

station /стэйшн/ n вокзал; станция (радио и т.п.); остановка (автобуса)

stationary /стэ́йшнэри/ adj неподвижный

stationery /стэ́йшнэри/ n канцелярские товары

status /стэ́йтэс/ n статус

status quo /стэ́йтэсквбу/ n статус-кво

statute /стэ́тьют/ n статус; закон; pl устав

staunch /стоонч/ adj стойкий

stay /стэй/ n пребывание; vi оставаться, гостить

stead /стед/ n: in my ~ /ин май ~/ вместо меня

steadfast /стэ́дфэст/ adj прочный; непоколебимый

steady /стэ́ди/ n устойчивый, твердый

steak /стейк/ n стейк, бифштекс

steal /стиил/ vt воровать, красть; vi красться, подкрадываться

stealing /сти́илинг/ n кража

steam /стиим/ n пар; vt варить на пару

steamer /сти́имэ/ n пароход; котел для варки на пару

steel /стиил/ n сталь; adj стальной

steep /стиип/ adj крутой

steeple /стиипл/ n шпиль; колокольня

steeplechase /стииплчейс/ n скачки с препятствиями

steer /стиэ/ vt править

steering /стиэринг/ n управление; ~ wheel /~ виил/ руль

stellar /стéлэ/ adj звездный

stem /стем/ n стебель; ствол; (грам.) основа; vt: ~ from /~ фром/ происходить от

stencil /стенсл/ n трафарет

stenographer /стенóгрэфэ/ n стенографист(ка)

step /степ/ n шаг; ступенька; pl стремянка; take ~s /тэйк ~с/ принимать меры; vi шагать; ~ aside /~ эсáйд/ сторониться; ~ on /~ он/ наступать на

stepchild /стéпчайлд/ n пасынок; падчерица

stepfather /стéпфáазэ/ n отчим

stepmother /стéпмáзэ/ n мачеха

steppe /степ/ n степь

sterile /стéрайл/ adj бесплодный; стерильный

sterilize /стéрилайз/ vt стерилизовать

stern /стёрн/ adj строгий; n корма

stew /стьюю/ n тушеное мясо; vti тушить(ся)

steward /стьюэд/ n управляющий; (ав.) бортпроводник

stewardess /стьюэдис/ n (ав.) стюардесса

stick /стик/ n палка, трость; vt втыкать; vi липнуть; ~ to /~ ту/ придерживаться; ~ out /~ áут/ высовывать(ся)

sticking plaster /стúкингплáастэ/ n липкий пластырь

sticky /стúки/ adj клейкий, липкий

stiff /стиф/ adj негибкий; жесткий; застывший; окоченевший; чопорный

stifle /стайфл/ vt душить, подавлять; vi задыхаться

still /стил/ adj тихий, неподвижный; adv до сих пор, еще, однако; ~ better /~ бéтэ/ еще лучше; n кадр

still-born /стúлборн/ adj мертворожденный

still life /стúллайф/ n натюрморт

stimulate /стúмьюлэйт/ vt стимулировать

stimulus /стúмьюлэс/ n стимул

sting /стинг/ n жало; укус; ожог (крапивой); vt жалить

stink /стинк/ n вонь; vi вонять

stipulate /стúпьюлэйт/ vt обусловливать

stir /стёр/ n движение, суматоха; vti шевелить(ся); ~ up /~ ап/ размешивать; возбуждать

stirrup /стúрэп/ n стремя

stitch /стич/ vt стежок; петля; шов; vt шить; ~ up /~ ап/ зашивать

stitching /стúчинг/ n сшивание

stoat /стóут/ n горностай

stock /сток/ n запас; акция; in ~ /ин ~/ в наличии; vt иметь в продаже; снабжать

stock-breeder /стóкбриидэ/ n животновод

stock-broker /стóкбрóукэ/ n биржевой маклер

stock exchange /стóкискчéйндж/ n фондовая биржа

stockholder /стóкхóулдэ/ n акционер

stocking /стóкинг/ n чулок

stock-jobbing /стóкджóбинг/ n биржевые сделки

stock-taking /стóктэйкинг/ n инвентаризация

stole /стóул/ n меховая накидка

stomach /стáмэк/ n желудок; живот

stone /стóун/ n камень; косточка (в ягодах); adj каменный

stool /стуул/ n табуретка

stoop /стууп/ vi сутулиться, наклоняться

stop /стоп/ n остановка; put a ~ to /пут э ~ ту/ положить конец; vt останавливать; прекращать; затыкать; пломбировать (зуб); interj стой!

stoppage /стóпидж/ n прекращение

stopper /стóпэ/ n пробка; затычка

stopping /стóпинг/ n зубная пломба

stop-press /стóппрэс/ n экстренное сообщение

stop-watch /стóпвоч/ n секундомер

storage /стóоридж/ n хранение; склад

store /стор/ n запас; магазин; универмаг; vt хранить (на складе), запасать

store-room /стóорум/ n кладовая

storey /стóори/ n этаж

stork /сторк/ n аист

storm /сторм/ n буря, гроза; vt штурмовать; vi бушевать

stormy /стóрми/ adj бурный

story /стóори/ n рассказ; повесть; (разг.) выдумка

story-teller /стóоритэ́лэ/ n рассказчик

stout /стáут/ adj прочный; стойкий; дородный; n крепкий портер

stove /стóув/ n печка; печь; плита

straight /стрэйт/ adj прямой; adv прямо; ~ away /~ эвэ́й/ сразу

straighten /стрэйтн/ vti выпрямлять (ся)

straightforward /стрэ́йтфóрвэд/ adj прямой, честный, простой

strain /стрэйн/ n напряжение; натяжение; переутомление; vi напрягаться, переутомляться

strained /стрэйнд/ adj натянутый

strainer /стрэ́йнэ/ n сито

strait /стрэйт/ adj тесный; pl пролив

strait-jacket /стрэ́йтджэ́кит/ n смирительная рубашка

strand /стрэнд/ n прядь (волос)

strange /стрэйндж/ adj странный; чужой, незнакомый

strangeness /стрэ́йнджнис/ n странность

stranger /стрэ́йндже/ n незнакомец

strangle /стрэнгл/ vt душить

strap /стрэп/ n ремешок; полоска; (воен.) погон

strategic /стрэти́иджик/ adj стратегический

strategy /стрэ́тиджи/ n стратегия

straw /строо/ n солома; соломинка

strawberry /стрóобери/ n земляника, клубника

stray /стрэй/ adj заблудившийся, бездомный; ~ bullet /~ бýлит/ шальная пуля

streak /стриик/ n полоса; черта (характера); vi проноситься

stream /стриим/ n поток, струя, течение; vi струиться

streamlined /стри́имлайнд/ adj обтекаемый; хорошо налаженный

street /стриит/ n улица

streetcar /стри́иткар/ n трамвай

street-walker /стри́итвóокэ/ n проститутка

strength /стренгс/ n сила

strengthen /стрé́нгсен/ vti усиливать (ся)

strenuous /стрé́ньюэс/ adj напряженный; требующий усилий

stress /стрес/ n напряжение; (грам.) ударение; vt подчеркивать; (грам.) ставить ударение на

stretch /стреч/ n растягивание, протяжение; at a ~ /эт э ~/ в один присест; vt вытягивать; ~ one's legs /~ ванз легз/ разминать ноги; vi растягиваться, простираться; ~ oneself /~ вансэ́лф/ потягиваться

stretcher /стрé́чэ/ n носилки

strew /струу/ vt разбрасывать, усыпать

strict /стрикт/ adj строгий

strictness /стри́ктнис/ n строгость, точность

stride /страйд/ n шаг; make great ~s /мэйк грэйт ~з/ делать успехи; vi шагать

strife /страйф/ n борьба, раздор

strike /страйк/ n удар; забастовка; vt бить, ударять; чеканить (монеты); открывать (месторождение); заключать (сделку); vi бастовать; бить (о часах); ~ up /~ ап/ начинать

strikebreaker /стрá́йкбрэ́йкэ/ n штрейкбрехер

striker /стрá́йкэ/ n забастовщик

striking /стрá́йкинг/ adj поразительный

string /стринг/ n веревка; шнурок; (муз.) струна; ~ of pearls /~ ов пёрлз/ нитка жемчуга; vt нанизывать; ~ together /~ тэгéзэ/ связывать

strip /стрип/ n полоска; vt сдирать; раздевать; vi раздеваться

stripe /страйп/ n полоса; (воен.) нашив-
ка, лампас
striped /страйпт/ adj полосатый
stroke /строук/ n удар; штрих; поглажи-
вание (рукой); (мед.) удар; ~ of luck /~
ов лак/ удача; vt гладить, ласкать
stroll /строул/ n прогулка; vi прогуливаться
strong /стронг/ adj сильный, крепкий;
прочный
stronghold /стронгхоулд/ n крепость,
твердыня, оплот
structure /стракче/ n структура; устройство
struggle /страгл/ n борьба; vi бороться
stub /стаб/ n пень; огрызок (карандаша);
окурок (сигареты); корешок (чека)
stubborn /стабэн/ adj упрямый, упорный
student /стьююдэнт/ n студент (ка)
studio /стьююдиоу/ n студия
studious /стьююдьес/ adj прилежный
study /стади/ n изучение; очерк; этюд;
кабинет; vt изучать; vi учиться
stuff /стаф/ n вещество, материал; vt делать чучело из; начинять; засовывать;
vi объедаться
stuffing /стафинг/ n начинка
stuffy /стафи/ adj душный
stumble /стамбл/ vt спотыкаться; ~ing
block /~инг блок/ камень преткнове-
ния
stump /стамп/ n пень, обрубок; vt ставить
в тупик; vi ковылять
stumpy /стампи/ adj коренастый
stun /стан/ vt ошеломлять
stupendous /стьюпендэс/ adj изумительный; колоссальный
stupid /стьююпид/ adj глупый
stupidity /стьюпидити/ n глупость
stupor /стьюю пэ/ n оцепенение
sturdy /стёрди/ adj крепкий, твердый
sturgeon /стёрджн/ n осетр
stutter /статэ/ n заикание; vi заикаться
stutterer /статэрэ/ n заика
sty /стай/ n свинарник; ячмень (на глазу)

style /стайл/ n стиль, фасон; in ~ /ин ~/ с
шиком; set the ~ /сет зэ ~/ задавать тон
stylish /стайлиш/ adj модный, шикарный
subconscious /сабконшес/ adj подсознательный
subdivide /сабдивайд/ vt подразделять
subdue /сэбдьюю/ vt подчинять
sub-editor /сабэдитэ/ n помощник ре-
дактора
subject /сабджикт/ adj подчиненный;
подверженный; подвластный; подлежащий; n подданный; предмет, тема;
субъект; (грам.) подлежащее; /сэб-
джект/ vt подчинять; подвергать
subjective /сабджектив/ adj субъектив-
ный
subjunctive /сэбджанктив/ n сослага-
тельное наклонение
sub-let /сабле́т/ vt передавать в субаренду
sublime /сэблайм/ adj возвышенный
submarine /сабмэрин/ adj подводный; n
подводная лодка
submerge /сэбмёрдж/ vti погружать (ся)
submission /сэбмишн/ n подчинение, покорность
submissive /сэбмисив/ adj покорный
submit /сэбмит/ vt представлять (на рассмотрение); vi подчиняться
subordinate /сэбординит/ adj подчиненный; /сэбординэйт/ vt подчинять
subpoena /сэбпиинэ/ n повестка в суд; vt
вызывать в суд под угрозой штрафа
subscribe /сэбскрайб/ vt жертвовать
деньги; ~ to /~ ту/ подписываться на
subscriber /сэбскрайбэ/ n подписчик
subscription /сэбскрипшн/ n подписка
subsequent /сабсиквент/ adj последующий
subsequently /сабсиквентли/ adv впоследствии
subside /сэбсайд/ vi убывать; оседать (о
земле)
subsidiary /сэбсидьери/ adj вспомогательный

subsidize /сáбсидайз/ vt субсидировать

subsist /сэбсúст/ vi существовать; кормиться

subsistence /сэбсúстнс/ n существование; средства к жизни

substance /сáбстнс/ n вещество; сущность; имущество; состояние

substantial /сэбстэ́ншл/ adj существенный; питательный

substantive /сáбстэнтив/ n имя существительное

substitute /сáбститьют/ n заместитель, заменитель; vt замещать, заменять

subtenant /сáбтэ́нэнт/ n субарендатор

subterfuge /сáбтэфьюдж/ n увертка

subtitle /сáбтáйтл/ n подзаголовок

subtle /сатл/ adj тонкий; неуловимый; утонченный

subtract /сэбтрэ́кт/ vt вычитать

subtraction /сэбтрэ́кшн/ n вычитание

suburb /сáбёб/ n пригород

suburban /сэбё́ёбн/ adj пригородный

subversive /сабвё́ёсив/ adj подрывной

subway /сáбвэй/ n метро

succeed /сэксúид/ vi добиваться, преуспевать; ~ to /~ ту/ наследовать; vt следовать за

success /сэксэ́с/ n удача, успех

successful /сэксэ́сфул/ adj удачный, успешный; преуспевающий

succession /сэксэ́шн/ n последовательность; преемственность; in ~ /ин ~/ подряд

successor /сэксэ́сэ/ n преемник, наследник

succumb to /сэкáм ту/ vi уступать

such /сач/ adj такой; ~ as /~ эз/ как например; pron таковой; ~ is life /~ из лайф/ такова жизнь

suck /сак/ vt сосать; ~ing pig /~инг пиг/ молочный поросенок

sucker /сáкэ/ n сосунок; леденец; паразит, тунеядец

suckle /сакл/ vt кормить грудью

suckling /сáклинг/ n грудной ребенок

sudden /садн/ adj внезапный; all of a ~ /оол ов э ~/ вдруг

suddenly /сáднли/ adv неожиданно

sue /сьюю/ vt преследовать судебным порядком

suede /свейд/ n замша

suffer /сáфэ/ vi страдать

suffering /сáфринг/ n страдание

sufficient /сэфúшнт/ adj достаточный

suffix /сáфикс/ n суффикс

suffocate /сáфэкейт/ vi задыхаться

suffrage /сáфридж/ n избирательное право

sugar /шýгэ/ n сахар

sugar-basin /шýгэбéйсин/ n сахарница

suggest /сэджéст/ vt предлагать

suggestion /сэджéсчн/ n предложение

suicide /сьюисайд/ n самоубийство, самоубийца; commit ~ /кэмúт ~/ покончить с собой

suit /съюют/ n костюм; (юрид.) иск; тяжба; ухаживание; (карты) масть; vt приспосабливать; устраивать; быть удобным; быть к лицу; vi ладиться; подходить

suitable /съюютэбл/ adj подходящий

suit-case /съююткейс/ n чемодан

suite /свиит/ n свита; комплект; гарнитур; гостиничный номер-люкс

suitor /съюютэ/ n проситель; ухажер

sulk /салк/ vi дуться

sulky /сáлки/ adj надутый

sulphur /сáлфэ/ n сера

sultry /сáлтри/ adj знойный

sum /сам/ n сумма, итог; do ~s /ду ~з/ решать задачи; vt: ~ up /~ ап/ подводить итог

summarize /сáмэрайз/ vt резюмировать

summary /сáмэри/ adj суммарный; n резюме

summer /сáмэ/ n лето; next ~ /нэкст ~/ будущим летом

summit /сáмит/ n вершина; ~ meeting /~ мúитинг/ встреча на высшем уровне

summon /сáмэн/ vt созывать; вызывать

summons /са́мэнз/ n вызов (в суд)

sumptuous /са́мтьюэс/ adj роскошный

sun /сан/ n солнце

sunburn /са́нбён/ n загар; in the ~ /ин зэ ~/ на солнце; vi греться на солнце

Sunday /са́нди/ n воскресенье

sunflower /са́нфла́уэ/ n подсолнечник

sunrise /са́нрайз/ n восход солнца

sunset /са́нсэт/ n закат

sunshine /са́ншайн/ n солнечный свет

sunken /са́нкэн/ adj затонувший; впалый (о щеках)

sunny /са́ни/ adj солнечный

superb /съюпёрб/ adj великолепный

superficial /съюпэфи́шл/ adj поверхностный

superfine /съю́юпэфа́йн/ adj высшего качества

superfluous /съюпёёфлуэс/ adj (из)лишний

superintend /съю́юпринтéнд/ vt заведывать

superintendent /съю́юпринтéндэнт/ n управляющий; старший (полицейский) офицер

superior /съюпи́эриэ/ adj высший, превосходящий; n начальник

superiority /съюпи́эриóрити/ n превосходство

superlative /съюпёрлэтив/ adj превосходный

superman /съю́юпэмэн/ n сверхчеловек, супермен

supermarket /съю́юпэма́ркит/ n универсам

supernatural /съю́юпэнэ́чрл/ adj сверхъестественный

supernumerary /съю́юпэньюóюмрэри/ n сверхштатный работник; (театр.) статист(ка)

supersede /съю́юпэси́ид/ vt заменять, вытеснять

superstition /съю́юпэсти́шн/ n суеверие

superstitious /съю́юпэсти́шес/ adj суеверный

superstructure /съю́юпэстра́кче/ n надстройка

supertax /съю́юпэтэ́кс/ n налог на сверхприбыль

supervise /съю́юпэва́йз/ vt наблюдать за; руководить; надзирать за

supervision /съю́юпэви́жн/ n надзор; руководство

supervisor /съю́юпэва́йзэ/ n надсмотрщик, надзиратель; руководитель; контролер

supper /са́пэ/ n ужин; have ~ /хэв ~/ ужинать

supplement /са́плимент/ n дополнение, приложение; vt дополнять

supplementary /са́плимéнтэри/ adj дополнительный

supply /сэпла́й/ n поставка, снабжение; pl запасы, продовольствие; ~ and demand /~ энд дима́анд/ спрос и предложение; vt поставлять, снабжать

support /сэпóрт/ n поддержка, опора; подпорка; vt поддерживать; содержать

supporter /сэпóртэ/ n сторонник

suppose /сэпóуз/ vt предполагать

supposed /сэпóузд/ adj предполагаемый

supposition /са́пэзи́шн/ n предположение

suppress /сэпрéс/ vt подавлять; замалчивать (истину)

suppression /сэпрéшн/ n подавление

supreme /съюпри́им/ adj верховный

surcharge /сёчардж/ n доплата

sure /шуэ/ adj уверенный; верный; a ~ place /э ~ плэйс/ надежное место; he is ~ to come /хи из ~ ту кам/ он обязательно придет

surely /шу́эли/ adv конечно

surf /сёрф/ vi кататься на волнах

surface /сёрфис/ n поверхность

surgeon /сёрджн/ n хирург

surgery /сёрджри/ n хирургия

surmise /сёма́йз/ n догадка; vt предполагать; подозревать

surmount /сёма́унт/ vt преодолевать

surname /сёрнэйм/ n фамилия

surpass /сёпáас/ vt превосходить

surplus /сёрплэс/ adj избыточный; n излишек

surprise /сэпрáйз/ n удивление; неожиданность; сюрприз; vt удивлять

surprising /сэпрáйзинг/ adj удивительный; неожиданный

surrender /сэрéндэ/ n сдача, капитуляция; vi сдаваться

surround /сэрáунд/ vt окружать

surroundings /сэрáундингз/ n pl окрестности

surveillance /сёвéйлэнс/ n надзор, слежка

survey /сёрвей/ n обозрение; осмотр; обзор; межевание; /сёвэ́й/ vt осматривать; исследовать; делать съемку

surveyor /сэвéйе/ n землемер; топограф; инспектор

survival /сэвáйвл/ n выживание; пережиток

survive /сэвáйв/ vt оставаться в живых, выживать

survivor /сэвáйвэ/ n уцелевший

susceptible /сэсéптэбл/ adj восприимчивый

suspect /сáспект/ adj подозрительный; /сэспéкт/ vt подозревать

suspend /сэспéнд/ vt подвешивать; приостанавливать; временно отстранять от должности

suspenders /сэспéндэз/ n pl подтяжки

suspense /сэспéнс/ n беспокойство; неопределенность; ~ novel /~ новл/ приключенческий роман

suspension /сэспéншн/ n временное прекращение; временная отставка; подвешивание; ~ bridge /~ бридж/ висячий мост

suspensory /сэспэ́нсэри/ adj подвешивающий; ~ bandage /~ бэ́ндидж/ суспензорий

suspicion /сэспи́шн/ n подозрение

suspicious /сэспи́шес/ adj подозрительный

sustain /сэстэ́йн/ vt поддерживать; переносить

sustenance /сáстинэнс/ n пища; средства к существованию

swab /своб/ n швабра; (мед.) тампон

swaddling clothes /свóдлингклóувз/ n pl пеленки

swallow /свóлоу/ n ласточка; глоток; vt глотать

swamp /свомп/ n болото

swampy /свóмпи/ adj болотистый

swan /свон/ n лебедь

swap /своп/ n обмен; vt обмениваться

swarm /сворм/ n рой; vi роиться

swarthy /свóози/ adj смуглый

sway /свэй/ n качание; колебание; власть; vt качать; склонять (на свою сторону); иметь влияние на; vi качаться

swear /свээ/ vi клясться; ругаться; ~ in /~ ин/ приводить к присяге

sweat /свет/ n пот; vi потеть

sweater /свéтэ/ n свитер

Swede /свиид/ n швед(ка)

swede /свиид/ n брюква

Swedish /свúидиш/ n шведский язык; adj шведский

sweep /свиип/ n подметание; трубочист; vt мести; (мор.) тралить; vi мчаться; ~ away /~ эвэ́й/ сметать; уничтожать; ~ past /~ пааст/ проноситься

sweeper /свúипэ/ n подметальщик

sweeping /свúипинг/ n подметание; pl мусор; adj широкий, с большим охватом

sweepstake /свúипстэйк/ n пари (на скачках), тотализатор

sweet /свиит/ adj сладкий; душистый; милый; have a ~ tooth /хэв э ~ туус/ быть сластеной; n конфета, сладкое

sweeten /свиитн/ vt подслащивать

sweetheart /свúитхарт/ n возлюбленный, дорогой

sweetness /свúитнис/ n сладость

swell /свел/ n выпуклость; (мор.) зыбь; adj (разг.) шикарный; vi разбухать, увеличиваться swelling /свéлинг/ n опухоль

swift /свифт/ adj быстрый; n стриж; ~ car /~ кар/ быстроходный автомобиль

swiftness /свифтнис/ n быстрота

swim /свим/ vi плавать, плыть

swimming /свúминг/ n плавание; ~ pool /~ пуул/ плавательный бассейн

swindle /свиндл/ n надувательство, обман; vt надувать, обманывать

swindler /свúндлэ/ n мошенник, плут

swine /свайн/ n свинья

swing /свинг/ n размах, качели; in full ~ /ин фул ~/ в полном разгаре; vti качать(ся), колебать(ся); ~ one's arms /~ ванз армз/ размахивать руками

swing-door /свúнгдор/ n вращающаяся дверь

swirl /свёрл/ n вихрь; vi кружиться

Swiss /свис/ n швейцарец, швейцарка; adj швейцарский

switch /свич/ n прут; (эл.) выключатель; vt переключать; ~ off /~ оф/ выключать; ~ on /~ он/ включать

switchboard /свúчборд/ n коммутатор

swivel /свивл/ vti вращать(ся), поворачивать(ся)

swollen /свóулэн/ adj раздутый

swoon /свуун/ n обморок; vi падать в обморок

sword /сорд/ n меч; сабля; шпага

sycamore /сúкэмо/ n платан

sycophant /сúкэфэнт/ n подхалим

syllable /сúлэбл/ n слог

symbol /симбл/ n символ

symmetry /сúмитри/ n симметрия

sympathetic /сúмпэсéтик/ adj полный сочувствия; благожелательный; симпатичный

sympathize /сúмпэсайз/ vi сочувствовать

sympathy /сúмпэси/ n сочувствие

symphony /сúмфэни/ n симфония

symptom /сúмтэм/ n симптом

synagogue /сúнэгог/ n синагога

syndicate /сúндикит/ n синдикат

synod /синэд/ n синод; собор духовенства

synonym /сúнэним/ n синоним

synopsis /синóпсис/ n конспект; резюме

syntax /сúнтэкс/ n синтаксис

synthetic /синсéтик/ adj синтетический

Syrian /сúриэн/ n сириец, сирийка; adj сирийский

syringa /сириúнгэ/ n сирень

syringe /сúриндж/ n шприц; пожарный насос; disposable ~ /диспóузэбл ~/ одноразовый шприц

syrup /сúрэп/ n сироп

system /сúстим/ n система

systematic /сúстимэтик/ adj систематический

T

T /тии/ n: to a ~ /ту э ~/ в совершенстве; точь-в-точь

tab /тэб/ n петелька; вешалка; ушко

table /тэйбл/ n стол; доска; таблица; расписание

tablecloth /тэйблклос/ n скатерть

tablespoon /тэйблспуун/ n столовая ложка

tableware /тэйблвээ/ n столовая посуда

tablet /тэблит/ n таблетка

taboo /тэбуу/ n табу

tacit /тэсит/ adj молчаливый

tack /тэк/ n гвоздик; кнопка

tackle /тэкл/ vt заниматься (чем-либо); решать

tact /тэкт/ n такт; тактичность

tactful /тэктфул/ adj тактичный

tactless /тэктлис/ adj бестактный

tactics /тэктикс/ n тактика

taffeta /тэфитэ/ n тафта

tag /тэг/ n ярлык, этикетка; бирка

tail /тэйл/ n хвост; пола; фалда; обратная сторона; ~ away /~ эвэй/ отставать

tailcoat /тэйлкóут/ n фрак

tailless /тэйлис/ adj бесхвостый

tail-on wind /тэйлонвинд/ n попутный ветер

tailor /тэйлэ/ n портной

take /тэйк/ vt брать; принимать (ванну, лекарство); занимать (место, время); ~ aback /~ эбэ́к/ ошеломлять; ~ care of /~ кээр ов/ заботиться о; ~ charge of /~ чардж ов/ брать на себя ответственность за; ~ cover /~ ка́вэ/ укрываться; ~ into consideration /~ и́нту кэнси́дэрэ́йшн/ учитывать; ~ off /~ оф/ (vt) снимать; (vi) взлетать; ~ out /~ а́ут/ вынимать; приглашать (в театр и т.д.); ~ part in /~ парт ин/ участвовать в; ~ place /~ плэйс/ иметь место; ~ the chair /~ зэ чээ/ председательствовать; ~ the trouble /~ зэ трабл/ брать на себя труд; ~ to task /~ ту тааск/ призывать к ответу; ~ up /~ ап/ браться за; he ~s after his father /хи ~с а́фтэ хиз фа́аэз/ он походит на отца; n улов, добыча; ~-off /~ оф/ взлет

tale /тэйл/ n рассказ, повесть, сказка; tell ~s /тэл ~з/ сплетничать

talent /та́лент/ n талант

talented /та́лентыд/ adj талантливый

talk /тоок/ n разговор; pl переговоры; vi говорить; ~ into /~ и́нту/ убеждать, уговаривать

talkative /то́окэтив/ adj болтливый

tall /тоол/ adj высокий

tally /та́ли/ n бирка, ярлык; vi соответствовать

tame /тэйм/ adj ручной, прирученный; vt приручать, укрощать

tamer /та́ймэ/ n укротитель

tan /тэн/ adj рыжевато-коричневый; n загар; vt дубить; vi загорать

tangible /та́нджебл/ adj осязаемый

tangle /тэнгл/ n смятение, путаница; vti запутывать(ся)

tank /тэнк/ n (воен.) танк; резервуар

tap /тэп/ n легкий стук; кран; затычка; vt стукать; ~ the line /~ зэ лайн/ подслушивать телефонный разговор

tape /тэйп/ n лента; тесьма; пленка; ~ recorder /~ рико́рдэ/ магнитофон

tapestry /та́пистри/ n гобелен

tar /тар/ n деготь; vt мазать дегтем

tardy /та́рди/ adj медлительный

target /та́ргит/ n мишень, цель

tariff /та́риф/ n тариф

tart /тарт/ adj кислый, терпкий; n торт, пирог; (разг.) проститутка

Tartar /та́ртэ/ n татарин, татарка; татарский язык; adj татарский

task /тааск/ n задача, задание; urgent ~ /ёрджент ~/ неотложное дело

taste /тэйст/ n вкус; ~s differ /~с ди́фэ/ о вкусах не спорят; vt пробовать, отведать; vi иметь вкус

tasteful /тэ́йстфул/ adj сделанный со вкусом

tasteless /тэ́йстлис/ adj безвкусный

taster /тэ́йстэ/ n дегустатор

tatter /тэ́тэ/ n лоскут; pl лохмотья

tattoo /тэту́у/ n татуировка

taunt /тоонт/ n насмешка, "шпилька"

taut /тоот/ adj туго натянутый, упругий

tax /тэкс/ n налог; vt облагать налогом

taxable /тэ́ксэбл/ adj подлежащий обложению налогом

taxation /тэксэ́йшн/ n обложение налогом

tax collector /тэ́кскэле́ктэ/ n сборщик налогов

tax-free /тэ́ксфри́и/ adj освобожденный от уплаты налогов

taxi /тэ́кси/ n такси; ~ stand /~ стэнд/ стоянка такси

taxpayer /тэ́кспэ́йе/ n налогоплательщик

tea /тии/ n чай

tea bag /ти́ибэг/ n мешочек с заваркой чая

teach /тиич/ vt учить, преподавать; I'll ~ him /айл ~ хим/ я проучу его

teacher /ти́ичэ/ n учитель(ница), преподаватель(ница)

teaching /ти́ичинг/ n учение; преподавание; педагогика

teacup /ти́икап/ n чайная чашка

team /тиим/ n команда; бригада; упряжка (лошадей); ~work /~ вёрк/ слаженность

teapot /тѝипот/ n чайник для заварки

tear /тээ/ n прореха; vt рвать, разрывать; vi рваться; ~ apart /~ эпа́рт/ разрывать на части; ~ off /~ оф/ отрывать

tear /тѝэ/ n слеза; ~ gas /~ гэс/ слезоточивый газ

tearoom /тѝирум/ n кафе-кондитерская

tease /тииз/ vt дразнить; n задира

tea set /тѝисет/ n чайный сервиз

teaspoon /тѝиспу́ун/ n чайная ложка

technical /тéкникл/ adj технический

technicality /тéкникэ́лити/ n формальность

technician /технѝшн/ n техник

teddy bear /тэ́дибэ́э/ n плюшевый медвежонок

tedious /тѝидьес/ adj скучный, неприятный

teem /тиим/ vi кишеть; изобиловать

teenager /тѝинэ́йдже/ n подросток

teens /тиинз/ n pl возраст от 13 до 19 лет; she is still in her ~ /ши из стил ин хё ~/ ей еще нет 20

teethe /тииз/ vi: the child is teething /зэ чайлд из тѝизинг/ у ребенка прорезываются зубы

teething troubles /тѝизинг траблз/ детские болезни (также образн.)

teetotal /титóутл/ adj непьющий

teetotaller /титóутлэ/ n трезвенник

telegram /тéлигрэм/ n телеграмма

telegraph /тéлиграф/ n телеграф; vti телеграфировать

telephone /тéлифоун/ n телефон; ~ booth /~ буус/ телефонная будка; vt звонить по телефону

teleprinter /тéлипрѝнтэ/ n телетайп

telescope /тéлископ/ n телескоп

television /тéливѝжн/ n телевидение; ~ set /~ сэт/ телевизор

tell /тэл/ vt рассказывать, говорить; приказывать; отличать; vi сказываться (на)

teller /тэ́лэ/ n рассказчик; кассир

temper /тэ́мпэ/ n нрав; настроение; гнев; loose one's ~ /лууз ванз ~/ выходить из себя; vt умерять; закалять

temperament /тэ́мпрэмент/ n темперамент

temperature /тэ́мпричэ/ n температура

tempest /тэ́мпист/ n буря

temple /тэмпл/ n храм; (анат.) висок

temporary /тэ́мпэрэри/ adj временный

tempt /темт/ vt искушать, соблазнять

temptation /темтэ́йшн/ n искушение, соблазн

ten /тен/ num десять; n десяток; (карты) десятка

tenancy /тéнэнси/ n аренда, наем

tenant /тéнэнт/ n арендатор; наниматель; съемщик; жилец

tend /тенд/ vt ухаживать за; vi иметь склонность

tendency /тéндэнси/ n тенденция, склонность

tendentious /тенде́ншес/ adj тенденциозный

tender /тéндэ/ n предложение, заявка на подряд

tender /тéндэ/ adj нежный

tenderloin /тéндэлойн/ n филей

tenderness /тéндэнис/ n нежность

tenement /тéнимент/ n арендуемое помещение (имущество, земля, квартира); ~ house /~ хáус/ многоквартирный дом, сдаваемый в аренду

tennis /тéнис/ n теннис

tenor /тéнэ/ n уклад (жизни); смысл (жизни); (муз.) тенор

tense /тенс/ adj напряженный; n (грам.) время

tension /теншн/ n напряжение

tent /тент/ n палатка

tentacle /тенткл/ n щупальце

tentative /тéнтэтив/ adj пробный, предварительный

tenth /тенс/ ord num десятый; n десятая часть

term /тёрм/ n термин; срок; период; семестр; pl условия; личные отношения; выражения; be on good ~s /би он гуд ~з/ быть в хороших отношениях; come to ~s /кам ту ~з/ приходить к соглашению terminal /тёрминл/ adj конечный; n конечная станция

terminate /тёрминэйт/ vi кончаться, истекать

terrace /тéрэс/ n терраса

terrible /тéрэбл/ adj ужасный

terrific /терúфик/ adj ужасающий; (разг.) потрясающий

terrify /тéрифай/ vt ужасать

territory /тéритри/ n территория; сфера

terror /тéрэ/ n ужас; террор

terrorism /тéрэризм/ n терроризм

terrorist /тéрэрист/ n террорист

test /тест/ n испытание; проба; экзамен; ~ tube /~ тьююб/ пробирка; vt испытывать

testament /тéстэмэнт/ n завещание; (церк.) завет; New (Old) ~ /нью (óулд) ~/ Новый (Ветхий) Завет

testify /тéстифай/ vi свидетельствовать

testimonial /тéстимóуньел/ n рекомендация, характеристика

testimony /тéстимэни/ n показание; доказательство

tetanus /тéтэнэс/ n столбняк

text /текст/ n текст

textbook /тэ́кстбук/ n учебник

textile /тéкстайл/ n текстильное изделие, ткань; adj текстильный

than /зэн/ conj чем; rather ~ /рáазэ ~/ скорее чем

thank /сэнк/ vt благодарить; ~ God /~ год/ слава богу!; ~ you! /~ ю/ спасибо!

thankful /сэ́нкфул/ adj благодарный

thankless /сэ́нклис/ adj неблагодарный

thanks /сэнкс/ n pl благодарность; ~ to /~ ту/ благодаря

thanksgiving /сэ́нксгúвинг/ n благодарственный молебен; благодарение

that /зэт/ pron тот, та, то, который, кто; conj что, чтобы; in order ~ /ин óрдэ ~/ для того, чтобы; adv так, до такой степени; ~ is (i.e.) /~ из/ то есть (т.е.)

thaw /соо/ n оттепель; vi таять

the /зыы/ - полная форма; /зэ/ - редуцированная форма; определенный артикль, в русском языке эквивалента не имеет; all ~ better /оол ~ бéтэ/ тем лучше; ~ more ~ better /~ мор ~ бéтэ/ чем больше, тем лучше

theater /сúэтэ/ n театр

theft /сефт/ n кража

their /зэ́е/ adj, theirs /зэ́ез/ poss pron их, свой и т.д.

them /зэм/ pron их, им и т.д.

theme /сиим/ n тема

themselves /зэмсэ́лвз/ pron себя и т.д., сами и т.д.

then /зэн/ adv тогда, потом, затем; now and ~ /нáу энд ~/ время от времени; conj тогда, в таком случае; since ~ /синс ~/ с того времени

theology /сиóлэджи/ n богословие

theory /сúэри/ n теория

therapeutic /сéрэпьюютик/ adj терапевтический

therapeutics /сéрэпьюютикс/ n терапия

there /зэ́е/ adv там, туда; ~ is /~ из/, ~ are /~ аа/ есть; here and ~ /хúэрэнд ~/ там и сям

thereabouts /зэ́ерэбаутс/ adv поблизости; приблизительно

thereafter /зэерáафтэ/ adv с того времени

thereby /зэ́ебáй/ adv тем самым

therefore /зэ́ефо/ adv поэтому

thereupon /зэ́ерэпóн/ adv затем

thermal /сéрмэл/ adj тепловой; горячий

thermometer /сэмóмитэ/ n термометр

thermos /сéрмэс/ n термос

these /зыыз/ adj, pron эти

thesis /сúисис/ n тезис, диссертация

they /зэй/ pron они

thick /сик/ adj толстый; густой; in the ~ /ин зэ ~/ в самой гуще; through ~ and thin /сруу ~ энд син/ несмотря ни на какие препятствия

thicken /сикн/ vti сгущать(ся); утолщать(ся)

thicket /сúкит/ n чаща

thick-headed /си́кхе́дыд/ adj тупой, бестолковый

thick-lipped /си́кли́пт/ adj губастый

thick-set /си́ксэ́т/ adj коренастый

thick-skinned /си́кски́нд/ adj толстокожий (также образн.)

thief /сииф/ n вор

thigh /сай/ n бедро

thimble /симбл/ n наперсток

thin /син/ adj тонкий; редкий (о волосах); жидкий; vi худеть, редеть

thing /синг/ n вещь; the only ~ /зэ о́унли ~/ единственное; it is a good ~ that /ит из э гуд ~ зэт/ хорошо, что; how are ~s? /ха́у а ~з/ как дела?

think /синк/ vti думать, мыслить; ~ over /~ о́увэ/ обдумывать

thinker /си́нкэ/ n мыслитель

third /сёрд/ ord num третий

thirst /сёрст/ n жажда; vi жаждать; be ~y /би ~и/ хотеть пить

thirteen /сёрти́ин/ num тринадцать

thirteenth /сёрти́инс/ ord num тринадцатый

thirtieth /сёртис/ ord num тридцатый; n тридцатая часть

thirty /сёрти/ num тридцать

this /зыс/ adj, pron этот; эта, это; ~ way /~ вэй/ сюда, вот так

thorn /сорн/ n колючка, шип

thorough /са́рэ/ adj тщательный, основательный

thoroughbred /са́рэбрэд/ adj чистокровный

thoroughfare /са́рэфээ/ n проезд, проход; магистраль

throughly /са́рэли/ adv вполне; тщательно

those /зо́уз/ adj, pron те

though /зо́у/ conj хотя; несмотря на; даже если (бы); хотя бы; as ~ /эз ~/ как будто; adv однако; тем не менее; все-таки

thought /соот/ n мысль

thoughtful /со́отфул/ adj задумчивый; заботливый

thoughtless /со́отлис/ adj необдуманный; невнимательный

thousand /са́узэнд/ num, n тысяча

thousandth /са́узэнс/ ord num тысячный; n тысячная часть

thrash /срэш/ vt пороть; (с.-х.) молотить

thrashing /срэ́шинг/ n взбучка; (с.-х.) молотьба

thread /сред/ n нитка; нить (также образн.); vt продевать нитку в иголку; нанизывать

threadbare /сре́дбээ/ adj потертый; (образн.) избитый

threat /срет/ n угроза

threaten /сретн/ vt угрожать

three /срии/ num три; n тройка

threshold /сре́шоулд/ n порог

thrice /срайс/ adv трижды

thrift /срифт/ n бережливость

thriftless /сри́фтлис/ adj расточительный

thrifty /сри́фти/ adj экономный

thrill /срил/ n трепет; vt сильно волновать; vi трепетать

thriller /сри́лэ/ n сенсационная книга или пьеса; (кино) боевик

thrive /срайв/ vi преуспевать

thriving /сра́йвинг/ adj процветающий

throat /сро́ут/ n горло

throb /сроб/ vi биться, пульсировать

throne /сро́ун/ n престол, трон

throng /сронг/ vi толпиться

through /сруу/ prep через; сквозь; из-за; adv от начала до конца; I am wet ~ /ай эм вет ~/ я насквозь промок; adj прямой (поезд)

throughout /сруа́ут/ adv везде; во всех отношениях

throw /сро́у/ n бросок; vt бросать, кидать; метать; ~ aside /~ эса́йд/ отбрсывать; ~ back /~ бэк/ отвергать; ~ in /~ ин/ добавлять; ~ off /~ оф/ сбрасывать; свергать; ~ open /~ о́упн/ распахивать; ~ out /~ а́ут/ выгонять; ~ up /~ ап/ извергать; вскидывать thrush /сраш/ n дрозд

thrust /сраст/ vt совать; толкать; вонзать; ~ aside /~ эсáйд/ отталкивать; ~ through /~ сруу/ пронзать

thug /car/ n головорез

thumb /сам/ n большой палец (руки); Tom T. /том ~/ мальчик с пальчик

thunder /сáндэ/ n гром; vi греметь; it ~s /ит ~з/ гром гремит

thunderbolt /сáндэбóулт/ n удар молнии

thunderstorm /сáндэстом/ n гроза

Thursday /сёёзди/ n четверг

thus /зас/ adv так, таким образом

tick /тик/ n тиканье (часов); отметка, "галочка"; in a ~ /ин э ~/ немедленно; vi тикать

ticket /тúкит/ n билет; ярлык

ticket-collector /тúкиткэлéктэ/ n контролер

tickle /тикл/ vt щекотать; it ~s! /ит ~з/ щекотно!

ticklish /тúклиш/ adj боящийся щекотки; щекотливый

tide /тайд/ n: high ~ /хай ~/ прилив; low ~ /лóу ~/ отлив

tidy /тáйди/ adj опрятный

tie /тай/ n галстук; (спорт.) равный счет; family ~s /фэмили ~з/ семейные узы; vt связывать, завязывать; ограничивать; vi сыграть вничью

tie-pin /тáйпин/ n булавка для галстука

tiger /тáйгэ/ n тигр

tight /тайт/ adj тугой; тесный

tighten /тайтн/ vti натягивать(ся); сжимать(ся)

tights /тайтс/ n pl трико; колготки

tile /тайл/ n черепица; кафель; ~d floor /~д флор/ кафельный пол; ~d roof /~д рууф/ черепичная крыша

till /тил/ vt возделывать; prep до; ~ then /~ зэн/ до тех пор

timber /тúмбэ/ n лесоматериал, (строевой) лес; ~ yard /~ ярд/ лесной склад

time /тайм/ n время; срок; период; раз, (спорт.) тайм; ~ and again /~ энд эгéйн/ неоднократно; one at a ~ /ван эт э ~/ по одному; at no ~ /эт нóу ~/ никогда; at the same ~ /эт зэ сэйм ~/ в то же время; at ~s /эт ~з/ временами; for the ~ being /фо зэ ~ бúинг/ до поры до времени; from ~ to ~ /фром ~ ту ~/ время от времени; in good ~ /ин гуд ~/ своевременно; in ~ /ин ~/ вовремя; have a good ~ /хэв э гуд ~/ хорошо проводить время; what ~ is it? /вот ~ из ит/ который час?

timeless /тáймлис/ adj вечный

timely /тáймли/ adj своевременный

timetable /тáймтэ́йбл/ n расписание

timid /тúмид/ adj робкий

timidity /тимúдити/ n робость

tin /тин/ n олово; жесть; консервная банка

tinfoil /тúнфойл/ n оловянная фольга

tin-opener /тúнóупэнэ/ n консервный нож

tinge /тинж/ n оттенок; привкус; vt слегка окрашивать

tinsel /тинсл/ n мишура (также образн.)

tint /тинт/ n оттенок

tiny /тáйни/ adj крошечный, малюсенький

tip /тип/ n верхушка; кончик; чаевые; vt давать на чай

tiptoe /тúптоу/ n цыпочки; on ~ /он ~/ на цыпочках

tipsy /тúпси/ adj подвыпивший

tip-top /тúптóп/ adv превосходно

tire /тáйе/ n шина

tired /тáйед/ adj усталый

tiredness /тáйеднис/ n усталость

tireless /тáйелис/ adj неутомимый

tiresome /тáйесэм/ adj утомительный; недоедливый

tissue /тúсью/ n ткань; бумажный носовой платок

tit /тит/ n синица; ~ for tat /~ фо тэт/ "зуб за зуб"

title /тайтл/ n заглавие; титул; звание; vt называть; озаглавливать

titter /ти́тэ/ n хихиканье

tittle-tattle /ти́тлтэ́тл/ n сплетни, тары-бары

to /ту/ prep в, на, к; ~ and fro /~ энд фро́у/ туда и сюда; a quarter ~ three /э кво́ртэ ~ срии/ без четверти три; ~ my mind /~ май майнд/ по моему мнению; ~ the right /~ зэ райт/ направо; the road ~ New York /зэ ро́уд ~ нью йорк/ дорога в Нью-Йорк; ~ order /~ о́рдэ/ на заказ

toad /то́уд/ n жаба (также перен.)

toast /то́уст/ n гренок; тост; vt поджаривать (хлеб); пить за здоровье

toaster /то́устэ/ n тостер; тамада

tobacco /тэбэ́коу/ n табак

tobacconist /тэбэ́кэнист/ n торговец табачными изделиями

toboggan /тэбо́гн/ n тобогган, сани

today /тудэ́й/ adv сегодня, в наше время

toddle /тодл/ vi ковылять

toddler /то́длэ/ n ребенок, начинающий ходить

toe /то́у/ n палец ноги

toffee /то́фи/ n тоффи (конфета типа ириса)

together /тэгэ́зэ/ adv вместе, сообща

toil /тойл/ n тяжелый труд; vi трудиться

toilet /то́йлит/ n туалет, уборная

toilet paper /то́йлитпэ́йпэ/ n туалетная бумага

token /то́укн/ n подарок на память; знак; символ; as a ~ of /эз э ~ ов/ в знак

tolerable /то́лерэбл/ adj сносный

tolerate /то́лерейт/ vt терпеть, допускать

tolerance /то́лернс/ n терпимость

toll /то́ул/ n пошлина; колокольный звон; ~ bridge /~ бридж/ платный мост

tomato /тэма́атоу/ n помидор

tomb /туум/ n могила; мавзолей

tomorrow /тэмо́роу/ adv завтра

ton /тан/ n тонна

tone /то́ун/ n тон

tongs /тонгз/ n pl щипцы; клещи

tongue /танг/ n язык; hold one's ~ /хо́улд ванз ~/ держать язык за зубами

tonight /тэна́йт/ adv сегодня вечером

tonnage /та́нидж/ n тоннаж

tonsil /тонсл/ n миндалина

tonsilitis /то́нсила́йтис/ n тонзилит; воспаление миндалин

too /туу/ adv также, тоже; слишком

tool /туул/ n инструмент; станок; орудие (также образн.)

tooth /тууc/ n (pl teeth) зуб; зубец; false teeth /фоолс тиис/ вставные зубы

toothache /ту́усэйк/ n зубная боль

toothbrush /ту́усбраш/ n зубная щетка

toothless /ту́услис/ adj беззубый

toothpaste /ту́успэйст/ n зубная паста

toothpick /ту́успик/ n зубочистка

toothy /ту́уси/ adj зубастый

top /топ/ n верх; верхушка (дерева); вершина (горы); макушка (головы); волчок; at the ~ of one's voice /эт зэ ~ ов ванз войс/ во весь голос; ~ secret /~ си́икрит/ совершенно секретно; from ~ to bottom /фром ~ ту бо́тэм/ сверху донизу; on ~ of /он ~ ов/ сверх; adj верхний, высший; vt покрывать, быть первым среди

top-hat /то́пхэт/ n цилиндр

topic /то́пик/ n предмет, тема

topical /то́пикэл/ adj актуальный; тематический; ~ question /~ квесчн/ актуальный вопрос

topmost /то́пмоуст/ adj самый верхний; самый важный

topple /топл/ vt опрокидывать; свергать

topsy-turvy /то́пситёрви/ n беспорядок; adj хаотичный

torch /торч/ n факел; фонарь

torment /то́рмент/ n мука; /томе́нт/ vt мучить

tornado /тонэ́йдоу/ n ураган

tortoise /то́ртэс/ n черепаха

torture /то́рче/ n пытка; vt пытать

toss /тос/ vt подбрасывать; вскидывать (голову); vi метаться (в постели) total /тóутл/ adj весь, тотальный; n итог

touch /тач/ n прикосновение; контакт; штрих; примесь; чуточка; a ~ of the sun /э ~ ов зэ сан/ легкий солнечный удар; keep in ~ with /киип ин ~ виз/ поддерживать контакт с; vt трогать, касаться

touched /тачт/ adj "тронутый"; взволнованный

touching /тáчинг/ adj трогательный

touchy /тáчи/ adj обидчивый

tough /таф/ adj жесткий; крепкий; трудный; n бандит

tour /туэ/ n поездка, турне; vt совершать турне по

tourist /тýэрист/ n турист(ка); ~ agency /~ эйдженси/ бюро путешествий

tournament /тýэнэмент/ n турнир

tow /тóу/ n буксир; on ~ /он ~/ на буксире

towards /тэвóодз/ prep к, по направлению к; по отношению к; около; для

towel /тáуэл/ n полотенце

tower /тáуэ/ n башня; вышка

town /тáун/ n город

town hall /тáунхóол/ n ратуша

townsfolk /тáунзфоук/ n горожане

townsman /тáунзмэн/ n горожанин

toy /той/ n игрушка; vi играть

trace /трэйс/ n след; vt прослеживать, калькировать

tracery /трэ́йсри/ n узор

tracing /трэ́йсинг/ n скалькированный чертеж

tracing paper /трэ́йсингпэ́йпэ/ n бумажная калька

track /трэк/ n дорожка (также спорт.); колея (жел. дороги); трек; off the ~ /оф зэ ~/ на ложном пути

trade /трэйд/ n торговля; ремесло; профессия; Jack of all ~s /джэк ов оол ~з/ мастер на все руки; vi торговать

trademark /трэ́йдмарк/ n фабричная марка

trader /трэ́йдэ/ n торговец

trade union /трэ́йдъю́юньен/ n профсоюз

tradition /трэди́шн/ n традиция; предание

traditional /трэди́шнл/ adj традиционный

traffic /трэ́фик/ n движение (любого транспорта); сообщение; транспорт; торговля; ~ jam /~ джэм/ "пробка"; ~ lights /~ лайтс/ светофор

tragedy /трэ́джиди/ n трагедия

tragic /трэ́джик/ adj трагический

trail /трэйл/ n след; тропинка; vi волочиться; тащиться

trailer /трэ́йлэ/ n прицеп; анонс; реклама

train /трэйн/ n поезд; шлейф (платья); вереница; vt обучать; (спорт.) тренировать

trainer /трэ́йнэ/ n (спорт.) тренер

training /трэ́йнинг/ n обучение; тренировка

trait /трэй/ n черта; штрих

traitor /трэ́йтэ/ n предатель, изменник

traitorous /трэ́йтрэс/ adj предательский

tram /трэм/ n трамвай

tramp /трэмп/ n бродяга; vi бродяжничать

trample /трэмпл/ vt топтать; (образн.) попирать

tramway /трэ́мвэй/ n трамвай

tranquil /трэ́нквил/ adj спокойный

transact /трэнзэ́кт/ vt вести (дела)

transaction /трэнзэ́кшн/ n дело, сделка

transcend /трэнсéнд/ vt переступать пределы

transcript /трэ́нскрипт/ n копия

transcription /трэнскри́пшн/ n транскрипция

transfer /трэ́нсфё/ n перенос, перемещение; /трэ́нсфёр/ vt переносить, перемещать

transform /трэнсфóрм/ vt превращать

transformation /трэ́нсфэмéйшн/ n превращение

transformer /трэнсфóрмэ/ n преобразователь; (эл.) трансформатор transient /трэ́нзиент/ adj преходящий, скоротечный; временный

transistor /трэнси́стэ/ n транзистор

transit /трэ́нсит/ n транзит; ~ visa /~ ви́изэ/ транзитная виза

transition /трэнзи́шн/ n переход

transitional /трэнзи́шэнл/ adj переходный

transitive /трэ́нситив/ adj переходный

translate /трэнслэ́йт/ vt переводить; транслировать (по радио)

translation /трэнслэ́йшн/ n перевод; трансляция

translator /трэнслэ́йтэ/ n переводчик, переводчица

transmission /трэнзми́шн/ n передача

transmit /трэнзми́т/ vt передавать

transmitter /трэнзми́тэ/ n передатчик

transparent /трэнспэ́эрент/ adj прозрачный

transplant /трэнспла́ант/ vt пересаживать

transplantation /трэ́нсплантэ́йшн/ n трансплантация

transport /трэ́нспот/ n транспорт; /трэнспо́рт/ vt перевозить

trap /трэп/ n ловушка, западня, капкан; vt ловить (в ловушку)

trash /трэш/ n дрянь, хлам, мусор

travel /трэвл/ n путешествие; vi путешествовать

traveller /трэ́влэ/ n путешественник; ~'s cheque /~з чек/ дорожный чек

traverse /трэ́вэс/ vt пересекать, ехать через

travesty /трэ́висти/ n пародия, искажение

tray /трэй/ n поднос

treacherous /тре́чрэс/ adj предательский

treachery /тре́чри/ n предательство

tread /тред/ n поступь; vi ступать

treason /триизн/ n измена; high ~ /хай ~/ государственная измена

treasure /тре́же/ n клад, сокровище; vt ценить, дорожить

treasurer /тре́жрэ/ n казначей

treasury /тре́жри/ n казна; сокровищница

treat /триит/ n угощение; удовольствие; (разг.) очередь платить за угощение; this is my ~ /зыс из май ~/ сегодня я угощаю; vt угощать; (мед.) лечить

treatment /три́итмент/ n лечение; обхождение

treaty /три́ити/ n договор

treble /требл/ adj тройной; vti утраивать (ся)

tree /трии/ n дерево; родословная

tremble /трембл/ vi дрожать, трепетать

tremendous /триме́ндэс/ adj громадный; потрясающий

tremor /тре́мэ/ n дрожь, трепет

trench /тренч/ n канава, ров

trend /тренд/ n направление, тенденция

trespass /тре́спэс/ vi нарушать границу (чужого владения); совершать проступок

trespasser /тре́спэсэ/ n нарушитель

trial /тра́йел/ n испытание, судебный процесс; on ~ /он ~/ под судом

triangle /тра́йэнгл/ n треугольник

tribe /трайб/ n племя

tribunal /трайбью́юнл/ n трибунал

tribute /три́бьют/ n дань; pay ~ /пэй ~/ (образн.) отдавать дань

trick /трик/ n уловка, обман; трюк; vt обманывать

trickery /три́кери/ n надувательство

trifle /трайфл/ n мелочь, пустяк

trigger /три́гэ/ n курок; защелка

trilogy /три́лэджи/ n трилогия

trim /трим/ adj опрятный; vt подрезать; отделывать (платье); подравнивать (волосы)

trimming /три́минг/ n отделка (на платье); приправа (к еде); pl обрезки

Trinity /три́нити/ n Троица

trip /трип/ n поездка; экскурсия; "подножка"; vt подставлять ножку; vi спотыкаться

triple /трипл/ adj тройной; vt утраивать

triplets /три́плитс/ n тройня

triplicate /трѝпликит/ adj тройной; in ~
/ин ~/ в трех экземплярах
triumph /трѝйэмф/ n триумф, торжество; победа; vi торжествовать
triumphal /трайáмфл/ adj триумфаль-
ный
triumphant /трайáмфэнт/ adj торжеству-
ющий; ликующий
trolley /трóли/ n тележка
trolley bus /трóлибас/ n троллейбус
troop /трууп/ n отряд; pl войска
trophy /трóуфи/ n трофей, добыча
tropic /трóпик/ n тропик; ~ of Cancer /~
ов кэнсэ/ тропик Рака; ~ of Capricorn
/~ ов кэприкон/ тропик Козерога
tropical /трóпикл/ adj тропический
trot /трот/ vi бежать (рысью)
trouble /трабл/ n забота; хлопоты; беспокойство; беда; неприятность; беспорядки; авария; неисправность; take the
~ /тэйк зэ ~/ брать на себя труд; get into
~ /гет ѝнту ~/ попадать в беду; vt беспокоить, приставать к; ~ oneself /~
вансэлф/ беспокоиться
troublemaker /трáблмэ́йкэ/ n смутьян
troublesome /трáблсэм/ adj хлопотный;
назойливый
troupe /трууп/ n труппа
trousers /трáузэз/ n pl брюки
trout /трáут/ n форель
truce /труус/ n перемирие
truck /трак/ n грузовик
true /труу/ adj подлинный; правильный;
верный; ~ copy /~ кóпи/ точная копия
truly /трýули/ adv правдиво, искренне;
yours ~ /йооз ~/ искренне ваш (в конце
письма)
trump /трамп/ n козырь; vt бить козырем
trumpet /трáмпит/ n труба; vi трубить
trumpeter /трáмпитэ/ n трубач
trunk /транк/ n ствол (дерева); туловище; чемодан; хобот (слона); pl трусы;
swimming ~s /свѝминг ~с/ плавки

trunk-call /трáнккóол/ n вызов по меж-
дугороднему телефону
trust /траст/ n доверие; трест; кредит; vt
доверять; поручать; vi надеяться
trustee /трастѝи/ n опекун
trustworthy /трáствёзи/ adj надежный
truth /труус/ n истина, правда
truthful /трýусфул/ adj правдивый
try /трай/ n попытка; испытание; vt испытывать; пробовать; судить; vi пытаться; ~ on /~ он/ примерять (одежду)
tub /таб/ n кадка; ушат; ванна
tube /тьююб/ n труба; трубка; тюбик
tuberculosis /тьюбёкьюлóусиз/ n туберкулез
Tuesday /тьюóюзди/ n вторник
tuft /тафт/ n пучок; хохолок
tug /таг/ n рывок; буксир
tuition /тьюѝшн/ n обучение; плата за
обучение
tulip /тьюóюлип/ n тюльпан
tulle /тьюóюл/ n тюль
tumble /тамбл/ n кувырканье; падение;
vi кувыркаться; падать
tumor /тьюóюмэ/ n опухоль; malignant ~
/мэлѝгнэнт ~/ злокачественная опухоль
tumult /тьюóюмалт/ n суматоха, шум
tune /тьююн/ n мелодия; in ~ /ин ~/ в
тон; vt настраивать
tuneful /тьюóюнфул/ adj мелодичный
tuner /тьюóюнэ/ n настройщик
tunnel /танл/ n туннель
turban /тёрбэн/ n тюрбан, чалма
turbine /тёрбин/ n турбина
turbo-jet /тёрбоуджéт/ adj турбореак-
тивный
turf /тёрф/ n дерн; торф; скачки
Turk /тёрк/ n турок, турчанка
turkey /тёрки/ n индюк, индюшка
Turkish /тёркиш/ n турецкий язык; adj
турецкий
Turkman /тёркмэн/ n туркмен(ка)
Turkmen /тёркмен/ adj туркменский

turmoil /тёрмойл/ n беспорядок, суматоха

turn /тёрн/ n поворот; оборот (колеса); очередь; перемена; at every ~ /эт эври ~/ на каждом шагу; take a ~ for the better /тэйк э ~ фо зэ бётэ/ принимать благоприятный оборот; by ~s /бай ~з/ по очереди; vt вращать; вертеть; поворачивать; перевертывать (страницу); заворачивать (за угол); перелицовывать (платье); ~ back /~ бэк/ поворачивать назад; ~ down /~ даун/ отклонять; ~ inside out /~ инсайд аут/ выворачивать наизнанку; ~ off /~ оф/ закрывать (кран); выключать (свет); ~ on /~ он/ открывать (кран); включать (свет); ~ to /~ ту/ обращаться к; приниматься за; ~ up /~ ап/ засучивать (рукава); vi появляться, приходить

turner /тёрнэ/ n токарь

turning /тёрнинг/ n поворот; перекресток; ~ point /~ пойнт/ поворотный пункт

turnip /тёрнип/ n репа

turntable /тёрнтэйбл/ n проигрыватель

turpentine /тёрпентайн/ n скипидар

turquoise /тёрквэз/ n бирюза

turtle /тёртл/ n черепаха

turtleneck /тёртлнэк/ n высокий воротник (свитера); свитер с воротником "хомут"

tusk /таск/ n бивень; клык

tutor /тьюютэ/ n репетитор; vt обучать, давать уроки

tweed /твиид/ n твид

tweezers /твиизэз/ n pl пинцет

twelfth /твелфс/ ord num двенадцатый

twelve /твелв/ num двенадцать

twentieth /твёнтис/ ord num двадцатый

twenty /твёнти/ num двадцать

twice /твайс/ adv дважды

twig /твиг/ n веточка, прутик

twilight /твайлайт/ n сумерки

twin /твин/ n близнец

twine /твайн/ n бечевка, шпагат

twinkle /твинкл/ vi мерцать, сверкать

twinkling /твинклинг/ n мерцание; in the ~ of an eye /ин зэ ~ ов эн ай/ в мгновение ока

twirl /твёрл/ vti вертеть(ся), кружить(ся)

twist /твист/ vt крутить, изгибать

two /туу/ num два, две; n двойка, двое, пара; in ~ /ин ~/ надвое; put ~ and ~ together /пут ~ энд ~ тэгёзэ/ понять, что к чему

twofold /тууфоулд/ adv вдвое, вдвойне

type /тайп/ n тип; класс; род; шрифт; vt печатать на машинке

typewriter /тайпрайтэ/ n пишущая машинка

typewritten /тайпритн/ adj машинописный

typhoid fever /тайфоидфиивэ/ n брюшной тиф

typhus /тайфэс/ n сыпной тиф

typical /типикл/ adj типичный

typist /тайпист/ n машинистка

tyranny /тирэни/ n тирания

tyrant /тайерэнт/ n тиран

tyre /тайе/ n шина, покрышка

U

udder /адэ/ n вымя

ugly /агли/ adj безобразный, уродливый

Ukrainian /юкрэйньен/ n украинец, украинка; украинский язык; adj украинский

ulcer /алсэ/ n язва

ultimate /алтимит/ adj конечный; окончательный

ultimately /алтимитли/ adv в конечном счете

ultimatum /алтимейтэм/ n ультиматум

ultra-short /алтрэшорт/ adj ультра-короткий

ultra-violet /алтрэвайелит/ adj ультрафиолетовый

umbrella /амбрэлэ/ n зонтик

umpire /áмпайе/ n (спорт.) судья; третейский судья

unable /áнэ́йбл/ adj неспособный; be ~
/би ~/ быть не в состоянии

unanimous /юнэ́нимэс/ adj единодуш-
ный, единогласный

unarmed /áнáрмд/ adj невооруженный

unashamed /áнэшéймд/ adj наглый

unasked /áнáскт/ adj непрошеный

unauthorized /áнóосэрайзд/ adj неправо-
мочный

unavoidable /áнэвóйдэбл/ adj неизбежный

unawares /áнэвэ́эз/ adv врасплох

unbalanced /áнбэ́лэнст/ adj неуравнове-
шенный

unbearable /áнбéэрэбл/ adj невыносимый

unbecoming /áнбикáминг/ adj неприличный

unbiassed /áнбáйест/ adj беспристрастный

unbind /áнбáйнд/ vt развязывать

unbreakable /áнбрэ́йкэбл/ adj небьющийся

unbridled /áнбрáйдлд/ adj разнузданный

unburden oneself /анбёрдн вансэ́лф/ vt
открывать душу

unbutton /анбáтн/ vt расстегивать

unceasing /анси́исинг/ adj непрерывный

unceremoniously /áнсéримóуньесли/ adv
бесцеремонно

uncertain /ансёртн/ adj неуверенный

uncertainty /ансёртнти/ n неопределенность

unchangeable /анчéйнджебл/ adj неизменный

uncle /анкл/ n дядя

uncomfortable /анкáмфэтэбл/ adj неудобный

unconditional /áнкэнди́шенл/ adj безоговорочный

unconquerable /анкóнкрэбл/ adj непобедимый

unconscious /анкóншес/ adj бессознательный

unconventional /áнкэнвéншенл/ adj не-
шаблонный

uncork /анкóрк/ vt откупоривать

uncouth /анкýус/ adj грубый, неуклюжий

uncover /анкáвэ/ vt открывать

undecided /áндисáйдыд/ adj нерешительный

undeniable /áндинáйебл/ adj неоспоримый

under /áндэ/ prep под; ниже; меньше
чем; при; согласно; ~ the condition /~
зэ кэнди́шн/ при условии; adv вниз;
внизу; ниже; adj нижний; низший

under-age /áндэрэ́йдж/ adj несовершеннолетний

undercover /áндэкáвэ/ adj тайный

undercurrent /áндэкáрнт/ n подводное
течение

undercut /áндэкат/ n вырезка (часть туши)

underestimate /áндэрэ́стимейт/ vt недооценивать

undergo /áндэгóу/ vt подвергаться; испытывать, переносить

undergraduate /áндэгрэ́дьюит/ n сту-
дент(ка)

underground /áндэграунд/ adj подзем-
ный; подпольный; n метрополитен;
подполье

underline /áндэлайн/ vt подчеркивать

undermine /áндэмáйн/ vt подрывать

underneath /áндэни́ис/ adv вниз, внизу;
prep под

underskirt /áндэскéт/ n нижняя юбка

understand /áндэстэ́нд/ vt понимать

understanding /áндэстэ́ндинг/ n понимание; come to an ~ /кам ту эн ~/ найти
общий язык

undertake /áндэтэ́йк/ vt предпринимать;
обязываться

undertaker /áндэтэ́йкэ/ n предприниматель; гробовщик

undertaking /áндэтэ́йкинг/ n предприятие; обязательство

undertone /áндэтóун/ n полутон; in ~s /ин ~з/ вполголоса

underwear /áндэвэ́э/ n нижнее белье

underworld /áндэвёлд/ n преисподняя; дно общества

undesirable /áндизáйерэбл/ adj нежелательный

undisputed /áндиспью́ютыд/ adj бесспорный

undisturbed /áндистёрбд/ adj безмятежный

undo /андýу/ vt развязывать; расстегивать

undoubted /андáутыд/ adj несомненный

undress /андрэ́с/ vti раздевать(ся)

undrinkable /андри́нкэбл/ adj непригодный для питья

unduly /андью́юли/ adv чрезмерно

undying /андáйинг/ adj бессмертный

unearned /анёрнд/ adj незаработанный; ~ income /~ и́нкэм/ непроизводственный доход

uneasy /ани́изи/ adj беспокойный; неловкий

uneatable /ани́итэбл/ adj несъедобный

uneducated /анэ́дьюкéйтыд/ adj необразованный

unemployed /áнимплóйд/ adj безработный

unemployment /áнимплóймент/ n безработица; ~ benefit /~ бéнефит/ пособие по безработице

unequal /ани́иквэл/ adj неравный

uneven /ани́ивн/ adj неровный; нечетный

unexpected /áникспéктыд/ adj неожиданный

unfair /анфэ́э/ adj несправедливый

unfamiliar /áнфэми́лье/ adj незнакомый

unfasten /анфáасн/ vt расстегивать

unfinished /анфи́ништ/ adj незаконченный

unfit /анфи́т/ adj негодный

unfold /анфóулд/ vti развертывать(ся)

unforeseen /áнфоси́ин/ adj непредвиденный

unforgettable /áнфэгéтэбл/ adj незабываемый

unforgivable /áнфэги́вэбл/ adj непростительный

unfortunate /анфóрчнит/ adj несчастливый; неудачный

unfortunately /анфóрчнитли/ adv к несчастью

unfounded /анфáундыд/ adj необоснованный

unfriendly /анфрéндли/ adj недружелюбный

unfurnished /анфёрништ/ adj без мебели

ungentlemanly /анджéнтлмэнли/ adj не свойственный джентльмену

ungrateful /ангрэ́йтфул/ adj неблагодарный

ungrounded /áнгрáундыд/ adj беспочвенный

unhappy /анхэ́пи/ adj несчастливый, несчастный

unharmed /анхáрмд/ adj невредимый

unhealthy /анхéлси/ adj нездоровый

unheard-of /анхёрдов/ adj неслыханный

unhurt /áнхёрт/ adj невредимый

uniform /ю́юнифом/ adj единообразный; n форменная одежда

unilateral /ю́юнилэ́трл/ adj односторонний

unimportant /áнимпóртэнт/ adj неважный

uninformed /áнинфóрмд/ adj неосведомленный

uninhabited /áнинхэ́битыд/ adj необитаемый

uninjured /áни́нджед/ adj неповрежденный

uninsured /áниншýэд/ adj незастрахованный

unintentional /áнинтэ́ншнл/ adj непреднамеренный

union /ю́юньен/ n союз; объединение

unique /юни́ик/ adj уникальный

unit /ю́юнит/ n единица; воинская часть

unite /юнáйт/ vti соединять(ся), объединять(ся)

united /юна́йтыд/ adj соединенный, объединенный; U. Nations /~ нэ́йшнз/ Организация Объединенных Наций

unity /ю́юнити/ n единство; согласие

universal /ю́юнивёрсл/ adj всеобщий; всемирный; универсальный

universe /ю́юнивёс/ n вселенная, мир

university /ю́юнивёрсити/ n университет

unjust /а́нджа́ст/ adj несправедливый

unkind /анка́йнд/ adj недобрый, злой

unknown /а́нно́ун/ adj неизвестный

unlawful /анло́офул/ adj незаконный

unleash /анли́иш/ vt развязывать (войну)

unless /энле́с/ conj если не

unlike /а́нла́йк/ adj непохожий; не такой, как

unlikely /анла́йкли/ adj маловероятный; adv вряд ли

unlimited /анли́митыд/ adj безграничный

unload /анло́уд/ vt разгружать

unlock /анло́к/ vt отпирать

unlucky /анла́ки/ adj несчастливый

unmarried /а́нмэ́рид/ adj холостой; незамужняя

unmask /анма́аск/ vt разоблачать

unnatural /анна́чрл/ adj неестественный, противоестественный

unnecessary /анна́сисри/ adj ненужный

unnoticed /анно́утист/ adj незамеченный

unpack /анпэ́к/ vt распаковывать

unparalleled /анпэ́рэлэлд/ adj беспримерный

unpleasant /анпле́знт/ adj неприятный

unpopular /анпо́пьюлэ/ adj непопулярный

unprecedented /анпре́сидэнтыд/ adj беспримерный

unprejudiced /анпре́джудист/ adj беспристрастный

unprofitable /анпро́фитэбл/ adj невыгодный; нерентабельный

unprotected /а́нпрэте́ктыд/ adj беззащитный

unquestionably /анкве́сченэбли/ adv несомненно

unquotable /анкво́утэбл/ adj нецензурный

unreal /анри́эл/ adj нереальный

unreasonable /анри́изнэбл/ adj безрассудный

unreliable /а́нрила́йебл/ adj ненадежный

unrest /анре́ст/ n беспокойство; смута

unruly /анру́ули/ adj буйный, непослушный

unscientific /а́нса́йенти́фик/ adj ненаучный

unselfish /ансэ́лфиш/ adj бескорыстный

unshakable /аншейкэбл/ adj непоколебимый

unskilled /а́нски́лд/ adj неквалифицированный

unsociable /ансо́ушебл/ adj необщительный

unstable /анстэ́йбл/ adj неустойчивый

unthinkable /анси́нкэбл/ adj немыслимый

untidy /анта́йди/ adj неопрятный

untie /а́нта́й/ vt развязывать

until /энти́л/ prep до, до сих (тех) пор; not ~ /нот ~/ не раньше; conj (до тех пор), пока

untimely /анта́ймли/ adj несвоевременный

untiring /анта́йеринг/ adj неутомимый

untouched /анта́чт/ adj нетронутый

untrained /а́нтрэ́йнд/ adj необученный

untranslatable /а́нтрэнслэ́йтэбл/ adj непереводимый

untrue /антру́у/ adj неверный; it is ~ /ит из ~/ это неправда

unusual /анъю́южуэл/ adj необыкновенный

unwell /анвэ́л/ adj нездоровый; he's ~/хииз ~ / ему нездоровится

unwind /анва́йнд/ vt разматывать

unwise /а́нва́йз/ adj неблагоразумный

unworthy /анвёрзи/ adj недостойный

unwrap /анрэ́п/ vt развертывать

up /ап/ adj идущий вверх; the price is ~ /зэ прайс из ~/ цена возросла; time is ~ /тайм из ~/ время истекло; adv наверху, вверху; наверх, вверх; ~ and down /~ энд да́ун/ вверх и вниз, повсюду; ~ to /~ ту/ вплоть до; ~ to now /~ ту на́у/ до сих пор; she came up /ши кейм ~/ она подошла; well ~ in /вэл ~ ин/ хорошо осведомленный; what's ~? /вотс ~/ в чем дело?; prep вверх по, вдоль по; ~ the street /~ зэ стриит/ по улице

upbringing /а́пбри́нгинг/ n воспитание

upgrade /апгрэ́йд/ vt повышать (по работе); повышать качество (продукции)

uphill /апхи́л/ adv в гору

uphold /апхо́улд/ vt поддерживать

upholster /апхо́улстэ/ vt обивать (мебель)

upholstered /апхо́улстэд/ adj обитый (материей и т.п.)

upholsterer /апхо́улстэрэ/ n обойщик

upon /эпо́н/ prep на; ~ my soul! /~ май со́ул/ клянусь!

upper /а́пэ/ adj верхний, высший; ~ floor /~ флор/ верхний этаж; get the ~ hand /гет зы ~ хэнд/ брать верх

uppermost /а́пэмоуст/ adj самый верхний; наивысший

upright /а́пра́йт/ adj вертикальный; прямой; честный; adv стоймя

uprising /апра́йзинг/ n бунт, восстание

uproar /а́про́р/ n буйство, шум

uproot /апру́ут/ vt вырывать с корнем, искоренять

upset /апсе́т/ vt опрокидывать; расстраивать; нарушать; огорчать

upside down /а́псайда́ун/ adv вверх дном

upstairs /а́пстэ́зз/ adv наверху, в верхнем этаже

upstart /а́пстарт/ n выскочка

up-to-date /а́птэдэ́йт/ adj современный

uptown /а́пта́ун/ n жилые кварталы города

upward /а́пвэд/ adj двигающийся вверх, направленный вверх

up-wind /а́пвинд/ adv против ветра

urban /ёрбэн/ adj городской

urge /ёрдж/ vt побуждать; убеждать

urgent /ёрджент/ adj настоятельный; срочный

urine /ю́эрин/ n моча

urn /ёрн/ n урна

us /ас/ pron нас, нам и т.д.

usage /ю́юзидж/ n употребление; обычай

use /ююс/ n польза; употребление, it's no ~ /итс но́у ~/ бесполезно; make ~ of /мэйк ~ ов/ использовать; /ююз/ vt употреблять, пользоваться, применять; we often ~d to be there /ви офн ~д ту би зэ́е/ мы часто бываем там; ~ up /~ ап/ расходовать

used /ююзд/ adj привыкший; подержанный; использованный; get ~ to /гет ~ ту/ привыкать к

useful /ю́юсфул/ adj полезный

user /ю́юзэ/ n потребитель

usher /а́ше/ n билетер; швейцар

usual /ю́южуэл/ adj обыкновенный, обычный; as ~ /эз ~/ как обычно

usurer /ю́южерэ/ n ростовщик

usurp /юзёрп/ vt узурпировать

usurper /юзёрпэ/ n узурпатор

utensil /юте́нсл/ n посуда, утварь

utility /юти́лити/ n полезность; public ~s /па́блик ~з/ предприятия общественного пользования

utilize /ю́ютилайз/ vt использовать

utmost /а́тмоуст/ adj предельный; величайший; do one's ~ /ду ванз ~/ делать все возможное; of the ~ importance /ов зы ~ импо́ртэнс/ чрезвычайной важности

utter /а́тэ/ adj совершенный, абсолютный; vt произносить, издавать (звук)

utterance /а́тэрэнс/ n высказывание

Uzbek /у́збек/ n узбек, узбечка; n узбекский язык; adj узбекский

V

vacancy /вэ́йкэнси/ n вакансия

vacant /вэ́йкэнт/ adj вакантный; отсутствующий (взгляд)

vacate /вэке́йт/ vt освобождать

vacation /вэке́йшн/ n каникулы, отпуск

vaccinate /вэ́ксинэйт/ vt делать прививку

vacuum /вэ́кьюэм/ n вакуум

vacuum cleaner /вэ́кьюэмкли́инэ/ n пылесос

vacuum flask /вэ́кьюэмфла́аск/ n термос

vagabond /вэ́гэбонд/ n бродяга

vagina /вэджа́йнэ/ n влагалище

vague /вейг/ adj неясный, смутный

vain /вейн/ adj напрасный; тщетный; тщеславный; самодовольный; in ~ /ин ~/ тщетно

valerian /вэли́эриэн/ n (мед.) валериановые капли

valet /вэ́лит/ n камердинер, слуга

valiant /вэ́льент/ adj доблестный, храбрый

valid /вэ́лид/ adj действительный, имеющий силу; веский

valise /вэли́из/ n саквояж

valley /вэ́ли/ n долина

valour /вэ́лэ/ n доблесть

valuable /вэ́льюэбл/ adj ценный, дорогой

valuables /вэ́льюэблз/ n pl ценности

value /вэ́лью/ n ценность; стоимость; цена; значение; vt оценивать; дорожить

valve /вэлв/ n клапан (также анат.)

van /вэн/ n фургон; авангард

vanguard /вэ́нгард/ n авангард

vanilla /вэни́лэ/ n ваниль

vanish /вэ́ниш/ vt исчезать, пропадать

vapour /вэ́йпэ/ n пар

variant /вэ́эриэнт/ n вариант

variation /вэ́эри́йшн/ n изменение; вариант

variety /вэра́йети/ n разнообразие; ~ show /~ шо́у/ варьете

various /вэ́эриэс/ adj различный, разный

varnish /ва́рниш/ n лак; лоск; vt лакировать

vary /вэ́эри/ vti менять (ся); vi отличаться

vase /вааз/ n ваза

vast /вааст/ adj громадный; обширный

vat /вэт/ n бак; чан; бочка; кадка

vault /воолт/ n свод; погреб, подвал; склеп; прыжок; pole ~ /по́ул ~/ прыжок с шестом; ~ing horse /~инг хорс/ (спорт.) конь

veal /виил/ n телятина

vegetable /ве́джитбл/ n овощ; adj растительный

vegetarian /ве́джитэ́эриэн/ n вегетарианец

vegetation /ве́джитэ́йшн/ n растительность

vehement /ви́имэнт/ adj неистовый

vehicle /ви́икл/ n перевозочное средство; повозка; автомашина

veil /вейл/ n вуаль; завеса; vt завуалировать

vein /вейн/ n вена; жила

velocity /вило́сити/ n скорость

velours /велу́э/ n велюр

velvet /ве́лвит/ n бархат

veneer /вини́э/ n фанера

venerable /ве́нрэбл/ adj почтенный

venereal /вини́эриэл/ adj венерический

Venetian /вини́ишн/ adj венецианский; ~ blind /~ блайнд/ жалюзи

vengeance /ве́нженс/ n месть

venison /вензн/ n оленина

venom /ве́нэм/ n яд

venomous /ве́нэмэс/ adj ядовитый

vent /вент/ n отверстие; отдушина; give ~ to /гив ~ ту/ изливать

ventilate /ве́нтилэйт/ vt проветривать; обсуждать

ventilation /ве́нтилэ́йшн/ n вентиляция

ventilator /ве́нтилэйтэ/ n вентилятор

venture /ве́нче/ n рискованное предприятие; at a ~ /эт э ~/ наудачу; joint ~ /джойнт ~/ совместное предприятие; vt рисковать; vi отваживаться

Venus /ви́инэс/ n Венера

veranda(h) /верэ́ндэ/ n веранда, терраса

verb /вёрб/ n глагол

verbal /вёрбэл/ adj устный, словесный

verbatim /вёбэ́йтим/ n стенографический отчет; adj дословный; adv дословно; quote ~ /кво́ут ~/ цитировать дословно

verdict /вёрдикт/ n приговор

verge /вёрдж/ n край; обочина (дороги); (образн.) грань; край; on the ~ of /он зэ ~ ов/ на грани; vi: ~ on /~ он/ граничить с

verification /ве́рификéйшн/ n проверка; подтверждение

verify /ве́рифай/ vt проверять, подтверждать

veritable /ве́ритэбл/ adj настоящий

verity /ве́рити/ n истина, истинность

vernacular /венэ́кьюлэ/ n местный диалект

versatile /вёрсэтайл/ adj разносторонний

verse /вёрс/ n стих; строфа; поэзия

versed /вёрст/ adj опытный

version /вёршн/ n версия; вариант

versus /вёрсэс/ prep против

vertebre /вёртибрэ/ n позвонок

vertebrate /вёртибрэйт/ n позвоночное животное

vertical /вёртикл/ adj вертикальный

vertigo /вёртигоу/ n головокружение

verve /вéэв/ n энтузиазм

very /вéри/ adj настоящий; (тот) самый; adv очень; ~ much /~ мач/ очень много

vessel /весл/ n сосуд; корабль

vest /вест/ n майка; жилет

vet /вет/ n (разг.) ветеринар

veteran /вéтерн/ n ветеран

veterinary /вéтринэри/ adj ветеринарный

veto /ви́итоу/ n вето; vt запрещать, налагать вето на

vex /векс/ vt досаждать

vexation /вексэ́йшн/ n досада

via /ва́йе/ prep по маршруту через

vibrate /вайбрэ́йт/ vi вибрировать

vice /вайс/ n порок, зло; (тех.) тиски; клещи

vice-admiral /ва́йсэ́дмэрл/ n вице-адмирал

vice-chairman /ва́йсчéэмэн/ n заместитель председателя

vice-president /ва́йспрéзидент/ n вице-президент

vice versa /ва́йсивéрсэ/ adv наоборот

vicinity /виси́нити/ n окрестности; близость; соседство; in the ~ of /ин зэ ~ ов/ поблизости

vicious /ви́шес/ adj порочный, злобный; ~ circle /~ сёркл/ порочный круг

victim /ви́ктим/ n жертва

victor /ви́ктэ/ n победитель

victorious /викто́ориэс/ adj победоносный

victory /ви́ктэри/ n победа

video recorder /ви́диоурико́рдэ/ n видеомагнитофон

video tape /ви́диоутэ́йп/ n видеолента

view /вьюю/ n вид; мнение; in ~ of /ин ~ ов/ ввиду; with a ~ to /виз э ~ ту/ с целью; vt осматривать, рассматривать

viewfinder /вью́юфайндэ/ n видоискатель

viewpoint /вью́юпойнт/ n точка зрения

vigil /ви́джил/ n бодрствование; ночное дежурство

vigilance /ви́джилэнс/ n бдительность

vigilant /ви́джилэнт/ adj бдительный

vigorous /ви́гэрэс/ adj сильный, энергичный

vigour /ви́гэ/ n сила, энергия

vile /вайл/ adj низкий, подлый

vilify /ви́лифай/ vt поносить

villa /ви́лэ/ n вилла

village /ви́лидж/ n деревня, село

villager /ви́лиджэ/ n деревенский житель

villain /ви́лэн/ n мерзавец, злодей

villainy /ви́лэни/ n злодейство

vindicate /ви́ндикейт/ vt оправдывать, доказывать

vine /вайн/ n виноградная лоза

vinegar /ви́нигэ/ n уксус

vineyard /ви́ньед/ n виноградник

vintage /ви́нтыдж/ n сбор винограда; ~ of 1940 /~ ов на́йнти фо́рти/ вино урожая 1940 года

violate /ва́йелэйт/ vt нарушать (закон); применять насилие

violation /ва́йелэ́йшн/ n нарушение; насилие

violence /ва́йелэнс/ n насилие; сила

violent /ва́йелэнт/ adj насильственный; неистовый; сильный

violet /ва́йелит/ n фиалка; adj фиолетовый; лиловый

violin /ва́йели́н/ n скрипка

violinist /ва́йелинист/ n скрипач

viper /ва́йпэ/ n гадюка

virgin /вёрджин/ n дева, девственница; adj чистый; ~ soil /~ сойл/ целина

virginal /вёрджинл/ adj девственный

virtual /вёртьюэл/ adj фактический

virtue /вёртью/ n добродетель; by ~ of /бай ~ ов/ благодаря

virtuous /вёртьюэс/ adj добродетельный

virus /ва́йерэс/ n вирус

visa /ви́изэ/ n виза

visibility /ви́зиби́лити/ n видимость

visible /ви́зэбл/ adj видимый; очевидный

vision /вижн/ n зрение; проницательность

visit /ви́зит/ n визит, посещение; pay a ~ /пэй э ~/ наносить визит; vt посещать

visiting /ви́зитинг/ adj посещающий

visiting card /ви́зитингка́рд/ n визитная карточка

visitor /ви́зитэ/ n гость, посетитель

visual /ви́жьюэл/ adj наглядный; зрительный

visualize /ви́жьюэлайз/ vt мысленно видеть

vital /вайтл/ adj жизненно важный, насущный; ~ issue /~ и́шью/ важнейший вопрос

vitamin /ви́тэмин/ n витамин

vitiate /ви́шиэйт/ vt портить

vivacious /виве́йшес/ adj живой; оживленный

vivid /ви́вид/ adj яркий; четкий; ясный

vocabulary /вэка́бьюлэри/ n словарь, запас слов

vocal /во́укл/ adj голосовой, вокальный

vocation /воке́йшн/ n призвание; профессия

vodka /во́дка/ n водка

vogue /во́уг/ n мода

voice /войс/ n голос

void /войд/ n пустота; adj пустой, недействительный

volcano /волке́йноу/ n вулкан

volt /во́улт/ n вольт

voltage /во́ултыдж/ n вольтаж

volume /во́льюм/ n том; объем

voluntary /во́лэнтэри/ adj добровольный

volunteer /во́лэнти́э/ n доброволец; vi идти добровольцем; предлагать (свою помощь, услуги)

voluptuous /вэла́птьюэс/ adj сладострастный

vomit /во́мит/ n рвота; vi рвать

voracious /вэрэ́йшес/ adj прожорливый

vote /во́ут/ n голос; голосование; vi голосовать

voter /во́утэ/ n избиратель

voting /во́утинг/ n голосование

voting paper /во́утингпэ́йпэ/ n избирательный бюллетень

vouch /ва́уч/ vt ручаться

voucher /ва́уче/ n расписка; квитанция

vow /ва́у/ n клятва, обет; vi клясться, давать обет

vowel /ва́уэл/ n гласный (звук)

voyage /во́идж/ n путешествие (морское или воздушное)

vulgar /ва́лгэ/ adj вульгарный

vulnerable /ва́лнэрэбл/ adj уязвимый

vulture /ва́лче/ n гриф; (образн.) хищник

W

wad /вод/ n кусок ваты

wade /вэйд/ vi переходить вброд

waffle /вофл/ n вафля

wag /вэг/ vt махать; вилять (хвостом)

wage(s) /вэйдж(из)/ n заработная плата; vt вести; ~ war /~ вор/ вести войну

wag(g)on /вэ́гэн/ n повозка; goods ~ /гудз ~/ товарный вагон

wail /вэйл/ vi вопить

waist /вэйст/ n талия

waistcoat /вэ́йскоут/ n жилет

wait /вэйт/ vti ждать; ~ a second! /~ э сэкнд/ подождите!; ~ on /~ он/ прислуживать за столом

waiter /вэ́йтэ/ n официант

waiting /вэ́йтинг/ n ожидание

waiting room /вэ́йтингру́м/ n зал ожидания; приемная

waitress /вэ́йтрис/ n официантка

wake /вэйк/ vt будить; vi просыпаться

walk /воок/ n ходьба; походка; прогулка пешком; go for a ~ /го́у фор э ~/ гулять; ~ of life /~ ов лайф/ профессия, сфера деятельности; vi идти; ходить; гулять; ~ about /~ эба́ут/ прогуливаться; ~ out /~ а́ут/ объявлять забастовку

walk-over /во́око́увэ/ n легкая победа

wall /воол/ n стена

wallpaper /во́олпэ́йпэ/ n обои

wallet /во́лит/ n бумажник

walnut /во́олнэт/ n грецкий орех

walrus /во́олрэс/ n морж

waltz /волс/ n вальс; vi вальсировать

wander /во́ндэ/ vi бродить, странствовать

wane /вэйн/ n убывание; ущерб (луны); vi убывать

want /вонт/ n нужда; недостаток; pl потребности; vt хотеть; нуждаться в; недоставать; wanted /во́нтыд/ требуется... (в объявлениях)

war /вор/ n война; W. Office /~ о́фис/ военное министерство (Англии)

ward /ворд/ n палата (госпиталя); опека; подопечный; vt: ~ off /~ оф/ отражать (удар); отвращать (опасность)

wardrobe /во́рдроуб/ n гардероб

wardship /во́рдшип/ n опека

warehouse /вэ́эхаус/ n склад

wares /вээз/ n pl изделия, товары

warfare /во́рфээ/ n война, военные действия

warlike /во́рлайк/ adj воинственный

warm /ворм/ adj теплый; сердечный; горячий; I'm ~ /айм ~/ мне тепло

warmonger /во́рма́нгэ/ n поджигатель войны

warmth /вормф/ n теплота; сердечность

warn /ворн/ vt предупреждать, предостерегать

warning /во́рнинг/ n предупреждение

warrant /во́рэнт/ n ордер; полномочие; гарантия; vt гарантировать; ручаться за; оправдывать

warranty /во́рэнти/ n гарантия; ручательство

warrior /во́риэ/ n боец, воин

warship /во́ршип/ n военный корабль

wart /ворт/ n бородавка

wary /вэ́эри/ adj осторожный

wash /вош/ vti мыть(ся); умывать(ся); обмывать (берега); стирать (одежду); ~ away /вэ́эй/ смывать(ся); I ~ my hands of it /ай ~ май хэндз ов ит/ я умываю руки; ~ up /~ ап/ мыть посуду; n мытье; стирка; прибой

washbasin /во́шбейсн/ n умывальная раковина

washhouse /во́шхаус/ n прачечная

washerwoman /во́шеву́мэн/ n прачка

washing /во́шинг/ n мытье; стирка; белье; ~ machine /~ мэши́ин/ стиральная машина

washstand /во́шстэнд/ n умывальник

wasp /восп/ n оса

waste /вэйст/ vt тратить; терять (время); портить; n излишняя трата; отбросы; отходы

wasteful /вэ́йстфул/ adj расточительный

waste pipe /вэ́йстпайп/ n сточная труба

watch /воч/ n часы, наблюдение; be on ~ /би он ~/ нести вахту, стоять в карауле; vt наблюдать за, следить за, сторожить; ~ out /~ а́ут/ берегись!

watchful /во́чфул/ adj бдительный
watchmaker /во́тчмэ́йкэ/ n часовщик
watchman /во́чмэн/ n сторож
water /во́отэ/ n вода; vt поливать; his
  mouth ~s /хиз ма́уф ~з/ у него слюнки
  текут; ~ down /~ да́ун/ разбавлять
water bottle /во́отэбо́тл/ n грелка
water-can /во́отэкэн/ n бидон; фляга
water closet /во́отэкло́зит/ n уборная
watercolour /во́отэка́лэ/ n акварель
water-cooled /во́отэкулд/ adj с водяным
  охлаждением
waterfall /во́отэфол/ n водопад
waterless /во́отэлис/ adj безводный
watermark /во́отэмарк/ n водяной знак
watermelon /во́отэмэ́лэн/ n арбуз
watermill /во́отэмил/ n водяная мельница
waterpower /во́отэпа́уэ/ n гидроэнергия
waterproof /во́отэпруф/ adj водонепроницаемый
water supply /во́отэсэпла́й/ n водоснаб-
  жение
watertight /во́отэтайт/ adj герметический
watery /во́отэри/ adj водянистый
watt /вот/ n ватт
wave /вэйв/ n волна; vt махать (рукой,
  платком и т.д.); завивать (волосы)
waver /вэ́йвэ/ vi колебаться
wax /вэкс/ n воск; vt вощить; vi прибывать (о луне); становиться
waxwork /вэ́ксворк/ n восковая фигура
way /вэй/ n дорога; путь; направление;
  манера; способ; образ действий; ~s and
  means /~з энд миинз/ способы и средства; by the ~ /бай зы ~/ кстати; be in
  the ~ /би ин зы ~/ мешать; in a friendly
  ~ /ин э фре́ндли ~/ мирным путем; on
  the ~ /он зы ~/ по пути; make ~ /мэйк
  ~/ уступать
wayside /вэ́йсайд/ n обочина; adj придорожный
we /вии/ pron мы
weak /виик/ adj слабый; болезненный; ~
  point /~ пойнт/ слабое место; ~ tea /~
  тии/ жидкий чай

weaken /виикн/ vt ослаблять; vi слабеть
weakling /ви́иклинг/ n слабак
weakly /ви́икли/ adv слабо
weakness /ви́икнис/ n слабость
wealth /вэлф/ n богатство, изобилие
wealthy /вэ́лфи/ adj богатый
weapon /вэпн/ n оружие
wear /вээ/ n носка; одежда; lady's ~
  /лэ́йдиз ~/ женская одежда; vt носить
  (одежду); ~ out /~ а́ут/ изнаши-
  вать(ся)
weariness /ви́эринис/ n усталость; скука
weary /ви́эри/ adj утомленный, усталый
weather /вэ́зэ/ n погода
weather-beaten /вэ́ззэби́итн/ adj обветренный
weather cock /вэ́зэкок/ n флюгер (также
  образн.)
weather forecast /вэ́ззэфо́ркаст/ n прогноз
  погоды
weave /виив/ vt ткать, плести
weaver /ви́ивэ/ n ткач
web /вэб/ n паутина; перепонка
wed /вед/ vi вступать в брак
wedding /ве́динг/ n свадьба
wedding dress /ве́дингдрэс/ n подвенеч-
  ное платье
wedding ring /ве́дингринг/ n обручальное кольцо
wedge /ведж/ n клин
Wednesday /ве́нзди/ n среда
wee /вии/ adj крошечный
weed /виид/ n сорняк; vt полоть
week /виик/ n неделя; ~'s wage /~с
  вэйдж/ недельный заработок
weekday /ви́икдэй/ n будний день
weekend /ви́икэнд/ n уикэнд
weekly /ви́икли/ adj еженедельный; adv
  раз в неделю; n еженедельник
weep /виип/ vi плакать
weigh /вей/ vt взвешивать; vi весить,
  иметь значение
weight /вейт/ n вес; штанга; бремя
weightless /ве́йтлис/ adj невесомый
weightlessness /ве́йтлиснис/ n невесомость

weightlifting /вéйтли́фтинг/ n поднятие тяжестей

weighty /вéйти/ adj увесистый; веский

welcome /вэ́лкэм/ n приветствие; (радушный) прием; adj желанный; vt приветствовать, (радушно) принимать; ~! добро пожаловать; Thanks! - You're ~! /сэнкс! ю а ~!/ Спасибо! - Пожалуйста!

welfare /вэ́лфэə/ n благосостояние; пособие по безработице; ~ state /~ стэйт/ государство всеобщего благосостояния

well /вэл/ n колодец

well /вэл/ adj хороший; здоровый; all is ~ /оол из ~/ все в порядке; I'm ~ /айм ~/ я чувствую себя хорошо; adv хорошо; вполне; очень; ~ done! /~ дан/ хорошо!, молодец!; interj ну!; as ~ /эз ~/ тоже, также; as ~ as /эз ~ эз/ так же, как

well-balanced /вэ́лбэ́лэнст/ adj уравновешенный

well-being /вэ́лби́инг/ n благополучие

well-bred /вэ́лбрэ́д/ adj воспитанный

well-disposed /вэ́лдиспо́узд/ adj благосклонный

well-informed /вэ́линфо́рмд/ adj хорошо осведомленный

well-off /вэ́ло́ф/ adj состоятельный

well-read /вэ́лрэ́д/ adj начитанный

well-timed /вэ́лта́ймд/ adj своевременный

well-wisher /вэ́лви́шə/ n доброжелатель

well-worn /вэ́лво́рн/ adj поношенный; (образн.) избитый

Welsh /вэлш/ n валлийский язык; adj уэльский, валлийский

Welshman /вэ́лшмэн/ n валлиец

west /вэст/ n запад; adj западный; adv на запад, к западу

western /вэ́стəрн/ adj западный; n вестерн

wet /вет/ adj мокрый, влажный; ~ fish /~ фиш/ свежая рыба; соленая рыба; "~ paint" /~ пэйнт/ осторожно, окрашено!; ~ through /~ сруу/ промокший до нитки

wetness /вéтнис/ n влажность, сырость

whale /вэйл/ n кит

whalebone /вэ́йлбоун/ n китовый ус

whaler /вэ́йлə/ n китобой

wharf /ворф/ n пристань

what /вот/ pron что, сколько, какой; ~ for? /~ фо/ зачем?; ~'s up /~с ап/ что происходит?; conj что; he knows ~'s ~ /хи но́уз ~с ~/ он знает, что к чему

whatever /вотэ́вə/, whatsoever /во́тсоуэ́вə/ adj какой бы ни, любой; pron что бы ни; все, что; ~ he says /~ хи сэз/ что бы он ни говорил; nothing ~ /на́синг ~/ абсолютно ничего

wheat /виит/ n пшеница

wheel /виил/ n колесо; руль; vt катить, везти; three-wheeled /сри́иви́илд/ трехколесный

wheelbarrow /ви́илбэ́роу/ n тачка

wheel-chair /ви́илчéə/ n кресло-каталка

when /вэн/ adv, conj когда

whence /вэнс/ adv откуда

whenever /вэнэ́вə/ conj когда бы ни; ~ you like /~ ю лайк/ в любое время

where /вэə/ adv, conj где, куда

whereabouts /вэ́эрэбáутс/ adv где, в каких краях; n местонахождение

whereas /вэ́эрэз/ conj тогда как

whereby /вэ́эбай/ adv посредством чего

wherefore /вэ́эфор/ adv для чего; conj по той причине, что

wherein /вээри́н/ adv в чем?

whereupon /вэ́эрэпо́н/ conj после чего

wherever /вээрэ́вə/ conj где бы ни

whet /вэт/ vt точить; возбуждать (аппетит)

whetstone /вэ́тстоун/ n точильный камень

whether /вэ́зə/ conj ли; ~ it's true or not /~ итс труу о нот/ правда ли это или нет

which /вич/ pron, conj который; что; adj какой

whichever /вичэ́вə/ pron какой бы ни, какой угодно

while /вайл/ n время, промежуток времени; for a ~ /фор э ~/ на время whim /вим/ n каприз, прихоть

whimper /ви́мпэ/ vi хныкать

whine /вайн/ vi выть; хныкать; скулить

whip /вип/ n кнут, хлыст; vt хлестать; погонять; сбивать (крем)

whirl /вёрл/ vti вертеть(ся), кружить(ся)

whirlpool /вёрлпул/ n водоворот

whirlwind /вёрлвинд/ n вихрь

whisker /ви́скэ/ n pl бакенбарды; усы; усики (у животных)

whisky /ви́ски/ n виски

whisper /ви́спэ/ n шепот; vt шептать

whistle /висл/ n свист; свисток; vi свистеть

white /вайт/ adj белый; седой (о волосах); n белый цвет; белизна; белок (глаза, яйца); turn ~ /тёрн ~/ бледнеть

whiten /вайтн/ vt белить

white-hot /ва́йтхо́т/ adj раскаленный добела

whither /ви́зэ/ adv, conj куда

Whitsuntide /ви́тснтайд/ n Троица

who /xyy/ pron кто; тот, кто; который

whoever /хуэ́вэ/ pron, conj кто бы ни

whole /хо́ул/ adj весь, целый; n целое; on the ~ /он зэ ~/ в целом

wholehearted /хо́улха́ртыд/ adj искренний, от всего сердца

wholesale /хо́улсэйл/ adj оптовая торговля; adv оптом

wholesome /хо́улсэм/ adj благотворный

whom /хуум/ pron кого, которого

whore /xop/ n шлюха

whose /xyyз/ pron чей, чья, чье, чьи; которого, которой, которых

whosoever /ху́усоэ́вэ/ pron кто бы ни

why /вай/ adv почему; interj ну!

wick /вик/ n фитиль

wicked /ви́кид/ adj злой

wide /вайд/ adj широкий; adv повсюду; far and ~ /фар энд ~/ повсюду

widespread /ва́йдспрэд/ adj распространенный

widen /вайдн/ vt расширять

widow /ви́доу/ n вдова

widower /ви́доуэ/ n вдовец

width /видф/ n ширина

wife /вайф/ n жена

wig /виг/ n парик

wild /вайлд/ adj дикий, неистовый; be ~ about /би ~ эба́ут/ быть без ума от

wilderness /ви́лдэнис/ n дикая местность; пустыня

wile /вайл/ n уловка, хитрость; обман

wilful /ви́лфул/ adj своенравный

will /вил/ n воля; сила воли; завещание; at ~ /эт ~/ по желанию; vt велеть, хотеть; v aux: служит для образования будущего времени

willing /ви́линг/ adj готовый, согласный

willingly /ви́лингли/ adv охотно

willow /ви́лоу/ n ива

willy-nilly /ви́линийли/ adv волей-неволей

win /вин/ n выигрыш, победа; vti выигрывать, побеждать

wince /винс/ vi вздрагивать

wind /винд/ n ветер; get ~ of /гет ~ ов/ пронюхивать

wind /вайнд/ vi виться, извиваться, крутиться; ~ up /~ ап/ заводить (часы и т.д.)

window /ви́ндоу/ n окно

windowsill /ви́ндоусил/ n подоконник

window pane /ви́ндоупэйн/ n оконное стекло

windscreen /ви́нскрин/ n ветровое/переднее стекло; ~ wiper /~ ва́йпэ/ "дворник"

windy /ви́нди/ adj ветреный

wine /вайн/ n вино

wine cellar /ва́йнсе́лэ/ n винный погреб

wineglass /ва́йнглас/ n рюмка

wineskin /ва́йнскин/ n бурдюк

wing /винг/ n крыло; флигель

wink /винк/ vi моргать; ~ at /~ эт/ подмигивать; смотреть сквозь пальцы

winner /ви́нэ/ n победитель

winter /ви́нтэ/ n зима

wintry /ви́нтри/ adj зимний

wipe /вайп/ vt вытирать; стирать

wire /вайе/ n проволока; vt телеграфировать

wireless /вайелис/ n радио

wire-pulling /вайепулинг/ n интриги

wiry /вайери/ n жилистый

wisdom /виздэм/ n мудрость

wise /вайз/ adj мудрый

wish /виш/ n желание; best ~es /бест ~из/ наилучшие пожелания; vti желать; ~ a Happy New Year /~ э хэпи нью йее/ поздравлять с Новым Годом

wistful /вистфул/ adj задумчивый

wit /вит/ n ум; остроумие; остряк

witch /вич/ n ведьма

witchcraft /вичкрафт/ n колдовство

witch-doctor /вичдоктэ/ n знахарь

with /виз/ prep с, вместе; у; при

withdraw /виздроо/ vt отдергивать; брать назад; отзывать; vi удаляться; (воен.) отходить

withdrawl /виздроол/ n изъятие; удаление; (воен.) отход

wither /визэ/ vt увядать

withhold /визхоулд/ vt удерживать; утаивать

within /визын/ prep в, внутри; в пределах; в течение; ~ a year /~ э йее/ в течение года; ~ call /~ коол/ в пределах слышимости

without /визаут/ prep без, вне, за; do ~ /ду ~/ обходиться без; ~ fail /~ фэйл/ непременно; it goes ~ saying /ит гоуз ~ сэйинг/ само собой разумеется

withstand /визстэнд/ vt противостоять

witness /витнис/ n свидетель; свидетельство; bear ~ to /биэ ~ ту/ свидетельствовать; vt быть свидетелем; заверять (подпись)

witty /вити/ adj остроумный

wizard /визэд/ n чародей

wolf /вулф/ n волк

woman /вумэн/ n женщина

womanly /вумэнли/ adj женственный

womb /вуум/ n (анат.) матка; чрево; утроба

wonder /вандэ/ n чудо; изумление; no ~ /ноу ~/ неудивительно; vi интересоваться; ~ at /~ эт/ удивляться

wonderful /вандэфул/ adj чудесный

wont /вонт/ n привычка

woo /вуу/ vt ухаживать за

wood /вуд/ n лес; дерево (материал); дрова

woodcut /вудкат/ n гравюра на дереве

woodcutter /вудкатэ/ n лесоруб

wooden /вудн/ adj деревянный

woodshed /вудшед/ n сарай

wool /вул/ n шерсть; go ~-gathering /гоу ~гээринг/ витать в облаках

woollen /вулин/ adj шерстяной

word /вёрд/ n слово

work /вёрк/ n работа; труд; произведение; pl завод; out of ~ /аут ов ~/ безработный; complete ~s /кэмплиит ~с/ полное собрание сочинений; vi работать, действовать; ~ out /~ аут/ разрабатывать, выйти, удаться; ~ over /~ оувэ/ перерабатывать

workable /вёркэбл/ adj осуществимый

worker /вёркэ/ n рабочий

working day /вёркингдэй/ n рабочий день

workmanship /вёркмэншип/ n мастерство

workshop /вёркшоп/ n мастерская

world /вёрлд/ n мир, свет

worldly /вёрлдли/ adj мирской

worldwide /вёрлдвайд/ adj всемирный

worm /вёрм/ n червь; глист; ничтожество

wormy /вёрми/ adj червивый

worry /вари/ n беспокойство; vi беспокоиться

worse /вёрс/ adj худший; adv хуже

worship /вёршип/ n почитание, богослужение; vt обожать

worshipper /вёршипэ/ n почитатель

worst /вёрст/ adj наихудший; adv хуже всего

worth /вёрс/ n стоимость; ценность; adj
    стóящий; be ~ /би ~/ стоить; it's ~ notice
    /итс ~ нóутис/ это достойно внимания
worthless /вёрслис/ adj никчемный
worthy /вёрзи/ adj достойный
wound /вуунд/ n рана; vt ранить
wounded /вýундыд/ adj раненый
wrangle /рэнгл/ n пререкания; vi прере-
    каться
wrap /рэп/ vt завертывать; запутывать; ~
    it up /~ ит ап/ заверните
wrapper /рэ́пэ/ n обертка; упаковщик,
    упаковщица
wrath /рооф/ n гнев
wreath /рииф/ n венок; кольцо (дыма)
wreck /рэк/ n авария, крушение; vt то-
    пить (корабль); разрушать
wreckage /рэ́кидж/ n обломки
wrench /рэнч/ n дерганье; вывих; гаеч-
    ный ключ
wrest /рэст/ vt вырывать (силой); выдер-
    гивать
wrestle /рэсл/ vi бороться
wrestler /рэ́слэ/ n борец
wrestling /рэ́слинг/ n борьба
wriggle /ригл/ vi извиваться, увиливать
wring /ринг/ vt выжимать, вымогать, ис-
    торгать
wrinkle /ринкл/ n морщина
wrist /рист/ n запястье
wrist watch /ри́ствóч/ n наручные часы
writ /рит/ n повестка
write /райт/ vti писать; ~ down /~ дáун/
    записывать; ~ off /~ оф/ вычеркивать
writer /рáйтэ/ n писатель
writing /рáйтинг/ n писание; in ~ /ин ~/
    в письменной форме
writing desk /рáйтингдэ́ск/ n письмен-
    ный стол
writing paper /рáйтингпэ́йпэ/ n писчая
    бумага
wrong /ронг/ adj неправильный; не тот;
    изнаночный; ~ side out /~ сайд áут/
    наизнанку; ~ side up /~ сайд ап/ вверх
    дном; n неправда; ошибочность

wrongly /рóнгли/ adv неверно
wry /рай/ adj кривой; ~ face /~ фэйс/
    гримаса

X

x /экс/ n (матем.) икс
xerox /зи́эрокс/ n ксерокс; vt размно-
    жать на ксероксе
Xmas /кри́смэс/ n Рождество
X-ray /э́ксрэй/ n рентгеновский луч; vt
    делать рентген
xylograph /зáйлэграф/ n гравюра на де-
    реве
xylophone /зáйлэфоун/ n ксилофон

Y

yacht /йот/ n яхта
yachting /йóтинг/ n парусный спорт
Yankee /йэ́нки/ n американец, амери-
    канка; янки; adj американский
yap /йэп/ vi тявкать
yard /ярд/ n двор; склад; ярд (мера)
yarn /ярн/ n пряжа
yawn /йоон/ n зевок; vi зевать
year /йее/ n год; this ~ /зыс ~/ в этом году
yearly /йéли/ n ежегодник; adj ежегод-
    ный; adv каждый год, раз в год
yearn /ёрн/ vi тосковать
yeast /йиист/ n дрожжи
yell /йел/ n пронзительный крик; vi виз-
    жать
yellow /йéлоу/ adj желтый
yes /йес/ part да
yesterday /йéстэди/ adv вчера; ~ morning
    /~ мóрнинг/ вчера утром; the day
    before ~ /зэ дэй бифó ~/ позавчера
yet /йет/ adv еще; все еще; as ~ /эз ~/ до
    сих пор; not ~ /нот ~/ еще нет; conj
    однако
Yiddish /йи́диш/ n идиш
yield /йиилд/ n урожай; добыча; доход;
    vt приносить (доход, результат и т.п.);
    vi уступать, поддаваться

yielding /йи́илдинг/ adj уступчивый

yoga /йо́угэ/ n йога

yoghurt /йо́гёт/ n йогурт, простокваша

yogi /йо́уги/ n йог

yoke /йо́ук/ n ярмо, иго

yokel /йо́укл/ n деревенщина

yolk /йо́ук/ n желток

you /ю́ю/ pron ты, вы

young /я́нг/ adj молодой; ~ people /~ пиипл/ молодежь

younger /я́нгэ/ adj младший

youngster /я́нгстэ/ n мальчик, юноша

your /йоо/ poss pron твой, ваш

yours /йо́оз/ pron твой, ваш; ~ faithfully /~ фэ́йсфули/ с уважением (в конце письма); ~ sincerely /~ синси́эли/ искренне Ваш

yourself /йосэ́лф/ pron сам, себя (2 л., ед. ч.); you are not ~ /ю а нот ~/ ты сам не свой

yourselves /йосэ́лвз/ pron сами, себя (2 л., мн.ч.)

youth /ю́юс/ n молодость, юность; юноша; молодежь

youthful /ю́юсфул/ adj юношеский, юный

Yugoslav /ю́югосла́ав/ n югослав(ка); adj югославский

zodiac /зо́удиэк/ n зодиак

zone /зо́ун/ n зона

zoo /зу́у/ n зоопарк

zoological /зоэло́джикл/ adj зоологический

zoologist /зоо́лэджист/ n зоолог

zoology /зоо́лэджи/ n зоология

zoom /зу́ум/ n гул, рев; жужжание; vi реветь; жужжать

Zulu /зу́улу/ n зулус(ка); зулусский язык; adj зулусский

Z

zeal /зии́л/ n рвение, усердие

zealot /зе́лэт/ n фанатик

zealous /зе́лэс/ adj рьяный, усердный

zebra /зи́ибрэ/ n зебра

zenith /зе́нит/ n зенит

zero /зи́эроу/ n нуль

zest /зест/ n "изюминка"; энтузиазм, пыл

zigzag /зи́гзэг/ n зигзаг

zinc /зинк/ n цинк

Zionism /за́йенизм/ n сионизм

zip fastener /зи́пфа́аснэ/ n застежка-молния

zither /зи́сэ/ n цитра

INDEX OF GEOGRAPHICAL NAMES

Abu Dhabi /эбу́уда́аби/ г. Абу-Даби

Accra /экра́а/ г. Аккра

Addis Ababa /э́дисэ́бэбэ/ г. Аддис-Абеба

Admiralty Islands /э́дмирэлтиа́йлэндз/ о-ва Адмиралтейства

Adriatic Sea /э́йдриэ́тикси́и/ Адриатическое море

Aegean Sea /иджи́иэнси́и/ Эгейское море

Afghanistan /эфгэ́нистэн/ Афганистан

Africa /э́фрикэ/ Африка

Alabama /э́лэбэ́мэ/ Алабама

Aland Islands /а́алэнда́йлэндз/ Аландские о-ва

Alaska /элэ́скэ/ Аляска

Albania /элбэ́йнье/ Албания

Albany /о́олбэни/ г. Олбани

Aleutian Islands /элю́юшьена́йлэндз/ Алеутские о-ва

Alexandria /э́лигза́андриэ/ г. Александрия

Algeria /элджи́эриэ/ Алжир

Algiers /элджи́эз/ г. Алжир

Al Kuwait /элкувэ́йт/ г. Эль-Кувейт

Alma Ata /а́алмээта́а/ г. Алма-Ата

Alps /элпс/ Альпы

Altai /элтэ́ай/ Алтай

Amazon /э́мэзэн/ р. Амазонка

America /эмэ́рикэ/ Америка

Amman /эма́ан/ г. Амман

Amsterdam /э́мстэдэ́м/ г. Амстердам

Amu Darya /эму́удэрья́я/ р. Аму-Дарья

Amur /эму́э/ р. Амур

Andes /э́ндииз/ Анды

Andorra /эндо́рэ/ Андорра

Angara /ангара́а/ р. Ангара

Angola /энгэ́улэ/ Ангола

Ankara /э́нкэрэ/ г. Анкара

Antarctic Continent /энта́рктикко́нтинент/ Антарктида

Antarctic Region /энта́рктикри́иджн/ Антарктика

Antigua and Barbuda /энти́игээнбарбу́удэ/ Антигуа и Барбуда

Antilles /энти́илиз/ Антильские о-ва

Antwerp /э́нтвэп/ г. Антверпен

Apennines /э́пинайнз/ Апеннины

Appalachian Mountains, Appalachians /э́пэлэ́йчьенма́унтинз, э́пэлэ́йчьенз/ Аппалачские горы, Аппалачи

Arabia /эрэ́йбье/ п-ов Аравиа

Arabian Sea /эрэ́йбьенси́и/ Аравийское море

Aral Sea /а́арэлси́и/ Аральское море

Ararat /э́рэрэт/ Арарат (гора)

Archangel /а́ркéйнджл/ = Arkhangelsk

Arctic Ocean /а́рктикэ́ушн/ Северный Ледовитый океан

Arctic Region /а́рктикри́иджн/ Арктика

Argentina /а́арженти́инэ/ Аргентина

Arizona /э́ризэунэ/ Аризона

Arkansas /а́рктикэ́усн/ Арканзас (река и штат)

Arkansas City /а́ркэнсоси́ти/ г. Арканзас-Сити

Arkhangelsk /арха́ангильск/ г. Архангельск

Armenia /арми́инье/ Армения

Ashkhabad /э́шкэба́ад/ г. Ашхабад

Asia /э́йше/ Азия

Asia Minor /э́йшема́йнэ/ п-ов Малая Азия

Assyria /эси́риэ/ ист. Ассирия

Astrakhan /э́стрэкэн/ г. Астрахань

Asunción /эсу́нсиэ́ун/ г. Асунсьон

Athens /э́финз/ г. Афины

Atlanta /этлэ́нтэ/ г. Атланта

Atlantic City /этлэ́нтикси́ти/ г. Атлантик-Сити

Atlantic Ocean /этлэ́нтикэ́ушн/ Атлантический океан

Auckland /о́оклэнд/ г. Окленд

Australia /острэ́йлье/ Австралия

Austria /о́стриэ/ Австрия

Azerbaijan /э́зэбайджа́ан/ Азербайджан

Azores /эзо́оз/ Азорские о-ва

Azov, Sea of /си́иэва́азов/ Азовское море

Bab el Mandeb /бэ́белмэ́ндэб/ Баб-эль-Мандебский пролив

Babylon /бэ́билон/ ист. Вавилон
Baffin Bay /бэ́финбэ́й/ Баффинов залив
Bag(h)dad /бэгдэ́д/ г. Багдад
Bahama Islands, Bahamas /бэхáамэáй-
    лэндз, бэхáамэз/ Багамские о-ва
Bahrain, Bahrein /бэрэ́йн/ Бахрейн
Baikal /байкáал/ оз. Байкал
Baku /бакýу/ г. Баку
Balearic Islands /бэ́лиэ́рикáйлэндз/ Ба-
    леарские о-ва
Balkan Mountains /бóолкэнмáунтынз/
    Балканские горы, Балканы
Balkan Peninsula /бóолкэнпини́нсьюлэ/
    Балканский п-ов
Baltic Sea /бóолтикси́и/ Балтийское море
Baltimore /бóолтимор/ г. Балтимор
Bamako /бамáакэ́у/ г. Бамако
Bangkok /бэнгкóк/ г. Бангкок
Bangladesh /бэ́нглэдэ́ш/ Бангладеш
Barcelona /бáрсилэ́унэ/ г. Барселона
Barents Sea /бáаренцси́и/ Баренцево море
Basel, Basle /бáазэл, баасл/ г. Базель
Basra /бэ́зрэ/ г. Басра
Batumi /батýуми/ г. Батуми
Beirut /бейрýут/ г. Бейрут
Belfast /бéлфаст/ г. Белфаст
Belgium /бéлджем/ Бельгия
Belgrade /белгрэ́йд/ г. Белград
Bengal, Bay of /бэ́йэвбенгóол/ Бенгаль-
    ский залив
Benin /бени́ин, бéнин/ Бенин
Bering Sea /бéрингси́и/ Берингово море
Bering Strait /бéрингстрэ́йт/ Берингов
    пролив
Berlin /бёли́н/ г. Берлин
Bermuc: Islands, Bermudas /бемьюю́дэ-
    áйлэндз, бемьюю́дэз/ Бермудские о-ва
Bern(e) /бёрн/ г. Берн
Bhutan /бутáан/ Бутан
Bikini /бики́ини/ атолл Бикини
Birmingham /бёрмингэм/ г. Бирмингем
Biscay, Bay of /бэ́йэвбискэ́й/ Бискай-
    ский залив
Bishkek /бишкéк/ г. Бишкек
Black Sea /блэ́кси́и/ Черное море

Bogota /бóгэутáа/ г. Богота
Bolivia /бэли́виэ/ Боливия
Bombay /бомбэ́й/ г. Бомбей
Bonn /бон/ г. Бонн
Bordeaux /бордэ́у/ г. Бордо
Borneo /бóрниэу/ о-в Борнео; см.
    Kalimantan
Bosporus /бóспэрэс/ Босфор
Boston /бóстэн/ г. Бостон
Botswana /ботсвáанэ/ Ботсвана
Boulogne /булóйн/ г. Булонь
Brahmaputra /брáамэпýутрэ/ р. Брахма-
    путра
Brasilia /брэзи́лиэ/ г. Бразилия
Brazil /брэзи́л/ Бразилия
Brazzaville /брэ́зэвил/ г. Браззавиль
Brest /брест/ г. Брест
Bridgetown /бри́джтаун/ г. Бриджтаун
Brighton /брайтн/ г. Брайтон
Bristol /бристл/ г. Бристоль
Britain /бритн/ см. Great Britain
Brittany /бри́тни/ Бретань
Bronx /бронкс/ Бронкс
Brooklyn /брýклин/ г. Бруклин
Bruges /брууж/ г. Брюгге
Brunei /брунэ́й/ Бруней
Brussels /браслз/ г. Брюссель
Bucharest /бьюю́окэрéст/ г. Бухарест
Budapest /бьюю́одэпéст/ г. Будапешт
Buenos Aires /буэ́нэсáйриз/ г. Буэнос-
    Айрес
Buffalo /бáфэлэу/ г. Буффало
Bug /бууг/ р. Буг
Buhkara /букáарэ/ г. Бухара
Bulgaria /балгэ́эриэ/ Болгария
Burma /бёрмэ/ Бирма
Burundi /бурýнди/ Бурунди
Byelorussia /бьéлэрáше/ Белоруссия
Byzantium /бизэ́нтиэм/ ист. Византия

Cadiz /кэди́з/ г. Кадис
Cairo /кáйэрэу/ г. Каир
Calais /кэ́лэй/ г. Кале
Calcutta /кэлкáтэ/ г. Калькутта
California /кэ́лифóрнье/ Калифорния

Cambridge /кéймбридж/ г. Кембридж

Cameroon /кэмерýн/ Камерун

Canada /кэ́нэдэ/ Канада

Canary Islands /кэнэ́эриáйлэндз/ Канарские о-ва

Canberra /кэ́нбэрэ/ г. Канберра

Cannes /кэн/ г. Канн

Canterbury /кэ́нтэбэри/ г. Кентербери

Cape of Good Hope /кéйпэвгу́дхэуп/ мыс Доброй Надежды

Cape Town, Capetown /кéйптаун/ г. Кейптаун

Cape Verde Islands /кéйпвёёда́йлэндз/ Острова Зеленого Мыса

Caracas /кэрэ́кэс/ г. Каракас

Cardiff /кá́рдиф/ г. Кардифф

Caribbean (Sea) /кэ́рибúэн(сúи)/ Карибское море

Carpathian Mountains, Carpathians /карпэ́йфьенма́унтынз, карпэ́йфьензʼ/ Карпатские горы, Карпаты

Carthage /кá́рфидж/ ист. Карфаген

Caspian Sea /кэ́спиэнсúи/ Каспийское море

Caucasus, the /кóокэсэс/ Кавказ

Cayenne /кэйéн/ г. Кайенна

Central African Republic /сэ́нтрэлэ́фрикэнрипá́блик/ Центральноафриканская Республика

Central America /сэ́нтрэлэмé́рикэ/ Центральная Америка

Chad /чэд/ Чад

Chad, Lake /лэ́йкчэ́д/ озеро Чад

Channel, the /чэнл/ см. English Channel

Channel Islands /чэ́нлáйлэндз/ Нормандские о-ва

Cheshire /чéше/ Чешир

Chester /чéстэ/ г. Честер

Chicago /шикá́агэу/ г. Чикаго

Chile /чúли/ Чили

China /чá́йнэ/ Китай

Chomolungma /чéумэлу́нгма/ Джомолунгма; см. Everest

Chuckchee Sea /чу́кчисúи/ Чукотское море

Cincinnati /сúнсинэ́ти/ г. Цинциннати

Cleveland /клúивлэнд/ г. Кливленд

Cologne /кэлэ́ун/ г. Кёльн

Colombia /кэлó́мбиэ/ Колумбия (страна)

Colombo /кэлá́мбэу/ г. Коломбо

Colorado /кó́лэрá́адэу/ Колорадо

Columbia /кэлá́мбиэ/ Колумбия (город и река)

Commonwealth of Independent States /комэнвэлф ов индепендент стейтс/ Содружество независимых государств

Conakry /кó́нэкри/ г. Конакри

Congo, the /кó́нгэу/ р. Конго

Connecticut /кэнэ́тикет/ Коннектикут

Constantinople /кó́нстэнтинэ́упл/ ист. Константинополь

Constantsa /констá́анце/ г. Констанца

Copenhagen /кэ́упнхэ́йгн/ г. Копенгаген

Corfu /кофу́у/ о-в Корфу

Corinth /кó́ринф/ ист. Коринф

Cornwall /кó́рнвэл/ Корнуолл

Corsica /кó́рсикэ/ о-в Корсика

Costa Rica /кó́стэрикэ/ Коста-Рика

Cote d'Ivoire /кэ́утдивуá́ар/ Кот-дʼИвуар

Coventry /кó́вэнтри/ г. Ковентри

Crete /криит/ о-в Крит

Crimea, the /краймú́э/ Крым

Cuba /кьюю́бэ/ Куба

Cumberland /кá́мбелэнд/ Камберленд

Curaçao /кьюэ́рэсэ́у/ о-в Кюрасао

Cyprus /сá́йпрэс/ Кипр

Czechoslovakia /чéкэслэвэ́киэ/ Чехо-Словакия

Dacca /дэ́кэ/ г. Дакка

Dakar /дэ́кэ/ г. Дакар

Dallas /дэ́лэс/ г. Даллас

Damascus /дэмá́аскэс/ г. Дамаск

Danube /дэ́ньюб/ р. Дунай

Dardanelles /дá́рдэнэ́лз/ пролив Дарданеллы

Dar es Salaam /дá́рэссэлáам/ г. Дар-эс-Салам

Dartmouth /дá́ртмэф/ г. Дартмут

Daugava /дá́аугава/ р. Даугава

Dead Sea /дэ́дси́и/ Мертвое море
Delaware /дэ́лэвээ/ Делавэр
Delhi /дэ́ли/ г. Дели
Denmark /дэ́нмарк/ Дания
Denver /дэ́нвэ/ г. Денвер
Devon (shire) /дэ́вн(шиэ)/ Девон (шир)
District of Columbia /ди́стриктэвкэлáм-
биэ/ Округ Колумбия
Dnieper /дни́ипэ/ р. Днепр
Dniester /дни́истэ/ р. Днестр
Dominican Republic /дэми́никэнрипáб-
лик/ Доминиканская Республика
Don /дон/ р. Дон
Dover /дэ́увэ/ г. Дувр
Dover, Strait of /стрэ́йтэвдэ́увэ/ Па-де-
Кале
Dublin /дáблин/ г. Дублин
Dunkirt /данкёрк/ г. Дюнкерк
Dushanbe /дьюшáамбэ/ г. Душанбе

Easter Island /и́истэрáйлэнд/ о-в Пасхи
East Indies /и́исти́ндьез/ ист. Ост-Индия
Ecuador /э́квэдо́р/ Эквадор
Edinburgh /э́динбэрэ/ г. Эдинбург
Egypt /и́иджипт/ Египет
Elba /э́лбэ/ о-в Эльба
Elbe /элб/ р. Эльба
Elbrus, Elbruz /элбру́уз/ Эльбрус
El Salvador /элсэ́лвэдор/ Сальвадор
England /и́нглэнд/ Англия
English Channel /и́нглишчэ́нл/ Ла-
Манш
Equatorial Guinea /э́квэто́ориэлги́ни/
Экваториальная Гвинея
Essex /э́сикс/ Эссекс
Estonia /эстэ́унье/ Эстония
Ethiopia /и́ифиэ́упье/ Эфиопия
Etna /э́тнэ/ Этна
Eton /иитн/ г. Итон
Euphrates /юфрэ́йтиз/ р. Евфрат
Europe /ю́эрэп/ Европа
Everest /э́верест/ Эверест

Falkland Islands /фо́оклэндáйлэндз/
Фолклендские о-ва

Faroe Islands, Faroes /фэ́эрэуáйлэндз,
фэ́эрэуз/ Фарерские о-ва
Federal Republic of Germany /фéдерлри-
пáбликэвджёрмэни/ Федеративная
Республика Германии, ФРГ
Fiji /фиджи́и/ Фиджи
Finland /фи́нлэнд/ Финляндия
Florence /фло́рэнс/ г. Флоренция
Florida /фло́ридэ/ Флорида
Formosa /фомэ́усэ/ Формоза; см. Taiwan
France /фраанс/ Франция
Franz Josef Land /фрэ́нцджéузифлэ́нд/
Земля Франца Иосифа
Freetown /фри́итаун/ г. Фритаун
Frunze /фру́унзэ/ г. Фрунзе; см. Bishkek
Fujiyama /фу́уджияямэ/ Фудзияма

Gabon, Gaboon /гэбо́н, гэбу́ун/ Габон
Galápagos Islands /гэлэ́пэгэсáйлэндз/
Галапагосские о-ва
Gambia /гэ́мбиэ/ Гамбия
Ganges /гэ́нджиз/ р. Ганг
Gdansk /гдаáньск/ г. Гданьск
Gdynia /гэди́нье/ г. Гдыня
Geneva /джини́ивэ/ г. Женева
Genoa /джéноуэ/ г. Генуя
Georgetown /джо́джтаун/ г. Джорджтаун
Georgia I /джо́оджье/ Джорджия (штат
США)
Georgia II /джо́оджье/ Грузия
Germany /джёрмэни/ Германия
Gettysburg /гéтисбёрг/ г. Геттисберг
Ghana /гáанэ/ Гана
Ghent /гент/ г. Гент
Gibraltar /джибро́олтэ/ Гибралтар
Glasgow /глáасгэу/ г. Глазго
Gobi, the /гэ́уби/ Гоби
Gorki /го́орьки/ г. Горький; см. Nizhni
Novgorod
Great Bear Lake /грэ́йтбээлэ́йк/ Боль-
шое Медвежье озеро
Great Britain /грэ́йтбри́тн/ Великобри-
тания
Great Slave Lake /грэ́йтслэ́йвлэ́йк/
Большое Невольничье озеро

Greece /гриис/ Греция
Greenland /гри́инлэнд/ Гренландия
Greenwich /гри́нидж/ г. Грин(в)ич
Grenada /гренэ́йдэ/ Гренада
Guadeloupe /гва́адэлу́уп/ Гваделупа
Guatemala /гвэ́тима́алэ/ Гватемала
Guinea /ги́ни/ Гвинея
Guinea-Bissau /ги́нибиса́у/ Гвинея-Би-
сау
Guyana /гайа́анэ/ Гайана

Hague, The /хейг/ г. Гаага
Haiti /хе́ити/ Гаити
Hamburg /хэ́мбёрг/ г. Гамбург
Hampshire /хэ́мпшиэ/ Гемпшир
Hanoi /хэно́й/ г. Ханой
Havana /хэвэ́нэ/ г. Гавана
Havre /хаавр/ г. Гавр
Hawaii /хава́йи/ Гавайи (острова и
штат)
Hebrides /хе́бридиз/ Гебридские о-ва
Hellas /хе́лэс/ ист. Эллада
Helsinki /хе́лсинки/ г. Хельсинки
Herat /херэ́т/ г. Герат
Himalaya(s), the /хи́мэлэ́йе(з)/ Гима-
лаи, Гималайские горы
Hindu Kush /хи́ндуку́уш/ горы Гинду-
куш
Hindustan /хи́ндуста́ан/ п-ов Индостан
Hiroshima /хиро́шимэ/ г. Хиросима
Ho Chi Minh /хэ́учи́ими́н/ г. Хошимин
Holland /хо́лэнд/ Голландия; см.
Netherlands
Hollywood /хо́ливуд/ г. Голливуд
Honduras /хондью́оэрэс/ Гондурас
Hong Kong /хонко́нг/ Гонконг
Honolulu /хо́нэлу́улу/ г. Гонолулу
Honshu /хо́ншу/ о-в Хонсю
Horn, Cape /ке́йпхо́рн/ мыс Горн
Houston /хью́юстэн/ г. Хьюстон
Hudson /хадсн/ р. Гудзон
Hudson Bay /ха́дснбэ́й/ Гудзонов залив
Hudson Strait /ха́дснстрэ́йт/ Гудзонов
пролив
Hungary /ха́нгэри/ Венгрия

Huron, Lake /лэ́йкхью́оэрэн/ озеро Гурон
Hwang Ho /хвэнгхэ́у/ р. Хаунхэ

Iceland /а́йслэнд/ Исландия
Idaho /а́йдэхэу/ Айдахо
Illinois /и́лино́й/ Иллинойс
India /и́ндье/ Индия
Indiana /и́ндиэ́нэ/ Индиана
Indian Ocean /и́ндьенэ́ушн/ Индийский
океан
Indonesia /и́ндэни́изье/ Индонезия
Indus /и́ндэс/ р. Инд
Ionian Sea /айэ́уньенси́и/ Ионическое
море
Iowa /а́йэуэ/ Айова
Iran /ира́ан/ Иран
Iraq /ира́ак/ Ирак
Ireland /а́йэлэнд/ Ирландия
Irtish /ирты́ш/ р. Иртыш
Isfahan /и́сфэхэн/ г. Исфахан
Islamabad /изла́амэба́ад/ г. Исламабад
Israel /и́зрэйл/ Израиль
Istanbul /и́стэнбу́ул/ г. Стамбул
Italy /и́тэли/ Италия

Jaffa /дже́фэ/ г. Яффа
Jakarta /джека́ртэ/ г. Джакарта
Jamaica /джемэ́йкэ/ Ямайка
Japan /джепэ́н/ Япония
Java /джа́авэ/ о-в Ява
Jersey /джёрзи/ о-в Джерси
Jerusalem /джеру́усэлем/ г. Иерусалим
Jibuti /джибу́ути/ г. Джибути
Jidda /джи́дэ/ г. Джидда
Johannesburg /джехэ́нисбёрг/ г. Йохан-
несбург
Jordan /джоодн/ 1) Йордания 2) р. Йор-
дан
Jutland /джа́тлэнд/ п-ов Ютландия

Kabul /кообл/ г. Кабул
Kalahara Desert /ка́алаха́аридэ́зэт/ пустыня Калахари
Kalimantan /ка́алима́антан/ о-в Калимантан

Kaliningrad /кэли́инингра́д/ г. Калинин-
град
Kama /ка́амэ/ р. Кама
Kamchatka /кэмчэ́ткэ/ п-ов Камчатка
Kansas /кэ́нзэс/ Канзас
Karachi /кэра́ачи/ г. Карачи
Kara Sea /ка́араси́и/ Карское море
Karlovy Vary /ка́алэвива́ари/ г. Карло-
ви-Вари
Kashmir /кэшми́э/ Кашмир
Katmandu /ка́атманду́у/ г. Катманду
Kattegat /кэ́тигэ́т/ пролив Каттегат
Kaunas /ка́унас/ г. Каунас
Kazakhstan /ка́азахста́н/ Казахстан
Kent /кент/ Кент
Kentucky /кента́ки/ Кентукки
Kenya /ке́нье/ Кения
Kerch /керч/ г. Керчь
Kharkov /ка́арькэф/ г. Харьков
Khart(o)um /кату́ум/ г. Хартум
Kiev /ки́иеф/ г. Киев
Kilimanjaro /ки́лимэнджа́арэу/ Кили-
манджаро (гора)
Kinshasa /кинша́асэ/ г. Киншаса
Kirghizstan /кеги́зстан/ Кыргызстан
Kishinev /ки́шинёф/ г. Кишинёв
Klaipeda /кла́йпидэ/ г. Клайпеда
Klondike /кло́ндайк/ Клондайк
Korea /кори́иэ/ Корея
Kuibyshev /ку́йбышеф/ г. Куйбышев;
см. Samara
Kuril(e) Islands /кури́ила́йлэндз/ Ку-
рильские о-ва
Kuwait /кувэ́йт/ Кувейт
Kyoto /киэ́утэу/ г. Киото

Labrador /лэ́брэдор/ п-ов Лабрадор
Ladoga /лэ́дэгэ/ Ладожское озеро
Lahore /лэхо́р/ г. Лахор
Lake District /лэ́йкди́стрикт/ Озерная
область
Lancashire /лэ́нкэшиэ/ Ланкашир
Laos /ла́уз/ Лаос
Laptev Sea /ла́аптьефси́и/ море Лапте-
вых

Latvia /лэ́твиэ/ Латвия
Lebanon /ле́бэнэн/ Ливан
Leeds /лиидз/ г. Лидс
Leghorn /ле́гхо́рн/ г. Ливорно
Leipzig /ля́йпзиг/ г. Лейпциг
Lena /ле́йнэ/ р. Лена
Leningrad /ле́нингрэд/ г. Ленинград; см.
St. Petersburg
Lesotho /лэсэ́утэу/ Лесото
Lhasa /ла́асэ/ г. Лхаса
Liberia /лайби́риэ/ Либерия
Libya /ли́биэ/ Ливия
Liechtenstein /ли́ктэнстайн/ Лихтен-
штейн
Liège /лиэ́йж/ г. Льеж
Lima /ли́имэ/ г. Лима
Lisbon /ли́збэн/ г. Лис(с)абон
Lithuania /ли́туэ́йнье/ Литва
Liverpool /ли́вэпул/ г. Ливерпул(ь)
Loire /луа́а/ р. Луара
London /ла́ндэн/ г. Лондон
Los Angeles /лосэ́нджилиз/ г. Лос-Анд-
желес
Louisiana /луи́изиэ́нэ/ Луизиана
Luanda /луэ́ндэ/ г. Луанда
Lusaka /луса́акэ/ г. Лусака
Luxembourg /ла́ксэмбег/ г. Люксембург
Lyons /ла́йенз/ г. Лион

Madagascar /мэ́дэгэ́скэ/ Мадагаскар
Madeira /мэди́эрэ/ о-в Мадейра
Madras /мэдра́ас/ г. Мадрас
Madrid /мэдри́д/ г. Мадрид
Magellan, Strait of /стрэ́йтэвмэге́лэн/
Магелланов пролив
Maine /мэйн/ Мэн (штат США)
Majorca /мэджо́окэ/ о-в Мальорка, Май-
орка
Malay Archipelago /мэлэ́йа́ркипе́лигэу/
Малайский архипелаг
Malaysia /мэлэ́йзиэ/ Малайзия
Malta /мо́олтэ/ Мальта
Managua /мэна́агвэ/ г. Манагуа
Manchester /мэ́нчистэ/ г. Манчестер
Manhattan /мэнхэ́тн/ Манхаттан

Manila /мэни́лэ/ г. Манила
Manitoba /мэ́нитэ́убэ/ Манитоба
Maputo /мэпу́утэу/ г. Мапуту
Marmara (Marmora), Sea of /си́иэвма́р-
мэрэ/ Мраморное море
Marseilles /масэ́йлз/ г. Марсель
Marshall Islands /ма́ршла́йлэндз/ Мар-
шалловы о-ва
Martinique /ма́ртини́ик/ о-в Мартиника
Maryland /мэ́эрилэнд/ Мэриленд
Massachusetts /мэ́сэчу́уситс/ Массачу-
сетс
Mauritania /мо́оритэ́йнье/ Мавритания
Mauritius /мэри́шес/ Маврикий
Mecca /ме́кэ/ г. Мекка
Medina /меди́инэ/ г. Медина
Mediterranean Sea /ме́дитэрэ́йньенси́и/
Средиземное море
Melanesia /ме́лэни́изье/ Меланезия
Melbourne /ме́лбэн/ г. Мельбурн
Memphis /ме́мфис/ г. Мемфис
Mesopotamia /ме́сэпэтэ́ймье/ ист. Месо-
потамия
Mexico /ме́ксикэу/ Мексика
Mexico (City) /ме́ксикэу(си́ти)/ г. Ме-
хико
Mexico, Gulf of /га́лфэвме́ксикэу/ Мек-
сиканский залив
Miami /майэ́ми/ г. Майами
Michigan /ми́шигэн/ Мичиган
Michigan, Lake /лэ́йкми́шигэн/ оз. Ми-
чиган
Milan /милэ́н/ г. Милан
Milwaukee /милво́оки/ г. Милуоки
Minnesota /ми́нисо́утэ/ Миннесота
Minsk /минск/ г. Минск
Mississippi /ми́сиси́пи/ Миссисипи (река
и штат)
Missouri /мизу́эри/ Миссури (река и
штат)
Moldova /молдо́ва/ Молдова
Monaco /мо́нэкоу/ Монако
Mongolia /монго́улье/ Монголия
Montana /монтэ́нэ/ Монтана
Montreal /мо́нрио́ол/ г. Монреаль

Morocco /мэро́коу/ Марокко
Moscow /мо́скоу/ г. Москва
Mozambique /мо́узэмби́ик/ Мозамбик
Munich /мью́юник/ г. Мюнхен
Murmansk /муэма́анск/ г. Мурманск

Nagasaki /нэ́гэса́аки/ г. Нагасаки
Nairobi /на́йэро́уби/ г. Найроби
Namibia /нэ́мибье/ Намибия
Naples /нэйплз/ г. Неаполь
Nauru /нау́уру/ Науру
N'Djamena /нджаме́нэ/ г. Нджамена
Nebraska /нибрэ́скэ/ Небраска
Neman /не́мэн/ р. Неман
Nepal /нипо́ол/ Непал
Netherlands /не́зелэндз/ Нидерланды
Neva /нэ́йвэ/ р. Нева
Nevada /нева́адэ/ Невада
New Guinea /нью́юги́ни/ Новая Гвинея
New Hampshire /нью́юхэ́мпшиэ/ Нью-
Гемпшир
New Jersey /нью́юджёёзи/ Нью-Джерси
New Mexico /нью́юме́ксикоу/ Нью-Мек-
сико
New Orleans /нью́юо́рлиэнз/ г. Новый
Орлеан
Newport /нью́юпот/ г. Ньюпорт
New South Wales /нью́юсаусвэ́йлз/ Но-
вый Южный Уэльс
New York /нью́юйо́рк/ Нью-Йорк (город
и штат)
New Zealand /нью́юзи́илэнд/ Новая Зе-
ландия
Niagara /найэ́гэрэ/ р. Ниагара
Niagara Falls /найэ́гэрэфо́олз/ Ниагар-
ский водопад
Nicaragua /ни́кэрэ́гьюэ/ Никарагуа
Nice /ниис/ г. Ницца
Nicisia /ни́кэси́иэ/ г. Никосия
Niger /на́йдже/ Нигер
Nigeria /найджи́риэ/ Нигерия
Nile /найл/ р. Нил
Nizhni Novgorod /ни́жнино́вгород/
г. Нижний Новгород
North America /но́осэмэ́рикэ/ Северная
Америка

North Carolina /но́оскэ́рэла́йнэ/ Северная Каролина
North Dakota /но́осдэко́утэ/ Северная Дакота
North Pole /но́оспо́ул/ Северный полюс
North Sea /но́осси́и/ Северное море
North-West Territories /но́освéсттéритериз/ Северо-Западные территории
Norway /но́овэй/ Норвегия
Norwich /но́ович/ г. Норвич
Noumea /нумэ́йе/ г. Нумеа
Novosibirsk /но́вэсибьи́ирск/ г. Новосибирск
Nuremberg, Nurnberg /нью́эрэмбёг, ньюю́юрнбэрх/ г. Нюрнберг

Oakland /о́уклэнд/ г. Окленд
Oceania /о́ушиэ́йнье/ Океания
Ohio /оиха́йэу/ Огайо
Oklahoma /о́уклэхо́умэ/ Оклахома
Oman /оума́ан/ Оман
Ontario /онтэ́эриоу/ Онтарио
Ontario, Lake /лэ́йконтэ́эриоу/ оз. Онтарио
Oregon /о́ригэн/ Орегон
Oslo /о́злоу/ г. Осло
Ottawa /о́тэвэ/ г. Оттава
Oxford /о́ксфэд/ г. Оксфорд

Pacific Ocean /пэси́фико́ушен/ Тихий океан
Pakistan /па́акиста́ан/ Пакистан
Palestine /пэ́листайн/ Палестина
Panama /пэ́немáа/ Панама
Panama Canal /пэ́немáакэнэ́л/ Панамский канал
Papua New Guinea /пэ́пьюэнью́ги́ни/ Папуа - Новая Гвинея
Paraguay /пэ́рэгвай/ Парагвай
Paris /пэ́рис/ г. Париж
Pearl Harbor /пёёлхáабэ/ Пирл-Харбор
Peking /пики́нг/ г. Пекин
Pennsylvania /пéнсилвэ́йнье/ Пенсильвания
Persian Gulf /пёёшнгáлф/ Персидский залив

Peru /пэру́у/ Перу
Philadelphia /фи́лэдéлфье/ г. Филадельфия
Philippines /фи́липинз/ Филиппины
Pittsburgh /пи́тсбёг/ г. Питсбург
Pnompenh /номпéн/ г. Пномпень
Poland /по́улэнд/ Польша
Portugal /по́отьюгэл/ Португалия
Prague /прааг/ г. Прага
Pretoria /прито́ориэ/ г. Претория
Puerto Rico /пвёётоури́икоу/ Пуэрто-Рико
Pyongyang /пьёнгйáнг/ г. Пхеньян
Pyrenees /пи́рэни́из/ Пиренеи

Quebec /квибéк/ Квебек

Red Sea /рэ́дси́и/ Красное море
Reims /риимз/ г. Реймс
Republic of South Africa /рипáбликэвсáусэ́фрикэ/ Южно-Африканская Республика, ЮАР
Reykjavik /рéйкьевик/ г. Рейкьявик
Rhine /райн/ р. Рейн
Rhode Island /ро́удáйлэнд/ Род-Айленд
Richmond /ри́чмэнд/ г. Ричмонд
Rio de Janeiro /ри́иоудэджени́эроу/ г. Рио-де-Жанейро
Rockies, the /ро́киз/ = Rocky Mts
Rocky Mts /ро́кимáунтинз/ Скалистые горы
Romania /румэ́йнье/ Румыния
Rome /ро́ум/ г. Рим
Rotterdam /ро́тэдэм/ г. Роттердам
Russia /рáше/ Россия

Sahara /сэхáарэ/ Сахара
Saint Lawrence /сэнтло́рэнс/ р. Св. Лаврентия
Saint Louis /сэнтлу́ис/ г. Сент-Луис
Sakhalin /сэ́кэли́ин/ о-в Сахалин
Salonika /сэло́никэ/ г. Салоники
Samara /сэмáрэ/ г. Самара
Samoa /сэмо́уэ/ о-ва Самоа
San Francisco /сэ́нфрэнси́скоу/ г. Сан-Франциско

San Salvador /сэнсэ́лвэдо/ г. Сан-Сальвадор

Santiago /сэ́нтиа́агоу/ г. Сантьяго

Santo Domingo /сэ́нтэдоуми́нгоу/ г. Санто-Доминго

São Paulo /са́унпа́улу/ г. Сан-Паулу

São Tomé and Principe /са́унтэмэ́йэнпри́нсипэ/ Сан-Томе и Принсипи

Saudi Arabia /са́удиэрэ́йбье/ Саудовская Аравия

Scotland /ско́тлэнд/ Шотландия

Seattle /сиэ́тл/ г. Сиэтл

Seine /сэйн/ р. Сена

Senegal /се́ниго́ол/ Сенегал

Seoul /со́ул/ г. Сеул

Sevastopol /сивасто́пэл/ г. Севастополь

Shanghai /шэнгха́й/ г. Шанхай

Siberia /сайби́эриэ/ Сибирь

Sicily /си́сили/ о-в Сицилия

Singapore /си́нгэпо́о/ Сингапур

Sofia /со́уфье/ г. София

Somalia /соума́алье/ Сомали

South America /са́усэме́рикэ/ Южная Америка

South Carolina /са́усќрэла́йнэ/ Южная Каролина

South Dakota /са́усдэко́утэ/ Южная Дакота

South Korea /са́ускэри́иэ/ Южная Корея

South Pole /са́успо́ул/ Южный полюс

Spain /спэйн/ Испания

Sri Lanka /сри́лэ́нкэ/ Шри-Ланка

Stockholm /сто́кхоум/ г. Стокгольм

St. Petersburg /сэнпи́итэзбёг/ Санкт-Петербург

Sudan, the /суда́ан/ Судан

Suez /су́из/ г. Суэц

Suez Canal /су́изкэ́нэл/ Суэцкий канал

Swaziland /сва́азилэнд/ Свазиленд

Sweden /сви́идн/ Швеция

Switzerland /сви́тсэлэнд/ Швейцария

Sydney /си́дни/ г. Сидней

Syria /си́риэ/ Сирия

Tadjikistan /таджи́киста́ан/ Таджикистан

Tahiti /тахи́ити/ о-в Таити

Taiwan /тайвэ́н/ о-в Тайвань

Tanzania /тэ́нзэни́э/ Танзания

Tashkent /тэшке́нт/ г. Ташкент

Tatarstan /та́тарста́н/ Татарстан

Tbilisi /тбили́си/ г. Тбилиси

Teh(e)ran /тиэра́ан/ г. Тегеран

Tel Aviv /те́леви́ив/ г. Тель-Авив

Tennessee /тэ́нэси́и/ Теннесси

Texas /тэ́ксэс/ Техас

Thailand /та́йлэнд/ Таиланд

Thames /тэмз/ р. Темза

Tibet /тибе́т/ Тибет

Tierra del Fuego /тиэ́рэде́лфуэ́йгоу/ о-в Огненная Земля

Tirana /тира́анэ/ г. Тирана

Tokyo /то́укьоу/ г. Токио

Toledo /тэли́идоу/ г. Толедо

Toronto /тэро́нтоу/ г. Торонто

Trinidad and Tobago /три́нидэдэнтэбэ́йгоу/ Тринидад и Тобаго

Tunis /тью́юнис/ г. Тунис

Tunisia /тьюни́зиэ/ Тунис

Turkey /тёёки/ Турция

Turkmenistan /тёкмениста́ан/ Туркменистан

Tver /твер/ г. Тверь

Uganda /юг э́ндэ/ Уганда

Ukraine, the /юкрэ́йн/ Украина

Ulan Bator /у́уланба́атэ/ г. Улан-Батор

Ulster /а́лстэ/ Ольстер

Union of Soviet Socialist Republics, USSR /ю́юньенэвсо́увьетсо́ушелистрипа́бликс, ю́юэсэ́са́р/ Союз Советских Социалистических Республик, СССР

United Arab Emirates /юна́йтыдэ́рэбэми́эритс/ Объединенные Арабские Эмираты

United Kingdom of Great Britain and Northern Ireland /юна́йтыдки́нгдэмэвгрэ́йтбри́тэнэнно́озэна́йэлэнд/ Соединенное Королевство Великобритании и Северной Ирландии

United States of America, USA /юнáйтыд-
стэ́йтсэвэмéрикэ, ю́юэ́сэ́й/ Соединен-
ные Штаты Америки, США
Urals, the /ю́эрэлз/ Урал
Uruguay /у́ругвай/ Уругвай
Utah /ю́юта/ Юта
Uzbekistan /у́збекистáан/ Узбекистан

Vancouver /вэнку́увэ/ г. Ванкувер
Vatican /вэ́тикэн/ Ватикан
Venezuela /вéнезвэ́йлэ/ Венесуэла
Venice /вéнис/ г. Венеция
Vermont /вёмóнт/ Вермонт
Victoria /виктóориэ/ г. Виктория
Victoria, Lake /лэ́йквиктóориэ/ оз. Вик-
тория
Vietnam /вьéтнэ́м/ Вьетнам
Virginia /вэджи́нье/ Виргиния
Vistula /ви́стьюлэ/ р. Висла
Vladivostok /влэ́дивóсток/ г. Владиво-
сток
Volga /вóлгэ/ г. Волга

Wales /вэйлз/ Уэльс
Warsaw /вóосо/ г. Варшава
Washington /вóшингтон/ Вашингтон (го-
род и штат)
Waterloo /вóотэлу́у/ Ватерлоо
Western Samoa /вéстэнсэмóуэ/ Западное
Самоа
West Virginia /вéствэджи́нье/ Западная
Виргиния
White Sea /вáйтси́и/ Белое море
Wisconsin /вискóнсин/ Висконсин
Wyoming /вайóуминг/ Вайоминг

Yalta /йэ́лтэ/ г. Ялта
Yellow Sea /йэ́лоуси́и/ Желтое море
Yemen /йэ́мен/ Йемен
Yenisei /йэ́нисéй/ р. Енисей
Yerevan /йэ́ревáан/ г. Ереван
Yugoslavia /ю́югоуслáавье/ Югославия
Yukon /ю́юкон/ р. Юкон

Zaire /зайэр/ Заир

Zambezi /зэмби́изи/ р. Замбези
Zambia /зэ́мбиэ/ Замбия
Zanzibar /зэ́нзибáа/ о-в Занзибар
Zimbabwe /зимбáабви/ Зимбабве
Zurich /зьюэрик/ г. Цюрих

APPENDIX I

RUSSIAN-ENGLISH BUSINESS TERMS

авиафрахт /ávia'fraht/ m
air freight

авизо /a'vizo/ n advice

акцепт /ak'tsept/ m acceptance

арбитраж /arbit'razh/ m arbitrage

аудитор /au'ditor/ m auditor, certified public accountant

банк данных /bank 'dannyh/ m data base

бартерный /'barternyi/ barter

бизнес /'biznes/ m business

бизнесмен /biznes'men/ m businessman

биржа фондовая /'birzha 'fondovaya/ f stock exchange

биржа ценных бумаг /'birzha 'tsennyh bu'mag/ f securities exchange

биржа чёрная /'birzha 'chernaya/ f black market

бонус /'bonus/ m bonus

брокер /'broker/ m broker

букировка груза /buki'rovka 'gruza/ f booking of cargo

бюро услуг /bju'ro us'lug/ n service center

валюта конвертируемая /va'ljuta konver'tiruemaya/ f
hard currency

ваучер /'vaucher/ m voucher

ввоз товаров беспошлинный /vvoz to'varov bes'poshlinnyi/ m duty free importation

вексель на предъявителя /'veksel' na predja'vitelya/ m bearer bill

вес брутто /ves 'brutto/ m gross weight

вес нетто /ves 'netto/ m net weight

взнос страховой /vznos straho'voi/ m insurance premium

взыскание налогов /vzys'kanie na'logov/ n tax collection

виза ввозная /'viza vvoz'naya/ f export permit

виза вывозная /'viza vyvoz'naya/ f export permit

виза многократная /'viza mnogo'kratnaya/ f multiple visa

вклад до востребова'ния /vklad do vost'rebovaniya/ m call deposit

возврат кредита /voz'vrat
kre'dita/ m repayment of
a credit

возмещение затрат /voz-
me'shchenie zat'rat/ n
reimbursement of expenses

**вознаграждение комис-
сионное** /voznagrazh'denie
zat'rat/ n commission payment

война цен /voi'na tsen/ f
price war

выплата авансом /'vyplata-
a'vansom/ f payment in ad
vance

выручка /'vyruchka/ f receipts,
returns, proceeds

вычеты налоговые /'vyche-
ty na'logovye/ m tax deductions

габарит /gaba'rit/ m overall
dimensions

грузооборот /gruzoobo'rot/
m freight turnover

грузополучатель /gruzo-
polu'chatel'/ m consignee

дебитор /debi'tor/ m debtor

декларация таможенная
/dekla'ratsiya ta'mozhennaya/
f customs declaration

демерредж /'demerredzh/ m
demurrage

демпинг /'demping/ m dumping

деньги наличные /'den'gi
na'lichnye/ pl cash

депонент /depo'nent/ m depositor

дефляция /def'lyatsiya/ f deflation

диверсификация /diversifi-
'katsiya/ f diversification

дивиденд /divi'dent/ m dividend

дилер /'diler/ m dealer

дисконт /dis'kont/ m discount

диспач /'dispatch/ m dispatch
(money)

договор аренды /dogo'vor
a'rendy/ m lease agreement

договор о найме /dogo'vor
o 'naime/ m contract of employment

**документы бухгалтер-
ские** /doku'menty buh'ga-
lterskie/ pl accounting records

досмотр багажа /dos'motr
baga'zha/ m inspection of luggage

**доход облагаемый нало-
гом** /do'hod obla'gaemyi
na'logom/ m taxable income

дубликат /dubli'kat/ m duplicate, copy

единица денежная /edi-
'nitsa 'denezhnaya/ f monetary unit

единица товара /edi'nitsa
to'vara/ f piece

жиро /'zhiro/ n endorsement

задолженность по
счёту /za'dolzhennost' po
'schetu/ f arrears

заказ пробный /za'kaz
'pro bnyi/ m trial order

запас золотой /za'pas zolo-
'toi/ m gold reserves

затраты прямые (скрыт-
ые) /zat'raty prya'mye (sk'ry-
tye)/ f pl direct (hidden) costs

заявка на кредит /za'yav-
ka na kre'dit/ f request for
credit

знак товарный /znak to'var-
nyi/ m trade mark

зона беспошлинная /'zona
bes'poshlinnaya/ duty free
zone

изготовитель /izgoto'vitel'/
m manufacturer, producer,
maker

изделья готовые /iz'deliya
go'tovye/ n pl finished goods

издержки производства
/iz'derzhki proiz'vodstva/ f pl
manufacturing costs

износ /iz'nos/ wear and tear

импортер /impor'ter/ m importer

инвестиции /inves'titsii/ f pl

investments

инкассация /inkas'satsiya/ f
collection

инфраструктура /infra-
struk'tura/ f infrastructure

каботаж /kabo'tazh/ m coastal
trade

капитал оборотный /ka-
pi'tal obo'rotnii/ m circulating
capital

карго /'kargo/ m cargo

касса /'kassa/ cash department

кассация /kas'satsiya/ f 1)
cassation 2) appeal

К и Ф C & F, Cost & Freight

квота импортная /'kvota
'importnaya/ f import quota

квота экспортная /'kvota
'eksportnaya/ f export quota

клиринг /'kliring/ m clearing

книга образцов /'kniga
obraz'tsov/ f sample book

книга приходно-расход-
ная /'kniga pri'hodno-ras-
'hod`naya/ f cash receipts
and payments book

колебания курсовые /ko-
le'baniya kurso'vie/ n pl
exchange rate fluctuations

компания совместная
/kom'paniya sov'mestnaya/
joint company

компания частная /kom-

'paniya 'chastnaya/ f private company

комплектность /komp'lektnost'/ f completeness

консалтинг /kon'salting/ m consulting

консигнация /konsig'natsiya/ f consignment

контрагент /kontra'gent/ m contracting party

контракт купли-продажи /kon'trakt 'kupli-pro'dazhi/ m sale-and-purchase contract

копия заверенная /'kopiya za'verennaya/ f certified copy

котировка /koti'rovka/ f quotation

кредит под залог /kre'dit pod za'log/ m mortgage credit

курс акций /kurs 'aktsii/ m stock (share) price

курс дня /kurs dnya/ m rate of the day

курс покупателей /kurs poku'patelei/ m buyers' rate

курс продавцов /kurs pro dav'tsov/ m sellers' rate

курс ценных бумаг /kurs 'tsennih bu'mag/ m rate of securities

куртаж /kur'tazh/ courtage

лизинг /'lizing/ m leasing

лист закладной /list zakla d'noi/ m mortgage bond

лицензия /lit'senziya/ f license

маркетинг /'marketing/ m marketing

налог на прибыль /na'log na 'pribyl'/ m profit tax

наценка розничная /nat'senka 'roznichaya/ mark up

номинал /nomi'nal/ m nominal value

ноу-хау /'nou-'hau/ know-how

образец подписи /obra-'zets-'podpisi/ m sample of a signature

объём закупок /ob'jem za'kupok/ m volume of purchases

объём перевозок /ob'jem pere'vozok/ m traffic volume

обязятельства платёжные /obia'zatel'stva pla'tezhnie/ n pl payment obligations

овердрафт /overd'raft/ m overdraft

оговорка о форс-мажоре /ogo'vorka o fors-ma'zhore/ f force majeure clause

окупаемость /oku'paemost/
f recoupment

операции биржевые /ope-
'ratsii birzhe'vie/ f pl exchange business

опцион /optsi'on/ m option

ордер кассовый /'order
'kassovyi/ m cash order

отгрузка /ot'gruzka/ f shipment

отправка груза /otp'ravka
'gruza/ f dispatch of cargo

отступные /otstup'nye/ pl
smart money

отчёт балансовый /ot'chet
ba'lansovyi/ m balance sheet

отчисления от прибыли
/otchisleniya ot 'pribyli/ n pl
deductions from profit

оферта /o'ferta/ f offer

парцель /'partsel'/ m parcel

перевод денежный /pere-
'vod 'denezhnyi/ m transfer of
money

перевозчик /pere'vozchik/ m
carrier

передача прав /pere'dacha
prav/ f transfer of rights

перетарка /pere'tarka/ f
repacking

переучёт векселя /pereu-
'chet 'vekselya/ m second

discount of a bill

перечисление безнали-
чное /perechis'lenie bezna-
'lichnoe/ n transfer by clearing

письмо гарантийное
/pis"mo garan'tiinoe/ n letter
of guarantee

письмо заёмное /pis"mo
za'emnoe/ n acknowledge-
ment of debt

письмо залоговое /pis"mo
za'logovoe/ n letter of deposit

письмо наложнным
платежом /pis"mo s na'lo
zhnym plate'zhom/ n letter to
be paid on delivery

плата арендная /'plata
a'rendnaya/ f rent

платёж в рассрочку /pla-
'tezh v rass'rochku/ m install-
ment payment

платёж наложенный /pla-
'tezh na'lozhennyi/ m cash on
delivery, COD

платёж отсроченный
/pla'tezh ots'rochennyi/n post-
poned payment

погашение кредита /po-
ga'shenie kre'dita/ n paying
off a balance

покрытие аккредитива
/po'krytie akkredi'itva/ n
payment of a letter of credit

полис комбинированно-
го страхования /'polis
kombi'nirovannogo strakh-
o'vaniya/ m comprehensive
policy

получатель денег /polu-
'chatel' 'deneg/ m payee

пользователь добросо-
вестный /'polzovatel' dob-
ro'sovestnyi/ m bona fide user

пометка в коносаменте
/po'metka v kona'samente/ f
detrimental clause

поощрение экспорта
/poosh'chrenie 'eksporta/ n
export promotion

порт по выбору покупа-
теля /port po 'vyboru po-
ku'patelya/ m port of buyer's
choice

посредничество /pos'red-
nichestvo/ n agency

поставка на условиях
СИФ-ФОБ /po'stavka na us'lo-
viyah sif-fob/ f delivery CIF-
FOB

пошлина единовремен-
ная /'poshlina edino'vre-
mennaya/ f final fee

право авторское /'pravo
'avtorskoe/ n copyright

право первой руки /'pravo
'pervoi ru'ki/ n first option

право подписи /'pravo 'pod-
'pisi/ n authority to sign

прайм-рэйт /'praim-'reit/ f
prime rate

предложение комплекс-
ное /predlo'zhenie 'komp-
leksnoe/ n package proposal

предприятие оптовое
/predpri'yatie op'tovoe/ n
wholesaler

прейскурант базисный
/preisku'rant 'bazisnyi/ m base
price-list

премия поощрительная
/'premiya pooshch'ritel'naya/
f incentive bonus

претензия встречная
/pre'tenziya vstrechnaya/ n
counter-claim

прибыль объявленная
/'pribyl' ob'yavlennaya/ f declared profit

прима-вексель /'prima-
'veksel/ m first bill

притязания патентные
/pritya'zaniya pa'tentnye/ n pl
patent claim

проверка кредитоспо-
собности /pre'verka kre-
ditospo'sobnosti/ f verification of credit standing

прогнозы коньюнктур-
ные /prog'nozy konyunk'tur-
nye/ m pl marketing forecasts

продажа на вес /pro'dazha
na ves/ f sale by weight

продление кредита /pro-
d'lenie kre'dita/ n extension
of a credit

продукция наукоемкая
/pro'duktsiya nauko'iemkaya/
f high tech products

продуцент /produt'sent/ m
producer

производство серийное
/proiz'vodstvo se'riinoe/ n
serial production

происхождение товара
/proishozh'denie to'vara/ n
origin of goods

пролонгация страхова-
ния /prolon'gatsiya straho-
'vaniya/ f renewal of expiring
coverage

просрочка   платежа /pros-
'rochka plate'zha/ f delay in
payment

протокол приёмки /proto-
'kol pry'emki/ m statement

of receipt

проформа /pro'forma/ f pro
forma

процент банковский
/pro'tsent 'bankovskii/ m bank
interest

процент по овердрафту
/pro'tsent po over'draftu/ m
overdraft rate

процент прибыли /pro'tsent
'pribyli/ m profit ratio

процент учётный /pro'tsent
u'chetnyi/ m discount rate

пул лицензионный /pul
litsenzi'onnyi/ m licensing
pool

пункт доставки груза
/punkt dos'tavki/ 'gruza/ m
point of delivery

разрешение на ввоз /raz-
re'shenie na vvoz/ n import
permit

разрешение на вывоз
/razre'shenie na 'vyvoz/ n
export permit

расписка ломбардная
/ras'piska lom'bardnaya/ f
pawn ticket

распределение риска
/rasprede'lenie 'riska/ n distribution of risk

расходы амортизацион-
ные /ras'hoddy amortiza-
tsi'onnye/ m pl depreciation
costs

расходы капитала /ras-
'hody kapi'tala/ m pl capital
outlay

расходы командирово-
чные /ras'hody komandi-
'rovochnye/ m pl travelling
allowance

расходы накладные /ras-
'hody naklad'nye/ m pl overhead expenses

расчёт в кредит /ras'chet v
kre'dit/ m commercial credit

регламент /reg'lament/ m
order of business

редисконт /redis'kont/ m
second discount

реимпорт /re'import/ m reimport

рейтинг /'reiting/ m rating

рекламация /rekla'matsiya/ f
claim

ремитент /remi'tent/ m remitter

репрессалии /repre'ssalii/ f
pl reprisals

ретратта /ret'ratta/ f redraft

рефакция /re'faktsiya/ f price
discount

рефляция /re'flyatsiya/ f reflation

реэкспорт /re'export/ m
reexport

римесса /ri'messa/ f remittance

риск кредитный /risk kre-
'ditnyi/ m credit risk

рынок товарный /rynok
to'varnyi/ m commodity market

сальдо /'sal'do/ n balance

санкции торговые /'sank-
tsyi tor'govye/ f pl trade sanctions

санкции штрафные /'sank-
tsyi shtraf'nye/ f pl fines

сбор гербовый /sbor 'gerbo-
vyi/ m stamp duty

сбор страховой /sbor straho'voi/ m insurance fee

свидетельство складс-
кое /svi'detel'stvo sklad'skoe/
n warehouse certificate

свинг /sving/ m swing

свитч /svitch/ m switch

своп /svop/ m swap

сделка аукционная
/'sdelka auktsi'onnaya/ f auc-

tion sale

сделка банковская
/'sdelka 'bankovskaya/ f banking transaction

СДР SDR

сертификаты денежного
рынка /sertifi'katy 'denezhnogo 'rynka/ m pl money
market certificates

сеть дилерская /set' 'dilerskaya/ f dealer network

СИФ CIF, Cost Insurance
Freight

скидка бонусная /'skidka
'bonusnaya/ f bonus rebate

скидка торговая /'skidka
tor'govaya/ f trade discount

склад консигнационный
/sklad konsignatsi'onnyi/ m
consignment warehouse

смета сводная /'smeta
ras'hodov/ f estimate costs

спот /spot/ m spot

спрэд /spred/ m spread

средства замороженные
/'sredstva zamo'rozhennye/ n
pl borrowed funds

средства привлечённые
/'sredstva privle'chennye/ n pl
borrowed funds

срок льготный /srok
l'götnyi/ m grace period

срок службы /srok 'sluzhby/
m service life

ссуда беспроцентная
/s'suda bespro'tsentnaya/ f
interest-free loan

ссуда целевая /s'suda tsele'vaya/ f purpose-oriented
loan

ставка льготная /'stavka
'lgötnaya/ f preferential rate

статья актива /sta't'ya
a'ktiva/ f asset

статья баланса /sta't'ya
ba'lansa/ f item

стоимость добавочная
/'stoimost' do'bavochnaya/ f
extra cost

стоимость рыночная
/'stoimost' 'rynochnaya/ f
market value

стокнота /stok'nota/ f stocknote

сторнирование /stor'nirovanie/ n reversing an entry

страхование убытков
/straho'vanie u'bytkov/ n
insurance against losses

субаренда /suba'renda/ f
sublease

сумма чистая /'summa 'chistaya/ f net amount

счёт дисбурсментский /schet disburs'mentskii/ m disbursement account

счёт-фактура /schet fak'tura/ f invoice

тариф единный /ta'rif e'dinyi/ m uniform tariff

тариф сквозной /ta'rif skvoz'noi/ m through rate

товаровед /tovaro'ved/ m commodity export

трансферт /trans'fert/ m transfer

тратта срочная /'trata 'srochnaya/ f time draft

удержание налога /uder'zhanie na'loga/ n tax deduction

условия отгрузки /us'loviya ot'gruzki/ n pl terms of shipment

уступка права /us'tupka 'prava/ f ceding a right

участие в прибылях /u'chastie v priby'lyah/ n profit sharing

учёт бухгалтерский /u'chet buh'galterskii/ m bookkeeping

факторинг /fak'toring/ m factoring

фирма подрядная /'firma pod'ryadnaya/ f contractor

фонды ликвидные /'fondy lik'vidnye/ m pl liquid funds

форфейтинг /for'feiting/ m forfeiting

франшиза /fran'shiza/ f franchise

фрахтование /frahto'vanie/ n chartering

хеджирование /hed'zhirovanie/ n бирж. hedging

цена договорная /tse'na dogo'vornaya/ f contracting price

цены сопоставимые /'tseny soposta'vimye/ f pl comparable prices

чек бланковый /chek 'blankovyi/ m blank check

чек туристский /chek tu'ristskii/ m travelers' check

экспорт бросовый /'eksport 'brosovyi/ m dumping

эмиссия ценных бумаг /e'missiya 'tsennyh bu'mag/ f issue of securities

ярмарка всемирная /'yarmarka vse'mirnaya/ f world fair

APPENDIX II

ENGLISH-RUSSIAN BUSINESS TERMS

acceptance n /экс'эптенс/
акцепт

accounting records n /э'ка-
унтинг 'рекодс/ доку-
менты бухгалтерские

acknowledgement of debt n
/экн'оледжмент оф
дет/ письмо заёмное

advice n /адв'айс/ авизо

agency n /'эйдженси/ по-
средничество

air freight n /эр фрейт/
авиафрахт

appeal n /эп'иил/ касса-
ция

arbitrage n /'арбитрадж/
арбитраж

arrears n /ар'иэрс/ задолженность по счёту

asset n /'эсэт/ статья актива

auction sale n /'окшн 'сэйл/
сделка аукционная

auditor n /'одитор/ ауди-
тор

authority to sign n /о'тори-
ти ту сайн/ право
подписи

balance sheet n /'бэлэнс
шиит/ отчёт балансо-
вый

balance n /'бэлэнс/ сальдо

bank interest n /бэнк
'интэрист/ процент
банковский

banking transaction n /'бэн-
кинг трэнз'экшн/ сде-
лка банковская

barter n /'бартер/ бартерный

base price-list n /бэйс
прайс лист/ прейску-
рант базисный

bearer bill n /'бээрэ бил/
вексель на предъяви-
теля

black market n /'блэкмар-
кит/ биржа чёрная

blank check n /блэнк чек,
чек бланковый

bona fide user n /'бона
'фиде 'юзэ/ пользова-

220

тель добросовестный

bonus n /'боунэс/ бонус

bonus rebate n /'боунэс ри'бэйт/ скидка бонусная

booking of cargo n /'букинг оф 'каргоу/ букировка груза

bookkeeping n /'буккипинг/ учёт бухгалтерский

borrowed funds n /'бороуд фандс/ средства замороженные

borrowed funds n /'бороуд фандс/ средства привлечённые

broker n /'броукэ/ брокер

business n /'бизнес/ бизнес

businessman n /'бизнесмен/ бизнесмен

buyers' rate n /'байес рэйт/ курс покупателей

C & F n /си энд эф/ К и Ф

call deposit n /коол ди'позит/ вклад до востребования

capital outlay n /'кэпитл 'аутлэй/ расходы капитала

cargo n /'каргоу/ карго

carrier n /'кэриэ/ перевозчик

cash n /кэш/ деньги наличные

cash on delivery n /кэш он ди'ливэри/ платёж наложенный

cash order n /кэш 'ордэ/ ордер кассовый

cash receipts and payments book n /кэш ре'сиитс энд 'пэйментс бук/ книга приходно-расходная

cash department n /кэш ди'партмент/ касса

cassation n /кэ'сэйшн/ кассация

ceding a right n /'сиидинг а райт/ уступка права

certified public accountant n /'сэртифайд 'паблик а'каунтант/ аудитор

certified copy n /'сэрти-'файд 'копи/ копия заверенная

chartering n /'чартэринг/ фрахтование

CIF, Cost Insurance Freight n /си-ай-эф кост ин-'шуэрэнс фрейт/ СИФ

circulating capital n /'сёркью'лэйтинг 'кэпитал/ капитал оборотный

claim n /клэйм/ рекламация

clearing n /'клиэринг/ клиринг

coastal trade n /'коустл трэйд/ каботаж

COD n /си о ди/ платёж наложенный

collection n /кэ'лекшн/ инкассация

commercial credit n /комёршл 'кредит/ расчёт в кредит

commission payment n /ко'мишн 'пэймент/ вознаграждение комиссионное

commodity market n /кэ'модити 'маркит/ рынок товарный

commodity export n /ко'модити 'экспорт/ товаровед

comparable prices n /'компэрэбл 'прайсес/ цены сопоставимые

completeness n /ком'плиитнес/ комплектность

comprehensive policy n /'компри'хенсив 'полиси/ полис комбинированного страхования

consignee n /'консай'нии/ грузополучатель

consignment n /кэн'сайнмент/ консигнация

consignment warehouse n /кон'сайнмент 'вээ-

хаус/ склад консигнационный

consulting n /кэн'салтинг/ консалтинг

contract of employment n /'контрэкт оф им'плоймент/ договор о найме

contracting price n /'контрэктинг 'прайсес/ цена договорная

contracting party n /'контрэктинг 'парти/ контрагент

contractor n /конт'рэктор/ фирма подрядная

copy n /'копи/ дубликат

copyright n /'копирайт/ право авторское

Cost & Freight n /кост энд фрэйт/ К и Ф

counter-claim n /'каунтер'клейм/ претензия встречная

courtage n /кёртадж/ куртаж

credit risk n /'кредит риск/ риск кредитный

customs declaration n /'кастэмз 'дэклэ'рэйшн/ декларация таможенная

data base n /'дэйта бэйс/ банк данных

dealer network n /'диилер 'нетвёрк/ сеть дилерская

dealer n /'диилэ/ дилер

debtor n /'дэтэ/ дебитор

declared profit n /дик'лээ/ прибыль объявленная

deductions from profit n /ди'да-кшнс фром 'профит/ отчисления от прибы-ли

deflation n /диф'лэйшн/ деф-ляция

delay in payment n /ди'лэй ин 'пэймент/ просрочка платежа

delivery CIF-FOB n /ди'ливэ-ри си-ай-эф эф-оу-би/ поставка на усло-виях СИФ-ФОБ

demurrage n /димь'юэредж/ демерредж

depositor n /ди'позитэ/ де-понент

depreciation costs n /ди'прии-ши'эйшн/ расходы амор-тизационные

detrimental clause n /детри-'ментал клооз/ помет-ка в коносаменте

direct costs n /ди'рект костс/ заявка на за-траты прямые

disbursement account n /дис-бёрсмент а'каунт/ счёт дисбурсмент-ский

discount of a bill n /дис-'каунт оф а бил/ пере-учёт векселя

discount rate n /дис'каунт рэйт/ процент учёт-ный

discount n /'дискаунт/ дис-конт

dispatch (money) n /дис'пэч/ диспач

dispatch of cargo n /дис'пэч оф 'каргоу/ отправка груза

distribution of risk n /дистри-'бьюююшн оф риск/ рас-пределение риска

diversification n /дайвёрси-фи'кейшн/ диверсифи-кация

dividend n /'дивиденд/диви-денд

dumping n /'дампинг/ экс-порт бросовый

dumping n /'дампинг/ дем-пинг

duplicate n /'дьюпликит/ дубликат

duty free importation n /'дьюı ти фри импор'тэйшен/ ввоз товаров беспош-линный

223

duty free zone n /'дьююти фри 'зоун/ зона беспошлинная

endorsement n /ин'дорсмент/ жиро

estimate costs n /'эстимит костс/ смета сводная

exchange business n /икс-'чейндж 'бизнес/ операции биржевые

exchange rate fluctuations n /икс'чейндж рэйт 'флактью'эйшнс/ колебания курсовые

export permit n /'экспорт пёрмит/ разрешение на вывоз

export promotion n /'экспорт про'моушн/ поощрение экспорта

export quota n /'экспорт 'квоутэ/ квота экспортная

export permit n /'экспорт пёрмит/ виза вывозная

extension of a credit n /икс-тэншн оф а кредит/ продление кредита

extra cost n /'экстра кост/ стоимость добавочная

factoring n /ф'экторинг/ факторинг

final fee n /файнл фи/ пошлина единовременная

fines n /файнс/ санкции штрафные

finished goods n /'финищд гудс/ изделья готовые

first option n /фёрст опшэн/ право первой руки

first bill n /фёрст бил/ прима-вексель

force majeure clause n /форс мажёр клооз/ оговорка о форс-мажоре

forfeiting n /'форфитинг/ форфейтинг

franchise n /'фрэнчайз/ франшиза

freight turnover n /фрэйт тёрноувер/ грузооборот

gold reserves n /'гоулд резёрвс/ запас золотой

grace period n /грейс 'пиэриэд/ срок льготный

gross weight n /'гроус вейт/ вес брутто

hard currency n /хард 'карнси/ валюта конвертируемая

hedging n /'хэджинг/ хеджирование бирж.

hidden costs n /'хиден костс/
заявка на затраты
скрытые

high tech products n /хай тек
'продуктс/ продукция
наукоемкая

import quota n /'импорт
'квоутэ/ квота импорт-
ная

import permit n /'импорт пё-
рмит/ разрешение на
ввоз

import permit n /'импорт пё-
рмит/ виза ввозная

importer n /им'портэ/ им-
портер

incentive bonus n /ин'сентив
'боунэс/ премия поощ-
рительная

infrastructure n
/'инфра'стракче/ инфра-
структура

inspection of luggage n /ин-
'спекшн оф 'лагидж/ до-
смотр багажа

instalment payment n /инс-
'тоолмент 'пэймент/
платёж в рассрочку

insurance premium n /ин'шуэ-
рэнс/ взнос страхо-
вой

insurance fee n /ин'шуэрэнс/
сбор страховой

insurance against losses n /ин-
'шуэрэнс э'гейнст
'лоссес/ страхование
убытков

interest-free loan n /'интрист
фри 'лоун/ ссуда бес-
процентная

investments n /ин'вест-
ментс/ инвестиции

invoice n /'инвойс/ счёт-
фактура

issue of securities n /'исью оф
сикь'юэритис/ эмис-
сия ценных бумаг

item n /'айтем/ статья баланса

joint company n /'джойнт 'ка-
мпани/ компания сов-
местная

know-how n /'ноу-хау/ ноу-
хау

lease agreement n /лиз эг-
'риимент/ договор
аренды

leasing n /'лиисинг/ лизинг

letter of deposit n /'летэ оф
де'позит/ письмо зало
говое

letter of guarantee n /'летэ оф
'гэрэн'тии/ письмо га-
рантийное

letter to be paid on delivery n
/'летэ ту би пэйд он

ди'ливэри/ письмо на-
ложнным платежом

license n /'лайснс/ лицензия

licensing pool n /'лайснсинг
пуул/ пул лицензион-
ный

liquid funds n /'ликвид
фандс/ фонды ликвид-
ные

maker n /'мэйкэ/ изготовитель

manufacturer n /'мэнью'фэк
черэ/ изготовитель

manufacturing costs n /'мэнью-
'фэкчеринг костс/ из-
держки производства

mark up n /'маркап/ наценка розничная

market value n /'маркит
'вэлью/ стоимость ры-
ночная

marketing n /'маркитинг/
маркетинг

marketing forecasts n /'марки-
тинг 'форкэстинг/ про-
гнозы коньюнктурные

monetary unit n /'монетэри
'ююнит/ единица денеж-
ная

mortgage credit n /'мооргидж
'кредит/ кредит под
залог

mortgage bond n /'мооргидж
бонд/ лист закладной

multiple visa n /'малтипл
'виизэ/ виза много-
кратная

net weight n /нет вейт/
вес нетто

net amount n /нет а'маунт/
сумма чистая

nominal value n /'номинл
'вэлью/ номинал

offer n /'офэ/ оферта

option n /опшн/ опцион

order of business n /'ордэ оф
'бизнес/ регламент

origin of goods n /'ориджин
оф гудс/ происхожде-
ние товара

overhead expenses n /'оувер-
хэд икс'пенсес/
расходы накладные

overall dimensions n /'оуве-
рол ди'меншнс/ габа-
рит

overdraft n /'оуве'драфт/
овердрафт

overdraft rate n /'оувер-
'драфт рэйт/ процент
по овердрафту

package proposal n /'пэкидж
про'поузл/ предложе-
ние комплексное

parcel n /'парсэл/ парцель

patent claim n /'пэйтент клэйм/ притязания патентные

pawn ticket n /поон 'тикит/ расписка ломбардная

payee n /пэй'и/ получатель денег

payment in advance n /'пэймент ин эд'ваанс/ выплата авансом

payment obligations n /'пэймент 'обли'гэйшн/ обязятельства платёжные

paying off a balance n /'пэймент оф а 'бэланс/ возврать кредита

piece n /пиис/ единица товара

point of delivery n /пойнт оф дэ'ливэри/ пункт доставки груза

port of buyer's choice n /порт оф 'байэс чойс/ порт по выбору покупателя

postponement of a credit n /пост'понмент оф а 'кредит/ платёж отсроченный

preferential rate n /префе-'рэншл рэйт/ ставка льготная

price discount n /дис-'каунт фром зе прайс/ рефакция

price war n /'прайс вор/ война цен

prime rate n /прайм рэйт/ прайм-рэйт

private company n /'прайвит 'кампани/ компания частная

proceeds n /'проусидс/ выручка

producer n /про'дьююсэ/ изготовитель

producer n /про'дьююсер/ продуцент

profit sharing n /'профит 'шээринг/ участие в прибылях

profit tax n /'профит тэкс/ налог на прибыль

profit ratio n /'профит 'рэйшиоу/ процент прибыли

pro forma n /проу'форм/ проформа

purpose-oriented loan n /пёрпэс 'оори'ентэд 'лоун/ ссуда целевая

quotation n /кво'тэйшн/ котировка

rate of securities n /рэйт оф сикь'юэритис/ курс ценных бумаг

rate of the day n /рейт оф зе дэй/ курс дня

227

rating n /'рэйтинг/
рейтинг

receipts n /ри'сиитс/ выручка

recoupment n /ре'купмент/
окупаемость

redraft n /ри'драфт/
ретратта

reexport n /'сэкэнд
'экспорт/ реэкспорт

reflation n /реф'лэйшн/ рефляция

reimbursement of expenses n
/'риим'бёрсмент оф икс-
'пенсес/ возмещение
затрат

reimport n /ри'импорт/ реимпорт

remittance n /ри'митнс/ римесса

remittance of a certified check n
/ре'митэнс оф а сёти-
файд чек/ покрытие
аккредитива

remitter n /ре'митер/ ремитент

renewal of expiring coverage n
/ри'ньюэл оф экс'пай-
ринг 'кавэридж/ про-
лонгация страхова-
ния

rent n /рент/ плата арендная

repacking n /ри'пэкинг/ перетарка

repayment of a credit n /ри-
'пэймент оф а 'кредит/
погашение кредита

reprisals n /ри'прайзлс/ репрессалии

request for credit n /ри'квест
фор 'кредит/ кредит

returns n /ритёрнс/ выру-
чка

reversing an entry n /ри'вёр-
синг ан 'энтри/ стор-
нирование

sale by weight n /сэйл бай
вейт/ продажа на вес

sale-and-purchase contract n
/сэйл энд 'пёрчес/
контракт купли-про-
дажи

sample of a signature n
/саампл оф а 'сигначе/
образец подписи

sample book n /'сэмпл бук/
книга образцов

SDR money market certificates
n /эс-ди-ар мани мар-
кит сэ'тификит/ СДР
сертификаты денеж-
ного рынка

second discount n /'сэкэнд
дис'каунт/ редисконт

securities exchange n /сикь'ю-эритиз икс'чейндж/ биржа ценных бумаг

sellers' rate n /'сэлэс рэйт/ курс продавцов

serial production n /'сириел про'дакшн/ производство серийное

service life n /сёрвис лайф/ срок службы

service center n /сёрвис 'сэнтэ/ бюро услуг

shipment n /'шипмент/ отгрузка

smart money n /смарт 'мани/ отступные

spot n /спот/ спот

spread n /спред/ спрэд

stamp duty n /стэмп 'дьюю-ти/ сбор гербовый

statement of receipt n /'стэйтмент оф ре'сиит/ протокол приёмки

stock exchange n /'стокикс-'чейндж/ биржа фондовая

stock (share) price n /сток шер прайс/ курс акций

stock-note n /сток 'ноут/ стокнота

sublease n /'саблис/ субаренда

swap n /своп/ своп

swing n /свинг/ свинг

switch n /свич/ свитч

tax deduction n /тэкс ди-'дакшн/ удержание налога

tax collection n /тэкс кэ-'лэкшн/ взыскание налогов

tax deductions n /тэкс ди-'дакшн/ вычеты налоговые

taxable income n /'тэксэбл 'инкэм/ доход облагаемый налогом

terms of shipment n /тёрмс оф 'шипмент/ условия отгрузки

through rate n /сруу рэйт/ тариф сквозной

time draft n /тайм дрэфт/ тратта срочная

trade mark n /'трэйдмарк/ знак товарный

trade discount n /трэйд дискаунт/ скидка торговая

trade sanctions n /трэйд 'сэнкшнс/ санкции торговые

traffic volume n /'трэфик 'вольюм/ объём перевозок

transfer of rights n /'трэнсфё

оф райтс/ передача
прав

transfer of money n /'трэнсфё
оф 'мани/ перевод де-
нежный

transfer n /'трэнсфё/ трансферт

transfer by clearing n /'трэнсфё бай 'клиринг/ пере-
числение безналич-
ное

travelers' check n /'трэвлэс
чек/ чек туристский

travelling allowance n /'трэв-
линг э'лауэнс/ расхо-
ды командировочные

trial order n /'трайел 'ордэ/
заказ пробный

uniform tariff n /'ююнифом
'тэриф/ тариф единный

verification of credit standing n
/'верифи'кейшн оф
'кредит стэндинг/
проверка кредито-
способности

volume of purchases n /'воль-
юм оф 'пёрчесес/ объ-
ём закупок

voucher n /'ваучер/ ваучер

warehouse certificate n /'вээ
хаус сэ'тификит/ сви-
детельство склад-
ское

wear and tear n /вээ энд
тээ/ износ

wholesaler n /'хоулсэйл/
предприятие оптовое

world fair n /вёрлд фээ/
ярмарка всемирная